It was obvious at ~~~~~~~~~~~~~~
The plant had a ~~~~~~~~~~~~~~
marked with galls, and here and there turning yellow,
as if autumn had already come; and the few fruits
were small and poor.

Laure looked at the two men. Monsieur Delisle's
face was grave, even sombre; Philippe's had a frowning pallor that filled her with foreboding, for it suggested emotions fiercely suppressed, as her father's
had been when he told her the house was burnt
down.

'Is it – the phylloxera?'

Philippe nodded.

A THREAD
OF GOLD

Helen Cannam

SPHERE BOOKS LIMITED

SPHERE BOOKS LTD

Published by the Penguin Group
27 Wrights Lane, London W8 5TZ, England
Viking Penguin Inc., 40 West 23rd Street, New York, New York 10010, USA
Penguin Books Australia Ltd, Ringwood, Victoria, Australia
Penguin Books Canada Ltd, 2801 John Street, Markham, Ontario, Canada L3R 1B4
Penguin Books (NZ) Ltd, 182–190 Wairau Road, Auckland 10, New Zealand

Penguin Books Ltd, Registered Offices: Harmondsworth, Middlesex, England

First published in Great Britain simultaneously
by Michael Joseph Ltd and Sphere Books Ltd, 1989
1 3 5 7 9 10 8 6 4 2

Made and printed in Great Britain by
Richard Clay Ltd, Bungay, Suffolk

For Tim,
who first introduced me to the
golden wine of Monbazillac;
and to so much else besides

ACKNOWLEDGEMENTS

It will be clear from the dedication that I have based both the wine and the situation of Casseuil on Monbazillac in the Dordogne; but in every other respect the commune of Casseuil and its inhabitants are entirely products of my imagination.

I have had a great deal of help with my research for this novel not only from family and friends in England and France, but also from many people who have no connection with me at all. Among these, I should like to mention Monsieur and Madame Gilles Cros of Clos Fontindoule, Monbazillac, whose 1970 Monbazillac was a positive inspiration! Thanks are particularly due to Madame Cros for answering my many questions concerning the traditional methods used in their vineyard.

At the Domaine du Haut-Pécharmant, near Bergerac, Monsieur Roches showed us some of the processes within the *chai*. At Berrie near Saumur on the Loire, Monsieur Guy Naveau gave us an enjoyable and informative afternoon in his *caves*. At the Cave Coopérative at St Vivien de Vélines (Dordogne) Monsieur Jean-Hughes Fourcaud proved a wonderful guide, demonstrating very clearly that even with the most up-to-date wine making methods there is still room for a thoroughly traditional enthusiasm. Thanks are also due to Monsieur and Madame Serge Fourcaud for making us so comfortable in their *gîte* in the midst of their vineyard.

Away from the vineyards, at the Archives Départementales in Bordeaux, Monsieur Beyriac generously gave up his time to tell us about many aspects of nineteenth century vine growing. In Bergerac the staff of the tourist office were most helpful. On quite another aspect of the book, General Robert

Bassac of the Service Historique de l'Armée de Terre at Vincennes kindly supplied details of the First World War experience of the 108th regiment of infantry.

In this country, the staff of Crook library have always been a great help. Last, but by no means least, thanks to Charles Eve M.W. of Peter Dominic and Mark Savage M.W. of Windrush Wines, Cirencester, who between them directed me to Mr Robert Brunck of the Great American Food and Wine Company in Purley, who was able to supply me with a sample of New York State wine, so that I could taste its distinctive flavour for myself.

CHAPTER
ONE

i

Laure gazed critically at her reflection in the mirror and could find little fault with it: a beautifully poised head upon a long neck, on the nape of which her smooth honey-gold hair was gathered loosely into a net beneath the wreath of white roses. She smiled at the perfect oval face, the brown eyes set off by delicately arched brows, the straight nose and small exquisite mouth. A pity – she stood up now, the smile fading a little – a pity there was not more of the tall and statuesque about her figure, graceful though it was. Even the modest *décolletage* and the closely fitting bodice failed to make her appear anything but regrettably slight.

She half turned, so that the inadequate curve of her breasts was less visible, and looked back over her shoulder at the tiny waist and the great sweep of satin and lace that spread out from it over the carpet behind. That was better! She smiled again.

'Thank you, Florestine. You may go now.'

Her voice was clear and authoritative, yet warm, with, she thought, just the right note of firm friendliness. She did not look round as the girl crossed the room and closed the door softly behind her, though she watched in her mirror until the tall figure had passed out of sight. She tried to suppress the distinct feeling of relief that followed Florestine's departure. The maid might be a few years older than herself, a good deal taller, and endowed with a daunting air of superiority; but Laure Frémont was now Madame Naillac, wife of the most handsome and delightful man in all France, and *châtelaine* of the beautiful and celebrated Château de Casseuil. And although she was only just eighteen, she had been well brought up and knew exactly what her responsibilities were.

1

Tonight, of course, her duty was to charm and delight her new neighbours and relations at this first meeting with them following her marriage; and for that her appearance was supremely important. She dropped a mocking little curtsey at her reflection in the mirror, smiling as she might at one of Philippe's friends.

A faint laugh, deep and richly masculine, made her turn sharply.

'Philippe! I did not hear you come in!'

He stood just inside the door, watching her with an expression in which admiration was very slightly tempered by amusement; the affectionate amusement of the mature man of the world towards the innocent vanity of his young bride. 'I was allowing myself the luxury of looking at you, for a little while. You are a joy to the eyes, *ma chérie*.'

He came to her and took her hands in his, pausing a moment to hold her there just before him, where he could look down at her. His eyes, like hers, were brown, but darker, with a gravity in their depths which his lightest mood could never quite dispel. It was one of the things that had first attracted her to him, that hint of something sombre and troubled hidden beneath the surface charm and the polished manners. Perhaps she hoped that one day, by the warmth of the love that he returned, the sweetness of her nature, she would be able to drive it away.

'They will begin to arrive very soon. We ought to go down. But first—' He drew her to him, released her hands and held her against his body, bending his head to bring his mouth down on hers, gently at first, and then with an insistent warmth to which she responded with enthusiasm. Her heart beat wildly, her limbs felt as if only the wide supporting hoops of her crinoline kept her standing, for they seemed to have no power left of their own.

That had been the thing that had surprised her most about marriage, the new sensations unlike anything she had ever known before. The wedding night, just under a week ago in Paris, had been frightening at first, and then, ultimately, quite pleasurable in a wholly unexpected way. It had left her filled with a new excitement at what might lie ahead, what exper-

2

iences and fulfilments her body might now hope to enjoy. It had also made her look at her mother (when they met at breakfast next day) in an entirely new way, and with a distinct curiosity. Madame Frémont had spoken, vaguely, of the pleasures and duties of marriage, but that was all. It was odd to think that this woman she had thought she knew so well had perhaps felt these very same delightful sensations many times in her married life. Until then, the only thing Laure had ever been sure about, concerning her body, was that it must be kept pure and untouched – much of her upbringing had been directed to that end. And now, in an instant, all that had completely changed.

She pressed her hands against Philippe's back, feeling its breadth and strength beneath the black cloth of his evening coat, closing her eyes the better to savour every delicious sensation shivering through her. She felt sorry when Philippe brought his thorough kiss to a conclusion and raised his head to look down at her.

'Well, *ma petite*, we have no time for this just at the moment.' He ran a finger down the curve of her cheek, setting her trembling even more delightfully. 'Later, *chérie*,' he whispered. Briefly his lips brushed her forehead, his hands ran up her arms to the shoulders. 'We must go down.'

He moved to her side, drew her arm through his and led her across the warm red hexagonal tiles of the landing to the broad stone staircase, worn from centuries of use. Below them, on the half-landing where the stairs turned for the final descent to the hall, a high wide window offered a breathtaking view; but it was already beginning to grow dark, and Laure was in any case too nervous now to appreciate its grandeur. Her attention at the moment was wholly concentrated on what awaited her beyond the turn of the stair.

The hall of the Château de Casseuil was simple, austere, dimly lit, its only customary adornments a sparsely carved chest of great age, two solid chairs and a small walnut table: no pictures, no carpets, no ornaments. But today against the bare stone walls great banks of flowers reached from the flagged floor almost to the oak beams of the ceiling, a mass of colour lit by candles set in carved stands. Late roses, chrysanthemums, gladioli, dahlias, sunflowers, lilies and a dozen other

3

kinds of flower, filled the air with their perfume, banishing the customary odours of ancient wood and weathered stone with the heady fragrance of early autumn. Even now, at this very last moment, Philippe's mother was giving imperious orders to a servant bearing a final hurried arrangement of flowers, though quite where he would find a space for them it was difficult to see.

Imposing, rather forbidding, in her grey corded silk with a little black lace cap on her grey hair, the old lady turned as the couple began to descend, and watched them gravely. Laure, conscious of a critical light in the sharp eyes, assumed her brightest and most confident smile. She was still not wholly sure of Madame Marie-Louise Naillac, for all that her mother-in-law had several times expressed her satisfaction at her son's marriage, and even claimed some credit herself for bringing it about.

Laure smiled steadily all the way down the stairs, aware that she and Philippe, dramatically contrasted, made an arresting couple – she so slight and fair in her bridal white, he so tall with his dark curling hair and magnificent moustache, his olive complexion and fine figure in the sombre evening coat. They were like two people in a fairy tale, Cendrillon and her Prince perhaps, or Sleeping Beauty just awakened from a hundred years of slumber, claimed by her hero.

Such fanciful thoughts were very far indeed from Madame Naillac's mind as she came forward to greet them. Not that she would have been surprised to know how Laure's imagination had taken flight – the girl was still very young, scarcely more than a child. That, of course, had been part of her appeal as a bride for Philippe, from Madame Naillac's point of view. An unformed girl could be directed, schooled, trained in the right way, like a young vine plant not yet ready to bear fruit. The best plants, rightly tended, came in time to bear the richest fruit, as one day this pretty convent-reared girl must do, both in a physical sense, as the mother of Philippe's sons, and, of course, morally and spiritually as well. Left entirely to herself, Madame Naillac would not have chosen Laure Frémont as her son's bride. She would have preferred at least a hint of noble blood, and a more unambiguously Catholic background: Monsieur Jules Frémont was, at best, indifferent

4

to religion, perhaps even, beneath the discreet and courteous surface, as anti-religious as his son Marcel had already shown himself to be. But he was also a highly placed official in the Ministry of Finance of the Emperor Napoleon III, a man of considerable wealth in his own right, and his wife was the sole heiress of a highly successful manufacturer from Lorraine, now deceased. Laure was their only daughter. If Philippe had to marry for love, better Laure Frémont than someone wholly unsuitable. He was over thirty now, after all, and it could have been a good deal worse. She permitted herself a carefully measured smile, conveying her approval to her daughter-in-law.

'You look charming, *ma chère* Laure. Come into the *petit salon* until the guests arrive. Monsieur and Madame Silvine are already here.'

Madame Naillac opened the door for them to pass into the room overlooking the gravelled courtyard on the south side of the château. It was panelled, simply furnished in the good solid local style, and occupied by her own brother, a thin, grave-looking man – like their father before him, a wine merchant from Bordeaux, now retired – and his plump overdressed wife with her little moustache and fussy effusive manner. Laure had already met them at the wedding in Paris a few days ago.

Fending off the even more rapturous greeting of Philippe's two pointers, until then recumbent before the fire, Laure smiled politely at Madame Silvine's gushing torrent of words, endured her hairy kiss, and raised her cheek to receive Auguste Silvine's cooler salute. He bore a daunting resemblance to his sister, which made Laure instantly nervous in his presence. Philippe, busy shutting the dogs into the adjoining library, was no help at all.

She smiled, slipped in what she hoped was an appropriate remark when Madame Silvine's volubility allowed, and was greatly relieved when her parents and her brother Marcel, who had accompanied them to Casseuil from Paris after the wedding, came downstairs in their turn. With them, at least, she could be wholly comfortable. At ease again, Laure became all sparkling laughter and talk, and by the time the first carriage could be heard rolling to a halt on the gravel outside, she was at her most irresistible, and sufficiently aware of it for the thought to add the final spice to her enjoyment.

The dinner was superb, served in the beautifully proportioned *grand salon*, since the dining-room was not quite large enough for so great an occasion. Beneath the delicately carved and painted beams of the ceiling, and the watching eyes of Philippe's ancestors looking down from their portraits on the wall, the guests sat at a long table, spread with starched damask, white as Laure's gown, glittering with silver and crystal and candlelight amongst lavish flowers and twisting fronds of ivy. Laure was placed at Philippe's left hand, at the centre of the table with her back to the massive stone fireplace, its carved coat of arms forming an appropriate heraldic backdrop to their marriage feast. She exerted herself to charm and to win over all these strangers, whom she must, for Philippe's sake – because they were his friends and neighbours – make into her friends too.

It was not difficult. Before even the soup course was over, Monsieur Henri Séguier (seated on her left) was already half way to enchantment with his neighbour's new wife. Laure listened attentively to all he said, greeted his rather heavy witticisms with a delicious gurgling laugh, and turned upon him now and then a smile of such dazzling sweetness that it almost left him speechless. If only he could have found a wife like this – oh, lucky Naillac, to have found her first! But then he, Henri Séguier, was already married, to poor colourless Aurore, seated silently beside him and taking half-hearted sips at the aromatic soup. It was easy to forget her depressing presence with this captivating little creature hanging on his every word. Aurore never showed such a warm appreciation of his conversational abilities – and this charming woman was a Parisienne, used to the best company that the capital could offer, the most brilliant examples of wit and intelligence. If Henri Séguier, talking of such simple, countrified matters as the regional cuisine, the shooting season just begun, the various facets of the life of a *vigneron*, could so interest the new Madame Naillac, that only bore out his long-held view that Aurore greatly undervalued him.

'We are already in the middle of the *vendange* at Trissac,' he informed his neighbour at one moment. Laure was not

6

surprised, because she knew, since Philippe had told her, that Casseuil's grapes were always harvested much later than those of most other vineyards.

'Is it a good harvest, *monsieur*?' Her brown eyes, flecked – in some lights – with green and gold, were raised brightly to his face, alive with courteous enquiry. In his excitement he had drunk rather more of the sherry that accompanied the soup than was wise, and his strong-featured face was rather flushed, so that its bright colour contrasted oddly with the pale hazel-blue of his eyes – fringed with fair lashes – and almost seemed to clash with the small light chestnut beard that decorated his chin: it lifted and fell again, spade like, as he put down his glass and beamed at her.

'Not bad, *madame* – not bad at all. Better than we feared at one time. Though you know of course that we are not quite so much at the mercy of the weather as is Monsieur Naillac.'

'Ah yes, what of the Château de Casseuil, *monsieur*?' someone broke in from across the table. The doctor, thought Laure, searching her mind for his name. That was it, Doctor Rossillon! 'Will this be a good year for you?'

Laure watched Philippe as he paused to rest his fork on his plate, the long brown fingers of his right hand curved about the stem of his glass. She felt sure that she would never in all her life tire of watching him. So tall, so assured, so much the natural leader of men here in his ancestral château – and out of all the women in the world he had chosen her!

'You should ask our good Monsieur Delisle that question,' Philippe replied, with a smile towards the lean dark man seated further down the table. Jean Delisle, *régisseur* of the château, was responsible for the day to day running of the vineyard and the *chai*. 'He is the expert.'

'But even he is not an oracle,' the *régisseur* reminded his employer good humouredly. 'We are all, in the end, at the mercy of the weather. This summer has been rather too unreliable so far, with insufficient sun. On the other hand, if the conditions are right in the autumn, the most unpromising year can end in a great vintage. If I were compelled to prophesy, I would say that, if this fine spell continues, 1866 will not be an exceptional year, but possibly a very acceptable one.'

'If not quite worthy to mark this great occasion in my life,' added Philippe, glancing at Laure. His eyes were warm and admiring as he raised his glass a little from the table in a silent and intimate toast; and Laure laughed softly and smiled back.

'You have not after all found the oïdium too much of a problem?' said the Abbé Lebrun, *curé* of Casseuil, seated – to Laure's initial dismay – rather too close to her father, whose anti-clerical views she knew only too well. But to her relief Jules Frémont seemed to be on his best behaviour tonight. He was after all devoted to Laure, and would not have wanted to spoil her triumph. Fortunately Marcel – who was thoroughly indiscreet and whose opinions were far more uncompromising – was seated well down the table between deaf Madame Rossillon and her very plain daughter. He looked, Laure thought, bored beyond words. She remembered fleetingly the Paris friends of whom their father so disapproved, the group of artists and idealists with whom he would gather in the cafés of Montmartre or Montparnasse to talk the nights away; and felt a certain amused compassion for him in this very provincial company.

'Oh, with sensible preventive measures one need no longer fear that,' Philippe was saying, a little dismissively it seemed to Laure. 'Is that not so, Monsieur Séguier? We are fortunate that these new diseases have waited until now to show themselves, when science is sufficiently advanced for us to combat them at once.'

'The recent problems with mildew have proved more difficult of course,' Laure's neighbour pointed out, although he did not look unduly troubled about it, 'and I heard of some new outbreak – in the Gard, I think it was: something that withered the vines just before harvest – was it last year now?'

'Yes,' Jean Delisle joined in earnestly, 'there have been a few cases, I gather – something quite new. I understand they called in the experts to investigate it at once.'

'Then it will only be a matter of time before they provide us with a remedy,' said Philippe with confidence.

'I've been reading Doctor Pasteur's new work on fermentation,' the *curé* broke in again, with the manner of one eager to please. 'I could not understand it all of course, but I found it fascinating, absolutely fascinating. As I was saying only yesterday to Monsieur Chabry here,' (that was the Mayor of the commune of Casseuil, seated opposite the *curé*) 'to think wine has been made since the earliest days, yet we never knew until now what secrets lie behind that simple and changeless process, such complexity, so many wonders!'

'I have not read the work, of course. My free time is limited.' Again the tone was just a shade dismissive. 'But certainly no *vigneron* could disagree about the complexity of our craft. We live always with the possibility of disaster as much as of triumph. One cannot make wine as if it were a product of industry; there are so many factors, known and unknown, so much still beyond our control – such as the weather, for example. But science does at least give us the hope of being able to control more and more for ourselves.'

Laure, who was interested in the conversation, but was beginning to feel just a little excluded, laid a hand on Philippe's arm and closed her fingers about it, squeezing it gently. He turned to smile at her and his dark eyes seemed to look deep into hers. She felt her whole inside give a leap of delight. She wanted to say, 'I wish it was bedtime,' but knew that would never do; besides, it would not be entirely true. After all the evening had scarcely begun.

The salmon (fresh from the Dordogne) which followed the soup was exquisitely decorated, its accompanying sauce perfectly designed to enhance rather than mask the delicate flavour. As the waiter carried the dish from guest to guest so that each one could help himself, a little procession of servants brought the wine that was to go with it: four bottles set upon a silver tray, which they placed at Philippe's elbow. As they did so, the candlelight caught a gleam of gold, a deep clear gold, lit with sparks of fire.

'Ah, the 1847 – sunlight imprisoned in a glass,' murmured the *curé*, who knew what to expect and, something of a connoisseur, appreciated his infrequent visits to the château as an experience to be relished in a life largely devoid of such indulgences.

Laure watched as Philippe himself poured the wine for his guests – the best Château de Casseuil was too good to be entrusted to a servant. She was reminded at once of their first meeting, in the cool dimness of the long, low *chai* that formed the western boundary of the courtyard, on the day when Philippe had brought out just such a bottle as he poured now, to tempt her father.

They had called at Casseuil on their way to Biarritz, making a leisurely tour of the holiday journey south. 'Today we shall taste one of the finest wines in France,' her father had promised that morning. Laure had known what he meant from the moment she first tasted it, but the memory, the flavour, that honeyed fragrant sweetness, would be linked for ever in her mind with other sensations, because of Philippe.

His dark eyes had watched her from the candlelit shadow as she tilted the glass to her lips, full of an intent interest, with something questioning in their depths. Do you feel the attraction too? Do you feel as I do now? And she had, from that first intoxicating moment.

She drank now, slowly, each sip held in her mouth for as long as possible, savoured to the full, the taste and the memory inextricably linked, equally resonant with sweetness, delight, a pleasure that aroused and satisfied the senses at once. No one else at this table – not her father, not the *curé*, not even Philippe himself – could know quite that depth of pleasure, no matter how appreciatively they drank.

For five long hours one sumptuous course followed another, of the best that the region could offer; wonderful pâtés, game of all kinds, goose and pork and an abundance of vegetables – served with delicious sauces enhanced with the delicate, enticing fragrance of truffles – salads, sorbets, lavish desserts, luscious fruit. Laure loved good food – good food and wine, talk and laughter, beautiful clothes, and to be the centre of admiring attention; tonight she had them all. Even when at last the meal came to an end, her enjoyment was not over, for there was dancing in the dining-room. In a haze of happiness, she turned about the room in Philippe's arms, feeling his nearness and the lilt of the music as one intoxicating sensation. Once, he said, 'Are you tired, *ma chérie*?' and she shook her head fiercely, astonished that he should even need to ask; and then wondered a moment after if he had simply been seeking an excuse to take her up to bed. But that would perhaps have been a discourtesy to their guests; and a little

10

later, mindful of his responsibilities as host, Philippe took her arm and guided her away from the dining-room towards the *petit salon*, where those who were disinclined for dancing could play cards and talk. There, he led her from one group to another, manifestly proud of the impression she made on everyone.

They came at last to where her father stood on the edge of an animated group of men. 'May I leave you to your father for a moment, *chérie*?' Philippe murmured. 'I want a word with my mother.'

Jules Frémont, overhearing, turned to smile at Philippe and then, as his son-in-law moved away, reached out to draw Laure's arm through his. 'I am so proud of you tonight, *ma chère fille*,' he murmured softly, below the fiercely arguing voices of his companions.

'. . . all sausages and bombast, that's what the Prussians are, nothing more!' That was Henri Séguier, good humoured but emphatic. Mayor Chabry, beside him, was clearly far from good humoured; but before he could say anything, Doctor Rossillon broke in.

'Perhaps, in the interests of our own army, one ought to investigate the power of the sausage,' he said cheerfully. 'Its effect on the Prussian troops seems to have been startling in the extreme, if the defeat of Austria is anything to go by.'

'We have been discussing the Austrian war,' Laure's father whispered to his daughter, by way of explanation.

'A matter of pure luck, that's all,' said Henri Séguier airily.

'Pure luck, to inflict a crushing defeat within six weeks?' exclaimed the doctor. 'Oh, come now, *mon ami*! Prussia is a force to be reckoned with, there can be no denying that. As I said just now, that is where the power will lie in Europe in future, if we're not careful. The Emperor has seen to it that France's pride has been trampled in the dust.'

At that, the Mayor could restrain himself no longer. '*Monsieur*, I will not stand by and hear the Emperor so insulted! Think what glory the Crimean war brought us! And remember *we* also beat Austria, in Italy, under our Emperor's leadership, before anyone had heard of Prussia. Think what prosperity we enjoy!'

'Think of Mexico,' added the doctor maliciously. 'I have no

11

need to insult the Emperor – his own actions have humiliated him quite enough in the eyes of the world.'

It was at this point that Henri Séguier noticed Laure, standing attentively at her father's side. '*Mes amis*, I am sure that Madame Naillac is not interested in foreign policy.'

'On the contrary, *monsieur*,' said Laure sweetly, 'I enjoy a lively argument as well as anyone.'

Henri Séguier looked surprised. 'Is that so, *madame*? But tonight, I am sure . . .'

Doctor Rossillon smiled at Laure. 'The Emperor should have sent you to rule Mexico, *madame*, instead of the hapless Maximilian.' He glanced round at his companions. 'Don't you think Madame Naillac would have been much more acceptable to the Mexican people? They could have sunk their differences in admiring her beauty.'

The men could, of course, only agree, but Monsieur Frémont tightened his hold on his daughter's arm. 'I shudder to think of her facing such dangers: revolution, the firing squad.' He shivered. 'No, far better to content herself with her little kingdom here.' He looked about the crowded comfortable room.

Compliments flowed over Laure, and the talk became light and amicable, and eventually Jules Frémont led her away to where her mother sat watching an intense game of cards.

'You didn't join in their argument,' Laure said to her father in some surprise as they crossed the room. 'Yet you were just as angry about the Emperor's Mexican policy as Doctor Rossillon.'

'So I was – and am still. But it is one thing to express your views amongst known and trusted friends in your own home, quite another to give reckless voice to them amongst near strangers. Mayor Chabry is clearly an ardent Bonapartist, the Emperor's man to the backbone. What if he should report to some higher authority on the subversive opinions openly expressed by a member of the government? It's not impossible.'

'But you make no secret of being a Republican.'

'Nor do I shout it from the rooftops. I am not wholly without discretion, *ma chère*. Did you not hear me being the soul of courtesy to the *curé* at dinner?'

'No, but I'm sure you were . . . He seems a pleasant man.'

'Perhaps, for a priest. Your mother liked him, but then that is different.' In Jules Frémont's eyes, piety was a weakness natural to women and as such acceptable, so long as it was not carried to excess. That was perhaps just as well, since his dislike of superstition (by which he meant Catholicism) had not been able to dim the faith of his much-loved wife, nor to prevent her from passing it on to her daughter. 'However,' he went on, 'I was gratified to note that your Philippe seems to have his reservations, although his mother appears to be a great deal more in the *curé*'s pocket than I suspected.' They reached Madame Frémont, who took Laure's hand in hers.

'You look so happy, *ma chérie*. I am glad.'

Laure kissed her and sat down beside her; and was content for a little while simply to be silent in the company of these two people she loved so much. She thought of the years they had shared: the early years, when she had learned to read and write at her mother's knee, and listened to her songs and stories; when she had been rocked and tossed in her father's arms, shown off before his friends with loving pride, her innocent infant remarks delighting and charming the company. She remembered family visits to her maternal grandparents' country house in Lorraine and – looking back with the experience of her womanhood – realised now how her father had been loved and welcomed there as warmly as was her mother. She remembered her school days in the tolerant, affectionate atmosphere of the carefully selected convent school. And holidays with Marcel as her closest companion and friend, but her parents too as a constant presence, assuring them both of security and love. Those three people – her mother, her father, Marcel – had been the heart of her life until now; a life full of friends and laughter and good talk, rides, walks, shopping expeditions, balls and dinners, visits to theatre and ballet and opera, which yet had a core of joyful serenity, sometimes troubled, but always there. And that life now had to come to an end. For the first time since she had met Philippe she felt not fear or apprehension or uncertainty, but a sharp pang of regret. For a moment tears rose in her eyes. And then she was conscious only of a tender gratitude. Her parents had given her so much, and above all the qualities that would enable her to shape for herself, here at Casseuil, a new life as rich and rewarding as the old.

She turned to look from one to another of them, holding a hand of each in her own. 'Thank you,' she whispered. 'Thank you both for all you have done for me since I was born.'

When – some time later – Philippe came to reclaim her, they were arguing good humouredly about wine – or rather, about one wine, the wonderful Château de Casseuil of tonight's meal.

'. . . You realise you are making the most revolutionary of suggestions, clean against all the accepted customs of generations of *vignerons* and wine drinkers?'

'With such a rebel for a father, what do you expect?'

'What has she been saying?' Philippe asked, looking tenderly down at his young bride.

'Only that she thinks Château de Casseuil should be drunk with something other than fish. Can you imagine it? Sacrilege, is it not?'

Laure laughed. 'It's such a huge wine you see. I just thought it might be better drunk alone, or with something much more strongly flavoured than fish.'

She realised that Philippe did not share her father's amusement, though he did smile faintly. 'You will learn, *ma chérie*. Experience counts for so much. Is that not so, *monsieur*?'

'Of course,' agreed Jules Frémont comfortably. 'And after all, she cannot help but learn all there is to know about wine, here at Casseuil.'

ii

The Frémonts, mother, father and son, were to return to Paris two days after that triumphant dinner. On the morning of their departure Laure woke early, disturbed by Philippe turning in the wide curtained bed to put his arms about her. She snuggled close, enjoying the feel of his chest – all coarse, dark, curling hair on hard muscle and bone beneath her cheek – the smell of him, the strength of his hold about her, the pressure of the kiss he placed on her averted head. She made some sleepy indecipherable murmur of contentment, and then realised this was not after all a preliminary to some greater closeness.

14

'I must get up now, *ma petite* Laure,' he said softly. 'I can't leave everything to Monsieur Delisle for ever – and there is a broker coming from Libourne this morning, to be tempted to buy. If I go now I can be back in time to say goodbye to your parents.'

'Let me come with you,' she pleaded into the warm hollow of his throat. She expected him to say 'yes' at once, and felt a little deflated when he did not.

'It would be very tedious for you, *chérie* – and besides you will want to spend the time with your parents. Lie in bed a little longer until they are about. There's no hurry.'

She moved just far enough away from him to free herself to look into his face. 'I think I've been idle long enough. Isn't it time I began to take my part in running our household? Your mother must be wondering what kind of a lazy wife you've brought home.'

'Oh, don't worry your head about that, *ma petite*. You can be sure that my mother will continue to hold the reins in her hands for a long time yet.'

For a moment she said nothing, being aware only of a sudden plunging sense of disappointment, almost of dismay. Was she not after all to be mistress of Casseuil, not even perhaps in name? 'But I ought to be relieving her of some of the burden. She's not a young woman. Surely she will be glad to rest after all these years?'

'Oh, by all means go to her, watch and listen and ask questions and learn all you can. She'll be delighted to teach you, so that one day, when she really does feel her age, you will be able to run things as smoothly as she has done.'

'But it's my duty, surely, as your wife. Maman always said . . . and I thought . . .' She faltered, troubled by this unexpected misunderstanding between them, the floundering feeling that she could not make him see her point of view.

Apparently quite unaware that she was suffering from anything more than a faint qualm of conscience, Philippe kissed her lightly, on the eyes, the nose, the mouth. 'Laure, *ma petite*, all you need to do is to enjoy yourself, delight my friends as you did the other night, and stay just as you are, sweet and happy and carefree. My mother likes being in

15

charge, and she's very good at it; very efficient and vigilant. If you want to learn from her, ask her for some hints to put by for the future, but don't worry your lovely head over anything else. After all, there may soon be other things for you to care about, if we're fortunate.'

A baby, she supposed, a little cheered. Yes, she wanted to bear his child, as soon as possible. But a little disappointment lingered all the same, though she responded to his final, long kiss before he slipped from the bed and went to his dressing-room.

She dozed a little after he had gone, and then woke again. It must still be early, for she did not think the angelus had sounded yet from the village church, and beyond the shuttered windows there was silence, and Florestine had not yet come to bring chocolate and let in the daylight.

Laure slid out of bed, padded across the cool floorboards to the nearer window, and folded back the shutters. Below there was only whiteness, a dense, milk whiteness packed down into every crook and hollow of the landscape, muffling every sight and sound. She could see the pale grey stonework of the wall beneath the window, and the edge of the slope rising away from the dry moat that surrounded the château; the short grass that covered it beaded with moisture. Beyond that there was nothing but the mist, and silence.

She was about to return to the comforting warmth of her bed when the silence was sharply broken by the sound of a door opening and then closing again, down there in the mist to her right, where a low entrance of recent date gave access to the kitchen and cellars of the château. The next moment a fair head came into view immediately below, the hair tousled and unprotected by any hat. It moved quickly, a little bent, along the moat to where the mist in a moment would once more swallow it up. Laure shot the window open.

'Marcel!' The head was thrown back, a fair fine-boned face turned up, a pair of brown eyes looked questioningly at Laure. 'Wait there. I'm coming down!'

She dressed herself quickly, as she used to do when she was a girl (before marriage and Florestine) pulling on a gown of tartan wool and a black velvet Zouave jacket, and hurried softly downstairs, meeting no one on her way, to let herself

16

out by the same little door Marcel had used – it was the only way out of the château apart from the great front door, still locked and barred at this early hour.

Marcel was waiting exactly where she had seen him last, below her window. He had a rumpled untidy look about him, as if he had dressed even more quickly than she had, and with less care. He looked as if he had not slept a great deal. With a sense that he needed comfort, Laure slid her arm through his, smiling at him. She did not have to look up to do so, as she did with Philippe, for though Marcel was two years her senior they were much of a height.

'I've not had one moment alone with you for weeks,' she said. 'I was so afraid you'd be off to Paris today before we could talk.'

'What do you expect? You're always surrounded by people,' Marcel complained mildly.

'I have responsibilities now, you know,' she reminded him. He grinned at her, clearly unconvinced.

'You know you love having such a fuss made of you. You can't fool me, *ma chère sœur*.'

She laughed, and then tugged gently at his arm, steering him to where a short flight of steps led out of the moat into the wall of mist. 'Let's go this way.' They moved on until the mist closed them in, their isolation complete. 'It's been such a busy time, in Paris before the wedding with so much to do, and since . . . But I have noticed, you've been in a strange mood.'

'What do you expect, with my sister going out of my life for ever?' The tone was light and teasing, but he did not look at her and she sensed the underlying constraint. Was that really all it was? They had always been close, close enough for anger and jealousy, often, in the past, but in recent years linked by a deep and trusting friendship. For the most part, however, they had different interests, different friends, sought different things from life. To be parted by her marriage ought not to be enough to depress him.

'Don't be silly,' she said now. 'I shall come back to Paris often. Where else am I to have my clothes made, after all? I doubt if Bergerac or even Bordeaux has anyone to match Worth. And I might just take a fancy to exchange a word or two with my parents, and my brother.'

17

He shook his head. 'No, not with me, not after next month.'

The sound of a fountain splashing into its bowl broke in on them, just beyond sight, oddly loud in the muffling stillness. One step more, and it was there in front of them, a solitary melancholy sight, splashing away to itself alone. Its very pointlessness seemed to strike at Laure's heart, as if it was that and not Marcel's words that had dismayed her. She stared at it and then, abruptly, at Marcel. 'What do you mean?' Without question she could see now the shadows about his eyes, the troubled line to his mouth. As she studied him he looked down, avoiding her eyes, and watched his right foot as if it had nothing to do with him down there, disordering the careful pattern of the gravel path with an inconsequential movement.

'I'm going away.'

'Away? Where to? Why?' And then before he could say anything her face lit up and she swept on, 'Has Papa allowed you to study art after all? But where will you go for that? What better place is there than Paris?'

He shook his head. 'No – no, things are still exactly as they were there. I cannot understand why he can so admire the most modern and radical styles of art, and yet not allow me to take it up as a career. It's not as if he thinks I'm no good. He's said himself . . . but you've heard all that before. What's the use of going over it again?' The momentary burst of indignation subsided, but the anger and bitterness in his tone had reminded Laure only too well of the fiercely argued disputes between father and son which at intervals in the past three years had so disrupted their once united family. For the most part their father was a man of great warmth and understanding, open to new ideas, wide in his friendships and interests; but even his considerable tolerance had its limits, and Marcel, by wanting to follow so precarious a career, had threatened to breach them. 'I suppose if I painted Romantic historical subjects worthy of the Salon he'd look at it quite differently: there's money in that!' So Marcel generally went on to say, to which his father's riposte was that he had no objection to Marcel's painting as a hobby; he simply did not want a son of his to follow it as a career. Now, however, Marcel abandoned that line of conversation. 'It's not that

18

anyway.' His foot continued its restless to and fro on the path, but it was the only sound beside the flat splashing of the fountain.

Laure's anxiety exploded in exasperation. 'Marcel, tell me! What's happened? Are you in trouble?'

He did look up then, briefly, with a rueful hint of a smile. 'In a way.' He paused again, but this time to find the right words before going on. 'You know the friends I go around with at home; Octave Bruard and the others?'

Laure nodded, with a hollow realisation growing in her as to what was coming. 'Disorderly riff raff, bad company,' was her father's view of that particular circle, not all of them artists (Bruard was not), but all linked by extremist political views and dubious morals. She had met most of them, and they had always behaved impeccably towards her, but she knew that as a loyal, if sometimes critical, member of the Imperial administration her father could only view them with disfavour.

'Yes, I know,' she said, and waited.

'Bruard's in prison again.'

'Again! I didn't know he'd been in prison.'

'Oh yes, it's not the first time. I don't quite know what it is this time, but something political of course. There was something else too. I was involved. I suppose you could say we've been indiscreet.'

'Oh Marcel, you fool! Is it a police matter?' She clasped his hand in hers; it felt cold, and she rubbed it between her palms absently, her eyes intent on his troubled face.

'Not yet, I think, but we'll be watched. You know how it is.'

'No I don't. I only know even you agreed that things were much better than they used to be, that the Emperor allows a degree of freedom undreamed of a few years ago. I remember you and Papa were of the same mind about that, for once.'

'I was wrong – it was all an illusion, or most of it.' He turned abruptly from her to stare at the unending aimless fall of the fountain. 'I can't stay here any longer. It is not my home now, not as it was. Everything feels wrong. I want to breathe, freely, without someone watching every step, laying out my path for me. I want to make my own way, as I choose. I know I can't do that if I stay in France.'

Laure stared at his rigid back in its coat of fawn cloth, furred with tiny beads of moisture. She felt as if the chill clamminess of the mist had settled somehow about her heart. 'What you're really saying is that you're bored and restless. It's not the Emperor's police you want to escape, it's Papa.'

After a moment he shrugged. 'I don't know. Perhaps. Whatever it is, I'm going.'

'Where will you go?' she asked dully, from her sense of misery. 'To England?'

'At first perhaps. Where else is there for we French exiles? But I have thoughts of going on to America later.'

She was appalled. 'Oh no! Marcel, it's the other side of the world! We'd never see you again.' She clutched at his arm. 'Oh, don't go! Change your mind, stay here, come and live at Casseuil if you like. I'm sure Philippe wouldn't mind.' She was by no means sure and almost instantly wished the words unsaid, praying that Marcel would not take her up on it – yet she could not bear it if he were to go—

'Don't be silly.' He gave a dry little laugh. 'What on earth would I do with myself here, buried in the country, miles from Paris?'

'It's nearer to Paris than America.'

He shook his head. 'Not really.' It sounded illogical, but she knew what he meant.

'You'll break your heart, so far away.'

'No, I shall simply learn to breathe again – to live for myself, in my own way.'

'But how will you live? You've no skill but your painting.'

He smiled then with a sudden cheerful unconcern, his hands expressive. 'Who knows? We shall see. I shall live somehow, that's all I know.'

She felt as if he had already taken one step on the journey away from her and their shared childhood. 'What of Papa, and Maman? Do they know?'

'Yes.'

The abruptness of his reply told her that the thought hurt him, with memories perhaps of pain on both sides; for the parents he loved and for himself too. It would not be possible, she thought, to tear up your roots so ruthlessly without doing some kind of damage.

'They've accepted it — they know my mind's made up. I told them I wanted to tell you about it myself, but not until after the wedding. I didn't want to spoil it for you. I meant to say before now, but it wasn't easy.'

Laure thought then of the weeks just before her marriage, when she had explained her mother's sudden tears, her father's occasional uncharacteristic gravity, simply as expressions of the natural emotion of parents about to see their only daughter wed. With shame, she realised that she had been so full of herself that she had not even guessed at the unhappiness beneath the celebratory surface.

Marcel stood looking at her, reading on her face how far his news had thrown her from the buoyant mood of the past days; and regretting it. He put an arm about her shoulders. 'Let's walk on a little if you like. Or shall we get lost and never find our way back?'

She had a little vision of herself walking on and on into the mist for ever, quite alone, with no familiar landmark to guide, no loved companion to comfort, no sound, nothing but the completeness of her solitude about her. It was a horrible vision, worse than a nightmare, and she shook it quickly away, moving closer to Marcel, feeling the warmth of his nearness. She was not alone, and the mist would soon lift to let in the sun.

They left the fountain behind, its sound falling away at last, and crossed wet grass under dripping trees, crunched over the gravel of the courtyard, passed beneath the stone arch beside the range of stable buildings onto the track beyond. It was an ordinary workaday track of hard packed earth, pale grey-brown and scattered with paler stones, wide enough for carts to pass along beside the regimented ranks of the vines that marched away from it into the mist, separated from the track only by an edging of low growing rose-bushes.

'We could be anywhere,' Marcel commented as Laure turned aside and led them between the vines. 'One vine looks exactly like another.' After a little while something loomed at them out of the whiteness, something grey, as high as a man. 'What in the name. . . ? Oh, it's this. I remember seeing it yesterday from the road. It looked like a tomb to me. What is it, do you know?'

It *was* a tomb, a solid simple edifice of stone set at the point where the vines ended and the land sloped down to the road that marked the boundary of the Naillac vineyards. They walked round it, reading the simple inscriptions, noting the faded and withered flowers laid upon it, inside the little wall that hemmed it in.

'The Naillac family vault – is that right? But why here, and not in the cemetery like everyone else?'

'Not quite like everyone else,' Laure pointed out. 'Haven't you seen other vaults like this around here? They're Protestant family graves, of course; there have always been many Protestants in the area. Didn't you think of that?'

Marcel's look of puzzlement faded. 'Of course. I was forgetting the Naillacs were Protestants. Though I did wonder to see the *curé* there the other night, and not the Protestant pastor, if there is one.'

'I don't think Philippe's very religious really, nor was his father. Perhaps they needed persecution to keep their faith alive. It's just a family tradition now. But of course Madame is a Catholic. I expect she wanted the *curé* there.'

Marcel gazed a little longer at the tomb. 'I suppose that's why the Naillacs kept their lands – and their heads – at the Revolution. Papa said the Catholic nobles in this region were much hated, on the whole. But most of the Protestants welcomed the Revolution, didn't they? Or perhaps they just kept their heads down and went on quietly tending their vineyards, and no one noticed them.'

Laure laughed. 'Let's go on.'

They walked on, skirting yet more rows of vines, gnarled stems whose heavy foliage was trained on neat wooden supports, the leaves already turning to gold, the fruit heavy beneath their sheltering brightness.

'Tell me,' Marcel asked, 'why do they harvest so late at Casseuil? The *vendange* is well under way everywhere else.'

There were so many deeply important things clamouring to be said. Laure kept thinking, He goes today, I may never see him again. Yet in some odd way it was a relief to avoid those important things, to skim over the surface talking of things that scarcely mattered at all.

'Oh, it's something to do with the kind of wine Philippe

22

makes. To be good, it must be harvested late – it's sweeter that way, I think – and the greatest wines are the ones that are harvested latest of all, so I understand. But it depends on the weather of course. Rain or frost in late autumn could ruin everything.'

'He must have strong nerves then,' said Marcel with feeling. 'If the grapes are ripe, why not harvest them as soon as possible? He said it wasn't going to be a great year anyway.' He stopped to examine the fruit on the nearest vine, the pale gold grapes heavy and full in their skins.

'Oh, I don't know. But there's good reason, Philippe says.'

They crossed the road and the vineyard beyond – not the château's, for these grapes were already picked – and came to a little wood, whose branches reached out suddenly from the mist to clutch at them.

'I think the mist's lifting,' Marcel commented at last. They looked about them. It was lighter, and a tiny breeze was just faintly discernible, stirring the whiteness so that far above they thought for a moment they glimpsed a hint of blue.

A few steps more, and by some weird silent magic the mist wavered, hovered, fled. And it was as if they stood on the edge of creation, watching the world take shape before them. Endlessly it seemed, far into the distance, far below the long slope on which they stood, the plain stretched, scored with vineyards, dotted with windmills and clustered villages and still green ponds, enlivened here and there by the darker mass of a wood, the high vertical spires of Lombardy poplars; on to the line of the Dordogne river marked by what remained of the mist, to the red-grey roofs of the town of Bergerac on its farther bank; on and on beyond until, hazily blue, the hills rose again in the north. From behind, the sun slanted golden over the nearer fields, gold on gold, firing the autumn leaves of the vines, the moisture-hung webs that bound them, the pale earth from which they drew their nourishment, all gold beneath a sky of a blue so pure and so brilliant that it hurt the eyes.

Turning, they could look back at the château itself, set just below the brow of the hill. So Laure had seen it for the first time on that summer morning just over a year ago, and felt then an inexplicable excitement, a sense that here was something important to her, of great significance, though of course she had not known that she was about to meet Philippe. It was a perfect fairy-tale castle, built during the Renaissance just at the moment when men no longer built first and only for defence against an enemy. So it had a hint of battlements, but delicate, ornamental ones edging the steeply pitched roofs of faded red tiles; and towers, four graceful round towers, one rising at each corner of the main mass of the house; and small-paned windows, too wide for defence, but just right to light and air the simply decorated rooms and give fine views from indoors of this vista of vineyards and woods and the distant shining river. Just behind the château the low buildings housing stables and *chai* reached to the little wood that crowned the hill. Out of sight beyond it was the village of Casseuil.

All the last traces of gloom fled from Laure's spirits as if the mist had taken them, as it had first brought them. She felt a joyous beating of the heart, a sense of well-being and rightness so complete that it was almost too much for words.

'I love it here,' she said. 'It's like coming home, as if I'd been meant to live here all my life.'

Marcel looked, a little wistfully, at her radiant face. 'I envy you, Laure. It's so easy for you.'

She slid her arm about his waist. 'It will be for you too, you'll see,' she assured him, all at once supremely confident, about everything.

CHAPTER
TWO

i

'That's right – steady now – good, good . . .' Jean Delisle
nodded approvingly as the golden liquid ran smoothly from
the oak *fût*, in which it had lain slowly maturing for the past
three years, into the clear glass bottle held in the careful hands
of young Aubin Lambert. The lad had come to work as a
labourer at the château only a few months ago, at the age of
fifteen; but he had already shown such intelligence and
promise that the *régisseur* had taken him under his wing and
begun to teach him just a few of the essential processes that
took place within the *chai*. Of course, the boy's father made a
little wine, but most of it was simply for his own consumption
– and, besides, with four older brothers and sisters at home
Aubin's opportunities for learning the craft there must be
slight.

Once the bottle was almost full, the boy turned off the tap
and topped up the liquid from a jug standing nearby, very
gently and carefully, so that there should be no danger of a
sudden overflow. Then the bottle was passed to Moïse
Delmas, his cousin (the people of Casseuil were almost all
interrelated) who operated the gleaming brass-trimmed
machine that inserted the long cork. It was then passed
through the open door to the next room, where Monsieur
Naillac stood at a table supervising the group of men adding
the final touches: the lead capsule that covered the mouth of
the bottle and the elegantly simple label that proclaimed the
name of the château and the date of the vintage. Beyond them,
another man packed the completed bottles into a wooden
crate ready, in due course, to be transported, along with
several crates already packed, down the hill to the quayside

warehouse of Teyssier et Fils, the brokers at Bergerac who were the chief dealers in the château's wines.

'Right now, that's the last. Get yourself off home. You're shaping up nicely.'

The boy nodded, colouring faintly at the praise, and pushed his hat on his curly hair and walked away, running at last up the long flight of steps that led to the door into the courtyard – for the sake of coolness the *chai* was sunk well into the ground. A gleam of light from outside shone briefly white and brilliant, diminishing the brightness of the candle flames by which the remaining men were working, and then was shut out again. When, a moment later, the light gleamed once more, Monsieur Delisle looked up and saw young Madame Laure descending the steps.

'I hope I'm not disturbing you,' she greeted her husband, a little uncertainly, as if something she saw in his expression made her feel herself less than wholly welcome. Jean Delisle found himself wondering sometimes these days . . . She was as pretty as ever, her slender figure exquisite still – as today, in the high-necked princess gown of blue-grey silk, fastened with tiny silk-covered buttons from its braided hem to its demure white collar. Her hair was as gleamingly gold, her skin as creamy fair as when she first came to Casseuil three years ago. Yet there was just a hint of a shadow about the brown eyes, just a suggestion of strain about the pretty mouth and the smooth forehead. Three years, and no sign yet of a child – that, thought Monsieur Delisle, might well be enough to explain it all; and the occasional suspicion of coolness towards her in Monsieur Naillac's manner . . .

'Not at all,' her husband reassured her politely, continuing with deft fingers to apply a label to a bottle. 'We have almost finished, *chérie*. If you return to the house I shall soon be with you.'

If she was aware of it, Madame Laure did not take the hint. Smiling a little defensively, she came slowly towards the table and stood, far enough from it to be out of the way of the men, watching the work in progress. Jean Delisle was struck, as on many occasions before, by the look of attentive interest on her face. For his part, it needed only the faintest gleam of enquiry in the eyes of another to bring all his life-long enthusiasm for

26

his craft to the surface. More than once he had tried to impart some of this enthusiasm to Madame Laure, not without effect, he thought. Sadly, Monsieur Naillac did not seem to notice his wife's eagerness to learn, if such indeed it was. Now, unable to allow any opportunity to pass, Monsieur Delisle moved to her side.

'A good order for Holland,' he explained in a low voice. 'The '65 vintage. It's scarcely ready for bottling, but it will never be a great wine, and our friend in Bergerac seemed to like it. We have a good deal of trade with Holland, you know. Many of our people went there in the 1680s to escape religious persecution, and the links have stayed.'

The last two bottles were labelled, put carefully into the crate, and then one of the men gently hammered the lid into place.

'Does it go to Bergerac first?'

'That's right: in a week or two when it's had time to rest from the bottling. From there it will go by river to Libourne, by means of a *gabarre*, of course.' They had talked before of the wide flat-bottomed boats used for transport down the Dordogne. Laure had watched them often from the quayside in Bergerac. 'From Libourne, they'll be shipped by sea. A long journey, but a Château de Casseuil can take it, of course. A rest at the other end, a little longer to come to full maturity, if our buyer can bear to wait, and there you are.'

'And how long before it's at its best?'

'Ah now, *madame* – that depends. To be sure, one has to try, to taste often, to judge the moment for oneself.' He grinned, and spread his hands. 'But of course, that is not always possible, and one might still miss the moment. This wine I think will be good at seven or ten years. The very best will live and grow for perhaps as long as a man's lifetime, if kept in the very best conditions and securely corked and bottled, naturally. Though at fifteen years or so it may be ready.'

'Like the '47.'

'Like the '47 indeed, *madame*. We have, alas, found an occasional bottle of that vintage which had maderised – turned a little burnt in flavour, darkened to brown – but most of it is still excellent even now.' On impulse, he reached for the jug from which Aubin had topped up the bottles, and poured the remaining wine into a glass.

'Here, *madame* – taste. You will I think see the difference from the '47.'

She held the glass so she could smell the wine, and even before she put it to her lips she knew there was a difference. This lacked the depth of colour, the full honeyed fragrance of the '47. It was brilliantly golden still, and aromatic, but somehow thinner. Sipping, taking in air as she held the wine in her mouth in the way her father had taught her, she found that the flavour was like the scent, good, sweet, greatly pleasurable, but without the heady lusciousness of the other. She swallowed, nodded, drank a little more. 'Yes, I see.'

'Now try just a little of the '67 here. Tell me what you think.'

He drew some from a *fût* further along the orderly row, and waited, watching her intently as she tasted.

'It's – not bad . . .' she said cautiously after a moment. Jean Delisle's mouth twitched into a faint smile, but he said nothing. 'I like the '65 better. This seems very thin. It's not very sweet either, and that's not good when it's young, is it? It needs the sweetness to age well.'

The smile broadened to fullness, and the *régisseur* nodded. 'Exactly so. If you remember, the harvest was poor in '67. We have already sold off most of the vintage for blending, or for making brandy. A wine that is "not bad" is not good enough to carry our label.' He felt, spreading through him, much the same warm sense of pleasure he had when watching young Aubin at work, the pleasure of a good teacher recognising qualities even beyond his expectation in a favourite pupil. 'You know, of course . . .' he was continuing, when a sudden burst of light from the door outlined the figure of Aubin, coming almost as if in answer to his thoughts, his face alight with some excitement, his wooden *sabots* clattering a joyous rhythm down the steps.

The men, clearing away the last of the equipment prior to going home, looked round with interest. Monsieur Naillac retraced his steps from the far doorway, which led to the office of the *chai*, where the vineyard records were kept – each day's work had to be entered there, and each transaction.

'*Monsieur!*' Aubin came to a halt and looked from the *régisseur* to his employer and back again. He was out of breath with running, but very pleased with himself. 'The grapes, the ones near the *caveau* most of all, even since this morning—today has made all the difference . . . I think it's time . . .'

Laure saw the same look of excitement reflected on Monsieur Delisle's face and, with more restraint, in Philippe's dark eyes.

'I'll come,' said Philippe. Monsieur Delisle came too, and Laure, full of curiosity, followed, since everyone appeared to have forgotten about her.

They crossed the courtyard, under the arch, along the track, through the vines where she had walked on that misty morning with Marcel. It was misty today too, but with the gentle autumn haze that bounded each of these late October days, silver moisture shot through with the gold of an apparently eternal sun. Even now, when the sun was low, it had none of the chillness of autumn, only a sweet freshness.

They came to the edge of the field, marked by the roses that bordered all the Casseuil vineyards, and the *caveau*, the family tomb on its little rise above the road. Aubin stopped, bending here and there amongst the vines, pointing eagerly to where the grapes were massed just above the stems, sheltered by the golden autumn foliage. Philippe and Monsieur Delisle moved around too, examining the grapes, exclaiming softly from time to time. Then Laure realised that she had not after all been unobserved, for the *régisseur*, crouching low, turned his head suddenly. 'See, *madame*.'

He had his hand crooked with great gentleness beneath a bunch of grapes, lifting it a little so that she could see it better, and there was such a note of excitement in his voice that she stooped to look with concentrated attention. What she saw brought not pleasure, but a sweeping sense of dismay.

Here were not the smooth rounded golden fruit she expected to see at this time of year, replete with sweetness, although most of the grapes had that familiar reassuring appearance. But among them whole clusters of fruit had an appalling look of disease and decay, some soft and purple in colour, some dark purple-brown, the worst shrunk, shrivelled, covered with a dusting of ugly grey-brown spores.

29

A strong smell rose from them, not unpleasant perhaps, heady and sweet, but with the inevitable taint of decay.

'Oh, what is it? Is it mildew? Or – oh, it's not, is it? That new disease, the phylloxera.' She gazed at Monsieur Delisle with eyes wide and appalled, and saw him smile. Behind him, Philippe, overhearing, laughed aloud, though not unkindly.

'*Petite idiote*, of course it's not! It's what we long for year after year.'

Monsieur Delisle stood up. 'A gift from God, *madame*,' he said with reverence in his voice. 'The one thing that makes a great wine, but comes alas too rarely – and even then cannot always be won for our use. It comes only when we have such an autumn as this, and if the weather holds, for three weeks, four, longer perhaps – then . . .' He broke off, his hands gesturing the inadequacy of words to express his feelings.

Laure shook her head in continued bewilderment. 'But what is it? They look rotten to me.'

'So they are indeed, *madame*. But this is no common rottenness. This is the *pourriture noble*, the noble rot. *Botrytis cinerea* the scientists call it. But whatever you call it, from this alone comes the great wine of Casseuil, and only from this. These grapes alone will be gathered first.' He pointed to the most shrivelled fruit. 'Then each day as more fall to the rot they will be harvested, until we have them all.'

'So the *vendange* begins in the morning.' Philippe's tone invested the words with all the resonance of a trumpet call. Aubin grinned and, looking round, Laure saw that the other men, who had followed at a distance, were grinning too.

When the men had gone on their way, the three of them remaining began to walk slowly back towards the house. Philippe slipped his arm about Laure, and she felt a tremor of happiness. It was so long since he had shown such spontaneous warmth towards her, so long since she had felt he wanted her.

'I knew this had to be a good year, right from the start,' he told her, though she wondered on what he could have based such optimism. 'Here at last, if the weather holds – and it will, it must! – we shall have a wine to pass on to our children and our grandchildren!'

The overflowing infectiousness of his delight, already

reaching her, fell short then, leaving her cold. She looked away from him, so that he should not see the hurt in her face. How could he! Did he not know what he was saying?

The sense of failure that lately had become, like the pain of a decaying tooth, a constant nagging part of her, returned in force, flaring into new and bitter life. Angry and hurt, she shook off Philippe's enclosing arm. He came to a halt, allowing Monsieur Delisle to walk on ahead a little way.

'Laure, what is it? What's wrong?'

She shrugged. Surely he must know: he was not stupid. Careless perhaps, or had he spoken like that because he deeply resented her failure, subtly reproaching her because she had not given him the longed-for son? He could not really believe there was much hope now of children. Three years was a long time, and there had been not the slightest sign. Barren, she thought, close to tears. I am barren. Stiffly, she walked on, saying nothing; and Philippe seemed to attribute her mood to some inexplicable quirk of the female temperament, which he could not begin to understand, for when she had said nothing for some little time he shrugged in his turn and hurried on to discuss tomorrow's arrangements with Monsieur Delisle.

ii

The household woke earlier than usual next day, stirred into life well before the morning angelus. By the time Monsieur Naillac was sitting down to breakfast in the *petit salon*, great pots of *saugrenade*, a rich stew of bacon, beans and garlic, were already bubbling away gently over the fire in the kitchen, ready to sustain the *vendangeurs*. The air was stinging with the scent of mounds of onions and garlic chopped for the *tourin*, the traditional soup; noisy with the clatter of feet on stone and the calling of instructions from one to another of the hierarchy of kitchen staff, under the watchful and astringent eye of old Madame Naillac. Simple red wine was set in jugs on a table here; bread, crusty and warm, laid ready there; the dairy had been checked to ensure there was cheese enough; the round cellar room beneath the south-east tower opened to reveal hams and other meats waiting in the coolness until they should be needed.

Outside in the misty dawn the *vendangeurs* came, men and

31

women and a few older children, about eighty in all, members of the same families that for generations had supplied the château with skilled labourers at harvest time: the Delmas's, the Lamberts, the Vergnolles, the Martins, the Foussacs, the Bertauds, the Frangeas's, the Chassaings, the Coudercs; wives and children and grandchildren of peasant farmers and small-holders, proud of the part they played in making a renowned wine, and glad too of the annual opportunity to add to the family income. In the courtyard they gathered and talked quietly, but with an air of subdued excitement, waiting for the moment when the sun should disperse the mist and dry the dew from the grapes. Nearby, carts were already laden with the *comportes*, the deep two-handled wooden containers into which the picked grapes would later be poured, and two men were leading out the oxen to be yoked. In the *chai*, Monsieur Delisle made his last checks on the condition of the press – clean and working smoothly, as he knew it would be – and of the *cuves*, empty, scrubbed, purified with sulphur candles some weeks ago. He wandered restlessly about in the unbear-able tension of these moments before work could begin, as of every idle moment through the coming weeks, until the *vendange* should come to an end. Monsieur Naillac, equally as tense, glancing out of the window now and then with anxious and fearful eyes, turned to a new page in the record book, entered the date, Tuesday October 12th 1869, and gnawed at his pen. Perhaps, thought Jean Delisle, watching him through the open door of the office, he was remembering an earlier entry in his father's writing, at just this moment many years ago. 'Rain', it had said. That was all, just 'rain'. Nothing had followed, because there had been nothing to follow, only more rain. And that, after just such an autumn as this, so full of promise. In a matter of days the grapes had moulded and rotted, not nobly, but disastrously, beyond any hope of using them even for distilling or blending. It was, Jean Delisle reflected, a mad way to make wine, so precariously that each step was a gamble, the dream of perfection weighed against the only too real possibility of no harvest at all – nothing; or everything. Years like '67 were easier of course, in a way. The cool unsettled weather of summer and autumn had left no doubt that there would be no *pourriture noble*, and

32

there could be no disappointment, because there had been no expectations. Yet even now in this moment of greatest anxiety the *régisseur* remembered the sense of depression he had felt as they had embarked on that *vendange*. No, for him there was no other way . . .

Outside, the sky was clear, the oxen yoked. Monsieur Naillac looked up from his books, glanced towards the *régisseur*, who nodded; and the two of them walked together into the yard where the *vendangeurs* waited. 'Let us begin,' said Jean Delisle.

Florestine, Madame Laure's maid, who regarded herself as rather above the hurly burly, crossed the hall some hours later taking one of her mistress's gowns back upstairs after giving it a brief airing out of doors. Sylvestre, the *valet de chambre*, with whom she carried on a kind of routine flirtation without substance, greeted her cheerfully. 'We find ourselves a little unwanted today, do we not? All this activity, and you and I are forced into idleness.'

'I could bear a little idleness, if you couldn't,' Florestine retorted. 'Just give me the chance, that's all.'

'Madame Laure keeps you busy then?'

'You'd be amazed how much work it requires to ensure the leisure of one fine lady.'

'A very lovely sweet lady though,' observed Sylvestre thoughtfully, looking down at the garment the maid held and fingering the lavish folds of dove grey tulle falling over a silk under-robe of a soft rose colour. 'She looked delicious all dressed up in this to go out to dinner last week.'

'Oh, she looks very fine, no doubt about that. A great ornament to the château with all her pretty clothes. But what else is she, tell me that? Nothing. If she went away tomorrow no one would even notice the difference, would they now?'

Sylvestre shrugged. 'You have a point perhaps. But it's not her fault. Think how it was last winter when Madame was ill – just a day or two, and then all at once Madame Laure took charge as if she was born to it. Not like Madame upstairs, of course – quieter, more gentle – but you knew she was in control, and everything went smoothly.'

'It didn't last did it? No sooner was Madame about again

than my mistress went back to her sitting about and her shopping – and that though Madame has never been quite as well as she used to be.'

Sylvestre grinned ruefully. 'Would you like to try opposing Madame when she wants to do something? Besides, I heard Monsieur Naillac tell Madame Laure it was good for his mother to be active and occupied again, and that she should be glad to hand back her duties to the old woman. Admit it, Florestine, you're just put out because old Antoinette can look down on you. She's Madame's maid, and Madame's in charge, so she's superior, she thinks. It makes you feel unimportant.'

'So what? Don't I have a right to complain? You know Antoinette, with her high and mighty ways; she thinks she's better than any of us. I think she models herself on Madame.'

Teasingly Sylvestre ran a finger down her cheek. 'Ah, poor Florestine! Never mind, maybe Madame Laure's day will come, and you will be able to turn the tables on Antoinette. If there should be a child now . . .'

Unwilling to be soothed, Florestine tossed her head. 'Then I'd have a nursemaid to put up with too. Anyway, it's not likely to happen. It's my belief she doesn't really want children. How could she wear all these expensive gowns with a big belly? And as for little fingers clinging to her skirts – can you imagine it?'

'Oh, now you are being unfair! Anyway, if children come, they come.'

'That's what you think.' Her expression was arch. 'There are ways of stopping them, you know.'

'Have you no work to do, that you stand gossiping in the hall?'

Florestine turned sharply, disconcerted to find that Antoinette had come soft-footed down the stairs. She wondered how much the other maid had heard of what was, after all, a most improper form of gossip about her employer. 'Mind your own business,' she retorted, but did nevertheless set off towards the stairs. She had scarcely reached them before Sylvestre called her back.

'I forgot. There's a letter for Madame Laure. You could take it up to her.'

'It's not just my mistress I keep in idleness,' Florestine complained with a grudging smile. But she took the letter and walked past Antoinette with her head high.

Laure had not wanted to be idle today. She had got up when Philippe did, certain that there must be something for her to do now the harvest had begun. In previous years there had not, but then this was an exceptional year. The *vendangeurs* would be picking with the laborious selectivity that Monsieur Delisle had described, working day after day to bring in only the most rotted fruit, each day's small store to be pressed of the little juice that remained to it after the mould had done its work: the long patient careful toil of weeks to come. Surely there would be no idle hands at Casseuil this year?

She was wrong.

'This is not the moment for inexperienced people to be underfoot,' Madame Naillac said firmly. 'We shall none of us have time to instruct you. Better to occupy yourself usefully in your room.'

Laure did not say, 'But what is there for me to do in my room?' She knew there was no point. Arguing with Madame Naillac led nowhere and only brought Philippe's disapproval on her head. So, her bitter sense of failure increased just that little more, she retreated to her room, to read and draw and gaze out of the window at the small figures of the *vendangeurs* moving amongst the vines on the slopes below the garden, their robust singing reaching her faintly on the sunlit air.

I am nothing, she thought. A spoilt child who is not a child any more. Only I am not allowed to be a woman.

She had come here with such hopes. Her mother had instructed her carefully in her wifely duties, warmly and with tenderness. 'You will be your husband's partner and companion, as well as the woman he loves. Do your best to understand his work and help and support him in it all you can. That is important, just as much as the smooth running of the household. It will strengthen your marriage and make it truly happy. I know, *chérie*, for I have found it so myself.'

It should have been easy, for everything about the vineyard fascinated her, from the tiny fragile rooted cuttings, planted out in the spring to replace, in the course of time, those vines that had grown too old to be productive, to the row upon row of bottles stored in the darkest recesses of the *chai*, full of the golden wine for which they all toiled. All except herself, that is.

She did not even have the comfort of Philippe's passionate lovemaking these days; or not very often. It was still good, when it came. But she knew her failure to give him a child had offended him, cooled his passion, turned him away from her. She wondered if he still loved her at all. He was kind to her, and polite, but there was a distance between them. Perhaps it had always been there and she had not noticed it before, when he had been so lovingly attentive. Sometimes these days she felt it was almost like living with a stranger. What did they have, when physical passion had gone? In her worst moments she found herself thinking, A lifetime like this, so empty, and she grew frightened.

She could not keep her mind on her reading this morning and she did not feel like drawing. At the best of times she hated sewing, and to look out of the window only made her sense of uselessness the more intense. Downstairs in the *grand salon* stood the piano upon which she could play inaccurately but with vigour – that often helped. Or the dogs might be there, bored too like herself, and enthusiastically responsive to any sign of affection. 'That's more use than sitting up here,' she told herself, crossing to the door.

Florestine, coming in at that moment, was at the door before her. 'A letter, *madame*,' she said.

From her parents, in Paris: Laure took it eagerly, opening it, reading with a sudden upsurge of cheerfulness. She had not told them of her unhappiness, for she did not quite know where to begin, and when she thought of putting it into words it seemed nothing very much, coming down only to the simple, sad fact of her childlessness. She did not want to write about that. So she told them about her rides, and her sketching expeditions, and her talks with Monsieur Delisle, and the dinners and dances at the houses of neighbours; and the gossip, and the occasional shopping trips to Bordeaux, which Philippe visited often both on wine business and because the family lawyer, an old friend of his mother, lived there. 'Bordeaux is much better than I expected,' Laure had written to her parents after her first visit. 'Such magnificent buildings, and excellent shops. I have three lovely new gowns; not quite like those of Worth, perhaps, but very pretty,' and she had gone on to describe them in detail. A new gown could sometimes, she found, distract her briefly from her unhappiness, and Philippe liked to see her looking her best and was full of compliments when she did so.

Her parents, in their turn, kept her informed about all her friends in Paris, and about the art exhibitions and the concerts, the opera, the good talk, the political events – it was like being again at their table in the elegant house in the rue St Honoré. Today, though, they had news of Marcel. He was not a good correspondent, so they heard from him rarely and briefly. He had, Laure knew, spent very little time in England on leaving France – 'The climate is terrible,' he had said. 'It rains all the time – and the people! So cold, so polite!' – and had soon set sail for America. Apart from a brief note from New York, full of uninformative high spirits, that was the last anyone had heard of him for over two years.

Now, wrote Laure's mother, they had another letter at last. '. . . And can you imagine, *chère* Laure, he has become a countryman! He met with André, a fellow Frenchman, in New York, who told him there was land to be had for the asking in the southern states since the Civil War left so much devastation. And so there they are, partners on a small farm on the northern borders of Arkansas, close to Missouri. They even think of growing vines. But you know our dear Marcel. I detect a little discontent with the unvarying horizons. He writes of an improvement he has made to a plough much used over there. He has great hopes, he says, and plans a trip to New York to see if he can find someone willing to invest in it. I have a feeling that once there he will find he is, after all, a city man – but perhaps I misjudge him. It all sounds so unlike our dear Marcel.'

It did indeed, thought Laure, bemusedly trying to imagine her brother, the painter, the idealist, the eager talker, as either farmer or businessman. For a moment the little sadness that his absence had left her with grew and intensified to a swamping sense of loss. He had gone for ever, the Marcel she knew, her companion and friend. If only she had found someone to take his place it would not matter so much.

But taken all in all, the letter cheered her, and she was almost at her brightest when lunch-time came.

Her companions, unfortunately, were not. Philippe, restless and ill-at-ease away from his vines at this crucial time, was irritable and abstracted and said little; whilst his mother was at her most forbidding. Now and then, Laure caught a critical stare directed at her from her mother-in-law's sharp eyes, which made her wonder what offence she had committed. It was possible to offend in all innocence, for even now there were times when youth and inexperience caused her to overstep some invisible boundary of Madame Naillac's making. The easy tolerance of her home, where manners were based simply on consideration for the feelings of others, was not enough for Philippe's mother. At Casseuil, the rules were more rigid, and far more numerous, almost as if she were back at school again. One kept a 'proper' distance from the servants, and one never performed for oneself any menial task that could be done by a servant; one did not wander alone and uninvited into the *chai* or through the vineyard (a rule that Laure disobeyed as much as she dared); one did not sit idly talking when one's hands could be occupied with needlework; one did not (if one was a woman) intrude one's own opinion when the men discussed politics or religion or some other serious matter; in fact one must exert oneself to conceal any trace of intelligence or learning (not, Laure suspected, that Madame Naillac thought her daughter-in-law possessed either of these attributes).

And then, of course, there was her greatest offence of all, her childlessness: very likely that was the trouble now. Laure braced herself inwardly for one of those barbed remarks that scattered the older woman's conversation from time to time. Wistfully, 'Oh, to hold my grandson in my arms!' Casually, talking of the plain and sensible daughter of a neighbouring Protestant family, 'She was considered as a bride for Philippe, but there were obstacles. However, he could have done worse, as it turns out. She has already given her husband three fine sons.' Sharply (and mystifyingly) 'You think too much of clothes, Laure. Perhaps if your mind had been more profitably occupied you might have given Philippe a son by now.'

But today the conversation remained general and uncontroversial, if chilly. It was only at the end of the meal when, normally, they would have retired to the *grand salon* for coffee, that Madame Naillac said suddenly, 'I wish to talk with you in my room, Laure.' Her tone permitted no argument.

Laure glanced towards Philippe, but he was already on his way to the *grand salon* and did not even appear to have heard his mother; or perhaps he chose not to. Full of foreboding, Laure followed the severe figure of Madame Naillac up four flights of stairs to the second floor where the older woman had established herself at her husband's death in the south-west corner under the roof. From the landing a door led into her sitting-room, from which a long window opened onto a narrow walk right round the battlements of the château. Beyond the sitting-room her bedroom gave access to the little tower room where Antoinette slept.

To enter these rooms from the unadorned simplicity of the rest of the château, where the ornaments were few and classical in style, the paintings chiefly family portraits, the furniture solid and a little rustic, was to enter another world. Not that Madame Naillac indulged herself as far as furnishings were concerned: there were no concessions to comfort in the hard wooden chairs, the oak cupboards and wardrobes, the polished uncarpeted floorboards, the uncurtained bed of finely grained walnut. But everywhere, on walls, shelves, wherever one looked, were reminders of the fervent Catholicism so alien to Casseuil: paintings full of frenzied activity, tormented saints, angelic choruses, madonnas with eyes raised heavenwards; crucifixes of many styles and sizes hung above a prie-dieu here, over a writing desk or a doorway there; missals and a variety of devotional works, many beautifully bound, ranged on shelves or laid on a bedside table for nightly contemplation; little statues, carved and painted and set in a niche or on a shelf with flowers and candles before them. The overpowering emotional impact of it all made an odd contrast, Laure had often thought, with the chilly austerity of its occupant.

The full force of that coldness was turned upon her now. Madame Naillac led the way into the sitting-room, crossed to the fireplace – empty, since she lit a fire only on the coldest winter day – and there, very upright, as if her silver-topped ebony cane was an ornament and not a support, she turned to face her daughter-in-law. 'Close the door, if you please. I have something to say which is not for other ears.'

Laure, obeying her, wondered if Antoinette might be listening from the bedroom. Whatever Madame's views on the treatment of servants, it seemed sometimes as if she regarded Antoinette as in some way a kind of extension of herself, exempted by nature from the usual rules. The next moment, as she faced her mother-in-law, holding her head high to conceal any sign of apprehension, all thought of Antoinette was driven from her mind.

'Are you taking measures?'

The question was abrupt, the tone hostile in the extreme, and Laure had no idea at all what Madame Naillac was talking about. She stared at her, trying to make sense of the words, wondering even to what area of her life the older woman was referring. After a time, Madame Naillac seemed to realise she had not made herself clear, for she repeated the question in more explicit terms.

'To prevent a child – are you taking measures to that end?'

Dimly, still not quite understanding, Laure began to wonder if she might indeed have 'taken measures' unknowingly, if something she had done could explain her childlessness. 'I don't think so, *madame*. I want a child so much.'

'What do you mean, you don't think so? You must know whether or not you have done anything to prevent a child. I know many young women do so, whatever the Church may have to say on the matter. Utter selfishness and depravity, to want their own comfort before children. I know you have your little vanities, and coming from Paris as you do, one never knows.'

Shocked, appalled at what the older woman seemed to be saying, Laure felt her colour grow and spread, and then slowly fade again, leaving her paler than usual. Looking at the severe features before her she felt an unaccustomed distaste at these indications of a knowledge of secret practices previously undreamed of, at the disgust in the other woman's eyes, at the realisation that Madame Naillac could think so of her. And then she felt a furious upsurge of anger.

'I would never, never do that! I want a child more than anything else in the world – more than you do, more than Philippe does – and not just so Casseuil has an heir: for itself, to love, to have something of my very own.' Then not waiting to be dismissed she turned and ran, stumbling, half blinded by tears, down the stairs to seek sanctuary in her room.

The tears were not so much of pain as of anger, a stinging anger at the hostile probing which had so cruelly exposed the most vulnerable part of herself. 'How dare she think that of me! How dare she ask! How can she not see how much I care?'

She flung herself on the bed weeping and drumming on the pillow with her fists in a furious outburst that had in it all the hurt and loneliness and bitter resentment of the past months, so long suppressed and held in check.

At last, exhausted, she lay still, face down, the anger succeeded by a sudden weary depression of spirits that left her without the will to move or even to think. She had not stirred when, a little later, Philippe came to change into his working clothes to return to the vineyard. With a murmur of concern he sat down on the bed beside her and put his arm about her. '*Chérie*, what is it? Are you ill?'

The warmth of his tone set her tears flowing again, but she sat up and tried to bring herself under control. This time at least, she thought, he must be on her side. So she told him all that had happened upstairs – a little shyly, because she was not used to discussing intimate matters with him – and waited for his arm to close further about her, to draw her to him so that she could find comfort against his chest, held in his strong embrace.

Instead, he heard her in silence and then moved back a little, setting his hands on her shoulders, and looked down at her. He spoke very gently, very kindly, but with just a hint of reproach in his voice. 'You must not speak of my mother like that, *chérie*. She acts always from the highest principles and the warmest feelings, and you must never forget the respect you owe to her. She wants the best for us both, you know.'

He had failed her. She stood up, her tears dried now to

nothing but stains upon her cheeks. 'For you perhaps, yes,' she said bitterly. 'But not for me.'

She turned away and walked to her sitting-room and closed the door behind her, shutting him out. And then she changed into her riding habit – a new one, of bright blue-green trimmed with black velvet – wondering all the time if in a moment Philippe would come to make his peace with her. But he did not, and so when she was ready she left her room by the other door.

There seemed to be no one about in the stables – presumably everyone was busy elsewhere; but in any case Laure, taught by her father, knew quite well how to saddle a horse herself. Madame Naillac would not have approved, but then that was not a consideration that was likely to carry very much weight with Laure just at the moment. It gave her some satisfaction too to know that the older woman would likewise not have approved of her intention to ride alone. But she could not have borne with any company in her present mood; or only the affectionate welcoming company of her beloved Fine Fleur, the beautiful dappled grey mare she had brought with her from Paris. It was a pain to think now of those Sunday rides with her father in the Bois de Boulogne, talking, arguing, laughing . . .

She rode out under the archway and along the road over the crest of the hill. The village was emptied today of half its population; the animals – chickens, geese, a couple of goats, a stray pig – wandered and grazed and scratched their way as usual over the uneven surface of the market place, but the café was deserted and no human being crossed the road or gathered to talk by the stream where the women did their washing. The hazy sunlit air was heavy with the fragrance of fermenting fruit, overpowering the customary everyday odours of dung heaps and cooking and woodsmoke. It was not only the Naillacs who made the precious Casseuil wine; many smaller vineyards within the boundaries of the commune did so as well, though never with quite the same success, so it was said. But as she left the village behind, Laure could see other workers amongst the vines that covered the slopes on all sides, some still lingering over their midday meal, others already at work again along the rows.

A windmill stood on the highest point of the undulating ridge of which Casseuil was a part, and there Laure drew rein to gaze out over the vast expanse of countryside below. Even in her unhappiest moments she never tired of this view. Here, a tiny speck gazing into the blue distance, she could almost imagine that somewhere to the east, if it were just a little clearer, she would be able to see the Dordogne river springing to life as a tiny mountain stream; or to the west, flowing wide and tranquil into the estuary of the Gironde and so on into the turbulent waters of the Atlantic. Somehow it put everything into perspective, exhilarating and consoling her at once.

Below the mill the road wound its way steeply down to the plain, passing the long low house at Trissac where Henri Séguier lived. Gently she urged her mare on.

Henri Séguier was riding too; or, rather, mounted on a big brown gelding he was instructing his five-year-old son Victor as the child sat solemnly astride a tiny white pony. He had been only two when his father had first lifted him into the saddle, and from the beginning had been entirely unafraid. Henri was proud of what he saw as a natural aptitude in his son. Today, having spent a little time correcting the boy's posture, he and Victor set out side by side along the straight poplar-shaded drive towards the road. They reached it just as Madame Laure Naillac was passing the Trissac vineyards.

Henri, who had been intending to turn left ahead of her, drew rein instead to wait for her to come up, removing his hat, smiling a welcome. Delicious little woman, that tiny waist emphasised by the close fitting jacket, her small breasts swelling enticingly beneath the bright fabric! He felt desire stir in him, as it always did in her presence, but more strongly than ever. Of course, since Victor's birth his wife had become progressively more unwell and was now wholly bedridden, and he had long since had to make other arrangements to satisfy his needs – a pretty young chambermaid here at Trissac, a girl in Libourne, another tucked away on a farm somewhere north of Bergerac – but that was not quite the same, for they were common sense transactions, more routine and mundane even than the selling of a cask of wine. Oh to have Philippe Naillac's luck, and find himself night after night with little Laure in his bed! He'd soon give her back the sweet glowing softness that had once been so much a part of her and now had faded a little – give her a child too, if that was what she wanted, for he'd proof right here beside him of his own potency.

'Good day, *monsieur*. How is Madame Séguier?'

Startled, confused because his thoughts had become very specific, pleasurably so, he coloured a little, realising that she had halted before him and turned upon him that entrancing smile . . . What a delicious little hat, that concoction of black velvet and blue-green feathers set on her golden hair. . . ! With an effort he assumed an expression of mournful regret.

'Sadly, she is no better, *madame*. Dr Rossillon is not optimistic, but we do not lose hope.'

Her dark eyes were warmly sympathetic. 'Oh no, you must never do that.' Her glance moved (a pity!) from Henri to the child. 'Is this your little Victor I've heard so much about? You ride very well, *mon petit.*'

Victor, a sturdy child with thick brown hair and eyes of a flat light brown colour, looked back at her without enthusiasm, as if resenting her interruption of their ride.

'Say thank you to Madame Naillac, Victor!'

'Thank you, *madame*.' To Henri's regret it was the only response Victor would make to her friendly attempt at conversation; Henri wanted everything about him to make a good impression on Madame Laure.

'The *vendange* has begun at Casseuil then? It could be a good year if the weather holds, one of the best even.' He did not really mind what he found to talk about, so long as he was able to keep her here with her attention focused on him. 'Of course, for me with my red wine it's been a little too hot for the very best – the grapes were a trifle scorched. But as I don't claim to make a great wine, that's no particular loss to me.' He asked after old Madame Naillac, and Monsieur Philippe, even after Philippe's new horse, Grand Turc (that was another possession of Philippe's he would give a king's ransom for) and finally, having exhausted every possible topic and realising that Laure – surely she could not be a little bored? – was about to ride on, he reached out and took her free hand in his. She wore no gloves and the hand was tiny, slender, beautiful: he stroked it as he talked, thrilling to the sensation, imagining

44

how the rest of her skin must feel, so white, so soft and smooth to the touch.

He was disappointed when, gently but firmly, she freed her hand; but then perhaps he had, a little, exceeded the bounds of propriety, and she was a well brought up young woman. He resigned himself to accepting her words of parting and watching her ride away. He knew the thought of her would feed his imagination for a long time to come.

iii

As if by a miracle – and to Jean Delisle it was always a miracle, however often it happened – the weather held, on past Le Toussaint (the feast of All Saints on November the first) and on, and on. One night down on the plain there was a touch of frost, but it did not reach Casseuil, and the next day the very last grapes were picked and carried in the *comportes* to the waiting press.

There were still a few late roses on the bushes edging the vineyard, and the *régisseur* cut one and handed it to Madame Laure when, wanting to share in the general rejoicing, she came into the *chai* on that last day.

'To celebrate the ending of the *vendange, madame*,' he said.

She laughed and took the rose and tucked it into a buttonhole at her breast, where it glowed against the blue watered silk of her gown. 'I've often wondered why we grow all those roses – now I know!'

'Ah no, *madame* – they have a serious purpose. Did you not know? You see, the rose is perhaps the only plant even more susceptible to disease than the vine, so if we find an ailing rose in the vineyard then we know we must take measures quickly to protect the vines.'

'I see! And I thought it was just because they looked pretty!'

'We are not quite such dreamers, *madame* – even here at Casseuil.' He smiled at her, a smile full of his overflowing joy in the *vendange*, lighting up his lean dark face, transforming it. 'If you have come in search of Monsieur Naillac, I believe you will find him in the office. Aubin, perhaps you would go and tell Monsieur that Madame is here.'

Aubin, looking resentful, let his arms fall from the high, heavy beam which he – together with two others – was turning to work the *pressoir*; but Laure said hastily, 'No – no, please – I'll go and find him in a moment,' and the boy returned thankfully to his laborious but satisfying task.

Laure stood looking down at the aromatic juice – the must – collecting in the trough below the *pressoir*, and then, in a logical progression of thought, across at the great oak *cuves* that marched in solid ranks into the dim recesses of the *chai*. 'Will the fermentation have begun?'

Aubin cast her a glance full of contempt for the silly ignorance of Paris-bred women. Jean Delisle merely smiled with gentle amusement. 'Come and see,' he said.

He propped a short ladder against one of the *cuves* and held it steady while she climbed up and looked in. The smell – a curious fierce smell, quite unlike the fragrance of mature wine – caught at her throat; but it was what she saw that held her mesmerised. The solid boards of the *cuves*, bound round with whiplash cords made from sappy young wood, had given no hint in their solidity of the turmoil within. Below her eyes a seething turbulent mass of pale froth whirled about the *cuve* like a living thing, with such force, such wild vigour that she would not have believed it possible had she not seen it for herself. She balanced there on the ladder gazing and gazing in utter fascination; and when at last she began to descend her eyes were bright with excitement. 'It's wonderful, *monsieur*!' She accepted his support for the last step. 'How long does it go on for?'

'That depends, *madame*, on the temperature, the quality of the must, many factors; and of course it will continue to ferment more gently even after the first fury has subsided. But it will remain like this for several days.'

'And do you just wait for it to stop?'

'Not always. A good *vigneron* must be always watchful, tasting, checking that nothing goes wrong – too much fermentation, you see, and we have dry wine, or even vinegar. But in a good year like this, with such an abundance of sugar in the grapes, then there is no risk of that – '

'Be careful. There are those who say women in the *chai* endanger the wine.' She turned to see Philippe coming towards them, but he was smiling with all the relaxed and tender charm of the old days, and she smiled back at him.

'Do they?'

'Ah, but Madame's presence can only have the most beneficial of effects!' said Monsieur Delisle gallantly.

Philippe took his wife's arm. 'Of course – how could it be otherwise?' Laure's heart was singing when, a little after, they walked back to the house together.

iv

'What shall I wear, Philippe? This gown might be best.' She tugged at the soft heavy folds of green velvet which hung in the wardrobe. 'But I wore it for last year's harvest supper.'

Philippe's smile of amusement was tinged, just a little, with irritation; or so it seemed to Laure. 'Do you suppose anyone will remember – or care?' he asked. 'After all, the peasants only ever have one best outfit to their name.' But he came to her side and lifted out a more recent acquisition, of heavy silk in a warm, soft blue, trimmed with cream lace. 'Wear this. The weather's warmer than it was last year, and it'll be hot in that crowd. Besides, it's a more sensible style for dancing.'

'Shall we dance then, this year?' Laure's eyes sparkled. In previous years they had gone to bed as soon as the supper was over, leaving the *vendangeurs* to dance alone.

'Of course, if you think you can manage a bourrée or two.' The brief hint of ill humour had gone; his eyes, meeting hers, were full of a bright intimacy that made her heart beat faster.

'You'll have to teach me,' she said, a little breathlessly, as if she implied something much more tender and personal than lay on the surface of the words.

Then Philippe rang for Florestine to help her dress, and the moment passed.

In the kitchen the *vendangeurs* were already gathering at the long tables where each day's lunch had been served. The vaulted roof echoed with the noise of their laughter and talk, and the air was hot and heavy with the aromas of close-packed bodies, southernwood (the plant used to preserve stored clothes from moths), and the various dishes waiting over the fire or on adjacent tables to be served. At a chilly distance, Madame Naillac supervised the arrangements for the evening,

47

but Philippe – pausing only to greet his mother with a light kiss – led Laure to the vacant seats beside Monsieur Delisle, right in the middle of that happy throng.

Laure felt more than a little bewildered. She had been three years at Casseuil now, and she knew most of the permanent vineyard workers by sight, and several by name; but she knew none of them well, and the many extra workers who were employed at busy times throughout the year – and especially now, for the *vendange* – were almost completely unknown to her. As she took her seat on the bench, smiling brightly, a chorus of comment greeted her from the men and women closest to her. Their expressions were friendly, their tone warm and welcoming, but since most spoke in the incomprehensible local patois (a little like Spanish to her northern ears) and the few who spoke French had an accent almost as impenetrable, she had no idea what was being said. She laughed a little nervously, and smiled the more, and then glanced at Philippe, imploring his help; but he was engaged in conversation on his own account and did not look her way. She was beginning to feel just a little hurt by his neglect of her, when Jean Delisle, on her other side, leaned over to murmur a translation or two; and from then on appointed himself both interpreter and guide.

'. . . That's Jacques Lambert, brother of Aubin, whom you know,' he whispered, as a well-made, bronzed young man, his eyes openly appreciative, said something to her, laughing as he did so. 'He says you are fit to be queen of the *vendange*, with your hair the colour of the wine.'

As Laure blushed a little and smiled her appreciation of the compliment, she saw how the girl next to Jacques nudged and scolded him good humouredly. Laure did not need the *régisseur*'s, 'That's Jacques's girl, Nanon Foussac' to tell her that the large, rather plain young woman was a little jealous.

'Over there, that's Aubin's sister, Suzanne – she's just married to Robert Martin, beside her there.'

'The man who runs the café?'

'That's right. And that's Jeanne Vergnolles, his sister, with her husband – the one with the baby. You may have seen her with the child in the vineyard.'

The supper began with soup, hot and richly flavoured,

ladled into wide soup plates, without rims so that the diners could, afterwards, as they said, *'faire chabrol'*. That local custom, as Laure knew by now, involved pouring wine into the last remnants of the soup, stirring it about and drinking it all from the bowl. Now and then some unfortunate guest at their table in the dining-room upstairs had shown his ignorance of social niceties by enjoying a *chabrol* under the cold eye of Madame Naillac, who wholly disapproved of bringing such peasant customs into polite company.

The *vendangeurs*, of course, had no such inhibitions. Exuberant, noisy, happy; they talked, laughed, shouted, and above all ate with wholehearted enjoyment. A *pot au feu* of meat and vegetables followed the soup, and then a fricassée of rabbit, roast mutton fragrant with garlic and herbs, cheese and the lavish local tart of flaky pastry and fruit soaked in armagnac. Laure savoured them all and learned from her neighbour and began to understand a little of what was said to her. The mass of strange and scarcely-known faces began to separate into a gathering of individuals, people much like Madame Naillac and Philippe, tied to this place by kinship and work and tradition, rooted here for generations, as she alone was not.

It was not, now, the *vendangeurs* who made her feel a lingering sense of isolation, but Philippe himself. Throughout the meal he talked to those around him, often with animation; but he addressed scarcely a remark to Laure, except when absolutely necessary.

Afterwards, as they crossed the courtyard in the damp chill of the night to where lamps glowed in the carriage house, Laure murmured to him, 'Why are you so cold to me? Everyone must have seen.'

He came to an abrupt halt and looked down at her in mild surprise. 'There was nothing to see. I am not cold at all. You imagine it.'

She shook her head vehemently. Suddenly, all the miseries and resentments of the past months bubbled to the surface and she knew she would even risk a quarrel to bring them into the open. She had borne it all in silence for too long.

'I imagine nothing, Philippe. You are so moody and distant, for days and days sometimes. I don't know what to do

49

to please you. I thought it was going to be better today; I thought you were happy and loving again. And then – now – ' She broke off, feeling close to tears.

'It is all in your imagination, Laure. I am very busy; I have a great deal to do – I can't always be hanging around you. I have a duty to others, you know.' Then he added gently, 'That doesn't mean I'm angry with you, or that I don't love you.'

That last assurance moved and consoled her. Perhaps he was right, and she was imagining things. She stood on tiptoe to kiss him, and he put an arm about her and said with sudden eagerness, 'Let's go and dance – listen, they've already started. You will love this dancing.'

The vigorous wheezy music of vielle and bagpipe came to them from the carriage house, and by the time they reached it the lamplit air was already hazy with the dust thrown up by the stamping, tripping feet of the dancers.

It was nothing like any other dancing Laure had ever known. Here was no lilting, drifting round the room in one's partner's arms, excited by his touch and his nearness, intoxicated by his whispered compliments. She found herself joining hands with girls and women she did not know; then forming an alternating chain – facing Philippe for a moment, moving towards him and away; and then finding her hands seized by some other partner – Jacques Lambert once, gentle Moïse Delmas another time – caught up in a single chaotic and yet ordered movement that drew in all the dancers together, clapping, stamping, laughing and shouting with the music. When, now and then, she hesitated, not knowing what to do next, someone would take her hand, laughing, and pull her back into the dance.

Yet in some strange way, cut off as she was from Philippe's embrace, touching his hand only now and then, meeting his eyes briefly and momentarily through the crowd, she felt all at once closer to him than she had for a long time, linked to him by happiness, joined with him in this celebration of the wine that gave life to Casseuil. Once, when a polka-like dance brought them together for the first time, his arms about her were urgent with an emotion she had not felt in him so freely for a long time. He could not speak to her, of course, or not tenderly, for the noise around her was too great; but as the dance ended he took her face in his hands and kissed her full on the mouth, as openly and warmly as any country boy kissing his sweetheart; and she knew what promise it held for later, when they should go at last to bed.

Long after midnight they lay in the dark in one another's arms, warm, contented, and heard the first soft falling of the rain.

'Let it do its worst,' Philippe murmured against her hair. 'The wine is safe. A year to remember – I was right, wasn't I, *chérie?*'

CHAPTER
THREE

i

'Your words this morning went straight to the heart, *mon père*. Thank you.' Monsieur Chabry bent his head gravely and held the *curé*'s hand in his own, all solemn approval.

The Abbé Lebrun smiled up at the Mayor. 'I am glad,' he said simply, since that seemed the most appropriate response. He had no illusions – as *curé* of Casseuil he had lost them long since – as to the reasons that brought his tiny congregation to mass on Sundays. Monsieur Chabry, of a Catholic family in a staunchly Protestant area, had nevertheless been an infrequent attender until the death of the previous mayor some years ago. As a fervent Bonapartist – his father had been a loyal soldier of the first Emperor Napoleon Bonaparte; he himself a vocal supporter of the present Emperor in his successful bid for power in 1851, and many times since then – César Chabry was a natural choice to succeed to the vacant post. Once the Imperial appointment had been confirmed, Mayor Chabry had apparently become very conscious that he was in a position of authority and that the eyes of all were upon him; and he had begun, ostentatiously, to attend mass every Sunday and Holy day. The Abbé Lebrun suspected that his piety amounted to very little, underneath. But then it was up to a good priest somehow to try and touch the hearts of his congregation, whatever brought them to church in the first place.

About Madame Naillac – who followed the Mayor and his wife into the porch with a chilly 'Good day, *monsieur – madame –* ' since she did not like them – the *curé* had no doubt at all. Her religious faith was very real and very deep; all she lacked was that essential and saving grace of charity. Sometimes religious people were more of a problem to him

52

than the bulk of his parishioners who never came to church at all.

Madame did not say that his words had reached her heart. She merely asked after his health and moved on into the hot June sunshine. With a sense of relief the *curé* turned to beam at little Madame Laure, as always exquisitely dressed, a sight to turn every head in the church – as her arrival at mass each Sunday invariably did. Astonishing how she seemed somehow to be wearing a different ensemble every time. Clearly she enjoyed the sensation she caused; but then she was young, and no doubt came to church because it was expected of her and because she had always done so. But he liked her, sensing in her – beneath the little vanities – much the same unappreciated intelligence as his own: unappreciated in his case because of his peasant origins, in hers because she was a woman and a young one at that.

'Monsieur Naillac returns this evening, I believe?' He knew the answer of course, for he had dined at the château last night, as he often did when Monsieur Naillac was absent.

'Yes, *mon père*. In time for dinner we hope.'

'Do mention the book I told you about. I am sure he would find it most interesting.' Very likely, since the *curé* had recommended it, the young man would not even look at the book; but the Abbé Lebrun lived in constant hope of gaining Philippe's friendship as a means of winning his soul at last for the church. No matter how often he was rebuffed he would not give up.

'I'll tell him, *mon père*.' She smiled and followed the sombre upright figure of her mother-in-law across the market place to where a little gate led into the *parc* of the château. He watched her until she had disappeared from sight. She's lost weight, he reflected. She has a nervous unhappy look under that pretty surface. He had thought so last night, but in daylight the change was more marked. He must, he decided, seize an opportunity – casually – to see her alone, in case something troubled her and she wished to talk to him about it.

Following her from the church came old Veuve Foussac, who took in washing, and her daughter Nanon, a big cheerful young woman, and his own patient elderly housekeeper, all three devout with a simple fervour that put the rest of them to

53

shame. And that was it: seven people, the usual Sunday congregation at Casseuil, unless you counted the two Chabry boys who put in an occasional appearance when not away at school. He made his slow way back to the vestry to remove his vestments, feeling, as so often, humbled and a little depressed. Eight years of ministry here, and his congregation had increased by two: it was not much to show for all his work. He sighed, made sure everything was in order, and left the church by the side door. Outside the café the men sat drinking and talking, ignoring him. Monsieur Vergnolles' goat, apparently with deliberate intent, blocked his path and slowly added yet another contribution to the dung that littered the market place, but did not move aside, so that he had to make a detour round it. A group of young men and women, giggling and chattering, dragged wood and vine prunings right under his nose, past the church towards the open hilltop site near the windmill – for the midsummer bonfire, the *curé* knew, which would be lit next Friday, along with a good many profane ceremonies against which he had been preaching in vain for years. There were always one or two girls pregnant as a result of this pagan event.

Beyond the *mairie* stood the tumbledown presbytery. Since the commune was supposed to maintain it and most members of the municipal council had no time at all for the Church, he had to put up with the leaking roof and crumbling plaster. Monsieur Chabry had tried to stir the council to action, but even he had failed.

The *curé* went inside to the little rooms that, always, struck damp and chill, and the cabbage soup and hard bread and cheese waiting for him; and thought wistfully of last night's splendid dinner and the excellent wine – an 1841 Haut-Brion it had been this time. But then, he told himself, few of his parishioners ate much better than he did – it was only right that he should live as one of them. He settled more cheerfully to his soup, enlivening its dregs with the sour red wine that was all he could afford.

Hercule heaved a massive sigh and settled his long soft nose on Laure's foot, so that she could no longer move it without an effort. She smiled and bent down to fondle his ears. The older dog, sensing favouritism, lifted his head to see what was going on, and then subsided again, evidently deciding that it would require too much energy to drag himself up and pad his way across the hearth to where Laure sat.

'It's all right for you,' she murmured to the dogs. 'You like doing nothing.' Besides, she added to herself, even the dogs had a part to play, their sleepy indolence able to turn in an instant to alert intelligence the moment Philippe took up his gun.

She glanced at the ornate gilded clock that stood on the massive sideboard in the *grand salon*: three o'clock – only three o'clock, and Philippe could not possibly be home before six! It was not so much that she wanted him to be here with her, as that his return would at least be a diversion, an incident to make a little ripple on the dreary surface of her day. For the rest, she would have to wait and see what his mood was when he returned. She had no great hopes. He had been withdrawn, almost unceasingly difficult through the long months of winter and spring, as if that joyous day of harvest celebration had never been. He ought to be happy. The good vintage last year had brought so much more extra business, so many orders, and necessitated so many trips to Bordeaux, even though it would be several years before the wine was ready for bottling.

Weary of being left at home, Laure had longed to go to Bordeaux with him again. In the early days of their marriage he had always taken her with him, proud to show her off to friends and acquaintances, clearly delighted with the impression she made on everyone. Together they had attended the opera at the beautiful Grand Théâtre, walked in Bordeaux's streets and gardens, even shopped together for the new clothes that Philippe liked to see her wearing. But later on – ashamed perhaps of her childlessness and the fading beauty that went with it – he had almost always put her off. 'I shall be very busy – you'd be bored,' he would say; or, 'This will be all business, no time for pleasure,' or, 'The roads are most unpleasant at this time of year, if not dangerous – much better stay here.' It was never an outright refusal, but somehow he made it very plain that he did not want her with him; and so, hurt, she did not force the issue. She knew that, if she had insisted, he would have allowed her to come; but she knew too that his silent resentment of her victory would have poisoned the atmosphere for the entire stay. So her only compensation must be the small gift he always brought back with him, like a sweet to console a disappointed child. It was not quite enough.

This time it was a brooch, very pretty, with sapphire droplets falling from an ornate silver bar. 'It's beautiful!' she exclaimed warmly, pinning it to the neck of her gown and raising her face for his kiss. But her pleasure would have been much greater had the kiss been longer, or accompanied by an embrace: it was all so formal. And the severe look was still on his face, the look that so effectively shut her out.

He had evidently been observing her in his turn, for as they lingered at the table after dinner he said suddenly, 'You're getting thin, Laure – and you look tired.' Laure was about to retort with an attempt at lightheartedness that he too looked tired, his eyes red rimmed and his cheekbones starkly prominent; but his mother broke in.

'I think Laure should see a doctor. Doctor Vignet in Bordeaux would be best perhaps. Doctor Rossillon is a good enough doctor – though the least said about his qualities as a man the better – but in specialised matters like this, barrenness and so forth, one wants something more. And if Laure's out of sorts it's all part of the same thing. A thorough investigation is what is needed.'

'There is nothing wrong with me!' Laure rose to her feet and stood angrily, trembling a little, beside her chair, clasping the back. 'I am only bored and tired and sick to death of being criticised for something that is not my fault!' She had meant to sound indignant and angry, but in her near tearful state succeeded only in sounding petulant.

Philippe came behind her and put his hands on her shoulders. 'Come, Laure, I think it's time for bed. Say good-night to Maman, and then we'll go.' He might have been talking to a child. Laure wanted to scream her rage at him, but she sensed that it would only make him patronise her the more. She went, obediently, to place a kiss somewhere near her mother-in-law's gaunt extended cheek, and then allowed Philippe to steer her to their room.

He did not send for Florestine, but saw Laure into bed

56

himself with a gentleness belied by the severity of his expression. He was kind, she supposed, but it was hard at this moment to believe that he had ever been the passionate lover who had brought her so much delight.

'If you're as cold as this to me, how will I ever conceive?' she reproached him. He looked genuinely surprised.

'Cold? I'm not cold – but I am tired, and so are you. Why else would you have indulged in that outburst downstairs?'

'If you don't see why then there's no point in my trying to explain.' She turned from him and lay with her face half buried in the pillow. Philippe stood looking down at her.

'Your nerves are bad, Laure. Maman is right, you ought to see a doctor. We must arrange something.'

'I am *not* going to see her precious Doctor Vignet. Madame Chabry saw him once for some such thing as this, and she told me the most terrible things.'

'You know Madame Chabry is a foolish old gossip. I don't know why you listen to her,' said Philippe impatiently; and then, to Laure's surprise, he added, 'But this time I think you're right. There are better doctors in Paris. There's Doctor Lescaut, for instance; he specialises in women's troubles, I believe, and he's from Bergerac too – ' Before he could finish, Laure was sitting up in bed, transformed as abruptly as if the pale nervous creature of the past weeks had never existed, her eyes bright, her face glowing with colour.

'Go to Paris for a few weeks,' Philippe concluded. 'See your parents, have a little holiday, and consult this doctor while you're there. It will do you good.'

She knelt up on the bed and reached up to put her arms about his neck. 'Oh, Philippe, yes! I should like that so much – and I want some new clothes before next winter: I can go to Worth.'

He disengaged her arms, patting her briefly on the head. 'Of course, if that's what you want.' She would have preferred him to be more warmly enthusiastic, but she let it pass. He dropped a light kiss on her forehead. 'That's decided then. Good-night, *chérie*.' He began to move towards the door.

'Aren't you coming to bed too?' Her voice was dismayed, the glow subsiding a little within her. Tonight, after this, they might have come together again.

'I have some things to do first,' was all he said, in the same level voice; that of a mature man maintaining his calmness and self-possession in the face of his wife's rather juvenile volatility.

For all her excitement, she was asleep by the time he came to bed.

ii

'There's something badly wrong, *chérie*. It can't all be put down to her failure to bear a child – don't you agree?'

Marguerite Frémont looked up at her husband from the Louis XV sofa on which she sat in their elegant *salon*; she was smiling a little sadly. 'Oh Jules, you have little understanding of women, if that's what you think. I have known the most intelligent and level headed of women driven to insanity by childlessness – do you remember poor Félicie, for instance?'

With an obvious effort, her husband did so. 'Was that her trouble then? *Mon dieu!* I didn't know.' He gave a visible shudder. 'Our poor little Laure – if I thought she would end like that – hysteria, delusions, suicide – no, that would be unbearable!'

Marguerite rose and put a comforting hand on his arm. 'Please God it won't come to that. Philippe was right to contact Doctor Lescaut: he has an excellent reputation. If anyone can help her, he can. And four years isn't so very long, after all. It just seems it, when you're waiting and hoping and nothing happens.' Her voice was calm and sensible, but Jules knew she felt her daughter's trouble as keenly as he did; it was only that, understanding its roots more clearly, she'd had time to grow used to the situation.

'And she sees the doctor tomorrow? Once that's over we must do our best – ' He broke off as they heard Laure descending the stairs; and then went on casually, 'I heard this morning that Bismarck's candidate has accepted the Spanish throne after all.'

Laure came in with a bright tense smile on her face, which dissolved the next moment as her parents, by turns, embraced her, as warmly as if they had not already embraced and wept over one another at the station.

'Oh, it's so good to see you again!' Laure hid her face

against her mother's shoulder, abandoning herself to the demonstrative affection she had missed so much.

Later, a little calmer, they went to dinner.

'What was that you were saying when I came in, Papa?' Laure asked. 'About Spain, and Bismarck – oh, it seems so long since anyone talked about anything but vines and vineyards and what *monsieur le maire* is doing.'

Her father smiled. 'Ah, but those things are important too – what could be more interesting than to know that we can expect wonders from the '69 Casseuil?'

'Philippe promises you a case as soon as it's ready.'

'I shall look forward to that with eager anticipation – and wish him many more such vintages.' He raised his glass. 'Here's to that, and down with the phylloxera and all his evil works!'

Laure drank too, laughing; and then raised a spoonful of soup to her mouth – her favourite lobster soup, to be savoured slowly, each mouthful as rich with memories and associations as with flavours. 'Philippe says they are sure to have a remedy against the phylloxera very soon. I think he's more worried about mildew.'

'Certainly, from what I've heard, the research into the phylloxera is progressing quite well, now that Doctor Planchon has isolated the insect responsible. But it'll sadly be too late for very many vineyards. I'm glad you've escaped. Did you hear that they believe the insect came from America? One could almost believe it to be some kind of revenge for the Emperor's Mexican adventure.'

'Yes, I heard the United States was very angry about that.'

'Oh, then some news does reach you, even in your provincial backwater!'

'Not much, Papa – and Madame Naillac – ' She tried to say the name casually, so that none of the emotions it evoked would be revealed, but it was not easy. 'She does not think it's quite right for women to talk politics, so mostly they talk of other things when I'm there.' Again her smile was bright, too bright. 'But I must catch up with all the news. Tell me about Spain!'

'It's simple really. Spain needs a king, or thinks she does, and Chancellor Bismarck of Prussia has come up with a close

59

kinsman of his own king as a candidate for the vacant throne. You know, I expect, how powerful Prussia is now. There was the defeat of Austria of course – and since then nearly all the German states have come under Prussian control. In place of fragmented, quarrelsome little states, we now have a strong and united neighbour – and an ambitious one at that. And now we are threatened with a Prussian dominated state on both sides of France. We are in danger of being crushed between the two of them.'

Laure's eyes widened. 'Is that possible, do you think?'

'Not at present, of course. We still have the most powerful army in the world, given good leadership. But unfortunately, France has few friends left in Europe. The Emperor's policy has alienated Italy, just when she too has become united and perhaps strong enough to be a useful ally. The English mistrust us totally – though that's nothing new of course. Russia doesn't like our support for Poland. Austria is now too weak to be of any use as an ally. The United States has not forgiven us for the foolish Mexican adventure – even Marcel mentioned it when he wrote.'

That distracted Laure at once from the problems of foreign policy. 'Oh, you must show me his letter. Is he still in Arkansas on his farm?'

Marguerite smiled. 'No – we were quite right: that didn't last. He's moved to New York. You know how little he ever tells us in his letters, but we gather he's involved in some kind of business venture. He seems to be doing quite well.'

Laure shook her head wonderingly. 'Marcel the business man! What became of his political principles in all this?'

'I always suspected they were no more than skin deep,' said her father. 'It wasn't what he believed so much as the company he kept – which was why I was so opposed to the lot of them. There's no sense in risking imprisonment for beliefs that are not really yours in the first place.'

'Does he still paint, do you know?'

'He doesn't say – you shall see the letter after dinner. I imagine he has little time for painting now.'

'I should be sorry to think that. I do like his paintings. Philippe has hung the one he gave us in the *petit salon* – it looks very well there.'

'Two of his friends have some works in a new exhibition that opened the other week – you must see them while you're here – very much in the new style, painted out of doors, full of light and colour – very fine, I think, though they're not much to the public taste. I can't think anyone can make a living that way. But I'm considering making a purchase or two, simply because I like the work.'

But no amount of talk about art or Marcel or public affairs or all the things Laure had so longed to hear again over her parents' table could take from her mind the one thing that exclusively obsessed it; which was the one thing of which she did not speak at all – tomorrow's impending visit to Doctor Lescaut. It was that which took from the evening all the relaxed enjoyment to which she had so looked forward; it was that which kept her awake all night, her stomach churning with fear. 'What will he do to me?' Or, worst of all, 'Will he say there will be no chance, ever, of bearing children?' How could she go home and say that to Philippe – or to his mother?

The doctor's examination was long and embarrassing, though not quite so bad as she had feared. She did not know how to interpret his occasional grunts and murmurs and when, afterwards, all comfortable reassurance, he sat back in his chair, she thought, Is this how he breaks bad news to his patients?

The doctor smiled gently. 'There is absolutely no reason that I can find why you should not conceive. Eat and sleep well, avoid tightlacing (you are fortunate that your figure does not need that kind of help), take moderate exercise, enjoy your good country air and don't be anxious: that will be enough. Unless of course there is something amiss with Monsieur Naillac . . .'

Laure stared at him, for a moment not quite able to grasp what he was saying. Somehow that had never occurred to her as an explanation for her childlessness. She thought of Philippe – his height, his strength, his air of commanding masculinity, the passion of his lovemaking – and almost found herself smiling at the very idea. And then she imagined how Madame Naillac would receive such a slur on her son's virility and she did smile. But she said only, 'Oh, I'm sure there's not.'

The doctor smiled in his turn. 'Then go home and bear your child.'

Outside the summer sun seemed to shine with a greater brightness, the Seine glittered and sparkled as it flowed beneath trees whose leaves had a new brilliance of colour, as if the first freshness of spring had touched them all over again. Laure wanted to run and skip and sing, to go to a ball and dance all night, to meet all her friends at once and throw herself into an ocean of talk and laughter and high spirits; and she longed most of all to rush to the Gare d'Orléans and catch the very first train back to Casseuil, and Philippe – to tumble into bed with him and there and then without delay create the child they both wanted so much.

Her mother, watching her face as they walked away from the doctor's, understood. 'I expect you won't want to stay in Paris long after this, though I hope you'll let us enjoy your company for a few days more.'

Laure laughed, because a simple smile would have required too much restraint. 'I do want to go home – and I want to stay too – oh, I don't know what I want!'

Since it was expected of her, both by Philippe and her parents, she did prolong her stay; in any case, there were the new gowns she had promised herself.

Only, somehow, faced with an enticing array of exquisite gowns in Worth's fashionable salon, it no longer seemed to matter so much, as if, with something to look forward to at last, she no longer needed the consolation of new clothes. Still, fashion had moved on since she was last in Paris, so she had to buy three gowns – one for the day and two for the evening – in the very latest style, with all the emphasis of the skirt behind, gathered into folds and frills in contrast to the smooth rather severe line of the front. And then, of course, she must find jewellery to go with them, and try a new perfume or two. At home, she asked Florestine to dress her hair in the new way, drawn back over the ears and falling in heavy soft curls from the crown to the nape of the neck.

Then there were dinner parties at the houses of friends long missed, and balls, and visits to the theatre and to art galleries. It was enormously enjoyable, yet her years at Casseuil seemed to have given her a wholly new perspective on all that once had been so familiar.

'Everyone at Casseuil thinks Paris is full of vice and immorality,' she confided to her mother one day, laughing at the idea. Yet unexpectedly she had found herself a little shocked by things she had never really noticed before: the open prostitution for instance, not only in the poor streets, but between the rich and fashionable courtesans – the *grandes horizontales* – and the most prosperous and apparently respectable of gentlemen. The Emperor himself, they said, had always set the tone, and it filtered down from him to permeate the whole of society. Not that her father or mother or any of their friends moved in the most frenetically pleasure-seeking circles, on the whole, but it was impossible not to be touched by it somewhere, somehow. Perhaps the people at Casseuil had a point, after all.

Her mother, as so often reading what lay behind her words, said, 'It's strange – I remember feeling exactly as you do, only in reverse, when I was first married. Coming from provincial quietness to Paris, it all seemed very wild and noisy and immoral – and then I went home again, and suddenly everything there was so dull.'

Laure remembered childhood visits to her grandfather's country house in Lorraine, all tranquillity and sunshine and simple pleasures, and wondered that anyone could have thought it dull. Yet sometimes during the past years at Casseuil she too had been bored. Only this time when she returned it would be different, because at last there would be a child.

It was not only her attitude to Paris that had changed of course. Physically the city itself had indeed altered, as it did constantly these days under the guiding hand of the city Prefect, Baron Haussmann, commissioned by the Emperor to transform his capital. At last the work was almost done, the chaos of demolition and rebuilding at an end. The Paris of Laure's childhood, all narrow cobbled streets, dark alleyways, low overhanging decaying houses – picturesque, exciting and dangerous – lingered only here and there, in little pockets between the straight wide lines of the new boulevards that thrust in a pre-ordained pattern through the city's heart, bordered with trees, lit with gas, smoothly macadamed, set on either side with high grand houses of uniform design, a model of order, grandeur, modernity: a fit capital for the centre of the civilised world.

One hot Sunday afternoon well into July, Laure walked with her father along the shining new splendour of the avenue de l'Opéra not far from their home, admiring the expensive shops, the ambling Sunday crowd making for the parks and the boulevards. 'Julie – ' that was the schoolfriend whom Laure had visited most often since coming to Paris, ' – Julie doesn't like all the changes. She says the old Paris was much more romantic. But I like it – it's so clean and airy and beautiful – much pleasanter to live in I should think.'

'If you can afford the rents,' agreed her father a little drily. 'Many of the poorer people have had to move out to Belleville or Ménilmontant or even further, and those areas have become more insanitary and overcrowded than ever – even the police think twice before setting foot in them. But it's pleasanter for the well-to-do not to be living pell-mell with the poorer classes, as in the old days.'

Laure shot a look at him. 'You don't approve of the changes then?'

He shrugged. 'I have mixed feelings. On the whole they are for the best perhaps. But perhaps the social as well as the policing aspects should have been taken more into account.'

'What has policing to do with it?'

'Well, many of the old nests of crime have been done away with. More to the point, the wide straight streets make it difficult for malcontents to build barricades, there are few paving stones left to be torn up for use as missiles or defences, and access for troops and police is much improved.'

'Is there a danger of uprisings like that then?' Laure asked, disturbed.

Her father smiled. 'To be honest, I hardly think so. Even I have to admit that we've had relative peace and stability for twenty years now – that is quite an achievement, given our turbulent history. No, however regrettable that may be seen to be in some quarters, we Parisians are more concerned these days to put our energies into other less disruptive matters than revolution – modernisation, commerce, industry and so forth. It's a good thing on the whole.'

'Marcel didn't think so,' Laure pointed out. 'But perhaps he's changed his mind now.' She thought of his letter. 'You laughed when he suggested you should go out there and join him, but are you not just a little bit tempted? America is a republic after all.'

'Ah, but not a French republic, *mon enfant*. Yes, I may have some discreet reservations about our form of government, but I have to acknowledge we have never prospered as we do today. And now we even have a ministry of Republican sympathisers ruling us with the Emperor's approval. All that, and the benefits of the most civilised country in the world. No, why should we wish to uproot ourselves and leave everything we have here? Perhaps when Marcel has made his fortune he'll come back to his own land again – we hope so.'

Laure enjoyed walking with her father, so fair and handsome, and proud of the small and exquisite figure of his daughter leaning on his arm. He was well known, and much liked and respected by his wide circle of acquaintances, and would pause often to exchange a greeting with this man or that woman, to discuss health or family matters or – most of all – the prospects for war with Prussia.

It seemed astonishing to Laure that in so short a time this cloud should have blown across an apparently cloudless sky. At first it had seemed as if it would all come to nothing. Bismarck's protégé for the Spanish throne had – under French pressure – tactfully withdrawn his candidature, and Laure's father had smiled with relief. 'You see, the Prussians know France is a different proposition from Austria – they don't want to risk trouble with us after all.'

But to his exasperation many members of the government, encouraged by the Empress Eugénie, insisted on demanding guarantees of future good conduct from Prussia. The Prussian King Wilhelm politely declined, but his chancellor Bismarck made sure that, in the newspaper reports of the incident, it seemed that France had received a humiliating rebuff.

'This must mean war,' commented Jules Frémont grimly.

'There are too many people who want to teach Prussia a lesson for us to let that go.'

But there was no grimness in the mood of the Parisians: war might be a game, Laure thought, judging by the atmosphere of happy excitement that hummed over the city on that bright Sunday. 'Do you think we should go to war?' she asked her father.

He smiled at her. 'My chief fear is that a brilliant military victory will only entrench the Empire more firmly than ever. Without it – who knows? – we might one day drift towards a republic. But a victorious Emperor Napoleon would regain all his waning popularity. On the other hand, Prussia is becoming dangerously powerful. A swift blow against her by France would help restore the natural balance in Europe. A united and aggressive Germany on our borders is something we cannot tolerate.'

'You think war is certain then?' Laure asked a little anxiously.

'I think it would have much to recommend it. Our armies could be in Berlin within a matter of weeks, if we act swiftly and with resolution. Prussia would not forget the lesson in a hurry.'

Before the week was over France had declared war. Laure and her mother stood on the balcony of the *salon*, listening to the distant sound of cheering and, further off, a sudden snatch of song – '*Allons enfants de la Patrie, le jour de gloire est arrivé . . .*' – the 'Marseillaise', that forbidden hymn of war and revolution. Marguerite Frémont put an arm about her daughter's shoulder and hugged her close; she was shivering a little, perhaps with apprehension as well as excitement.

'*Chérie,*' she said after a moment. 'I think perhaps you should go home.'

It was all so exciting in Paris, here at the hub of the world; yet at Casseuil in that country quietness Philippe was waiting, and the child still unconceived – even the feverish atmosphere of a city going joyfully to war could not quite silence the hope and longing in her heart.

'Of course, Maman,' she said.

Going home on the train Florestine complained bitterly of the chaos and discomfort. It seemed as if half France was on the move; or the younger male portion of it at least. Carriages and stations were crowded with noisy groups of bewildered looking young men in uniform, many of them strung about with parcels and packages, gifts of food or clothes from the mothers or sisters or sweethearts who waved tearfully from platforms, or clung for a last lingering embrace through a carriage window. The armies of France – inheritors of the splendid traditions of Condé and Turenne, of the forces of the Revolution, of the great Napoleon – were mobilising for the advance into Prussia, to answer the call of the motherland and crush the pretensions of the newly emergent power on her borders. How could anyone be anything but proud and happy to be French at such a time?

And then at Libourne there was Philippe coming through the throng to meet her, a warm breathing reminder that it was not the war that mattered most now, but this – her homecoming. Laure had scarcely time to read the emotion on his face, the tenderness of his smile, before she found herself folded into a great warm suffocating embrace, her face covered with kisses each one of which told her as words never could how much he had missed her and how glad he was at the good news she had told him in her letter.

If it had been left to them, Laure and Philippe would have tumbled straight into bed together the moment the carriage came to a halt in the courtyard at Casseuil. But Madame Naillac, smiling with all the warmth she could muster, had a magnificent dinner ready for them and they had to wait. But not too long: there was approval in her eyes as they kissed her good-night while it was still scarcely dark.

It was like the early days of their marriage, all joyous passion; and, later, lying awake because she was too happy to sleep, Laure thought: Everything is going to be all right. The long winter was over: summer had come again.

iv

Two weeks later, her period began. She wept a little, with bitter disappointment. When, in bed that night, she told

Philippe what had happened, he was consoling. 'Never mind, *chérie*, we shall just have to try harder. Don't worry – remember what the doctor said.'

She remembered, then, something else the doctor had said, which she had until now kept to herself. But should it not be told after all? Might there be something in it, however unlikely it had seemed at the time?

'Philippe,' she began, glad that the darkness hid her embarrassment. 'Philippe, is it possible. . . ? Dr Lescaut asked – I don't think it, not really – but – '

'But what?'

'If it is not because of me that we have no child – could it be, might it be – because of you – ?'

She knew it was a terrible thing even to suggest to a man, an imputation against his manhood. She expected indignation, anger even. But instead, to her astonished relief, Philippe simply laughed, softly, easily, comfortably. And then his lips moved over her forehead.

'No, *chérie*, it's not that, I assure you.'

'But how can you be sure? Have you seen a doctor too?'

This time there was a little hesitation. Then after a moment he said, 'Yes – yes, of course I have seen a doctor – in Bordeaux once when I was there. So you see, there is nothing to fear, nothing at all.'

CHAPTER
FOUR

i

The Trissac vines looked reassuringly healthy, the grapes full and purple, as one would expect in early September after a summer of burning heat punctuated by sudden showers, never so long or so heavy as to cause any damage. In a week or two, Henri Séguier thought as he finished his inspection, they could hope to begin the *vendange*, and it might well be a good one. He was aware, as he walked back to the house, of a sense of relief: another year almost behind him, another harvest almost safe, and still there was no sign of the phylloxera which had already attacked three vineyards uncomfortably close to Trissac. He had – like most *vignerons* – increased the frequency of the sulphur spraying that had for some time been a routine measure against oïdium. It was said that it might also be effective against the phylloxera louse; it was certainly beginning to look as if that were true. Up at Casseuil, Philippe Naillac had taken the same precautions, and they too had escaped. But one could never quite be sure.

He went to his room to wash and dress for dinner, feeling all his usual good humour return with the warm water, the scented soap, the soft towels. There was an agreeable evening ahead of him, a good dinner and good company; he began to hum to himself as he eased his powerful arms into the starched shirt held out for him by his manservant. Tonight Laure Naillac would grace his table.

He had scarcely seen her since her return from Paris, but at least he knew she was safely back. He had been a little surprised himself to find how much he had minded her absence: knowing she was not at Casseuil, that there was no chance of an unexpected meeting to brighten his day – that had been the worst part of it, burdening him for weeks with an

69

uncharacteristic sense of depression. He had missed her far more than he had ever missed his wife since her unregretted death last December.

Once dressed, he went to sit on the edge of Victor's bed, prodding the child teasingly in the chest. 'And how did you like dining with such a pretty little companion, *mon vieux*? I'll bet you couldn't keep your eyes on your food for one moment!'

The child giggled in the slightly knowing way that pleased his father, suggesting an understanding between them, man to man. Usually when there were no guests they dined together; but tonight Victor had eaten in his room with his new nursemaid – like all Henri Séguier's female servants chosen for her looks and a certain acquiescence of temperament. Victor had not minded his banishment too much, since he knew his father would come and talk to him before saying good-night, as he always did. He adored Henri, and liked nothing better than to be treated with this genial camaraderie, even if he did not always understand what was said to him.

When they had talked and joked and laughed a little more, Henri kissed the boy, gave the giggling nursemaid a parting fondle, and was already descending the graceful curved staircase as the first guests were admitted. Of course! he thought, with a twinge of irritation, as he saw who had stepped into the hall, trust César Chabry to be first, punctual to the minute. But he assumed a friendly manner and went, hand outstretched, to greet that dour, moralising, self-important man and his disagreeably plain wife. After all, as Mayor of Casseuil, the commune whose borders took in the hamlet of Trissac, Monsieur Chabry was a man to be cultivated, however reluctantly. 'Ah, our valiant and over-burdened Mayor – welcome, my dear Chabry!'

By the time Monsieur and Madame Naillac arrived, Henri had begun to fear that they might have been unavoidably detained. But he could forgive them even that anxiety, with Madame Laure looking so enchantingly pretty in a confection of apple-green satin whose clinging smoothness over breast and waist and stomach drew his eye on down from the low, frilled neckline to the simple hem and up again over the gentle exquisite curves of her body. A new fashion, he realised, leaving the figure of its wearer, and that alone, to provide all the interest in front. 'Ah, Madame Naillac, you are more lovely every time we meet!' he said fervently, his eyes lingering over her as he bent to press a kiss on her hand. His only regret was that she withdrew the hand so quickly, but perhaps the sweetness of her smile, the low softness of her voice were some compensation for that.

It was inevitable – despite the mixed company and the good food and wine – that at some stage during the evening the conversation should turn to the war, for which there had been little enthusiasm outside Paris.

'And is there any more news of our Emperor's "*Grande Armée*"?' Doctor Rossillon's sarcastic tone was not lost even on Monsieur Chabry, who was not quick witted; but in any case the doctor's Republican views were well known, and his mocking disapproval of the policies that had led to the war.

'I have no very recent news,' the Mayor replied rather stiffly. 'But once we have mobilised the reserves there will be ample reinforcements – the Prussian defeat is only delayed, as we all know. It will come.'

The doctor raised his eyebrows but refrained from commenting on that optimistic remark. What news had filtered through during the past weeks had been dismal in the extreme. The armies sent to deliver the swift and salutary blow to Berlin had apparently not even crossed the border into Germany, but were bogged down in confused and largely unsuccessful manoeuvres in Alsace and Lorraine. 'What amazes me,' the doctor went on, 'is why we haven't had a spate of marriages in Casseuil since war broke out. Or do we have no young men on the list for the reserve?'

'None of mine, I hope, just before the *vendange*,' said Henri.

'No, Monsieur Séguier, I believe you will escape, unless there is some move to extend the call-up. No, there are only two or three from within the commune – young Jacques Lambert is one, I do know.'

'If I were him I'd get Nanon Foussac to the *mairie* as quickly as possible. I wonder why he hasn't? They've been promised to one another for I don't know how long.'

'They're a careful family, the Lamberts,' said Philippe.

'They wouldn't think of marriage until they were quite ready – and perhaps they believe the war will be over before the reserves can be mobilised.'

'Considering what terms we'd be likely to get if we made peace now, I hope they're wrong,' said the doctor.

'Yet we all thought it would be over quickly.'

'*You* did,' Henri corrected him. 'All those Paris connections of yours, Philippe *mon ami* – they were so sure of a brilliant victory. Out of touch with reality and too many heads in the clouds, that's Paris for you.'

'Do you forget that I am a Parisienne, *monsieur*?' That was Laure Naillac, all pretty sparkling indignation.

'Of course not, *madame* – but it is to your credit that you had the good sense to leave Paris and come and live among us. And of course you are a woman – it is the privilege of your lovely sex to be as empty headed and fanciful as you please – it was not for your intellect or your judgement that you were created, thank goodness, but for other softer attributes—'

He was surprised to see from her heightened colour that he had annoyed her, though he could not think why.

'From the way the war has apparently been conducted it does not seem to me that your sex has any reason to claim superiority of judgement, *monsieur*.' Beside her, Doctor Rossillon gave an appreciative chuckle.

Henri stared at her, astonished at this sudden evidence of spirit – not entirely desirable spirit, he thought: Philippe Naillac should keep his wife under firmer control. But on the whole he liked her the better for it. A fight or two added spice to a relationship – if only he could have called their casual acquaintance by so warm a name!

'Ah, but perhaps it's the female influence that's to blame after all,' said Doctor Rossillon brightly. 'Is it not true that it is not the Emperor but his wife who is the real ruler of France?'

'Monsieur, you forget that our Emperor is a sick man!' César Chabry's voice was squeaky with indignation.

'All the more reason, *monsieur le maire*, for him to give up any pretence of trying to rule, and to return the power to the people, where it belongs, before it is too late.'

The Mayor burst out, 'Do you forget, *monsieur*, that it was the people who brought the Emperor to power?'

'Nineteen years ago – and only then because all possible opponents had been clapped in gaol. When since then have the people been asked for their opinion?'

'I am quite sure,' said Chabry with dignity, 'that the people would vote as their interests dictate – for government by the Bonapartist dynasty which has brought such glory and stability to France.'

'Glory? Stability? When we're up to our necks in a war we don't want, at the whim of an Emperor too weak to say no to his wife—! Come now, Chabry, we might as well have Louis XVI and Marie-Antoinette back at the Tuileries – it would be no different: Bourbons or Bonapartes, they're all the same at heart. What France needs is an end to personal government; and a return to free elections. When she is truly left free to choose, she has always voted for a republic.'

'The Republic means disorder and revolution, and you know it!'

'Rubbish! History shows that we resort to revolution only when stupid, stubborn, pig-headed rulers try to prevent the people from setting up the Republican form of government which best expresses its will for France.'

'History also shows that France has twice had to call on a Napoleon Bonaparte to save her from the chaos of Republicanism!'

The atmosphere was alive with hostility, mayor and doctor glowering at one another across the table. Henri enjoyed a little lively argument, but this was another matter. 'Madame Naillac, I believe I have heard you say that you have a brother in America – you have good news of him I trust?'

But despite Henri's best conversational efforts, Monsieur and Madame Naillac did not linger very late at his table. They left on the heels of the Chabrys, giving him no time to enjoy their company without the irritating presence of the least welcome guests. He kissed Madame Laure's hand as slowly and thoroughly as he decently could – and as she would allow, coy little woman that she was! – and then he assisted her into her carriage and stood back to watch that fortunate young couple drive away.

*

It was a relief to be free of the necessity to smile and talk and look full of cheerful interest in everything and everyone. Laure leaned back and closed her eyes. Oh, it had been such a long day!

She felt Philippe's hand close about hers. 'You are tired, *ma chérie*?'

'Yes – no – oh, it's only—' She felt the tears rise in her throat and fell silent.

His grasp tightened. 'I know – it's another disappointment. But don't be downcast about it.'

'How can I help it? It's taking so long!'

'You've been home scarcely six weeks – that's not long.' He reached out and drew her close to him. 'You need other things to think about – some distraction. We could go away somewhere, to the sea perhaps—'

There was a sudden violent jolt. They were thrown sharply forward. Philippe banged his head, Laure fell against him in a confusion of limbs. The carriage had come to a halt.

Philippe, righting himself as quickly as he could, opened the window and leaned out. 'Aristide – what is it?'

Laure could not make out the coachman's reply, half drowned as it was by distant raucous sounds – shouting, she thought first; and then realised it was singing, to a tune faintly familiar, though she could not quite place it. Philippe continued to stare out into the night; full of curiosity, Laure moved to his side.

The coach had stopped some way below the church, and just beyond Philippe's head Laure glimpsed the market square and the solid front of the *mairie*, not in sober darkness as she would have expected, but lit both by a dim glow from the café, and by the lanterns held in the hands of a small group of men gathered before it. Striding across the dusty ground towards them – his voice anxious, remonstrating, high-pitched above the singing – was Monsieur Chabry, whose stationary coach had blocked their path. Madame Chabry, white with apprehension, was leaning out to watch.

The next moment Philippe jumped down, and Laure followed him to the shelter of a buttress against the church wall where – half-concealed from view – they could see more

74

clearly. 'I wonder what's going on?' Philippe murmured. 'I can see Jean Lambert there – what is he doing?'

He was, Laure realised in a little while, climbing onto a ladder placed against the wall of the *mairie* and reaching upwards with something heavy and soft falling back from his hands; up towards the communal flag pole that was used only on occasions of celebration. The men were silent now, watching intently. The lantern light touched on a splash of bright colour.

'Oh, he's hanging the flag! But why, at this time of night?'

The heavy tricolour folds fell into place and a cheer broke out from the watching men. '*Vive la République!*' That was clear enough, and so was the singing that followed; this time Laure recognised it at once – of course, the 'Marseillaise'.

Gesticulating wildly, Chabry broke into a run. '*Messieurs! – mes amis!* – what is this? Monsieur Lambert, I beg you—!'

The singing died away to a few uncertain phrases; at least some of the men were clearly very drunk. Jean Lambert descended from the ladder and turned to face the Mayor: Laure could make out the shadowy figures of his sons Jacques and Aubin behind him. 'Robert Martin here,' he gestured towards the man at his side, village cabinet maker and café owner, 'he's just come from Bergerac. The Emperor's finished, done for – the Prussians have him prisoner. There's talk of a Republic.'

Laure held her breath. In the midst of the wild cheering that followed, Mayor Chabry stood absolutely motionless, his sense of shock clear in every rigid, appalled line of his body. Robert Martin slapped him – rather too vigorously – on his back, and he tottered as the noise grew louder. They had begun singing again, when he pulled himself free and shouted at the top of his voice for quiet.

They did not give him what he wanted, but after a moment or two Jean Lambert gestured to them and the noise grew a little less. Chabry burst out, with all the dignity and authority he could muster, 'Until and unless I have official notification of what you say, you will refrain from seditious gatherings of this kind. Disperse, if you please, and remove the flag.' He stood, soldier-like, to attention. '*Vive l'Empereur!*'

A jumble of angry jeering sounds rose from the men, from

which two evidently disconnected words emerged clearly – 'Merde!' and 'République!'

The Mayor, his arms beating the air, shouted for order and respect; Jean Lambert, with studied insolence, spat in the dust at his feet.

'You're finished too, Chabry – you and your Emperor both. From now on . . .' he stabbed the man's chest with an emphatic finger: 'the people are in charge – and that's us, Chabry – us! Do you hear?'

The men growled agreement, the sound swelling, full of rage and menace. They moved forward, closing in on the Mayor's solitary figure. From somewhere a stone flew across, just missing Chabry's head. He ducked; and then, arms thrashing, pushed his way forward and laid hands on the ladder, fighting off the men who clutched and dragged at him.

Madame Chabry, behind them, screamed. Laure said urgently, 'Go and help him, Philippe, quick!'

'Who? Chabry? He deserves all he gets.'

She had no time to be shocked at such callousness (though she did not much like the Mayor herself). Suddenly, from the direction of the presbytery, the curé came running, shouting in his turn.

'That will make matters worse,' said Philippe, as a scattering of stones greeted the curé's arrival. Chabry's coachman, passing them, ran to his master's aid.

The market place was full of shouting and anger and black struggling figures; above the din, Chabry called, 'Naillac – I implore you – go to the gendarmerie – quickly!' and then he disappeared somewhere below the gesticulating mass of angry men.

Philippe did not move. 'Go on, Philippe – you must! Someone will be hurt!'

With some reluctance, Philippe turned back to their coach; where Aristide said, 'Not you, monsieur – I'll go. You take madame home – if you don't mind walking this little distance. But quickly, monsieur, before things get worse.' He turned the coach and drove away; and Philippe put his arm about Laure.

'He's right – let's go home. We'll go by the road, then we don't have to pass through the market place.'

'No,' said Laure firmly. 'I'm not going so long as Madame Chabry's here by herself. What if they should turn on her?'

Philippe glanced at the Mayor's coach and the pale face still just visible at the window. 'She's safe enough. No one even knows she's there.'

'They're coming this way!'

A stone shot towards them, falling just short. Philippe pulled Laure back. 'Come! It's stupid to stay!'

She shook herself free. 'No!'

Philippe, exasperated, cried, 'Laure, don't be so foolish! Come home! . . . See, Chabry's all right.'

The Mayor had somehow broken free: dishevelled, his clothes torn, blood trickling black from a gash on his forehead, he was limping quickly towards his coach, the *curé* (in little better shape) following, the coachman pausing only to hurl a stone at their pursuers, before scrambling onto his seat and gathering up the reins. Without glancing at Philippe, the other two jumped inside and the coach drove away.

The pursuing men flung missiles after the coach until it was out of sight; and then they turned, and saw Philippe and Laure. For a moment they stared at one another: the angry men, stones in their hands, their jeers dying away to quietness; and the tall man, anxiously clasping his wife's arm, as she stood straight and unafraid, watching them. Then the men shrugged, exchanged derisive comments, and turned and made their way back towards the market place. They began to sing again; and a little after came the sound of breaking glass.

'The Presbytery windows,' said Philippe. 'A favourite holiday sport.' He steered Laure along the road towards the main gate of the château.

'How could you just let it happen?' she reproached him. 'They would have listened to you.'

'Do you really think so? I don't. See how much notice they took of the *curé*.'

'But they don't like him. You're different.'

'Exactly. I mind my own business and don't interfere.'

They were crossing the courtyard when they heard the horsemen passing in the distance. 'The *gendarmes*,' said Philippe. 'Aristide was quick. But I'd wager anything they'll

77

find the market place miraculously empty. A few peaceful drinkers in the café, that's all.'

It was only as they went into the house that the full significance of tonight's incident struck Laure. She came to a sudden halt.

'Philippe, do you suppose they were right?'

'Right about what, *ma chérie*?'

'About the Emperor being a prisoner. And . . .' Her voice took on an excited, happy note. 'A Republic . . . Do you think a Republic really has been declared?'

Philippe shrugged. 'Who's to say? We'll hear soon enough, I suppose.'

Still Laure did not move. 'Wouldn't that be wonderful?'

Philippe laughed. 'And this is the little Republican who wanted to go to Chabry's rescue! Do be a little more consistent, *ma chère*.'

'Oh, it's not that I like his politics. But no one should be attacked for what they believe. He was only doing his duty. Think if he'd been killed!'

'Chabry's not the kind to end up as a martyr, Laure – don't you know that by now? And before you rejoice too much in a change of government, remember the defeat of the Emperor might well mean the defeat of France.'

'Oh no, not if we have a republic to carry on the fight. Isn't that what you want too?'

He shrugged again. 'Perhaps. It doesn't make that much difference, does it? So long as we have peace.'

How could anyone care so little about something so important? Laure wondered, with a trace of exasperation. Excitement had driven away much of the depression that had settled on her since this morning, when she had realised for the second time that she was still not pregnant. As they made their way upstairs to bed, she felt no trace of weariness.

The next morning César Chabry, bruised and aching, was faced with the most painful official duty of his proud career, that of conveying to the commune the news of the Emperor's defeat at Sedan in north-east France, along with a large portion of his army – all now in Prussian hands. What made it more bitter still was to have to announce – to the unreserved delight of almost all his hearers – that a republic had been declared in Paris and a government of National Defence set up to oversee the future conduct of the war.

The announcement duly made – proclaimed at the beat of a drum to the cheering villagers, carried in person to his supposedly more sympathetic hearers – César Chabry returned home and paced up and down his *salon* and poured out his feelings, bitterly and at length, to his two sons, Louis Napoléon and Eugène, and to his wife.

'I have given my life, my loyalty, all I have to the Bonapartist cause! I have served the Emperor in everything, unswervingly, in the face of ridicule and vilification. I have been accused of corruption and tyranny, of all manner of vile things, quite without foundation, and I have borne it all in silence, with dignity, for the Emperor's sake, as his representative here. And now, how am I repaid for my loyalty? By this shameful betrayal – I can call it no less! Such cowardice, such – yes, treason, one must almost call it that! – to surrender to the invader with scarcely a show of resistance! I put my trust in him and he has proved himself utterly unworthy of that trust! How can I hold my head high after this? How can I face the people over whom I am supposed to have authority?' He stopped in his tracks and fell briefly silent, remembering one particularly painful episode from this morning, and then added, 'I saw the look on Madame Naillac's face when I told her – even her, whom I thought my friend! It was triumph, naked triumph! I know what she hopes for now – that son of hers in my shoes, so she can have her finger in all the commune's business!' Trembling, he sat down and bent his face in his hands. His wife came to put an arm about him.

'You are too fine a man, *mon chéri*, to be tainted by the Emperor's dishonour,' she murmured consolingly.

ii

By the end of the week there was a letter from Laure's mother. 'We expect to have to face a Prussian attack here in Paris, but do not be anxious, *chère* Laure, we are prepared, and spirits are high. In fact I cannot remember such a feeling of joy and unity as there is in Paris at the moment. Your father has joined our local unit of the *Garde Nationale*, like all good citizens – he is very assiduous in his duties and you would not believe how handsome he looks in his uniform! Everywhere, there are signs of readiness – flocks of sheep and oxen herded into the Bois de Boulogne – the Champs Elysées and the Champ de Mars hidden beneath tents and wagons and bright with the uniforms of the regular soldiers encamped there. If necessary we can withstand a siege of as much as eighty days, so we are told – but of course before the end of November (that is where we will be in eighty days, is it not?) we hope we shall be relieved.'

'And who is going to relieve them, do they suppose?' demanded Philippe when he read the letter. 'The reserves aren't fully mobilised yet and most of them are untrained. And who's going to organise it all, if the government's shut up in Paris?'

'There is a delegation at Tours, is there not?' put in Laure.

'A few old men long past inspiring resistance in anyone? Oh, come now, *chérie*, what good can they do?'

'Maman says no one really believes the Prussians can cut off Paris entirely.'

'Since there's no army left to prevent them, I imagine they will be able to do so quite easily. No, they should be making peace, not building up their defences.'

'But you heard the terms the Prussians are asking! They want all of Alsace and most of Lorraine. How could any government agree to that?'

'Oh, I expect they're just bluffing,' said Philippe amiably. 'Besides, better two provinces than the whole of France defeated.'

'You wouldn't say that if you came from Lorraine!'

'As you do not, Laure.' Madame Naillac had come into the room behind them. 'Your mother's connection with that province does not make you an authority. Lunch is served, and I trust you will refrain from any further discussion of public affairs.'

iii

Moïse Delmas hurried to catch up with his young cousin Aubin, walking with head bent against the rain towards the château. The boy said nothing as Moïse reached him, his only indication that he had seen his cousin a swift uncommunicative glance in his direction.

'There'll be nothing doing outside today,' Moïse said after a moment, by way of conversation, speaking, as always among family and friends, in the local patois. 'Nothing much doing anywhere, I reckon.'

Aubin shrugged. 'I'll go home if I can. My dad wants help.'

Yes, he would, Moïse thought: the small family farm was not only a vineyard, but also included fruit trees, goats, chickens, a few cattle, a little maize, as well as a profitable business cutting and shaping false acacia wood for vine posts, supplied to most of the local vineyards. For that, Jean Lambert needed the extra hands his older son supplied, especially since the first of his three daughters was married now, the third slow-witted and not much use about the place. Until now Aubin's small wage from the château had been more use than his presence would have been; but with Jacques called up for the reserves – the *Gardes Mobiles* – Aubin was needed at home.

'There'll not be much of a harvest this year, unless the weather picks up. This rain's upset all the good the summer's done.'

'There'll be no harvest at all at this rate.' Aubin spoke with the confidence of knowledge. 'We can't pick in this, and if it goes on we'll have grey rot setting in, and that'll be that.'

'War – bad weather – ' Moïse shook his head. 'A bad year this.' He glanced at Aubin's grave young face. 'Was Nanon Foussac at your place last night?'

Aubin shot him a look, guarded, slightly questioning. 'Yes, she was.'

'She'll be hoping the war's over soon. They say she's good reason, better than most.'

'If you mean she's pregnant, yes, that's right. Dad had me write to Jacques and tell him.'

'Ah!' Moïse gave a sigh of satisfied curiosity. 'Maybe they'll let him come back and wed her then. Pity they couldn't have been wed before. If I could find a woman who'd have me I'd be at the *mairie* today. Still, at least he knows she's not barren.'

'He didn't want to be wed too young.'

'Better that than the army – still, they'll not be waiting now, longer than they can help.' The rain swept across the courtyard, lashed by a bitter wind from the north; at the well a girl shivered as she filled a pail; and beyond her a slight figure shrouded in a cloak and hood ran towards the *chai*. Aubin gave an exclamation under his breath.

'What does she want there on a day like this?'

'Madame Laure? Maybe she's looking for Monsieur.'

'She's always around. Silly woman.'

Moïse smiled wryly. 'You shouldn't talk of her like that, Aubin. She's your employer's wife, you know.'

'Dad says why couldn't he have chosen some nice girl from a local family, someone with her feet on the ground, not a silly Paris woman all fine clothes and empty hands – under the *curé*'s thumb too, like Madame Naillac.'

'Maybe the old woman had a say in it. They say it's never been the same since she wed old Monsieur Naillac – in the old days they didn't have all these ideas above themselves. Still, there it is – times change. We have to make the best of it. Monsieur Philippe's all right now.'

Aubin shrugged. 'I suppose so. You'd hardly know, mind. He's never here.'

He was there today though, standing with the *régisseur* at the top of the office steps as they entered the *chai*, looking down at Madame Laure, who was coming towards him with a letter in her hand.

She had that worn strained look again, Jean Delisle thought as he watched her; though at the moment she was smiling and excited. But he had troubles enough of his own, without concerning himself with hers. He put her from his mind and went to meet Aubin and Moïse. 'You still with us, Moïse? No news?'

'Not yet, *monsieur*. But we expect it any day, my brothers and me.'

'Let's make the most of you while we have you then – not that there's much we can do today.' He was smiling, but his spirits were lower than they had been for a long time. If it hadn't rained they might have started on the *vendange* today. It was one of those frustrating years when more conventional wines were full of promise, for the weather had broken only with the late autumn.

'In that case, *monsieur*, can I go home?' Aubin's French was careful and precise. 'My father wants help – he has vine posts to prepare for Monsieur Chabry. And with Jacques away . . .'

Jean Delisle looked at the boy with a sudden flash of anger rising in him. Damned war, damned weather, disrupting life like this! 'I don't see why not, just for today,' he said slowly, his tone markedly reluctant. 'But, Aubin!' as the boy turned to go, 'remember, there's a future for you here, a good one, more than you'll ever have at home. One day I'll be too old for this job, you know – and it could be sooner, who knows?' he put in gloomily; adding, 'I can't promise anything, but I've got my eye on you.'

A rare grin, sudden, joyous, broke across Aubin's habitually impassive face, setting a spark alight in his eyes. 'Yes, *monsieur*. Thank you.'

The *régisseur* went to report Aubin's absence to Monsieur Naillac, who was reading the letter his wife had brought.

'You see this?' he greeted Jean Delisle, waving the thin travel-stained paper. 'It comes from Paris. Now how do you suppose it reached us?'

Monsieur Delisle, in no mood for guessing games, shook his head. 'I can't say, *monsieur*. I thought Paris was cut off – unless it was posted before the end of September, but that would be four weeks ago now. A long time for a letter, even allowing for the war.'

'And this was written last week, by my mother-in-law in Paris. Here's what she says, "If this letter reaches you safely it will be thanks to our new form of aerial transport – the hot air balloon. We all gather to see them set out from Montmartre or the Gare d'Orléans or the Gare du Nord – where one may also watch these modern wonders being made in great numbers. We watch them rise majestically into the air with their brave crews aboard, and pray that the wind may keep them safe from the Prussians and all other dangers. They look so fine, carried away over the roofs and spires of the city into the blue distance. On 3 October we saw our intrepid Minister of the

Interior, Léon Gambetta, take flight, and we all cheered and wished him well – he looked a little pale, I thought, but well he might, for it is a dangerous enough means of transport even without the threat of Prussian guns trained on one. But he was cheerful and full of enthusiasm for the task ahead of him. We hope you will have heard of his courageous journey, for he was bound for Tours, there to organise the war effort and the relief of Paris – but we have no firm news of his safe arrival." *We* have, of course,' Philippe interposed wryly. 'If the army takes you, Delisle, I shall personally wish our new Minister of War had landed slap in the middle of Prussian headquarters.'

Jean Delisle gave a thin smile. As an unmarried man without ties he was technically liable to be drafted into the newly constituted National Guard (established on the same lines as that already in force in Paris) but at forty he was almost over the age limit, and they all hoped that might save him from the call-up. As it was the three Delmas brothers were sure to go; the only question was how soon.

'I hope Monsieur and Madame Frémont are suffering no hardship?' Monsieur Delisle asked politely, because he felt he ought to. The troubles of Paris seemed slight against his own.

'They are very well,' put in Laure. 'My mother says that the worst thing is the boredom and the lack of news – she says they almost wish for a bombardment or an attack, so that there will be something to talk about.'

iv

There had been a slight frost last night, and today it was raining again. But Philippe had long ago resigned himself to a poor harvest, and by now, early in November, all the useable grapes had been gathered. There would be no 1870 Château de Casseuil.

'I suppose,' Jean Delisle had said the day after the Delmas brothers had left for training camp, 'it's just as well we can't hope for much when we're so short of men. Imagine how it would have been if we'd had a vintage wine to make and no one to do it!' But the thought did not seem to cheer him much, even though the call-up had spared him and the arrival of his forty-first birthday had now put him firmly beyond its reach.

The *régisseur* was not good company these days; but then

neither was Philippe. This morning a visit to the office by Monsieur Chabry – which appeared to give the Mayor a certain malicious pleasure – had not helped matters either.

He found Laure sitting on a stool close to the fire in the *petit salon* with the dogs stretched out on a rug beside her. She was fondling their ears by turns and gazing into the fire, her expression as sombre as Philippe knew his own to be.

'Where's my mother, do you know?'

Laure turned her head. 'Upstairs I think. She had letters to write. Has something happened?'

He came and stood looking down at her. 'I've just heard. The call-up has been extended – there are to be no exceptions. They're taking the married men now too.'

She said nothing for a moment; then asked in a voice that sounded strangled somehow, 'No matter what age?' She had gone very pale.

'So long as they're between twenty-one and forty, no.'

She swept to her feet and clung to him with a desperate fierceness. 'Oh Philippe, I don't want you to go – I couldn't bear it!'

He put his arms about her, holding her firmly but gently. 'Who wanted France defended then, and no talk of a dishonourable peace?'

'That was different – and aren't there enough, without you?'

Philippe tried to make his tone as casual and reassuring as possible. 'They may not get round to me until it's over; it depends how quickly the authorities move. Monsieur Chabry had only been informed of Gambetta's decree yesterday and came to tell me of it – he has no definite instructions yet. We must be prepared, that's all.'

At lunch a little later Laure could scarcely eat, and now and then found herself weeping openly. All those summer hopes, where were they now? The war that would be over in days, the child that would come to them, the new life in their marriage – was that all to end like this, with Philippe going away to fight?

Madame Naillac, more sombre and austere than ever, observed her daughter-in-law critically for some time, and then said with asperity, 'Control yourself, Laure. If Philippe is called to do his duty, it is not for us to undermine his courage.'

Then, as they rose at the end of the meal, she said suddenly, 'I shall call on Monsieur Chabry this afternoon.'

Philippe, half way to the door, turned and stood quite still. 'Indeed, Maman? Why, may I ask?'

For a moment Laure thought Madame Naillac looked almost flustered. 'I should like to be sure of the terms of the decree. It may be that you are not eligible after all – and one knows that the discretion of the authorities can sometimes be exerted in favour of one or another individual.'

'No!' Shocked, Laure stared at Philippe, astonished to hear him contradict his mother. 'No, Maman, I forbid you to call on Chabry! No member of my family will go crawling to him.' Realising perhaps what effect this unwonted defiance must have on his mother, he came and took her hands in his and went on more gently, 'Besides, Maman, it would do no good – on the contrary, Chabry would only be more inclined to make sure that the terms did include me.'

'Surely not, *mon cher*! Do you forget that there is talk of allowing mayors to be chosen by election? He will do all he can to curry favour with the electors, for fear he loses his post when the election comes.'

'But the mayor is to be elected by the municipal council,' put in Laure, 'and they won't vote for someone who favours the well-to-do. Can you imagine Jean Lambert voting for a mayor who took his son and his nephews and kept Philippe safe at home?'

Madame Naillac turned cold eyes on Laure. 'What do you know about it, pray?'

'I've heard the men talking to Monsieur Delisle – I know what they think of Monsieur Chabry, and of the war, and the injustice of military service.'

'Have you nothing better to do than listen to peasant gossip?' The retort silenced Laure, the more especially as it was accompanied by a reproving glance from Philippe. But Madame Naillac did not, after all, call on the Mayor that afternoon.

Laure did not want to let Philippe out of her sight, not for a moment. Now she knew she might lose him, all the frustrations, the resentments, the ill feeling that, sometimes, had come between them, faded to nothing. All that mattered was that she loved him, and he was hers, and they might have so little time left together. When he returned to the *chai* that afternoon, saying, 'No, Laure, stay here – you will only distract me,' she watched him go with a pain as great as if he were indeed marching to war. That night in bed she knew that some at least of her mood was shared by him. He turned to her without hesitation, and with an eager hunger that was quite new; and she responded with all the longing of her heart. For that little time, carried beyond themselves by desire, they could forget everything. For the next few weeks as they waited, tense, fearful, for the blow to fall, they clung to one another, together as often as they could, seizing every moment that came their way to make love with that same desperate passion.

I know how Nanon felt when Jacques had to go, Laure thought. I know why she gave in to him. She watched the young peasant girl in church, on the day the *curé* celebrated mass in thanksgiving for the victory at Coulmiers near Orléans a few days before. Nanon's eyes were shining, full of pride and tears, as the Abbé Lebrun spoke of the valiant young soldiers of the Armée de la Loire whose patriotic fervour had given them victory over the ruthless invader. Jacques Lambert, they all knew, had been one of that number. 'Oh, let the war be over soon, very soon!' Laure prayed. 'Before Nanon's baby is born – before they send for Philippe – soon, soon!'

It must be soon, because her mother had said Paris could only hold out to the end of November, and that was just a few weeks away. Winter had come early here, with bitter cold. What must it be like in Paris, so much further north?

'It is cold, so cold, and there is so little fuel for the fires, even if one has money to buy it. For the poor it is very hard, and they are hungry too, although thank goodness those who serve in the National Guard have their pay to keep themselves alive, and their families. But do not fear for us, *chère* Laure, you would be amazed at how high our spirits are still, and how ingenious one can be with the oddest food. We have not yet tried rat, although I am told that with the right sauce it is not unpleasant. I must admit my conscience was not easy about it, but we did find cat to be very palatable, and dog too – and if one has the means, one can buy camel, or monkey, or even elephant – the animals from the Jardin des Plantes have, alas, come to serve us only too well! Horsemeat too is common, though I do not care for it much. But one must eat! It is still news of which we are most starved, for it is only what the occasional carrier pigeon brings in that tells us what goes on out there where you are, *chère* Laure, and no pigeon brings us news of you!'

They had that second balloon-borne letter from Laure's parents on the bleak December day when news came of the defeat of the Armée de la Loire at Orléans, now once again – after a taste of liberation – in Prussian hands. 'So, the war's not going to be over soon,' Laure said mournfully.

'Not unless we suffer total defeat,' agreed Philippe.

'Which we must not – not ever!'

'Even if it means I have to go and fight?'

She moved further into his arms.

'I've heard the delegation at Tours is moving to Bordeaux. It's further from the enemy, and so much safer.'

She looked up at him. 'So Gambetta will be in Bordeaux?'

'When he's not rushing around inspiring everyone to greater efforts, yes, I suppose so. Would you like to go to Bordeaux for a few days? War or not, it should be lively with the government there – and I have to go on business anyway.'

Laure bent her head, concentrating for no apparent reason on Philippe's top waistcoat button, her fingers tracing its shape, round and round. 'Let's wait and see, after tomorrow.'

'Why tomorrow? What's happening tomorrow?'

'Nothing.' Her colour rose, and she was smiling a little, but still she shook her head. 'Wait – wait and see.'

When Philippe returned to the house for lunch next day he found Madame Naillac alone in the dining-room.

'I don't know where she is,' said his mother stiffly, in answer to his question. 'She slipped out without a word to anyone – except, I suppose, Aristide, since she took the carriage. I shall speak to her about it when she returns.'

But when, moments later, Laure did return and stood poised in the dining-room doorway looking at them, something in her face silenced them. Rosy, smiling, her eyes brimming with unshed tears, she seemed unable to speak.

It was Philippe, coming to her, who found his voice first. 'Laure?'

Her hands clasped together in her little fur muff, her shining eyes raised to his beneath the brim of her pretty tilted hat, she stood there smiling and smiling. And then at last she whispered huskily, 'Oh Philippe, I've been to see Doctor Rossillon. It's what I thought! I'm going to have a baby.'

CHAPTER
FIVE

i

Aubin stood alone in the centre of the *chai*, very still, very white in the face. No one yet had dared to go to him, or to touch him, or to say anything, as if they feared the consequences of shattering that unnatural immobility. Instead they stood a little distance away, watching him.

After a moment, Robert Martin who, as Aubin's brother-in-law, had brought the news, took a step forward, and then thought better of it. In the end it was Jean Delisle who put an arm about the boy. 'Go home with Robert, *mon enfant*. There is no need to come back until you wish to.'

'Of course not,' added Philippe.

'And if there is anything your father needs – or anyone . . .'

'Yes, *monsieur*. Thank you.'

They were going with the boy to the door when it opened. Philippe looked quickly up, and then mounted the steps and gently drew Laure out again into the cold January rain. 'No, Laure, don't—'

'I heard – they said Aubin's brother—'

Philippe patted her hand. 'I know, I know, but you mustn't come in, not in your condition. You know what I said.'

'I thought, at a time like this—'

'All the more reason not to upset things. They have very strong feelings about pregnant women in the *chai*. I know it's superstition, but I don't want any trouble. Come now, back to the house. It's much too cold for you.'

Ever since her pregnancy had been confirmed, Philippe had been obsessively protective, cossetting her as if she were the most fragile thing ever created. On the whole she liked it – but not today, when she wanted so much to share in the tragedy

90

that had hit Casseuil; her village now, her corner of France as much as Philippe's. Besides, it was not so much Philippe's concern for her that kept her from the *chai* as the firmly held local belief that the presence of a pregnant woman would turn the wine to vinegar. Sometimes she wondered if, for all his education, Philippe half believed it too.

'Can't I speak to Aubin?'

'Better not.' Philippe steered her inexorably back to the house. 'It's not sunk in yet, I think. He's better with his own people.' He shook his head. 'It'll hit them hard. Jacques was a fine young man. And Aubin's hardly of an age to take his place.'

'Poor Nanon.'

It seemed to take him a moment to realise who she meant. 'Yes. Though perhaps the child will help, when it comes.'

Instinctively, Laure's hand moved to her own stomach, still scarcely rounded. 'I suppose it must, a little.' She stepped into the hall, glad to be out of the rain. Behind them Sylvestre closed the door on the sad little group making its way across the courtyard back to the village. 'As if it wasn't enough to have suffered such a defeat, without this too.' They had heard some days ago of the overwhelming Prussian victory at Le Mans, but that it had any more personal bearing on them no one had realised until word came this morning of Jacques Lambert's death in the battle.

'They're saying the Prussians are bombarding Paris now too.' Sylvestre's voice had the indefinable note of a man who takes a certain grim satisfaction from adding to the general sense of doom.

Laure gave a little cry and Philippe, furious, put an arm about her. 'Sylvestre, have you taken leave of your senses?'

The *valet de chambre* observed the new pallor of Laure's face and was instantly contrite. 'Forgive me, *madame – monsieur* – I did not think.'

'That is patently obvious.' Philippe's tone was withering. He held Laure to him and stroked her hair. 'Come upstairs, *chérie*. Rest a little, and don't be afraid. No harm will come to your parents. They are civilians, after all.'

'Papa's in the *Garde Nationale*.'

'I don't suppose they'll have much to do, with regular

troops there too. You must calm yourself, for our child's sake.'

'For the child's sake.' The phrase echoed constantly in her ears these days, expressing the loving concern of Philippe and his mother. Irritated sometimes, yet grateful, Laure could only yield to it, and wish that her anxiety for her parents did not cast such a shadow over her present happiness. Now, meekly, she allowed Philippe to lead her upstairs.

ii

'*Chérie*,' said Philippe from the doorway, with such a note of concerned tenderness that Laure looked up sharply from where she lay on the sunlit sofa in the *petit salon*. 'I have just read, in the paper . . .' He raised his hand with the newspaper clutched in it.

She waited, studying his face: a little pale, expressionless, it told her nothing, except that he found it difficult to choose the words for what he had to say.

He came into the room, placing the newspaper carefully on the table, beyond her reach. Then he seated himself on the chair beside her, transferring the muddle of books and discarded needlework that scattered it on to the floor. He took her hands in his.

'*Chérie*,' he said again, very gently. 'Paris has capitulated.'

For a moment she felt nothing. In her head, a detached little voice said, 'It is over'. No more cold and hunger within that suffering city; no more thundering guns.

Philippe passed her the paper and she read, slowly, seeing everything as clearly as if she were there. The past weeks: the constant boom of the bombardment, while children died of starvation and old people shivered and froze to death, and the numbers of the injured mounted daily . . . And at Versailles, in the great Hall of Mirrors of the ancient palace of the kings of France, the Prussian King had himself proclaimed Emperor – Kaiser – of all the Germans, and feasted his courtiers and generals in pompous celebration.

Now the guns were quiet, the long – unbelievably long – resistance over. 'Eighty days,' Laure murmured. 'They said they could hold out for eighty days, at the most. That's less than three months. And they held out for four.' Her voice had

92

an unmistakable note of pride. Then she thought, at what cost? What must it be like now, in Paris?

As if reading her thoughts, Philippe reached over to show her a paragraph in the paper. 'You see, they brought food in at once. The English have been very generous, they say.'

Laure should have felt relief. Instead, she felt only a great sadness, like a weight settling about her middle, heavy and oppressive. She tried to fight it: 'Paris is not France,' she said aloud. 'Gambetta still has an army in the field.'

Philippe took her hand in his and stroked it gently. 'We must not delude ourselves, *ma chérie*. The Emperor chose to take on the might of Prussia. The only lesson *that* has taught us is that Prussia is now the master of Europe – no, it's Germany now, isn't it? The new great power. Everything has changed. We are nothing any more, just a defeated enemy.'

He sounded so despondent that Laure longed to comfort him. 'It won't always be so,' she said. 'France will be great again, you'll see.'

'Perhaps it would be better for us all if she didn't try to be,' he suggested. He forced a smile, and then bent to kiss her. 'We shall have peace now; we must be thankful for that.' He took her in his arms. 'Do you realise, your parents have no idea that you are going to have a baby? I'll bring you paper and a pen and you must write at once and tell them our news. And then you must ask them to come and stay for as long as they like.'

The letter went on its way, and Laure waited, and feared, in case there should not be a reply at all.

The very next day a letter came from her mother, sent the moment the siege ended, but written at intervals during the last terrible weeks of desperate hunger and incessant bombardment, a letter of high courage and wild hopes, ending with an account of a meal eaten the previous night which in its lovingly detailed description of fairly ordinary ingredients told Laure more than anything else what her parents must have endured. Madame Frémont concluded, 'I cannot write more now, but I will send this so you know we are well. You will hear again very soon.' Laure's own letter had not of course reached them by then.

Her father's reply followed swiftly after; and it proved to be shockingly different from what she had anticipated, a total contrast with her mother's cheerful account of danger. She had not thought her father capable of such bitterness and anger. 'I have resigned from my post in the Ministry of Finance. I felt honoured to serve the Republic; now I feel only disgust that a government in which I have a part, however small, should so have dragged the honour and pride of France in the dust. You will have heard the terms of the armistice agreed with the Prussians; you will know that to win a spineless and cowardly peace we are to give up two of our fairest provinces to the conqueror and pay two thousand million francs as a bribe to free the rest of our soil from occupation. You will say that the terms are not yet ratified by an elected assembly, that there are still Frenchmen in arms against the invader – but if you believe that in the end that will make any difference, then you are fortunate in not yet having learned the bitter lesson that has been forced upon us at the hands of those in whom we placed our trust.'

At the end, briefly, he spoke of their joy at her news, thanked Philippe for his invitation, and declined it. 'For the time being we prefer to remain here. Casseuil is rather far to come at this time of year. Perhaps in the summer you may expect a visit.' And that was all.

Laure was disappointed, even a little hurt; and greatly distressed by her father's outpouring. 'He's not quite fair, I think,' commented Philippe carefully. 'France needs peace, and I don't imagine we could have won it on any other terms. I know not everyone agrees – Gambetta resigned too, so your father's in good company; but I think most people will accept it, however regretfully. The elections will tell.'

iii

'You have finished the pruning very quickly, considering that we are still so short of labourers,' Madame Naillac said, as they sat at dinner some days later.

Philippe, emerging from some private thoughts of his own, smiled faintly at his mother, but made no comment.

'When will the Delmas brothers come home, do you think?' Laure asked.

Philippe shrugged. 'When the government decides, I suppose.'

'Or the Prussians,' suggested Laure. 'Don't they say we have to reduce our army to nothing?' She half expected Madame Naillac to rebuke her for talking politics, but no rebuke came.

Instead, the old woman said, 'That is natural enough, *ma chère* Laure. After all, we can have little use for an army now.' These days, astonishingly, it was always '*ma chère* Laure'. Laure had decided after a time that Madame Naillac's new warmth towards her was no pretence. By becoming pregnant, Laure had at last shown herself worthy of Philippe, and so she had won the right to his mother's affection.

'It is humiliating all the same,' Laure pursued, rather rashly, she thought; but Madame Naillac seemed as inclined as she was to discuss the latest news.

'The elections showed a clear wish for peace,' she pointed out. 'In ratifying the peace terms the Assembly was simply carrying out the will of the people.'

'Sometimes I wonder about the will of the people,' observed Laure, whilst imagining how her father would exclaim at such a heretical statement. 'I find it very hard to believe the majority of the people really want the Bourbon kings to rule us again.'

'Yet the vast majority of the deputies elected are Royalists of one kind or another,' said Philippe. 'Even Adolphe Thiers, who leads them, is said to have some Royalist leanings. But Doctor Rossillon is of the opinion that the election result was more of a protest than anything else. The Royalists are the only ones who had nothing to do either with the war or the defeat. The Bonapartists and the Republicans are both discredited now.'

'But which king do the Royalists want – there are two claimants aren't there?'

'That is for them to sort out,' said Madame Naillac. 'I do not imagine it will have any great effect upon us here.'

'Unless it leads to civil war.'

'Pray do not be melodramatic, *ma chère* Laure!'

'But there's already trouble in some of the big cities, isn't there – in Lyon, for instance?'

'Just the usual left wing rabble,' said Madame. 'And the cities are not France, after all. France is pre-eminently the countryside – you must remember that. I think that is one great advantage in having the Assembly meeting in Bordeaux – it helps the deputies to remember that Paris is really of no importance at all.'

'So they agreed that the Prussian army should occupy Paris for two days!' Laure exclaimed. 'You know what the Parisians think about that.' Her father's letter, received this morning, had told them plainly enough: 'Now we must endure the humiliation of Prussian feet marching where our own armies have trod – the boots of a slavish and despotic nation profaning the soil from which liberty sprang. What more can there be for us to suffer now?'

'It is simply a token gesture, that is all – one of those things that the defeated must endure.' Madame Naillac's uncharacteristic tolerance came to an end at last. 'It seems to me, *ma chère* Laure, that you should not be worrying about such things at this time. I remember well when I was carrying Philippe that I took care always to keep my thoughts only on what was beautiful and calming to the spirit.'

Amused, Laure glanced at Philippe, but he showed no sign of sharing her reaction, or even that he had heard what his mother had said. He was gazing rather sombrely towards the window where the February rain dashed relentlessly against the glass: the shutters had not yet been closed.

Later, when they rose from the table to adjourn to the *grand salon*, Philippe went to close them. Madame Naillac frowned. 'Leave that. I will ring for a servant to do it, in a moment.'

His hands fell, and he moved towards the door, following Laure, who was already crossing the hall.

'Wait!' said his mother. 'I want to speak to you.' Philippe halted, silent, while she closed the door and turned to face him. 'You saw Doctor Rossillon today.' It was not quite a question.

'Yes.'

'Then you spoke of the matter we discussed the other day. What was his reaction?'

'If you mean: did we discuss the municipal elections? No, we did not.'

She frowned. 'But why not? I understood that was your purpose in going to see him.'

He shrugged. 'May is a long way off.'

'Oh, Philippe, what is the matter with you? If you are to stand for election as mayor, then you have to gather your supporters together, draw up a plan of campaign, make a list of names to present to the people. That can't be done overnight.'

'You are supposing that I wish to stand as mayor.'

'That was what we agreed.'

'It was what you suggested. I have not yet decided.'

'But surely you don't want Chabry to be elected, now that there's a chance to oust him?'

A smile briefly lit the sombreness of his face. 'I don't think there's much danger of that, even if I don't stand at all. He has few friends in the commune.'

'But you must stand! Can't you see?'

He put out a hand to silence her, his expression once again gloomy and withdrawn. 'Have you not thought, Maman? You know what it is like at election time – the dirt scraped up, the way everyone seeks out every little tiny weakness, every breath of scandal, anything to discredit his opponent. And Chabry has never had any scruples, whatever impression he may like to give on the surface.'

'You are surely not afraid of him? Your conscience is clear!'

He hesitated, biting his lip; then said, 'That would not stop him, and . . .' After another pause, he added, 'I would not want Laure to be subjected to such unpleasantness, at this time.'

'We can protect her from it, between us – you know that.'

He turned away from her to stand with his fingers tapping on the window sill. 'I don't know . . . I feel . . .'

She laid a hand on his arm. 'It is your right, Philippe, your place, to be mayor of Casseuil. It is expected of you.'

He glanced at her. 'By whom, Maman? You – or the voters? I don't know. I have no real interest in it, especially not now.'

'That is only a passing mood. You are anxious, of course. But later, once the child is born, things will seem different, I assure you. You *must* stand!'

He sighed. 'Let it rest, Maman. I'm meeting with Doctor Rossillon and the others next week. We shall see then.'

Relieved, she gave one of her rare smiles. 'Then that is all right. They will convince you that you must stand, I know.'

iv

The château garden changed little through the year: only its lawns, crossed by the neat gravel paths, decorated by the fountain and a stone seat, showed a brighter green in spring, and in summer—everywhere but under the shade of the walnut and chestnut trees – a parched dun colour. But then the glory of the garden was its view, beyond the low stone wall that edged the slope into the valley. Down there, on this late March day, was all the colour and sweetness of springtime, the dazzling white of blossom on orchard trees, the pale green of poplars, the pink haze of new life smudging the outline of oak and chestnut, dandelions spreading gold on roadside and meadow, hawthorn and wild rose edging the woods, the willows veiling the water of pools and streams with a more lively green. Near at hand the vines still had a wintry look about their gnarled black stems, but Laure knew that if one studied them closely one would see the new buds bursting their brown sheaths. Between the rows Aubin Lambert guided the plough behind the plodding oxen, turning the soil to aerate it and free the bases of the vines from the protective covering that had kept frost at bay through the winter months. If his brother's death had affected him deeply he showed little sign of it, Laure thought; much less than poor Nanon Foussac who, heavily pregnant, came to mass each Sunday leaning on her mother's arm, and often disturbed the little congregation with her weeping. Laure, full of fervent thankfulness for her own happiness, was distressed that anyone at all should have reason to grieve.

Today, though, her serenity was untroubled. She smiled to herself, her mind empty of anything much more than a general sense of contented well-being, enlivened by the burgeoning of spring around her. The trickling of the water, the rippling song of a bird somewhere in a tree far across the garden, the gentle rustle of the wind, all seemed to flow through her with a rhythmic vibration right to the depths where the growing child lay curled in darkness, still, quiet, waiting.

No – no, not still – with a sudden leap of wonder she looked down and laid both hands over the gentle swell of her stomach. No, she had not imagined it. There had been something there, a faint distinct fluttering, quite unlike the ordinary internal rumblings of her digestion. The baby had moved.

She laughed softly to herself, felt the sensation again, even thought it rippled against her palm. She glanced around, longing to see someone she could tell; but the garden was deserted. She began to hurry towards the house, all eagerness; and then remembered that Philippe had gone to Bordeaux the day before yesterday and would not be home until dinnertime. He went there much less often these days, but he could not of course wholly neglect his work because she was pregnant, especially since she was so well – only it would have been good to tell him. There was Madame Naillac, of course, but even in her new, more approachable frame of mind Laure did not quite want her to be the first to know. Then Florestine came to tell her that Doctor Rossillon was here, so she hurried indoors and poured out her joy to him.

He must have heard it all many times before from the women he had attended through twenty years of medical practice, but his reaction was all she could have wished. 'Excellent, my dear *madame*, excellent! Just as it should be. Everything is going very well indeed.'

She liked Doctor Rossillon. He was a warm kindly man without airs and graces. He might perhaps lack the city doctor's acquaintance with the latest medical knowledge, or his sophistication, but he was a sympathetic listener and unfailingly reassuring.

'You speak of the infant as "he" I notice,' he commented with a smile. 'You're quite sure it's a boy?'

She smiled serenely back at him. 'Quite sure. I've felt sure from the first moment. Philippe says it doesn't matter, and I mustn't be disappointed if I'm wrong, but I shan't be, because I *know*.'

'What matters is that you bear a healthy infant of whatever kind and remain in the best of health yourself,' said the doctor briskly, 'and I'm glad to say that, at least, looks a certain prospect.' He examined her rather cursorily, by way of final confirmation of his view – Florestine was present of course, as she always was during the doctor's visits. 'Monsieur Naillac is in Bordeaux, I gather?'

Laure nodded. 'Yes.'

'He'll find it very quiet then, now the Assembly's gone. We shan't know what to do with ourselves after all the excitement. Though it looks as though there'll be fireworks in Paris in the near future. The deputies were wise to settle on Versailles as the seat of government and not Paris itself.'

Laure had not even glanced at a newspaper for some time, nor heard from her parents since her father's last bitter letter. The inward-looking lassitude of pregnancy had taken her over, protecting her more surely than Philippe and his mother ever could from the troubles of the world outside. 'What do you think is going to happen then?'

Doctor Rossillon gave her a keenly questioning glance. 'You know some of the Parisian hotheads have declared a Commune?' She shook her head, a little puzzled. 'Not like our little commune here, of course, worrying about the state of the roads and whether to let the presbytery fall down. As I'm sure you know Paris has had no elected governing body since her commune gave such trouble during the Revolution. Now they have one again. Its members make some wild claim to be speaking for the whole of France, the way Parisians do. There's a good deal of talk about the government's betrayal and so forth. I expect you've heard the kind of thing.'

'Yes, from my father.'

The doctor smiled wryly. 'This new lot in control in Paris make us stolid Republicans look positively right wing, I fear – a motley crew of revolutionaries, old and new, with goodness knows how many years of prison and exile between them. Though one has to admit, the people of Paris did elect them, hard though it may be to believe. In my opinion hurt pride's at the root of it; but we shall see. There have been one or two nasty incidents, but I don't doubt Monsieur Thiers will have order restored in no time – he has a name for firmness.' He studied the growing anxiety on her face, and added quickly, 'I wouldn't have brought it up, only I thought you'd know. Don't worry about your parents. The papers say things are normal enough for ordinary people, whatever odd goings-on there may be at the Hôtel de Ville.'

Laure remembered Baron Haussmann's wide new streets built to prevent barricades and to allow easy access by police or troops, and was reassured, a little. Her father had been quite certain that the old revolutionary days of fighting in the streets were at an end, and he knew his Paris as well as anyone. As much as anything to distract herself from the inevitable tremor of anxiety, Laure changed the subject. 'I hear you're standing as mayor at the local elections in May.'

Instinctively, Doctor Rossillon drew himself up to his full height, smiling with happy pride. 'Yes, that's right. Someone has to oppose Chabry. I tried to get your husband to add his name to my list for the municipal council, but he wasn't interested.'

'I didn't know that!' She felt momentarily a little hurt that Philippe had not mentioned this approach and then was a little consoled to think that he had apparently not told his mother either, since she had said nothing about it.

'I thought he might be offended that he wasn't heading the list himself. I suspect Madame Naillac would like to see him as mayor. I would have been quite happy to take second place to him, but I was overruled by my colleagues. In any case, Monsieur Naillac assured me he has no interest in public affairs at all. I had the impression he has more personal worries at present, but you'll know about that. Perhaps quite simply he doesn't want any further responsibilities before this child of yours makes his appearance. You've been through so much to get you to this point. You tell him there's absolutely nothing to worry about, won't you?'

She told him, of course, but Philippe's protectiveness towards her did not lessen in the least. It was made worse by news that could only increase Laure's anxiety about her parents.

Within a matter of weeks Paris was once more under siege, and this time by her own fellow countrymen. Terrible rumours reached them as time passed, so that Laure found it impossible not to be deeply troubled; rumours of arrests and shootings by the revolutionary Commune, of all kinds of excesses towards those who did not share its views. The small unpleasantnesses of their own municipal elections, which resulted in a sweeping success for Doctor Rossillon and his supporters, came as light relief, in contrast to the news from Paris.

At the end of May the government troops finally entered the capital and found that the days of barricades were not after all at an end. They were met, so the papers said, by a desperate resistance from men and women who deliberately set Paris burning around them in a kind of bitter spite at their defeat. The most terrifying *Communards* of all were the *pétroleuses*, a force of women 8,000 strong (so it was said) who rampaged through the streets hurling improvised petrol bombs into any building not yet alight.

Then it was over, the rebellion crushed, thousands of prisoners in the hands of the government at Versailles; and a brief letter came from Laure's parents. 'May we come and visit you for a little while? We have reached a decision that we wish to discuss with you face to face. We are well.'

Laure was puzzled by the curtness of the letter, so unlike her parents' usual effusive style; but she was too relieved to worry about it unduly. Probably they were, quite simply, exhausted, after all they had endured through the past year. Philippe would be delighted to welcome them, she wrote in reply; and so of course would she.

v

It was a day of intense heat when Philippe went with the carriage to meet the train at Libourne and bring Laure's parents back to Casseuil. Laure, listening restlessly from her couch, heard the rumble of wheels on the gravel outside and flew into the hall to greet them. Madame Naillac, more dignified, waited until the fervent embraces had subsided a little, and then said, 'I've ordered tea to be brought. I'm sure you will be glad of some immediate refreshment after your journey.' She led them into the *grand salon* and ushered them to chairs. 'You must have had a terrible time at the hands of those bloodthirsty monsters. How glad we are that you are safe.'

Laure, looking from her mother to her father and back again, thought that the past weeks had indeed left their mark. In the hall it had been too dim to see clearly, but now it was only too obvious how grey and exhausted they both looked.

'Which bloodthirsty monsters had you in mind?' returned her father, with such an odd dry note in his otherwise expressionless voice that Laure was startled.

Madame Naillac too seemed a little surprised. 'Those *Communards*, of course, with their dreadful women – we heard all about it. But that's not the same as living through it of course. One gathered that they made short shrift of their enemies. Since one supposes that meant anyone of means and respectability, we did fear for your safety.'

Was Madame Naillac simply being polite, Laure wondered, or had she indeed been more anxious than she had allowed Laure, in her pregnant state, to see? She noticed now that Philippe exchanged a glance with his mother; and decided with some alarm that the latter was the case. It must indeed have been bad.

'Oh, I was taken in for questioning once in the early days, but very soon released,' said Monsieur Frémont casually; although again Laure had that uncomfortable sense of something lying suppressed beneath his words. 'After that we moved in with friends, judging it wiser not to make ourselves too conspicuous. It was inconvenient, but no worse.' He looked round the comfortable, solidly furnished room, and added, 'We shall be glad of the quiet of Casseuil for a little time.'

After that, the conversation languished, and when Madame Naillac suggested that the Frémonts might like an hour or two of rest in their room before dinner, the suggestion was eagerly seized upon. Laure insisted on going up with her parents, driven by an increasing conviction that something was very badly wrong, something more than mere exhaustion.

She was completely sure of it when she stepped into the room after them, pausing just inside the door, and they turned in silence to look at her. She thought they would begin to speak at once. Perhaps that was what they intended, for they both had a strained poised look, and her mother raised a hand in a weary, almost imploring gesture, and then let it fall again as if she could not begin to find the words for what she wanted to say; and sat down on the window seat. Jules Frémont glanced at her, closed his hand upon her shoulder, and then explained quietly to his daughter, 'Your mother needs rest, Laure. It's been a terrible time, for everyone. I never thought—' He broke off there, as if afraid that, in going on, his voice might give way altogether, allowing through all the emotions that Laure knew lay underneath. As it was, the impassivity that had been in his tone downstairs had quite gone, leaving it harsh and rasping.

Madame Frémont turned her head to look out of the window; with the light full on her face the quivering of her lip was clearly visible. 'It's so quiet here,' she said in a whisper. And then she gave a single choking cry, bent her face in her hands and burst into tears.

Laure ran and knelt on the floor beside her and put her arms about her. 'Oh, Maman, don't! What is it? Tell me – oh, don't cry so!' She felt her mother cling to her, felt her rest her forehead on her shoulder, felt her body shake with every sob; just with such abandon had she herself wept sometimes in her mother's arms, a child seeking comfort in the most natural place in the world. But now it was her mother who was broken with grief, and she the daughter who offered the shoulder and the comforting arms. And her father stood by with desolate eyes as if he too wanted somewhere to turn for help. It was an odd unpleasant reversal of the order of things, making Laure feel as if a sudden chill wind had somehow found its way into a warm and shuttered room.

After a time, as her mother's weeping grew a little less, Laure looked round at her father, standing rather helplessly behind her. 'You said you had reached a decision about something. Is this to do with that?'

Her father hesitated, looked down and up again. Like his wife just now, he made a silent gesture with his hand, expressive of the inadequacy of words. Then he cleared his throat vigorously and said, 'The house is burned, you know.' His tone was oddly matter of fact, as if the destruction of the house was no more than a trivial accident. But his restless eyes never met Laure's for more than a moment and hinted at things unspoken, things that held the real horror, whatever it was, behind her mother's sobs and the tension that afflicted them both. Yet if the burning of their house was not the real horror, what was? Nothing surely could be worse than that? She stared at her father, while her hand continued tenderly to stroke her mother's hair.

'So of course is the Tuileries,' her father went on, 'and my old ministry in the Louvre, and the Hôtel de Ville, and most of the new Opéra, and a hundred other buildings large and small. Paris is in ruins.' He moved uneasily away, and then nearer again to rest one hand against the folded shutters by the window. 'But buildings can be reconstructed. Some things cannot.'

Laure felt a shudder, warning of a fresh outburst of sobbing, run through her mother. 'I shall never go back, never!' She raised her head then, so that Laure could see the ravaged tear-stained face; and she went on in a rapid painful near-whisper, as if compelled to speak, though every word cost her some agony of recollection. 'Laure, there are corpses under the streets now, just anyhow where they crushed the barricades and rebuilt the roads on top. They buried some alive, so they say. The Seine ran blood; we saw it, a great smear in the water, like oil . . . and the wagons, full of corpses, a whole load just from one courtyard, you could smell the burning afterwards.' The words trailed away in renewed sobbing, and Laure murmured the soft tender little phrases that once would have comforted her in some childish grief.

'I did not know it was so bad,' she said in distress, when her mother was calm enough for her to give her attention again to her father. 'We heard some things. The papers said they'd tried to burn down Paris. They said there was an army of women.'

To her surprise her father smiled, a tiny, bitter, mirthless smile that hardly deserved the name. 'The *pétroleuses*? Yes, it made a good story: we heard it too. There may have been a few, acting alone – I don't know.'

'There was Madame Paulin.' Her mother's voice broke through on a sob.

'Madame Paulin? The washerwoman from around the

corner?' Laure looked puzzled: surely her mother could not be implying that the quiet respectful elderly widow was one of that fanatical band?

'Yes, that's the one.' Jules Frémont nodded grimly. 'She was on her way to the dairy with an empty milk bottle. Poor old soul, she wasn't to know how that would look to suspicious minds seeing incendiary devices on every side. They shot her as a *pétroleuse*. And Jean her son, you remember him, a bit slow in the head? When he saw what they'd done he flew at them in a rage. They shot him too.'

'Who? Who shot him?' For the first time it began to dawn on Laure that it was not after all the excesses of the *Communards* that had so appalled her parents.

'The soldiers from Versailles; the government troops, of course. Who else?'

Laure was silent for a moment. 'But terrible things had been done, hadn't they? People said there must be no mercy for the guilty.'

'There was no mercy for anyone, Laure.' Abruptly he pulled up a chair and sat down close to his daughter, talking earnestly. 'Oh, certainly there were wrongs done by the *Communards*, arbitrary arrests, murders – you will have heard of the Archbishop's murder, of course. They were a rabble, many of them, but what they did was nothing, nothing at all set against the revenge of the Versailles troops.' After a pause, as if gathering strength to draw breath, he asked, 'Do you know how many fell under the guillotine during the period of the Great Terror during the Revolution?'

Laure shook her head, leaving him to answer for her. 'Two thousand, perhaps three, they say: an appalling figure in a few short months. The very thought of it still makes us tremble with fear and shame.' He almost smiled again at the puzzlement in her eyes; and then he concluded harshly, 'Early estimates suggest that in our week of blood just past, our enlightened and civilised government was responsible for the deaths of at least fifteen thousand of its own citizens – and I think that may well prove to be a gross underestimate.'

The figure was too vast to mean anything to Laure. She could think only of little Madame Paulin and her slow good-natured son; and of her mother weeping in her arms. She said carefully, as if clutching at some kind of excuse, 'They said the fighting was desperate.'

'So it was, but very many of those killings were in cold blood: prisoners, passers-by, anyone who offered any excuse. As for the real *Communards*, they fared worst. You remember Octave Bruard?'

Marcel's friend, the agitator of whom her father so strongly disapproved, imprisoned more than once by the Emperor: 'Yes.'

'They had him with others in a line of prisoners bound for Versailles. We saw them being marched through the streets near the Champs Elysées, through crowds howling for their blood – well-to-do people like ourselves, who'd lost a great deal, as we had, and were angry – but I can find nothing in that to excuse them. They were like animals, not human beings at all. Someone must have known Bruard, and perhaps had some grudge against him, for there was a sudden rush from the crowd to seize him. The soldiers intervened, dragged him clear – and then beat him to death themselves with their rifle butts. I know that is true, because I saw it.'

Laure shivered, as her mother was doing now, and knew they shared the same appalling vision of what might have been. 'Thank God Marcel went away,' she whispered. Her parents had no need to say any more.

There was a long interval of silence, while they all followed similar grim trails of thought. Then Jules Frémont said, 'So we have reached a decision, as we told you. We are going to join Marcel.'

Laure stared at him, gave a little dismayed cry.

'Once I said I had no wish to leave the most civilised country in the world. Since then I have seen an Empire end in dishonour, a Republic accede to a disgraceful peace – and now this.' His voice was pulsating with indignation and bitterness; there were tears in his eyes. 'I have seen into the heart of our civilisation, Laure, and found only barbarity and horror. The city of lights, they called it, but the lights are those of its burning buildings, and of the corpses on their pyres. I want no part of it any more. America may be raw and new, but it lays no claim to civilisation. That is enough for me, and for your mother.'

Laure reached out a hand towards him. 'Come and live here, Papa – you would be welcome here. We're a long way from Paris.'

He shook his head. 'Casseuil is still France; and from here – God forgive you for it – that horrible vengeance looks like justice. I've heard what Philippe and his mother have to say. Besides,' he added more calmly, 'you have your own life to lead, and every reason to be happy. For you we hope that there will never be the kind of disillusionment that we have suffered, or for anyone else in France perhaps. We have no wish to take the risk any more, but for you it is different. We don't want you to have to face the possibility of a conflict of loyalties, because of us. No, our decision is made, and as soon as all the arrangements are concluded, we shall go. It shouldn't take long.'

CHAPTER
SIX

'Here, *chérie*, I thought you would like to have it at once.' 'It', Laure saw, looking up from the hot chocolate that, indolently propped on pillows, she had been sipping with luxuriant slowness, was a letter; what was more, a letter from America.

'Maman! Oh, Philippe, thank you!'

He sat down on the edge of the bed (having removed the breakfast tray to safety) and waited while she read. It was the first time she had heard from her parents since the day in mid-June when, deaf to all sensible, rational arguments, they had left Casseuil – and France – for ever. Secretly, Philippe had thought them more than a little hysterical, but there it was. He hoped that now Laure would be reassured as to their well-being.

She was. She read quickly, giggling now and then at some remark of her mother's, some lively or amusing anecdote, and at the general tone of relieved high spirits that permeated the letter. 'We have everything, *ma chère* Laure, and we miss nothing – except, of course and always, you alone. But we know at least that all is well with you, and that must be our consolation.'

She finished reading and handed the letter to Philippe, and as he read she thought, with a sense of surprise, My mother is right: all is well now, and I don't mind any longer that they are gone. I shall always miss them, always love them, but I know I can be happy without them. In the lonely days when her marriage had been at its most difficult she had clung to the thought of her parents as the one sure, safe place; the only people who would never fail her, who would always be there in her moments of greatest need. Now she recognised that the need had gone. She had her own life, her own duties separate from theirs, her own future to look forward to.

She smiled at Philippe as he folded the letter, waiting for him to return the smile, all intimate tenderness. He did return it, but only briefly, and then he said, 'I'm glad they are settling down well.' He laid down the letter and stood up, going to look out of the window. 'I have to go to Bordeaux.'

'Oh, not again!' She tried very hard to sound as if she did not really mind. 'When, today?'

He came back to the bedside and she saw that he was frowning, with something of the withdrawn look she had dreaded so much in the past. 'No, I've one or two things to do before I go. I'll leave first thing tomorrow.' He studied her face. 'I don't like to leave you so near your time.'

She smiled reassuringly. 'There are several weeks still to go, and I'm very well, and you won't be long, will you?'

'Three days, four at the most; no more than that.' She could almost see the effort he made to drive his gloomy mood away and smile at her. He pushed her hair from her face and kissed her. 'Then I promise I shall stay here until the baby comes.'

The next morning Laure did not take her breakfast in bed, as she had been accustomed to do for some weeks now. She rose when Philippe did and went down to breakfast with him, so as to see him on his way.

She was sorry that Madame Naillac was there too, although she did not really resent it; relations between them were daily growing immeasurably better. They were, almost, friends. But her mother-in-law's presence did make it impossible for her to talk to Philippe in the tender intimate way that she had planned, seeing it as a loving wifeliness to send him from her wanting only to be home again as soon as possible. In fact, conversation this morning was difficult and strained, as if Philippe's thoughts were already occupied with the impending business.

Once, Madame Naillac said, 'You'll call at the bank too, when you've seen Maître Perrard?' Maître Perrard was, Laure knew, the family lawyer. It surprised her just a little that Philippe should have told his mother more of his business than he had his wife, but then very likely she had questioned him about it. In any case, it was at Laure he glanced first before he replied, rather curtly, 'Yes, of course,' and began to pour himself some more coffee.

They were not even able to finish the meal in peace. Halfway through, Monsieur Delisle came to the house to ask for a word with Philippe, who excused himself and left.

Madame Naillac began to talk in a desultory way to Laure, as if good manners required her to entertain her son's wife in his absence, and then suggested that Laure should take her morning rest sooner than usual, in view of her early start to the day. Politely non-committal (since she did not feel in the least tired) Laure finished her breakfast as quickly as she could and wandered out into the garden.

It was already very hot; by mid morning it would be unendurable. But for now it was pleasant to wander slowly past the fountain and on to the far side of the garden. There was no wind, but at least it seemed a little fresher here. She stood still for a moment or two, looking over the shimmering valley; and then she saw Philippe not far away among the vines, deep in conversation with Monsieur Delisle. She decided to walk down to them.

They did not see her coming, and when she spoke suddenly beside him Philippe looked round with a start of surprise. 'What are you looking at so earnestly?' she asked lightly; for they had been gazing with some concentration at one of the vines.

She thought for a moment that Philippe was angry with her, and regretted having come: it was not her business after all. If he had wanted her to come he would have brought her with him. But though he said nothing, he stood aside with a gesture for her to come and look too.

She knew what to expect at this time of year, something like all the other plants in this row, which varied only very slightly one from another – the Sémillon larger and rougher and brighter in leaf than the Sauvignon Blanc, which occurred at intervals; or the rarer Muscadelle. But all, now, should be flourishing, waist high, lush with foliage beneath which the tiny green clusters were already forming.

And then she looked.

It was obvious at once that something was wrong. The plant had a sad look, the leaves sparse and marked with galls, and here and there turning yellow, as if autumn had already come; and the few fruits were small and poor. Nearby, one or two other plants had the same appearance. Someone had scraped the soil away at the base, so as to expose the roots, although at a glance Laure could not tell if anything was wrong with them.

She looked from one to another of the two men on either side. Monsieur Delisle's face was grave, even sombre; Philippe's had a frowning pallor that filled her with foreboding, for it suggested emotions fiercely suppressed, as her father's had been when he told her the house was burnt down.

'Is it – the phylloxera?'

Philippe nodded. Monsieur Delisle said, 'I fear so, *madame*, though I shall seek expert opinion to confirm it.'

Laure slid her hand through Philippe's arm and pressed it, trying to give comfort, though he did not appear to notice it. He stirred suddenly from a momentary grim reverie, and said to Monsieur Delisle, 'I must go. We'll talk about what's to be done when I return.' And then he turned and began to walk back towards the courtyard, where his horse Grand Turc was already saddled and ready. Laure had to walk very fast to keep up with him.

His parting from her was hurried and preoccupied, as if he scarcely knew what he was doing, though he did embrace her briefly. 'Go in out of the sun and rest,' he instructed her with a rather abstracted concern, before gathering up the reins and turning his horse towards the road – he preferred to ride when he went to Bordeaux. Laure felt a little oppressed by his gloom, regretting that they should have parted like this, even for so short a time. She did after all go and lie down, feeling suddenly very tired.

The days went by very slowly, so heavy with heat that it was difficult for Laure to find any way of passing the time, since the simplest of exertions left her exhausted. Only in the early mornings and late in the evenings did it grow cool enough for her to wish to venture out of doors.

The third day of Philippe's absence was the worst of all, oppressively, overwhelmingly hot. When she stepped outside soon after breakfast she found that the sun already had a burning intensity about it, so that she felt as though she were stepping into a furnace that stifled all breath and threatened to shrivel her skin and hair and eyes. Even indoors with every window flung wide there did not seem to be any tiny current of air stirring anywhere. In the end, burdened by carrying so great a weight in such concentrated heat, Laure found it easier to give in and lie on the sofa in the *grand salon*, dressed only in a fine lawn wrap, and wait for the sun to go down.

Dusk when it came hung heavy over the vineyard, turning the sky to a strange, livid yellow-grey, an evil colour, Laure thought, as if somehow the disease that lurked in the vegetation below had seeped into the whole atmosphere, poisoning and polluting everything it touched. She felt exhausted, even a little sick, and her head throbbed. It was still unbearably hot, the tense air vibrating with the shrill frenzied chorus of crickets and cicadas.

'There'll be a storm soon,' Madame Naillac commented from the shadowy corner of the room where she sat no longer able to see her book. 'That will clear the air.'

In her early days at Casseuil Laure had loved the fierce dramatic intensity of the frequent electric storms, the dark sky riven by the piercing, white hot ferocity of the jagged lightning, the earth trembling on and on at the deep crashing roar of the thunder. But perhaps her impending motherhood made her less able to find enjoyment in such elemental things, bringing out instead all the protective instincts, the longing for security, for what was familiar and gentle and safe. Whatever the reason, today she felt not exhilarated but edgy, wishing the storm would come if it must, and then be at an end so that the cool night could follow and allow her the refreshment of sleep, and help her to pass the time until Philippe's return.

'He'll not be back today, or he would have been here by now,' Madame Naillac had said at dinner-time.

The storm came at last, with a sudden fierce gust of wind that slammed the door of the *grand salon* with a sharp crack, and a tremendous united burst of thunder and lightning that set the dogs cowering beneath Laure's couch, whimpering with fear. Calmly Madame Naillac rang for a maid and asked her to close windows and shutters and pull the curtains across them. The storm receded, shut firmly outside, while their world, safe and warm and lamplit, was reduced to the space of that beautiful room, with its pictures and ornaments and quiet but restless dogs.

They knew, without other signs, when the storm had finally eased, for the younger of the two dogs (the older was too lazy) went to the door, tail wagging and eyes imploring, and asked to go out. Laure knew how he felt; she had a sudden longing herself for quietness and cool air after the heat of the day.

'I'll see him out,' she said to her mother-in-law. 'I should like a breath of air before bed.'

She thought for a moment that the older woman was about to protest; but Madame Naillac was inclined these days to indulge most of Laure's whims, attributing them, at worst, to her delicate condition. 'Take a lantern with you then,' was all she said.

The storm had receded to a distant growling flicker of light beyond the far hills; the rain that had followed it had all but ceased, leaving the air sweet with the scent of damp earth and crushed vegetation. With the dog obediently at her heels, Laure set out across the courtyard, slowly, breathing in great gulps of the refreshing air.

She had reached the well when she realised that the dog had disappeared. She raised the lantern high and looked about her: there was no sign of him. She called, softly, and then again a little louder. The dog barked sharply from some way off, from the direction of the stables, she thought. A little exasperated she called again, but still drew no other response than an answering bark. Perhaps the dog, usually obedient, was tormenting the stable cat. Since that animal, like herself, was heavily pregnant, Laure went with fellow-feeling to investigate, and go to the rescue if necessary.

The dog whimpered as she came up to him, and she began to think he must have met with some accident; but as the light fell on the animal she saw he was simply standing at the closed door of the furthermost stable, asking to be let in. 'No, you bad dog, you shan't go and chase poor Ninou. Come on now!'

The dog merely whimpered again, and raised a paw to scrape imperiously at the door. From inside the nervous

114

muffled whinny of a horse, uneasy perhaps at the unfamiliar sound outside, answered briefly.

Still the dog would not come. Then, from the corner of her eye, Laure saw a black shape, sinuous in spite of the bulging belly, move across the yard just beyond the reach of the lantern light. The dog, with the sharp instincts of an animal, must have seen the cat, but he did not stir from his post, only turned his head to look at Laure and whine again more imploringly still.

'What is the matter with you? What have you heard?' She supposed that she ought to investigate. If she had given the matter some thought she might have woken Mathieu the stable lad, asleep (presumably) in his hay loft above the carriage house. He was a big strong lad, ready for any emergency. But she did not think of intruders, only that perhaps one of the horses was sick, for she could hear that troubled whinnying again, and was struck by something odd in its sound. Philippe cared very much for his horses and would not forgive neglect; and her own beloved Fine Fleur was stabled there too.

She grasped the dog's collar, just in case, and laid down the lantern while she opened the door, and then took it up again and held it high as she went in. Fine Fleur snorted a greeting at her from somewhere in the shadows; Philippe's Grand Turc gleamed black in the light. It was him she had heard, then. He looked magnificent, as always, a beautiful specimen of healthy horse-flesh.

She came to an abrupt halt. Grand Turc, whom she had seen three days ago trotting with contained grace and power along the road away from the château with Philippe on his back – how could he be here now?

Frowning a little, trying to make it out, she went to him, reaching over the door of his stall to run a hand along the muscular arched neck. He had been rubbed down after a fashion, but there was moisture still on his mane, and his coat had a touch of dampness about it. But then it would, if he had been out in that storm.

Philippe must be home! Perhaps he had somehow passed her in the dark. She must go back to the house, quickly. Her heart light, she called, 'Hercule!' Where was that dog? The wretched animal had gone again. She heard a rustle of straw, a sharp bark, an agitated whimper. What now? she thought, following the sound to the far end of the stall.

She almost tripped on the gun, half concealed in the straw near the outstretched hand with its open palm, its relaxed fingers. Her breath caught somewhere in her throat, she lifted the lantern high. There by the whimpering dog he lay stretched on the straw, his head a bloody pulp of bone and shattered flesh, and something worse –

Philippe.

Somewhere a scream seared the night, and another and another. There was a clatter, a flash of light; and then only darkness and roaring, and a terrible wrenching pain.

CHAPTER
SEVEN

Mathilde Marie Françoise Naillac was born at dawn on the day after her father's suicide, and baptised at once by the *curé* summoned in haste from the village, for she was a tiny and sickly infant.

Afterwards, the Abbé Lebrun did his best to give what consolation he could to the stricken household. Old Madame Naillac, rigid with shock, was yet utterly controlled, not for one moment forgetting what behaviour was seemly in the circumstances. She heard the *curé*'s words in an attentive silence and knelt at his side while he recited prayers for the dead over the still body of her son, laid out on a bier in the *grand salon* with candles at each corner and a gold-embroidered pall covering the ruin beneath. Yes, the *curé* had told her, suicide was a sin: but Philippe had not of course been a Catholic, and God alone knew the secrets of men's hearts. He alone must be left to judge.

Young Madame Naillac, newly delivered of her child, was too ill to be reached by the *curé*'s words. Doctor and midwife and Florestine the maid hovered over her heavily drugged form; and her mother-in-law confided to the *curé*, without visible emotion (she had shown little emotion of any kind throughout the night) that the young widow was not expected to live. The *curé* administered the last rites with an aching sense of pity for the bright youth and vitality quenched in the grey-faced figure on the bed; then left the château, taking the infant Mathilde with him. The Lord gives – the Lord takes away, he thought sadly, as he made his way to the cottage where Nanon Foussac lived with her mother. Just two days ago Nanon's infant Jacques, her sole consolation since her fiancé's death, had ended his brief and sickly existence.

Perhaps little Mathilde would bring some comfort to the young mother for that second most bitter loss; but in any case the child needed milk and Nanon, a good Christian woman, had milk enough and to spare. It was a sadly appropriate solution.

Laure did not want to recover. She did not want to return to any kind of consciousness, glad as she was of the drug that held her in a merciful darkness, out of reach of recollection or understanding. When at last its hold began to lessen, and some cold hand came to drag her towards light and consciousness, she fought it all the way, pulling against it back into the dark, in search of a greater darkness without end.

But she could only fight so long before her body won; and then she knew where she was – in her bed, in her room, with the summer sun filtered by the heavy curtains – and how she came to be there, and all, *all* that had happened.

The screams had been hers. The crash, the lantern falling. The pain, the agony of a labour no longer wanted, or welcome. That much she knew, though as yet she had not been able to understand why it was so. At the end of the long anguished night there had come a cessation of bodily pain, which only made it possible for that other, crueller, pain to course fiercely and with white heat along her veins to every part of her. Somewhere a tiny feeble cry had broken out, though she had not wanted to hear it. A voice, far off, grave, had said, 'A little girl.' Someone had swayed into view, holding towards her something tiny, wrapped in a shawl, like a doll, and as still and motionless; but she had not wanted to see and had closed her eyes again. She had not opened them when a voice, several voices, had remonstrated, pleaded, begged; she had not even taken in what they said. In the end, there had been the cup held to her lips, the bitter taste and that blessed oblivion.

She had no idea how long it had lasted, only that now it had come to an end, though she ached for its return. As far as she could she kept her eyes closed and lay still, only allowing them to give her water from time to time and dose her with medicine that sometimes brought sleep. And all the while as the hours passed, and then the days, she knew that her body, her hateful rebellious body, was growing stronger, fighting its way against all the passionate longing of her mind and spirit back to health and wholeness, and the full relentless awareness which still she resisted with all her might.

And then one day she knew she could fight it no longer. Youth and health and some will that was a part of her, yet unacknowledged, had won. That other lesser will – for an end, for death – had been, at the last, defeated.

But if life had won, she had no intention of allowing it to enjoy the victory. When anyone tried to talk to her, she would turn away from them, especially if it was Madame Naillac, haggard and stern with grief, her voice reproving, scolding, commanding by turns; or the *curé*, infinitely gentle, talking of her child's need of her, and of God's love and mercy, in a way which made her want to scream in his face with hysterical derision.

But she could not shut out thought any longer, now her body was recovering. The fleeting disjointed images, disturbing enough, began to take shape, fit together, form a pattern that hammered cruelly at her understanding. Philippe is dead, they told her, Philippe is dead, and by his own deliberate choice. Though you loved him, though you were carrying his longed-for child, he turned in despair to the darkest secret corner and put his gun to his head and blew out his brains, because somehow in some inexplicable way the world offered him nothing worth living for any more – not you, nor Casseuil, nor his unborn child.

She could make no sense of it. There had been the disease in the vines, that terrible disease for which no one had yet found a remedy; was that enough, of itself? No, no, the relentless voice in her head told her in reply, it would not have been enough, if the rest had been right.

Tears came, not to bring comfort or release, for they were harsh uncontrollable tears which slid beneath her closed lids and poured down her cheeks and brought no relief. 'Why, Philippe, why?' she cried in silence through the endless flowing tears. But she saw only the smashed face, and it could give her no answer, only a thousand questions more.

'Why?' she whispered aloud to Madame Naillac, when she sat next at the bedside. 'Why did he do it?'

It was the first time she had spoken to anyone since that

terrible night. Madame Naillac withdrew still further into the grave sternness to which her whole personality seemed to have been reduced. The dark eyes – so like Philippe's, yet somehow with nothing of Philippe in them – studied Laure's face, coldly, without sympathy. Only the length of her silence, and the dry harshness of her tone when she spoke at last, indicated the depth of a grief held under tight control.

'When he saw Maître Perrard that day, he learned that matters were very much worse than he had anticipated.'

Laure had resented the return of clarity to her mind, yet now it failed her, for she could make no sense of what the other woman was saying. 'What was worse? I don't understand.'

'No.' Madame Naillac's expression was all cold reproach. 'You would not understand, of course,' it said. She waited a little while, and then went on in that same clipped unemotional tone, 'He had been in financial difficulties for some time. A good vintage this year might have helped. In the circumstances, given what Maître Perrard had to say—' She spread her hands in an expressive gesture.

Laure swallowed hard and took a deep slow breath, as if that might somehow clear her head and make understanding easier. 'You knew about it then?'

'I knew a little. Not the full extent of it. I tried to do what I could to help, as far as it was in my power – a few little economies.'

Laure had a sudden burning recollection of those expensive gowns made in Paris, of the other luxuries, large and small, with which she had indulged herself, confident of Philippe's wealth. Yet he had admired the gowns, shown no trace of disapproval. 'Why did he not tell me?' she burst out in an agony of shame and distress.

'Because he could refuse you nothing – nothing at all!' The emotion showed through now, cracking the smooth cold surface to release a flood of anger and bitterness, setting the hard old voice quivering in a thin fiery thread of words. 'He adored you, blind fool that he was! He didn't see your selfishness, your vanity, your indifference to anyone but yourself. He would have bankrupted himself to keep you happy. Oh yes, he knew very soon that it was not love and a good husband that would make you smile for him, but pretty clothes, trinkets, flattery. It is you who killed him, you with your cold vain heart, and you could not even give him a son to bear his name! A puny girl, only a puny girl who if she lives will marry one day, so there will be no more Naillacs at Casseuil. He is dead and gone and his soul is lost for ever, and you did it!'

Laure lay flattened against the pillows, battered by the onslaught, faint and trembling and unable to move or speak or think. She watched the old woman force herself to her feet, leaning heavily on her stick, with the uncharacteristic tears, unshed, sharpening the angry glare of her eyes. For a moment she stood looking down at the daughter-in-law who had so brutally failed her; and then she turned and left the room.

For a time shock numbed Laure, leaving her unable to weep or take in those cruel words. And then, slowly, the tears returned, pouring out as before, only this time with all the shame and guilt behind them. She could see it all so clearly now – the selfishness and vanity of which she had been accused. 'But it's not fair,' she protested inwardly. 'How could I know how things were, if no one told me?' But the signs had been there; looking back, she saw them now, quite clearly, the long silences, the moodiness, the irritability, all the marks of worry. If she had cared as a good wife should she would have questioned him about it, probed until he confided in her, given him the help and support he needed so desperately. She would never for one moment have bought those things, the gowns, the jewellery, if only she had known. 'Yet how could I have questioned him, being so young myself, and he so old and wise, or so I thought? Only I could have done—'

Anger, resentment, guilt, reproach tossed her back and forth, with no way out, no conclusion, no final peace of mind. 'He could refuse you nothing.' '*You* killed him, with your cold vain heart.'

'I am not cold and vain!' she protested inwardly; yet she had behaved as if she were, and in his despair he had not thought for one moment of turning to her. And now he was dead, and she could never show him that he could depend on her after all; that she was not shallow and selfish and frivolous.

She wept for a long time with a helpless abandoned misery

that brought her no relief, but simply came to an end because the tears had run their course and she was too weak to cry any more. Exhausted, she lay with closed eyes while the sense of guilt swept through her again, tormenting her. The old woman's words echoed and re-echoed in her head, stirring her once more to anger. 'You could not think that of me, Philippe! You could not have thought it!' But there was only silence and emptiness, and no one replied.

The long hours of the day and the following night were filled only by her own painful recollections, disturbed scarcely at all by the ministrations of the doctor and Florestine. The three connected yet warring emotions battered her, fighting and succeeding one another in a relentless progression: grief, guilt, anger, over and over again, endlessly. Some time around the middle of the night, wearied by the bright accusing vision of all those pretty gowns she had loved so much, hidden in the wardrobe where somehow she could see them as clearly as if Florestine had paraded them before her, she tried to send her mind out into the dark, to wherever Philippe's spirit wandered now.

'I'm sorry, Philippe – so sorry, *mon chéri* – forgive me!' Only there was no sense of forgiveness, only a darker and more horrible vision, of Philippe riding home that night through the storm, too despairing to care that the rain drenched him, or to think of seeking shelter. Why had he come back, if it was only to die? So that she could find him, and know what she had done? 'No, no, not that; don't let it be that!' More likely because he could not do it in Bordeaux, amongst all the crowds; and because he wanted Grand Turc to be safely stabled first – he was always considerate of his horses. Perhaps he had no gun with him, and so came home to find the one he kept in the office. Perhaps he had not intended to take his life, not at first, but only during the course of that last lonely journey found he could no longer face the bleakness of his existence. One thing only was certain : a despair beyond anything Laure had ever known had crouched on his back like some evil night wraith and brought him at last not home to her arms, but to the dark corner of the stable where the thunder had drowned the noise of his solitary death.

If only she could somehow go back, if only there could be a

second chance! How she would love him, another time; how she would insist on sharing his anxieties, console and support him in everything, show him that her vanities were trivial, inessential things, easily cast aside in the moment of need! Only there was to be no second chance; he had gone for ever. Now, when she knew how little the material things really meant to her, he had gone and she could never show him that he had misjudged her, that she was not an empty-headed childish plaything, undeserving of the love that she had sometimes even dared to doubt, but a woman of strength and character and good sense, fully worthy to be his wife.

She wept again as dawn came, and with the tears came a new sense of purpose, taking slow shape, hardening, telling her what she must do. She could not turn to Philippe and say, 'I am not like that; watch me, hear me, and you will know.' But perhaps somewhere his spirit could tell; and in any case Madame Naillac was still there to be proved wrong; and she herself, full of guilt and self-doubt. She would prove to them all that they had misjudged her, that beneath the frivolous exterior stripped from her for ever on that stormy night was a woman of quite another kind. She would grieve – she would grieve for ever – but she would not allow herself to be crushed.

When Florestine came in, she astonished the maid by declaring that after breakfast she would get up. The skirt and bodice were ready for her, made while she lay ill, in the heavy black crêpe-draped bombazine that proclaimed her widow-hood. She put them on with a kind of savage relish, because they seemed to symbolise her altered frame of mind. For her there would be no more fine fashionable clothes, no soft colours and shining floating fabrics, no ribbons or frills or lace, only the sombre enveloping gown over the drab black underwear, the cap confining her hair, the bonnet and veil and black cashmere shawl for outdoor wear. In Philippe's memory, for love of him, she would wear these outward signs of her widowhood for ever, long after the two and a half years that convention demanded, flaunting them like a banner.

She found that it took all her strength and all her resolution to dress (even with Florestine's help) and then walk to the chair by the window, which was frustrating in the extreme, for there was so much she wanted to do. But it was a start, and with that she had to be content.

Each day, a little at a time, she made herself stand and walk for a little longer, a little further, building up her strength. Madame Naillac had not come near her since the morning of her angry outburst, nor did she now, which was a relief, for Laure did not feel able yet to confront her. As soon as she was ready, she would seek her out.

When, a week later, she pushed open the door of the older woman's room in answer to her imperious '*Entrez!*', Laure saw the surprise on Madame Naillac's face. If she had known the young widow was about again, she had not realised she was strong enough yet to consider mounting the stairs to her room. Laure was, certainly, more than a little breathless, and still very thin and pale, but she was fully in command of herself. She would not sit down unasked – and Madame Naillac did not ask – but stood coolly just inside the door with her hands lightly clasped in front of her, steadily confronting this woman whom she had once thought her friend, but who now, sharing her grief, had shown herself to be her enemy.

'I wish to know exactly what the position is, the debts, the assets of the estate, everything. Then I can judge better what I must do.' Her voice was as clipped and cool as that of her mother-in-law. Madame Naillac, looking up from her table in utter astonishment, was fortunately unaware that beneath Laure's cool exterior lay a turmoil of emotions – apprehension, guilt, along with a lingering bodily weakness that demanded of her a considerable effort of will to remain standing there.

There was what seemed to Laure an interminable silence before Madame Naillac spoke at last. 'The affairs of the estate are in my hands. That is as it should be, for you are not competent to handle them in any way. You will receive an appropriate allowance, sufficient for your needs – your real needs, that is. A pity your parents are not still in Paris; you could have returned to them. That would have been the best solution.'

A safe, comfortable solution: yes, Laure had to acknowledge that. And at the same time she was glad it was not possible. She did not want safety and comfort. Somehow she had to make expiation for what she had done to Philippe, try to do what she could to put things right. He had loved Casseuil, as he had loved her; she would show his spirit, if it looked on still, that his heritage was safe in her hands. 'I wish to know everything,' she repeated.

Madame Naillac reached for a ledger from the shelf behind her, laying it on the table as if ready to begin work on it, and impatient to do so. 'I have a great deal to do, Laure. Don't waste my time. You have neglected your piano practice of late, naturally enough. Perhaps you should give that some attention.'

'If you will not tell me then I shall go to Bordeaux and see Maître Perrard. I think he would not refuse to talk to Philippe's widow.'

The old woman's hard eyes studied her face, penetrating in their scrutiny, and not liking what they saw: the answering glint in Laure's once gentle eyes, the firm set of her pretty mouth. As if uncomfortably aware of being put at a disadvantage, Madame Naillac stood up. 'Very well,' she said icily. 'Come tomorrow morning at ten. I shall have the papers ready by then.'

Madame Naillac had no intention whatsoever of relinquishing control of any part of Casseuil to her daughter-in-law. She had managed the household since her marriage to Philippe's father thirty-seven years ago. She had guided and advised her son when he had inherited the vineyard at his father's death, and often afterwards, and since that dreadful night three weeks ago she had been in sole charge of everything, dealing with all the complicated arrangements for the funeral (Why had Philippe not died a Catholic?) and then making herself fully conversant with every detail of the estate's business. She had in any case always kept herself informed about what was going on, and had supposed that Philippe confided fully in her; but she had found at his death that there was a good deal he had kept hidden, perhaps to spare her anxiety, and it had been a painful task investigating the full extent of Casseuil's difficulties.

She could, of course, have continued to refuse to tell Laure anything. Maître Perrard was a trusted family friend and could be asked to say nothing to Philippe's widow. But on reflection Madame Naillac thought that it might be to her advantage to be open with Laure. Confronted with the complex problems that lay before her, it was unlikely that the young woman would pursue the matter any further. She was not strong willed or disciplined enough for that; the temptations of luxury and idleness, however limited for now, would in the end be too much for her. Moreover, once she saw clear evidence of her own folly, and how it had contributed to the present disaster, she would very probably be so overcome with shame and an abject sense of her own unworthiness that she would be entirely willing to allow herself to be guided in future by Madame Naillac.

In any case, whether Laure allowed it or not, Madame Naillac intended that she should be so guided. She prepared herself well for the interview, choosing her tactics with care, planning exactly what she would say, and how and when.

The meeting began as she had anticipated with the two women seated facing one another across the table in the hot overcrowded room, Laure silent and attentive as Madame Naillac turned the pages of account books, demonstrating and explaining in carefully selected detail. But then, all at once, without quite knowing how it happened, the older woman realised that the interview was no longer entirely under her control; was even threatening to veer off in some highly undesirable direction. Laure began to ask questions, and they were disconcertingly intelligent and perceptive questions. Worse, she seemed to realise at once when Madame Naillac had carefully omitted to mention some point or another, supposing the omission would go unnoticed. With a grudging resentment, the old woman had to recognise that though Laure might be weak and frivolous, she was certainly not a fool. Afraid of losing control of the situation altogether, Madame Naillac became at once alert and watchful, ready to deflect any undesirable line of enquiry.

Casseuil's situation was not wholly bleak; but it was bad enough. Most of Laure's dowry – the capital of which was still legally her own – was untouched, and the château still held in the *chai* a good stock of its finest wines, which could be sold as necessary. And there might be some kind of harvest this year, despite the first inroads of the phylloxera. But they could not hope for an immediate income anywhere near high enough to pay off the appalling total of unpaid debts. They were not all Laure's debts, for Philippe too had spent unwisely from time to time, though often enough on some lavish gift for his wife. There were so many of these, in fact, that Laure to her shame could not now remember receiving them all. But it was her own spending, on the gowns from Worth, the perfumes and jewellery, which formed a great part of the debts. Laure saw it, and felt the reproach of it like a new fever in her veins. How could she have let it happen?

'Clearly the first thing to do is to pay off the debts,' she said, swept by a longing to put them all behind her at once, without delay. 'My dowry will see to that.'

'Nonsense. That is quite unnecessary. I shall agree an allowance with you, as I said – that will come from your dowry. The debts will be paid off as it becomes possible. A proportion of my own money – I have something for myself, of course – that will be used to keep the estate running smoothly, as far as possible. I shall make decisions as to where the economies will fall, in due course.'

'I suggest,' said Laure with a careful politeness belied by her imperious tone, 'that you do nothing until I have had time to study the figures further. Then we can discuss it together.'

She saw the dark eyes flash defiance at her; but Madame Naillac said nothing, simply turning to replace the ledgers on the shelf. She said eventually, 'My brother is coming tomorrow. He may well have views on the matter.'

Then I shall have to fight him too, if we do not come to the same conclusions, Laure thought, with a certain unacknowledged weariness.

Ending the interview on that unsatisfactorily inconclusive note, she descended the stairs and made her way across the landing to go to her own room, aching for rest and quiet. Below in the hall she could hear some kind of altercation taking place between Sylvestre and someone whose voice she did not know. She went to the turn of the stairs to investigate.

A woman stood just inside the massive front door, a woman with all those voluptuous curves that Laure had so much desired in the days when such things still mattered to her (it

127

seemed a lifetime ago now). She was pretty in an obvious sort of way, rosy cheeked, with curling hair of a rather unnatural blondeness. Like Laure, oddly enough, she too was dressed in black, but somehow on her the sober colour had a glossy, jaunty look, emphasising her figure, decorated with shiny jet buttons and knots of velvet ribbon. Holding her hand – or rather, held by hers and looking as if in some way he did not quite belong to her – was a small boy, also dressed in black. He was tiny, little more than a baby, a slight frightened-looking toddler with delicate features and soft brown hair, bleached in streaks where the sun had caught it.

Laure stared at them. She had made many new acquaintances and met many new people since coming to Casseuil; but she knew she had never seen these two before.

The woman caught sight of her – alerted perhaps by some unconscious movement on Laure's part – and stepped forward, pushing aside Sylvestre's resistant figure. 'Madame Naillac?'

So used was she to deferring in this house to her mother-in-law, that Laure was on the point of denying the designation. But just in time she thought, I have a right to that name, after all. And she said quietly, 'Yes, I am Madame Naillac.'

She began slowly, but with dignity, to descend, indicating to Sylvestre by a gesture that he could go.

As she reached the hall the woman pushed the child forward and crouched down with her arm about him, holding him close to her side. He wriggled a little as if he did not quite like the contact, his eyes never leaving Laure's face; strange eyes, light hazel-green with flecks of gold and brown, set in a fringe of thick dark lashes. Laure shivered a little, though she did not quite know why. The woman's perfume, heady and expensive, threatened to overwhelm her.

'This is Frédéric – Frédéric Brousse. Brousse is my own family name, and he is my son. But his father was Philippe Naillac.'

How Laure remained on her feet at that moment she did not know. But somehow she did so, though she knew she had gone very white and the roaring in her ears threatened imminent faintness. Through it all the same powerful will that had fought against her wish to die; that had driven her from her bed the other day; that had given her the courage to face her mother-in-law on equal terms: that same will must have helped her when all else failed.

It was more than she could do, though, to say anything, even to marshal her thoughts or find words to express them. But then the woman hardly paused to note her reaction before she went on in a voice breaking with emotion. 'I read of his funeral in the paper, just like that, with no warning. I knew then I had to come and beg for your help – there is no one else, you see. He did everything for me: paid the rent on my apartment in Bordeaux, gave me enough to live on, and clothes too, and of course money for the child, to pay for the boarding with the wet nurse. And now he is dead and I have nothing. He told me what a good woman you are – I know you will have pity on his son.'

His son – Philippe's son – this fragile-looking little boy with the disconcertingly direct gaze! She stared at the child, seeing nothing of Philippe in him. How could he have anything to do with that great tall dark strong man in all the pride and splendour of his prime? Yet why otherwise should this woman have come, to a house of bereavement threatened by financial disaster – though perhaps she did not know about that?

'How can I believe you? He is nothing like Philippe.'

'Yes, yes, there is Philippe in his face. Look at the cheekbones, the set of the jaw – when Philippe was just such a little boy—'

There was so great a flood of emotion in the voice that Laure did not realise who was coming down the stairs behind her until she turned and saw her mother-in-law. The old woman's face was transformed, her mouth twisted into a tremulous smile that took all the harshness from it.

She descended with astonishing speed, clinging to the rail with both hands, and passed Laure. Then she bent to take the child by the shoulders, holding him for a moment before her hands moved up to close about his small frightened face so that she could more easily study it. Laure saw that she was weeping, as she had never seen her weep before, her body heaving, the tears pouring down her lined cheeks. Then she drew the child in against her skirts and looked at his mother

129

and spoke in a ragged uneven voice quite unlike her usual controlled tone. 'You gave him a son, and for that, whatever kind of woman you are, there are no words warm enough to tell you what I feel. The pity of it is that the child can never bear his father's name; but he has his father in him all the same, I can see that. Of course you need have no fear that he will not be cared for, most tenderly, and you too, of course. Come into the *petit salon*, then we can talk.'

As if Laure were somehow invisible, Madame Naillac led mother and child away and closed the door behind them. Laure stood staring at the door, at its dark heavy surface, shut, firmly shut, right in her face, excluding her, with a horrible finality. 'You are nothing now,' the gesture seemed to say. 'Your life is over, as surely as Philippe's.' She had never in all the years felt so defeated, so alone, as she did now; not even in those first moments of awareness after Philippe's death. Could it be true? Was it possible that the one thing she had clung to, the one thing that even Madame Naillac had conceded, 'He adored you', had after all been an illusion? There was nothing unusual in a man keeping a mistress; on the contrary, it was entirely normal. But even when things were at their worst she had thought she and Philippe were different.

A renewed faintness reminded her that long ago she had known she needed rest. She moved, somehow, to one of the carved and uncomfortable hall chairs and sat there, seeing nothing, trying by searching her memory to find the truth.

All those business trips to Bordeaux; she had accepted them as such even when, latterly, he had refused to take her with him. That was not proof, of course, but it made it possible.

Then there were the little trinkets he had bought, so many of them that she had not been able to remember them all. If they had not all been bought for her, then of course she would not have remembered.

And his certainty that it was not his fault that they had no child, and the slight hesitation when she had asked how he knew . . . Oh yes, he knew, for that girl had borne him a son to prove it!

I did not know him at all, she thought bitterly. He was a stranger all along, the man I married. And I was simply his wife, chosen for my fitness for the position, like a housemaid or a stable boy. All that devotion, all that care – it was only what any man owes to his wife, a husband's duty.

In three short weeks she had been stripped, relentlessly, piece by piece, of everything: of love, of security, of trust, of belief in herself, of all that was known, all that was safe, all that life had meant to her from infancy, even her longed-for child.

Her child: the despised girl who was the mark of her failure. She had been baptised Mathilde, Madame Naillac had said, because it was the name of a dead sister, much loved in life; and she had been put out to nurse with a woman in the village where she might, or might not, survive. Laure had not asked anything more, because she had not felt the remotest interest. She supposed her daughter was still alive, since no one had told her otherwise, but she did not even know where to find her.

Now she knew that it was imperative that she did so. If nothing else, she and Mathilde had one thing in common – they were both alone and rejected. They needed one another.

Laure reached for the bell and summoned Sylvestre to order the carriage for her, and Florestine to bring her shawl and bonnet: she knew she could not find the strength to go herself in search of them. And then she set out alone for the bleak little presbytery.

The *curé* welcomed her – courteously masking his surprise but not his pleasure – into his book-littered living-room, clearing three leather bound volumes and a couple of pamphlets from a worn chair so she could sit down, and offering her a little coffee, or brandy, anything she liked. She declined, and came at once to the point, '*Monsieur le curé*, I want to see my baby.'

For the Abbé Lebrun the whole business of Philippe Naillac's death had been unrelievedly depressing. It was not just the fact of the suicide – a natural enough cause for doubt about the eventual fate of the young man's soul – but there had been a great deal of unpleasantness afterwards, over the funeral. Doctor Rossillon, supported by other friends of Philippe's, had insisted that the burial should be conducted according to Protestant rites, in the family *caveau*. When Madame Naillac had objected coldly that her son had never once set foot in the Protestant *temple* at Bergerac, they had suggested a secular funeral instead. Madame Naillac had argued fiercely for a Catholic burial in the village cemetery. As her parish priest, the Abbé Lebrun might have been expected to agree; but the young man had been both a suicide and a non-Catholic, for whom the rites of the Church must be a mockery. In the end, under the old woman's ceaseless pressure, he had given in, but his conscience was still not easy about it. And all the time the widow had lain beyond the reach of his spiritual guidance, showing no interest at all in the child who should have been her consolation.

Now, suddenly, here she was sitting very upright in his living-room and showing all the interest he could have wished for in the fatherless infant. He could almost have wept with thankfulness.

Instead, he said quietly, 'Of course, *ma fille*. She is with Nanon Foussac. You knew the poor girl had lost her baby? I will take you there at once.'

The news of Mathilde's whereabouts shook Laure a little. She had not known of Nanon's second loss. Now, learning of it, she was not sure that she wanted to face the bereaved young woman. Yet were they not in some way equal in their loss? It could even be said that Nanon was the more fortunate, because she had been sure of Jacques's love; but Laure doubted very much if Nanon would see it like that.

She walked with the *curé* along the street towards the poor little cottage on the eastern edge of the village, and thought, What must it feel like to be forced to nurse a stranger's child, when your own has just died? Would you hate that child, as it took the milk meant for your own infant, and thrived with the life denied to the one whose place it had usurped? Oh yes, Mathilde needed her, she was certain of that.

The cottage had one room with a loft above, reached by a ladder. There was little light, except what was shed by a small fire over which a cooking pot bubbled gently. But it was enough to show Laure the one bed, which Nanon shared, presumably, with her mother; whom they had seen in the distance washing clothes in the stream that ran not far from the house. There was a table too, a rough wooden chest, two chairs, and a stool on which Nanon sat, with a wooden cradle at her feet and the baby in her arms. The gentle sucking noise of the feeding infant filled the room.

Laure came to a standstill just inside the door, struck by a sudden disinclination to go any further. I should not have come, she thought. What can I possibly do, or say?

The young peasant girl had not looked up. Dressed in the black everyday wear of her kind, with a large apron covering her skirt and a plain white coif on her brown hair, she sat there with all her concentration focused on Laure's little daughter. There was light enough for Laure to see the tenderness on Nanon's face, and the way the child's little toes, just visible beneath the folds of the shawl, curled with contentment and her tiny fingers kneaded blissfully at the full breast.

I was wrong, Laure thought. She does not need me after all.

The *curé* pulled a chair near to the fire, facing Nanon, and turned to summon Laure to sit down. She did so, with a sense that she was wasting her time, but managed to force a smile when Nanon at last raised quiet grey eyes to her face. It was quite a long time before the girl returned the smile, and then only faintly, for a brief moment, before turning her attention again to the child.

Mechanically, Laure asked how Mathilde was doing – was she thriving, was she sleeping and feeding well? It was clear enough that she was, of course. She was very small, too small for a three-week-old child, but there was a warm colour on the rounded curve of her cheek, a soft gold down on her little head, dimpled flesh on her small hands.

Nanon had little French, and it took some time, and considerable help from the *curé*, before she was able to reply; and as she spoke Laure sensed her hostility, not strong, but real enough, based perhaps on the fear that one day she might lose this child too.

Laure felt a new hopelessness. Would she ever find it in herself to tear Mathilde from Nanon? Had she already lost Mathilde, even before she knew she wanted her, to this young woman who could give her the one thing she needed, which her mother could not give?

No, she thought. No, she is mine, and one day she will have no need any more for milk, but a great need for other things: education, guidance, protection, love, for they are a part of her heritage as surely as is the château itself. Then she will need me.

And meanwhile Laure did still have a task to perform. Above all, she must do all in her power to make sure that when Mathilde came of age there would still – in spite of the phylloxera, in spite of little Frédéric Brousse – be a great name at Casseuil, an inheritance her daughter could take on with pride and confidence.

When she had seen the baby tucked up asleep in the wooden cradle rocked by the peasant girl's bare foot, she made her way slowly home, full of a painful tangle of emotions amongst which only a renewed determination gave her any comfort at all.

CHAPTER
EIGHT

i

Auguste Silvine was quite unprepared for the news that greeted him when he arrived at Casseuil. At the time of the funeral, that sad, almost furtive affair, he had agreed that on his return to Bordeaux he would carry out a few errands for his sister, conclude some necessary formalities with Maître Perrard (also present at the funeral) and come back to Casseuil in a few weeks time to report on his progress and give whatever other help might be necessary. On the whole (since Marie-Louise was quite well able to take care of all practical matters for herself) he saw his visit largely as a way of showing his sympathy with his sister in her loss.

The sympathy was real enough. There was nothing warm or effusive about their relationship, but in his way Auguste was genuinely fond of her, and he understood as perhaps no one else did how deeply her son's appalling death had affected her. There had never been any room in her heart for anyone but Philippe, and his passing must inevitably leave a terrible emptiness, the more so as the longed-for heir had turned out to be a mere daughter after all.

So, full of concerned affection, he stepped out of his carriage in the courtyard, scrunched across the gravel to the little stone bridge over the moat, through the door held open by Sylvestre; and in the hall met, coming down the stairs, all rosy cheeks and too-bright hair, a young woman he had never seen before, holding by the hand an equally unknown little boy. She paused, turned a rather knowing smile upon him, and then disappeared into the *petit salon*, with all the confidence of someone entirely at home. Auguste stood still for some time after they had gone, as if he could not quite bring himself to believe the evidence of his own eyes; then he turned to Sylvestre. 'Who was that . . . lady? And the child?'

'Mademoiselle Brousse, *monsieur*,' said Sylvestre smoothly, his expression giving nothing away, 'and her son Frédéric.' After a moment he added, 'They came yesterday, *monsieur*.'

Since that would seem to be all Sylvestre was willing to tell him without further questioning, Auguste decided to save his questions for his sister, and made his way upstairs. Why, he wondered, not for the first time, did Marie-Louise choose to live at the very top of the house? Surely, infirm as she sometimes was, she would be much better off nearer the ground floor? Not that he would ever dare to put such an argument to her.

His sister was able, very quickly, to satisfy his curiosity about the mother and child downstairs. But what she told him left him in a state of shock, which was quietened only after a long interval of calm discussion (on her side at least). Who would have thought it, of his dutiful, respectable nephew? In any other circumstances he might have smiled at the piquancy of the situation; but for such a reaction, at the present time, his sister would not readily have forgiven him. Instead, he tried as best he could to give his attention to the sensible proposals she was putting before him.

They were interrupted by a sudden peremptory knock on the door; and very soon young Laure came in, full of a brisk impatience quite unlike her usual manner. 'If the future of Casseuil is to be discussed,' she said, 'then I should like to be present.'

Her tone contrasted so oddly with her pathetic appearance that Auguste once again had that sensation of disbelief, as if things were suddenly all out of place. For one so used to an orderly routine as he was, this was proving an uncomfortable visit.

Marie-Louise looked Laure up and down in chilly surprise, and then said, 'What we are discussing is none of your business. For the time being the future of Casseuil must wait.'

What, Auguste wondered, did Philippe's widow make of all this upheaval – the mistress, and the bastard at whose name a curious expression, a kind of devouring hunger, came into Marie-Louise's eyes? He could not see Laure's face clearly

the simple practical question, gave him a little shock, as if he had been temporarily transported back to those happier days of a few weeks ago.

'Are they still healthy, those vines?'

He had been trying to find appropriate words of condolence with which to greet her. Now, with relief, he answered her question instead. 'So far, I think, *madame*, but I have only just begun to look.' He paused, looking back at the sturdy little plants; and then burst out, 'It was all part of the annual cycle, planting them. As the oldest plants grow too old, the young ones take root – cuttings from the best stock to ensure our future. And now, now, *madame*, I ask myself if there will be a future.' He regretted at once his selfish intrusion of his own bitter feelings: this was no time to impose his troubles on a young widow with far greater reason to grieve.

But before he could frame an apology she said vehemently, 'There *must* be a future, *monsieur*. Believe me, if it's in my power to make it possible, then there will be, and one worth striving for.'

It was an extravagant claim from someone apparently so weak and powerless, but it touched him all the same. 'If only it were as easy as that, *madame*: simply to want it to be so.'

'I know it can't be that easy. All I am sure of is that there must be a way, some way, to keep the vineyard alive. But I know so little. You must have some ideas yourself as to what is possible. How bad is it so far?'

'Bad enough, *madame*. As perhaps you saw, we have found yet more affected plants, hence the bonfire there. We have increased the sulphur spraying, but too much of that will be as fatal as the phylloxera.' He became aware as if for the first time of the heat of the sun – it was close to midday now – and of the fragility of the young woman beside him beneath those heavy black folds. '*Ma chère madame*, this heat cannot be good for you. I am glad to see you so much recovered, but should you not be indoors, in the shade?'

'I want to know exactly how things stand, *monsieur*. That's why I came. I am quite well, you know.'

'Then come to the office and allow yourself to be seated while we talk.'

She shook her head. 'No, it's better to see for oneself.'

He had always suspected that there was a hidden strength in Madame Laure; now he was sure of it. He did not argue any further, but simply said, 'There is little enough to see, I think. But if you feel able to walk with me for a short distance I can show you where the affected plants were found; you will see the gaps in the rows.'

They walked on, and she saw what he meant. So far the gaps were few, not enough to have any major effect on this year's harvest. 'Can you be sure that other plants are not already affected?'

'Not at all, alas, *madame*. The early signs are hard to see.'

'Are there any other preventive measures that can be taken, apart from the sulphur?'

'Certainly, one can try. I understand that an injection of carbon disulphide into the earth at regular intervals can help.'

'Will you try that?'

His mouth had a wry twist to it. 'One requires 150 grammes per square metre, *madame*. I have done some calculations. The cost would be something in the region of three to four hundred francs per hectare, and Casseuil has twenty hectares of vineyard, a large area. I think perhaps . . .'

He did not need to finish. Laure remembered the debts, and the limited resources left to them.

'Of course,' he added, 'the sulphur too is expensive. We have stocks still, but they will not last for ever.'

Perhaps, thought Laure, Madame Naillac was right to think that some of the debts must be left unpaid for the time being. Though even then there would not be enough. 'Are there any other treatments?'

'There is one that has been shown to work, without any doubt.' He saw her head lift and was uncomfortably aware of the bright light in the eyes turned upon him. 'That is to flood the roots with water, and to leave them submerged for a period of forty to fifty days. That kills all traces of the insect on the root.'

Instantly, he sensed her disappointment. 'That's not practicable then: not here on the hillside.'

'No, only on the plain, *madame*, and only then when there is access to an ample water supply. It is ironic, is it not? It has long been recognised that the best wines come from the hills;

yet the surest treatment can only be used on inferior vines.'
They came to the point near the road where the *caveau* stood
on its height above the valley, and gazed out over the serene
sunlit landscape. 'They have found too that vines grown on a
sandy soil seem to have a natural resistance to the insect.'

'Then one could perhaps make changes to the soil?'

That brought a defiant light to Jean Delisle's eyes. 'In
theory, perhaps, though it would be difficult.' His tone was
curtly dismissive. 'For my part, I believe that if Casseuil is to
be reduced to making an inferior wine without distinction,
then she might as well cease to make wine at all.'

Laure looked puzzled. 'Of course, I agree, but what has
that to do with the soil?'

For once the *régisseur* was disappointed in her. 'Oh
madame, how can you even ask that? You must know that the
soil is everything – *everything*! It is true that there are many
factors that go to the making of a great wine; the types of vine
that are grown, the manner of their growing, the nurture that
is lavished upon them, the weather of course, so important to
us here at Casseuil, the skill and judgement of the *vigneron*.
But there is above all, first and foremost, one thing alone
without which nothing else would be possible: the soil. You
could take the vines, the skill of the ablest *vigneron*, even
arrange the weather. But transplant them all to a different soil,
even a few kilometres away, at Trissac, for example, and you
would have a wine of quite another kind. It might just
possibly be a good wine, or more likely it would not; but it
would not be a Château de Casseuil. In this soil below our feet
are many things that one may study and analyse – the chalky
clay that so often makes a good wine, the right proportion of
moisture, a variety of minerals of many kinds, but also
something more, something beyond analysis, the subtle
unknown factors that for centuries have combined to transmit
to our vines exactly that quality that makes them like no other
in the world. Upset that perfect balance, and you might
destroy the phylloxera, but, without doubt, you would also
destroy the wines of Casseuil. If ever that course is decided
upon here, then I could not stay and watch it happen.'

'Nor I, I think, *monsieur*,' said Laure quietly. 'Forgive my
ignorance. I understand now.'

When, some time later, Laure parted from Monsieur Delisle in the office, carrying with her a copy of Doctor Planchon's recent work on the ways of the phylloxera louse, the *régisseur* realised that they had not once spoken of her loss. He regretted it. He knew that all the conventions, as well as common consideration, had required him to make some sympathetic allusion to her circumstances. Yet he felt, oddly, a little comforted. For the first time since that dreadful day some weeks ago he began to feel that he had not after all been left to fight on alone. Old Madame Naillac had indicated her trust in him and assured him of her support; but from the young widow he had a sense that someone else shared his vision and his determination. He even began, just a little, to hope again.

Laure went downstairs to dinner that night, for the first time since her illness. She was desperately tired and longed to give in to the urging of her body to sink into bed and wait for Florestine to bring her a tempting supper on a tray. But she was determined that Madame Naillac should be reminded that in everything she had Laure to contend with now, that she could not simply ignore her existence. Even if Frédéric should prove to be Philippe's son (and Laure still could not quite believe that he would), the old woman must not under any circumstances be allowed to forget that Laure's daughter was her father's rightful heir.

So she forced herself to descend the stairs and take her seat facing the frigidly silent figure across the table, and even tried very hard to eat some of the food for which she had no appetite. What she found she could not do was to talk to Madame Naillac; in her exhausted state she could think of nothing to say.

At the end of the meal, eaten in total silence, she said, 'Good-night, *madame*,' and went to kiss the old woman as she always used to do. But Madame Naillac drew sharply away, as if any kind of closeness with Laure was an offence to her. Then, unexpectedly, she said, 'Mass is being offered each morning this week for Philippe's soul, at my request. It would perhaps be fitting if you were to be present in church yourself, to add your prayers to those of myself and *monsieur le curé*.

After all, it is largely your doing that they are so desperately needed. It is the least you can do.'

Laure opened her mouth to speak, but could not think what to say. She felt only a kind of revulsion from all that the old woman implied.

'Mass is at seven. I will arrange for you to make your confession first. I am sure you see the necessity.'

'No!' Laure found she was trembling. She had spoken more sharply than she had intended, but it was very hard to bring her voice sufficiently under control to continue in a quiet and reasonable tone, 'No, *madame*, thank you. I am not, I think, quite well enough yet for that.'

She knew it was a lie, or at the least an excuse. The very thought of going to mass to pray for Philippe when her whole spirit saw no justice, no purpose, no sense in his death, when she felt that all that had happened to her was far worse than she could possibly have deserved; no, the very thought of it was repugnant to her. And as for going at Madame Naillac's bidding to confess her guilt, even if it was real—

She realised as she dragged her slow way upstairs that the simple logical reason why the whole idea was so abhorrent to her was that something had gone from her forever, with Philippe's death: the last traces of the simple happy faith of her girlhood.

Next morning, awake too early and unable to sleep again, Laure went to her dressing-room to find a book, and from the window saw Madame Naillac crossing the courtyard on her way to mass. At her side, head solemnly bent, missal clasped in her gloved hands, walked Rosaline Brousse.

Laure stood quite still, watching them; two black figures moving on past the well, through the gate in the delicate wrought iron fence that edged the northern side of the courtyard, across the track and into the little wood that led up to the village, where the trees at last hid them from view. Her hands clenched tight at her sides, she thought, How soon before there is news from Bordeaux? Oh, let her be an imposter – please God, let her be an imposter!

'Doing a flit, Florestine?'

The maid gave a start, pressed her free hand agitatedly to her breast, and turned to see Sylvestre coming towards her from the kitchen stairs. 'Oh, don't frighten me like that, you!' A hint of a smile belied the scolding words.

Sylvestre came and took the heavy leather bag from her hand. 'No pretty woman should burden herself like this. You'll develop muscles in all the wrong places, and that would never do.' She giggled. 'Jean-Baptiste' – he was the cook – 'said the carriage was out there. Is that where you're going with this?'

Florestine put a finger to her lips. 'Hush! Madame Laure doesn't want the old woman to know.' He opened the door and together they crossed the bridge.

'Where's she going then? And what's she got in here? The family silver?'

'Near enough – it's her jewels. We're going to Bordeaux.'

Sylvestre stopped, head on one side, and eyed her quizzically. 'Without Madame's permission? Not wise, Florestine, not wise at all. Or is your mistress running away? If she's not coming back I suppose it doesn't matter what she does, though Madame might jib just a bit at losing Aristide as well.'

'I don't know why she's going, though I'd guess she means to sell this lot.' She touched the bag. 'But it's my belief that's just an excuse. I think she wants to make enquiries about Mademoiselle Rosaline.'

'I thought Madame was doing that already?'

'Maybe she's tired of waiting to hear, or maybe she doesn't trust Madame. All I know is she's been in a funny mood ever since that one came.'

'Can you blame her? You'd not exactly be jumping for joy in her position, would you now?'

Florestine was wrong. Impatient though she was to know the truth – even, so she told herself, if it supported Rosaline in every respect – Laure's chief aim in going to Bordeaux was to find out exactly where she stood and to see if there was anything she could do, even at this early stage, to ease the difficult situation facing them. If, somehow, she were to find herself stumbling upon any information about Rosaline, then that would be a bonus; but she was too weak still, and too shaken by Philippe's death, to feel able to undertake a search herself.

At Bordeaux she found accommodation in a quiet and respectable hotel and next morning made her way – with Florestine rather grudgingly carrying the bag – to the most prestigious jewellers' in the city. Here, at least, she owed no money; and here, in a back room, she spread on a table every piece of jewellery she owned, apart from a ring and necklace and earrings of gold hung with pearls that Philippe had given her at their marriage, which she had kept to pass on one day to Mathilde.

She left the shop some time later with the bag much lighter, but containing now a considerable sum of money.

She went next to call on Maître Perrard with whom – by means of the hotel messenger – she had already made an appointment for that morning.

It was here at last that her resolution faltered. It was odd that she should not have anticipated just such a reaction; but it was not in fact until an obsequiously attentive clerk was showing her into the rich gloom of the lawyer's office (leaving Florestine in the waiting room) that she remembered that Maître Perrard must have been one of the last people to see Philippe alive. She kept herself under control only until the lawyer had welcomed her and urged her to be seated in his most comfortable chair; and then to her extreme embarrassment she began, helplessly, to weep.

If the lawyer was equally embarrassed, he hid it well. He behaved in fact as if women's tears were a normal feature of a lawyer's existence (as perhaps they were), and went to a cupboard in the wall, took out a bottle of brandy and a glass, and poured some for Laure, who took it with a stifled 'Thank you.' It was some time before she was sufficiently calm to take a sip, though she did feel a little steadier for it afterwards. 'Forgive me,' she murmured. 'I did not mean . . .'

He reached across his desk, at which he had been seated while he waited for her to stop crying, and took her hand in both his, patting it consolingly. 'I understand, *madame*. You have suffered a sad loss. I was deeply grieved to hear of it.

Little did I think, that day . . . I have asked myself since if I could have done anything to soften the blow, if it would have made any difference.'

'Did he . . . did he seem distressed then, when you told him how things were?' She wanted desperately to know all she could. So much had been hidden from her, and it was important for her now to understand exactly what kind of man Philippe had been, and why he had acted as he did.

'He could not take it lightly, of course; but no, I did not gain an impression of despair. But then, what does one ever know of the mind of another human being? So much must remain unseen. I do know, however – I have heard of it since – that he passed several hours after leaving this office in a desperate search for solutions. He was trying to raise additional funds, of course, but he was too wise to involve himself in any deal of a dubious kind, and no more straightforward arrangement came his way; things had gone too far for that. I am only deeply sorry that it should have been so. Without the phylloxera outbreak it might have been different; there would not then have been quite the urgency. In the circumstances I believe that was, as they say, the last drop that caused the vase to overflow.'

The last drop in the bitter cup, the one that had sent him home in the storm to die. Laure sat there seeing, not the office with its books and ledgers and stacked metal chests, but Philippe riding alone out of the city as the lightning tore the sky in two. She wondered fleetingly how often one of Maître Perrard's calm dry statements had sent a client away with all hope destroyed. Not perhaps that one should blame him simply for doing his job.

With an effort she switched her mind from Philippe and gave her attention to what had brought her here.

It was harder than it might have been, because that unfortunate display of emotion had made it more difficult for her to present the level-headed and sensible appearance that she had intended. But she took a deep breath, folded her hands loosely in her lap in a gesture of deliberate relaxation, and said quietly, 'Maître, please will you tell me exactly what is the position with regard to my dowry? I know that while – my husband – lived I could not spend it without his guidance and his agreement. Am I now free to do with it what I choose?'

The lawyer cleared his throat and rested his hands, fingertips just touching, upon the table. 'Ah now, *madame* – there, I regret that your position has not materially changed. As always, the dowry remains your property, although now of course your husband's proportion of the interest belongs to your daughter. But responsibility for it since the decease of your husband rests with Monsieur Silvine and, in the absence of any other close male relative of Monsieur Naillac, with Madame his mother, advised, in theory at least, by myself.'

Laure tried not to show her dismay. She swallowed hard. 'Then I can do nothing without their agreement?'

'No, *madame*. It is for your protection, you see. You are very young, a young widow, alone in the world. You must see the need for your interests to be fully protected.'

She made no comment on that. 'And the estate, my daughter's property?'

'That too is under the care of Monsieur Silvine and his sister.'

'So they can do what they like with it?'

'Only in the best interests of your daughter, of course. But then I am quite sure you have nothing to fear on that score. And I am sure too that you will be fully informed as to what decisions are taken, and even consulted about them should you wish to be.'

I wish I could be so sure, thought Laure bitterly. 'Is there anything I am free to do, without advice or consultation?' she asked.

'You may bring up your daughter as seems best to you, guiding her morally and spiritually, taking all necessary steps for her welfare. So long as you do that well, then no one will have the right to interfere.'

And what, wondered Laure, was the legal definition of 'well'? How easy would it be to fall short of Madame Naillac's no doubt rigorous standards, and what then would become of her independence as a mother? She did not need to ask; it was quite obvious what the answer would be.

She looked across at the lawyer's grave face, seeing there a certain amount of sympathy for her position, but no hope of escape from it. There was really no more to be said to him about it.

'Then may we come to the debts please – the ones my husband left. I wish to know which require most urgent payment, and to make arrangements for those at least to be settled – with this.' She lifted the leather bag on to the table. 'I have sold some jewellery.'

There at least it appeared there was no difficulty, and, by the time she was ready to leave, the money had gone and the lawyer had agreed to pay off a considerable number of the debts, including all those that had reached the stage of a threatening letter. It was, Laure felt, a small step in her otherwise doomed fight for independence.

But there was still one thing more. As she rose to her feet she said with studied casualness, 'Maître, if Frédéric Brousse is indeed my husband's son, has he any legal claim to his estate? Could my daughter lose anything because of him?'

She was a little surprised to see that the lawyer was clearly much embarrassed by her sudden question; he even blushed quite deeply. 'Ah!' He cleared his throat. 'I see! I did not realise you knew.'

'How could I fail to know, with that woman and her child under my roof?'

Her indignation moved him. 'Of course, *madame*. I regret deeply that you should have had to suffer such . . . such an insult. It must have been distressing in the extreme.' He paused, and Laure thought: He spoke in the past tense – then Rosaline *is* an imposter, and it will all come to an end!

'I understood you were making enquiries.'

He looked deeply unhappy. 'They are completed, *madame*. I have just this morning written a letter to Madame Naillac, which I was about to ask you to deliver to her. If you will please be seated again then I will tell you what I have found.' He came round the table and held the chair for her to sit down. Then, after a further pause to gather his thoughts, while Laure's heart beat fast with hope, he went on slowly, 'This is not easy for me, *madame*. Believe me, I regret—' Then with sudden vehemence, 'It should not have happened, no indeed it should not! However, the past cannot be undone. My enquiries were as thorough as I could make them, as, I

148

gather, were those of Monsieur Silvine, to whom I spoke yesterday. I regret, *madame*, that we reached the same conclusion. Forgive me if the details pain you, but I think you ought to know. It seems beyond doubt that Mademoiselle Rosaline Brousse had an association with Monsieur Naillac from at least 1862. Both were well known in the neighbourhood of her apartment, which was rented from that period in the name of Monsieur Naillac. Further, the child Frédéric Brousse, whose birth was registered in February 1869, was acknowledged by Monsieur Naillac as his son on that date. Furthermore, Monsieur Naillac paid for him to be boarded thereafter in the care of a decent woman some miles away, out in the country.' Again, he pressed her hand. 'I am so sorry, *madame*. It seems there can be no possible doubt. Of course, there is no question of an illegitimate child having any rights of inheritance – it is perhaps a small consolation for you.'

It was scarcely any consolation at all, set against the new knowledge, which, though she had expected it, still shook her deeply. Before ever they had met, Philippe had loved another woman, loved her enough to set her up in comfort and independence, with no great attempt at concealment. It was possible that, on meeting Laure, his feelings for Rosaline had lessened; it was possible that he had loved Laure as much as, perhaps even more than, his mistress. But he had not ceased to visit her. He had gone to her again and again, deceiving his wife to do so. And in the end, when it seemed that his wife had failed him, Rosaline had given him not only a child but a son, living proof of Laure's inadequacy and his own potency.

As the coach carried her home to Casseuil Laure thought back to that spring of 1869 when Frédéric was born, trying to bring to mind any indication that for Philippe this had been a momentous time in his life. She remembered well enough that for her it had been one of the bleakest periods of their marriage, when her sense of failure had swamped her with a desperate misery, and Philippe had hardly ever been at home, and when he was with her seemed preoccupied and uncaring, as if she hardly interested him any more. Had he shown any signs of joy, or satisfaction? She could remember none now. But it had been the year of the last great vintage and she recalled only too well his words as the *vendange* began, 'I knew this had to be a good year, right from the start.' A good year, because it had begun with the birth of his son – yes, she understood now what he had meant, in full.

So much for love, and trust, and loyalty. She mourned him, missed him dreadfully, longed to go back and find he was still alive. Yet, she wondered now, who was this Philippe she missed so much? A tall handsome man who treated her with lofty tenderness, as if she were both fragile and very young; looking back, had there ever been anything more? Passion, yes; a tendency to moodiness; but that was all. What had she ever seen of the real Philippe? She was right to think that he had been a stranger, and how can you mourn a stranger? Had Rosaline known him any better? It seemed only too likely. Perhaps then his mistress had more right than his widow to weep for his passing. It was a bitter thought. The only faint crumb of comfort was the little angry voice that said, 'Why should you feel such guilt for what you did, when all the time he was doing this to you?' Only she could not keep out the insidious retort that if she had been a better, more loving wife then perhaps he would not have needed to go to Rosaline.

Madame Naillac emerged from the *petit salon*, just as Laure crossed the hall on her return from Bordeaux; she might almost, Laure thought, have been listening for the sounds of her arrival.

'Laure!' She waited, Laure watching her from the foot of the stairs, until Sylvestre had secured the front door and gone away, and then she said, 'Where have you been?'

'To Bordeaux,' Laure told her coolly. She remembered the letter and drew it from her pocket. 'Maître Perrard sent this for you.'

Madame Naillac took it and Laure saw her hand tremble as she opened it.

'He told me what was in it,' Laure added. 'It's all true. Rosaline Brousse was exactly what she claims to be.'

'That is what I expected. I did not know he had a mistress, of course. He would not have thought it proper to talk of such things to his mother. But he was a man, with a man's needs – it was to be supposed he satisfied them somehow. One must be practical about these things.' And then she read the letter, and Laure saw the glow of pleasure spread over the hard face. 'So, Frédéric is his son, beyond all doubt. I knew it in my heart.' Once again there were traces of tears in her eyes; but sentiment did not linger for long. She read the letter again, folded it, and then looked sharply at Laure. 'It is most improper for you to be gallivanting about the countryside so soon after Philippe's death. Have you no respect for his memory? What must Maître Perrard have thought of you?'

'It did not appear to trouble him. Besides, I had to go.' She braced herself for the next disclosure. 'I have sold my jewellery and arranged for the most pressing debts to be settled.'

Madame Naillac's eyes glittered angrily. 'What right had you to do that without consulting me? You knew what I intended in that matter. You had no business to go directly against my wishes, behind my back.' She looked Laure over as if she found nothing in her appearance for which she did not feel the greatest possible distaste. 'Well, you will have to take the consequences. It will be no good running to me when you realise you've no pretty baubles left to wear. I shall have Frédéric to provide for, and have no intention of paying for your little frivolities.'

'There will be no frivolities, only what Casseuil needs.'

'Then you should have left the debts and kept your jewellery to hand. Casseuil will get nothing from my own funds, not if Philippe's son is to be raised as his father would wish – there is his education to consider.'

It seemed to Laure that here, as if by a miracle, was her opportunity. 'I shall ask you for nothing. Do what you like for Frédéric. All I want is to look after Mathilde's interests. I am quite able to take responsibility for the house and the vineyard; and of course, for what is left in its accounts.' Could it really be as easy as that?

It could not.

'Never! As long as I live, I shall be mistress of Casseuil. Do you really think for a moment that I would allow an incompetent like you to have free rein in my house, under my very nose? No, whilst I am alive the house and the vineyard will be in my care, and mine alone. You needn't fear that they will suffer at my hands. I shall do my best for Casseuil, not because it belongs to your daughter, but because it is my home. After I am dead, then you can do what you like – that's if Mathilde hasn't already married by then. If she has there'll be a stranger in charge here, so it won't matter what anyone does. I just hope I don't live to see that day.' She glanced down at the folded letter. 'If only Frédéric were legitimate, and could inherit!'

There was no answer to that, or none that would not be unforgivably rude or hurtful, so Laure said nothing and began to move towards the stairs. Seeing her go, Madame Naillac concluded sharply, 'I shall not tolerate any further interferences of the kind you indulged in today. As soon as possible I shall arrange a figure for your allowance. You may do what you please with that. For the rest, you will leave everything to me.'

Laure, trying to sound reasonable, made a last desperate attempt to win some right to a say in her life. 'I think that we should work out some kind of plan together. Obviously we need to cut back on our expenses, perhaps manage with fewer servants. I have a few thoughts on the subject. May I come and discuss them with you in the morning?'

'Have I not made it clear that I have nothing to discuss with you, that matters concerning the house and the estate are my concern alone? I want to hear no more talk of this kind.' She half turned away, and then remembered something. 'Oh, your parents wrote. A letter came today.'

Whilst Laure had been ill Madame Naillac had written briefly to the Frémonts to tell them of Philippe's death and Mathilde's birth, as well as their daughter's ill health. Later, when Laure recovered, she had written at greater length herself, indicating that she was as well as could be expected in the circumstances. No one, of course, had mentioned financial problems, and even the fact of suicide had been brought in only obliquely. But they could not yet have received Laure's letter and so they had replied to Madame Naillac, clearly deeply anxious about their daughter and including a host of anguished messages for her, in the hope that she was in some kind of fit state to receive them. Laure took the letter that Madame Naillac handed to her and went to compose a reassuring reply for that distant family. It was odd, she thought, that they seemed part of a past long vanished that had nothing to do with her any longer. She did not even consider telling them of her present unhappiness.

Coming down for dinner that evening, Laure reached the hall just as Madame Naillac emerged from the *grand salon* on her way to the dining-room. She was not alone. Shining with satisfaction, Rosaline Brousse accompanied her, attentive to every word she was saying; though she spared a moment to shoot a triumphant glance that was not quite a smile in Laure's direction.

Laure halted just where she was at the foot of the stairs. Until today Rosaline and her child had taken their meals in their room upstairs, living largely separate lives discreetly apart from the rest of the household. But today of course everything had changed; and here Rosaline was walking to the dining-room as if nothing could be more natural.

Was that how it was to be now? Was she, Laure, to sit at table with Philippe's mistress, to watch her basking in all the approval that once, for a little while, had been enjoyed by Philippe's wife? She knew she could not – would not – take the last few steps to Rosaline's side, not even when Madame Naillac paused and turned coldly towards her. 'Ah, Laure! I was afraid you were going to be late.'

Very pale, trying to control the trembling that affected her voice as much as her limbs, Laure said, 'I think after all I am not as well as I thought. I shall dine in my room this evening, if you will excuse me.' She did not wait for a reply, but retreated upstairs and there sank shivering on the bed.

She had ample time that night to think over all that had happened; too much time, for she slept very little. But when the ringing of the morning angelus broke into her dazed half-sleeping state she had come to no particularly helpful conclusion. One thing only was certain: she depended, always and for everything, on Madame Naillac. If she was to have any hope, ever, of any kind of freedom, then it must be granted to her by her mother-in-law. That Auguste Silvine was also responsible for her and for Casseuil was insignificant; he would without doubt support his sister in everything.

She had to accept then that whatever Madame Naillac chose to do must be endured. And that the only way in which she could gain any influence herself was by somehow winning back the support and friendship that she had lost at Philippe's death. She could not hope to act alone, but she could perhaps work to achieve some kind of partnership.

Yet that seemed at the moment to be an impossible goal. She knew instinctively that the older woman's hatred of her was deeper than reason, perhaps beyond recall. Once, fear of offending Philippe had kept her from fighting his mother's unkindness; now, when it was so much the greater and when every impulse she possessed urged her to fight, Laure recognised that she could not do so without risking the loss of all the last faint traces of freedom that remained to her. But she could not meekly accept everything that the old woman asked of her. She had to fight somehow, even if the weapons she used must be deliberately blunted or subtly disguised.

After breakfast she made her way up the stairs to Madame Naillac's rooms. To her surprise the door stood open, revealing a bustle of activity: much moving of furniture, with the authoritative tones of the old woman directing operations. Laure went to the doorway and paused there – apart from anything else her way was barred by a narrow wooden bed tipped on its side. The focus of all this activity seemed to be the tiny, round tower-room beyond Madame Naillac's bedroom, which itself was just visible through the open door facing her across the sitting-room. Until now, Antoinette had slept there, but at present it appeared to be empty and in the process of being thoroughly cleaned. Aristide, who had been pressed into furniture removing duties, murmured to Laure as he came to collect a stool from nearby, 'The little boy's to have that room, I'm told.'

Madame Naillac, hearing his remark, turned with a rebuke on her lips, and saw Laure. She crossed the room at once.

'This is not the most convenient moment, but since you are here I would like a word with you – about your behaviour last night.'

Laure glanced at the servants, pausing full of curiosity to

154

listen: she guessed well enough what a great source of entertainment the whole business of Rosaline's arrival, and its effect on them all, must be providing. 'Then may we speak in private, *madame*?'

After a momentary hesitation, the old woman ordered Aristide to move the obstructive bed and emerged onto the landing. She led the way across to what was evidently to be Antoinette's new room: many of the maid's belongings were already there, and her narrow bed, although she herself was fully occupied with the others.

There, as Madame Naillac closed the door and turned to face her, Laure quickly intervened. '*Madame*, if you believe that my indisposition last night was a fabrication, then you are quite right, and I make no apology for it. All I ask is that so long as Mademoiselle Brousse remains at Casseuil I shall not be required to sit at table with her. That does not seem to me to be an unreasonable request, in the circumstances.'

'Then you will have a very restricted life. I choose that Mademoiselle Brousse eats at my table, at least when there is no other company. You must accustom yourself to that, or take all your meals in your room.'

Laure was temporarily diverted by the realisation that Madame Naillac's approval of Rosaline was not after all so wholehearted as to extend to being willing to display her before friends and neighbours. The thought gave her a certain malicious amusement, short-lived perhaps, but for that instant almost consoling. It hinted too at a certain underlying insecurity in the old woman's attitude to the whole affair, which might, Laure thought, be to her own advantage.

'Do you really think Philippe would have wanted his wife to be forced to live under the same roof and eat at the same table as his mistress?' She knew it was a cruel question to put to a bereaved mother, and regretted the bitterness that had made her stoop to ask it, but she was too hurt to be considerate.

The next moment she realised that her regret was wasted. She had not touched Madame Naillac at all.

'What you have done removes any claim you might have had to be treated with respect; I am quite sure that Philippe would agree with me. As surely as any murderer, you killed him. Can you ever forget that? Can you think that any hurt, any humiliation you may suffer will ever be expiation enough for that?'

Once Laure too had thought as the old woman did, hating herself for her blindness, her selfishness, her lack of love. But that had been before she knew about Rosaline. She had not forgiven herself, but she had learned that Philippe too had been guilty, and that made all the difference. 'You are unjust, *madame*! You know as well as I do, you must know, that Philippe bought gifts for Rosaline too. How do you know that she did not make unreasonable demands on him? At the very least, he had her rent to pay, and her keep, and the money for the child.'

'Yes, the child: that's just it. Would you have had him turn his back on his son, pretend perhaps that he did not exist? He had responsibilities, and being a man of honour he met them in full. I have seen no evidence that Rosaline asked any more of him than was her due, as the mother of his son.'

No, you would not, thought Laure wearily. If you do not want to see, then nothing will make you do so.

Once again she found herself brought up short by the stone wall of her mother-in-law's hatred, which offered no crack, no chink through which to make any appeal for justice or consideration, a smooth impervious surface that barred her way wherever she turned.

'And what about Mathilde? She may not be a boy, but she is Philippe's legitimate heir. Surely you do not really want her to grow up in the same house as her father's mistress! What will I say, when she asks about Rosaline?'

'She is not even in the house at present,' said Madame Naillac impatiently. 'She is in any case much too young to ask questions.'

'But she will, one day. What kind of atmosphere is that for a child to grow up in? Is that really what you want for your granddaughter?'

'My concern is with my grandson. How you bring up Mathilde is your business: I shall not interfere. And you are, of course, quite at liberty to live apart from the rest of us, keeping to your rooms. I would raise no objection to that.'

Laure opened her mouth; and then, abruptly, closed it

again, letting her hands – raised to support her argument – fall back to her sides. What was the use? If the censorious and devout Madame Naillac was impervious to all argument from morality, then Laure had no choice but to admit defeat.

As she made her way downstairs again she derived a tiny grain of comfort from the realisation that her mother-in-law had not, after all, scolded her for refusing to eat with Rosaline last night. It was hardly a victory, but it was perhaps a tiny concession to Laure's battered feelings.

iii

During the next few days Madame Naillac took final and total control of her grandson. She had him moved from the guest-room where he had slept with his mother to the little tower-room, where a narrow bed, a bookcase filled with carefully selected books, a table and a chair were put ready for him. In this austere little room he slept alone and passed the large part of each day, busy with some activity decided upon by his grandmother. At other times, for hours together, she kept him at her side, teaching him with fierce concentration to read and write and count, instructing him in deportment and table manners, forcing him to pronounce his hesitant baby words with no trace of the country accent that, in her eyes, deformed them, reading to him from some improving work.

Laure, gathering something of this ruthless régime from her occasional glimpses of it, wondered if the poor child had any understanding of what was happening to him, or was simply utterly bewildered. He was certainly submissive. Sometimes she would see him taking his daily walk about the garden in the company of his grandmother or Antoinette and she was struck by the air of gravity that hung about him, quite unlike the bright chirping curiosity proper to a two-year-old.

There was nothing rigorous about Nanon Foussac. Her life, her world, were bounded by Mathilde and her needs. For her, she would have given up anything at all. A willing slave, she answered every slightest cry with the comfort of her arms or her breast, or the rough gentleness of her singing. All her other duties were pushed aside, fitted in only if time allowed. She had no scruples at all about leaving to her mother all the cleaning and the cooking, the tending of the garden and the chickens and the goat, and the mounds of washing by which they had earned their keep since her father's death. She was paid for her care of Mathilde, of course; but that was beside the point. This fragile little creature whom at first, bitter with grief, she had hated for living at all when her own little one was dead, had become the whole reason for her existence.

One morning, when Laure made her daily visit, Nanon tried to explain her feelings – on this occasion the *curé* was present too, so she had an interpreter. In his absence any conversation between the two women must of necessity be limited.

'You see,' she said earnestly, 'what we did, me and Jacques, it was a sin, when all's said and done. Maybe he didn't look at it like that, and I didn't either at first; and of course when he died I was glad about the baby – I had something left, you see. But then God took my baby too, and I knew how it was: I'd done wrong and I had to pay for it.' She spoke with a calm gravity, as one stating a sober fact, and then the next moment smiled suddenly, the emotion lighting her large, rather ungainly features to a kind of radiance. 'But God was good after all, and he gave me this little one to show I was truly forgiven.'

Afterwards, as they left the house together, Laure said vehemently to the *curé*, 'That was terrible, what Nanon said – horrible! How could anyone believe it?'

'It gives her comfort, *ma fille*. Would you deny her that?'

Laure wondered how far the Abbé Lebrun had influenced Nanon to think as she did, but she parted from him at the château gate without asking him. He was useful to her as a go-between in her dealings with Nanon, and she recognised, however reluctantly, that he cared about her. But he was too much Madame Naillac's friend for her to want to encourage him in any way.

As for Nanon, Laure could not grudge her the consolation she found in Mathilde. But today, as so often, she had wanted to cry out, 'Mathilde is my daughter, *mine* – never forget that, for one day I shall take her home, and you will not have her any more.' There was in the thought both concern for Nanon, and an expression of her own pain.

The visits to the little house were the one thing that gave purpose to her days, the one thing she had left to look forward to; but they did not make her happy. She was fiercely jealous of Nanon, whose tender nourishment of the child had earned her the first gurgles and smiles of Philippe's daughter, the first love of her infant heart. Yet Laure pitied her too, recognising her need for Mathilde and acknowledging the comfort the baby brought her. It was tormenting to want Mathilde so much to be hers alone, and yet at the same time to shrink from the pain which that move would bring to Nanon.

As she let herself into the wood by the little gate, closing it again behind her, she thought, How can they all be so smug about things? The *curé* with his soothing words, Nanon today, smiling like that, my parents, full of how wonderful America is: do they remember nothing, any of them? The world is a dark and horrible place, full of pain and suffering wherever you look, full of the dreadful cruel things we do to one another. How can anyone see any cause for hope, except by shutting his eyes and his ears and his heart?

Her eyes were open now, seeing the path that led down to the château, dappled with sunlight, shaded with trees afire with the flame colours of autumn, a glowing frame for the distant honey-pale walls of her home, the glimpse of blue sky beyond.

A beautiful day; and running into view across the path was a little child, in laughing pursuit of a butterfly. There was delight on his small face, wonder in his outstretched hands, so much unthinking happiness that for a moment she did not recognise him.

Then a tall figure emerged slowly from the trees behind him, leaning on her cane, all measured dignity, and called sharply, 'Frédéric!'

The child turned, looked up at his grandmother's expression, unfrowning but severe, and came trotting meekly back to her side to walk there as obediently as a little dog, with all the light gone from his face.

Laure waited until they had disappeared from sight before going on her way again. She was smiling slightly now, but not with pleasure – rather, with the sour satisfaction of someone who has just had her most bitter prejudices confirmed.

*

Rosaline, a little bored, had wandered out into the vineyard in search of entertainment. She enjoyed the comforts of Casseuil, the good food and luxurious surroundings and the unaccustomed pleasure of having a host of servants to wait upon her. She was glad too that she had been relieved so completely of the care of Frédéric. Having had almost nothing to do with him from the moment of his birth until his father's death two months ago, she had found on the journey from Bordeaux that he aroused in her no maternal feelings whatsoever. Philippe had been a doting father, of course, and often visited the child; but she had rarely accompanied him. She had discovered with some regret that she did not even like Frédéric very much, perhaps because she sensed that he did not like her. She had now and then had to fight an urge to punish him in some way for his indifference to her. At least now that responsibility no longer hung over her. Madame Naillac had made it very plain that although Rosaline was welcome at Casseuil, the separation between mother and son was to be complete.

It required, however, a considerable effort on Rosaline's part to maintain the appropriate demeanour before Madame Naillac; knowing her place, never for a moment stepping beyond the bounds of what was allowed. She had always been good at suiting her behaviour to the company she kept, but the old woman's standards were high and it was only too easy to fall beneath them; to use her fish knife for the meat, perhaps, or talk with her mouth full, or employ some slightly vulgar expression (she knew when she had done that by the just perceptible stiffening of Madame Naillac's features) or laugh too loudly at quite the wrong moment. She was learning fast, but she felt that one did need a rest now and then.

She was also growing more than a little tired of exclusively female company. She had never before found herself in a situation where the only men about her were servants from whom she was expected to keep her distance. She had enjoyed an occasional brief exchange with Sylvestre – when no one was about – which had reassured her that she was not losing her touch; but that was unlikely to lead anywhere, and besides, he was not very attractive, a bit pale and soft and plump for her taste.

The young man who worked out in the vineyard, seen from her window from time to time, was another matter altogether. Only a boy, of course, and thus much younger than she was, but well made, the muscular strength of his body visible through the thick loose folds of the blue country smock and and the unappealing black trousers. Under the worn black felt hat sprang luxuriant chestnut curls, framing a strong tanned face in which his teeth now and then flashed brilliantly white. Yes, on the whole Rosaline thought she would enjoy coaxing a smile from those rather daunting features. He might be a mere boy, but her own early background had been much like his, an obvious basis for sympathy.

Unfortunately, when she came within sight of him this morning she saw that he was not, as she had thought, alone, but working with the much more unprepossessing older man who was probably a relation. Worse, Monsieur Delisle was there too, and she knew from her single encounter with him that he disapproved wholeheartedly of her.

At that moment Rosaline saw Laure cross the track from the wood and reach up to open the gate into the courtyard, and, abandoning her original plan, she came running to join her.

'Good morning, *madame*. How is the little one?' She spoke in gasps, being out of breath, but her tone was friendly and her smile warm.

Laure said nothing and deliberately moved faster. She did not slam the gate shut in Rosaline's face, but it was obvious that she would have liked to do so.

'*Madame*, please – I would like to speak to you.'

'I can't think why: we have nothing to say to one another.'

'I do understand how you feel, oh be sure I do.'

At that Laure swung round, her eyes very dark and angry. 'How can you understand, even for a moment? If you had any tiny grain of sensitivity in you, any respect for Philippe's memory or his wife's feelings, then you would never, never have come near Casseuil!'

Rosaline held out her hands in a gesture of entreaty. 'You, who are a mother too, can you not see why I came? Would you have let your child starve without lifting a finger to help him? Do you think it cost me nothing to come begging to the woman who has every reason to hate me?'

There were, Laure saw with astonishment, real tears brimming in the brown eyes facing her, and the attractive voice was quivering with emotion.

She would not allow herself to be moved. 'You got what you wanted, didn't you? You don't need my pity any more, if you ever did.' Again she turned away, and this time Rosaline laid a hand on her arm.

'I'm not asking for your pity.' Laure shook off the hand, but Rosaline knew she had her attention, and went on, 'We loved the same man. If he were still alive, then that would be reason enough for us to hate one another. But he's dead, and we both miss him. Surely that should bring us together?' She paused, looking thoughtfully into the hostile face before her. 'Don't you ever wish you could talk about him to someone? Memories to share, perhaps . . .'

'With you? Never!'

Laure walked quickly away, on into the house. Only once did she glance round, and then she saw that Rosaline was blowing her nose, as if to restrain her tears. Laure thought, Did she love Philippe? Does she really care that he's dead? There was, of course, no way of discovering the answer without asking Rosaline; and that Laure had no intention of doing.

iv

A few curled bronze leaves floated gently down from the chestnut tree near the stables to lie on the gravel beneath. As Aristide led him out into the sunlight, Grand Turc shied at them, more from high spirits than from fear. He stood there, tossing his head, stamping his feet, as if fully aware of his gleaming magnificence, at which Henri Séguier was looking now with a new pride of ownership.

At last! After all this time! Henri thought to himself, but he did not, of course, put it into words: that would hardly have been tactful, suggesting that in some way he regarded the death of Philippe Naillac as a stroke of good fortune, which of course it was not . . . But it was sweet all the same to find himself the owner of his late neighbour's coveted horse. He tried not to think of that other possession of Philippe's which

162

he coveted far more; but a natural train of thought led him all the same to say casually to Aristide, 'What of the other horse – Madame Laure's mare, that is?'

'Oh, she's not to be sold. They're keeping that one, and the pony for the trap.'

'Not the carriage horses? Nor the others?'

'No, *monsieur*. They're all sold.'

Things were bad then, worse perhaps than rumour had suggested. 'Pity about Madame Laure's mare. I'm looking for a new mount for my son. That one would have done very well I think. Perhaps if I spoke to her . . .'

'I'm sorry, *monsieur*. She sees no one at the moment, except *monsieur le curé*. And Madame Naillac was very clear – Fine Fleur is to stay, for the use of Madame Laure when she's able to ride again.'

Henri shrugged. 'There we are then.' He looked again at Grand Turc and felt his good humour return. 'Let's get this one home.' His own ageing horse stood patiently nearby, held by the Trissac groom, whom Henri called to lead Grand Turc away.

He himself delayed his own departure as long as possible, in the faint hope of catching a glimpse of Laure, even perhaps engineering a chance meeting. When his desultory conversation with Aristide could not sensibly be prolonged, he wandered out into the vineyard, down the slope by the garden wall, in some slight hope that Laure would be outside, enjoying the autumn air. The garden was empty; but amongst the thinning vines two women were removing the heavy lower leaves from the plants, so that the sun could more easily reach the grapes. Once that would have been work for ten women or so, but now, presumably, the château could no longer afford to employ so many. Soon, Henri supposed, they would not have vines enough left to occupy even two women at these routine tasks.

Further on, he saw another woman, all in black, her hair gleaming gold in the sunlight. For an instant his heart missed a beat; and then she moved, gracefully, but in a manner which even at this distance was full of a blatant and calculated sexuality. Not Laure Naillac, then; but who could it be? He thought he knew all the women with any claim to beauty in the region; and that this one came into that category was clear.

She was talking to Aubin Lambert, and he appeared to have forgotten all about the work which, presumably, he should have been doing, and was staring at her like a man besotted.

The next moment, Aubin had his arms about her and was kissing her; and she meanwhile, with her pretty white hands, was doing things to his young body which only a woman very experienced in these matters would think of doing. Watching them, Henri felt excited at the very thought of it. A pretty woman, the kind who would make a quite delightful mistress . . .

And then he realised who she must be: there had been gossip enough about her, after all. At that moment, Jean Delisle passed him – greeting him as he did so – and the young woman, seeing the *régisseur* coming, pushed Aubin from her, with some giggling excuse, and turned and hurried back towards the house.

Full of curiosity, and something else, Henri stayed where he was until she reached him. She paused as she came near, and smiled, quite winningly. She *was* pretty, even if the gold of her hair owed less to nature than did Laure's. She was a little older than Laure, and had a quite undeniable sexual allure, much more obvious and yet less overwhelming than anything Henri had ever felt in Laure's presence. Yet there were a thousand other women like this, and nothing about her that would linger in the mind once she had gone. If Philippe Naillac's wife had been like her, he might have tried to get her into his bed (it would certainly be easier with this one than with Laure), but he would not have found himself cursed with this eternal and tormenting desire.

'Good day, *monsieur*.' Even the words sounded knowing, full of hidden meanings. He raised his hat to her and watched her go. How could Philippe Naillac possibly have been interested in her, when he could have had Laure in his bed every night?

He turned and walked slowly back to the courtyard and his waiting horse. As he rode away he saw that behind the stables, where Aristide and his wife lodged in an adjacent cottage, a cart was being loaded with the coachman's modest belongings. It was not only the horses that were leaving Casseuil.

*

164

That afternoon Laure sought out Madame Naillac in the *petit salon*; Frédéric always slept after lunch, so his grandmother in her turn took a rest then, and Laure knew she would be alone, without even the dogs for company, since they too had gone to new homes.

Laure saw at once that the old woman resented her intrusion into this moment of quiet, but she did not hesitate. '*Madame*, why have you ordered all the horses to be sold except Fine Fleur?'

'That is no concern of yours. I do as I see fit.'

'If you had consulted me, then Fine Fleur could have been sold too.'

She saw genuine surprise on the older woman's face. 'Don't be ridiculous. I see no reason for that. You will need something to ride when the first period of mourning is over.'

'I can walk or take the trap, like everyone else.'

'I have no wish to ask more of you than is reasonable. You must have your little pleasures. What else otherwise will you do with your time?'

Laure clenched her hands tight, trying hard to keep her anger under control. She was not a spoiled child to be humoured and pampered. Why could Madame Naillac not see that she wanted to be treated like a responsible person, to be asked to bear her share of the economies that necessity forced upon Casseuil? 'If Fine Fleur is sold, there will be more to spend on other things, on labourers for the *vendange*, for instance. Monsieur Delisle is very worried . . .'

'Ah, that's another thing – you will please refrain from visiting the *chai* or wandering about after Monsieur Delisle. Have you forgotten that it is scarcely three months since Philippe died?'

Laure nearly exclaimed, 'Is that all? It feels like years!' But instead, remembering as always how powerless she was, she returned meekly, 'You know I do not forget. But I want to help, and you will not tell me what needs doing. Let me sell Fine Fleur.'

'Your horse is paid for from your funds, not those of the estate.'

'Is that any reason why they should not be spent on the estate?'

'I suppose not, if it pleases you.' The old woman's shrug indicated her complete indifference to the matter.

Laure felt immoderately elated at this unexpected concession. She knew, because a message had come from Aristide through Sylvestre, that Henri Séguier was interested in buying her mare; although she was glad that convention made it possible for her to carry out the transaction by letter, without seeing him. It was painful enough losing her beloved horse, without having to endure Henri's attentions in the process.

Over the past weeks she had steadily paid off one after another of the outstanding debts from her regular allowance. Now, she thought, the last debts could wait a while, until the *vendange* was over. One franc fifty a day would hire a labourer.

There was another step she could take too, with no regrets at all. She summoned Florestine to her.

'I find it necessary to dispense with the services of a maid,' she said quietly. 'You will of course be assured of the best references and every help in finding a new post.'

She sweetened the pill of dismissal still further by giving Florestine almost every one of those exquisite gowns that once had meant so much to her. Later, she watched the bemusedly ecstatic maid pack them away in her own bags, and was glad that they would no longer hang in the wardrobe to reproach her every time she opened its doors with her vanity, and her thoughtlessness, and her lack of love.

CHAPTER
NINE

i

It could not be put off any longer, he knew that. Fighting the sense of reluctance that tugged almost irresistibly at him, whispering to him to work instead on tomorrow's sermon, or to go and see César Chabry (which would mean listening to the man's unending complaints against the Empire and the Republic together, and their relative injustices in relation to himself; but that was preferable nevertheless to the alternative) the Abbé Lebrun brushed the stains from his *soutane*, tidied his hair, and set out unhappily through the wood towards the château.

Yes, Madame Laure was at home and would see him, if he would just take a seat in the *petit salon*. There was no escape that way then; but he had not really expected it. He had after all chosen this time because he could more easily see her alone, in the morning, while her mother-in-law was occupied with the child upstairs.

Laure came in quietly. Although, after more than a year of mourning, she could by now have discarded some of the more hampering trappings of her widowhood, she had not done so. It was hard for the *curé*, confronted for so long with the subdued black-draped widow, to remember now the sparkling young wife of the old days. Yet he knew that somewhere within that meek and apparently pliable little person was a core of steel. It was that he most feared today.

She greeted him with cool brevity and took her seat facing him, hands loosely folded in her lap; they were very pale and thin, and yet looked warm and alive against the dead blackness of her skirts.

Since there seemed to be no appropriate way of leading gently up to what he had to say, the *curé* plunged straight in.

'I understand from Nanon Foussac that you plan to have your daughter brought here – next week, she said.'

Laure did not stir. 'Yes.' There was no expression in her voice, any more than in the still face below the ugly concealing cap.

'May I ask, why now?'

'She is weaned. This is her home.'

'You would not consider, perhaps, waiting a little? She is doing very well in Nanon's care, you know.' He could not now see Laure's face, for she had bent her head.

'There was sickness in the village last winter – if she should catch anything – and the house is not very clean, you must admit. She'll be safer here.'

'You know Doctor Rossillon keeps a careful eye on her.'

'He has less time now he's mayor.'

'You know he will always put his patients first. And . . .' he added a little awkwardly, as if aware of committing an indiscretion, 'he is I think rather more welcome at the Foussacs' house than beneath Madame Naillac's roof.' It was well known that only in the most extreme need would the old woman send for Doctor Rossillon, and then she made it plain he was admitted only and exclusively in his medical capacity; if there had been another doctor nearer to Casseuil than Bergerac, she would have turned to him instead. She had never forgiven Doctor Rossillon for allowing himself to be elected mayor, in what should, she believed, have been Philippe's natural place; and he had only made matters worse by his disagreement with her over the funeral arrangements. 'If it's cleanliness that troubles you,' the *curé* went on, since Laure's expression did not change, 'I can arrange for improvements in that respect – particularly if a little more money were forthcoming. It would not take much.'

Laure had raised her head again and was regarding the Abbé with a steady gaze that had something implacable about it. 'I am her mother. Her place is with me.' She spoke without emotion, as one stating an undeniable fact; as indeed, the *curé* had to acknowledge, it was.

He shifted uncomfortably in his chair, rearranging the musty folds of his *soutane*, black like those of his companion's dress: two quiet courteous figures in black discussing in civilised tones something behind which lay a world of anger and pain. The thought gave him an odd and unreal sensation.

'I think you know how much the child means to Nanon. You must do, of course.'

'Do you know how much she means to me?' Even now the question was put calmly; and the *curé* ignored it.

'Nanon lost everything – her man, her child. She was close to despair – not simply grief, you understand, but real despair, of a mortal kind. And then Mathilde came and she found every reason to live, and to go on living. Would you take that from her?'

'She has always known it was only until Mathilde was weaned.' There was, now, a sharp edge to Laure's voice, and a coldness in which the *curé* thought he could detect a hint of fear. 'That is the usual arrangement with a wet nurse, is it not?'

'By no means always. But that is not the point. For most wet nurses it is simply a profession, a matter of money. Nanon has never seen it like that.'

Laure rose suddenly to her feet and stepped towards the fire, looking down at the glowing logs; and now her voice was trembling. 'Then she should have done! You should have made sure she did. Why else did I go every day to see Mathilde, if not to remind them both who her mother was?'

'*Ma fille*, that alters nothing. It is not alas so easy as that to arrange the feelings of another person. I am not asking you to give up anything, you must see that, only to wait a little longer, to leave things as they are until Mathilde is grown enough to need schooling and so forth – then we would all I think agree that she would be better off here.'

'And do you think Nanon will find it any easier then to give her up? No, it will be worse.'

'She will be further from her sad losses of last year, better able to face a new loss – and, of course, Mathilde will be more independent and, living so near, well able to come and visit her often.'

Sharply, Laure turned. 'Have you forgotten that I too lost something last year? Am I to give up all I have left, to comfort Nanon? Don't I have needs too, like her?'

'Of course, *ma fille* – no one would deny that. But as I said, you will not be giving up anything at all.'

Laure sat down again, leaning forward with her hands giving expressive emphasis to her low insistent words. 'Do you know what it's been like for me this past year? Always, waiting and waiting, with nothing to do, nothing to hope for but this one thing. Mathilde is all *I* have, *mon père*. I do not even have work to do to occupy my days, because that is not allowed. Nanon always had things to do, she can have them again, and they will help her forget.'

'You think washing clothes is a good cure for heartache, *ma fille*?'

The pale hands were twisted together, their tense fingers eloquent of pain. 'No—' She stopped abruptly, and the *curé* could see how much she was trembling. When she spoke again it was obvious that it cost her a great deal to keep her voice under control. 'Mathilde is my child, mine alone – if I leave her there she will not even know me or want me, and I shall lose her for ever.'

'Do you forget, *ma fille*,' the *curé* put in sternly, 'that she is not your child alone, but first and before all a child of God, entrusted to your care?'

'To *my* care, yes – not Nanon's.'

'And it is up to you to decide what is best for her – for *her*, *ma fille*, not for you.'

Laure stood up. 'I have decided. She is coming home on Monday. I have told Nanon so, and she will I am sure be prepared.' There was dismissal in her tone and the *curé*, heavy-hearted, recognised it. He rose to his feet too; and then was struck by a sudden inspiration.

'There is another way, *ma fille*. Yes, bring Mathilde here; but bring Nanon with her. She would come, I know – and make herself useful to you in many ways, I'm sure. You would both of you gain from it.'

'No! Mathilde must know that I am her mother, I alone. It was not my fault I could not nurse her when she was born. Now that she no longer needs that, then I can give her everything. I may perhaps take her to see Nanon sometimes, indeed I'm sure I shall, but I will not have her brought up torn two ways, not knowing who she must love first of all. I'm sorry if Nanon is distressed by it, but I can't help that.'

'I am sorry too, *ma fille*, deeply sorry.' He turned and

crossed the room and made his way along the hall and out of the house, not attempting to hide the dejection that bowed his head and hunched his shoulders. There was only prayer left, and sometimes even he wondered what use that was, set against the intensity of a woman's grief, or the anguish of loss, or the hardness that grew out of too much suffering.

Nanon gave up the baby very quietly. The little girl was ready when Laure arrived on Monday morning, shining with cleanliness and dressed in the exquisitely simple white dress that her mother had provided for her. She took a few unsteady steps across the hard earth floor towards Laure, and then laughed and tottered back to Nanon, and clung to the peasant woman's heavy none-too-clean skirts, her brown eyes peeping shyly round at her mother. Without a word Nanon bent down and picked her up and handed her to Laure. She stood with her hands by her sides saying nothing as Laure murmured some kind of awkward thanks and then, anxious to be away, turned and left the cottage. There was no sound from Nanon as the door closed on her motionless figure.

Mathilde took her thumb from her mouth and began to cry.

ii

> Il était un' bergère,
> Et ron, ron, ron, petit patapon
> Il était un' bergère
> Qui gardait ses moutons,
> Ron, ron,
> Qui gardait ses moutons . . .

Round and round they danced, hands joined, Laure's sweet clear voice punctuated by her daughter's infectious gurgling laughter. Then Mathilde tripped, wobbled, sat down, and laughed all the more. Laure sank down facing her and laughed too.

Madame Naillac, coming into the *grand salon* at that moment, gazed in astonished disapproval at the spectacle of her daughter-in-law, cap awry, face flushed and laughing, spread on the floor as if she had not a care in all the world.

Laure looked round and saw her, and with a kind of intuitive gesture of protection reached out and drew Mathilde into her arms, where the child nestled close, all at once quiet and a little solemn. Like that, unsmiling, her brown eyes – more intensely dark than her mother's – bore a quite devastating resemblance to Philippe's. For Laure, often, that wistful brown gaze had set her heart turning with regret and pain and all the ambiguous sense of loss that Philippe's death had left to her. Now she saw that Madame Naillac too had been struck by the likeness; for a moment her mouth had an odd twist to it and she reached out for the additional support of a nearby chair, though she had her cane to lean on, as always.

She's aged terribly, Laure thought suddenly. It was the first time for a long while that she had looked with objective eyes at her mother-in-law. Madame Naillac had every reason to look old, of course; but there was a greyness and strain about her face that Laure did not remember having seen before. She wondered if Philippe's mother was ill. Sobered, even stirred to something that was not quite pity, she put Mathilde from her and rose to her feet, though she kept an arm about the child.

'So this is how you spend your Sunday mornings when the rest of us are at mass.'

All Laure's new-born sympathy vanished in an instant. She took Mathilde's hand and moved to pass Madame Naillac. 'We are going out to enjoy the sunlight until lunch-time.'

'The child was always at mass when Nanon Foussac had charge of her. *Monsieur le curé* was asking after her this morning.'

Laure did not say, as she very much wanted to, 'Then *monsieur le curé* should mind his own business.'

Perhaps Madame Naillac read the words in her eyes, for she went on, 'The welfare of her soul is in your care, as well as that of her body. But I suppose it is of little use to talk to you of such things. You are clearly much more your father's daughter than I ever suspected.'

The thought of her father, so suddenly and unexpectedly, brought a painful lump to Laure's throat, adding hurt to her anger. She reached down and swept Mathilde into her arms and almost ran from the room. She had meant to go upstairs for coats for the two of them, but Antoinette was on the stairs, leading Frédéric, very correct in his Sunday best; so, wanting to prevent any contact between Mathilde and her half-brother, Laure led her daughter straight outside. So far she thought the little girl was quite unaware of the presence of another child in the house. It helped that Madame Naillac too clearly wished to preserve that ignorance for as long as possible.

Mathilde, a naturally happy child who had quickly accepted the new life thrust upon her so suddenly, moved along the track with the unpredictable irregularity of the very young, trotting slowly beside her mother at one moment, the next darting off, laughing and full of excitement at something she had seen, or just for the pleasure of being caught breathless and giggling in her mother's embrace. It was at just one such moment, as Laure kissed the flushed happy little face, that they came on Jean Delisle, not seeing him until Mathilde's sudden silence alerted her mother to his presence.

Laure straightened, and he smiled at her with the gentle, rather melancholy smile that was his most optimistic expression nowadays.

'A charming sight, *madame*. It cheers the heart.'

Laure thought he did not look much cheered. It was a long time since she had spoken to him. Madame Naillac's disapproval alone might not quite have been enough to deter her from seeking him out, but her frustrating sense that she was powerless to help him in any way, however clearly she might see what ought to be done, deprived her of any satisfaction she felt in talking to him. So she had limited herself to contributing what she could from her allowance to the needs of the estate, and kept away from the *chai* and the vineyard.

During the past month of course she had been so absorbed by Mathilde that she had not given a thought to anything else at all. It was only now, meeting Jean Delisle and reminded by his expression of the gravity of the situation, that she saw how sparse were the vines growing here beside the track, how many more had gone since she had last walked this way. She realised too that beneath the fiery foliage of the remaining plants the Sémillon grapes were already showing signs of the *pourriture noble* that indicated the imminence of harvest.

'We begin work tomorrow, *madame*,' said Jean Delisle, as if he read her thoughts.

'It looks as if it may be quite a good harvest.'

'Yes, there is some *pourriture noble* – not one of the best years, but moderate. Except that the vines have diminished by perhaps a quarter since last year, in spite of all we could do.'

Laure dived to retrieve Mathilde, who was toddling off towards the vines with a mischievous backward glance at her mother, and held her firmly in her arms. The child reached out a hand to the *régisseur*'s sombre face, and at last woke a reluctant smile from it. He took the hand and kissed it.

'Ah, *ma petite*, how I hope all this lasts long enough for you to enjoy it one day!'

'Have you enough men for the *vendange*?'

He shook his head. 'No, *madame*. I'm sorry to say that even with your generous contribution we shall not be able to hire many additional hands this year. So, it's up to Aubin Lambert and the Delmas brothers, and your humble servant here, with perhaps twenty others.'

'Then there can be no question about it – I shall help too. You cannot possibly manage with so few.'

He looked doubtfully from her to Mathilde and back again, but it was a measure of his desperation, and his relief, that he did not argue.

The next morning, without a backward thought for her resolution to wear full mourning to the end of her days, Laure put on the simplest and least hampering of her black dresses, bound her hair up beneath a plain cotton bonnet as did the local women in the fields, and set off for the vineyard with Mathilde on leading strings.

As quickly as she could she set herself to follow Jean Delisle's instructions, as he showed her how, with the small pointed shears provided, she must cut from the vine only the ripest grapes, those in which most of the juice had turned to sugar and left only the richest concentrated moisture behind. These were then laid carefully in a basket, which, when full, was carried to be emptied into one of the *comportes* on the cart at the edge of the field. It was slow, laborious, back-breaking work, and Mathilde's lively presence did not make it any easier. Once, fleetingly, Laure thought of Nanon, who would surely have loved to watch over the child during the long hot days of the *vendange* – but no, she had determined that no one ever again should come between herself and Mathilde. So she distracted the little girl with a doll, a book, with pebbles or flowers, anything that might give her some hope of peace; and persevered at her work.

They broke off for soup and bread and wine, after what seemed like a whole day, though it was still scarcely mid-morning. It was a long time since Laure had been as hungry as she was now. She ate the fragrant *tourin*, relishing the simple pungent flavours of onion and garlic, finishing it as the others did with a *chabrol*, and finally mopping up the dregs with a chunk of bread. Beside her at the table in the kitchen Mathilde ate from her own small bowl, enjoying the doting attention of their fellow *vendangeurs*.

Afterwards, returning to the vineyard in a sun that seemed already as hot as if it were August and not October, Laure was brought to a sudden halt. There, waiting beside the piled-up baskets at the edge of the vines, was Rosaline.

After a moment's hesitation, Laure took a firm hold of both the leading reins and Mathilde's hand, and walked forward, deliberately not looking at the intruder. Since that one approach from Rosaline last year Laure had managed almost wholly to avoid her. She was furious now that the girl should be here; and her anger grew when Rosaline calmly took up a basket and began to work along the adjacent row, picking with a skill that suggested she had done this before.

It was inevitable that they should pass close to one another. Laure looked up and met Rosaline's gaze, as unsmiling as her own, but calm and matter of fact. 'You need all the help you can get,' said Rosaline quietly. 'My father had a vineyard once, you know. I'm used to this kind of thing. You won't know I'm here.'

How could she help but know, even if she did not look round to see that blonde head in its cheeky black hat bent over the vines? She felt Rosaline's presence as if it were some kind of painfully irritating substance rubbed into her skin, setting all her nerves on edge and taking from her any last shred of pleasure in the work. But Rosaline was right: they did need all the help they could get. So she endured it all as best she could.

She noticed, as a kind of additional irritation, though it touched her too, that Jean Delisle was more than usually kind to her, as if he wanted to show that he took her part.

Laure had to acknowledge that Rosaline worked unobtrusively and very hard, and much more effectively than Laure herself, inexperienced and hampered by Mathilde, could hope to do. Now and then Rosaline smiled at the little girl over the vines, or waved at her. Laure wanted to tell Mathilde not to smile back, but she could not bear the thought of teaching her child to hate or mistrust anyone, however much they might merit it. She could only try as best she might to keep the little girl's attention turned away from Rosaline. Once the *vendange* was over she would make sure that they did not meet again, although she was not quite sure how.

At lunch-time Laure, exhausted now, went indoors to eat in her room, and, afterwards, like Mathilde, to sleep a little. It took an enormous effort on her part to force her weary body back to the vineyard for the afternoon's work.

As dusk fell the *vendangeurs* dispersed to their homes, and Laure hurried ahead of Rosaline so they would not have to walk to the house together. In the hall Madame Naillac, alone and purposeful, was waiting for her.

'What do you think you are doing, coming in like some brazen peasant girl?'

'You know quite well what I am doing,' Laure replied wearily. 'I owe you no excuse.'

'How dare you speak to me like that! You are not even properly dressed.' Her disapproving gaze took in the light frilled bonnet, the absence of the concealing veil and shawl.

'One can't pick grapes in full widow's weeds, *madame*. And the grapes must be picked.' She did not want to argue tonight. She wanted only to sink into bed, and to sleep. She was too tired even for hunger.

'First you destroy my son by your frivolity, then you insult his memory by working like a peasant.'

Laure felt Mathilde shrink against her skirts, frightened by the tall severe figure and the cold voice. She knew exactly how Mathilde felt. Tonight she herself seemed to have lost all her courage. 'You must see, *madame*, that I had no choice.'

Perhaps after all Madame Naillac did see that, for she gave Laure a last icy sweeping glance and then made her way to the *petit salon*. Laure, not able at the moment to face the stairs, sank onto the nearest chair and gathered Mathilde on her knee, resting her cheek against the heavy warm gold hair. It was only then that she realised that Rosaline had followed her into the hall, although how long she had been there she did not know.

'She's not fair, always throwing that at you,' said Rosaline in a low voice.

'Throwing what at me? I don't know what you're talking about.' She wished she could find the energy to walk quickly away, but it had abandoned her.

'What she always says – that you're to blame for Philippe's death. It's nonsense, and everyone else can see it if she can't. All right, he bought you fine clothes and things, just like he did for me, but it wasn't your fault he couldn't afford them. He should have said no and told you why, if things were that bad. His trouble was that he never could say no, not to anyone. I loved him, of course I did, but I was never blind – I saw him for what he was. Weak, too weak, under the thumb of his mother and anyone else who wanted to lead him by the nose. Anything for a quiet life, that was Philippe.'

Laure was so startled by this wholly new view of her late husband that she forgot for a moment to be offended by Rosaline's presence. She gazed up at what she could see of the other woman's pretty face, its expression thoughtful in the dimness of the unlit hall, and felt only curiosity. 'You thought him weak?' All that strength, that masculinity, that sense of power: surely that could not have been an illusion?

'Of course, didn't you? No, perhaps not. You were very young when you married him, I suppose, and raised very sheltered too. Maybe you believed what the old woman's always saying about how he'd have been a real leader of men if only he'd been a Catholic or a Bonapartist or even a Republican, or if it hadn't been for the treachery of some of his friends. But she's wrong, you know. The only one who would have led would have been her, through him. He never could free himself of her, and he never would have done I reckon. You're stronger than he ever was, a hundred times stronger.'

177

Strong — while she sank here exhausted on a chair in the house in which she had no freedom and no power, with her slighted child held in her arms and her husband's mistress, whose presence she was forced to endure, standing over her? Stronger than Philippe, who had owned the house and the vineyard and whose very air of strength had first attracted and then won her? She could almost have laughed at the very idea, with a kind of bitter amusement. But she did not laugh. Instead, thinking hard, she stood up and cast a last curious glance at Rosaline and made her way slowly upstairs, carrying the sleepy Mathilde.

Henri Séguier rode through Casseuil and past the château whenever he could, even if it meant going out of his way to do so. He knew quite well what drew him there, and he recognised at the same time that the whole thing was a piece of foolishness. Laure Naillac was, of course, technically free to marry again; but she was mourning a much loved husband, and the heavy folds of her widow's weeds and the demands of convention that cut her off from all contact with the world, could not keep her from him more surely than her grief for Philippe. It would be a very long time before she would be receiving guests again in a normal way, even longer, if ever, before she could be invited out to a dinner or a party — particularly now that her financial circumstances made any return of hospitality impossible. No, in a way Henri Séguier had lost all hope of her more conclusively than if Philippe were still alive. But all the same he continued to ride that way.

They were at work in the château vineyards, he saw: a handful of workers busy along the thinning vines. He could not see Jean Delisle, but presumably he was busy with the pressing in the *chai*.

One of the women looked up and Henri, gallant as ever, raised his hat, and then realised with a shock that it was Madame Laure herself. The shock gave way the next moment to a joy that was almost overpowering. Without a second thought he dismounted and led his horse over to where she was — fortunately she was working near the edge of the vineyard beside the road.

He did not see the child until he had reached her, seated on the stony ground solemnly rearranging a little heap of pebbles; but, beyond registering that this small creature must be Casseuil's new owner, he did not give her a second glance. His eyes were all for Laure, this new frail thin Laure whose eyes seemed too large for her delicate face, her slender hands too small and soft to be forced to such heavy work. But still that gold hair, that beauty a man could feast on and never tire – he gazed at her quite unable for some time to find any words even for the simplest of greetings. She did not help him either, but looked at him gravely, without any great interest, as if more than anything she was glad of an excuse to straighten her back and rest for a while.

'Good day, *madame*,' he said at last, although even to his ears his voice sounded strange. 'May I wish you a good harvest?' He was aware that this was probably the most inept of greetings.

'As you please, *monsieur*,' was all she said, with none of the sweet conscious charm of the old days. But she could have told him to drown himself and he would have thought her charming still.

She looks exhausted, he thought; and for the first time into the turbulent passion of his feelings for her crept something that was almost protective. With it, more forcefully, came indignation, at the circumstances that had forced this exquisite creature to work like a peasant in the fields. She was made to be pampered, to live in luxury, for the delight of some fortunate man – not for this drudgery. Bad as things were at the château, this depth of degradation was surely unnecessary. 'Did Monsieur Delisle tell you?' he said. 'I've been advising him to give up on the vines.'

He had her full attention now, even if it had in it an element of hostility. 'To give up?'

'Yes, as I've done at Trissac.'

'Have you? Did the phylloxera reach you too then?'

'Yes, last year, about the same time as it struck you. I could have fought it, I suppose, but it's my view that would just be money down the drain. There's no fighting this one in the end. No, I had the whole lot pulled up and I've gone over to tobacco – now that's the crop of the future, I'd say.' It was hardly an appropriate form of conversation for his first meeting with a newly widowed lady of good family. But Laure Naillac was not like other ladies (if she had been, she would not so have possessed him). Further, she was following all he said with considerable interest – perhaps, even, he had begun to convince her.

'It's different for you. Your wine was never like ours.'

'True, *madame*, very true. But sad though it may seem I think we may be seeing the end of wine making in France.'

'No! That I could never accept!'

'I could be wrong. But if I'm not, then the wise man won't leave it too long before he acknowledges defeat. That way lies bankruptcy.' He was desperate to convince her; for her sake, of course, so he told himself.

But there was something else too, a part of him wanted to gain some kind of authority over a woman whom he knew, by instinct as much as by experience, to be wilful and independent to an unusual degree. Master *her*, and one would have achieved something indeed – something more even than the mastery of the spirited horse at his side. The very thought excited him.

'You must excuse me, *monsieur*. I have work to do.' She did not sound offended at his frankness (as she might have been, in the circumstances), merely businesslike. So, since she left him no choice, he took his leave of her and watched from the road as she gathered up the child and moved on to the next row.

Near her, a blonde woman, pretty and a little older than she was, paused to speak to her. Henri knew who that was, for he had seen her once or twice already, and gossip, full of delighted scandal, had filled in the rest: Philippe Naillac's mistress, welcomed under the château roof because of the son she had borne him. Henri had felt indignation on Laure's behalf when he had heard it; now he was surprised to see that they appeared to be on quite good terms.

That day, at intervals, when they were working within earshot of one another, Laure had learned a great deal about Rosaline. That odd conversation last night in the hall had aroused her curiosity about her rival and even, just a little, cracked the barrier of hostility that she had erected against her. Coolly, without any hint of friendship, she had made the first approach to Rosaline the next morning, asking, 'How did you meet Monsieur Naillac?' It was something she had often wondered, but until now she had always hated Rosaline too much to ask. Not, even now, that she could put the burning question that had tormented her at intervals since Rosaline's arrival: 'Why her and not me? What did he see in her?'

'I was a dancer at the Grand Théâtre in Bordeaux,' Rosaline replied simply, as if that explained everything. And then, realising perhaps that it did not, added, 'He used to come backstage sometimes. That was a long time ago now, eleven years or so, I suppose. We got talking and that's how it started. I think I made him laugh, you see.'

Laure found to her surprise that she did see. She had heard how Sylvestre laughed when Rosaline paused on her way through the hall to talk to him; and she had even seen Aubin Lambert grin once at something she said, as she could not remember him doing, ever, for anyone else. It was, even so, difficult to imagine Philippe laughing in the carefree and uninhibited way Rosaline's words conjured up. It had not occurred to her before that Philippe had never laughed very much, even in the early days of their marriage. It was not a comfortable sensation, to suspect that in a few moments of talk with Rosaline Brousse she had learned more about her husband than she had ever known in five years of living with him.

To stave off the cheerless implications of that reflection, she asked Rosaline, 'But you said your father had a vineyard; how did you come to be a dancer?'

'Oh, it was never much of a vineyard, and my father was just a peasant, you know, and a poor one at that. He drank and got into debt. He had to sell up. Then he took us to Bordeaux to look for work. I learned to dance, and it was me that kept him some of the time, until he died – fell in the river one night when he was drunk, and drowned.' She sounded as though his passing was unregretted. 'So you see, I'm well used to debts.'

'Then why did you come here? I should have thought you'd want to avoid that ever happening again.'

'I had no choice, had I? I depended on Philippe for

181

everything. Besides, I didn't know how things were until I got here.'

'Then why stay?'

Rosaline's smile was rueful. 'You'd like me gone, wouldn't you? I can't blame you for that. I stay because I've nowhere else to go, and there's no other man I want after Philippe, not just yet.' For an instant, fleetingly, emotion did show on her face, and Laure found an answer to one unasked question: yes, Rosaline had loved Philippe. The next moment the customary cheerfulness had returned. 'Besides, things may seem bad to you here, but believe me they could be a lot worse. You've still got the house and the land and some money of your own. And the old woman's got money too, you know.'

Was that what Rosaline was after? 'She hasn't very much.'

'More than you think, I'd guess.'

'But there's Frédéric.'

'He's my son – have you forgotten that?'

Laure did not ask what exactly she meant to imply. Tired of the conversation, distracted by a sudden restlessness on Mathilde's part, she returned to her work. But now and then through the day she found herself talking to Rosaline, as one might to any new and not yet quite trusted acquaintance.

iii

It was close on midnight and out in the November darkness a fierce wind dashed the rain against the low tiled roof of the house at Trissac. But inside, behind closed shutters and drawn curtains, the *salon* was warm, and bright with firelight and candle flames, and Doctor Rossillon, enjoying a rare interlude of relaxation in an increasingly busy life, sat back in a comfortable chair with a glass of brandy in one hand and a cigar in the other, and considered the possibility that by next year the last of the German occupying forces might have been removed from French soil. 'I'm told there are hopes of paying off the remainder of the indemnity in the next few months.'

Henri Séguier shook his head. 'I'd have thought it impossible, if I hadn't seen what's been done already. Pity we can't hope to regain Alsace and Lorraine so easily.'

'Just so long as we don't sell out to the Royalists – but

support for the Republic is growing, there's no doubt of that.'
A bell, clamorously ringing, broke in on their talk and jerked the dozing Madame Rossillon abruptly awake.

'Someone needing the doctor, or the mayor,' predicted Henri with a grin.

'It'll be the doctor at this time of night,' his guest decided.

He was right. 'Mathieu from the château is here, *monsieur*,' Henri's servant told him. 'He asks for *monsieur le docteur*, as quickly as possible. Madame Naillac is very ill.'

Doctor Rossillon was already on his feet, and his wife gathered up her shawl and her glasses and made ready to follow him. But Henri, struck by a sickening lurch of the stomach, stood still where he was, gazing at the man with dismay.

'That'll be old Madame Naillac, I take it?' the doctor pursued; and with an overpowering sense of relief Henri saw the man nod.

After that it took only a matter of minutes to have the carriage at the door and see the guests into it.

At his own house the doctor ushered his wife inside, seized his medical bag, and returned to the carriage for the last stage of the journey.

Antoinette was frantic with anxiety. She had never seen her mistress so ill, so feverishly unaware of what was going on around her. Barring the door to everyone else (except Frédéric, of course, who was innocently asleep in his own room), she admitted the doctor with tearful relief.

He was there for some considerable time, and at the end of it was gravely reassuring. 'She has a strong constitution, you know. But you're going to need help – it'll be a long business.'

'It's the grief, caught up with her at last,' said Antoinette. 'Or that's what I think.'

'You are probably right,' the doctor conceded.

He said the same a little later to Laure and Rosaline, in the *petit salon* where he found them waiting together and in silence for him to come down. 'She's tried to hide her feelings for too long. That's against nature and bad for the health; but there we are – it's the way she's made. What the outcome will be I just don't know. What I do know is that old Antoinette

183

will be ill herself if she's left to cope alone. There's no danger of infection, of course, so either of you ladies can venture into the sick-room without fear. I've left instructions with Antoinette for now. I'll be back in the morning.'

When he had gone, Rosaline said emphatically, 'I hate illness – I can't bear sick-rooms. I'll help all I can downstairs, but I'm not going up there until the old woman's better.'

So that left Laure, the least acceptable nurse from Madame Naillac's point of view; but there was no one else. The chief difficulty was Mathilde. Laure did not want to leave her downstairs, not trusting the un-maternal Rosaline to supervise adequately a lively inquisitive toddler; but equally the child would be in the way in the sick-room. Regarding it as a temporary situation born of desperation, Laure despatched Mathilde that first morning to keep her half-brother company in the little room so conveniently adjacent to Madame Naillac's bedroom. She had not wanted the children to meet, under any circumstances, but it could not be helped.

To her astonishment the arrangement seemed to work very well. The sounds of infant chatter and the answering gurgles of baby laughter that reached her from time to time were wholly reassuring. When now and then she looked in on them she found them absorbed and happy with Frédéric's few toys and books, playing together like any normal, good natured brother and sister. Poor little Frédéric, it'll do him good to enjoy being a child for once, she thought, temporarily softening towards him.

For the time being Madame Naillac was in no condition to know, or to care, who was nursing her. The frail pathetic figure crying out in delirium for her dead son seemed to have nothing left in it of the forceful woman Laure had come to hate. Yet, oddly, that did not make her task any easier. She felt a grain of rather grudging pity; yet what struck her most of all was a sense that this total dependence of the old woman on her was somehow unnatural, even a little repugnant to her. She washed and changed the patient, administered the medicines, sat at the bedside, all with a kind of revulsion quivering beneath the calm efficiency of her manner. She did her duty, but she felt no warmth and no affection: how could she, when Madame Naillac had given her no cause, ever, to love her?

The careful nursing and Madame Naillac's resilience together brought recovery at last. The first clear sign that the old woman was over the worst came when, without pausing to offer any thanks, she banished Laure, and Mathilde, from her room. Frédéric's days of freedom were at end; even before she could stumble from bed to chair, she had taken control once more of her grandson's life. Very soon, thought Laure dismally, she would be making her way downstairs again, gathering up the threads briefly laid down.

But she was wrong. Madame Naillac made a rapid recovery that astonished Doctor Rossillon; but it was by no means complete. It was very clear that she would never again be well enough to walk much further than the length of her two rooms, certainly not to negotiate the stairs or make a supervisory tour of the kitchen or the servants' quarters; still less, venture outside. She could rule Frédéric as firmly as ever; but she could no longer rule the château.

'I'm afraid you're going to have to take on far more responsibility than before,' Doctor Rossillon told Laure with regret. 'Madame Naillac has enough to keep her alert and occupied, with the boy to care for. But I'm afraid anything more would be too much for her. I know how difficult it will be for you, in the circumstances – but I can't see what else is to be done.'

Holding her breath with a mixture of hope and apprehension Laure made her way upstairs and asked to see her mother-in-law. There, quietly, politely, without explanation, she asked for the household account books.

Upright in her chair, the old woman subjected her in silence to a long cold scrutiny; and then without a word gave a sign to Antoinette to bring the books to her. Laure was tactful enough to accept them with a meek, 'Thank you, *madame*,' and no sign of triumph on her face. On the first floor landing she met Rosaline, who smiled at her with an expression that said as clearly as any words, 'Did I not say you were strong? You see, I was right. You have won at last.'

Laure spent twenty-four hours studying the books and making her plans; and then she began at once to put them into effect. As she had long thought, much more drastic measures

185

were required than Madame Naillac had ever set in motion. First, Laure shut off almost all of the house except the occupied bedrooms, the kitchens and the *petit salon*. She put ornaments away, covered furniture with dustsheets, and locked the doors on the shrouded rooms. Then, coolly, allowing no personal feelings to intrude, she gave notice to Sylvestre and Jean-Baptiste and all the other servants except Mathieu and Antoinette, who was in any case paid by Madame Naillac. And then she set out for the village, taking Mathilde with her.

Nanon Foussac was outside her cottage scattering corn for the chickens. She saw Laure coming from some distance away and stood still, watching, her face expressionless. Laure could not help but notice how drawn and dejected she looked, almost shrunken within the big-boned frame.

Then Nanon saw Mathilde and colour flooded her face, and she laid down the basket of corn and ran forward with a cry; so far and no further, for she stopped abruptly, as if all at once afraid.

Laure halted too and released Mathilde's hand. The child stood gravely looking at Nanon for a moment; and then as her nurse slowly and uncertainly held out her arms she ran laughing into them. Laure fought fiercely to crush the sharp pang of jealousy that shot through her. 'I've come,' she said, her voice dry, even a little harsh, 'to see if you would be willing to come and work at the château, cooking and so forth, anything that needs to be done. You would be paid well, of course. And . . . and you could help me care for Mathilde, when I am busy.'

The answer was a long time coming, but Laure saw the tears and the trembling incredulous smile and knew what it would be long before Nanon gave it.

CHAPTER
TEN

Another spring, the third since the phylloxera came to Casseuil and Monsieur Naillac died: 1874. Twenty years ago almost to the day Jean Delisle had taken up his post as *régisseur* for Philippe Naillac's father – so full of hope and enthusiasm, those two qualities that, amply rewarded, had scarcely diminished in him throughout the years. Until now.

Jean Delisle closed the book that offered so cheerless an account of the past few months and crossed to the window. Out there in the May sunshine the ordered rows of vines looked to the casual observer much as they had always done at this time of year. Cut right back by the winter pruning, the twisted stems were already covered with buds just beginning to open. How many this year would put forth leaves and fruit for the last time, destroyed by the hidden plague at their roots? Nothing, nothing at all seemed able to halt the slow inevitable progress of the disease.

Anything else he could have fought: the death of Casseuil's owner, the financial difficulties – with Madame Laure in charge now there should have been a hopeful future. She learned so quickly, with a kind of intuitive intelligence, understanding almost before she was told. It had been a delight to have her working beside him – at once employer and pupil – during the past year or so. Or it would have been, had the knowledge of the phylloxera not gnawed at his heart and his spirit just as surely as it destroyed the once healthy roots of Casseuil's great vines. Many of those vines had been there for longer than he had, and they gave the best grapes of all – it was like tearing out his own heart to pull them up and burn them.

Tears came, misting the sunlit landscape, blurring the rows

of vines so that he could no longer make out the great yawning gaps where the wooden supports stood exposed, and empty.

He swung round and made his way briskly down the steps and into the dusky coolness of the *chai*; on to the furthermost part of the building where the bottles gleamed faintly in the arched bins where they lay maturing. Some of this wine was twenty, thirty years old, the residue of the great vintages of the past. For how many centuries now had the Naillacs made wine at Casseuil? Three at least, very possibly more, centuries of unrest, of religious wars and oppression, of persecution and revolution, while Monarchies and Republics and Empires came and went; and only this one thing remained constant, the endless striving for the very best the vines could give.

'Monsieur Delisle.'

He had not heard her come, but he was not surprised that she was there. He turned slowly, gradually focusing his sad dark gaze upon the pale gleam of her face. '*Madame* – forgive me, I did not hear you.'

There was a little silence. He knew why she had come, and he guessed that she had no wish to rush into what she had to do. 'Shall we go to the office, *madame*?' he said at last. 'I find that this place does not raise the spirits after all.'

They walked to the office without speaking, and there the *régisseur* held a chair for Madame Laure to sit down, though he remained standing, facing her across the desk, bracing himself for what she had to say.

'*Monsieur*, you said once that if the day came when Casseuil was no longer able to produce anything but an inferior wine you would not wish to preside over it.'

He felt his mouth twitch at the corner, but not with amusement. 'As I recall, *madame*, those were not my exact words. It was the deliberate destruction of the quality of our wine that I said I could not bear to contemplate. But I am not so stupid as not to know what you are going to say.' He did not help her by saying it himself, because he could not.

'Deliberate or not,' she said sadly, 'the effect is the same, or it will be. You know better than I do that the disease has not been checked, that unless someone somewhere finds a remedy very soon there will be no healthy vines left at Casseuil, or very few at best. Until then the most we can hope for is an ever smaller quantity of wine probably of declining quality. We have cut back everywhere we possibly can, so as to have the means to try any new remedy. But now . . .'

'You can no longer afford to employ a *régisseur* to preside over a declining vineyard – I know that, *madame*. I have known it for a long time. I was in fact trying to find the courage to come and tell you myself that this must happen, but—' He bent his head and pressed his fingers to his eyes. 'I have worked at Casseuil since I was twenty-four – it has been my life.'

'I know. I know how you must feel – what we owe you – I only wish there were some other way.'

He could hear that she too was fighting back the tears. It gave him strength enough to bring himself under control and look up again, although his voice was still unsteady and a little rough. 'There is not, *madame*: I know that. I heard last week that one of the lesser Sauternes châteaux is seeking a *régisseur* – the methods used there are much the same as we use here. They have the means to fight if the phylloxera reaches them, as it has not yet. I thought I might try my luck there – one never knows.'

'You are of course welcome to stay until you have found somewhere to go.'

He forced a faint smile. 'Oh, I shall not put that burden upon you. I have enough saved, in case things turn out badly for me – I shall not starve. Fortunately I have no family.' He shook his head. 'Sometimes I wonder what will become of us all – not just here at Casseuil, but all over France. Every day somewhere new succumbs to the disease. If it goes on like this there will be no vineyard left untouched. Can you bear to think of that, *madame*? No vineyards in Périgord or Bordeaux, none on the Loire, or in Burgundy or Champagne or on the Rhône – all our greatness eaten away by a creature so small we can hardly see it. It is too terrible to contemplate.'

'It hasn't reached Burgundy yet, has it? Or Champagne, or the other more northern vineyards?' Her tone suggested rather that she was trying to stave off her own despair than to comfort him.

'Not yet – but it will only be a matter of time, I fear.'

'Perhaps they will find a remedy.'

'It will be too late for Casseuil.'

After a little pause he cleared his throat and assumed a tone of brisk practicality. 'Keep young Aubin Lambert on for as long as you can. He'll be called up for military service this year, but I advise you to make it clear there'll be a job for him here when he comes back. He's a good lad, intelligent, learns fast. If, some day, there should be some change for the better, then you'll need someone like him. You can always find casual labourers – but men with judgement, that's another matter. There is one other thing – you'll have my house and its land to sell. You'll not get much for it in present conditions, but use what you get to try the carbon disulphide treatment I mentioned. Just on a few plants, to keep something alive – it would cost too much to treat them all, of course. And the '69 wine is ready for bottling – you have that to fall back on still. Don't rush to sell it though – prices for good wine are sure to rise, and you will have it to turn to as a last resort.'

She thanked him. 'You see, you do still hope, just a little.'

He shook his head. 'No, *madame*, not really. I'm not sure I shouldn't be advising you to do what they've done at Trissac and go over to tobacco or some other crop. I believe Monsieur Chabry for instance, is intending to replant with fruit trees. Something like that – it would be the sensible course.'

'Would Casseuil wine ever have been made at all, if we did the sensible thing?' He smiled very faintly, acknowledging the truth of what she said. 'No, I pray it won't come to that. Believe me, *monsieur*, so long as there is one healthy plant left at Casseuil then I shall fight for it – and even if the very worst happens I shall not admit defeat until I know beyond doubt that we could never, never have the faintest, remotest hope of making good wine here ever again. And then, even then, I think I shall not give up. I don't know how I shall do it, but I am determined that somehow we shall survive.'

Moved almost beyond words he bent and took her hand in his and pressed his lips to it. 'I honour you for your courage, *madame*,' he said huskily. 'If there is any hope, any justice—' He broke off; and then a moment later paid her the ultimate compliment. 'Monsieur Naillac would have been proud of you.'

CHAPTER
ELEVEN

i

The *curé* had scarcely reached the door of the church before Antoinette was there with the boy. They were always the first to leave after mass. As if by some prior agreement no other member of the congregation ever made a move to rise from his bench until the maid and her charge had left the seat they occupied at the very front of the church and walked up the centre aisle and out of the building. By the time anyone else reached the porch they would be crossing the wood on their way back to the château. Something about them made sure that no one ever intruded on their isolation on that front bench, by sitting beside them or speaking to them; though what it was, the *curé* was not quite sure. Certainly Antoinette's severe black-clad figure was daunting enough in itself; and combined with the gravity of the child in the equal severity of his Sunday clothes there was nothing encouraging of familiarity about the pair. Even so –

'Good day, *monsieur le curé*.' The two voices, the one rough with age, the other clear and piping, both cool and expressionless, greeted the Abbé Lebrun in passing. He smiled, returned the greeting, sought as always for something to say; and realised as usual that he was already too late: they had gone. He sighed. He ought by now to have found some way to reach out to the child. A boy of seven, to whom he had been giving lessons at the château every weekday for the past year – how could he fail to have established some kind of relationship with him by now? But he had failed, completely. Frédéric was intelligent, startlingly so at times, a model pupil in a superficial sense, and he worked as hard as his demanding grandmother could have wished. Yet never once had the *curé* felt that he had come anywhere near to touching the child beneath the grave, obedient surface – if indeed there was a child there somewhere. He did not think he had ever seen Frédéric smile.

There was a little interval while the rest of the congregation rose, moved to exchange a greeting here or there, made its way slowly towards the door. First was Monsieur Chabry, who did not smile much these days either, with his wife and his eldest son Louis Napoléon (no one used the Napoléon now, especially since his father had begun to drift towards Royalism). A nervous young man, Louis Chabry was to be married soon to a Catholic girl of good family from Bergerac – his father's choice rather than his own, the *curé* suspected.

For a moment there was a smile, fleeting but real, on Chabry's long face. 'We hope you will allow us to have the pleasure of welcoming you to dinner at our house tomorrow night, *monsieur le curé*. Monsieur and Madame Lacroix will be with us for the evening, and Mademoiselle Lacroix too, of course.'

There were in these difficult times few tables to which he was ever invited which offered any very enticing prospect; but Chabry's was one of them, since he still had a very able cook, and an excellent cellar which he could afford to enjoy. The *curé* beamed. 'I shall be delighted to come, *monsieur*, *madame*,' he replied with a fervour that was wholly sincere.

'Good day, *monsieur le curé*.' That greeting again, spoken once more in a lisping childish treble – yet how different this time! Accompanied by a delightful dimpled smile and a pair of dancing brown eyes the words had a sunny warmth about them that was almost tangible even on this cold morning.

'Good morning, Mathilde, *ma petite*. And how are you this morning?'

She giggled, wriggling a little in the way small children often do when they are just a little shy; but she did not lower that direct and happy gaze. 'Very well thank you, *monsieur le curé*.'

Tall for her five years, fast losing the plumpness of babyhood, she was a charming child. The *curé* touched her soft cheek for a moment. How easy she was to love, as easy as her half-brother was difficult! He watched her go on her way, skipping along between her mother and Nanon, a hand held by each, all the last traces of Sunday dignity gone. That had worked out for the best after all, the *curé* reflected; far beyond his expectations. Nanon was blissfully happy now, usefully employed at the château and sharing Mathilde's love with Madame Laure in a way that seemed to cause neither of them any heartache or jealousy, nor to face the child with any painful conflict of loyalty. As Mathilde learned to talk, so Nanon had learned with her, until now she could speak French quite well, if with a strong accent; and at the same time a warm and surprisingly equal friendship had grown up between her and Laure. Her coming to the château had even brought Laure back to church, though perhaps old Madame Naillac's inability to come to mass herself had helped there, as well as Laure's concern that her daughter should have the very best upbringing. The *curé* had seen it all and rejoiced. His only sadness about the situation these days was that – except when in the company of her child – Madame Laure had a look of near desperation. She had done so much, struggled on with such courage; but everyone had a breaking point. The *curé* feared that she must now be very near to hers.

The lunch – soup, bread and a pot of meat and vegetables put to cook slowly over the fire early this morning – was ready for them when Laure and Nanon reached the château. In the dim warmth of the kitchen, Rosaline – who only went to mass occasionally, when the mood took her – had set the table with four places. She had a sleek shining look about her, not unusual these days. Laure wondered sometimes what brought it on, but had no wish to pry. Presumably there was a man somewhere, but as long as Rosaline was discreet Laure supposed it did not matter much. They had learned to adjust to one another surprisingly well after all. They were not friends exactly – they were too dissimilar for that – but Rosaline's cheerful willingness to turn her hand to almost anything that needed doing had been an undeniable asset through the last difficult years; just as her unsentimental clearsightedness about Philippe's shortcomings had helped Laure to come to terms with his death. Since Mathilde accepted those around her with a happy lack of curiosity there had been no need for uncomfortable explanations either.

The three women were already at table, Mathilde beside her mother, who kept a watchful eye on her manners, when Antoinette's dark presence intruded. Rosaline, smiling, went to bring a tray and set on it enough food for the three people upstairs.

'Madame seemed better this morning when I looked in,' she told the maid: for two days now Madame Naillac had been troubled by a slight cold.

'So she is, *mademoiselle*. She never ails for long, thank God. She was only anxious for the boy, in case he should be infected.'

'Colds are nothing to children,' said Rosaline carelessly. When Antoinette had gone, she added, 'Anyone would think it was the plague. Madame blames me for it, you know, because I sneezed over her one day last week. She almost refused to see me yesterday.'

Doubtless, as usual, Rosaline had talked her round, thought Laure. She had a way with her that few could resist in the end, and Madame Naillac, surprisingly perhaps, had resisted less than most. 'It's only because she loves him,' Laure pointed out. Obsessive, a single-minded passion such as perhaps even her son had not aroused in her: yes, Madame Naillac's love for Frédéric, however little the child himself saw of it, was the sole consuming purpose of her life now that Philippe had gone. For her now no one else existed, least of all the little girl who should have had the first claim on that love.

Rosaline shrugged and sat down again, eating with the rather affectedly refined manners that Laure tried very hard to counter by her own example to Mathilde. 'Do you know what I heard this morning? Monsieur Chabry's buying up the land down at La Borie – you know, where the man shot himself last year.' Philippe's had not been the only suicide in the neighbourhood since the phylloxera struck. Many peasant farmers, already burdened by the habitual debts that were a part of their lives, had found this final blow too much for them. If they had not all been driven to suicide, many had sold up and moved to the towns in search of work.

'Well, he's got a rich wife for his son – he can afford to,' said Nanon.

'Yes, I heard her family weren't very happy about that marriage – they have noble connections somewhere, and the Chabrys are a bit beneath them.' Laure never ceased to be amazed by how much local gossip Rosaline knew, despite having, apparently, few contacts with the village. 'Still, they say Mademoiselle Lacroix is very plain and rather stupid, so perhaps they're glad to get someone to take her.'

Laure allowed the talk to pass over her, bemusedly wondering how it must feel to be able to contemplate buying land – even land at the ridiculously low prices that the present crisis had made inevitable. She could not even remember now what it had been like to be able to buy what one wanted without having to think twice about it – no, not twice, but three, four, five, six times; and then in the end almost always being forced to decide against it.

She was glad when the meal was over and she could be alone for a while. Mathilde curled up on her little bed in what had been her parents' bedroom – Laure now slept in her sitting-room overlooking the courtyard – and, once the washing-up was done, Nanon settled down in a chair near the bed to doze over the mending, although if Mathilde woke she would at once be alert, ready with a song or a story to delight her beloved charge. Rosaline had undertaken to begin digging over the small plot where, later, they would plant their summer vegetables – tomatoes, courgettes, aubergines. They had to be self-sufficient now in everything they could grow or raise themselves – milk and cheese from the three goats, eggs from the hens, maize to feed the animals, fruit and vegetables for the household.

'I always knew you were a peasant at heart,' Madame Naillac had said venomously to Laure, when she first realised how Philippe's widow was living – which was very soon after the changes had been made, for the old woman knew almost everything that went on.

Laure had been wryly amused by the charge. She had nearly retorted, 'What about the empty-headed Parisian frivolity you were for ever throwing in my face?' But she did not waste her breath in argument. Sure of herself, confident that she was doing the best she could for Casseuil, carried along by an overriding sense of purpose, she had been untroubled by the old woman's criticism. She had cut everything to the bone, paid off the last of the debts, made each sacrifice with uncomplaining cheerfulness. Madame Naillac's aim had been to ensure that Casseuil survived for her lifetime; Laure was building for a future for her child, her grandchildren, for endless generations yet undreamed of. For that any present hardship was a tiny price to pay.

So it had seemed in those early days when, in spite of everything, she had been happy, because she was free to take her own path towards her chosen goal.

Today though, as so often lately, there was no heady sense of freedom to bear her up. As she made her way across the courtyard towards the vineyard – watched, she was sure, by Madame Naillac or Antoinette from the windows under the roof, or even from the battlemented walk that bordered them – she wondered what was the point of continuing to plan or to look ahead, as, in some sense, she was doing now. She went to the tiny plot – less than a quarter of a hectare – that had been set aside for the protective treatment suggested by Jean Delisle, where the vines still flourished untouched by the phylloxera, and finished the pruning almost completed by Aubin, putting aside the best cuttings to be rooted and eventually planted out, to provide new stock for the vineyard. But it would be two years before these cuttings would fruit at all, five before any wine could usefully be made from them, and only after twenty years or more of careful nurture would the grapes they gave be at their best. Meanwhile, if she did not maintain the laborious, dangerous and expensive treatment of the soil at their roots, they would have no hope of lasting so long – and her resources were dwindling fast. In a year or two perhaps she would have nothing left, even for the routine spraying. But if she were to stop planning as if there were a future then she would have reached the end, admitting defeat. And that she would not do, not yet.

The wind was bitingly cold. Laure's velvet jacket, rubbed to a shine in places, did little to protect her from it. She tried to tell herself that it was already February, that it would soon be spring. There were buds on the apricot trees in the orchard beyond the *chai*, giving promise of the mass of delicate pink blossoms that in a few weeks would open against the pale honey colour of the surrounding wall, and before long there would be primroses in flower on the bank at the far side of the wood and along the road near the *caveau*. But no feeling of growth or rebirth sprang up in her to fortify her against the cold and the greyness and the weary sense of hopelessness which seemed all of a piece with the bleakness of the world around her. Not even the thought of Mathilde could cheer her today.

She remembered suddenly the odd little vision that had come into her mind all those years ago, when she had walked with Marcel into the mist; of herself trudging through a featureless grey landscape in a desperate solitude. That feeling was with her now, a part of her life, intrinsic to each wearying day.

I mustn't give up, never, never! she told herself; but at the same time she was wondering how long it would be before she did.

The next day Laure set Aubin on the second racking of the new wine, the 1875 vintage. The weather had been reasonable, but the balance of the wine had been wrong – too much Muscadelle, too little Sémillon – because the progress of the phylloxera had been uneven; and the entire yield had not been much more than five hectolitres to the hectare, about half the output of the old days. Of course the greatest vintages had always resulted in a smaller quantity of wine, because the *pourriture noble* robbed the grapes of juice, but there had been little *pourriture noble* last year.

Still, the routine tasks had to be done, and the new wine drawn off into a new *cuve*, leaving the impurities in the old one, and inhibiting further fermentation. Once Laure had given her instructions, Aubin set to work.

He smiled to himself as he did so, amused by the signs of agitation Madame Laure had shown again this morning – all that blushing and breathlessness, and a distinct snappiness of tone when she spoke to him. He knew quite well what caused it, too. He knew he was attractive to women, a fine made young man of twenty-three; and it gave him more than a little satisfaction to find himself with this unexpected power over his employer. Not that he fancied her particularly: she was pretty of course, even beautiful, but she did not stir him to any real interest. Not like Rosaline did – his smile broadened and his thoughts went back to yesterday morning in the seclusion of the little upstairs room in what had once been the coachman's cottage – very fortunately Aristide had left a mattress behind. Rosaline, now, *did* stir something in him, and knew all kinds of unguessed-at ways of making the most of the feelings she aroused. He had learned a very great deal from her during the past year or two, one way and another. Not that, in any sense, his emotions were involved, as he was quite sure hers were not either.

Aubin's strongest feelings he kept for far more important things, above all for his ambition one day to own land for himself; not the small share in the family farm that would eventually come to him, but real land, enough to live on, and all of it exclusively his. Even with his brother Jacques dead, there were still three sisters to share the inheritance, the eldest married to Robert Martin who, being practically landless himself, had every reason to want his wife to hang on to her portion. If only he had the money now, when land was so cheap! He had saved hard during his months of military service, putting aside all he could from his meagre soldier's pay. He could have signed on for a further term, with the promise of rising quickly from the rank of sergeant with which he had left the regiment. But he preferred to be his own man and continue to strive for his dream of total independence; and so he had come back to Casseuil and his old job here at the château. If something more lucrative had offered itself he would have taken it. But unfortunately work of any kind was not easy to come by in the countryside these days, even for a young man with his skills. So, as long as Madame Laure continued to pay he would stay on here, pleasing her with the conscientious thoroughness of his work, and embarrassing her with the assertive masculinity of his young body. Poor lady, he thought, with a rare twinge of compassion, she'll not have had a man in her bed for five years now, and it's not so easy for a lady in her position to put that right.

The real trouble for Laure had been a dream a few weeks ago. Where it had come from she did not know, though she supposed at some unconscious level she must have found

Aubin attractive even before then. There had been earlier dreams too, so intensely and unmistakably sensual that she had blushed to think of them; but at least in them the desires aroused, stirred and ultimately satisfied had been unfocused and solitary. It was when at last they found only too clear an object in the young man she saw almost every day, that her problems began. She knew Aubin saw her embarrassed self-consciousness, and that only made it worse. I need a lover, she thought ruefully now, as she crossed the courtyard on her way back to the house, the rain rapidly cooling her too hot face. That was what men did, after all: a practical solution to a practical problem. But she was not a man, and she had a young daughter in her care, and a censorious mother-in-law watching over her; and besides for her it could never be simply a practical problem. She could not really imagine herself, outside her dreams, giving herself to a man she did not love.

A rider was turning in under the archway towards her, a big square figure on a muscular brown horse: Henri Séguier. What a pity I don't find him attractive, she thought ruefully, as she went to meet him. But she did not, nor did she have any inclination to speak to him this morning; if she could have avoided him she would have done so. She wondered what today's excuse for calling would be. There was always some ostensible reason, but usually of so transparently invented a nature that it did not deceive her for a moment.

He had scarcely troubled to find an excuse at all this time. He murmured something not quite coherent about last year's tobacco prices and the prospects for this year, and pressed into her hand a cutting from a newspaper suggesting that tobacco was indeed the crop of the future.

It was too wet for them to stand talking outside, so she opened the door into the house and entered, saying quickly, 'It's good of you to trouble to call. I wish I had time to discuss all this with you at greater length, but I'm afraid you find me very busy today.'

He followed her inside, closing the door after him, and then took her hand in both of his and stood looking down at her with a disconcerting expression that had in it something that was not quite tenderness nor yet lasciviousness, but contained a little of each. '*Chère madame*, it distresses me that you

199

should be so burdened.' He stroked her hand, turning it palm upwards. 'This pretty hand was not made for peasants' work.'

'It has to do whatever is necessary,' she returned crisply, trying to pull free from his grasp, without success.

'Ah, but is it indeed necessary? Consider—'

'Maman!' Mathilde, all untidy golden hair, rosy cheeks and vast apron stained with the results of her morning's 'helping' in the kitchen, flew across the hall. 'I've made a honey cake, and Nanon says—'

Henri did release Laure then, and she turned to gather the smiling sticky child into her arms, grateful for the interruption. 'Mathilde, say good day to Monsieur Séguier now.' Dutifully, all demureness, Mathilde did so. Though she had deprived him by her coming of his wished-for tête à tête with her mother, Henri beamed down at her.

'She'll break a few hearts one day,' he predicted. 'Just like her mother.'

The next moment Laure saw his eyes move from her face to some point behind her shoulder. She turned and saw Frédéric coming down the stairs towards them. Although he was slightly made and scarcely taller than his half-sister he had an unchildlike air of self-possession; a cool exterior, veiling what lay beneath. Laure always felt uncomfortable in his presence, though she was not quite sure why. Certainly it had something to do with his strange eyes, at once reproachful and knowing, like those of a hungry cat.

'*Madame*,' he began (he was always impeccably polite), 'Madame my grandmother asks if Monsieur Séguier would be kind enough to call on her, if he feels able to spare the time.' He recited the words as if he had learned them by heart, as perhaps he had.

'But of course, I shall be delighted to do so.' The summons to Madame Naillac's presence was becoming almost routine, whenever, which was seldom, a visitor called to see Laure, any visitor. Some sixth sense, or acute observation from the window, always told the old woman who was here, and it was usually Antoinette who would come to invite the guest upstairs: Frédéric was rarely seen by anyone but the *curé*.

Now the boy bowed his head. 'Thank you, *monsieur* – please to come.' He was about to stand aside to gesture Henri to go ahead, when Mathilde gave a little wriggle, and then a jump. Having successfully attracted his attention, she turned the full force of her enchanting smile upon her brother. For a moment Frédéric gazed at her with his usual impassivity; and then, faintly, the thin mouth tilted a little at the corners and he coloured to the roots of his brown hair, though whether from pleasure or embarrassment Laure could not have said. In any case, in the next instant he was once more all coolness, ushering Henri ahead of him up the stairs. Mathilde watched him a little wistfully, her head on one side. 'I want Frédéric to play with me,' she said, as if she had suddenly recalled that one time three years ago when they had played together while Madame Naillac was ill; but it was unlikely that she did, for she had been very young then. She had not referred to it since.

'Frédéric lives upstairs,' was all Laure could think of to say now, and she distracted Mathilde with the promise of a story, leading her to the *petit salon*.

It was already occupied. Rosaline was there, on her knees before the hearth coaxing the newly lit fire into life. She stood up, rubbing her hands carefully on her black skirts, where the marks would not show: the white apron she wore was spotless. 'Did I hear Monsieur Séguier out there?'

Laure took up the copy of La Fontaine's fables lying on the table and sat down, drawing Mathilde onto her knee. 'He's upstairs, calling on Madame.'

'Oh, she's checking up on you again is she?'

Laure said nothing, because there was nothing to say. Rosaline was quite right, and they both knew it. Madame Naillac had no intention of allowing infirmity to keep her in ignorance of what was happening downstairs. All her visitors were closely questioned about everything they had seen, and if she did not like what she heard she would summon Laure upstairs and tell her so. It was just one more of life's many irritations.

Rosaline seated herself on a chair facing Laure. 'If you played your cards right you could have Monsieur Séguier just where you wanted him.'

Laure looked at her a little coldly. There were times when she found herself unpleasantly out of sympathy with Rosaline's view of life. 'I am not aware that I want him anywhere

201

but where he is,' she said, pointedly opening the book. She hoped that would silence Rosaline, but it made no impression at all.

'Oh, come now, Laure – give him just the very tiniest encouragement and he'd propose to you; even you must see that. And then, goodbye to all your worries! Why break your back in a struggle you can't win when you could snare yourself a rich husband? I wouldn't.'

'Then perhaps you'd better try and win him for yourself, because I certainly have no intention of marrying again.'

She began briskly to read aloud, scarcely noticing the words.

'*Maître corbeau, sur un arbre perché . . .*'

Rosaline shrugged, but fell silent, listening to the fable for a while; and then she gave a sudden exclamation and burst out, 'Oh, I forgot – there was a letter.' She brought it from the mantelpiece. 'From New York,' she added, turning it in her hand.

Laure left Mathilde to look at the pictures in the book and opened the letter, irritated by the way Rosaline sat down and watched her, eager with curiosity.

There was the usual news from her mother, cheerful, optimistic, pleasantly eventful. Marcel's invention had not after all done very well, but he had nevertheless made a favourable impression on Frank O'Brien, the wealthy banker who had financed his entrepreneurial efforts. Laure's brother, to her astonishment, was by now a trusted employee of the bank, and a friend to the whole O'Brien family – including, Laure gathered, his only daughter Eileen, whose name dotted Madame Frémont's accounts of picnics and boat trips, theatre visits, balls and dinners. 'We could be entirely happy, *ma chérie*, if only we could be sure that all was well with you. It is not that we doubt your assurances – yet you say so little. Your tales of Mathilde's little ways delight and amuse us, and she must indeed be a joy and a consolation to you. But what of you yourself, and your circumstances? That they are not as easy as we could wish is clear enough, and we have heard from others too how devastating is the spread of the phylloxera in France at present. Oh, if only we could see you again and talk to you, then I'm sure our minds would be set at rest! Why do you not come out here to see us? Just for a little while, for a holiday; though – who knows? – you might well find like us that you never wanted to leave New York again, once safely here. Bring Mathilde too, of course. We could send you the money for your passage, if that would be a difficulty, as I fear it might. Oh, do come, *chère* Laure – we all so *long* to see you again . . .'

Laure read to the end and then, in silence, folded the letter and slipped it into her pocket.

'Are they well, your parents?'

'Yes, thank you.'

'I should so love to see America. Wouldn't you?'

'I don't know . . . They want me to go out there, for a holiday.'

Rosaline's eyes shone as if the prospect had been offered to her rather than to Laure. 'Oh, you must go!' Her expression sobered. 'I suppose it would cost too much.'

'They would pay.'

'Then indeed you must go. Just think what an opportunity it will be! Half across the world, a new country, new people – oh Laure, I wish I could come with you!'

'How can I go? I can't leave Casseuil as things are.' But behind the casual dismissive words she felt a longing so intense that it hurt. Oh, to turn her back on all this, just for a little while! To be among people who loved her and cared for her, completely and without reserve, and in whom she could confide without mistrust; to be free of the endless hard work, and, worse, the constant gnawing anxiety; to be away from jealousies and tensions and the continual humiliating reminders that the ultimate power still rested with Madame Naillac, if she should choose to exercise it. To be in a place where Philippe's daughter would be accorded all the love and recognition that were her due, which, at Casseuil, Philippe's bastard had so completely usurped. To let go of the burdens and responsibilities that tied her here and allow herself to rest on the undemanding love of her mother and father and Marcel.

'Of course you must go. What could possibly go wrong in a few weeks? The rest of us can look after things: Nanon in the house, Mathieu outside, Aubin in the vineyard and me to give a hand wherever it's needed. And whatever differences you may have with Madame upstairs, she's not interested in stirring things up down here. She'll let everything go on as you want. If you don't trust the rest of us, ask *monsieur le curé* to keep an eye on us. Go as soon as you can, and you'll be back well before the *vendange*.'

Laure would not allow herself to yield at once to the overpowering impulse to say yes to her parents' invitation. But she knew that in time she would, because it was without question exactly what she needed. She had come dangerously close to giving up the daily burden which was becoming too much for her. A breathing space, a pause to reflect and take stock at a safe distance from Casseuil, would allow her either to return refreshed and invigorated knowing better what she must do; or to recognise that there was indeed no future for Casseuil.

And there was Mathilde, whom, lately, she had found so little time to enjoy. It would be good for them both to go away together and learn to know one another again, sharing an adventure.

To Laure's surprise Madame Naillac did not oppose the plan when, tentatively, it was put to her. 'Do as you please,' she said. 'With things so run down here I can't see that your absence will make any difference.'

'I should be back before harvest,' Laure promised.

'Oh, do you think there will be a harvest then? There can't be many more now, surely. You realise I suppose that I am not able to run things in your absence. Will you leave Mademoiselle Brousse in charge? She is an intelligent young woman.'

'I shall consider the matter.'

Somehow, smoothly, inevitably, it was settled. In June she and Mathilde would leave for America, and spend perhaps six weeks there. A brief letter from her mother enclosed funds for the passage for herself and the child, and concluded longingly, 'Oh how wonderful it will be to have all the family together again at last!'

Laure went to Bordeaux to buy tickets for the crossing and to instruct Maître Perrard in her absence to pay Rosaline an allowance at regular intervals to cover the wages and other necessary expenses of the estate, and to make extra payments, at his discretion, should they become necessary. At Casseuil, the *curé* promised to keep a paternal eye on everyone. 'Have no fear, *ma fille*, all will be well. I'll do my best to comfort Nanon and see that young Aubin looks after your vines. And Rosaline's promised to keep careful accounts and let me check them every week. So now you just enjoy yourself and come back to us truly refreshed.'

ii

'This, *ma chérie*, is the Atlantic ocean!'

As she stood on the deck with an excited Mathilde jumping up and down beside her and watched the coast of France dwindle away to a thin grey line and then to nothing, Laure knew that this time at least she had made the right decision. Already she felt incredibly light-headed, almost exhilarated, as if all her cares were slipping one by one swiftly and surely into the water, to be carried in the ship's wake back towards the distant coastline fast merging into the uniform grey of sea and sky.

She had broken free. No ties bound her now to the past or to its cares or to that disappearing land on the far horizon. No one now could call her back or burden her with decisions and anxieties. She was without responsibility, except for Mathilde, who was no burden at all. For days, weeks now, there would be nothing to do but eat and sleep and walk about the deck and enjoy the companionship of her child. She could even avoid the other passengers if she chose, for she had dressed herself for the voyage in the full hampering folds of her widow's weeds, although convention would have allowed her by now to dispense with them altogether. It was not just that these clothes of her early widowhood were the least worn and mended, since they had not been subjected to hours of work in the vineyard or the house; but she had learned too that for a woman alone they afforded excellent protection. No one would risk intruding upon a new widow, and everyone treated her with sympathetic respect. With Mathilde at her side in the sombre greys and blacks that could never quite dim her brightness, they made a touching pair, and Laure was free

205

to choose whom to approach among the passengers and whom to avoid, without fear of suffering unwanted attentions.

They enjoyed every moment of the voyage. When the weather was wild, they both stood on deck clinging for support to the nearest railing and laughing into the wind and the spray. It was perhaps as well that there was no one about, or they would have been thought mad. But their fellow passengers, frightened or seasick, remained firmly below deck.

For the most part the voyage was calm and they could pass their days gazing into the dark green-grey-blue depths of the water looking for fish, watching the birds soaring and weaving over the ever-changing surface of the sky; once, the enchanted spectators of a whole joyous host of dolphins leaping and playing just a short way off from the ship. Other passengers might grow bored with the endless vistas of sea and sky, but for Laure, taught by a child's vision, every day brought some new wonder or delight.

By the time the coast of the new and unknown continent came into sight, a faint smudgy line far off in the morning light, she felt young again, alive and happy and full of hope, eager for adventure and new experiences, as excited as Mathilde herself.

An age seemed to pass while the ship slowly edged its way nearer to the shore, allowing the details of landscape, settlements, buildings, to unfold themselves before the eyes of the watching passengers. And then all at once everything happened in a bewildering rush, and in no time at all Laure found herself somehow on the wharf with an awestruck, almost silent Mathilde clutching her hand and whispering, 'Maman, my legs feel funny.' And then her mother, her father, Marcel were there, embracing her by turns, all tears and laughter and lavish kisses. Mathilde was swung in the air, hugged and exclaimed over, excited into wild happy laughter.

'Oh, Laure, *ma chérie*, after so long!'

'Maman! Oh, Maman, it's so good to see you again!'

'What a beauty, little Mathilde, our first dear grandchild, and how like your Maman you are!'

'Marcel, I do believe you've put on weight!'

'It's so good to see you again!'

'So good.' And then, the next moment, in the midst of the joyous confusion, Laure found herself held at arm's length while her mother studied her, and she saw the dismay that shadowed the beloved face.

'Oh Laure, *ma chérie* – those terrible clothes!' Marguerite Frémont gave a little shudder. 'I had not expected . . .'

Now, if ever, was the time for Laure to tell them the truth, to confess her poverty and her loneliness, and find the comfort they would surely give. But instead she lifted the veil from her face and said quietly, 'I want to wear them still, for Philippe's sake.' It was only a tiny lie, and it had been true once; but she felt a little chill as she spoke, and at that very instant wished the words unsaid. But there was no going back. She might tell them the truth later perhaps, and confide in them as openly as she had intended to do; but that could not alter the fact that in this very first moment of reunion she had allowed a kind of deceit to come between herself and her parents.

Marguerite Frémont drew Laure into her arms again and hugged her in silence, trying to communicate the depth of her sympathy for Laure's long grief; only it was not that grief for which Laure now needed sympathy.

Somehow Laure and Mathilde and their luggage were transported through bewilderingly busy streets to the comfortable Manhattan apartment where the Frémonts lived, close to Central Park. There, slowly, Laure was able to draw breath, to steady herself and to realise that she was here on a new continent thousands of miles from everything that was known and familiar; and yet surrounded as she had not been for many years by those who loved her most and knew her best in all the world. It was an odd, disorientating state of affairs.

Later, as she brushed Mathilde's hair before dinner, the child said to her, 'Maman, is that my grandmother too? Like Madame at home?'

Laure's hand stilled, and she half-turned the little girl, so she could look into the thoughtful face. 'Yes, *ma petite*, of course.'

'She's different,' said Mathilde wonderingly. 'She likes me.'

Laure hugged the child, resting her cheek on the soft hair.

'Yes, *minette*, indeed she does.' And she felt a surge of happiness. There might be a shadow over this reunion, even a strangeness, but that could not do more than temper a little the joy of meeting again, nor could it destroy the enduring love she had for those three people she had not seen for so long.

As she made her way to the dining-room, Mathilde skipping happily at her side, she thought, I was foolish to think everything would be exactly as it used to be. How could it, after all that has happened? In the past years she had been widowed, borne a child, struggled and suffered, and all this, far away from her family, living through experiences that she had been unable then to share with them. She had not even tried to do so for the most part. How, after all, do you describe across half the world the arrival of your dead husband's mistress and son, without causing a distress you have no means of assuaging? Nor had she told them of Madame Naillac's hostility, nor done more than hint at the near-ruin of Casseuil. How unreasonable of her to expect that the moment they were together again all the old easy confidence would immediately return between them, as if the years of separation had never been!

After all, their lives too had moved on, and they had been changed too, by experiences which she could only share at second hand.

As they sat down to dinner she studied them all, lovingly but with detachment. Her parents looked older, but not much older, and both had an air of happy prosperity about them. They knew, they told her, that they had been absolutely right to come to the United States; they had not suffered a moment's regret. As for Marcel, he had changed almost beyond recognition: not physically perhaps, though he had lost some of the slender boyishness she remembered. With it though had gone the air of slightly diffident charm, the Bohemian grace, the careless clothes that proclaimed his artistic leanings. In its place was a self-confident young man, elegantly but discreetly dressed by New York standards, given to assertive pronouncements, with a bright-eyed thrusting air about him: a young man on the make. He no longer painted, and was surprised when she asked him about it.

The individuals she knew and loved so well were there still, beneath all the changes; but she was going to have to renew her acquaintance with them, as they were with her. And that meant, she realised, accepting that the years had separated them and that there was no going back. For the moment at least she must put aside the past as best she could, and begin with today. So she fended off many of their questions with the briefest of replies, and diverted them with questions of her own. That was in any case not difficult to do, for they were brimful of their own wonderful piece of news, announced by her mother as they sat at dinner.

'You couldn't have come at a better time, Laure. Just two days ago it was decided – Marcel is to be married. Now you will be able to stay for the wedding.'

Her delight was real and wholehearted. She set down the glass she was about to raise to her lips and cried out, 'Married! Marcel! Oh, *mon cher*, do tell me – who is she?' No wonder, she thought, that her brother had that warm happy look about him.

'Eileen O'Brien, old man O'Brien's daughter.'

Laure felt, obscurely, cheated. Marcel, her idealistic brother, about to marry the boss's daughter, and so doubtless further an already prospering career: it all had a chilly calculating ring about it, emphasising how very far removed he was from the Marcel of her girlhood.

'Marcel will become a partner in the bank when he's married,' her father put in with pride, as if to confirm that unfavourable impression.

'And when is that to be?' Laure asked carefully.

'At the end of September. It has to be a very grand wedding, you see, so it can't be hurried.'

She had not meant to be away from Casseuil for so long, but it would be silly to come so far and not stay for this important occasion in her brother's life.

'You will meet Eileen tomorrow. You'll like her, I know.' Marcel sounded entirely confident.

Laure managed a faint smile and raised her glass again; and then her attention was caught, abruptly, by the oddity of the smell that met her, even before she could drink. She looked down at the glass: a red wine, almost crimson from the side, but with paler brown tints from above, and that strange smell. She sniffed: very sweet, with a fragrance like that of wild strawberries, without the delicacy. Cautiously, she tasted; and it did not need the palate so carefully trained by Jean Delisle to tell her that this was like no other wine she had ever known. The taste seemed to fight with the sweet, assertive aroma; it was assertive too, but in a wholly different way, fruity perhaps, but thin, with little body and with a rank, almost animal aftertaste that lingered long on the tongue.

'What *is* this wine?'

Her father laughed at the suspicious tone. 'Ah, I wondered if you'd notice anything. It's one of our own New York wines.'

'We made much the same sort of wine in Arkansas, my friend André and I,' put in Marcel, 'when we first came to America.'

Laure sipped again, wrinkling her nose a little. 'It's – strange,' she said carefully. 'It's nothing like anything I've ever tasted at home.'

'No, it wouldn't be,' said her brother. 'Our vines are quite different. We grow our native *Vitis labrusca* and so forth, not the *Vitis vinifera* which you European *vignerons* grow.'

Laure was not yet sufficiently at her ease to say outright that she did not think the native vine was worth the effort of cultivating, if this was the result. Instead, she was more guarded. 'Does no one here grow European vines? I think I would if it were me.'

'No you wouldn't, *ma sœur*, for one simple reason with which you ought to be only too familiar: the phylloxera louse.'

'What has that got to do with it?'

'Do you forget that monstrous little insect first came from America? Anyone who tries growing European vines soon gives up – the phylloxera always gets them in the end. But the *Vitis labrusca*, being a native plant, has a natural resistance to phylloxera. Maybe you should take some back with you.'

Laure looked down at her glass with a wry expression. 'I don't think so,' she said. With a sudden sense of depression she wondered if, in the end, this odd wine with its unpleasant aftertaste would be all that was left to them: no Bordeaux, no

Casseuil, no Burgundy or Champagne, just this, the product of the new world that, here as everywhere, had swept all its rivals before it, a wine as unrefined and assertive as the people from whose land it came. I'm tired, she thought. Things will seem more cheerful tomorrow.

They did, for she met Eileen O'Brien and was, as Marcel had promised, enchanted by the pretty, lively Irish-American girl and realised that this was, first and foremost, a marriage of the heart. Marcel clearly adored her. He had even found some previously undiscernible religious yearnings within himself and become devoutly Catholic like his bride. Her father the banker, a big man whose shrewdness was well hidden beneath a laughing fast-talking exterior, was not as she had expected either, and she saw that the mutual respect and liking between himself and Marcel were real and open; she sensed it even though the older man spoke no French and she little English.

There was no mistaking the warmth of her welcome in New York. Not only her family but all their friends (and they were astonishingly many) did all they could to entertain herself and Mathilde as lavishly as they knew how. It was a bewildering city, her stay there exhausting and exhilarating at once. It was like the port area of Bordeaux magnified a thousand times. Everywhere there was a babel of tongues, English, German, Yiddish, Italian and innumerable others; a medley of faces, black, white, brown, yellow; a jostling thrusting atmosphere, rough and raw and noisy and yet always with that exuberant warmth that almost overpowered her. Mathilde was cosseted, caressed, cooed over, showered with presents and compliments that threatened to turn her head; she loved every moment of it, and became adept at displaying just the right degree of infant charm to win over everyone she met.

It was all more than a little exhausting and very far removed indeed from the quiet period of restoration and reflection that Laure had wanted so much. The days passed, then the weeks, and she had scarcely found time to draw breath. In a week from now Marcel was to be married.

Then one hot Sunday afternoon, leaving Mathilde in the doting care of her grandparents, Laure went at her brother's suggestion to walk with him in Central Park, and for the first

211

time she had a sense of quietness and sympathy and of a moment offered to her, open to confidences and sharing.

Only she did not know where to begin or even, now, if she wanted to begin any more. After all, everything she had suffered seemed so far away, even rather unimportant, and much of it anyway was past and done with. What point was there in talking of it? Yet it seemed something of a waste to be walking in silence, however companionable, at Marcel's side.

It was her brother who broke the silence. 'You've changed, Laure. I expected you to be very much the same, but you're not. You don't laugh like you used to.'

She looked at him, and did laugh then, a little ruefully and with some surprise, that he should have expected anything else. 'Don't I? Perhaps I've not had much to laugh about just lately.'

'No, I suppose you would not have – poor Laure. Has it been very bad? You haven't said much, you know.'

She shrugged. 'Bad enough at times. But at least I've always had Mathilde. Besides,' she went on brightly, sheering away from his sympathy, 'you've changed too – much more than I have, I'm sure.'

'Have I?' He looked startled, and she laughed again.

'Of course; isn't it obvious? Where's the revolutionary young painter of the old days? Do you ever remember now what it was like, all that passionate talk far into the night, the cafés and the absinthe – everything?'

He smiled reflectively. 'Ah yes, all that – it seems a long way away now.' His gaze sharpened. 'In any case, what did you ever know about it?'

'Oh, more than you realised, *mon frère*, I assure you.' She slid her arm through his, drawn close by memory. 'And now, what do I find? A respectable man of affairs just like Papa. No, not just like, more respectable, more conformist even – and not even wholly French any more, chattering away in English all day like you do.'

'Of course. I'm an American citizen, and proud of it.' He grinned at her. 'But I'm Marcel still – perhaps I have just found the real Marcel at last.'

'Did you know you speak French with an American accent now?'

'Do I really?' He gave a shout of laughter. 'Oh, Laure, it's good to have you here – I'm so glad you could come. You've been the one thing I've missed, living here.' He came to a halt and studied her face intently. 'You've said nothing, but you know we hoped you'd come for good – that you'd stay here with us?'

She looked away from him. 'I know. But I can't say yet. It's all been so strange. I need time. It's like coming to a whole new world quite different from the old, and I haven't grown used to it yet.'

'That's just the charm of it, that it is a new world, nothing like poor, tired old Europe. A new world, and a new life – doesn't that tempt you?'

She shook her head with a smile. 'I don't know, Marcel, I just don't know. I'm not used to all the city bustle. I find it hard to think.'

It was true; but she knew that she would very soon have to force herself to face the alternatives. Before she came to New York she had never really believed she would want to stay; now she was not so sure. What, after all, was there to tempt her to go back? The same endless desperate struggle towards a goal that daily receded further beyond her reach into an infinite distance? Now that she was – for a time at least – free from that struggle, able to look at it from the outside, she found that she no longer had any real hope left of restoring Casseuil, or even of staving off for much longer the moment when the disease would reach the last of the vines. Then what would there be for her to work for? A good tobacco harvest? Even had that been a possibility for someone with no capital to invest, she could summon up no enthusiasm for so purely mercenary a business. A wine made from the tough native American vine? No, she thought, not at Casseuil, not ever.

And if she stayed, what then? She would have the loving companionship of her parents and Marcel and the many new friends she had already begun to make; new opportunities; a clean break with the past and all its troubles.

'American women have a great deal more freedom than you have at home,' Marcel told her. 'It's a good country for children too.'

That was true: she had seen it for herself. It suggested to her

213

as well a possibility that she had not seriously considered until now – that she might marry again. At Casseuil that was, at best, unlikely. Who, there, would she ever wish to marry? And what hope had she of ever meeting a man she could love, not as she had loved Philippe, but deeply, and truly, and enduringly, with the maturity gained by bitter experience? Even if the impossible were to happen, and she were to meet someone and fall in love, the possibility of being able to allow the relationship to flower and develop, watched as she was by Madame Naillac, was slight in the extreme. Here it would be different. Here, she could move freely in whatever company she chose, in a society where every simple and natural remark of a woman to a man was not automatically seen as an invitation to something more; where one could make friends without compromising oneself and committing oneself to something one did not want. And she was sure that it was that kind of easy friendship which was the most likely to blossom into love.

I am twenty-eight, she thought. I have been a widow – a chaste widow – for seven years. My body has needs which only find an outlet in dreams. Leave them unsatisfied, and there will be more uncomfortable situations, like that with Aubin. And it is not only my body; I want companionship too, so that I can share my life in every way with the person I love.

Was that kind of love a possibility? She did not know; but she was quite sure that at Casseuil she would never find it. Yet was that enough to persuade her to stay – the hope that she might fall in love again? Did her life not need some other purpose as well? Could she really tear herself completely and for ever from all the responsibilities she had carried for so long?

I don't know, she told herself again and again. I just don't know.

The wedding preparations, and then the uproarious splendour of the wedding itself, enabled her to put the problem aside again. It was indeed a grand wedding, she acknowledged, as she stood with Mathilde at her side amongst the glittering congregation at the nuptial mass. She had given in to her parents' pleading and allowed them to buy new clothes for

214

herself and Mathilde, so that the sombre mourning clothes would not cast a shadow over the proceedings. For herself, she had chosen a silk dress of unrelieved simplicity, in a steel grey that was one of the approved colours of half-mourning; and she wore it with a kind of regret, not because of Philippe, but because (rather to her own surprise) something in her still felt ashamed at the possibility that she might take any pleasure in new clothes. For Mathilde she was not sorry at all, and was delighted that her little girl should be a picture of bright youthfulness in rose pink, with a silken sash and a matching bow in her hair.

It seemed to her that all of fashionable New York (if there was such a thing) was present today, the glowing colours of their wedding clothes outshining the lavish flowers, of a piece with the exquisite music. Yet for all the extravagant display of the wedding, there was something almost informal about it, which – remembering the tasteful magnificence of her own wedding – Laure found very strange. In the ballroom hired for the celebrations the multitude of guests were noisy, lively, uninhibited, and the dancing had a wild spirited quality, more like that of the peasants at Casseuil at harvest time than the graceful, restrained dancing Laure had known in Paris or Bordeaux. It had, undeniably, its endearing side, even if – though she did not dance herself – it left her at the end feeling as exhausted as if she had just spent a whole day picking grapes in the vineyard.

Picking grapes; it would soon be harvest time at Casseuil, and she ought to be going home. Autumn was coming, the mornings and evenings already crisp and chill, and even if she left now she might well be too late for the beginning of the *vendange*. Yet her parents, feeling a little bereft once the wedding was over and Marcel and his bride had left for their honeymoon, begged her to stay just a few days more, a week or two perhaps.

So she stayed, writing to Madame Naillac to let her know that she would not be home just yet; and there was a little peaceful interlude during which the arguments circled endlessly and inconclusively in her mind. And then Marcel and Eileen returned and, seeing them together, she felt a sharp pang of envy, for which she hated herself. Once, long ago, she had wished it were possible to go back to the first days of her marriage and begin again, guided by the wisdom she had learned since then. Now she realised that she did not want to go back, because Philippe had been, not a lover and friend, but a stranger whom she had shaped in her mind into something he was not. He had been – as she knew him – almost a figment of her imagination, for the real Philippe had been someone quite different. She wondered now if she could ever have come to love the real Philippe, had she found him in life.

No, what she envied now was the thing she had never experienced, the warm loving companionship, fired with passion but not limited to that, which linked Marcel and Eileen. They shared a delight in touching, kissing, embracing, but more than that they shared thoughts and laughter and experiences with an open friendliness she had never even caught sight of with Philippe. United by that closeness of spirit, they could look forward with confidence to a lifetime of happiness. Coming to America had given Marcel this gift. Could she find the same joy by staying here now?

A week after the young couple's return there was a grand dinner at Frank O'Brien's luxurious home, as noisily informal as the wedding had been, although the food and wine were excellent – no American wines here, Laure noted, as she sipped at the champagne with which the meal ended.

Later, weary of noise and laughter and a jollity that seemed always just beyond her reach, she retreated to the relative quietness of the small library, a spotless, beautifully appointed room that looked as if it was never used. There after a time Marcel found her, sitting in a deep winged chair with her face illuminated only by the light of the fire.

He closed the door and came to join her, pulling up a stool to her side and taking her hands in his. 'You're sad, *petite sœur*. I can't have that, you know – not when I'm so happy. Tell me, *ma chère*, what is it?'

She smiled faintly. 'I'm not sad exactly – it's just the usual thing: I don't know what to do for the best.'

'Then let me advise you: stay here with us and make a new life for yourself and little Mathilde. Then we'll all be happy. There – it's simple, is it not?'

'I wish it were. Sometimes it seems that it is. It would be *good* to stay. But I don't know – to leave everything behind for ever – to know I would never see Casseuil again: that's a big step.'

'If it's the right one that doesn't matter.'

'I know.' She smiled suddenly. 'Perhaps it is. Sometimes I am sure that it is – but always there is that doubt.'

'Have you heard from Casseuil?'

'Once, from Madame Naillac. She said everything was going well.' The old woman had not been any more informative than that, but the crisply uncommunicative letter had been enough to reassure Laure that there was no urgent need for her to return; if she decided to return.

There was a little silence. Laure knew Marcel was trying to think of something to say that might cheer her. 'Can I get you anything to eat? Or some more wine? – good French wine, of course.'

She shook her head, smiling. 'No thank you.'

'Oh, that reminds me – I heard something today that might interest you. I got talking to a man who came into the bank, and we found we both knew my friend André in Arkansas – he of the vineyard, that is. We got onto the subject of wines and the phylloxera crisis and so forth, and he said they're talking of grafting cuttings of *Vitis vinifera* onto rootstock of *Vitis labrusca*, or *Vitis riparia* – whichever type of wild vine seems to do best. Apparently it's already been tried in a few places, with some success. André's been asked to supply a vineyard somewhere near Bordeaux.'

Slowly, Laure took in what he was saying. 'They grafted European vines onto American roots – is that what you're saying?'

He nodded. 'The best of both worlds – phylloxera-resistant roots with the highest quality grapes. Or so they hope. I don't suppose anyone's got any fruit out of it yet.' He caught sight of her expression, and fell abruptly silent.

The warm rose-gold of the firelight lit the creamy pallor of Laure's face, throwing the fine cheekbones into sharp relief, emphasising the hollows about her eyes, the clear line of her jaw, and adding a kind of visionary glow to the smile that softened the too-rigid mouth and shone from her brown eyes.

Still holding her hands, Marcel studied her and drew the inevitable conclusion.

'I wish I hadn't spoken,' he said ruefully at last. 'You're going back aren't you?'

She smiled steadily at him with the serenity of someone who has chosen her path and already set her foot upon it. 'Yes, Marcel. I'm going back.'

CHAPTER
TWELVE

i

Two days out from New York the first gales hit the ship. There was no question this time of standing on deck, laughing into the wind – that would only have been asking to be swept overboard. Even below deck it was almost impossible to keep upright without clinging fiercely for support to every possible protrusion. Laure learned, with some sense of humiliation, that the best travellers have their limitations. Furthermore, when the storm was at its height she was reduced to a state of abject terror, lying on her bunk with a frightened Mathilde in her arms praying desperately that it would be over soon, somehow, anyhow.

The gale slackened, a day of calm followed; and then the next storm struck and the ship, sails furled, could only brace itself and ride it out there in mid-ocean. That formed the pattern of their voyage, an endless succession of storms broken only by brief momentary periods of calm. It seemed like a miracle when at last on a quiet still day they came within sight of Bordeaux. Laure had chosen to go home, looking forward to her return; but her reaction now surprised even herself. She greeted the blissful vision of the coast of France with rapturous tears, and gathered Mathilde fiercely into her arms. 'We're home, *chérie* – home at last!'

There was no one to meet them at Bordeaux. Laure had not written to warn Madame Naillac of her arrival, thinking it likely she would reach home before any letter. So, alone and unaided, she and Mathilde caught the train to Libourne, from which there was now a line to Bergerac.

As the train moved slowly out of the station, Laure looked out on the familiar streets and the river, and the suburbs, and enjoyed the novelty of being able to understand the talk around her. I made the right choice, she thought. This was what was meant by homeland, *patrie*, this sense of having reached a place of rest and refreshment for the spirit, a place where one belonged. She leaned back against the hard seat with her eyes closed and a smile of contentment on her face, while Mathilde snuggled happily against her. And on her other side her hand rested on the battered black trunk that she had guarded so carefully all the way across the Atlantic.

In there, swathed in damp cloths and concealed in the folds of one of her nightgowns (it would never be the same after this, but she did not care) lay half a dozen healthy rooted cuttings of a wild American vine.

'I'll see what I can do with these first,' she had told Marcel. 'If the grafting works, then I can make plans.' She did not quite know what she would do then, for to import sufficient American vines to provide grafting stock for the entire Casseuil vineyard would cost more than she could ever afford, even if (as she had no intention of doing) she were to ask her parents to help her. Though they had a good income from investments made on their arrival in America, Laure guessed that there was little left over once the comforts of life were supplied. But for the sake of Casseuil she would find some way forward. So she had parted from her parents and Marcel, wept with them and waved from the ship until the dots on the wharf had faded from sight; and then she had turned her face to the future.

At the station at Bergerac she hired a cab to take them the last six kilometres to Casseuil, and all the way gazed out of the window for the first sight of home.

The château looked exactly as she remembered it, though somehow more welcoming, more lovely than ever there on the hill with the clear light of the winter afternoon on its honeyed walls. The cab swung round a bend, passing the green willow-fringed pool that marked the northern boundary of the château's lands, twisted its way sharply upwards, slowing as the horse laboured on the hill; there at last were the vineyards. Laure, peering out of the window, felt a sudden flutter of panic. Would there still be any healthy vines left?

They were there still, in the drabness of early December, but mercifully with no sign yet – at a glance anyway – that the

220

disease had reached any more of them. It was not that, then, which caught Laure's attention and made her lean across to look with astonished dismay out of the window.

For a long time now it had not been possible to keep the earth in the vineyard entirely free of weeds, as it had been in the old days. But she had never seen it so bad as it was now, with a sodden dark mass of weeds crowding the roots of those last precious vines, everywhere between the rows. Worse, no one had earthed up the vine roots against the winter frosts. She leaned further over and saw here and there withered bunches of grapes left on the plants, pecked at by crows that flew up as the coach passed; they ought to have been picked, long since. What was Aubin thinking of to allow things to come to this pass? She felt anger bubbling up in her, driving out the joy of her homecoming.

In the courtyard she wasted no time, lifting down Mathilde and the luggage, paying off the cab driver as quickly as she could. Here too there were clear signs of neglect, weeds pushing their way up through the gravel, dead leaves swirled by the wind into corners, accentuated by the mournful banging of an outhouse door left open somewhere beyond the *chai*. She went to close it, acknowledging that weeding the yard was of minor importance now labour was short; it would be unreasonable of her to expect anyone to attend to that. But the vines, they were another matter.

Mathilde, looking a little puzzled, had followed her. 'Maman,' she murmured anxiously. Laure smiled to reassure her and took her hand.

'Come, *ma petite*. Let's put my plants in water; then we'll go and find everybody.'

She unlocked her trunk, took out the plants and, filling two buckets at the well, plunged the roots into the water; then she carried the buckets carefully to the office and set them down.

There was no sign of Aubin. The office was empty and every surface was coated with dust, as if no one had been here for a very long time, although Aubin was supposed to keep regular accounts of work done and money spent. On the desk and scattered about the floor were letters, roughly opened before being cast aside – unanswered, she feared. Some were bills, others clearly queries about sales – the château's lifeblood in these difficult times, so long as they still had some good wine in the *chai*.

She pulled books and ledgers from the shelf and looked through them. The last entries of any kind had been made in August, in Aubin's careful rounded writing, recording the fourth racking of last year's vintage; but nothing more since then, nothing at all. She turned the pages rapidly, looked through all other possible books, seeking records of the recent harvest, any records. But there were none.

She explored the *chai* and found her growing fear too ominously confirmed. The 1875 wine, left untended (presumably) since that racking in August, had failed to clear – it should have been racked again, or failing that, treated with isinglass. It smelt unpleasant too, as if some impurity had been allowed to taint it. In the further room, where the vintages of '71 (*that* should have been bottled by now), '72 and '73 were slowly maturing – in '74 they had lost everything to storms and rain – the barrels had not been checked and topped up and the air had got into several of them and turned the wine to vinegar. None of it had been great wine, but the '72 at least might have merited the Château de Casseuil label – and now it had gone, all of it, ruined by carelessness. Finally, the *cuves* that should have held this year's fermenting wine were empty, scrubbed and purified since their last use, smelling faintly fruity, but grey with dust.

There had been no harvest.

What terrible thing had happened? She must have been wrong and missed the signs; the disease must have reached even the last plants by now, destroying the final hope for Casseuil – for where was she to find vines to graft onto her roots if all of them were dead or diseased?

She had to know the truth, without delay. The weight of grief about her heart was unbearable, dragging her limbs into weary slowness. She was scarcely aware of Mathilde at her side as she trudged out to the vineyard, afraid of what she might find there.

No, her first impression had not been wrong; the plants were still healthy, despite the weeds. There was no sign even that one of the more mundane problems had attacked them – grey rot, for example, which could sometimes ruin a whole promising crop of Sémillon grapes, if the balance of warmth and moisture were not exactly right. Relief flooded her; to be succeeded at once by renewed anger.

Neglect was all that was wrong, total criminal neglect. No one had lifted a finger to pick the grapes. Perhaps it would have been only a small harvest, but it would have been better than nothing, better than this. She turned furiously and stormed back towards the house. If she met Aubin now she would be greatly tempted to throttle him with her own bare hands.

The hall was empty, as dusty as the office had been, the stairs grey and dingy and crumbed with dry mud, what she could see of the great window festooned with cobwebs. There was no one about, but from below rose, clearly, the sound of voices raised in song: a woman's, lively and suggestive and rich with laughter; a man's raucous and more than a little tuneless with drink. Laure made a move towards the kitchen stairs; and then some instinct warned her against it: Mathilde first, just in case. 'Let's go and take our coats off.' She led the child upstairs.

Her room was exactly as she had left it (apart from the dust) and so was Mathilde's. She delayed just long enough to see the child settled into the rediscovery of long unseen toys and books, and to pull off her bonnet and shawl; and then she ran swiftly downstairs again.

There was in the kitchen no trace of the trim scrubbed orderliness that had marked Nanon's rule: dust and grease covered every surface, the floor was stained and littered with spilt food and discarded utensils, a rancid smell lingered beneath the fresher odours of alcohol and some kind of stew cooking over the fire. Close to the hearth sat a man Laure had never seen before, a long lean dark-eyed man who held Rosaline on his knee with one enclosing arm, whilst the other was busy somewhere inside her bodice. They had stopped singing, but they did not see Laure because he was attempting to kiss Rosaline whilst she shrieked with laughter, tossing her head, her mouth open beneath his pursuing lips and tongue. They swayed together on the unsteady stool, with the awkward uncoordination of drunks. Two half empty glasses stood on the table nearby and, precariously close to the edge, a bottle in which only the dregs remained of a liquid gleaming richly gold where the light caught it.

Laure gave a cry, and ran and seized the bottle – one of the last, the very last, of that wonderful vintage she had tasted first on the day she had met Philippe.

'How dare you! How could you!' She stopped, because there were no words strong enough for what she felt.

Rosaline, suddenly quiet, slid from the man's knee and stood there, smoothing her skirts, patting her hair, but looking rather defiant than embarrassed. 'What's the matter with you? If you come back without any warning you can't expect to find everything just so.'

'But this – to find you drinking this!' Furiously she raised the bottle high.

Rosaline shrugged. 'That's what it's for isn't it?'

'Do you even know what it is? Do you care?' She thought as she spoke how pointless the questions were. She looked about her, taking in the full extent of the disorder that filled the room. 'Where's Nanon? And Aubin – I want to see him at once.'

Rosaline shrugged again, spreading her hands to indicate how little she cared. 'How do I know? They went a long time ago.'

'Went? Went where? What do you mean?'

'Just that – they upped and left, months ago now. Or weeks anyway. Aubin and Mathieu went first, then Nanon.'

The man, still spread at his ease on the stool, his back resting against the grimy wall, burped and grinned. 'Better off without them, aren't we, *mon petit chou*?' He curved his hand caressingly about Rosaline's backside and she gave a delighted wriggle and shot him a grin.

'Who are you?'

Supporting himself on the wall with one hand, he half rose to his feet and managed a drunken derisive bow in the direction of Laure's indignant, unyielding figure. 'Achille Lemoine, at your service, *madame* – dear and much respected friend of Mademoiselle Rosaline here.' He hiccuped and bowed again before sitting heavily back on the stool.

'Who gave you permission to come here?'

'I did, of course.' Rosaline's head was high, her eyes

224

sparkling and defiant; clearly she was much less drunk than her companion. 'You left me in charge, remember. You didn't say I had to live like a nun.'

'I left you in charge – I did not give you leave to drive away my servants, neglect my vines, bring your lover into my house, drink my most precious wine.'

'*My* this, *my* that! The old woman upstairs might have something to say about that.'

'Don't tell me she knows what you're up to!'

Rosaline shrugged yet again. 'She knows Achille's here. She likes him: he amuses her. She has him up there to see her nearly every day. If you want him out, you'll not get her to back you up.'

'I run this place, not Madame Naillac.'

'Oh yes? Maybe you did once, but only because the old woman let you. I've been in charge for the past months remember, and I've got Madame's backing. I don't think you'll find it so easy to have your way now. In any case, who's in charge by law, if it comes to that? Not you, I'll be bound.'

No, Laure acknowledged bitterly to herself; Rosaline was quite right. She had control only on sufferance, at Madame Naillac's pleasure. If that pleasure were to be withdrawn, she could do nothing about it.

She stared at Rosaline, whom she had trusted to care for this place she loved; and wished bitterly that she had never gone away.

What could she say? She felt sick; deeply, coldly angry; and quite helpless. She looked from one to another of the two people facing her, taking in their hostility and defiance and – most painful of all to her pride – their derision; and then she turned and walked away. She heard them laugh as she closed the door behind her.

She looked in on Mathilde, who was reading a book with apparent absorption, but looked up as she came in. 'Can I go and see Nanon?'

'Very soon,' Laure assured her, and wondered whether there was any truth in her answer at all. Then she climbed the stairs to knock on Madame Naillac's door.

'*Entrez!*'

All was quietness here, and order. The old woman sat,

wrapped in shawls, in the heavily cushioned chair where she spent her days, well protected from draughts. Near her at the table her grandson worked with close attention at a piece of Latin translation; he looked up as Laure came in, and she was struck more than ever by the unchildlike impassivity of his expression, the veiled eyes that returned quickly to his book. He seemed quite unsurprised to see her, as if she had been gone only an hour or two.

His grandmother was less controlled, though only for a moment. The dark eyes widened, her hand crept to her breast, she exclaimed, 'Laure!' and then she was calm again, her voice cold and steady. 'So – you have returned.' She held out her cheek for the necessary brief kiss of greeting, and then turned to her grandson. 'Frédéric, go and find Antoinette. She will be in the garden, or perhaps the kitchen. Tell her you will go for a walk now, and then we shall take tea, at four o'clock.'

The boy did not move, beyond laying down his pen the better to give his full attention to his grandmother. His face had an odd shut-in look, not merely expressionless, but resistant, almost stubborn.

'Go along, *mon enfant.* Be quick now.'

He shuffled his books into a pile, arranged them to one side, rose to his feet; and then paused again. 'May I read in my room instead, Grand-mère?'

She stared at him, clearly amazed by such uncharacteristic self-assertion. 'What is the matter with you, Frédéric?' Her voice sharpened suddenly with anxiety. 'Are you ill?'

'No, Grand-mère.'

'Then hurry up. It's a fine day: make the most of it. Put on your hat and coat now. The wind is fresh today.'

Laure watched him go into the adjoining room, without further protest, but as slowly as was consistent with obedience. A little later, neatly dressed in his outdoor clothes, he made his way downstairs. She glimpsed his face as he passed and thought, He is afraid. But what was there out there that could possibly frighten a child?

Then she remembered his mother and Achille. It was only too possible that, sent on some errand by his grandmother, he had seen something between them, come across something – like that scene witnessed today, or worse – that no child ought

226

to be allowed to see. Or perhaps Achille was unkind to him . . . Madame Naillac was not the sort of woman in whom a child would confide in trouble or distress. Let me never fail Mathilde! she prayed.

'You will find some changes, I expect.'

Startled out of her reflections, Laure gave her full attention to the old woman, and was annoyed to feel herself colouring. After all, it ought to be Madame Naillac who was on the defensive, always supposing she had some idea what was going on – but then she had always had that uncanny ability to keep herself fully and thoroughly informed about the activities of the household. Cautiously, yet trying to eradicate all trace of hesitation from her voice, Laure said, 'I do not like what I have seen.'

There was a frigid little smile on Madame Naillac's face. 'You do not approve of Monsieur Lemoine perhaps. I did not know you were such a prude.'

Laure was astonished. She had been absolutely sure that Madame Naillac's tolerance of sexual irregularities in the male portion of humanity did not extend to those of any woman, excepting always the liaison that had produced Frédéric. But that Rosaline, who had been loved by Philippe, should take up with another man – surely she could not accept that with equanimity?

As if reading her thoughts, the old woman continued smoothly, 'Oh, certainly I was not pleased when I learned that Rosaline had invited her friend into the house. But having met Monsieur Lemoine I took rather a different view of the matter. He is a most thoughtful man, considerate and sympathetic – not refined or educated of course, but then neither is Rosaline, and there is nothing wrong with simplicity after all, if it is honest and unashamed. Rosaline has told me that she can never hope to meet Philippe's like again, nor does she believe she will ever love as she did then – the thought of him is still able to set her weeping.' She paused, moved herself by that evidence of long devotion. 'But a good, steady, respectable man with whom she can settle down in the security of marriage – that is not something to be lightly disregarded.'

These soothing reflections seemed to Laure to bear no relationship whatsoever to what she had seen and heard downstairs. She did not believe that either Rosaline or her lover had marriage uppermost in their minds; but it was not, of course, the moral aspect of the situation that really disturbed her. 'Do you realise that Nanon and Aubin have both gone, heaven knows where?'

'But of course – what need is there of them, when Achille is here to do the work? A fine strong man he is too. Rosaline has taken over the cooking, and does it very well, and he does what is necessary outside. He made it very plain he requires no payment, only a roof over his head and his keep. You should be grateful; think what he saves us in wages.'

'Saves us! Madame, he can have done nothing! There is neglect everywhere – they have even been drinking the '47 wine. I found a bottle on the table.'

She knew then, watching the old woman's expression set into icy rigidity, that she had no hope at all of making her see the truth; the poison had already done its work, thoroughly and completely, during her long absence.

'You never did like Rosaline, did you? You have always been jealous, because she gave Philippe the son he wanted – because she was the woman he chose out of love, not from duty or necessity. Well, she has shown her worth these past months. Remember, it was you who turned your back on your responsibilities here, of your own free will; no one forced you into it. I always knew you were unreliable. You can hardly complain now if someone else has shown herself more capable than you.'

For the moment, Laure could think of nothing to say to that, beyond a sharp 'We shall see,' which came nowhere near expressing what she was feeling. She knew that until she had made herself thoroughly familiar with everything that had happened in her absence she would not know where to begin her fight to restore things to normal.

She waylaid Antoinette first, as she came upstairs with the tea things; fortunately Frédéric had been sent on ahead up to his room, so that she was alone.

'You must see how things are down there,' Laure greeted her as they met on the landing: she tried not to sound too accusing. 'You know how angry Madame would be if she knew the truth. Why do you not tell her?'

Antoinette – who made no secret of the fact that she had never liked Laure – looked at her with eyes as cold and hard as those of her mistress had been. 'What she doesn't know can't hurt her. All that matters is that she's happy. Monsieur Lemoine makes her laugh, like I've never seen her laugh in years. Why upset things? It does no harm if there's a mess downstairs.'

'But the estate, the vineyard, everything: you can't really believe Madame Naillac would want things to be neglected like this!'

'She doesn't care about the vineyard any more; she knows it's finished. All she cares about is Monsieur Frédéric, and that she should be able to live at Casseuil until she dies. All *I* care about is that she has her way, and is happy too.'

'But can't you see? If the estate is ruined she won't be able to live here any more!'

'I can't see that what's happened has made any difference at all to the estate. It was ruined anyway. Nothing's any the worse, except for you. And you'll have to put up with it, that's all.'

Laure contained her fury, but only just, and only until the servant had disappeared from sight around the turn of the stair. Then she ran downstairs and out into the cold wind, not even noticing that she wore no coat; and taking a spade from the outbuildings made her way to the overgrown neglected field where the phylloxera had first made its appearance and began furiously to dig. She had thought they might plant maize here next spring, but now in the most favoured corner she set to work to clear the ground for the six American vines.

ii

'Watch out, *monsieur le curé* – they'll eat you alive down there this morning!'

The Abbé Lebrun, well used by now to the passing jibes thrown at him from the café, walked on with dignity, pretending not to hear. He had his hand on the gate leading into the wood of the château when Robert Martin, standing in his café doorway with Jean Lambert and two others, called again.

229

'There'll be fireworks, *curé* – she's back at last!'

This time the *curé* did turn round. 'Back? Who's back?' He took a step or two towards the men, ignoring the mocking chorus.

'Look how white he's gone!' 'Trembling at the knees, *curé*?' and a number of other cruder taunts reached him.

He waited calmly for the noise to subside, so that Robert Martin could give him a reply.

'Madame Laure, of course. She came back last night. I should go back home if I were you – she'll be waiting for you with a knife if I'm not mistaken.'

The *curé* was amazed that they should apparently know what he had thought to be a confidential matter – that he had any responsibility for the situation at the château. But then it was very difficult to keep anything quiet in Casseuil. He said nothing more, but simply continued on his way to give Frédéric his lesson, followed, until the trees had closed him in, by the derisive cries from the café.

He was far from taking the matter as calmly as his manner suggested. He knew well enough that Madame Laure had every cause to be angry, and – however unreasonably – he did feel a certain guilt about the way things had developed. He realised as he let himself into the hall of the château that he was more than a little apprehensive.

She was there and – if not obviously waiting for him, and armed with a scrubbing brush rather than a knife – did come towards him the moment she saw him. She had clearly chosen to scrub the hall floor first thing this morning so as to be sure of catching him when he arrived.

'Ah, they said you were back,' he put in quickly before she could speak. 'I'm very glad to see you. You are badly needed.'

'So I find.' Her voice was cold; he had not known Laure Naillac was capable of making him feel so small and so unworthy. 'What became of your promise to watch over Mademoiselle Brousse?' She did not wait for an answer. 'I trusted you – I trusted them all – and *this* is what I find—!'

'I understand your indignation, *ma fille* – and feel it too, believe me. If I could have done more, then be sure I should have done. But my hands were tied.'

'How?'

'As soon as I saw how things were going I remonstrated with Mademoiselle Brousse. When it seemed that this approach could not hope to succeed, then I put the matter before Madame Naillac. I – I regret to say that she did not believe me. I was simply upbraided for my pains. Even when Aubin and Mathieu left, and then Nanon, even then she would not listen. There is I fear no one so blind as the person who does not wish to see.'

Madame Laure studied him, no less angry than before, although he felt – or hoped – that the anger was no longer directed against him. 'And where are they now – Aubin and Mathieu and Nanon, I mean?'

'Nanon is at home. Whether she could be persuaded to return I don't know, but she would I am sure be delighted to see the little one again. I presume Mademoiselle Mathilde has returned with you?'

'She's upstairs. What about Aubin?'

'He too went home for a time, but he very soon quarrelled with his sisters and left – to seek work in the town, I believe, but where exactly he went and with what success I don't know. Mathieu is working for Monsieur Séguier and is, I think, unlikely to wish to come back here.'

'Did Rosaline dismiss them?'

'No: they went of their own free will. Largely, of course, because they had not been paid for some time. Nanon stayed longer than the other two, but in the end the situation became too difficult even for her loyalty.'

'Then Madame Naillac *must* be convinced of the truth somehow. Surely there is some way?'

'I wish I could believe that there was. As I see it your only possible course is to persuade Mademoiselle Brousse and this – er – her companion – to leave. Though how you would achieve that I do not know.'

Laure watched him go on his way upstairs. So much for his support; she had it, his words had implied, just so long as no action was expected of him. 'Thank you, *monsieur le curé*,' she murmured bitterly, as she returned with angry vigour to her scrubbing of the floor.

*

Nanon was ecstatic at seeing Mathilde again; but she was quite firm. 'I'm sorry, *madame*, but I'm not coming back while that woman's there.'

But at least next morning Laure was able to leave Mathilde in Nanon's care when she set out for Bordeaux to see Maître Perrard.

The lawyer was wholly unaware of the situation at Casseuil. The money for the wages had been paid regularly to Rosaline and, hearing nothing more, Maître Perrard had assumed that all was well. Listening now to Laure's account of what she had found on her return, he was as shocked as so cautious and impassive a man could be.

'Of course,' he warned, when Laure asked for his advice, 'if Madame Naillac wishes to leave the situation as it is, then she has the right, as I am sure you realise, unless perhaps her brother were to raise objections; that might make a difference. But – like you – I am sure that if she were to learn the truth she could not permit such a state of affairs to continue. Let me suggest that I contact Monsieur Silvine and arrange with him to come to Casseuil – without warning might be best perhaps. Then we can investigate the situation and, should we find ourselves in agreement with you, we will take steps to inform Madame Naillac of the truth. Will that content you?'

For the first time since her return to France Laure felt almost optimistic. She even managed a smile – knowing and rather malicious – for Rosaline when they met in the kitchen that evening, whilst Achille was upstairs charming Madame Naillac. Little do you know! she thought; and then realised that Rosaline, standing hands on hips with her back to the fire, was looking at her with just the same malicious little smile on her face, as if she knew exactly what Laure was thinking and had her answer ready.

'I suppose you went to Bordeaux today, to see that lawyer?' Laure said nothing, but continued to smile, although a little knot of apprehension tightened about her middle. 'You needn't think he'll help you. He's Madame's man first.'

'But of course. He will do nothing without her agreement.'

'And I'll tell you one thing, she'll never agree to send me away, or put you in charge again, no matter what anyone tells her – even if she believes every word of it.' She paused, just for

an instant, to let Laure take in what she had said; and to give
the greater emphasis to her concluding thrust. 'Not, that is,
when she knows that if I go, Frédéric goes with me.'

Laure stood very still, while hope drained away. She made a
last desperate attempt to stem the flow.

'You wouldn't – you couldn't do that!'

'Why not? You know she'd agree to anything rather than
lose him.'

'But you don't give a *sou* for Frédéric!'

'So what? He's still my son – and a bastard son at that. No
one else has any rights over him but me. I can do what I like
with him.'

Speechless, Laure stared at her, mesmerised by that triumphant look, the bright mocking eyes. How could any mother
care so little for her child as to use him as a pawn in a ruthless
bid for power? She felt sick, ashamed that she could ever have
been so blind as to trust Rosaline or confide in her; and
bitterly angry too, because she knew she could find no
weapon strong enough to withstand this final blow.

She went upstairs and wrote to Maître Perrard, instructing
him, with bleak brevity, to forget that their interview had ever
taken place, and to abandon any plans to come to Casseuil.
Then she set out for the village to post it.

Coming back, she met Rosaline in the hall, and turned her
eyes away from the malevolent smile that greeted her; they
were both making for the stairs, but she stood aside to let the
other woman go first, not wanting to feel that look of smug
satisfaction behind her all the way to her room. She was
aware, momentarily, of someone stepping on to the landing
from above just as Rosaline completed her ascent: Frédéric,
carrying his grandmother's tray back to the kitchen. She had
time to register surprise that Madame Naillac should have
asked him to do anything so menial, and to suggest to herself
that perhaps he chose the task to escape from the presence of
Achille; and then she saw him come to a halt and retreat
hastily to the shelter of the half-landing. Only when his
mother had gone – without any sign that she had seen him –
did he come down again, looking rather paler than usual. He
greeted Laure with a 'Good day, *madame*,' and then went on
down the lower stairs towards the kitchen.

She watched him go, struck by a new thought: if she was right, and Frédéric was afraid – for whatever reason – of meeting his mother or Achille, she could question him, find out what troubled him, what he had seen or suffered, and persuade him to confide in his grandmother. Surely then, faced with damning evidence against Rosaline, Madame Naillac would find a way to drive the woman away without losing Frédéric in the process? Laure began to follow the boy; and then, abruptly, thought better of it. If she was wrong, and he had nothing on his mind, then she would be troubling him unnecessarily, perhaps damaging his innocence; and it was in any case a delicate matter, an ugly one, to contemplate using a child as an informer against his own mother. Besides, she acknowledged bleakly that Rosaline was unlikely to allow herself to be deprived of that ultimate, powerful weapon she possessed, of her right to decide what should become of her son.

She had lost, and this time she could see no hope of victory. She went to her room and wept; and thought, Why did I come back? There's nothing for me here any more.

But that was not quite true. Rosaline and Achille had the run of the house, they had control wherever they chose to exert it; but they had no interest whatsoever in the remnants of the vineyard. Apart from making some attempt to cultivate the vegetables and care for the animals on which they depended, they did nothing out of doors. There, at least, Laure could do as she pleased.

She had new locks fitted to the doors of the *chai* and kept the keys about her person. She had been appalled to discover how much of the old Casseuil wine had gone in her absence. She had depended on those stocks to supply their needs when all else failed, for with the destruction of so many vineyards the finest wines fetched increasingly high prices. Now, that resource had dwindled alarmingly. But however bleak the present, however unpromising the future might look, there were still her American vines. She could not begin the grafting until spring, and she would not give up altogether before she had seen if the grafting would work. I didn't go to all that trouble for nothing, she thought.

It was desperately hard and came close, often, to breaking her spirit. Indoors, her room and Mathilde's were their only sanctuary from the constant presence of Rosaline and Achille. The two of them ignored her totally, unless forced to do otherwise, and when she remonstrated at food wasted, dirt uncleared, or questioned them about the disappearance of a number of valuable ornaments from the shrouded cupboards in the *grand salon* (discovered by chance when she went to look for something stored there), they simply laughed at her and turned away. She did not dare to allow Mathilde to wander freely about the house, for fear of what she might see: they had no inhibitions at all about how they behaved in the most public place, since they knew there was no likelihood of Madame Naillac coming downstairs. Laure wondered what threats or inducements they had used to make sure Frédéric did not betray them; perhaps his own natural reticence was protection enough.

She hated the enforced restriction, for her daughter's sake in particular. Mathilde will turn out like Frédéric, she thought bitterly; but she did not really believe it. In any case, when Mathilde needed greater freedom, she had Nanon to go to. Happy and carefree, the child showed no signs of a troubled spirit: she was Laure's sole consolation. If all else failed, if she had in the end to admit defeat and write to her parents to beg for her passage to America to join them there, she would still have Mathilde. Nothing could take that from her.

iii

'You must see, *mon ami*, that we cannot hope to entice the children of poorer families to school unless we can provide a fund to supply them with the necessary books. The council pays their fees, of course, but books are another matter – and these days so many of our families are poor.'

'You want me to contribute to your book fund, I suppose?' Henri Séguier, on horseback before the *mairie*, looked as if he was already regretting having paused to speak to Doctor Rossillon. These days his old friend seemed increasingly wrapped up in communal affairs, and Henri was not much interested in such things, unless they were likely to have some direct effect upon him.

'You are one of the few citizens within the commune who is actually in a position to do so,' the doctor pointed out.

'It's not books that are the problem, in my opinion,' said Henri. 'While the school's held in that miserable tumbledown shack you haven't a hope of increasing the numbers. From what I hear, a new schoolmaster wouldn't come amiss either.'

The doctor sighed. 'Indeed, no. But how can we hope to attract a good schoolmaster to the present building? And the municipal council has no funds for a new building at present. It should have been taken in hand long ago, when funds were more readily available.'

'You blame Chabry then?'

'Of course. The council was always ready to support a new school. But Chabry never did hold with educating peasants – the *curé*'s philosophy: teach them to recite the catechism in patois and you've done all that's required. So we have children growing up who can neither speak nor understand French, let alone read or write it. It is a deplorable situation. However, I feel that a fund for books would be a beginning – a small one, but significant.' He raised his eyes expectantly to the rider's face.

'Oh, you can count on me for something, you know that,' said Henri carelessly. 'But that's not much to be going on with.'

'No. A pity things are as they are at the château – I feel sure Madame Laure would be sympathetic, in the circumstances.'

'Perhaps she'll come back from America with a fortune,' Henri put in lightly.

'Oh, she's back already. Didn't you know?'

Henri was uncomfortably aware that he was blushing. He was momentarily so overcome with emotion that he relaxed his hold on the reins and Grand Turc stamped and sidled beneath him. 'Really?' he said as casually as he was able. 'No, I didn't know. When was that?' He calmed the horse as best he could.

'Oh, two weeks ago now. Not that anything much has changed since her return. I imagine she regrets bitterly ever having gone away. Poor woman, she has courage, but—' The doctor shook his head.

As soon as he could, Henri took his leave of the Mayor, and

then turned Grand Turc's head towards the road that skirted the west side of the church and ran down the hill a little way until it came to the drive of the château.

The great grey-gold building stood on a kind of natural shelf on the hillside, its vineyards radiating out from it in all directions, except to the south where the wood shielded it. Henri's eyes scanned the interrupted rows as he rode; and there at last he saw Laure, just at the point where the land began abruptly to slope down into the valley, a tiny solitary black figure silhouetted against the endless blue distance. He would have taken her for a peasant had he not been told she had returned.

He did not go to her at once, but first left the horse at the stable, shutting it into a stall himself, since there was no one to do it for him. Then he walked down to where he had seen her. By now she was bent low between the vines, laboriously clearing the ground of the withered remains of last year's weeds. It took him some time to find her.

She glanced round, saw him, and stood up, rubbing her earthy hands on her skirts before offering one to him. Without a thought for the dirt, Henri bent and kissed it. He was gratified to see her colour rise a little at the gallantry of the gesture.

'*Ma chère madame*, I have only just heard you were back.' He paused to study her – the slender figure, still somehow with a hint of elegance about it in spite of the dull threadbare black of the skirt and bodice and the windswept look about the gold hair beneath its little white cap. More than ever, she had the fined-down look he had observed in her since Philippe's death, as if everything that was inessential to her beauty had been scoured away by suffering. She looked tired and – for all her welcoming smile – more than a little anxious. Yet nothing in the end could detract from the exquisite moulding of cheekbones and chin, the perfection of nose, mouth and eyes; even in death, Henri thought, with a shiver at the very idea, she would be beautiful.

'You have troubles, I hear,' he said warmly. 'I want you to know that in me at least you will always find a friend.'

He did not think he had ever seen her so moved before. Her smile spread and there were tears in her eyes. He had to suppress a strong urge to gather her into his arms and kiss away those tears. Instead, he stroked her hand, while his eyes continued to gaze hungrily at her small exquisite person.

'Thank you, *monsieur*,' she said at last, fervently, in a voice trembling with emotion.

'If there is anything I can do – *anything*!'

'I wish there were, *monsieur*, but—' She shrugged expressively.

Now, he thought, was the moment to bring up the point that had first occurred to him some long time ago, but, then at least, had seemed a little irrelevant. Full of a gratifying sense of power, he said casually, 'You wish, I suppose, to rid yourself of that woman – Mademoiselle Brousse?'

'Of course; only—'

'Ah!' He folded both hands firmly about hers, and there was a note of satisfaction in his voice. 'Do you realise, *ma chère madame*, that if a man installs his mistress beneath his wife's roof, then the wife has good grounds for divorce?'

Laure was clearly puzzled. 'I didn't know that; but I don't see what it has to do with me.'

'There are similarities in your case, are there not? Your mother-in-law has installed your husband's mistress beneath your roof, and what is more has permitted her a freedom – a licence even – which is an insult to you. I think it very likely that you would have a good case in a court of law should you wish to force Mademoiselle Brousse from Casseuil. If Madame Naillac tries to insist that she stay, then you can claim that she is no worthy guardian of your interests or those of your child.'

He watched as wonder, hope – even, at the last, a faint delight – glimmered in her eyes, held in check yet still struggling through her doubts. 'But surely our lawyer Maître Perrard would have told me, if I were entitled to bring any such action?'

'Does he not represent Madame Naillac, rather than you? He would hardly give you advice you might employ against her, would he now? But my own lawyer – the best in Bergerac, I assure you – he would be happy to advise you.'

The next moment all the hope had gone. She pulled her hand free and half-turned away from him. 'It's no good anyway. Mademoiselle Brousse threatens to take her son with her if she goes — Madame Naillac would never let her go in those circumstances, whatever the cost.'

'She might have no choice, if the alternative was to lose all her power over the château.'

Laure shook her head. 'Frédéric means more to her than the château or anything else. I think she would sooner leave than lose him. And I can hardly make myself responsible for driving Philippe's mother out into the street.'

'Then use that as a threat. Make it clear she must find some way to persuade Mademoiselle Brousse to go voluntarily, or you will use the law against her. I suspect that's all you need.'

'But Rosaline won't leave, I'm sure of that.'

'Because of the boy?'

'No, not that at all. I think she's afraid of finding herself with nowhere to go and no means to live on. I suspect she knows full well that Achille Lemoine is no more than a bird of passage, and is only too likely to move on some day. Besides, he has no money. As things are, she can please herself how she lives and yet still be sure of a roof over her head at the end.'

'Yes, I heard the man already has a wife and children somewhere, so there's no hope there. But surely if Mademoiselle Brousse could be given enough to ensure her future security, then she'd go?'

Laure shook her head again, and he saw the regret in her eyes. 'Where would I ever find the means for that?'

'Would not Madame Naillac do so, if it bought her the boy?'

'I'm afraid Rosaline would want a good deal more than either of us could possibly afford.'

He caught at her hand again, holding it firmly. 'Then permit me, *ma chère madame* — a tribute from one who wishes only to be your most devoted servant. *I* have the means to pay Mademoiselle Brousse whatever she requires.'

'Oh, I could not—!' Her eyes, troubled, astonished, flew to his face. 'No, no. It is most generous of you even to think of it; but I could not put myself so much in your debt.'

'Then let us come to some more formal arrangement. For example, you could undertake to repay me little by little over the years. Or, better still, we can defer repayment until such time as your circumstances change – as, of course, I hope very much that they will.'

It took him some time to overcome her scruples, but in the end he did so, because she was desperate and he offered the only possible way out.

Within a week Rosaline had gone, and Achille with her. Henri had taken responsibility for the whole business. He had bargained with Rosaline, agreeing in the end to pay her just enough to ensure her uncomplaining departure, but no more. When Madame Naillac, furiously angry, blamed Laure for Rosaline's announced intention to leave, Henri warned her of the alternative, should she prove difficult. Terrified above all of losing Frédéric, the old woman added a sum of her own to Rosaline's discharge payment, and insisted on a written renunciation of the child. Henri had taken great care not to suggest in any way that Laure herself was, of her own volition, threatening to take legal action against her mother-in-law; but Madame Naillac was not stupid. And Laure knew that for this she could expect no forgiveness, ever. The old woman might have no choice now but to return control of the château to her daughter-in-law; but one day, if it lay in her power, she would have her revenge. Laure, untroubled, accepted that possibility as part of the price she must pay for ridding Casseuil of Rosaline and Achille.

Henri came to see them go. He stood beside a jubilant Laure on the little bridge in front of the château and watched them drive away in the pony trap that he had supplied, a final manifestation of a generosity that amazed Laure and filled her, a little, with foreboding. She owed him so much, more than the simple sum that she could not hope to repay for the foreseeable future; for ever now he would have a hold over her which in gratitude she could not deny or repel. She had an uneasy sense that she had bought her freedom at a price that might in the end bring her to a greater servitude. But today she was too happy to allow that to trouble her very deeply.

'We shan't see them again,' he commented with satisfaction as they disappeared from view. Veiling the warmth of her feelings with a certain constraint, Laure smiled at him.

'I don't know how I can thank you enough,' she said

quietly. 'You have been a true friend. I could not have rid myself of them without you.'

'A woman alone must always be at a disadvantage, however strong she is. You understand that now, I think. I do not need to explain to you the value of having a man to call upon in need. You have been too long alone, you know.'

His meaning was only too clear, but Laure pretended to misunderstand him. 'I have hopes of persuading Aubin to return, if he can be found. If not, then I shall look for someone like him – someone strong and reliable.'

'I was not thinking of a servant or a labourer.' He turned to face her, and one hand rested caressingly on her arm, moving slowly up towards her shoulder. 'No woman should live alone, without protection – least of all one so beautiful.' The hand reached her shoulder and crept on towards the narrow crêpe frill at her neck. 'You are alone, with a fatherless little girl to bring up – I also am alone, and my son is motherless. I have considerable wealth; you – undeservedly, sadly – you have little. It seems to me that the solution is inescapable. What could be more natural than that I should place at your disposal all that I have, in return for what would be to me a greater gift – your beautiful self?'

She could not then, brusquely, free herself from his insinuating touch, although the feel of his plump fingers on the bare skin of her neck repelled her; but she owed him too much for that. Instead, she stood very still, looking at him, and said quietly, 'I owe you so much, *monsieur* – gratitude, in particular – and I am moved by your proposal, very much moved. Whatever you may feel, I know I have little to offer as a wife; I can only feel honoured that you think otherwise. But I must refuse you. I am not yet ready to think of marrying again – perhaps I never shall be. I hope you will understand.'

Never, never would marriage to Henri Séguier be a possibility for her, but she could not tell him that. She knew that by evading the issue, turning aside from an immediate and blunt rejection, she made it only too likely that he would retain some hope for the future, and continue to pursue her. But this was not the moment to rebuff him. She even allowed him, lightly, briefly, to kiss her, before she gently freed herself and invited him to take some refreshment in the *petit salon*, where

Mathilde, a reassuring third party, was busy at her morning handwriting exercise.

When he had gone, Laure put on one of Nanon's voluminous aprons and went to the kitchen and set to work to scrub and wash and tidy. She sang as she worked, rejoicing in her isolation, in the certainty that no longer would Rosaline or Achille intrude on her, either here, or anywhere else in the château. She had left Mathilde upstairs, alone in the *petit salon*, reading; and she could do so knowing that the child would hear and see nothing that could trouble or distress her. The sense of liberation was wonderful and exhilarating. For the first time since Philippe's death she was free of Rosaline; she had broken with the unhappiness of the past. Today was a new beginning, the one she had dreamed of as she left New York, but better even than she could have imagined.

When, after two energetic hours, the kitchen bore at least some passing resemblance to Nanon's spotless domain, Laure went to find Mathilde. As she crossed the hall, Frédéric came downstairs in Antoinette's company, on his way outside for his daily walk. For a moment his eyes met Laure's: they were as remote and expressionless as ever. 'Good day, *madame*,' he said politely. She returned the greeting and stood still, watching, until the door had closed behind them both.

What was he thinking? Did he know what part she had played in driving his mother away? She did not even know if he had seen Rosaline before she left, or had any opportunity to say goodbye. Did he mind her going, or was he relieved, delivered from a burden no child should have to bear? She did not know, and very likely she never would. It was strange, to live day after day under the same roof as another human being – and that person a mere child – and not to know anything of what he was thinking or feeling. She shivered, and felt as if a shadow had fallen across her happiness. There was not after all to be a clean break with the past. Rosaline had gone, but she had left a part of herself behind; and who was to say that Frédéric might not in the end prove to be more of a threat to Casseuil than his mother? Once he was grown, and able to influence his grandmother for good or ill, might he not make a more formidable adversary than Rosaline had ever done? He was intelligent, cold, unknowable. Had she rid herself of one enemy, only to find herself, a few years from now, with a more dangerous one by far?

You're being ridiculous, she told herself firmly. He's just a child – an unhappy child. And by the time he's grown, there will be nothing he can do to damage Casseuil. I shall make sure of that. I shan't make the mistake of going away again, or trusting someone who is unworthy of trust. And besides, by then Mathilde too will be grown up, and I shall have an ally and a friend.

Singing softly, she opened the door of the *petit salon*. 'Go and put on your coat, *minette*. We're going to see Nanon. I think she might come back here today.'

CHAPTER
THIRTEEN

i

Auguste Silvine was in a far from happy mood as his carriage turned up the hill towards the château. He cast a disparaging eye over the blighted vineyard and reflected sourly that anyone with a grain of common sense would long ago have sold up and moved away. His sister was too infirm herself to manage so large an enterprise efficiently, and her daughter-in-law showed a stubborn, blind determination to ruin the whole family by refusing to relinquish her dream of restoring the vineyard. Without capital, faced with the worst catastrophe ever to hit the wines of France – and one that was confronting even the great wealthy vineyards with disaster – that goal had no hope of being reached. But Laure would not listen to the voice of reason and Marie-Louise declared that as long as she lived she would stay at Casseuil, and so the two stubborn women worked in a kind of conspiratorial rivalry to bring everything to ruin about them.

But it was not the plight of Casseuil that lay behind his present mood; if the two women wanted to struggle on in near penury that was their business. No, what he resented was Marie-Louise's insistence on involving him in responsibility for her son's bastard. In his opinion Frédéric's mother should have been paid off right at the outset and told to take the child with her, never to return. His presence at Casseuil hardly brought credit to Philippe's memory, and in Uncle Auguste's opinion the whole business was very unfair to charming little Mathilde, that delightful smiling golden-haired creature who never failed to win a laugh and a kiss even from his own rather austere self.

Perhaps if Frédéric had been something like his half-sister, he might have felt differently towards him. But nothing could make him warm to the stiff silent unchildlike boy whom he was now to be obliged to accompany to and from school at the beginning and end of each term, and entertain at his house on his free Sundays. In fact, if Marie-Louise had won her point, Frédéric would have lived with his uncle and attended the *lycée* as an *externe* – a day boy – but Auguste had at least managed to persuade her that, as a recent widower, he could not be expected to undertake such a responsibility. He had not at first seen why his sister wanted the boy to attend the *lycée* at all, in preference to one of the many excellent private religious *collèges*.

'It is what Philippe would have wanted,' was her reply, rather surprisingly perhaps. 'He went there himself. And I know he did not approve of boys being taught by priests. It was one thing he was very firm about.' The only thing, Auguste reflected to himself. 'I am glad to say, Frédéric has had an excellent grounding in religion, and now that he has made his first communion I think him sufficiently fortified against any unfortunate influences he may meet.'

Her confidence did not, unfortunately, extend to allowing him to travel unaccompanied to school, least of all on the train. So here Auguste was, several months later, driving to Casseuil to take the boy back to school after the New Year holiday, and looking forward without enthusiasm to the forthcoming hours of silent proximity.

I'm not a young man, thought Auguste resentfully. I shouldn't be expected to make long journeys in the middle of winter to act as guardian to a young boy with no claim on me. But somehow – though he was only two years her junior – Marie-Louise had always been able to make him do what she wanted, and so here he was sitting wrapped in rugs in his comfortable carriage as it drew to a halt before the door of the château, and trying to muster the will to stir himself to step out into the cold wind and face the long climb up the stairs to his sister's room, without even the assistance of a helpful servant.

It was some consolation to him to meet with Mathilde emerging from her room just as he crossed the first floor landing; in fact, for a moment, the sight of her tall slender prettiness drove all his discontentment away. She dropped a graceful old-fashioned little curtsey – 'Good day, *monsieur*' – and then turned that enchanting smile upon him, drawing one of his own rare smiles in return. He patted her cheek, even dropped a light kiss upon it, and thought how he would have liked just such a little girl as this, had he been blessed with children, which, thank goodness, he had not.

'How are you, *mon enfant*? They're not sending you away to school then?' The remark was simply by way of conversation, for he knew, of course, that there was nothing to spare for her education. He looked from her sweet glowing face to the threadbare wool of her winter dress – a severe dark garment, high necked, long sleeved, unflattering, cut perhaps from something of her mother's – and reflected that even its drabness failed to diminish her blooming ten-year-old prettiness.

'I shall begin lessons with Maman again tomorrow, *monsieur*.' He realised with a sense of astonishment that she was holding out her arm towards him. 'Shall I walk up the stairs with you, *monsieur*?' Charmingly put, it was an offer of assistance; clearly his painful breathlessness had not escaped her. He was very much touched, but said nothing and simply took the proffered arm and went with her towards the detested upper flight of stairs.

'I suppose you have come to take Frédéric back to school,' she went on conversationally. She had made sure that he was next to the handrail and she on the inside, supporting arm in place: so young, and such natural, graceful tact. Uncle Auguste, more moved than ever, could only manage a grunt in reply to her remark.

Mathilde frowned just a little, in no way disfiguring her face. 'He didn't look very happy when I saw him yesterday, nor the day before. I think perhaps he doesn't like school.'

Auguste was more impressed by her concern for this half-brother whom she had every reason to hate, than by what she told him. After all, when did Frédéric ever look happy?

On the landing outside her grandmother's door, Mathilde deposited her uncle, assured herself that he was not too out of breath, and left him, running down the stairs on light feet. He watched her go, and then squared his shoulders and braced himself to face his sister.

*

246

Mathilde was quite right; except that, loved and happy herself, she could have no conception of the depth of fear and loathing with which Frédéric faced the prospect of school.

Nothing in his life before had prepared him for it. His only close companions since early childhood had been his grandmother and, to a lesser extent, Antoinette and the *curé*: three old people who demanded – and received, always and unquestioningly – his respect and obedience in all things. He had of course been aware of Mathilde, but as a remote and privileged creature dancing golden and entrancing through that foreign and forbidden world beyond his grandmother's door, impinging only briefly and bewilderingly in the few moments when their paths crossed. She was not quite real somehow; rather a thing of fable, elusive and untouchable. He felt for her nothing so uncomplicated or so concrete as envy, more a kind of wistful admiring wonder, without comprehension; certainly no sense that she was in any way – in her youth, her parentage, her experience – like himself.

Intelligent, hard working, polite, obedient, reserved, he went in all innocence to school, dressed like a little soldier in the *interne*'s uniform, excited, feeling very grown up, looking forward to the wise teachers, the profound study that was promised him. The teachers were there, certainly, but far removed, like gods, from the extraordinary, noisy, turbulent schoolboy underworld that sucked him in until, by the end of his first day, he felt as if he was drowning in it.

There was nothing in his past to help him as he sat at his desk with the clamour of the other boys around him, appalled at the way they set traps for the teachers and the hated *pions* – the ushers responsible for discipline – plotted practical jokes, jeered at and vied for attention from one another; and tried to prod this peculiar new pupil into some kind of response. There was nothing to help him when he stood alone in the gravelled yard, not knowing how to join in the rough and tumble of play because playing had never been a part of his life. His sole defence, as always, had been the armour plating of reserve inside which he had learned long ago to hide himself; and that, very soon, had only served to turn curiosity to malice. He was a natural victim, and he quickly became one, verbally, physically, in every moment when the supervision of teacher or *pion* was absent; and even sometimes, more subtly, when it was not.

It had been a relief beyond words to come back for Christmas to the safe, grey, regulated world of his grandmother. He had accepted her disappointment at his unexpectedly low marks without excuse. He had no intention of telling her that his only concern at school had been, somehow, to get through each twenty-four-hour space in turn until term ended, and that work of any kind had become an irrelevant luxury. He was quite sure that if he had confided in her she would only have urged him to greater courage; and since he knew he had few reserves of courage left that was not what he needed. So he had tried to put all thought of school out of his mind, until the muted New Year celebrations reminded him how little time he had left and robbed him of sleep and appetite.

As he sat white and silent beside Uncle Auguste on the journey to Bordeaux, fear twisted and turned, a hard tangled knot in his stomach. It would be night when they reached the school, and waiting for him would be the barrack-like dormitory, the hard narrow bed in which he would lie after the lights were extinguished and the *pion* asleep, listening for the scuffles and whispering and smothered laughter that would mean that his torment was about to begin.

He had lived through it all in imagination, over and over, by the time the reality of it was upon him; and he discovered that the pleasant days of relaxation amongst friends and families seemed only to have renewed his tormentors' enthusiasm for their game. This term was going to be every bit as bad as the last.

He began, as before, to count the days. It had helped him to hang on somehow, by thinking, If I can just last until next Sunday. Sundays offered him the only hope of escape, to the cheerless haven of Auguste Silvine's house, where no schoolfellow could follow him.

'Now how about a nice walk?' Uncle Auguste would say to him often, with awkward brightness, once the midday meal was over. 'I generally have a sleep of an afternoon, and I'll be dull company for you. In fact, one Sunday perhaps you'd like to invite a friend along, to keep you amused. Now I suggest you go out and see some of the town while you have the chance.'

But he had no friends; and out in the city streets there would be other boys – *externes*, or other *internes* like himself – enjoying the unaccustomed freedom of a few unsupervised hours. So he did not go out, but spent the long Sunday afternoons seated on a hard chair in the dark but rather magnificent *salon* waiting with dread for the moment when he must return to school. He knew Uncle Auguste found his visits a great trial, and was sometimes tormented by the fear that the old man would suddenly refuse to let him come any more; but so far at least that had not happened.

On Thursday afternoons there was also a weekly holiday; or there was for the *externes* at least. For the *internes* there was a supervised walk, two-by-two through the city streets. Unfortunately, the *pion* attached to Frédéric's class seemed, like everyone else, to have taken a dislike to him and he appeared not to notice the jostling and kicking, the barbed remarks directed at Frédéric as they walked along; just as he noticed nothing during meals or study periods or playtimes, and slept on undisturbed through the dreadful night hours.

After lunch (of which Frédéric as usual ate little) on that first Thursday of term the customary drum beat out to summon the boys for their walk. The *pions*, arms waving, gestured their charges into line. '*Messieurs*, hurry now! Silence over there!'

At the latest possible moment, Frédéric ran to the latrines. It would almost certainly make him late, liable to lines or a detention, but that did not worry him. He quite liked the thought of a detention – quiet, solitary, closely supervised. In any case, it was only at times like this that he could be reasonably sure of finding the latrines unoccupied. He had learned from bitter experience that he was at his most vulnerable in this unsavoury environment, where there was no one to see what was going on.

Unfortunately today he was out of luck. Three of his classmates were leaving the latrines as he reached them. They stopped in their tracks, turned, closed in about him. One snatched his *képi* from his head, tossing it into the smelliest corner, another hooked a leg about his feet, tripping him up.

He slid free from them, darting to retrieve his *képi*; but they had barred the way to the door. He stood where he was, frozen within a cold fog of unreality, shrinking inwardly from what was coming next. He had learned long ago that, small and slight as he was, resistance only made matters worse. His only hope was that it would not take long . . . Surely the *pions* would notice their absence very soon?

And then, so suddenly that he jumped, an arm threw itself about his shoulders. 'Come on then, *mon vieux*! You're walking with me today, remember—'

The voice somewhere behind and above his left ear was jovial and assertive, and carried clearly to the waiting boys. Frédéric could see astonishment on the faces before him, but it was no greater than his own. He looked round, and up, and only grew more bewildered than ever. The voice – and the arm – belonged to Félix Petit, a classmate who had, until now, made no impression at all on his miserable existence, except as a splendid figure as remote as he was magnificent, like a mountain distantly glimpsed.

He had the most inappropriate of surnames, for '*petit*' this son of a country schoolmaster most certainly was not. At thirteen he towered over his fellows, a veritable giant, almost as tall as a man, broad and muscular, his head crowned with a thick mass of curling black hair, his dark eyes flashing fire; voice, gestures, spirit all of a largeness in keeping with his frame. Effortlessly, he dominated the other boys with an unquestioned authority, though he seemed always a little apart from the groups and cliques into which they divided, perhaps because his quick and lively mind made him popular with teachers as well as pupils, a fact that no one would have dared to resent.

The most amazing thing about today's incident was not that, almost at once, Frédéric's tormentors should abruptly and silently have melted away; but that Félix Petit should apparently have decided, for some inexplicable reason, to take Frédéric Brousse under his protection.

Frédéric was allowed no time to contemplate the wonder of it. His arm still about the smaller boy's shoulder, Félix steered him from the latrines, along the passage, out to join the waiting column of boys in the yard. It was a measure of the magical immunity from the common rules of humanity that seemed to set him about that no one said anything to them on the subject of their lateness.

Frédéric's first instinct, once they were out of the latrines, was to shake the arm from his shoulder. He was not used to being touched, least of all with any kind of affection. At home, his grandmother gave, and expected in return, a twice daily peck upon both cheeks; but that was the nearest he had ever come to a caress since his mother went away. Her caresses, lavish, soft, scented, he remembered with distaste, even nausea, associating them always with other things seen and heard and suffered, which he preferred not to bring to mind.

But Félix had just – miraculously – rescued him from a nightmare. At the very least, common politeness demanded that he endure the carelessly flung arm, out of gratitude, without complaint. So he did so, and it remained, sometimes a casual weight across his shoulders, sometimes tightening to clasp him more firmly and give emphasis to something its owner was saying; and Félix, it seemed, never stopped talking.

Slowly, bit by bit, Frédéric began to take in that flow of talk. It was as if they were alone, the other boys, the *pions*, the busy crowded streets, fading away around them. In fact they did fall behind a little, and no one seemed to notice. They walked along the broad quayside, amongst cranes and bustling men, exotic smells and raucous noises, where the ships rocked at anchor on the water, their masts like leafless winter trees pointing to the grey sky.

'*Mon cœur, comme un oiseau, voltigeait tout joyeux
Et planait librement à l'entour des cordages –* '

Félix spread out his free arm in a sweeping gesture towards the ships, his voice softly pouring out the words after it as if he too could send his heart hovering like a bird amongst the rigging. Frédéric laughed, not with amusement, but with excitement.

'What's that?'

'Baudelaire – "Les Fleurs du Mal" – I have it at school: I'll show it to you when we go back – it's wonderful!' His voice fell to a conspiratorial whisper. 'But don't let them catch you reading it!' He recited some more of the poem, and then phrases, verses from others in the same collection, and Frédéric saw what he had meant. This intense sensuous poetry was unlike anything his grandmother had ever read to him from those ancient volumes at Casseuil consecrated by a century at least of respectability; though he did not understand much of it, he knew she would not have approved at all. And he did not care, even exulted in the dangerous sense of a new and imminent freedom.

Tentatively, when Félix paused for long enough, Frédéric ventured a comment; and found to his delight that it was heard with attention and respect. The talk became a conversation, a mutual exchange lit by a sense of recognition, which hovered on the brink of friendship.

Next morning Frédéric woke in the dark to his usual black dread of another day; and then remembered with a flooding sense of relief that there was nothing, now, to fear; and the next moment could not believe it would be so easy. What if he doesn't like me today? What if it was just a mood?

The drum roll drove the boys from their beds at half-past five. He looked across the dormitory to where Félix stretched, a yawning giant, towards the high shadowed ceiling; and felt a nervous quiver of anxiety in his stomach. The next moment the great arms fell abruptly, the mouth snapped shut, and the black eyes reached him, bright and friendly, lit by a sudden grin. Shyly, but with the fervour of relief, Frédéric smiled back.

As they trooped down the stairs he felt that casually affectionate arm drape itself again about his shoulder, and was glad; he was beginning to like the feel of it. He had a strange sensation this morning, almost as if he were floating somewhere above the ugly mundane world of noisy boyhood. He was thankful that Félix seemed content to talk on without a response: he was sure that if forced to speak he would burst into tears, but from joy, not misery. It was as if something long frozen inside him had begun to thaw, forcing its way through the hard protective shell that had formed itself about his heart, allowing a new and unfamiliar warmth to spread

252

through him, bringing with it the capacity to feel, to respond, to love.

ii

There were buds forming already on the grafted vines. Aubin finished repairing the supporting posts and stood looking down at the hopeful signs of new growth. They were fully established now – this year, with care and good weather, they'd fruit well. But what use were half a dozen plants, however healthy? You couldn't make a vineyard out of that. He'd have been as pleased as anyone to see Château de Casseuil wine being made again, but there was no sense in pretending there was any hope of that now, not without the capital to restock with American roots and carry out an extensive grafting operation. Looking after these few plants in a tiny corner of the devastated vineyard was work for a lady gardener, not a *vigneron*.

He shrugged, and made his way up the hill to yoke the oxen to the plough. The brisk February wind had dried the soil enough to think of preparing the ground for the maize; that at least was a sensible activity, with a practical end in view. Monsieur Séguier at Trissac had the right of it, going over to tobacco when he did. Aubin had hoped now and then that he might be offered work at Trissac – Monsieur Séguier was at Casseuil often enough, and could see Aubin's capacities for himself. But though so many peasant families had left the land, the larger farmers too were cutting back, so that vacancies for skilled labourers were few. This was better than nothing of course, better than the city life he had tried and hated, but he knew there was no future in it for him, or anyone else come to that. Unless Madame Laure changed course the château was doomed – though if she were to marry Monsieur Séguier that might be another matter; everyone knew he was after her, and had been for years.

He was there now, taking his leave of Madame Laure in the courtyard, his manner (even viewed from this distance) all doting attentiveness. Aubin thought it odd that so level-headed a man should be so persistent, when he was clearly not wanted. It was not as if Madame Laure had anything to offer: she was pretty, of course, but so was many another; and she had no money, not even the land and the château, since they belonged to Mademoiselle Mathilde by rights. Aubin watched until Monsieur Séguier had mounted and ridden away, and then crossed the yard to the oxen stall.

Catch me chasing a woman who didn't fancy me! he thought to himself. All cats are the same at night – why waste time on one that's unwilling? Though if I were her— He shrugged again. There's no accounting for women, especially fine-bred Paris ones.

He was well into the ploughing when he saw the man again: he had been there yesterday, seated on the bank beyond the road working concentratedly at something. Aubin had decided, after some hours of discreet observation, that he must be a painter; though why anyone should want to paint blighted vineyards and windswept winter fields he could not imagine. When Laure came to find him to discuss the prospects for the sowing, he said as much to her.

'Perhaps he likes painting gloomy scenes,' suggested Laure, narrowing her eyes to try and make out more clearly the small figure on the far bank; though with little success. That he was a painter was clear, for he had a pochade box open on his knees, the lid holding the small canvas upon which he worked, just as Marcel used to do when he painted out of doors.

'Why should anyone want to look at things like that?' Aubin asked uncomprehendingly.

Laure did not feel equal to trying to explain; in fact, it did not make much sense to her either at the moment. She changed the subject. 'I'm going to Bergerac this morning – I'll take that broken harness to be repaired. Is there anything else that needs attention while I'm there?'

'Not that I can think of, *madame*.'

It was a walk of six kilometres to Bergerac, and Laure could not take the trap, with the harness broken and no other means of attaching the pony to the vehicle. But she was fortunate this morning, for the *curé*, passing the end of the drive as she reached it, was himself on his way to town in his own trap and offered her a lift. 'I can't bring you back, I'm afraid,' he said regretfully. 'I'm on my way to Périgueux – the Bishop, you know—'

*

254

Jean-Claude Arnaud completed his painting of the young peasant ploughman – jaunty red scarf at his neck a bright splash of colour against the sombre background – packed his pochade box away in his knapsack, folded his stool and tucked it under his arm, stamped a little to restore the circulation to his limbs, and set off down the hill with the swinging springy step of a man who has no claims on his time and no responsibilities.

The wind had risen and he was tempted simply to return to the warmth – and ample country cuisine – of the inn at Trissac where he was lodging. On the other hand, the air was bright and clear and he had as yet explored very little of this unknown countryside. He might not want to paint again today – sitting so long this morning had chilled him enough already – but he could make a note of any promising scene to which he might wish to return another day.

He paused at a *boulangerie* in the next village and, sniffing with appreciative nostalgia at the familiar smells, bought a small loaf, from which he tore pieces to eat as he walked on towards the distant river.

Laure had some time to wait while the harness was being repaired. She made her few purchases, all absolutely essential, and called by previous appointment on the office of Teyssier et Fils in the old town near the port, where she agreed a price for a crate of '69 Château de Casseuil – that would pay for the sulphur needed for this year's spraying of what was left of the vines, but not for the carbon disulphide needed to inject the soil around the roots. If some other means did not come her way, then she must cease that treatment altogether and almost certainly lose the last of the vines to the phylloxera – but she would not think of that now. She would find a way, somehow.

Afterwards, still with time to fill, she wandered down to the river, trying to ignore the rumbling emptiness of her stomach and the alluring smells from the town's cafés, busy serving lunch to their customers. At home, Nanon would have prepared one of her comforting soups, and it would be a wholly unjustifiable extravagance for her to waste precious money on food here in Bergerac: her stomach must wait.

The little port was quiet, because it was lunch-time, and also because these days there was little remaining of the bustle and activity that had proclaimed its prosperity. She remembered how it had been once, when the wide cobbled wharfs that sloped down to the water would be covered with barrels stacked ready for transporting on the *gabarres* that crowded the river. Wine had not been by any means the only commodity carried from here, but it had been far and away the main one, its importance to the town emphasised by the din of hammering and sawing and banging from the workshops of the *tonneliers* who supplied the local vineyards with vats and barrels. Then, it had seemed as if every other building near the port housed a *tonnelier*; now heartbreakingly many stood empty, the business gone or given over to some other trade. There had been boat builders too, adding their noise to the general clamour, stalls selling wine and grilled fish and meat to the men who loaded and unloaded the boats (though Laure, fighting her hunger, tried not to think of that now); and a constant coming and going at the little hut that housed the navigation office, where every transaction was recorded.

Today, only a few fishermen sat in sad tranquillity waiting for a catch and, further off, a group of washerwomen knelt at the water's edge: a line had been strung up from a lamppost on the wharf, and the muted colours of the garments already flapping there brought a cheerful if not quite festive note to the sombre scene. The women were singing too, but breaking off now and then to toss some remark amongst themselves in the lilting cadence of the local dialect – which now, sometimes, Laure could understand a little. Occasionally a shout of laughter rose in the quiet lunch-time air.

Laure moved slowly across the port and paused to watch the women, aware – surprisingly perhaps – of envy. She did not envy them their work, the hours of drudgery day after day, in burning heat or, as today, in a cold wind that reddened and chapped the hands that rubbed and rolled the clothes against the washboards. No, what she envied was the other intangible yet unmistakable thing that for a long time now had been wholly absent from her life: the companionship, the sense of lives indissolubly linked by shared work and hopes and dreams. She was, all at once, acutely and painfully conscious of her own isolation.

She was not, of course, actually, physically, alone; in fact, in some ways she had a great deal to be thankful for. Mathilde, first and foremost; and Nanon, even Aubin – and then, more uncertainly, there was the *curé* and Henri Séguier. But with none of these people could she talk more than at a very superficial level of the things that mattered most to her, the difficult decisions, the hopes and plans and desperate anxieties, for they were almost all, to some degree, dependent upon her. Even less could she share with them the long buried interests and enthusiasms of her girlhood, which had no place any more in the harsh reality of her present existence.

As for family, apart from Mathilde, Laure felt as if there was no longer anyone left to her. How can you still think of people as 'family' when all you ever know of them is from infrequent letters, which perhaps keep back as much as they tell? More than ever, those distant lives in America had moved on, away from her, in a way that could only emphasise her separation. Some time ago, Marcel's Eileen had given birth to a son, Michael. He would be five now, a little boy chattering away in an American English that very likely she would not be able to understand. Her mother sent loving accounts of him, which made Laure long all the more to see him; but he was not quite real to her, and even Marcel and her mother seemed in some way no longer to have an actual existence, as if they were simply figments of her imagination.

As for her father, he had indeed gone beyond her reach. She had heard of his sudden death last year with stunned grief. She could not even go to his funeral, or do more to console her mother than write the tenderest of letters. And she could never, now, let him know how much she had loved and valued him. Thinking of him often, she had realised how much of him there was in her; but since she could not talk of it to him there was no comfort in that. She tried to remember their last moment together, embracing in tears on the quayside in New York; but even that had been reduced to only the dimmest and most uncertain of memories, whose detail she might even have invented afterwards.

Her head bent, she turned away from the women and

walked on towards the tree-lined riverside path; and did not see the painter seated where, unobserved, he could paint the washerwomen, until she was passing just behind where he sat between the first two trees. Thinking suddenly with pain and love of Marcel, she paused to see what he was doing.

She expected something amateurish, mildly interesting at the most; what she saw was a canvas, vibrating with life and colour, which, bursting on her vision, brought a sense of shock and delight. 'It's wonderful!' she exclaimed. How had he found all that colour in the black figures bent against the smoothly flowing river and the stone bridge beyond? She looked up and saw that indeed it *was* there, if one studied it with other eyes.

He had neither moved nor turned round when she came to stand at his shoulder, nor did he show any sign now that he had heard her. His hand – broad, brown, the fingers short and square-tipped – moved the brush with deft strokes over the canvas, putting the finishing touches to the scene; not before time, for the women were going now.

'I think I saw you this morning at Casseuil,' Laure said after a moment, although she did not particularly wish to intrude on his painting. It was such a joy to watch an artist at work again after all this time, seeing how this touch of ochre or burnt sienna, that sure stroke, could in an instant bring the scene to life. The long forgotten yet familiar smells of paint and linseed oil reached her, richly evocative of long-ago summer days in Paris, of painting by the Seine with Marcel and his friends, her own efforts looked upon with slightly patronising kindness by the professional artists.

Then he looked up at her, and she forgot all about painting, Marcel, the past, the present; everything.

He was young, much younger than she was, little more than twenty perhaps. He was slim, but broad shouldered and muscular beneath the loose creamy smock (was he not cold in this wind?). His hair was dark and thick and curling, untidy because it was too long to be anything else out of doors on a day like this, framing a small lively face that narrowed from wide cheekbones to a neat round chin, deeply cleft. But it was his eyes that she noticed first, and last, and could not turn from. Set beneath heavy dark brows, fringed with long lashes, they were deep blue-grey, wide, with something in them that she felt rather than saw, something that ran through her as if he had touched her, and set her stomach turning as it had done when Philippe first looked at her over his raised glass. Only, even then it had not been quite like this, not with this devastating, overwhelming sensation that swamped her, suffocated her, so that she trembled and could not breathe but simply stood staring at him with parted lips and a mind empty of anything but those smoky, lazy eyes.

Then he smiled. His mouth was wide, supple, the smile full of mischief, charm, heaven knew what else. With those eyes it was almost too much—

'Ah, you are the lady from the château. You were pointed out to me, passing in the *curé*'s carriage. Madame Laure, they said.'

She might be lonely here in the country, but she was never alone; she had learned that long ago. But she gave only a moment to that reflection. What caught her attention more was his voice – warm and expressive yet casual and heavily accented, with an accent no longer familiar.

'You're from Paris, surely?' Her own voice, she thought, sounded at once squeaky and breathless, excited, not quite under control.

'Yes.' He looked surprised. 'How did you know?'

'The accent. I am from Paris myself.'

There was a hint of rueful amusement in his eyes now. 'But not from Belleville I suspect, *madame*.'

The polite tone, ironic but guarded, chilled her, bringing her suddenly to her senses. He had reminded her of the distance between them, shown her what he saw when he looked at her: a respectable widow past her first youth, her hair twisted into a severe knot on her head, her old-fashioned black dress much mended beneath the folds of the shawl, the fine lines beginning to appear beside her eyes and in the once smooth skin of her forehead.

'No,' she said soberly, without further comment.

It's like Aubin all over again, she told herself. Just a matter of imagination and too long without a man. But she knew it was not; for no one, ever, had affected her as this man did, like a sudden blow whose effect she felt still in her weak limbs and fast-beating heart. Some instinct – warning, protecting – told her to take her leave and go; but she made no move to do so. 'Are you on holiday here?'

'Not exactly. I am an artist by profession. I came here in search of new subjects. So I suppose this is work, though I must admit the people at home wouldn't dignify it with the name. However, I intend to return to Paris with a collection of masterpieces that will confound them all and instantly make my fortune.' He cast a swift, and devastating, grin in her direction. 'I am ambitious you see, *madame*. I dream of an exhibition and the acclaim of fashionable society. Unfortunately, fashionable society has always been slow to recognise merit. But it will, this time it will.'

His insouciant arrogance delighted her; there could be nothing offensive in it when it was softened with such charm, and that boyish grin. Boyish because he *is* a boy, she reminded herself, sternly but ineffectually.

'You have a distinctive style, all of your own; perhaps that will make it easier for you to be accepted. Your picture makes me think a little of that group they used to call Impressionists. My father used to admire them very much; but I know they didn't sell very well. Only your style is not quite like theirs – perhaps you'll be more fortunate. Still, I'm very out of touch with things now.'

'Some of the Impressionists have begun to sell – Auguste Renoir, for example. He created quite a stir at the Salon a couple of years ago – though that was with a portrait of course. Things are changing, but it is always slow.' He looked at her with a new interest. 'You know something of painting then?'

She could almost have wished him not to direct those eyes at her, so much did they make her colour rise and quicken her breathing. Yet— 'I used to paint a little for my own amusement,' she said, with some semblance of calmness. 'My father, as I said, was an admirer of modern painting. He was even brave enough to buy several – one wonderful canvas by Claude Monet I remember very well, which he bought just

260

before the war. Above all, my brother had ambitions as a painter and was much influenced by the artists of the Impressionist group. Monet once spoke well of his work.'

She had his full attention now, however disturbing that might be. 'Truly? He must have had merit then. What became of him?' His tone was gentle, in case the answer should be a painful one.

'He went to America and became a businessman.'

The painter commiserated laughingly. 'Ah, it's as I feared – a tragedy!' He began to clean his brushes. 'Do you not come to Paris at all now?'

'No. My parents went to America too, after the war; my father died there last year.' She paused, for it still hurt her to speak of that too recent grief. After a moment, she said, 'I think there would be few Paris friends left now from the old days, especially of my brother's circle – many of them died or went into exile in 1871 I think.'

The glance he directed at her then was unexpectedly sombre. 'Ah, the Commune – yes, that made a difference. Not that I remember much, except the noise of shooting and a great deal of fear and anger, and my uncle dead, and his wife and my cousin, and that we hid in the cellar for days. But I *was* only twelve.'

And I was a woman, almost a mother, when this boy hid from the bloody revenge of the Versailles troops; remember that, never forget it. When he looks at you, he does not need to remind himself that there is a gulf of years between you.

But even with that cautionary admonition niggling at her she still made no move to leave him, but waited as he packed away his materials and talked about his home and his friends; and found that they did after all have one or two acquaintances in common. More than that, he brought into the greyness of her life a sudden glimpse of the Paris she remembered, of artists and cafés and good talk; and laughter. And somehow, in spite of everything, she found herself forgetting her embarrassment and laughing and talking with him, suddenly as much at ease as if she had known him all her life.

Yet as they talked she noticed at the same time with what swift grace he rose to his feet; watched the curve of his body as it unfolded upwards, the movement of muscle beneath the rough smock. He was not tall, not much more so than she was, so that, standing up, their eyes were almost on a level. It was strange that she should feel at once at ease with and disturbed by him, excited by his body, refreshed by a mind that somehow seemed exactly, delightedly in tune with her own.

'Shall we walk on? Were you going this way?' He gestured along the riverside path; and Laure came abruptly back to reality. She realised uncomfortably how much time had in fact passed during what had seemed just a fleeting moment in the painter's company. The harness would have been ready long ago, and there were innumerable tasks awaiting her attention at Casseuil.

'No – no, I must not.' She thought she had never spoken with such reluctance. 'I have something to collect – and then I must go home.'

She felt a little hurt at his cheerful, 'Then *au revoir, madame*. I have enjoyed our meeting.' But even so, he stood in silence for a little while longer, looking at her, before he turned and walked away.

Laure felt as if some new brightness had gone from the day; in spite of the sun and the blue sky and the tossing branches of the trees, everything seemed suddenly more grey, more drab than it had ever been before. She collected the harness and set out for home, across the graceful bridge over the Dordogne, through the suburb of La Madeleine with its grandiose classical church and its many wine merchants' *chais*; and out onto the long straight road that ran across the valley floor towards Casseuil on its heights.

Once, vineyards had bordered the road for almost the whole way. Some still remained, sad looking, the rows like the teeth of an old man, unhealthy and full of gaps. Many were abandoned and overgrown; others, like those at Trissac, had given way to tobacco. She had come this way often, but now somehow it was all much more depressing than it had ever been.

Then, ahead, where a wall bounding a garden gave a little shelter from the wind, she saw a slim dark-haired figure sitting on the bank. Laure took in the cream smock, the knapsack thrown aside. There could be no doubt—

Her steps faltered; she stood still. She could feel her breathing quicken as her colour rose. Some little part of her did not want to meet him again, fearful of the depth of emotion he stirred in her; but it was not that part which, the next moment, drove her feet on again, quicker than before and with a new lightness of step.

He did not raise his head until she had reached him, but he looked so unsurprised to see her that she wondered if he had been watching her all the time.

He grinned. 'We meet again, *madame*. Permit me to walk with you.' She saw that he had been eating; a crust of bread and the remains of a goat's cheese lay on their wrappings on the grass beside him.

'Don't let me interrupt your lunch,' she said quickly. 'Mine will be ready at home – I ought to hurry.'

'You will be very hungry by the time you get there. Why not share what I have?'

It was preposterous that she should even consider accepting such an offer from a stranger. She was a respectable woman, with responsibilities and duties; such behaviour was simply inconceivable.

She sat down beside him on the grass, taking bread and cheese from his hand, smiling at his '*Bon appétit!*' before beginning to eat. Perhaps the simple explanation was that she was so hungry that she would do anything for food.

Afterwards, of course, they walked on together, talking with all the ease of familiarity she had known once with Marcel; only with Marcel there had not been this other dimension, which made her feel rather than see or hear his every word and gesture; each turn of his head, the neat proportions of his body, the clean golden-brown line of his cheek, the swiftly changing curve of his mouth – warm, friendly, ironic, grave, teasing – the glance of those disturbing eyes, the expressive resonance of that voice.

They came to the point where the Trissac road ran off to the right; and he had told her he was making his way back to Trissac. 'There's a cottage I saw yesterday, which I thought I'd like to paint,' he said casually. 'Come and see what you think.'

She went, unhesitatingly, feeling like a girl again, as young and carefree as he was. Did he feel it too, this intense attraction that set every nerve tingling and made her want to skip and dance and sing?

Just before they reached Trissac they followed a track that ran along the edge of a ploughed field to a tumbledown cottage set in the remains of an orchard and garden, weed grown and neglected: La Borie, whose land now belonged to César Chabry. There Jean-Claude came to a halt and studied the scene for a moment in silence, frowning a little. 'I think my memory must have been at fault – it looks less promising today. What do you think?'

'If you want a picture of desolation, you have it there, I suppose. But your painting by the river was so alive, so full of colour. This is dead – I can't think it's your style.'

'On the contrary: I make a speciality of misery.' He grinned, as if to belie his words. 'See.' He knelt on the ground and opened his pochade box and showed her a number of finished canvases.

Yes, she could see that this afternoon's happy scene was quite unlike these paintings. One after another showed the misery of a countryside devastated, decaying, depopulated. Yet it was not utter misery she looked at, but a starkness softened by a struggling life, resistant always to the worst that could happen, crying out perhaps in anger, pain or indignation, but never in despair or hopelessness. 'You have painted what I feel,' she murmured. 'Never to give up, never, whatever happens – that life and hope are always there, if we fight—'

He looked up at her, without smiling now. 'I'm glad you see it. That is what I feel too.' He gathered the paintings together, shut them away and stood up. 'But I can't feel it here today. It won't do, I think.'

'The man who lived here killed himself. His family went away.'

'Perhaps that's it.' He studied her face as, just now, he had studied the cottage. 'They told me your husband did the same.'

'Yes.' She felt cold suddenly, touched by some chill finger from the past, as if the despair she had so fiercely rejected was reaching out to her in warning: I am still here, waiting – one day you will acknowledge me, if I have my way. It cut ruthlessly through the threads of physical attraction and mental excitement that had begun so quickly to bind her to this man; and brought her uncomfortably to her senses – or what she supposed were her senses. 'I must go home,' she said, and began to turn away.

'Wait!' His hand closed imperiously about her arm. She swung round with a question in her eyes, but for a few moments then he said nothing at all; simply stood looking at her. She felt her heart thud harshly beneath the intentness of his gaze, all grave absorption. 'You are beautiful – did you know?' She wondered if he realised that he had dropped all at once into the familiar *tu* instead of the respectful *vous* he had been employing until now; she felt her colour rise. The next moment, respect uppermost again, he said with brisk matter-of-factness, 'I want to draw you before you go – stand there, just as you are: I'll be quick.'

He pulled sketchbook and charcoal from his knapsack and set to work, crouched on the ground. It was the artist in him that spoke like that, she told herself. It was that which gave his eyes their intent and searching quality, so that though they hardly left her face except to move over her slender figure in the dark dress, she responded to them as if they were not those of an artist, but of a lover, touching her whole skin with fire.

He was quick, as he had promised; and very soon he brought her the sketch to see. 'There.'

She saw, drawn with a sure economy of line, an eager woman, still young, vital, poised with glowing eyes against a windswept sky. The look on the face brought the colour once more to her cheeks. 'Oh!'

'You like it? Then take it.'

She was obscurely disappointed that he was so ready to part with it, but accepted the drawing with an appropriate show of gratitude. He had signed it in the corner, and she bent to study the name.

'Jean-Claude Arnaud,' he interpreted for her. 'You have not heard of him yet; but you will, one day.'

She laughed, a little unsteadily. 'If you can flatter a mature woman as gracefully as this you should go far,' she returned, deliberately mocking her own foolishness.

He did not laugh. 'No, *madame*, I do not flatter – ever. I draw only what I see; and what I feel—'

She had again, more strongly than before, that warning sense that she was stepping onto dangerous ground full of hidden crevasses into which she might fall endlessly to some unknown disaster. 'I ought to go. I should have gone long since.'

His eyes met hers with a seriousness that was like a touch of the hand. 'I shall see you again.' It was neither a promise nor a suggestion, but a simple statement of fact. She said no more, did not smile or wave, but turned and walked away, back to Casseuil. Once on the road, beyond his line of vision, she found she was trembling.

What a fool you are! Thirty-three years old, a widow with a daughter near enough to womanhood herself – and you behave like a schoolgirl! Why, a few more years and you'd be old enough to be his mother.

But not quite, whispered a fainter voice in her head, not quite; and the years that divide us are no more than between me and Philippe. Why should it make any difference? But it does, it does! echoed the first voice, in time with the relentless beat of her sensible country boots upon the road.

iii

The bell clanged loudly at the front door. Mathilde, perched on a stool at the kitchen table, dipping her final piece of bread into the remains of her coffee, looked at Nanon; and Nanon, briskly chopping onions, laid down her knife and muttered one of those colourful exclamations in patois whose sound so delighted Mathilde. She liked to display her knowledge of the country language – which was fairly extensive – but Nanon heartily disapproved of the accomplishment. It might make it easier for her to communicate with the child, but young ladies of good birth – in her opinion – should speak only the purest French.

'Who's that ringing at this hour? It's hardly day yet.'

'I expect it's Monsieur Séguier,' Mathilde suggested in a neutral tone, as she watched the last drop of moisture soak satisfyingly into the bread, leaving the inside of the bowl smoothly blue. It was her favourite bowl, this one.

'Not as early as this, I'd say – though maybe you're right.' Nanon rubbed her hands on her apron.

'Shall I go and answer the door for you?' Mathilde did not want to; she did not much care for Monsieur Séguier, though she could not quite have said why. It had something to do with the way he patted and fondled her, and the harsh roughness of his embraces; but then people fussed over her all the time, and mostly she did not mind in the least.

Nanon – dear kind understanding Nanon – seemed to know exactly how she felt. 'You finish your breakfast, *floreta*. I'll go.'

Mathilde sucked slowly at the bread, chewing the crust last of all; and then slid from the stool and took her bowl to the stone sink to wash and dry it and put it away with the other everyday dishes on the dresser – the best things were stored somewhere beneath the dustsheets in the locked dining-room, although bit by bit they were being sold off, whenever there was an unexpected bill or a poor harvest. Mathilde, in the constant company of her mother and Nanon, knew all about bills and poor harvests. They did not tell her everything, of course, but she knew when to be quiet and listen, so as to satisfy her curiosity.

Since Nanon had still not returned and she had nothing else to do, Mathilde set to work on the onions – they would be put in a pot with other vegetables and a piece of meat of some kind to cook slowly throughout the day and be ready for their dinner. Under Nanon's tuition, Mathilde was already quite a competent cook.

The onions were strong and she had to blink the tears from her eyes when Nanon came back, to be able to see her clearly. When she had the large kindly face in focus again, she thought it had an odd expression, as if something had surprised Nanon and she was considering it carefully.

'I've finished the onions,' said Mathilde. 'Was it Monsieur Séguier?'

'No.' Nanon's voice reflected her expression. 'It was some painter – he wants to paint from up here—' She broke off, as if the whole thing was somehow beyond her comprehension, much more complicated than it seemed on the surface; and then said in her usual matter-of-fact tone, 'Your maman says you're to tidy yourself up and go along to the *petit salon*. So hurry now, *floreta*.'

Mathilde washed her hands as best she could in the remains of the washing up water, drying them, as Nanon always did, on her apron, and then ran upstairs. What did her mother mean by 'tidying' herself up? Removing her apron was an obvious first step, and she supposed she ought to brush her hair and perhaps tie a ribbon round it. But what about her dress? She looked down, a little disparagingly, at its much mended sombreness, the lines marking the let-down hem, the sleeves that were a fraction too short. Sometimes – just for a moment – she found herself wishing for pretty clothes, for something light and colourful, with frills and ribbons perhaps, or a silken sash – like the much loved dress, long since worn out, which she had worn for Uncle Marcel's wedding.

She knew it was wrong of her; vanity was a sin, as the *curé* reminded them all very often at the first communion classes she attended each week; and besides it was not fair to Maman, who did the best she could; she had even promised that this summer, for her first communion, she should have a brand new dress as pretty as any worn by the other girls. She looked forward to that, remembering the delicate confections of lace and muslin, white as hoar frost, which the girls had worn at Frédéric's first communion last year. Not of course, that clothes were important – white was for purity and spiritual grace, not prettiness.

Still – she regarded herself in the mirror, without enthusiasm. Dark grey wool was not pretty, however you looked at it; there was also a distinct stain half-way down the skirt, right in front where everyone would see it. And Maman had asked for tidiness at least.

She changed quickly into her best Sunday and festival wear, not very much better, but a more cheerful dark blue, less mended. Unfortunately it was also becoming much too small for her, but there was nothing she could do about that.

In the *petit salon* her mother stood before the empty hearth looking up at Uncle Marcel's painting of the Seine on a winter's day, all frost and soft rosy light. Two things struck Mathilde about her then: the one, that her sombre dress was even more threadbare and unbecoming than her daughter's; the other that it made not the slightest difference, for her hair shone gold as a candle flame and her face even seemed to glow too, from some inner illumination. My mother is beautiful, thought Mathilde, with a kind of wonder.

Laure had been talking about the painting, pointing out some detail to the young man who stood beside her, and who was looking (understandably, Mathilde thought) not at the picture, but at Maman. The next moment he turned his head and saw her, and smiled: he had a lively attractive face, which Mathilde liked at once.

Laure looked round too, and for some reason blushed as she came to lay a hand on Mathilde's shoulder and lead her forward to greet the young man; who must, Mathilde supposed, be the painter Nanon had spoken of.

'This is Monsieur Arnaud from Paris, who is going to paint the view from our house. I was showing him your uncle's picture.' Maman sounded flustered, inclined to talk more than usual. She had been in an odd mood last night too, restless and unpredictably irritable; Mathilde could not quite make it out.

The young man took her hand and held it for a moment, and smiled charmingly. 'Mademoiselle Mathilde – I am enchanted to meet you. Your mother tells me you draw quite well.'

'It never comes quite right, *monsieur*; not as I should like it to.'

'Ah, that is the sign of the true artist – always to seek perfection, knowing you will never find it, yet refusing to give up the search.'

Mathilde smiled politely, since she was not entirely sure what he meant; and then – pressed to do so by her mother – showed him some of her drawings (a little shyly) and was flattered that he did not simply say, 'Very good, *mon enfant*,' and lay them aside, as most adults would have done. Instead he looked at them with great attention and gave her a few kindly hints for improvement, at the same time as he complimented her. It was pleasant to be taken seriously for once.

After that, he took up his belongings from the hall and went out into the soft spring morning, leaving Mathilde to her lessons. She was a little puzzled as to what all the fuss had been about.

That there was something odd going on was clear, however. Maman's mood of last night, her flustered manner, did not leave her even when the painter had gone. She set Mathilde to work at a handwriting exercise, copying out La Fontaine's fable of the fox and grapes. Usually that would have been fun, enlivened with conversation and her mother's encouragement to decorate the page, afterwards, with appropriate little drawings. But this morning Laure seemed remote and abstracted, wrapped up in some thoughts of her own. The restlessness of last night was still with her too, and an inclination to be impatient. Mathilde rarely minded that she had no playmates of her own age, for she loved her mother and enjoyed their close companionship; but today Laure might as well not have been there for all the difference it made. She was relieved when, half-way through the morning, her mother sent her to Nanon in the kitchen, where she knew she would be welcomed to help with the baking.

It took Laure some time to find Jean-Claude. He had not taken up his position near the fountain where she had expected to find him. 'I should be grateful, *madame*, if you would permit me to paint the view of the valley from your garden,' he had said to her with rather daunting formality when she had come to him in the hall at Nanon's summons. Since she had passed a sleepless night wondering if she had imagined the few hints yesterday that he might share her feelings for her, it was not an encouraging beginning.

After that, it had been easier for a little while – no, not just easier, but wonderful, making her feel again that she was once more a young girl in Paris, laughing and talking with friends who shared her interests and enthusiasms. Until, that is, Mathilde's arrival had thrust upon her the realisation that Jean-Claude was as near in age to her daughter as to herself. Up to that point she had been concerned only that nothing should be kept hidden from Mathilde, that there should be no guilty secrets. Now she had another anxiety niggling in her mind.

She found the painter at last at work near the stables, intently transferring that scene of neglect to canvas. 'I might have known the other view was too pretty for you,' she said with a note of asperity, which she regretted at once.

Jean-Claude grinned unconcernedly. 'I didn't think you'd mind if I took your permission to paint with some liberality.'

She stood at his shoulder watching as he worked, without really seeing what he did. His brush had scarcely paused since she came.

'A pretty little creature, your daughter,' he said after a moment or two. The 'little' was reassuring, as was the conversational tone, except that she was in no mood for idle conversation. She felt his nearness as a kind of pain, as if a rigid and impenetrable barrier kept her from reaching out to touch him, as with every instinct she longed to do. She stared at the thick curls of his hair, clustered loosely on his neck, the slight movement of his shoulder muscles as he worked, and then at the supple brown hands. It hurt her to hold back from stroking his hair, to keep herself from putting her arms about him, from reaching out to caress those hands.

To still the ache of it she moved away, round to his side, further off than before. 'I thought you might like some coffee,' she said abruptly, almost roughly. 'Or you can eat with us if you like. We shall be sitting down to lunch soon.'

'Thank you.' He did not even look up.

'Just come to the kitchen if you want anything.'

'Thank you.'

She knew, she had to accept, that for him work came first, before anything else; or was it rather that she was not of sufficient interest to him to tempt him from it? She was angry that she should even be asking herself that question. She had no claim on him after all; he had given her no real reason to suppose that she should. He had not told her, either, that he had come here today to see her. Perhaps he really *had* wanted only to paint.

She forced herself to turn away, walking briskly with her hearing tuned for the moment when he should call her back. It did not come.

*

She was searching for eggs in the various outbuildings beyond the *chai* when he came to her; she did not even know he was there until he spoke just behind her as she emerged into the sunlight. '*Madame . . .*'

She turned so quickly that she almost lost her balance and the basket slipped from her hand. He reached out and caught it and laid it carefully down, and then she felt his hands on her elbows, steadying her. 'I'm sorry if I startled you.'

They stood there, quite still, she breathing fast, her colour high; he very grave, with eyes intent upon her face. Then he raised one hand and ran a finger softly down her cheek, from eye to chin, crooking it gently there to draw her face to his, if she wanted it.

She wanted it, with every part of her she wanted it. His mouth was soft, warm, firm on her lips; and then exploring, eager as she opened hers to him. His hands slid to her throat above the little frill, round beneath her ear, until his fingers ran up through her hair and brought her closer still. She felt her body move, as if by no deliberate choice, against his, her arms close about him, her palms spread against the hardness of his back, feeling it there beneath the smock as she had so longed to do. She felt his other hand run over her shoulder, down, to close about her breast, and wished, achingly, that the heavy thickness of her dress did not part skin from skin, touch from touch.

Her foot moved, suddenly, striking something; there was a clatter on the flat stones near the doorway where they stood. The basket tipped, spilling the eggs; and Jean-Claude looked down and swore.

'Oh!' She moved away from him, but he held her and laughed.

'It's only the eggs – come!' His voice was warm and inviting, and her roused body urged her to return to his arms, to forget everything but that.

Only she remembered – suddenly, for no good reason – Rosaline in Achille's arms, and the look in Frédéric's eyes in those far-off days. Maybe Rosaline had felt for Achille what she felt now for Jean-Claude – it was an unpleasant thought, but salutary. True, Mathilde was older than Frédéric had been then, and quite a different child, her mother's loving companion; but—

'Someone might come,' she whispered. 'We mustn't—'

Still his hands held her, their clasp firm on her arms; but he was frowning now. 'Do you want me to go?'

No! No—!

'Yes,' she lied.

For a moment he hesitated, as if trying to gauge the truth from her expression; and then he nodded, kissed her once, briefly, on the lips, and turned and walked away.

She gathered up the three unbroken eggs and went in for the lunch for which she had no appetite at all, and the happy childish chatter which fell unheard against ears that echoed still with Jean-Claude's voice.

It was no passing mood. It was with her still at the end of that day, and the next, and the three that followed, this thing that the painter had woken in her.

It was more than just desire. That, after all, for the most part in an abstract undirected way, had troubled her often enough since Philippe's death, as was natural in the circumstances. But this was far more even than the embarrassing interlude with Aubin – not only focused, but rooted deep in herself, in some place she had never even guessed existed until now. She wanted Jean-Claude, and she wanted him with a hunger of mind and body so acute that it would not let her rest. It possessed her, obsessed her, filled her every waking moment; and her dreams when, fitfully, rarely, she slept. It gave a languid heaviness to the way she walked, for she was intensely conscious with every move she made of her body in its entirety, as if each nerve and muscle had its root in that new found secret core of her being. It slowed her speech, her reactions, shutting her off in a world apart, where her devouring need of him had become the only reality.

Four interminable days of this inner fire that tormented yet never consumed, and she could bear it no longer.

'I must see you,' she wrote, late at night in her room, her pen moving with the swiftness of the flame that fed her nerves and her muscles, 'I shall go to the ruined cottage at La Borie tomorrow (Thursday) afternoon. Please come. Laure.'

Thursday afternoon, when Mathilde went to the presbytery

for her first communion class, and there was no danger that she would find out where her mother was going, or why—

Laure folded the letter (her hands trembled as she did so), sealed it, addressed it to Jean-Claude at the inn where he had told her he was staying, put on her jacket and a hat with a veil and went out into the village. There she found a lad standing alone and idle round the corner past the church, and paid him to deliver the letter, hoping he would not recognise her; though it was a forlorn hope – the fact that she only knew him slightly by sight meant nothing. But her need for Jean-Claude was too great for caution.

She did not sleep at all that night. She lay turning this way and that in a vain attempt to find relaxation, now and then dozing a little, but always jerked awake very soon by some anguished question. What if he has gone away? What if the letter does not reach him, and he does not come, and I wait and wait? What if it *does*, but he will not come—?

Doubts grew and festered. What would he think of her, offering herself to him so blatantly? Would he not be disgusted and reject all thought of her? He was attracted, a little, that was clear – or he had been five days ago.

But now? She had sent him away – that alone might have turned him against her. And she had been right to do so, to protect her child, to keep herself from doing wrong.

Yet now she had abandoned all shame, all modesty, all morality, and begged him to meet her. I only want to see him again, that's all, she tried to tell herself, but she knew he would not read so innocent a motive into her note.

By the time the angelus rang out from the church tower to wake the village she was swept by shame at last night's impulse, and as she rose and dressed formed a new resolve: I shall not go. He may go to La Borie if he wishes, but I shall not be there. She felt calmer as she went down to breakfast, her decision made.

She took Mathilde to the presbytery herself that afternoon, exchanging some kind of greeting with the *curé* as she did so (it was difficult to concentrate on anything today). Then she turned back along the road towards the château. I shall write some letters this afternoon – a letter to go with the birthday present for Marcel's little Michael. Mathilde had laboriously knitted a pair of gloves for her small cousin, and it was high time they were sent off.

She reached the gate into the wood, put her hand on the latch; and paused.

Behind her the road continued on its way through the market place, between church and café. She was conscious even now of eyes watching her from the café window, full of curiosity. She tried to look like any casual passer-by going for an afternoon walk as she turned away from the gate and continued along the road, to where it forked just past the church; to the right lay the road to the château. Laure went steadily on, past the *mairie* and the new school building – nearly completed, thanks to a government subsidy – and on by way of the windmill down the steep winding road to Trissac. She passed Henri Séguier's low elegant house, walked through the village and a small wood beyond, and then turned left by the edge of the ploughed field.

There was no one there when she reached La Borie. It was very warm this afternoon, one of those still sunny spring days that bring the taste of summer to come, without the oppressiveness of summer heat. In the neglected orchard the buds were already well formed on the fruit trees, the grass showing new green around the gnarled roots. In the nooks and crannies of the crumbling stone wall that enclosed the orchard, small plants were struggling to life.

Laure sat down on a lichened wooden bench; but only for a moment. It was unbearable, sitting still with all her nerves stretched as they were. The only thing she could do was to stand up and walk about the overgrown garden, on the pretext of exploring, knowing she was doing so only because otherwise she would go mad.

It felt as though hours passed like that, in aimless agitated waiting. He won't come, she told herself at first. You shouldn't be here yourself – it was stupid, wrong, foolish.

Then, when a bird flew up suddenly, startled by some unseen threat, or she caught some distant inexplicable sound, she would find herself running to where she could look along the track by the field, half expecting to see a short dark figure coming this way; but there was always no one, just the sunlight gold on the still field and the trees faintly hazed with green.

What am I doing? I have seen him twice, twice only, and I do this – how can I so forget myself? Why did I come? I did not mean to, I had decided I wouldn't. Yet here I am.

After a time she pushed open the door of the cottage – paint peeling, hinges half broken – and went inside. It struck chill there, dark and damp with long neglect. There was no furniture left, except a broken stool, no sign that anyone had lived here, apart from long-dead ashes, a black heap, on the hearth. There were only two rooms, soon explored, with nothing to offer but a bleakness that deepened her own unease; and she made her way back out into the sunlight.

I shall go home, she thought. She rounded the corner of the cottage; and there he was, stepping out from among the cherry trees, so close that he almost collided with her.

They came to a halt at the same moment, without saying anything. She looked at him, and he at her, unsmiling, eyes held together in a single concentrated gaze. She felt as if she were being drawn into his eyes, those deep smoky eyes; imprisoned there, without escape. She wanted to say, 'Hold me – take me – now!' But instead she caught her breath, poised, keeping the explosion at bay.

Who moved first, or how, she did not know, but she felt his hands on her arms, their grasp running through her whole body, burning her, turning her limbs to ashes beneath her.

And then they were together at last, and his mouth had found hers with a hunger like her own and he was drawing her down with him to the grass below the trees. This time, abandoned without the faintest hesitation to the fire that was consuming her, she knew there would be no end but the one she wanted and needed with such an ache of longing.

Afterwards, she understood at last why Philippe had gone to Rosaline to find completion, why what he had known with her had not been enough. The pleasures that marriage had brought her had been just that and no more: pleasures – simple, agreeable, a little shallow, sweet and untroubled as a fine winter's day. This, now – this meeting of two bodies in the patterned sunlight beneath the trees – was fire and tempest, dazzling light and darkness deeper than any night, something fragile and elusive and tender as a new blossom, yet strong and wild and inexorable as the great Atlantic rollers beating on the western shore. It was Paradise, ecstasy; a man and his mate coming home together in peace. It was this she had recognised and sought; and found at last.

CHAPTER
FOURTEEN

i

It was the third Thursday afternoon in a row that Henri
Séguier had been turned away, disappointed, from the château. He had been delighted when Mathilde had begun to
attend her first communion classes, since it seemed to offer a
perfect opportunity for seeing her mother alone. In fact, he
had not often managed to do so, for when Mathilde was
absent Laure took care to find herself some task in the
company of Aubin or Nanon; but there was always the
chance –

And now, suddenly, she had been inexplicably away from
home every time he called. Nanon did not even seem able to
come up with an excuse, claiming she did not know where
Laure was; but Henri thought he detected some consciousness
in her eyes, as if she knew Laure's whereabouts quite well, but
had no intention of telling. 'Madame Naillac is at home,
monsieur,' she had told him, as if that offered some kind of
alternative. In the end, today, he had spent half an hour with
the old woman, in case she knew what her daughter-in-law
was up to; very little escaped her watchful eye. But this time
she seemed unaware even of Laure's absence, so there had
been no consolation for him there.

Riding away from the château, Henri asked himself, 'Is she
deliberately avoiding me?' It had never occurred to him that
any woman might find him unattractive, least of all one he
desired so passionately. But Laure Naillac owed him a great
deal – was it possible that she only continued to receive him at
all because of that debt? If she had not been grateful, would
she long ago have sent him packing? It was not a very
flattering thought. On the other hand, it was good to think
that, if he did not have her affection, he still had some

undeniable power over her. Since they no longer had any opportunity to meet socially, in a conventional sense (she was too poor for that) it did at least make it possible for them to continue to keep in touch.

As for love, and passion, if she showed none for him as yet, then his own feelings more than made up for that. In time, inevitably, he must begin to make some impression on her, and he was prepared (since he had no choice) to wait for the day when he would know that at last he had stirred to life in her the fire that lay hidden beneath the cool surface.

Only, if she was never there, how could he win her? True, she had been at home – weeding amongst the vegetables, with Mathilde's help – when he had called on Monday; but there had been something strange about her mood, something that eluded him more than usual, as if she were present only in the body, while mind and heart and spirit were voyaging elsewhere. Of course, it was her body above all that inflamed and tormented him, so that he longed to clasp it fiercely to him, to press wild kisses on that soft sweet mouth; as he did, often, in his imaginings, finding himself now and then murmuring her name to the plump, tediously acquiescent forms of Lucile or Suzanne – but it was exasperating all the same to have the distinct impression that she no longer heard a word he said to her, or even tried to listen. She always used to be so polite, so attentive.

As he emerged from the courtyard he met Aubin, leading the oxen back after the ploughing was done. On a sudden impulse he drew rein and greeted the young man. 'I am anxious to speak to Madame Laure,' he said, in the manner of one with urgent news to impart. 'Do you know where I might find her?'

Looking at Aubin's face, he felt suddenly hopeful. Quite clearly the young man knew something. But he hesitated a moment before replying and his answer was, initially, disappointing. 'No, *monsieur*,' he said; yet there was a note of uncertainty in his voice.

'You've no idea at all where she goes on Thursday afternoons? What if you need to find her in a hurry?'

Aubin shrugged. 'Then I can't, *monsieur*.' He was about to

return to his interrupted task when he said suddenly, 'Maybe you should look for the painter.'

Henri stared down at his curly head, already bent again over the lumbering beasts. 'Painter? What painter? What do you mean?'

Briefly Aubin glanced up at him before moving away. 'Nothing, *monsieur*; just that.'

It was then, enquiring fairly discreetly amongst his own servants and the country people around Trissac, that Henri learned that a young artist from Paris had spent some weeks in the area, painting local scenes and staying meanwhile at the nearby inn. Furthermore, Henri vaguely remembered passing just such a young man walking home one night along the Bergerac road. He had not paid him much attention, beyond registering that he was a stranger, and very young, not a great deal older than his own son Victor in fact. What on earth could he possibly have to do with Laure Naillac?

His informants told him. She had been seen walking and talking with him by the river in Bergerac; he had spent several hours painting up at the château; she had given young Daniel Vergnolles a whole franc to take a letter to him at his lodgings; and twice, on a recent Thursday, she had been seen inexplicably on the Trissac road, once in the early afternoon going that way, the other time coming back to Casseuil in the dusk. No one put it into words for him, but it was quite clear to Henri that everyone assumed that some kind of liaison had been formed between the two of them.

Fighting a furious jealousy, Henri tried to tell himself that he did not believe a word of it. Laure had always been interested in painting; like the painter himself, she came from Paris: what more natural than that she should go a little out of her way to notice him and talk to him? But when, next day, he rode to Casseuil and found her at home he was struck by the glow that hung about her, recognising it reluctantly – and with fury – for what it was, the look of a woman rapturous with love and satisfied passion. When he thought of all she owed him, all he offered still – that she should go for her pleasure to a penniless boy from Paris! He wanted to take her and shake her and shout at her for the humiliation of it.

If you want a man so much, then I am here! so he would say. How could you do this to me!

'I am not yet ready to think of marrying again,' you said. Poor grieving woman, I thought – and then you do *this*! How *could* you—!

But he knew that to allow her to see his anger unrestrained would only, in the end, defeat his object. He wanted to win her as his bride. Women liked to be mastered, certainly, but Laure Naillac was too proud a woman to submit without a fight. He enjoyed a fight, but if he was not careful, and gave his anger too free a rein, this fight might result in a permanent breach between them, which even her gratitude to him would not be able to heal.

So he suppressed his rage as best he could, and went to tackle her firmly, but with care. Even so, he was too angry to be truly tactful.

'People are talking about you,' he told her bluntly.

She coloured just a little, but continued to look steadily up at him. 'Oh? I cannot think why. What are they saying?'

He was annoyed that the directness of her question put him somehow on the defensive. 'It's that painter who's staying at Trissac. You know—'

'But I don't. Please tell me.'

Part of him wanted to be reassured by the guileless tone, but his common sense told him that this would be naïve in the extreme. Hoping to prod her to some definite admission, which he could then deal with as he saw fit, he said abruptly, 'I am told you have been meeting him.'

'Really? How interesting.'

'Then it's not true?'

'What do you think, *monsieur*?'

She had put him at a clear disadvantage, and he recognised that. He could hardly tell her, unreservedly, exactly what he did think; not if he hoped still to maintain the appearance of friendship between them. But he knew quite well that, admitting nothing, she had equally denied nothing. He had challenged her and she had slipped smoothly from his grasp, leaving him empty handed. The whole situation enraged him.

After that he kept his eyes and ears open. There was

never any final, concrete evidence of what she was doing. She and the painter were never seen together again, and no meeting place was discovered. But Henri knew enough at last to decide that a quiet word with Madame Naillac, when the opportunity arose, might not go amiss. He had not told her of his interest in Laure, but he was sure she knew of it and thought it likely, even, that she approved. He had not wanted to put it to the test until he had won Laure over; but he had no intention of sitting quietly by while she encouraged another man.

ii

The cherry blossom opened week by week to bridal splendour; and then slowly the petals fell soft as confetti from amongst the opening leaves, tenderly green. The tangled branches overhead became as much a part of the brief yet eternal hours Laure spent with Jean-Claude as the touch of his hand upon her body, or the softness of the spring air on her skin when she lay half-undressed in his arms. They would talk or fall silent as the mood took them, make love or simply give themselves up to the tranquil delight of an affinity so complete that it needed neither words nor caresses to sustain it.

There came a day – a Thursday, like all the others – when the fruit was already beginning to form amongst the darkening leaves above their heads and the shade of the orchard brought a welcome relief from the heat of the afternoon; and Laure looked up into the sheltering canopy and murmured, 'Cherry time – "Le Temps des cérises" – do you know the song? Everyone was singing it the summer of the war.'

Softly he sang a snatch of it, the sweet poignancy far removed from the blissful fulfilment they had shared just now. Then he turned his head and nibbled tenderly at her ear, and she laughed; and the next moment grew serious again.

'Mathilde will make her first communion in two weeks.'

'Mm,' he murmured with his lips on her throat. 'Charming – maiden piety. Do you believe in all that? I don't.'

'I know, you told me. And I told you I believed something, but I don't know what. But that's not what I was thinking of. I was thinking that soon we shan't be able to meet like this any more.'

He sat up then, abruptly, looking down at her with eyes darkened and dismayed. 'What are you saying? Why not?'

'Because Mathilde will not have her classes any more,' Laure explained patiently, but with an ache about her heart. Putting it into words made her realise the truth of it as she had not done fully until now. 'She will be at home, and I cannot risk her finding out about us.'

Fiercely he seized her shoulders. 'Why not? Are you ashamed of me then, or of this?'

She reached up and put her arms round his neck to draw him down to kiss her, but he would not come. 'Of course not; how can you ask that? But there are some things it is not good for a child to know. She's too young to understand. She's just been learning all about purity and holiness and truth – what would she think if she knew what we were doing? Can't you imagine?'

'What is impure about this, tell me that? Or wrong, or dishonest? I love you, you love me; we hurt no one, deceive no one. What could be more natural, or more right?'

'Nothing! Nothing.' She clutched at him. 'But she is only ten. What if she knew, and hated me for it?'

'Then it is quite simple. We must marry.'

Laure fell back, flat, limp on the grass. She stared up at him, thinking, Did he really say that? Did I imagine it?

After a time he grinned and said, 'What's wrong? Is it such an outrageous proposition? Surely that could not offend you?'

She laughed a little unsteadily. 'No – no, but – I had never thought—'

'Nor had I, until now. But it is obvious, is it not?'

She raised herself on one elbow and he moved away, doing the same, so that they half lay, looking at one another, no longer smiling. 'It's not obvious at all. You are scarcely twenty-two, far too young to think of marriage.'

'Why? Because I have no money, because I've not made a name for myself yet? I will, and you can share it all with me – or does it offend you to think of marrying a mere boy?'

'Of course not – but I'm more than ten years older than you. Even the youth and beauty I have will not last for ever: they'll be gone long before you grow old.'

'And then you think I will cease to love you?' He drew her

283

to him. 'No, Laure, never – you will always be beautiful and I shall always love you, never think otherwise. It is not your face I love, or your soft skin, not even just your body, but all of you, every part of you to your very soul. That will endure for ever.'

'If you marry me, you will have to take on Mathilde too – another man's child, whom you are too young to have fathered.'

'And you fear I might desire her one day, instead of you? No, *ma mie*, because she's not you, and never could be.'

She wanted so much to be convinced. Until now she had lived only for the present moment, looking ahead no further than the next meeting here at La Borie, afraid to allow herself to think of the future. She had shrunk from that as if from an inevitable pain that she dared not contemplate. Yet here was Jean-Claude offering her not pain or loss or separation, but a future of which she had never dared to dream. Even now she hardly dared to do so. She searched round, urgently, for some other argument to use against him; and found it.

'But what will we live on? You know my circumstances.'

'Then I must work and work and sell my paintings all the sooner, so that you can restore your vines and keep your château in repair and bring your daughter up as you wish. I have painted here as I have nowhere else – you've seen what I've done, you know that's true. What is more, my best work is still to come, and Casseuil will draw it from me, I know that. I shall need to go to Paris sometimes – it's the only way to become known and to sell – but always there will be you to return to, *ma chérie, ma mie, ma vie*—' He began to kiss her, softly, swiftly, his lips moving from eyes, to nose, to mouth and throat, and on over her body. She allowed him to distract her into passion, forgetful for a delicious space of time of anything but the fusion of their bodies.

Afterwards she knew as she lay with closed eyes in his arms that her spirit had already yielded to him, even before he whispered softly into her ear, 'Say yes, *ma vie*.'

'Tomorrow I shall come to the château and together we shall tell Mathilde, and your mother-in-law. Do you think she will devour me, for having the temerity to raise my eyes to Madame Laure?'

'Of course not. She has far too low an opinion of me for that.'

He gave a shout of derisive laughter. 'Oh, so I am just about disreputable enough for you, is that it? I look forward to tomorrow.'

Jean-Claude looked odd in a respectable suit, with a carefully knotted cravat and his hair smoothed into some semblance of tidiness; almost subdued, Laure thought, unlike himself. Feeling a little unexpected droop of the spirits she let him in, closing the door after him on the seductive warmth of the summer morning. No orchard today, no sweet air full of summer fragrance, only the dim coolness of the hall. Today's business was serious.

Then Jean-Claude took her in his arms and kissed her, and she saw the sparkle in his eyes and felt happy again. 'I've said nothing to anyone of course. Mathilde's at her piano practice.' From the shrouded *grand salon* the notes reached them, light and tripping, making the statement superfluous. 'I think we should see Madame Naillac first. I told her you would be coming, though she won't know why.'

The days passed slowly for the old woman whilst Frédéric was at school, which was perhaps why she received them with what was, for her, almost graciousness. She even asked Antoinette to bring coffee, and invited them to be seated. 'My daughter-in-law tells me that you have something you wish to say to me,' she said when the initial courtesies had been exchanged. 'You are a painter, I believe. You would perhaps like me to commission some work from you?'

Laure wondered if the old woman really thought that. Her expression was utterly impassive, giving nothing away, although her eyes as usual had an intent and penetrating look.

Jean-Claude, unperturbed, self-assured, smiled with all his easy youthful charm. 'Nothing would give me greater pleasure, *madame* – except what has brought us to you today – to invite you to share our rejoicing at our forthcoming marriage.'

There was a long silence. Laure had not known quite how Madame Naillac would react to the news. She had not expected pleasure, for that would not have been in character; the old woman was incapable of feeling glad because Laure was happy. What she had not anticipated was what she saw now in her mother-in-law's eyes, the look of appalled and frozen horror underlying a disbelief that was, almost, total.

'I do not understand.' The cold voice indicated not bewilderment but a sense that anyone capable of contemplating such behaviour was somehow beyond her comprehension.

'It is very simple,' said Laure steadily, with regret that any unpleasantness should intrude upon her happiness, and a wish to keep it at bay at all costs. 'We love each other, and we have decided to be married.'

'Love? What sort of talk is that?' Her eyes swept contemptuously over Jean-Claude, and then back to Laure again. 'I could give another name to what has been going on between you – the peasants already do so. I had intended to speak to you about it, and remind you of what you owe to your family name. I had not thought you wholly lacking in shame and a sense of honour.' So she knows, thought Laure; I suppose I should have guessed that she would. 'But this—!' the relentless voice went on. 'To think of marriage—' Her gaze again scoured Jean-Claude. 'What are you, young man? A penniless painter, I know – but your parents, what of them?'

Laure glanced at Jean-Claude and with foreboding saw the sparkle of anger in his eyes and the way he threw up his head before making a crisp reply. 'My father is a baker from Belleville.'

It was only too clear that Madame Naillac – a well-informed woman – knew perfectly well that Belleville was perhaps the most unsavoury and disreputable of the working-class areas of Paris. And whilst she was prepared to meet on friendly terms with people of all classes and backgrounds, her toleration did not extend to making close and irrevocable ties with such people; in particular when they combined dubious origins with a far from respectable profession. Laure could read all that passing over the old woman's face and felt a sense of hopelessness – not for her ultimate happiness of course, but for her over-optimistic desire to share that happiness with everyone and to be at peace with all about her.

The next moment she grew genuinely alarmed for the old woman. The knotted hands had tightened on the arms of the chair, the knuckles white; her face was suffused with colour, her mouth half open, her breathing harsh and rapid. It's her heart, Laure thought. The shock's brought on an attack. She looked about the room, wondering where she might find the drops the doctor had prescribed for just such an emergency.

Then Madame Naillac forced out in a hoarse whisper, 'Go! Leave me, now!'

Jean-Claude rose to his feet and stepped, head angrily high, to the door; but Laure, anxious still, took a step towards her mother-in-law. 'Both of you – go!'

So she followed Jean-Claude, because she could do nothing else; to stay might only make matters worse. She was relieved when, a moment after, she heard the bell ring out, summoning Antoinette.

If Jean-Claude had been aware of Laure's anxiety he did not show it. He slid an arm about her shoulder and grinned ruefully at her. 'It seems I am after all a little too much for her to stomach. Her opinion of you is not quite so low that she could approve a connection with a baker's son from Belleville.'

'Then she will have to accustom herself to the idea – somehow, we must make her.'

'He is a very good baker, my father. Perhaps he should undertake to send her some of the finest examples of his art.' He began to nibble at her ear.

'Jean-Claude, won't you be serious? She could make things very difficult if she chose.'

'Could she? Perhaps; but we will not let it hurt us, *ma très chère* Laure.' As they reached the first floor landing he kissed her caressingly on the mouth, drawing her into his arms; and she allowed herself to be comforted.

Later, when he had gone – postponing the interview with Mathilde for the time being – Antoinette came hobbling down the stairs to summon Laure to Madame Naillac.

This time there was no pretence at courtesy; and since she would not sit down without invitation, Laure stood facing the old woman and thought, So she has not begun to accept the idea of our marriage – or if she has, it is with reluctance.

When Madame Naillac spoke at last it was calmly, without warmth or a trace of the anger she had shown before. 'Laure, what I have to say is simplicity itself. It is to me incomprehensible that any woman of sensitivity who had been loved by my son could wish to marry another man, least of all one so wholly unsuitable – but, if that is indeed your wish, then I shall not prevent you from doing so.'

'No, *madame* – but then I had not supposed you would – or could, if it comes to that.' Her tone was not conciliatory, but then neither was that of her mother-in-law.

The old woman raised a hand in a warning gesture. 'I have not finished. I shall not prevent your marriage; but equally I refuse to continue to live beneath the same roof with you if you choose to do so.'

Laure stared at her in amazement. 'You will leave Casseuil?'

'On the contrary. *You* will leave, should you decide to throw yourself away on that painter.'

'May I remind you that I have as much right to live here as you have – more, perhaps, for it is Mathilde's house, and she is my daughter.'

'And my granddaughter, child and heir of my son. Have you forgotten that?'

Never, thought Laure; though you have, right from the start.

But before she could put the thought into words the old woman went on, 'Marry by all means, go where you will with this man; but you will not remain at Casseuil, and you will go alone. Mathilde remains here, under my guardianship. I will not permit some penniless painter of no doubt dubious morals and no breeding at all to have a hand in her upbringing.'

'You have no choice but to permit it. When I remarry, Mathilde becomes my husband's responsibility. He is a good man. He can be trusted to take care of her. You will have no cause to regret it.'

'I shall have no opportunity to do so.' The dark eyes studied Laure's face without kindliness or warmth. 'I do not think you quite understand,' she resumed with precision, enunciating each word with great care, as if speaking to a particularly slow-witted child. 'If you marry, then I shall take the matter to court. There will be no difficulty in convincing a judge that a penniless painter almost young enough to be your son is no fit guardian for an innocent young girl. My brother is fond of Mathilde – I can be sure of his support. We shall obtain custody of the child and full responsibility for Casseuil. There is no doubt at all that a court would decide in our favour, given the circumstances.'

Laure felt rather than heard the words, like a series of blows battering at her happiness and her pride. She stepped, blindly, towards the nearest chair and sank down on it, trembling violently. 'You couldn't do that to me!' Her voice came in a whisper, between dry lips.

'Why not? It would seem to me the only possible course, the only right one. You have already amply demonstrated the unreliability of your morals. This marriage would simply be the final confirmation of it.'

'But I love him!'

Madame Naillac made a derisive exclamation. 'You talk like some witless female in a novel! Have you no sense of what is fitting? A woman of your age, a widow with a distinguished name, should have more respect for her own dignity. You have responsibilities, or so you claim. If you wish to abandon them for some fleeting and disreputable passion, then do so by all means; but do not in that case expect to be allowed to retain those same responsibilities as if nothing had happened. That is only reasonable, it seems to me.'

'Only reasonable' – and the law, consulted in the person of Maître Perrard, summoned two days later to Casseuil along with Uncle Auguste, agreed, whatever the private feelings, unconsulted, of the two men might have been.

It was, as Madame Naillac had said, simplicity itself. If Laure chose Jean-Claude, she must leave Casseuil and Mathilde to the care of the two old people; if she wished to retain her position as mistress of Casseuil and mother to Mathilde, she must renounce Jean-Claude, completely and for ever.

She went to him at the inn at Trissac, heedless of who might see her go; what did it matter now, after all? She climbed the creaking wooden stair to his dim little room under the roof and sat on the bed beside him and told him everything.

'It is not just our marriage she objects to. She says she will go to court if we continue to meet at all.' Laure swallowed hard, trying to keep back her tears. She had need of all her courage if she was to hold on to some last shred of hope in this wreck of her happiness. 'We shall just have to be patient,' she went on with a bright little smile belied by the misery in her voice. 'One day . . . She might change her mind perhaps, and . . . She is old . . .'

Abruptly, Jean-Claude stood up. 'So we have to wait until she dies, is that it?' He spoke with such bitter harshness that she was shocked. 'How old is she? About seventy perhaps? She could live twenty years more! And two would be too many, can't you see that?' He seized her shoulders so fiercely that she cried out.

'Of course I do! I'm not young like you are – you have a lifetime left.'

'And I want to live every moment of it, not wait around for life to come to me, for some old woman to give me leave to be happy.' He pulled her into his arms, holding her close to him with all the urgency she could hear in his voice. 'No, you must come with me, at once – we'll go to Paris. Leave that tyrannical old woman, show her she has no hold over you any more.' He drew back a little, slid his hands about her face, tilted it so that he could look into it, and kissed her very gently. 'I know what you will suffer,' he murmured. 'I know how hard it will be for you. But when we are in Paris I will help you forget. Trust me, for that is my solemn promise. Never, never will you have cause to wish you had chosen otherwise.'

Momentarily bewildered, she stared at him. 'But – I can't come! If I take Mathilde with me they'll find some way to bring her back. And I can't leave her.' The whispered words were rough with pain.

'You must. I cannot wait. If you are not prepared to leave her, then it's over between us. Over, for ever.'

'Don't you understand – she is all I have?'

'All! What of me? Am I nothing to you then? How can you talk like that?'

She clasped his arm. 'Don't! Don't tear me apart more than you have already. I love you, you know that.'

'Then how can Mathilde be "all" you have? The two things are incompatible, Laure. I must be a part of that "all", or I am nothing.'

She sat very still, gazing at him, while the joy and the

passion and the exhilaration of the past weeks fell away, leaving only two unhappy people in a drab little room staring at one another in bewilderment and anger.

She loved him; yes, of course she loved him, as she had loved no other man in all her life, for why otherwise would she be eaten up by this terrible gnawing pain within her? He had brought her passion and ecstasy and laughter, a kind of new awakening after long sleep. Yet—

Set against everything that Casseuil meant to her, the years of work she had given to it, the burdens she had carried that it might thrive again; set against Mathilde her beloved child, heart of her heart, flesh of her flesh, whom she had cherished and worried over and given all that was hers to give – what was all that Jean-Claude offered, against them? One of them perhaps, with anguish and heart-searching, she might have renounced – but not both, not those two things that had been embedded for ever in her heart long before Jean-Claude came into her life: she could not do it.

She stood up, slowly, her lips pressed tightly together, her hands unconsciously, nervously, smoothing her skirts, tidying her hair. 'You are young. You have all your life ahead of you. One day you will make a name for yourself. There will be other women, much more suitable women. As for me, too much of my life has already passed; there is too much that has a greater claim on me than you could ever have. I cannot leave it all, even for you. Forgive me, if you can.'

She bent and kissed him on the forehead, and then turned and walked away from him, out of the room and down the stairs, without once looking back.

She had spoken calmly, with restraint. Her manner had been wholly controlled, even dignified, her face grave and quiet. She had told him – and believed it as she did so – that he had nothing to offer.

But as she walked back up the hill to Casseuil through the gathering dusk the tears ran unheeded down her cheeks and mingled with the soft summer rain that drenched her through and through, but could not wash away the agony that tore her in pieces endlessly, without respite.

CHAPTER
FIFTEEN

i

'Monsieur Brousse, *monsieur le censeur* wishes to speak to you.'

Frédéric looked round the considerable bulk of Félix, perched massively on the side of the desk and obscuring most of his view of the *pion* who had brought him the message; then he swung his legs over the bench and stood up, bringing his face level with his friend's teasing, derisive countenance.

'Discovered at last,' said Félix, 'it must be expulsion this time!'

Frédéric grinned. 'Not while you're still here, *mon ami* – in your impunity is my safeguard.' He smoothed his hair and pulled his jacket straight. 'I will deal with that last point of yours when I return. So, marshal your arguments or your defeat will be certain.'

Félix aimed a mock blow at Frédéric's head, slid off the creaking desk onto the bench; and sat there with the grin fading from his face as he watched his friend's slight figure follow the *pion* from the room.

Frédéric returned after a brief absence and came quietly to his desk and began to put his books away. His face was pale, with the withdrawn look that Félix knew so well. Since he said nothing, the large boy prompted him, though gently, in an undertone, 'What is it, *mon vieux*?'

'My grandmother – I have to go home.'

Félix reached out and clasped his arm for a moment, the pressure expressing his sympathy. Frédéric raised his eyes in silence; and then nodded, freed himself, closed the desk and abruptly walked away.

Uncle Auguste was waiting outside in the carriage, fussing a little; but he was very old now, like his sister nearly eighty, and easily tired, so that very soon he lapsed into a silence for which Frédéric was heartily thankful. He had no wish either to talk or to listen. He leaned away from the old man and stared out of the window at the fresh spring green of the passing countryside.

He thought, not of his dying grandmother to whose bedside he had been summoned, but of Félix with whom, on many a Sunday afternoon, he had walked through the city suburbs and the country beyond. But not for a long time now, not since . . .

His mind swerved away from that dark gulf, to settle more firmly on Félix himself. It had been several months after their first meeting before he had at last brought himself to ask, 'Why did you help me that day?' It was longer still before he realised that Félix's casual reply, 'Because I felt like it. I always do what I feel like doing' summed up his friend's whole philosophy of life. But that did not mean that his affection for Frédéric was not real, and enduring.

But it did not of course mean, either, that it did not change, as Frédéric had discovered on the day just over a year ago that still cast a shadow over their relationship. Félix – like his friend fifteen by then – had promised a new and mysterious entertainment for their Sundays together. Frédéric, who was entirely happy with the present state of affairs – the long walks, the talking and reading, the retreat (when rain or a sudden storm drove them to it) to some barn or outbuilding where they could spend an uninterrupted hour or two together – had followed him a little reluctantly, fearing some threat to the solitary and exclusive nature of their friendship.

At first he had not realised what kind of place it was to which Félix had brought him. It was a respectable looking house in a back street, with a cheerful curtained room rather crowded with an ill-assorted gathering of scantily clad laughing females, and boys and men of various ages and degrees of respectability, including a few of their fellow pupils. Then, all at once, Félix had disappeared somewhere upstairs with one of the women; and another, round and blonde and scented, with pale breasts curving out of a low frilled bodice and plump hands that pawed and kneaded him, had entwined herself about Frédéric as he sat uncertainly at the table where his friend had abandoned him. It was like his mother all over again, the too-blonde hair, frizzed and curled, the great breasts, the perfume heavy and nauseating in his nostrils –

He had torn himself free and run out into the street and been sick in a corner somewhere.

Later, back at school, Félix had sought him out, grinned at him ruefully, and put an arm about him in a brief gesture of understanding. He had said nothing more about it after that; but he went to the brothel quite often, and though they still spent many hours walking and talking together it had never been quite the same again. Félix had grown away from Frédéric, leaving him with an emptiness from which only the old frozen Frédéric could have protected him – if Félix himself had not driven out the old Frédéric for ever.

Still, they were friends, closer to each other than to anyone else in the world, and the thought of Félix was one which, when they were apart, Frédéric always found consoling. His grandmother, of course, knew nothing of his life at school, beyond being proud of his considerable academic achievements; now, he supposed, she never would. He was unable to decide exactly how he felt, knowing that she was dying. She had always been there, a part of his life, as fixed and unchanging as the rooms in which she lived. He could not imagine an existence without her. Perhaps he did not really believe that she could die.

It was Laure who came out to meet Frédéric as the carriage halted at the château. He had grown a little, she thought, although at seventeen he was not as tall as Mathilde, two years his junior; and he had a fair down on his upper lip – very soon he would be a man. She took him by the shoulders and kissed him lightly on both cheeks, and wondered what he felt. He looked calm enough, exactly as he always did, a slender youth with strange eyes and a remoteness which, though it had lessened a good deal since he went to school, she still found almost impenetrable.

'How is she?' he asked now, correctly. His voice had still not quite settled into the deeper tones of manhood, but was husky, a little rough edged.

'No better, no worse. Doctor Rossillon says she might go at any moment, or she might linger for days. We must be prepared for either eventuality.' One hand on his shoulder, she steered him gently into the house. 'Would you like something to eat before you go up?'

He shook his head. 'No, I'll go to her now, thank you.'

Madame Naillac had suffered a stroke yesterday afternoon, and since then had lain unconscious, her harsh and noisy breathing the only sign of life. The doctor, who had been at Casseuil almost without interruption since the attack, said it was only a matter of time. The *curé* had administered the last rites, so everything was prepared.

She died, without regaining consciousness, at dusk that day, with Frédéric standing beside her holding her hand; just as she would have wished had she known about it, Laure supposed. Mathilde, who had been there too, at a respectable distance, went to Frédéric as soon as the death was confirmed and put her arms about him with what Laure thought was a touchingly maternal gesture.

'I'm sorry, Frédéric,' she murmured tenderly. 'I know how you must have loved her.' For a moment, to Laure's surprise, the boy allowed his head to rest against his sister's shoulder, acknowledging her consolation; then, carefully and politely, he freed himself. It was the only time he showed any mark of grief, if such it was. There were no public tears for Madame Naillac from the grandson she had adored. He left that to Antoinette, and to Nanon, who knew what was proper to the occasion.

The funeral was conducted with appropriate ceremony, paid for from funds left expressly for that purpose by the old woman herself. It was just as well she had shown such foresight, Laure thought, for her own resources would not have been able to provide more than the very simplest of funerals, and that only with difficulty. As it was, the Abbé Lebrun managed to import a small boys' choir from Bergerac to sing the requiem, the church was packed to the door, not only with relations and prominent Catholic acquaintances like César Chabry, but also some like Doctor Rossillon who had never been known to set foot inside the building before; and outside, the entire village seemed to have assembled in the market place to pay its respects – or at least to satisfy its curiosity. The old woman had even left enough money to dress the chief mourners in new black garments for the occasion. Laure thought ruefully that it was ironic that the only new clothes she had acquired since Philippe's death had been mourning clothes, almost as if Fate were trying to force her to keep to that long-ago resolution to dress in widow's weeds for the rest of her life.

After the funeral, Maître Perrard read the will. It was short and simple and very clear: Madame Naillac had died possessed of just over twenty thousand francs; and, apart from a small pension for Antoinette, she left all of it, every franc, every last sou, to Frédéric.

All those years of economising, of scrimping and saving, of desperate anxiety, and all the time the old woman had held in her hands the means to pay for the regeneration of Casseuil, for the restocking of the vineyards – the one thing that Laure for all her courage and determination had lacked; and it had been here all the time, within her reach. Or had it? Would things have been any different if she could have made a friend of Madame Naillac, if she had not fought the old woman? She would never know; and now for ever it was beyond her reach, wasting away in trust for a cold-eyed schoolboy who could have little use for such a fortune.

Frédéric returned to Bordeaux, by his own choice, as soon as all the necessary formalities were over. Laure, fighting her resentment and anger, forced herself to reassure him. 'You know this is still your home, for as long as you wish it to be so.' After all, she told herself, without his grandmother he was powerless any longer to threaten her or Casseuil. By inheriting Madame Naillac's small fortune he had done his worst. She could not like him, but she had no need any longer to fear or mistrust him. She even felt a reluctant twinge of compassion as he thanked her and climbed into the carriage beside his grim-faced uncle. He seems dazed, poor boy, she thought; but then I suppose he has lost the only person who ever really loved him.

She did not herself make any pretence at grieving for the old woman. She showed a proper respect, but that was all. Her chief sensation, hourly growing, flowering, expanding, as cramped limbs spread and move into renewed vitality, was one of freedom.

Free – she was free. Free after all these long years to direct and manage Casseuil as she chose, without interference. Free to welcome whomsoever she pleased, openly, to the house. Free, if she wished (and could gain the approval of Maître Perrard and the near senile Uncle Auguste) to marry again.

Only that last freedom had come too late. Jean-Claude had gone from her life, and there could be no return to that golden spring of five years ago, before their bitter parting. She had not expected to hear from him ever again, and nor had she done so. Her only news of him had been gathered by chance last year from a newspaper thrown casually on a table in the office of Teyssier et Fils, where she was negotiating yet another sale of old Casseuil wine – this time in a desperate attempt to raise the funds to pay for some kind of remedy against the outbreak of mildew that had affected the last few vines. As if they hadn't enough with the phylloxera! The spraying had failed, and her chief recollection of that visit had been of what she saw in the newspaper. The art critic, in a floridly written passage, had described an exhibition recently opened in Paris – a new young artist, most promising – pictures of intoxicating colour and richness, full of emotion. Laure had read it hungrily, twice through, remembering the glowing phrases afterwards with a mixture of pain and triumph. He had been right then: he was making a name for himself. Perhaps he was married by now.

Only for a moment did she consider the possibility of writing to tell him that the only obstacle to their marriage had gone, for she knew that the greatest, the insurmountable obstacle was still there: her rejection of him on that day of summer rain just before Mathilde's first communion. For that, she sensed, he would have felt a bitter and unforgiving anger for many months, until time and other women diverted him from his pain. He had been a boy then; now he was a man, older, matured and changed in ways she could not guess at. No, she had made her choice then; she had known that she must live with it and had done so as the raw anguish faded to a more bearable ache, which she feared now to disturb in case it should flare to new life. Besides, she did not know his address.

No, her freedom was more a matter of feeling than of anything concrete or tangible. What use after all was freedom, when what she really lacked was money? Madame Naillac's death had, temporarily, prevented her from confronting the starkness of her predicament; now it only faced her all the more clearly.

It was two years since any wine, however inferior, had been made at the château. The mildew had taken the last of the old vines; and then, this spring, devastatingly, it had appeared on the cherished plants grafted on to the American roots. Laure might think of herself still as a *vigneron*, and Casseuil as a vineyard, but she knew that was a delusion. They produced a little maize, enough vegetables to allow for a small surplus, and they managed – just – to cover their needs from day to day; but that was all.

She hoped, daily, desperately, for a miracle, something that would make possible the regeneration of the vineyard. But all the time she lived with the dread that some unexpected demand on her resources would bring her to the end and confront her with the final, unavoidable realisation that she must sell the château.

She tried not to think about it, tried only to live – as she had done for so long – from day to day, staving off what she feared would in the end prove to be inevitable. Now she knew the time had come when she could no longer afford to pay anyone to work for her. She had been bracing herself to go and break the news to Aubin when Antoinette had come in distress to tell her of Madame Naillac's attack. Almost with relief, she had put that other matter aside, until a more appropriate moment.

The appropriate moment had come, with the funeral over, Antoinette retired to live with her niece, Frédéric gone and the house settling back into some kind of normal routine. Laure did not allow herself to consider how she would manage everything without Nanon and Aubin. The house perhaps would not be too difficult, now they used so few rooms, and Mathilde was old enough to take a part there. But to manage even with her daughter's help to till the fields, to plough and sow and reap and go to market – that would be another matter. It can't be helped, she told herself. We'll find a way.

In a sudden drenching downpour she crossed the courtyard and found Aubin in the office where once Monsieur Delisle had reigned supreme. He was bent over one of the worn ledgers laboriously recording the poultry and vegetables sold at market yesterday, the money having already gone towards arrears in his pay. He looked round as she came in, straightened, and said at once, '*Madame*, there's something I have to say to you.'

She stood facing him, thinking that he must have decided to take the initiative himself; perhaps, for the sake of his pride, it was just as well.

'I shall be leaving next week, *madame*. I am going to be wed.'

That did surprise her; and at the same time took all the bitterness from the situation. 'Oh, I'm so glad, Aubin! Who is she? Do I know her?' She could not remember ever having seen him with a girl.

He shrugged. 'Maybe – Marie Couderc from Le Petit Colin.' Suddenly expansive, speaking with a mixture of pride and satisfaction, he went on. 'She's a good few years older than me, of course, but not past child bearing – the best way, that; there'll be children, but not too many. She's a good strong sensible woman, and her father's only child, so there'll be a nice bit of land with no other claim on it. He's fit enough to give us a hand about the place still, but old enough to be glad to let someone else run things, so we should have a free hand. And I've managed to put a bit by, enough to make it worth her while to take me on. So it's all worked out for the best.'

Laure studied the handsome face and the strong body, the curly hair, the still-youthful air of confidence and good health. She did know Marie Couderc by sight; a plain, solid, dark woman, already past her first youth and ageing quickly as many peasant women did. Laure suspected that it was not just the 'bit put by' that made Aubin a good proposition from Marie's point of view.

As for Aubin himself, that was clearly another matter. He had said not a word about love or passion, nor had his tone or his manner suggested them; but for all that his clear pride in his forthcoming marriage had nothing defensive about it. He was making a good match, a sensible partnership with advantages on both sides. He would be doing well for himself, on his own terms.

Laure congratulated him and wished him well, and ran back to the house through rain that fell more heavily than ever. By the time she reached the hall she was drenched, too wet to tackle Nanon yet; or perhaps it was rather that she wanted to seize any excuse to put off what must be a far more painful interview. She made her way upstairs to change.

The door leading from her room to Mathilde's stood wide, and she could see her daughter seated at her little writing desk (Laure's once) by the open window, her pen moving busily over the paper spread before her. It was warm in spite of the rain and the air smelt sweet, flowing in to the accompanying rattle of the downpour.

Laure stood in the doorway momentarily forgetful of why she was there, and watched her daughter a little abstractedly, noting with tenderness the graceful way her small golden head was set upon her long neck, the lovely line of her slender body in the inevitable black dress. She wanted so much for this beautiful child of hers: happiness and love, but also pretty clothes; a good education, at school somewhere so she could make friends of her own age; a future untroubled by anxiety; the freedom to marry as she chose.

Mathilde, perhaps becoming aware of some small restless movement of her mother's, turned her head and smiled. 'You're wet, Maman.'

'So I am. I came up to change.' She threw off her gloomy mood and smiled in return. 'What are you writing so busily, *ma mie*?'

'I'm writing to Frédéric.' A frown gathered above her gentle brown eyes. 'You see, he has no one now. I thought it might comfort him to have a letter. I shall tell him he needn't answer if he doesn't feel like it.'

Young as she was, Laure thought ruefully, she knew Frédéric's capacity for rejection and was preparing herself for it. But her daughter's thoughtfulness touched her. She herself would never have been so concerned for Frédéric's feelings, and yet surely Mathilde, passed over by her grandmother in favour of her bastard half-brother, had more reason than most to think ill of him. Laure went, impulsively, and kissed her; and Mathilde laughed and caught her hand and held it and exclaimed, 'Ugh, you're soaked to the bone, Maman – go and change or you'll catch a cold.' But even then it was a little while before she would let her mother go.

Laure changed, gathered up the wet clothes to take them to the kitchen to be dried before the fire and had her hand on the door when something half-heard caught her attention, and she stood still to listen. The rain swished down outside the window, Mathilde's pen scratched over the paper; and somewhere overhead, insistently, rhythmically, something dripped. She listened a little longer, gazing up at the ceiling, and then laid down the clothes and went to investigate.

The top floor of the château had lain undisturbed for years now, the succession of attic rooms – once used by servants – emptied long ago of most of their furniture. It was only too easy to find the source of the noise: here and there, in this room and that, the rain dripped or poured through ceilings cracked and scarred and stained with damp and mould. In one room a great pool of water trickled through the floor into the room beneath, the one above Mathilde's. Everywhere, the air smelt of decay.

In the end, desperately fighting a growing panic, Laure summoned Aubin and together they squeezed through a trap door into the loft space right under the roof. There, her worst fears were emphatically confirmed. Even to the inexpert eyes of herself and Aubin it was clear that the entire roof was in a terrible, perhaps even a dangerous state of repair.

There is to be no miracle then, she thought, with a dull sense of despair. Only this, the last blow, the end of everything. Even the smallest respite for which she might have hoped had been taken from her. She looked round and caught Aubin watching her, with something in his expression that said, 'I got out just in time.'

As they came downstairs again Nanon met them with the news that Monsieur Séguier was waiting below.

'Oh not now!' Laure murmured aloud. 'Tell him I—' and then she paused.

She thought of Aubin's marriage, entered upon so coolly, so practically, as a sensible business proposition. It was the way most peasant marriages were arranged; and very many others too. Her own marriage to Philippe, founded on mutual attraction, had been, almost, something out of the ordinary, although even that could not have taken place had it not also been a good match from a worldly point of view. And here she was now facing destitution and the ruin of all her hopes; whilst the wealthy man who – infatuated – had pursued her for years waited downstairs.

'Tell him I shall be with him very soon,' she said steadily; and then she went to her room to dress with the greatest possible care.

ii

Laure reached to the back of the cupboard in the office and took out the rolled-up charts that had been hidden away there. Once, the latest of them would have been hung on the office wall, providing an up-to-date record of every single vine in the vineyard; but in the end Jean Delisle had found himself unable to go on recording the steady deterioration of the enterprise to which he had given so much of his life, and the charts had been put away well out of sight.

Laure had not wasted these three weeks before her wedding in making preparations for that event – or no more than were absolutely essential. Most of the time she gave to paying the bills (few enough, since she had lately been in no position to risk getting into serious debt); giving orders for extensive repairs to the château (to begin on her wedding day, when she and Mathilde would move temporarily to Trissac); interviewing labourers for the estate and making arrangements for them to begin work next month, to prepare the land for the new vines; visiting, with eager interest, one after another of the nurseries that had sprung up recently along the river on the fringes of Bergerac, ready to supply the local vineyards with healthy rootstock, for grafting or replanting; and cleaning, sorting and tidying all the records and other documents and equipment in the study, and in the office and workrooms of the *chai*.

Now at last the moment had come to make the firm plans for the future of the vineyard which she had feared would remain for ever just a dream. Smiling to herself, she unrolled the charts and spread them one on top of another on the desk and studied them with careful attention.

Each one, identical in outline, showed the twenty hectares of the château's land, divided into odd-shaped parcels, some with ancient names, others labelled according to a distinguishing feature – the *caveau* plot, for example. Reaching from the edge of the wood on the south-east side of the château, the land ran in a great sweep down the hillside to the valley floor, where the pool and a wood beyond it marked the northern boundary. From there, the road from Bergerac curved its way up the hill, watched over by the *caveau* and marking the western boundary of the vineyard until it reached its limit close to the village church.

Jean Delisle had been meticulous in his records. From the charts one could see how the different grape varieties had been arranged – the majority Sémillon, but every fifth one a Sauvignon Blanc, about one in twenty a Muscadelle. Beside each plot he had recorded the year of planting and the dates each year on which the first grapes of each variety had been harvested. The vines in the *caveau* plot always flowered and ripened first, Laure noted, and were always first to show signs of *pourriture noble*; the shady plot below the garden was generally the last to be ready; the field by the pool, where the land levelled on to the plain, was most often affected by frosts and produced abundant fruit that only in the best years was affected by the *pourriture noble* – down in that fertile spot the vines had no need to struggle, and a soft-living vine produced characterless fruit, as she knew.

Laure made notes as she studied the charts; and then took a large sheet of paper brought with her from the house and carefully copied onto it the outline of the land; and then she sat back and looked at it.

Land, empty of everything but weeds and dereliction, poisoned with disease, uncared for; yet with the potential still to nurture the very greatest wine, as great as any of those still stored in the bottles in the deepest recesses of the *chai*. Or was it? What kind of wine would they produce, these strange new plants with their alien roots? Would the fruit of the Sémillon and the Sauvignon Blanc and the Muscadelle retain their own distinctive, inimitable qualities, grafted onto a rootstock from

303

a vine whose own grapes made so strange a wine? She did not know; very probably no one knew for certain. Yet all over France *vignerons* were taking this step into the unknown, because it was the only way forward, staking all they had on the gamble that the grafted vines would serve them as well as the old ones had done. It was at once terrifying and immensely exciting; for Laure as much as anyone, since she had now none of the old vines left to which to turn. For her, this was in every sense a new step.

She studied her notes. Twenty hectares . . . She must leave room for new planting as the years went by, so that when at last the first vines grew too old there would be something to take their place (if she might not live to see it, she must still plan as if she would). Suppose then that she were to replant ten hectares to begin with, at a density of about 10,000 vines per hectare, the three varieties in the traditional proportions . . .

She made her calculations, pausing now and then to check some point against Jean Delisle's notes, trying to ask herself what he would have done in her place.

Certainly he would have restocked the *caveau* plot, at once, without hesitation. The field by the pool was another matter. If it had not already been planted when he came to Casseuil, would Jean Delisle have taken the decision to plant it at all? Laure doubted it. Much better to grass it and leave it as pasture, to provide grazing for the oxen and perhaps for some other animals, whose dung would be a useful source of nourishment for the vines; the only other grazing land they had was a small field near the Foussacs' house, too high and stony to provide good quality animal feed – in time, that might even prove to be good land for vines. But there was no hurry; all she had to decide now was where to plant the first vines, and that was an easy enough decision to make, given Jean Delisle's charts.

She pencilled in her suggestions on her new chart, and with each mark she felt her happiness grow.

iii

The news that Laure Naillac was to marry Henri Séguier reached the village on a Sunday morning, when it was assured of the swiftest possible publicity; and it caused a sensation.

'So it paid him to be stubborn after all,' Jean Lambert commented, as he sat at his customary table in the café amongst a congenial group of friends and relatives. 'He's got her in the end.'

Robert Martin, who had just brought drinks to the table, pulled up a chair and sat down. 'That's all he *has* got. As I see it, she gets everything else out of this bargain. Beats me why she didn't snap him up years ago.'

'She's a strange woman,' Aubin said. 'Not like the others.'

'What will they do with the château, do you know?' Robert Martin asked. 'Plant with tobacco?'

'Not on the hillside there, I'd say.' Jean Lambert shook his head. 'Not the best crop for that position. Fruit trees, perhaps—'

'She's replanting with vines.'

Every head turned in Aubin's direction, the eyes full of astonished enquiry.

'But how can she do that?' Robert Martin demanded. 'They'll only die, like all the rest. The ground must be crawling with the poisonous little creatures.'

'The phylloxera louse doesn't work quite like that.' There was a note of superiority in Aubin's tone. He glanced, half-smiling, towards his father, who stared at him for a moment and then asked wonderingly,

'Those American vines you were on about – is that it then?'

Aubin nodded. 'That's right. They've tried them in some places, so she said. Used as grafting stock, that is – they don't give good grapes by themselves. But the grape varieties will be the same, except for the roots.'

'And does it work – where they've tried it, I mean?' Robert Martin was clearly fascinated by the whole idea.

Aubin shrugged. 'No one knows for sure. They've not had long enough yet.'

'Rather her than me then!' said Jean Lambert with feeling. 'What a risk to take! She might lose everything.'

'Not her,' his son reminded him: 'Monsieur Séguier. Madame Laure knows *exactly* what she's doing. She won't lose a thing.'

Robert Martin smiled with reluctant admiration. '*What* a

305

woman! You have to hand it to her – she knows how to get what she wants.'

'Maybe,' said Aubin soberly. 'But what she really wants is a good Château de Casseuil again – and she may not get that, not ever. *That*'s the risk she's taking. If she doesn't get that, I suppose it may not seem such a good bargain after all.'

Aubin's sister – Madame Martin – came to extricate her husband from the company and overheard the last remark. 'She's getting a fine figure of a man, and a fortune; that can't be bad. And we'll have a grand big wedding to look forward to – a bit of feasting and drinking and some dancing maybe. It's time we had a bit of fun.' She prodded Robert Martin in the back. 'As for you, *mon bonhomme*, have you got nothing better to do than sit there gossiping like an old woman? I'm rushed off my feet, I can tell you.'

The people of Trissac and Casseuil, who – like Madame Martin – would have welcomed some kind of wholehearted festivity to brighten their increasingly cheerless lives, were to be sadly disappointed. The eagerly anticipated wedding took place very quietly and hurriedly and proved to be a thoroughly dry and legalistic affair. The family lawyers of the two households were seen arriving at Trissac for the signing of the marriage contract on the eve of the wedding – it was known that Madame Laure had been very careful to safeguard her daughter's inheritance and had inveigled a fine sum of money out of her bridegroom to spend on the château, over which she was to retain control.

No one expected that legal occasion to be public and festive, of course. But the civil marriage at the *mairie* next morning was equally uncelebratory: the men – the two lawyers, Victor Séguier, old Auguste Silvine and Monsieur Séguier himself, all dressed in dark suits; the women – Nanon Foussac, Mademoiselle Mathilde, Madame Laure, scarcely more cheerfully clad, being technically still in mourning for the old woman. The only bright splash of colour came from *monsieur le maire*'s tricolour sash, and a little posy of spring flowers carried by the bride.

Then, later, at the church, there was no singing, no attempt to decorate the building, only the simplest of ceremonies; and if Monsieur Séguier had the most satisfied of expressions, his bride looked solemn and Mademoiselle Mathilde positively miserable. Even the Abbé Lebrun looked as if it gave him no pleasure to officiate at the wedding. And no one but immediate friends and relations were invited to the celebrations at Trissac afterwards. It was all a very poor affair.

For Laure it was not a celebration at all, or not in any sense in which she understood the word. It was, simply, the other side of the bargain struck on the wet day in May when she had steered Henri towards proposing to her again and had then promptly accepted him. His part of the bargain had been to provide her with everything she needed for the future of herself, the vineyard and Mathilde; her part, now, was to remember that she had entered freely into this marriage and that she owed it to him to make him as happy as it lay in her power to do. She had what she wanted; Henri must feel that in return he had gained his heart's desire.

So she stood at his side in her high necked, much buttoned dress of lavender grey silk and talked animatedly, the picture (she hoped) of the happy bride, and tried not to mind that his hand constantly squeezed and fondled her waist and that his breath smelt, unappealingly, of stale tobacco and brandy; and wished that she could somehow forget the look on Mathilde's face when quietly, with a matter-of-fact simplicity that had in it a warning to make no comment, no objection, she had told her daughter of her forthcoming marriage. She had not until then realised how intensely Mathilde disliked Henri; but she knew now, although she had not discussed her motives for the marriage, nor permitted any discussion of it. Only she had not been able to forget that look, not for a moment.

She hoped it was her imagination that it was still there now, behind the brittle smile on the girl's face as she talked to Victor Séguier, who was large and foul mouthed and boorish as his father at his very worst was not. Four years older than Frédéric – who had not been invited to the wedding – he had spent a few unproductive years at the *lycée* at Bordeaux, until his father had removed him lest he gain any unhelpful intellectual ideas that might interfere with his inherited skills as a businessman. Laure doubted if he had ever been in any danger, for his schooling had given him not the remotest trace of polish. Now she was struck forcibly by the contrast between the two young people: her daughter, brought up in poverty and solitude with none of the benefits of education; her new stepson, born to wealth and comfort and every advantage that money could buy – yet it was Mathilde who was cultivated, intelligent, tactful, sweet natured, accomplished.

'A fine couple in the making, don't you think?' Henri's voice broke in suddenly on her thoughts and brought her, starkly, to a new realisation.

Laure had thought she was aware of all the possibilities, understanding Henri's passion for her, which had swept him – the most apparently calculating of men – into what was, for him, a marriage of the heart. But perhaps after all calculation had not been entirely absent from it. Perhaps he saw this union of their parents as a means to bring the children together. They had not been able to meet socially, because poverty had kept Mathilde and her mother almost wholly isolated, and Mathilde was too well protected for chance meetings to be a probability. But now they would be forced into an acquaintance of a most intimate kind. In time, one day, if Henri had his way, it might be more than that. A marriage between unrelated stepchildren might be unusual, but legally it was not an impossibility. Laure saw the prospect with Henri's eyes: he knew that for her to bear him a child was, at the most, a near-impossibility. She had conceived Mathilde only with the greatest difficulty, and she was now nearly thirty-eight. In any case, they neither of them wanted more children. For both of them, their hopes for the future must rest on Victor and Mathilde, the heirs of Trissac and Casseuil. Only, for Henri those hopes had clearly taken on a very concrete shape, which Laure saw only now: the two great estates of Trissac and Casseuil joined by marriage to form the most impressive property for miles around; the long traditions of Casseuil, the thrusting modernity of Trissac making a formidable unity. Laure looked at Henri, his complacent smile, his eyes resting on his son's large figure; and then her gaze moved to Mathilde's sweet smiling face and the hands clasped nervously before her. No! she thought. No

– as long as I live that *cannot* be! But today was Henri's day, and so she said nothing.

And then the feasting was done, the guests had gone, and it was time for bed; and Laure had a new prospect to face, the one which she had tried not to think of until the moment came when she had no choice but to confront it.

She had never in all her life gone to bed with a man for whom she felt neither love nor attraction, nor even a fleeting affection. It had never occurred to her to do so – that was something for women like Rosaline, who used their bodies for their own material ends. Except that even Rosaline had felt something for the men she had slept with; she was not simply a common prostitute.

It was only when she had walked before Henri into the bedroom, hearing him close and lock the door behind him, that Laure realised what she had done, what she was about to do. She was about to give herself to a man for whom she felt neither desire nor respect, to provide food for her family, a roof over their heads, a future: it was the last resort of every poor and desperate woman throughout the centuries. And she was no different in any way from them. She would even pretend to enjoyment, to please the man who had bought her.

Her hands were trembling as she undressed, and Henri saw it and laughed, coming from behind to slide his hands under her bodice and fondle her breasts a little roughly, as he did everything. She forced herself to stay where she was, and even rested her head against his chest, as if with pleasure.

'Timid as a virgin, *ma petite poule*? Come now, I'll show you how a man takes a virgin.' His hands moved outwards, tearing at the fabric and the lacing; and then he swung her round, lifted her off her feet and carried her to the bed and flung her down there. He was on her almost at once, a great heavy-breathing weight, all heaving flesh and hard hands that crawled all over her, tearing and kneading without gentleness.

It was worse than anything she would have thought possible. He did things to her that she had not dreamed anyone could do, would even want to do. In passion perhaps, tenderly, between two people swept by mutual desire, then it might, just might, have been different – but not like this, as if she were some kind of inanimate creature laid out for his gratification, to be mauled, invaded, used.

When he had finished – and that was not for a very long time, hours even – she lay on her back in the dark, aching and bruised and numb, and utterly sickened. She felt soiled, violated.

Beside her Henri had turned away and was already sleeping with deep contentment in the ruined bed, sheets and blankets in a tangled disorderly heap around him. Had it been like this for his first wife, poor dead Aurore, night after night of loveless passion, without tenderness? Perhaps Aurore had loved him, and not minded. But perhaps on the other hand she understood now why Aurore had always had such a look of cowed misery about her. Shall I look like that in a year or two? Laure wondered now.

She crawled from the bed and went to the dressing-room and pulled off the last torn remnants of her pretty bridal undergarments and washed herself, ruthlessly, all over, splashing and rubbing and rinsing, trying to rid herself of the taint of Henri's assault. All the time through her head ran words swift with anguished panic, 'What have I done – oh, what have I done?'

She knew, of course; and she knew she had no choice but to endure. 'As you make your bed, so must you lie on it,' they said. How very true, she thought bitterly.

CHAPTER
SIXTEEN

i

The evening angelus rang out, its sound muffled a little by the mist that clung damp and cold to the hillside and wreathed itself about every turret, every outbuilding of the château. The men walked briskly towards the glowing rectangle where the lamplight spilled from the open door of the office into the yard. There would be a fire in there today, for Madame Laure had been working at her desk since morning, finalising the year's accounts before the celebrations for Christmas and the New Year interrupted the business of the vineyard.

The men came, dark figures in the dusk, and gathered in the doorway, forming an untidy huddle before the table where Madame Laure was already looking up, smiling, and reaching for the ledger and the first of the little piles of cash counted out in a row in front of her.

'Moïse Delmas.' The man detached himself from the others and put out his hand to take his week's wage; not a vast sum, but enough to make it possible for him to go on living in his home village, at a time when so many had gone to the towns in search of work. He looked down at the coins in his palm, counting quickly – one franc fifty a day, six days – but lying there were fourteen one franc coins. He looked up again, startled.

'A little extra, as a gift for the new baby,' Madame Laure explained quietly. Moïse, whose second daughter had been born just yesterday, coloured, murmured his thanks, grinned as his workmates gave him appreciative thumps on the shoulders; and joined in the joking and laughter that all at once brought a festive holiday atmosphere to the bare, tidy little room.

He stood to one side and watched as Madame Laure called the men in turn to the table. His expression was wholly appreciative, not simply because of today's gift, but because she was such a pleasure to watch. Elegant in a closely buttoned grey silk jacket over a beautifully draped skirt, she bent her golden head five times over the ledger, five times raised it to turn those bright dark eyes on the man stepping towards her, five times reached out a hand – exquisitely framed in a little lace ruffle – with the coins held in her palm, five times took the pen to make a note, swiftly and neatly, of each man's name and the amount of his pay. When she had married Henri Séguier, everyone had approved. Now, they had all said, the château would not only have money spent upon it, but a firm hand in control at last. And so it had, both firm and undeniably competent; only to everyone's surprise the controlling hand had remained her own, that pretty little hand with its carefully trimmed nails and the faint scar just visible on the slender wrist, the sole reminder now of the hard days of the past. Even Moïse, who had known her in the old days, found it hard to remember how they had all scorned her Paris-bred ignorance and frivolity; or even how doubtful they had all been, two years ago, at the prospect of working for a woman – a woman, moreover, who was intending to bring a wholly new process into one of France's greatest vineyards. She had no choice, of course, if she was to have any hope that the vineyard might be great again. The old vines were all dead and one couldn't make a great wine – or any kind of wine – without vines. But she had taken a risk, and one that had still not shown its worth, though the vines looked healthy enough and already provided work for almost as many men as in the old days. Somehow they had all ceased to question what she was doing and saw in her now only the efficient mistress of a thriving enterprise.

When the last man had been paid, Laure asked them all to wait, unlocked the little corner cupboard and took out a bottle of brandy, which she set beside a row of glasses on the nearby window sill. Moïse Delmas, and others of the older men who remembered the days of Monsieur Delisle, grinned and moved expectantly forward: so he had always celebrated a special occasion or a forthcoming holiday. The men took the glasses she poured for them, drank to Christmas and the New Year – 1889 – and to Madame Laure herself.

'We'll meet again on January the seventh,' she reminded them. 'Good-night until then.' They nodded and smiled and called their last greetings, and trooped away, glowing and cheerful, into the night.

Laure tidied away bottle, glasses and ledgers, locked drawers and cupboards, lit a lantern and extinguished the lamp, and made her way back to the house. Tonight it was too dark and cold to tempt her to make a last tour of the fields, as she often did. She never tired of walking between the rows of young vines, noting their progress, willing them to grow and flourish. And they *were* growing and flourishing; even now in the dead of winter she was able to see the life in them, asleep, waiting for warmth and spring. There had been a tiny harvest this year; perhaps next year they might even make a little wine. But it would be years yet before they could begin to hope for anything more than the most ordinary vintage. Patience – patience to wait – that was all it needed. But Laure was not patient. She seethed with longing for these early years to be over, the plants matured, ready to give of their best – and for that best to be what she had dreamed of, like the best of the old days.

Warmth wrapped her round as she stepped into the house and Marius, the *valet de chambre*, came to take the lantern from her. Even here in the hall there was a fire today, as there had been only on the most festive occasions in the old days. In two years she had not quite grown used to the change that had come about: never to be cold, or hungry, or troubled by worn clothes and the constrictions of poverty. Still, coming in like this, she would be struck by the shining polished floors, the new gilded decoration of the beams of the *grand salon*, the rich curtains at the windows, the furniture restored and cleaned to its former beauty, the signs everywhere of wealth and luxury and comfort. Undeniably, it was good to be dressed with style and elegance, as she chose to dress; to eat well; to visit and be visited by friends and neighbours; to have leisure, if she wished, to read or paint or play the piano. It was especially good to think of the vineyard coming to life out there in the night; and to look at Mathilde as she came now to greet her mother in the hall, to note the poise and grace that two years of schooling had given her, the becoming blue of her demure but beautifully cut velvet dress, the look of health and happiness that clung about her.

'Is Monsieur Séguier back yet?'

'No, not yet.'

A simple question, simply answered; yet Laure felt relief pour over her, and thought, A little more time, a few hours perhaps.

As soon as the repairs and refurbishment of Casseuil had been completed, Laure and Henri and Mathilde had come to live here, leaving Victor alone at Trissac; but Henri had no claim on Casseuil and was still master of Trissac, and so he continued to spend almost every day with his son, concerned with the business of his own estate. Always though, always without fail, he would return to Casseuil at night, no matter how long he was delayed at Trissac; always, without fail, he would come back to his wife, and the bedroom they shared upstairs, at the other side of the house from Mathilde's little suite of rooms. That, Laure knew, was the price she paid for everything, for comfort and luxury, for the schooling Mathilde had so enjoyed, for the rebirth of the vineyard. Now, after more than two years, she found herself asking often if the price had been too high; and she could not find an answer.

Tonight the respite was brief. She had scarcely had time to change and join Mathilde in the *grand salon*, to wait until dinner should be ready, before he was there, coming in all smiles, full of Christmas good humour and self-satisfaction. He kissed them both, rang to demand that dinner be served at once, and regaled them with some story of an ill-fated courtship at Trissac, which they heard with restrained politeness. Does he never notice how unenthusiastically we listen to him? Laure wondered.

Yet on the surface he was kind in his way, generous even. He loved to give lavish presents: a new dress, a piece of jewellery, some unexpected treat. He did not seem to resent Laure's independence at Casseuil, although she steadfastly ignored his advice; nor did he appear to mind that she was well on the way to succeeding in spite of it. If it were not for the nights . . .

After dinner, Laure lingered as long as she could downstairs, knowing that Henri was impatient to go to bed. She only went up early if he was out late, or for some reason needed to stay up longer. In the end there was no more putting it off: Mathilde had long since gone upstairs, the fire was low, Henri yawning broadly – perhaps he would sleep tonight.

'High time that girl was married,' Henri commented as they passed the closed door of Mathilde's little sitting-room – once Laure's blissfully solitary bedroom – from which her bedroom led.

'She's only seventeen. There's no hurry.'

'Nonsense, much better to wed young. You were yourself, remember.' His hand was already making its way round her back to her breast, though she tried to hurry on ahead of him. 'What's more, it's high time Victor had a wife – he's twenty-four now, needs to settle down.' A little pause, carefully calculated for effect, though she knew what was coming. 'You know he has his eye on Mathilde. He was talking to me about it today. They'd be well-matched, don't you think?'

They had reached their room, and a sense of weary stoicism settled over Laure's spirits. 'If they were both in agreement about it, certainly,' she said diplomatically. 'Mathilde must be free to make her own choice.'

Now they were inside, with the door closed behind them.

'A fine young man like Victor – of course she'll want him. As for my boy—' He began to tear at her clothes, ignoring her protests, excitement giving a new eagerness to his grasping hands. 'Lucky young dog, to have the deflowering of a sweet, untouched little virgin like your girl.' The thought brought him swiftly to the peak of desire, and he threw Laure on the bed and set to work with more than his usual vigour.

Afterwards, she was sick, alone and shivering in the little dressing-room. Why do I let it happen? There must be some way out – next time . . .

But she knew the answer only too well. She let it happen because she could do nothing else. She had tried protests and struggles, coldness and anger: each in turn seemed only to fire Henri's passion the more, as if he believed she was simply teasing him. He was apparently incapable of realising that she did not want his advances. Once, she had locked herself in

315

another room, but his angry thumping on the door had attracted the servants, and with Mathilde in the house she dared not risk such a disturbance: she could not bear it if her innocent daughter should find out the truth. In the end there was nothing she could do. It was all part of the bargain, entered into with her eyes open. Besides, she dared not push Henri too far: she needed him still, at least until they were making wine again at Casseuil. She was trapped.

Laure rose late next morning, after Henri had left the room, but found she was even then too early, for he was still at the breakfast table, engrossed in his newspaper. But at least Mathilde was there too and came, smiling, to kiss her. She held a letter in her hand.

'Frédéric?' Laure asked, through a throbbing head. Mathilde nodded and handed her a neatly folded note that had been enclosed with her own. It was closely written in Frédéric's small exquisite writing; and informed Laure, with formal correctness, that he would be coming to Casseuil for Christmas, if that was not inconvenient.

'He's coming on Saturday,' Mathilde said happily, glancing again at her own letter.

Rather to Laure's surprise (and possibly to Mathilde's too), Frédéric had replied with reasonable promptness to his half-sister's first compassionate letter. His reply had been brief and uninformative, but not discouraging, and Mathilde had written again. Her letters, always, were warm girlish outpourings, full of lively accounts of all the things she was doing, the books she read, the music she sang or played, the people she met, the countryside through which she walked or rode. Frédéric's at first said very little, beyond the barest account of school lessons; but then, bit by bit, he began to write about the impression made upon him by something he had read, to express ideas and thoughts that had come to him; and he referred to Félix and to the things they talked about sometimes. Very soon, the correspondence became a two-way thing and Frédéric's letters almost matched Mathilde's for length. He suggested books for her to read, and she read them avidly and told him what she thought, and they would sometimes argue affectionately, at length, over some point or other – on paper, of course. When she went to school it made no difference: they continued to write, only now she had new experiences about which to confide in him.

Laure, who saw only a few of the early letters, realised all the same that Mathilde had somehow (miraculously, she thought) succeeded in establishing an easy, happy relationship with her half-brother. It showed itself on the few occasions when they met at Casseuil; it was as if they had grown up together, like any brother and sister. They talked and argued and laughed, and Laure was astonished to see Frédéric so much the normal young man – quiet, sometimes reticent, sometimes inclined to an acid sharpness of tongue, but very far removed indeed from the repressed child she remembered.

He had left the *lycée* having distinguished himself in the *baccalauréat*, the highly competitive end-of-school examinations, and then – a more notable achievement still – he had gained admission to the prestigious École Normale Supérieure in Paris. Félix, making some pretence at some kind of unspecified studies – enough, he hoped, to protect him from the demands of military service, from which students were exempt – shared the rooms Frédéric rented for them in the Boulevard St Michel.

Mathilde looked up again, smiling. 'He says we should go to Paris in July, for the Exhibition and the centenary of the Revolution.'

'If the Republic survives so long,' commented Laure drily, sitting down to pour herself a bowl of coffee. 'General Boulanger's antics look set to overturn the government if they're not careful.' The flamboyant General had won enthusiastic votes – including Henri's – in the Dordogne earlier this year, and his followers were clamouring for him to be brought to power.

Henri looked up from his paper. 'The General's a good Republican.'

'Frédéric says many of his followers are Royalists,' Mathilde pointed out. 'He says they hope he can be made to bring back the monarchy.'

'Oh, these Normaliens! They're all – what do they call them? – Socialists and so forth: you can't trust what he says.

We need a strong man at the helm. The country's gone to pot since the Empire ended – no firm government, no sense of direction.'

If it had not been for her headache Laure might have protested, but she could think only of the frosty morning outside, which might clear her head; and of the vineyard, where for a while she could escape Henri, even forget about him.

'Let's go to Paris in the summer, Maman,' Mathilde urged again. 'I'd like to see the new tower that's being built, all in metal – the Tour Eiffel. Frédéric says "It is unbelievably ugly, about as fitting as a factory chimney in the heart of Paris." And I've never been to Paris, Maman.'

'We shall see,' was all Laure would say, as she broke a piece from her croissant and began, without enthusiasm, to eat.

'Oh, you go – a good idea,' said Henri cheerfully. 'Just the thing for you both – shopping, a look at the sights. But there's no need for you to call on that wet hen of a Frédéric to escort you. Victor would enjoy a trip to Paris – he'll go with you.'

Laure caught Mathilde's expression, and then remembered a thought that had come to her at some time during the long sleepless hours of the night. If her daughter was to escape Henri's increasing pressure to marry his son, then an alternative must be found, and quickly; but as yet Mathilde knew few young men, and showed little inclination to enlarge her acquaintance. 'What do you think, Henri? Should we give a ball for the New Year? There always used to be one at Casseuil in the old days.'

She saw Mathilde's face brighten, and was thankful that Henri too – always hospitable and gregarious – was pleasantly distracted by the idea.

'Splendid – yes, why not? We've not much time. I'll set things in motion at once. And you too, *ma chérie*, today.' He folded his paper and laid it down, and left them to finish their breakfast in peace.

ii

Mathilde was smiling to herself as she sat by the fire in the *grand salon* after lunch on the following Saturday. She was alone, for Laure had gone to Bergerac to make final arrangements about the flowers for the ball, and Henri, as usual, was at Trissac. She worked in a rather desultory manner at redecorating a hat whose artificial flowers had grown worn and a little faded. There was no longer any need for frugality, of course, but she saw no point in throwing away perfectly good garments when a little judicious repair might restore them completely. Besides, it had been rather a fetching little hat and she was proud of her skill in making the best of the most unpromising materials.

Life had seemed, sometimes, just a little aimless since she left school. Far in the future was marriage, to a man who would sweep her off her feet and capture her heart in one swift moment of exhilaration; but that was all somewhat unreal, beyond her present experience, not even much wished for as yet. At the moment the relationship she most valued was that with Frédéric, the warm accepting companionship, the sense of being understood and listened to with sympathy. Bitingly intelligent himself, he assumed an equal intelligence in her and never patronised her as other men – in her slight experience – were inclined to do. And now, not only would he be here in time for dinner tonight, but there was the ball to look forward to – frivolous, conventional perhaps (she doubted if Frédéric would share her wholehearted enthusiasm at the prospect), but *fun*.

It was warm in the *grand salon*, for there was no wind today to fight with the heat from the fire. It would be dark soon. Mathilde found that her hands had fallen idle. The little blue net flowers rolled away, one by one, from her knee; her eyelids drooped.

Then, suddenly, there was someone behind her chair, two cool slim hands across her eyes, chilling her into wakefulness, and a laughing voice saying, 'Who is it then?'

With a cry she tossed the hat aside and sprang to her feet. 'Frédéric! Oh Frédéric. We weren't expecting you for hours yet!'

'I caught an earlier train.'

She did not run to him at once, preferring to stand lit with delight to look at him, to see what had changed in the months since they had last met – no, not simply months; more than a year, she realised.

She saw the slender young man she remembered, little changed, still not quite as tall as she was, an elegant young man in the height of Paris student fashion, with the same fine-boned face, a soft little moustache on his upper lip, his shining brown hair rather on the long side, his eyes – gold-green noticing eyes – studying her as she studied him. She felt in a strange way, suddenly, that she was seeing him for the first time, that she had never really seen him before. She was, after all, not able to run to him as she had intended, all sisterly warmth; but that was not because she did not want to.

To Frédéric, on the other hand, Mathilde was not exactly as he remembered her. His memory was of a girl, and this now was a woman, slim as a boy almost, with her breasts scarcely giving definition to the modest blue dress; but a woman all the same, straight and pure and fine, all creamy skin and cloudy golden hair, poised and beautiful. Only her eyes were the eyes he knew, gentle and brown and warm in the sweet oval of her face. He, too, who had only lately learned to receive and return the embraces she gave so lavishly and easily, found he could not go to her. He stood exactly where he was, very still, looking at her.

There was a silence that seemed to stretch into eternity, a great stillness holding them from somewhere outside themselves. Within it, somehow, it was as if the earth moved beneath them and they both felt it, and nothing would ever be the same again as long as they lived.

The spell broke, but not to give them release. Mathilde, conscious of strangeness, reached out a hand. Frédéric did the same, touching her just for an instant: that tiny momentary contact sent an impulse running swiftly right through her, from head to foot. She knew she was trembling.

'Come and sit down,' she said shakily. 'Warm yourself. It's cold today.' She did not really know what she was saying, but she had to break the silence somehow.

He came and seated himself, with uncharacteristic clumsiness, in the chair that faced hers across the hearth. She resumed her own seat. They looked at one another and then away, saying nothing. When they did speak it was abruptly, at the same moment.

'Did you—'

'I heard—'

They both laughed, breathless with awkwardness.

'You first.'

'No, you.'

Another silence, and they smiled ruefully at one another, acknowledging the embarrassment.

'Would you like some tea?' Mathilde asked brightly at last. 'Maman's gone to Bergerac, but she'll be back soon.' It was easier, being utterly practical and matter-of-fact.

He hesitated, then said quietly, 'Thank you. I should like some tea. Shall I ring?'

He stood up, just as she did the same. They were suddenly very close, facing one another, eyes level. She felt his hands move to touch her elbows, closing slowly about them. She knew she swayed nearer, towards the fine mouth beneath the soft moustache. Then she saw he had closed his eyes, as if to shut her out. A moment more, and he had released her. He swung round and walked briskly to the bell, sending its note clanging through the quiet house. He stayed there beside it until the maid came, although it was Mathilde, as pale as he was, who spoke to her. 'Would you bring the tea in now please, Françoise?'

To the relief of both of them – though it was not really relief, for there was disappointment in it too, as if something begun could not now be resolved, for the moment at least – Laure came in as the tea arrived, and Henri followed soon afterwards.

Frédéric was welcomed with varying degrees of warmth, his early arrival exclaimed over. A murmur of conversation filled the air. Feeling suddenly light headed, as if freed from some kind of intolerable restraint, Mathilde found she was almost at ease again. Over the tea, seated about the fire, she talked to Frédéric, asked him questions about his journey and his plans, laughed and teased him a little. With an equal sense of release he answered, questioned in return, parried her teasing. Never once, except for the tiniest fraction of an instant, did his eyes leave her face, or hers his. Their mood of slight delirium – put down, by Laure, simply to youthful high spirits – brought the company to life. Laure knew Mathilde could sparkle like this, but she had never dreamed that Frédéric was capable of being so exhilaratingly lively, so wickedly funny even, full of acid wit.

'How good to have Frédéric among us again,' Laure said to Mathilde with perfect sincerity when the time came at last to say good-night. 'It's been a lovely evening. Sleep well, *minou*.'

She did not guess that Mathilde would sleep even less than she did that night.

The atmosphere of slightly deranged hilarity continued, and marked the whole of that Christmas and New Year holiday. Laure, used to Mathilde and Frédéric preferring one another's company when at Casseuil together, was surprised to be asked, often, to ride with them when they went out, to play cards or sing with them, to join in their talk. It delighted her that they should not find her too old and tedious to share their pleasures, although she noticed, indulgently, that even when she was there they sometimes talked together as if they had forgotten about her; but it was mostly silly, giggling, childish talk, reminding her how very young they still were.

iii

'What a fortunate chance that you should be staying here at this time!' César Chabry was openly rubbing his hands together, already savouring the prospect of being able to include two such exalted guests in his party for the New Year ball at Casseuil.

'Oh, but Charles and Élisabeth are going home on Friday – are you not?' Émilie Lacroix turned a smile of deceptive innocence on her cousins, seated together at the card table in the *salon* of the Lacroixs' Bergerac mansion; but before there was any reply, Émilie's sister Catherine, heavily pregnant and very bored, broke in with a pleading note in her voice.

'But they would like to stay on for the ball – wouldn't you? Please say you will!' For Catherine marriage to Louis, César Chabry's eldest son, meant enduring, day in, day out, the company of people whose whole outlook and way of life was not at all of a kind she had been used to. She clutched hungrily at any opportunity to surround herself again with her own more refined and well bred relations.

322

'You'd find it very tedious,' Émilie countered. 'It'll just be one of those very countrified affairs. The Séguiers are not at all *comme il faut*, from what one hears.'

'You are a little unjust, *mademoiselle*,' César Chabry protested, though secretly not displeased to hear his neighbour so denigrated. 'Monsieur Séguier is the most hospitable of men, and his wife is charming – her daughter too. I am sure you would not be disappointed, Monsieur de Miremont – nor you, *mademoiselle*. Do, I beg of you, condescend to prolong your stay a little and grace our humble festivities with your presence.'

He looked anxiously from one to another of the two aristocratic young faces: that of tiny, lively, black-haired Élisabeth de Miremont, who was seventeen, and her brother Charles, four years older, tall and grave. The Lacroixs were a respectable and wealthy family of the upper bourgeoisie; their cousins the de Miremonts were unquestionably noble by birth, and breeding, and tradition. Since the dawn of time almost it seemed that the family had owned (amongst much else) the château and lands of St Antoine de Miremont in the rocky, densely forested countryside north-east of Bergerac. A de Miremont had occupied almost every one of the highest posts in Church and Army and Court under successive kings of France, serving always with unquestioning loyalty. During the Revolution, three of their number had died bravely beneath the guillotine, whilst others had fought long and hard against the Republic on behalf of the exiled Bourbons. Later, the family had somehow managed to regain possession of its lands and château, and had for the most part remained there quietly ever since, treasuring memories of a glorious past and hoping still for an eventual return of France to her rightful allegiance. Charles and Élisabeth were the two youngest of the Comte de Miremont's seven children. To César Chabry, now fully converted to Royalism, they were worthy of the utmost devotion.

There was a little silence, while everyone looked at Charles de Miremont, who was clearly giving the matter of the ball serious consideration, under subtle pressure from his sister, who was directing a fervent appeal at him with her eyes: she loved dancing, of all kinds. It was some time before his mouth relaxed into a faint smile and he bowed his head. 'Very well, Monsieur Chabry. I think there can be no objection to our remaining for the ball. Thank you.'

It had not been an easy decision for Charles. He cared very little for balls, although he danced well enough. But, serious minded and devout, with his head full of dreams and ideals, he found it hard to suit his manner and his conversation to the light-hearted frivolity of a ball. He was conscious too of his responsibility for Élisabeth's welfare, whilst they were away from home. What would his parents think of this ball? He had heard one or two things about the family at Casseuil that made him uneasy – there had been a suicide, for example, and one or two other doubtful matters. On the other hand, one should not be guided by gossip, and in any case César Chabry (whom he tried hard to like) would surely not invite respectable guests to a house that was less than respectable. And Élisabeth would so much enjoy an evening of harmless pleasure, and so would his cousin Catherine, who, he feared, was not at all happy in her marriage – and then there were his parents' wishes to consider. 'I *know* you are sure you have a vocation for the Church, Charles,' his father had said only a short time ago. 'But your uncle,' that was his uncle Cardinal de Miremont, 'has his doubts, and so have I. Should we in due course be proved wrong, we shall give you every encouragement. But in the meantime you must try a little normal social life. Meet a few young ladies of good family, mix in good company – and not half-heartedly, but with a real effort at enjoyment. That's all I ask.'

Charles had been little impressed by the girls his parents had paraded before him. Like his sisters, they seemed nice enough, but incomprehensibly obsessed with clothes and dancing and young men and gossip. It was hard to believe they belonged to the same planet as he did. It was a similar story with his fellow law students at Bordeaux. There, too, he was following his father's wishes, to a certain extent at least. Both his father and his uncle had pointed out that he had spent the whole of his schooldays in the fervently religious atmosphere of one of France's most prestigious private *collèges*, and so had little experience of the world outside. To that end, before committing himself finally and irrevocably to a monastery or other religious order, he was advised very strongly to try some other career. They would have preferred the army or even some minor political involvement (it seemed an auspicious time for Royalists to make themselves felt). But Charles, observing that a lawyer in the family might be useful, had surprised them all by taking up his studies in that field, with great seriousness. It was, sadly, proving much harder than he had anticipated, and not simply because he knew his vocation lay elsewhere. But perhaps that was all the more reason, now, to bear his father's wishes in mind and resolve to enjoy the ball at Casseuil.

For all his good intentions, however, his mood was not cheerful as he sat in the carriage with the giggling chatter of his sister and his cousins about him, driving through the darkness of New Year's Eve to Casseuil. It had been a cold day, and at dusk the rain began, steady and insistent. But the lanterns hung at the door of the château gave a festive brightness to the wet gravel and the pale shining stone of the walls, against which great jars of flowers and winter greenery framed the welcoming opening, from which more light – brighter, warmer – and the sweet distant lilting strains of the little orchestra enticed the guests inside.

Charles was agreeably surprised by the appearance of the hall. Its spotless austerity pleased him, and the ancient solidity of its simple furnishings; there was nothing vulgar or ostentatious here. The *grand salon*, of course, to which they were led once they had discarded their outdoor clothes, was brilliantly lit, warmed by a huge fire, perfumed with flowers and dauntingly full of people; but even here, beneath the trappings of the ball, there was the same unpretentious simplicity.

Monsieur Séguier was much as Charles had expected, a big man all shades of red from his grey-flecked hair to his welcoming outstretched hands; but his wife was indeed charming, a little graceful golden-haired woman in a gown of rose and dove grey, which might have looked matronly but somehow did not.

And then Charles was presented to Mademoiselle Naillac.

He had known always that one thing only would ever turn him from his intention to enter the Church; and that would be a meeting with the ideal woman of his dreams. Perfect, unblemished, all sweetness and purity, she did not – could not – exist, and so he had not given the subject more than a passing thought.

And yet here before him, smiling, blushing a little, in the simplest of white gowns with a single rose in her coiled golden hair, was a vision made real, his unattainable dream in human shape. Somehow – he did not quite know how – Charles managed to perform a little bow, even to kiss that slender white-gloved hand, which smelt of some delicious perfume that, for all its subtlety, seemed to go straight to his head. She said something to him in the lowest and sweetest of voices and he stammered an inarticulate reply and then stood like a fool gazing at her until his aunt, behind him, prodded him gently on his way.

He moved on, across the crowded ballroom, and stood near the long, curtained windows staring at the dancers yet seeing nothing but the vision no longer before his eyes. He tried to talk himself into common sense. One ought not to go by appearances – just because she was beautiful it did not follow that her soul too conformed to his image of perfection. She was human – like himself, like his sisters – and fallible, of course; and probably, like so many girls, light minded and given to gossip and spitefulness.

He contrived very soon to dance with her. It was the polka, his favourite dance, suddenly become exhilaratingly enjoyable; and with a growing sense of excitement and wonder which he could not suppress he found her just as she ought to be – warm, modest, ready to talk (but not too much), with a friendliness sweetened by that appealing hint of shyness. Her voice was sweet, clear and musical, her smile utterly entrancing. She listened with flattering attentiveness as he replied to her observations or – choosing his words with even more than his usual care – put his own in return. He wanted to sweep her right into his arms, not hold her at this decorous distance where one hand was light on her tiny waist, the other delicately supporting her own. He wanted to cry out, I love you – come away – marry me tonight! But that would have been ridiculous, and also reckless and quite improper; and even under the influence of this flood of wild and unaccustomed emotion he did not yield to it. Wait, he warned himself; take your time, as

326

long as you need. There is no urgency. You must be sure. Better patience now, than a lifetime of regret.

He danced with her again later, and this time thought her just a little abstracted – courteous, all sweetness still, but with a hint of vagueness in her manner, as if not quite all her attention was directed towards him. But that could not make her seem less than perfect.

Earlier, Mathilde had been intrigued by this tall young man with wavy black hair, neatly cut, above a rosy unremarkable face in which bright blue eyes looked out on the world with an expression that somehow mingled innocence and astonishment. He had an odd way of pausing after every question she asked or remark she made, as if carefully weighing his words before venturing anything so reckless as a reply; and then he would speak very deliberately, giving each word just the right amount of emphasis, so much and no more. She supposed it must be a result of his lawyer's training.

This second time, however, she scarcely heard anything he said, though she murmured what she hoped were appropriate replies, while her eyes – when he was not actually gazing full at her with his undeniably enraptured stare – searched the room behind his shoulder. Where was Frédéric? She had not seen him at all since they had gone upstairs to change after dinner; and even before then he had been more silent and evasive than usual. She was afraid he had not relished the prospect of the ball, but she had not supposed he would not even put in an appearance. Her spirits – high, soaring at first – had begun to droop a little. The past days had been shared with Frédéric and had been the more joyful for that; and if she could not share the ball too it would lose some of its glitter, for all the compliments and the heady sense that she alone was the focus of attention and admiration.

She was beginning, just a little, to grow irritated by the leaden nature of her partner's conversation. Disappointment nibbled away at her patience. And then, all at once, as her glance darted across the room, she saw Frédéric emerging from the *petit salon* – set aside for those who wanted a little quiet – looking as neat and self-contained as ever, as if he did not quite belong in this noisy excited throng of people. She kept her eyes on him, relieved that the dance ended almost at once and that, as young Monsieur de Miremont led her back to her seat, Frédéric saw her and slipped through the dancers towards her.

He greeted Charles with a nod of the head that was not quite a bow, which acted – as he had clearly intended – as a dismissal.

'Where have you been all evening?' Mathilde asked, fanning her glowing face with more than ladylike vigour.

'I did not think—' Over his shoulder, Mathilde saw Victor coming their way, with something ominously purposeful in his manner.

'Quick!' she broke in. 'I'm free for this dance – dance with me, or Victor will ask me. I can't bear the way he paws me.'

Frédéric wasted no time. He drew her to her feet, slid his arm about her waist, clasped her hand lightly and swung her into the waltz that was just beginning. He danced gracefully, but his expression was wholly at variance with the ease of his movements. Mathilde could not remember having seen such a thunderous look on his face before.

'Does he do that? Paw you, I mean?'

Mathilde felt a little alarmed, troubled by sudden visions of quarrels, duels even – and Victor was a large young man, without scruples. 'Oh, it's just his way,' she said mildly.

'He has no right! I can't bear to think of it!'

'Then don't think of it.' Her voice was gentle. 'I don't, any more than I have to. There are ways a woman can deal with a man of his kind, you know.' She smiled at him. 'If you scowl like that people will think we are quarrelling.'

The scowl vanished. 'I could never quarrel with you,' he said earnestly.

'No, you never have.' She sounded surprised, as if she had only just realised it. 'But then I suppose we haven't seen so very much of one another. It's difficult to quarrel by letter.'

His eyes moved from her face to her earlier partner, glimpsed a short distance away. 'Who was that you were dancing with just now?'

'Oh, he's one of Monsieur Chabry's party – one of the noble relations, I think. He's a law student.' She paused, watching the dancers for a little longer. Charles's present partner was a graceful languid young woman in green satin, whose dark glossy curls gleamed as she moved and whose figure, given emphasis by the cut of her bodice, had all the generous curves for which Mathilde longed so vainly. 'Don't you think his partner is the most beautiful creature you ever saw?' Her voice had a wistful note.

'She's not my type.' He held her with a sudden urgency. 'Don't ever want to be like that, Mathilde. Don't change, don't try to change. Stay just as you are. You have—'

He broke off abruptly, his face unusually full of agitation. Mathilde laughed, a little shakily. 'We all grow older, you know. We can't help but change one way or another.'

'But not like that, not ever.' His hold on her waist tightened still more.

She was very conscious of his nearness, the warmth of his hand where his fingers curved about her own; and of his face, close to hers. They ended the dance in silence, coming to a standstill even before the lilting tune reached its conclusion, their eyes held together in concentrated gravity. Afterwards, as the other couples jostled past to return to their places, Frédéric seemed to recollect himself. He drew away, let his hands fall, and walked back with her across the room, not touching her at all, not even looking at her. Yet they were too absorbed in one another to notice that Victor was waiting for her, until he stood up and reached for Mathilde's arm.

'Now, sister Mathilde – one half-brother has had his turn with you, and now it is mine.'

There was nothing she could do, except plead a tiredness she did not feel. Besides, she was conscious of a stifling sensation, as if increasingly it was difficult to breathe. She knew she must get away from Frédéric, quickly. She forced a smile for him as Victor led her away, but she was troubled by the stricken look in his eyes. Then another couple passed, shutting him off from her view; and when they had gone he had disappeared.

In his eagerness to secure her as his partner, Victor had led her onto the floor a little too soon, before the dance had begun. It gave him more opportunity than she liked to touch her, running a hand up her bare arm, fondling her waist. She wriggled free and tried – without much success – to put a safe distance between them.

'May I remind you that you are not in fact my half-brother,' she said sharply, agitating her fan before her face in case that might help to keep him at bay. 'We have neither father nor mother in common.'

It was a mistake. She realised that almost before she finished speaking, and saw the knowing smile that curved his full mouth. They said a full mouth denoted a passionate nature, which not a reflection she found reassuring; it was after all only a desirable attribute if one *wanted* to arouse that particular passion. 'All the better, *ma petite* Mathilde – there need be no barrier between us, need there?'

'On the contrary,' she retorted with the asperity that Victor always, somehow, managed to bring out in her, against all the usual gentle warmth of her nature, 'there should be a greater barrier between a single man and a single woman unconnected in any way, than between a brother and a sister.' Then, quickly, conscious that she was blushing, she changed the subject, making some inconsequential remark about the beauty of the flowers.

Mathilde danced that night until her feet ached, although she was never conscious of tiredness. When she was hungry, a host of young men clamoured to take her in to supper. When she was thirsty, there was competition to bring her wine or fruit punch. Compliments poured over her, she had never a moment alone, she knew the ball was, for her, an unqualified triumph. Yet underneath, all the time, was a troublesome agitation of spirits that would not let her enjoy herself wholeheartedly, without alloy. Something – she had no time, no inclination to think what – was missing.

At midnight the orchestra fell silent and the dancing stopped. Henri Séguier took up his position before the hearth and raised a hand for silence. Then he made a little speech wishing all the guests good health, prosperity and happiness for the coming year. There was much kissing and embracing, and a little gift for everyone, beautifully wrapped.

Mathilde sought out her mother and hugged her tenderly. 'I wish you all the love and happiness in the world, Maman. And the very best wine.'

Afterwards, she escaped as soon as she decently could from

330

the too-long embraces of Henri and Victor and went to bestow one of her most affectionate kisses on old Doctor Rossillon, sitting well wrapped up near the fire: he had been very ill last year, and his medical practice had now been taken over by his efficient son-in-law, Doctor Bonnet. He received her kiss with delight. 'Seventeen years ago I saw you into the world, *ma petite*,' he told her (he was much given to reminiscence these days), 'and looking at you today I'm proud to have had a hand in it.' Then there was Monsieur Chabry and his younger son, Eugène, whose roving eye and hand were a little more restrained than Victor's; and Louis and Catherine Chabry; and Émilie Lacroix, of whom she was already very fond, and pretty Élisabeth de Miremont, and her brother Charles, who raised her hand to his mouth as reverently as if it were some sacred relic. On and on about the room, Mathilde was embraced and kissed; laughed over and complimented and showered with good wishes; and all the time her eyes searched restlessly for Frédéric. Surely he would not let the New Year begin, without wishing her well?

But he did; and when the dancing resumed there was still no sign of him. Now at last Mathilde did begin to feel tired; once, for a moment, she felt a foolish inclination to burst into tears. But fortunately just then a young man from Bergerac who never failed to make her laugh claimed her as a partner, and the moment passed.

The older people, and those who had not planned to stay all night at Casseuil, were already leaving; there were not many hours to go now. There was in Mathilde a sense of anticlimax, of something incomplete, of waiting for an appropriate dénouement, though of what kind she could not say.

It was perhaps a little before three when Mathilde found she had torn the frilled train of her gown, quite seriously, so that the delicate lace trailed raggedly on the floor: it needed immediate attention. She excused herself to the laughing group of young people who surrounded her – among them of course the already inevitable Charles de Miremont – and made her way towards the stairs, intending to go to her room to find needle and thread.

Unfortunately, glancing round as she crossed the hall, she saw Victor Séguier coming steadily after her through the

crowd. Having drunk heavily this evening, he would probably have few scruples about following her upstairs. She
hoped he did not see her turn aside and run down the stone
steps to the passage that led to the cellars and the kitchen.

Only one solitary lamp burned there and it was very dim, so
that she did not see someone coming her way until, at the
point where a second, unlit, passage led to the garden door,
she ran into Frédéric. She gave a little startled cry; and then, to
cover her surprise – and another kind of agitation – began to
scold him.

'What do you mean by lurking in the dark like that? Where
have you been all this time?'

He shrugged, his expression indecipherable, though there
was something that was almost a smile hovering about his lips,
without warmth or humour. 'Here and there. In the dining-
room and the library. I went up to my room for a while.' He
spoke carelessly and his tone was light; and she realised with a
tremor that was not quite alarm that he had been drinking,
was even a little drunk. She had never known him drink too
much before. 'What are you doing here then? Have you tired
of husband hunting?'

Ignoring the faint malice of that last remark, she explained
at least about the necessary repair, and showed him the torn
lace. He bent to examine it, as far as he could see anything in
the near darkness, and then straightened again, looking at her
very intently. 'I'm going to kiss you,' he said suddenly.

'No,' she whispered; but she stayed where she was and, as
his arms closed about her, reached out to hold him. She felt his
mouth on hers, soft, warm, gentle. She closed her eyes and
gave herself up to his kiss, all of herself, without reserve. She
had known nothing like this, no joy; and no pain.

After a little while he drew away, though his hands still held
her. 'I love you,' he said softly. 'You know that.' He looked,
not content or happy, but distraught.

'I know,' she said. 'And I—' She broke off, for she could
not say it. She was not drunk as he was.

Abruptly he let his hands fall to his sides. 'I'm going out. I
need some air.'

'But it's dark, and cold. It's been raining all night.'

He brushed her cheek with his hand, the softest of caresses. 'Don't think of me. Enjoy your ball.'

All at once she was frightened. She thought he looked a little desperate. His father – their father – had been desperate . . . She reached out after him. 'Frédéric, don't . . .!' But he had gone, slipping silently away into the deeper shadow. She stood staring along the passage at the door she could not see, but which just now had opened and then closed again, shutting out the night and the bitter rain.

Laure was the first of the household to come downstairs next morning, apart from the servants soft footedly clearing away the debris of the ball. Excitement had kept her from sleeping very much, just as now it made her feel wide awake and alert. For once it was pleasurable excitement, because the ball had been a great success, enjoyed (she thought she could safely say) by everyone, and above all by Mathilde. That glowing smiling face had seemed everywhere last night, as her daughter talked and laughed and danced. Even at the end when she was quite clearly very tired she had been as animated as ever. Furthermore, she had made new friends and – Laure was certain – had conquered several hearts amongst the young men of the neighbourhood. For once, too, Henri had been too tired himself for anything but sleep, and he was still asleep now, well after dawn.

Relishing the quiet, glad of this time to herself, Laure asked Françoise to bring breakfast to her in the *petit salon* and went to the *grand salon* in search of a letter that had come yesterday from her mother, which in the general bustle she had found no time to read. She would enjoy it over her breakfast.

Then she realised she was not alone after all. Frédéric was there, standing very still near the newly lit fire, staring at nothing in particular.

'Are you up already? Perhaps you were very wise and went to bed early.'

When he turned to look at her she realised that was unlikely, for he looked not just tired but exhausted, with shadows like bruises about his eyes. He was very pale. 'I didn't go to bed.'

Laure was concerned, from the new and rather grudging

333

fondness for Frédéric that had been growing in her during the past days. 'Where have you been then?'

'Outside.'

'All night? In this rain?' The wind had risen and the rain was lashing the windows, where before it had simply fallen with a cold relentlessness.

'I have changed since I came in, as you see, *madame*.' He was indeed dressed with all his customary neatness.

She wanted to ask why he should have behaved so strangely, but something prevented her. This morning he was nothing like the charming, lively young man she had begun to know this Christmas time. 'I expect you're hungry after all that fresh air. There is breakfast in the *petit salon*, if you wish.'

'I am not hungry thank you, *madame*.'

She gazed at him in some perplexity for a little while, wondering what was wrong and what – if anything – she could do about it. He looked as if he had forgotten she was there, returning his attention to whatever it was that had absorbed him as she came in. Doubtless that was something internal, deep in his thoughts, though his eyes rested on the family photographs set out on the table, careful portraits of herself and Philippe just before their marriage, her parents with herself and Marcel in Paris, Mathilde demure and pretty in the flowers and lace of her first communion, herself and Henri with their guests in the garden at Trissac, stiffly posed.

She sighed, and turned to go; and as she did so heard him call, softly, 'Wait – please, *madame* – there is something I—'

She looked round, glad that he should have appealed to her. 'What is it?'

'I wondered . . . we . . . is it . . .' He cleared his throat and began again. '*Madame*, was there ever any doubt that Monsieur Naillac was my father?'

So that was what he had been staring at; the fading photograph of Philippe, looking as dark and handsome and assured as on their first meeting. It would be only natural if Frédéric found no trace of his slight fairness in that impressive figure, if he began to wonder . . .

She understood him: he had been happy here this Christmas, more attached than ever to his half-sister and her family,

334

accepted by them as never before. He wanted to be sure that this sense of belonging was not all an illusion.

'You don't look much like him, do you?' she said with a smile. 'But then neither does Mathilde. No, you can be sure there was no mistake. Monsieur Naillac acknowledged you from the beginning. We went into it all very carefully when you first came here.' She watched for the lines of strain to fade and the brightness to return to his eyes.

Instead, he turned away from her, and just in that fraction of a second she glimpsed such a look of anguish on his face that she cried out, 'Frédéric, what is it?' She took his arm and brought him round towards her again, and their eyes met.

And then, appallingly, she understood. What she saw in his eyes was not hope confirmed but hope destroyed, beyond recall; and some instinct told her exactly what that hope had been and what had destroyed it.

She caught her breath, held it, released it very slowly, trying to steady herself. She let go of his arm, and he straightened, as if bracing himself for a blow, although in that instant nothing was further from her mind. She was conscious only of a great pity; until she remembered Mathilde.

Dear God, what of Mathilde? What was her part in all this? Did she know? Worse, did she . . .?

She felt suddenly sick. At this moment, she thought she could almost have killed Frédéric with her bare hands, for the threat he posed. And yet, if indeed she had guessed right, she pitied him still, oh yes, she pitied him.

'I am going away tomorrow,' he reminded her quietly, out of the clamorous silence that had fallen. 'I expect it will be a long time before I come again.'

She wanted to say, 'Go now, at once, and never come back.' But that would have meant – obliquely at least – putting into words what she feared, and she could not bear to do that. It would only have made the terrible thing somehow more concrete, more real. So she said as calmly as she could, 'You'd better go and rest. I'll send Françoise up with some breakfast for you.'

She watched him go; but for a long time she did not move from where she stood. She tried, desperately, to realise the enormity of what she thought she had discovered, to explain it, to trace its development uncoiling like a snake beneath the happy surface of the past days.

Happy; too happy. She thought of the feverish hilarity of the two young people, the wild edge to their talk and laughter; their fear – was it fear? – of being alone together. If that was it, then Mathilde was in as deep as Frédéric.

'Let me be wrong. Oh God, let me be wrong!'

She tried to steady herself and look calmly at the situation. She might even be wrong about Frédéric, she might well have misread his unhappiness; he was a difficult young man to know. And if it *was* true, then there was cause for pity, and thankfulness that he was going away, but no real reason to suppose that Mathilde had been tainted. Could not her mood this Christmas be explained simply by a heady combination of happiness and excitement? She loved Frédéric, certainly; Laure acknowledged that. But only as I love Marcel, no more, she told herself.

That did not prevent her from watching Mathilde closely all that day, looking for the least sign to confirm or contradict her fears. Frédéric kept to his room, appearing only at dinner-time; Laure did not know whether to be relieved or disturbed that Mathilde seemed scarely to notice how withdrawn was his mood. She had distractions enough, of course. Several of last night's guests were still in the house, departing only at intervals through the day, and some of the nearer guests – among them the clearly smitten Charles de Miremont – called to express their thanks for last night. And of course there was still Victor.

If Mathilde seemed a little irritable, that could be attributed only too easily to Victor, who showed a marked reluctance to return to Trissac and scarcely left Mathilde's side all day. Laure, watchful and anxious, kept close to her daughter. Tired, afflicted a little by an inevitable sense of anticlimax, constantly troubled by Victor – it was no wonder that Mathilde was irritable.

Victor stayed at Casseuil that next night too, although he was not up when Henri and Laure and Mathilde stood at the door to see Frédéric on his way. Laure thought the young man looked every bit as strained and exhausted as he had yesterday morning; but he parted from them with correct good manners

– a restrained embrace, a light kiss on each cheek, as cool and emotionless for Mathilde as for Henri and Laure. But coming last of all to his half-sister, he held her for a moment longer, lightly, by the elbows, and said, '*Au revoir, petite sœur.* Find yourself a husband before I come again – but make sure he's a good one.' The tone was light, jocular (and Frédéric was never jocular), and he was smiling; but to Laure's eyes the smile had a bitter twist to it, and his voice was hard-edged with pain.

As for Mathilde, she only smiled faintly and murmured, 'Take care of yourself,' and then stood back to wave him away. Laure remembered how at their last parting she had hugged him unreservedly.

Yet, as the carriage rolled away, she did not cry or show any sign – more than a grave quietness – of grief or distress. If she felt anything more than a natural sadness at the departure of a brother, she was hiding it very well. Laure did not know whether or not to draw any comfort from that.

As they turned to go back into the house, Henri put an arm about Mathilde and hugged her to his side. 'He's got a point about that husband for you, *ma petite*. It's high time you were wed. And we know just the one.'

Laure saw Mathilde glance sharply up at her stepfather, with a question in her eyes which quickly dwindled and died as she read the answer. She slipped out of Henri's arm and excused herself a little incoherently, running on ahead of them. Henri, irritated, swore softly. 'What's the matter with the girl? You'd have thought she'd want to hear what I have to say.'

'I don't think this is the moment,' Laure said, all calm reasonableness. 'She's just said goodbye to a brother of whom she's very fond.'

'Then she needs someone to take her mind off him. There's a sure way to distract a woman from the loss of a brother, and that's to give her a lover. She's nearly eighteen and ripe for it.'

Laure was in no mood to take part in Henri's favourite game of hints and innuendoes, ending only when he had exhausted all the possible variations in the revelation of exactly what was on his mind; as if she had not known it all along. 'If you mean Victor,' she said briskly, 'then I think it's time you realised there's no future in that. She's had long enough now to show any interest in him, if she felt any.'

'Nonsense, Victor's hardly begun. Give him a free hand and he'd win her in no time. It would be a perfect match. I'm only considering her interests.'

'And do you think I, as her mother, do not have them at heart even more than you do?'

Henri smiled and pinched her cheek, his eyes knowing. 'We all know women look at things differently, don't we? You'd let sentiment get in the way. One has to be practical in these matters.'

In the circumstances, Laure thought it was a singularly inept observation, but she let it pass, saying only, 'Do you not consider happiness important, and love?'

'Oh, love! whatever that is! So long as a woman has a man to keep her satisfied in bed, that's all she needs. That lasts longer than any soft sentimental feminine feelings. That, and a careful eye for the material things. After all, make sure a woman has pretty clothes and flattery, and she'll not ask for more.'

Laure felt sick, the more because in so many ways his philosophy exactly matched her own behaviour. How could she begin to argue with him? At least he had married her because, passionately, he desired her; whereas she had gone into it open-eyed for the most basic and hard-headed of material reasons. She could not begin to explain that she wanted something quite different for Mathilde; that only if Mathilde was happy could she justify her own actions to herself.

Later that day, returning from the office where she had been sorting and tidying in this quiet period before pruning began, Laure passed Mathilde's door and thought she heard the sound of stifled sobbing.

She stood still, listening, while something seemed to tighten about her heart; and then she knocked, firmly, trying to push away her fear at what she might find. 'Mathilde!'

338

One sob more, and then silence. She knocked again.

'One moment!' She heard steps, the splash of water, Mathilde approaching, the key turn in the lock; and her daughter faced her, smiling brightly. 'What is it, Maman?'

There was a rim of red about her eyes, but it was the only trace Laure could see of recent tears.

'I thought I heard you crying. What's wrong?'

'Nothing. Why should there be?' The cool uncaring tone was like a slap in the face. This was her beloved daughter, her friend and confidante, warm, open, loving; and it was as if she had slammed the door shut against her mother. She was in trouble, but she did not want Laure, or anyone. Laure tried to hide her hurt; and succeeded, of course, with the skill born of long practice.

'That's all right then.' She paused, watched by Mathilde, all bright brittleness; and then added, 'I thought I might go for a ride before dinner. Will you come?'

'No thank you, Maman. I have a book I wish to read.'

Cursing Frédéric from the bottom of her heart, Laure turned away; and then felt a little flutter of relieved pleasure as Mathilde called her back. 'Maman.'

At last her daughter had allowed the unhappiness to show – not much, for it was still held in check, but her mouth had a tremulous line now that it was no longer forced into a smile. 'Maman, how long is Victor staying? I thought he would go back to Trissac today.'

So it was *Victor*! That was why she had been weeping! The flutter of relief became a flood, and Laure went and put her arms about Mathilde and held her, ignoring the faint resistance she felt still in the slim body. 'I thought so too, *chérie*: perhaps he will. Has he been troubling you again?'

Mathilde gave a little sob. 'He always does, whenever he's here; you know that.' It was the first time she had ever spoken of it. Laure had feared that her silence on the subject had been caused by a sense that Victor's presence, like so much else, was an essential part of the new life that had begun with her mother's marriage; and she knew that this was one subject she must never, ever talk about to her mother. Not that Laure had ever hinted at such a prohibition, after the first time they spoke of it; but she had not needed to. In some things mother and daughter had no need of words.

'Then you mustn't be alone with him, *chérie*. Perhaps we should try to find a suitable companion for you, or at the least a personal maid.' It was a pity, she thought, that last autumn Nanon had been forced by her mother's increasing ill health to return to her home in the village.

'You know I don't want that. I've not been used to such things. I never had any need for any company but yours and Nanon's and—' She began to weep in earnest again, and Laure kissed her and stroked her hair.

'Then make sure you have my company. Come with me when I go to the vineyard or the *chai*. After all, they belong to you and one day you may be glad to know something about what goes on there.'

'Perhaps,' was all Mathilde would say.

That night Laure decided that the time for tactful reticence was long past. She had once heard Henri advise his son that 'Women like to be mastered'. It was high time she disillusioned him, at least as far as Mathilde was concerned.

'You must speak to Victor,' she told Henri. 'No modest young girl should have to put up with the kind of attentions Mathilde endures at his hands.' She nearly added, 'Even you would not behave quite so crudely,' but stopped herself just in time.

'Nonsense, she's just playing at modesty; they all do that. She's lapping it up underneath.'

With an effort Laure remained calm. She knew anger only made Henri more obstinate than ever. 'Not Mathilde. I know her better than that.'

He chuckled and pulled her to him, roughly unbuttoning her bodice and thrusting his hand inside. 'Look at you – never more desirable than when you're pretending to detest it.'

She did not try to argue with such twisted logic, only said with an edge to her voice, 'Perhaps you forget that this is Mathilde's house. If she should choose not to be troubled by Victor, then that is her right. She can refuse to receive him here.'

The hand – thank goodness! – ceased its groping. He

pushed her from him, suddenly angry. 'Don't forget, if it wasn't for me she'd have no house. She'll make my son welcome here or have me to answer to.'

So Mathilde's peace of mind is part of the price too, Laure thought miserably.

CHAPTER
SEVENTEEN

The Easter sun was warm and languorous on Charles's back, the clear air alive somehow with tiny flecks of gold – gold dust scattered in celebration of the season. Beneath his horse's hooves even the earth seemed dazzling where the light picked out the pale sheen of the stones. All the earth dressed for the season: Charles, not on the surface a fanciful person, was being carried along still on a flow of exaltation from the religious celebrations of the last few days, augmented now by the prospect of seeing Mademoiselle Naillac again. That was, of course, a very much more worldly excitement; but for Charles it was tinged with the same radiance. He was almost moved to sing aloud, so happy was he; but having little musical ability and a strong sense of decorum, he resisted the temptation.

Casseuil looked like some castle in a dream, the heavenly city perhaps, as painted in one of those popular pious allegories displayed on the walls of many a peasant cottage, a golden castle on a hill patterned with the vines spread out in ordered richness on the slopes up which he rode. He could almost imagine flocks of angels hovering over those delicate little turrets, slender angels in blue, their dark eyes gently glowing in the grave loveliness of their faces.

At the château there was a blow to his joyous mood.

'Madame is not in the house at present, *monsieur*,' Marius told him. 'Nor is Mademoiselle Mathilde.'

Somehow that possibility had not occurred to Charles. He stood there not quite knowing what to do, turning his hat in his hands and staring rather blankly at the servant. 'When – when do you expect them to return?'

'Oh, they are only in the vineyard somewhere, *monsieur*. I expect you will find them if you care to walk that way.'

The day was lit up again, more gloriously than ever. Charles set out, his pace steady and measured, as he forced it to be against all the wild eagerness of his spirit, his eyes searching the rows of vines as he walked.

There were buds on the stems, already opening a little, so that the twisted lifelessness of winter had passed, promising growth and renewal. His own home district was too wooded and rocky for vines, and few had grown them even before the phylloxera outbreak: the black gold of Périgord, the truffles lurking hidden beneath the luxuriant oak trees, was what gave it its wealth, together with timber and chestnuts. But Charles had a considerable knowledge of wine, learned from his father, and a great interest in all aspects of agriculture. It was not only Mathilde that drew him to Casseuil; or not quite only.

Here, amongst the vines, men were at work ploughing and hoeing. He exchanged a greeting with them as he passed, gravely courteous, and wondered where the ladies were.

He saw them at last, in a far corner of the vineyard just beyond the point where the land dipped into the valley: two fair heads catching the sunlight, bent together in consultation or conversation. They saw him coming and he was gratified by the warmth of Laure's welcoming smile, reflected more faintly on her daughter's face. Laure came to him, holding out her hands.

'Monsieur de Miremont – what a pleasure! I didn't know you were in the neighbourhood.'

'I am spending a few days in Bergerac, before returning to my studies,' he explained. He made a stiff little bow over her hand. *'Madame – mademoiselle –* I hope I find you both in the best of health. My uncle and aunt asked me to convey their good wishes, should I see you.'

Laure murmured the appropriate response, asking after him in return.

'I am in the best of health, *madame*, God be thanked,' he replied, with all his usual careful gravity. She had noticed before – but forgotten until now, as they had not seen him since the New Year – that he had a tendency to bring the Deity into his conversation with unusual frequency, not casually or

343

as an exclamation, but with great seriousness. He was an odd young man.

'I am so glad to find you out here,' he went on now. 'On my last visit Monsieur Séguier told me of your great desire to restore the vineyard. I thought it a noble enterprise.' He paused for a moment, as if carefully selecting the right words before going on. 'I should be gratified if you, *madame*, and Mademoiselle Naillac too, were to feel able to give up a little of your time to show me something of your enterprise here. But of course, *madame*, if it would incommode you—'

'Not at all, *monsieur*,' returned Laure, steadfastly refraining from looking at Mathilde, whom she guessed to be as close to laughter as she was herself; but she did not want to risk hurting the young man's feelings by giving way to it. Ponderous, even pompous, his manner might be, but she sensed that beneath it lay a measure of sensitivity. 'It would be a pleasure.'

Oddly enough, it was exactly that, and not only because of the unconscious amusement Charles provided. He showed what was clearly a genuine interest in all she had to say. His regret at the ravages the phylloxera had made, his sympathy for her struggle to survive, both seemed real enough.

'You are perhaps too young to have tasted one of the great Château de Casseuils.'

'On the contrary, *madame*. My father still has in his cellar a few valued bottles of the vintages of '47 and '69, which we are able to enjoy when an occasion arises of sufficient importance to merit such a mark of honour.'

'Then you may be able to understand what I am striving for; though I fear Monsieur Séguier thinks I am, at best, misguided.'

'Ah there, *madame*, he must be wrong!' It was almost an outburst. He took her hand, looking solemnly down at her from his considerable height. 'I believe that the good Lord gives us his treasures to use only to his glory. Thus it follows that if the earth at Casseuil is so constituted as to bring grapes to perfection, then that is what it must be permitted to do.'

'He seems then to have overlooked the phylloxera in his calculations,' Laure could not help pointing out, a little mockingly. As she did so she glimpsed the hint of malice in

Mathilde's smile and rather regretted her words. She hoped she had not shocked the young man.

He was silent for a little longer than usual, as if at the least her remark required more than the average consideration. At last he said, 'Forgive me if I disagree, *madame*; but are we not all part of his plan – you yourself, *madame*, as much as anyone? As I see it he brought you here with a mind and a heart and hands to work for his purposes, just at the moment when such attributes were most greatly needed.'

Laure was genuinely intrigued by this novel point of view, though beside her she could sense Mathilde's growing restlessness. 'But what if I'd followed Monsieur Séguier's advice, and gone over to tobacco or fruit trees? It would have been a much more reasonable and businesslike decision.'

'That would have been to turn your back upon the particular gifts you were given, for simple material gain, which must always be contrary to God's plan. Or,' he concluded in a sudden moment of self-doubt, 'so it seems to me.'

What would he have said, Laure wondered, if she had told him the whole sordid story of the marriage that had saved Casseuil? She doubted if his naïve piety would have an answer for that. But in spite of everything she rather warmed to him. Ponderous, even irritating he might be, but there was a genuine sincerity behind it all that was both unexpected and a little touching.

Not that it was likely to appeal to Mathilde, at once amused and bored by this weighty conversation. Her attention had clearly wandered and she hung back a few paces behind her mother and their guest as they made their way up the slope towards the château. Realising this, Laure halted to allow her to catch up, and to bring that particular conversation to an end. 'We have seen a good deal of Mademoiselle Lacroix lately,' she told Charles, as Mathilde reached them. 'Mathilde has become very fond of her. They are much of an age you know.'

She saw Charles colour at this mention of Mathilde, a colour that deepened as the girl's attention returned to him.

'So my cousin tells me. And that brings me to the reason for my coming here today.' He reached into the pocket of his handsome checked coat and pulled out a letter, which he handed to Mathilde. 'For you, *mademoiselle*. My cousin, and her parents also, hope you will be so kind as to come and spend a few days with them.' Laure saw the pleasure light Mathilde's face and smiled a little ruefully to herself. She wondered if Charles himself had engineered this visit, coinciding so conveniently with his own. 'You know, *madame*,' he was reassuring her now, 'that Madame Lacroix will care for your daughter as you would yourself.'

No, better, thought Laure bitterly; for I cannot even protect her from Victor.

He came with increasing frequency to Casseuil and nothing she or Mathilde could do seemed to make any difference to his behaviour. Mathilde was never left alone with him, but that seemed scarcely to deter him at all. Laure had tried to reason with him in private and even resorted more than once to a public rebuke, which had served only to bring Henri's wrath down on her.

'How dare you humiliate my son before our friends!' he had upbraided her. So the knowing, offensive compliments, full of innuendoes, had continued, the lingering caresses on hand and arm, neck and waist from which Mathilde shook herself free in vain. Once, she had turned on him with a sharpness worthy of Frédéric at his most dismissive. He had looked startled, but it had seemed only to make him the more eager in his attentions, as if that show of spirit excited him. Avoidance was the only possible way out; and that was becoming increasingly difficult. 'Then let her wed him,' was Henri's solution. 'A few months of marriage and he'll be content to keep his hands off her; then it'll be Mathilde who'll be crying out for it instead.' Laure did not deign to reply to that.

He was here again today. The faint murmur from Mathilde, the bleak look in her eyes expressive of the misery that only too often these days found release in tears; these signs warned Laure even before she looked up and saw Victor riding towards the house.

He had seen them and they were only a short way from the arch into the courtyard, so there was no escape. He rode up to them, dismounted swiftly and came at once to cast a casual greeting at Laure and Charles before putting his arm lingeringly about Mathilde and kissing her, holding her the closer when she shrank away from him. 'Mm – sweet little sister.' He glanced at Laure. 'My father sent me over on an errand for him. I'll stay to lunch.'

'Then perhaps you would care to stay as well,' Laure invited Charles, who was gazing at Victor with marked distaste. It was a moment or two before he heard what she said, a little longer still before he overcame his astonished delight enough to accept the invitation with enthusiasm. Laure returned her attention to Victor. 'As it is almost lunch-time,' she said crisply, 'I suggest you do whatever you came for at once. I expect you will wish to return to Trissac as soon as possible afterwards.'

'Oh, there's no hurry.' But he did release Mathilde, with a last long caress of the arm; and she went at once to Charles, all smiles and warmth.

'There is just time for you to hear the new song I have been practising – if you wish that is, Monsieur de Miremont.'

Unmusical though he was, Charles could have asked for nothing more. He went with her, apparently blissfully unaware of Victor's scowl, or the fact that she was using him to demonstrate her detestation of Victor's behaviour. You see, said the impulsive sweetness of her manner towards Charles, this is how I reward a kind and considerate man. Laure hoped – without much conviction – that the lesson would not be lost on Victor.

Unfortunately, after lunch Victor showed no inclination to return to Trissac, whilst good manners compelled Charles to take his leave of them before he risked outstaying his welcome. In the *petit salon*, where they had been sitting over coffee, he came to bend over Mathilde's hand, not quite presuming to kiss it. 'I look forward to meeting you again very soon in Bergerac,' he said. She rose to go with him to the door, and Victor clutched at her arm.

'A moment, Mathilde.' She pulled herself free and made some confused and hurried excuse and ran away upstairs to her room, where even Victor would not follow.

It was Laure, alone, who went to the door with Charles.

'Forgive me if I presume, *madame*,' the young man said, once they were out of Victor's hearing, 'but I think that

Monsieur Séguier's manner towards your daughter is not always what it ought to be.'

'It is not at all what it ought to be,' Laure agreed grimly. 'Please do not think it is a matter of indifference to me.'

Charles was blushing now. 'I *have* presumed, *madame*; it is not my business, I know. But you see, a young girl of such . . . to see her treated so . . .' In his distress he seemed unable to find words to express what he felt.

Laure smiled gently. 'Then she will benefit from a few days respite in Bergerac, as I'm sure you understand. You have my note for Madame Lacroix safe, I hope? I shall bring Mathilde over tomorrow.'

'I look forward to it, *madame*, with the greatest possible pleasure.' They had reached the front door, where a groom had Charles's horse ready. 'Ah, *madame*, I recollect now. I am not sure, but when he rode to meet us before lunch I think I saw signs of wear on the girth of Monsieur Séguier's saddle. I could not be sure, but if I am right then it is something that should not be neglected. Perhaps you would be so good as to mention it to him for me?'

So now you've put us all to rights, she thought; but she was amused rather than resentful. 'But of course, *monsieur*,' she assured him cheerfully. '*Au revoir!*'

Much later, when Henri had returned and dinner was over and Victor – at last – had gone, Laure went to say good-night to Mathilde, and was distressed by the desperation with which the girl clung to her. 'I hate Victor so, Maman. What can I do? I know you don't want me to marry him, but—'

'But your stepfather does; I know. It makes it very difficult. Just have courage, *ma petite*, and patience, and one day they will both grow tired. They must realise at last that if ever Victor is to marry then he must look elsewhere.'

'I suppose so.' She drew back a little, standing now slumped against her mother, supported by that protective arm. 'Sometimes the days seem so long.'

The weary despair behind the words made Laure's heart twist painfully. At seventeen, with all her life before her, to feel like this – how could any man do that to her, knowingly, without scruple?

'You have your visit to the Lacroixs to look forward to, *minou*. You will enjoy that.'

'I suppose so.'

'And in July we go to Paris; don't forget that. Now all the unrest has died down there should be no problem about it.'

'Only, unless we can stop him, Victor will come too. It wasn't Victor I—' She turned abruptly away, and Laure caught little of what she said then, only, '. . . he can't . . .'

Frédéric, she thought, with the unpleasant lurch of the stomach that the thought of him had brought ever since that New Year morning. He had written only once, in reply to a rather restrained letter from Mathilde, and then simply to say that he would not, after all, be able to see them in Paris, since he would be too much occupied with his examinations at that time. Mathilde had accepted the excuse calmly, without comment, but what she really felt underneath Laure could only guess. She was, however, quite sure that if the alternative escort for their visit was to be Victor, then Mathilde would inevitably think of Frédéric with intense regret.

'We'll find a way to go without him,' she promised, though she had no idea how.

To her relief, the next moment Mathilde gave a sudden little laugh. 'What a strange young man that Charles de Miremont is, Maman! I do find it hard not to laugh out loud sometimes.'

Laure smiled; but added warningly, 'Be careful, *minou*. I think he could easily be hurt – and he's an agreeable young man, in his way.'

'Beside Victor, he's a paragon,' Mathilde agreed drily. 'But you are right; I will try to be kind.'

Laure kissed her again and left her, and went to her room to face her own private nightmare.

She had fallen asleep at last some time long after midnight when a sound jolted her awake. She lay listening, aware that beside her Henri was doing the same.

The sound came again: the wild clanging of a distant bell and with it an incessant hammering upon the front door. Laure glanced towards the window, shuttered and curtained;

there was no line of light marking its outline. It was still night then.

'*Mon Dieu*, what can all that be?' Henri rolled over, groaning, groping to light a candle. A little after, as the clamour continued, he left the room.

Laure pulled on a wrap and followed him. By now the noise had woken Marius, and by the time Laure had reached the half-landing he was hurrying, lamp in hand, a comical nightcapped figure, to reach the door just as his master did.

'Maman!' Mathilde came down the stairs behind her. Laure reached out an arm to draw the girl to her side. 'What is it?'

'I don't know.'

'Monsieur Séguier has a gun.'

'So he has.'

But when at last the door was unbolted and flung wide they saw that there was no need for guns. A man stumbled over the threshold, talking wildly, incoherently, in a confused mixture of French and patois. Behind him two others came more slowly carrying something heavy on a makeshift stretcher.

Laure could not hear all that was said after that, but enough of it reached her to make a deadly kind of sense. 'An accident, *monsieur* . . . a fall from his horse . . . a broken girth, it seems . . .'

They had found him, these three revellers, as they returned late from a convivial evening somewhere: Victor, lying by the roadside whilst his horse grazed unconcernedly nearby. His skull was broken.

When Laure next saw Charles de Miremont, sometime after the funeral, she said, 'It was my fault. I forgot to give him your message.'

He took her hand in both of his, looking down at her with his blue eyes full of compassion. 'You must not reproach yourself, *madame*. I too forgot, until the very last moment; and it was only by chance that I saw it at all. He might have checked it himself – indeed, he should have done so. It is the first rule for every horseman.'

But she wondered sometimes, If I had not been angry with

350

him, if I had not hated him for what he did to Mathilde –
would I have remembered then?

And whatever her feelings for Henri she would not have
wished even on him the wild grief that possessed him
now.

They did not go to Paris that year.

CHAPTER
EIGHTEEN

As the Abbé Lebrun crossed the market place the first of the village children were already making their way to school, though it was scarcely light and the last notes of the morning angelus had only just faded into silence.

The *curé* peered at the two figures coming his way through the mist: two quite large children, their sabots clattering on the newly paved surface. He might have known: the Martin boys, Jean-Jacques and Lazare, very tidy in their black smocks with their satchels on their backs. It was Robert Martin's way of demonstrating his fervent support for the commune's school, to ensure that his sons were always first in the playground in the morning. There was already a light in the café and very soon Robert Martin himself would leave his house and make his way, puffed up with importance, to the *mairie*. He had been elected Mayor of Casseuil following the death of Doctor Rossillon earlier this year.

The doctor had been bad enough, the *curé* thought. After all, the godless school with its mixed playground and its aggressively Republican teaching had been his cherished scheme. But at least he had been a well-educated man of civilised tastes, unfailingly good mannered. Robert Martin was another matter altogether, assertive, loudly hostile to the church, taking to extremes all the most unacceptable of Doctor Rossillon's principles. There were still, in one or two places about the market place, torn remnants of tricolour ribbon and bunting left from the lavish, noisy celebrations of July's centenary of the Revolution. They rustled and flapped when the wind blew, irritatingly reminding the Abbé Lebrun of all his failures.

Even his Church seemed to be deserting him these days, he reflected sourly. At the highest level it was being hinted that it was the duty of French Catholics to accept the Republic and work with it for the good of France. But then those Bishops with their modern ideas – and even the Holy Father himself, far away in Rome – didn't have to live day after day in a community where everything they held most dear was hated and reviled. *They* did not have first hand experience of the evil he was fighting.

The Church's supporters in Casseuil seemed to grow fewer by the year, despite the Abbé's strenuous efforts. There might be a new little Chabry to add his lusty crying to the prayers at mass, but for all that the congregation had dwindled depressingly. Mademoiselle Mathilde was still faithful, and so was Nanon Foussac; but since her marriage Madame Laure had come only very rarely to church and, when he called to remonstrate with her, refused obstinately to discuss the matter. His own housekeeper had died, and so had Nanon's old mother, who used to ring the angelus. He had been unable to find a replacement for either of them, which was why he had this morning, as usual, rung the bell himself.

As he reached the door of the presbytery, young Daniel Vergnolles passed him on his way to work. 'Good morning, *mon fils*,' said the *curé*, who never quite gave up. But I might as well be invisible, he thought, as the young man went on his way without even looking round.

The presbytery was in an appalling state of repair by now, almost uninhabitable. It would be cold too, and cheerless, for he had still to light the fire and prepare coffee for his breakfast. He pushed open the door.

'*Monsieur le curé!*' He turned, quite astonished that anyone should want him; and then was enormously cheered to see Mathilde Naillac coming across the road towards him, rosy and breathless. Suddenly it seemed much lighter. He realised that it was going to be a fine day.

'I hoped to catch you at church, but I was too late.'

'I did not know you had already returned from Bordeaux.'

'We came back last night. Maman had to be here for the *vendange*, and besides there was nothing to keep us once it was over.' She paused, and he realised she had something of great importance to tell him. '*Monsieur le curé*, he left me everything he had – and it is a great deal, a very great deal.'

He took her hand and patted it. 'Are you really surprised, *ma fille*?'

'Yes – yes, I am. I suppose there was no one else, except perhaps my mother, but even so—' She smiled a little sadly. 'Poor Uncle Auguste, he must have been very fond of me, and I did not even realise. That's why I've come, as soon as I could. I'd like you to say a mass for him, if you would.'

'Of course, *ma fille*. I shall do so gladly. On Thursday, if that will suit you . . . Did you perhaps meet with Monsieur de Miremont in Bordeaux?' The question was casually put, but Mathilde coloured and became at once rather reserved.

'No. We did not expect to do so.'

The *curé* regretted the question and immediately began to talk of something else. He did not want any misplaced intervention of his own to upset the delicate business of a courtship that might or might not lead to the happy outcome he so hoped for. He knew that Mathilde and her mother had recently spent some days as guests of the Comte de Miremont. That was an auspicious and very tangible sign of the way things were going. But nothing had been said yet, or decided. Only: a devout, aristocratic Catholic married to Mademoiselle Mathilde and living at the château – that would be an answer to his prayers, providing the Church with the strongest possible of allies. He must not allow himself to hope too much; one might so easily be disappointed.

Daniel Vergnolles was whistling as he made his way through the trees towards the château. Moïse heard him and turned to wait for him to catch up.

'You sound cheerful this morning, lad.'

Daniel grinned. 'Why shouldn't I? No more sitting around at home listening to the two old people going on at me – that's excuse enough to be cheerful.'

Moïse looked just a little disapproving. 'There must be plenty for you to do at home. There's only the three of you to look after the land.'

'That would be fine if there was enough land to feed three of us. Besides, I've had my fill of it, slaving away every hour God gives for no reward. That's no life.'

354

'You've only a week or two more, then it's the army for you. Couldn't you put up with it that long?'

'That makes it worse. They've done nothing but complain and wring their hands since I had word to go. My mother weeps all the time. I'm glad to get away, I can tell you. Another thing, once my military service is over, I'll not be back, not ever. It'll be Bordeaux for me, or some other town: money in my pocket and a nice indoor job with fixed hours.'

Moïse shook his head. 'Well, you won't be the first – or the last either, I reckon. You'd not have this job here now if so many hadn't gone already.'

'No, so Madame Laure said. She knows I can't stay till the end of the *vendange*. One thing I will say though – it's good to think of a real *vendange* at Casseuil again.'

The thought visibly cheered Moïse too. 'Aye, it is that. The first *vendange* since the blight – you can almost believe things are going to get better.'

'There'll be others too. They say Chabry's replanting with grafted vinestock now.'

'And my cousin Aubin's begun too, over at Le Petit Colin. They're all doing it. But Madame Laure was the first. I'm proud to think I had a hand in it. We weren't too sure, any of us, that first spring, when we grafted on to the new rootstock. It was strange to us then of course. Nowadays, we all learn how to graft the vines.'

'Or buy them ready grafted.'

'Or that. But it was new then, all of it. It's a funny feeling, knowing you're the first, and not knowing what will come of it. It must have been worst for Madame Laure, being the one who chose to do it. There were some who said she was mad – and some who thought she'd bring worse things than the phylloxera to Casseuil, on the foreign vines.'

'There isn't anything worse than the phylloxera,' said Daniel scornfully. '*And* there weren't any vines left in Casseuil by then, to be hurt by it.'

'That's right, there weren't. She's the one who brought them back.'

'Aye. Whatever's been said about a woman running a

vineyard, she's proved them wrong in the end. She knew what she was doing all along.'

Laure was already there when they arrived, looking very businesslike in her black serge skirt and jacket, softened by a fall of lace at the throat. It was just like the old days, the oxen being put to harness, the *comportes* carried out to the carts, the baskets ready, an air of happy expectancy over everything.

Laure was trembling with excitement. In the office she dropped the record book twice before she laid it open on the table; and when she entered the date she could hardly control her pen. 'Tuesday October 15th 1889 – commencement of the *vendange*.'

All thought of yesterday and Mathilde's astonishing legacy from Uncle Auguste, which had so delighted them both, had left her now. All that mattered was that at last it was here, the day she had longed for, the first day of her first real harvest.

She hoped she had thought of everything. The *pressoir* was ready and she had checked that it was in working order. The *cuves* were thoroughly cleaned and purified with sulphur. For the time being they would re-use the old *cuves*, but when there was a great wine again, then she would buy new ones. In the kitchen Nanon – for once supplanting Louis-Christophe, the self-important young chef – was lovingly preparing the *tourin* and the *saugrenade* for the *vendangeurs*' meals. And everyone was ready outside, waiting for the signal to begin.

Oh for Jean Delisle to advise her, to remind her of anything she had forgotten! But Laure had to manage without him, relying on all he had taught her and all she had learned since he left, from Aubin and the others. Was this how Monsieur Delisle had felt each year as they embarked on the *vendange*, with a fizz like champagne spreading out through his veins from some tight churning little knot deep inside?

The sun was up now, the early mist dispelled; a perfect day. Laure laughed aloud – she could not help it – as she went out to give the word to begin. She took up a basket herself and went with them, joining her voice to their songs, though she did not know the words of the patois; in recent years there had been too little singing at Casseuil for her to learn. The vines were too young for anything more than the most ordinary

356

wine to result, and the weather had been too changeable; there was only the very slightest hint of *pourriture noble* on a few of the Sémillon grapes this year. But what mattered was that they would be making wine again from the healthy plants on whose thin young stems the scars of the grafting were by now scarcely visible.

When the first cartload of *comportes* was ready, Laure went back with it to the *chai*, where Daniel, as instructed, was waiting to operate the *pressoir*. Together they lifted the *comportes* and carried them inside and emptied them into the *pressoir*; and the three men heaved on the great beam. Laure watched the must flow out, clouded with impurities as always at this stage, its fruity odour filling the air, a clean young smell with nothing of the rich heady fragrance of the must of the great years about it. For that she would have to wait, for many years yet. But she had begun.

So completely did her joy carry her through the day that she did not realise how tired she was until she went in after dark to change for dinner. But weariness only replaced joy with contentment. She hummed to herself as she washed and put on a pretty evening dress – in a delicate shade of lilac, because they were in mourning for Uncle Auguste – and coiled her hair high on her head.

In the room next to hers Henri, cheerful too, was whistling tunelessly, but she heard him without fear. This room overlooking the courtyard, no longer a guestroom, was her sanctuary, her solitary retreat. She did not quite know how or why it had happened, but since Victor's death Henri had ceased to make any demands upon her. Grief had been a part of it, a grief that was still only partially healed, although on the surface Henri showed few signs of it. Perhaps, also, the fact that she had disliked Victor had made her suddenly unattractive to his father. Whatever the reason, he had made no objection at all when she had quietly moved into the adjoining bedroom, and he had left her in uninterrupted possession of it ever since. She supposed he must have made other arrangements to supply his needs – the housekeeper at Trissac, perhaps, a fine looking woman – but that did not trouble her. Marriage to Henri had become bearable, now that the dark side of his nature was no longer forced upon her.

The easing of that particular burden had lately confronted her with quite a different concern. For she had realised at last – though in some sense she had always known it – that the possibility of Mathilde's marriage threatened the one thing that (apart from her daughter) she still cared about most deeply; her control of Casseuil. When Mathilde married, her husband, whoever he was, would replace Laure as master of Casseuil; he would even be able, if he wished, to turn her from the house – after all, Trissac was now her home, strictly speaking. But at least Auguste Silvine's legacy gave Mathilde the freedom to make her choice of marriage partner without pressure from Henri or anyone else. It even left her free not to marry, should she so decide. Laure pushed the unwelcome, intruding thought from her mind and concentrated again on today's joyous beginning.

She went downstairs, smiling as she heard the sweet notes of the piano floating up to her: Mathilde, occupying her time until dinner was ready with some new tune – or was it new? Something about its wistful sweetness tugged at her memory. Mathilde began to sing.

Laure stood quite still. It all came back to her in a rush: the summer sun, the cherries ripening overhead, and Jean-Claude's arms about her blissfully contented body. She pressed her hand to her mouth in a sudden gesture of anguish.

'She sings well, our little heiress, does she not?'

Laure shuddered and turned her head to look at Henri, coming down the stairs behind her. She hoped he did not see anything out of the ordinary in her expression.

'Let's go and join her. I'm hungry – I hope Louis-Christophe has been able to get into the kitchen long enough to prepare dinner. Lunch was terrible. I wished I'd stayed at Trissac.'

Laure went with him as if dazed; across the hall, into the *grand salon* where the notes of the music came like darts, each one shooting its way with agonising precision into her raw nerves.

'What's that you're singing?' Henri asked.

Mathilde's fingers came, mercifully, to a halt, and she stood up. She looked very happy. ' "Le Temps des Cérises" – don't you know it? It was republished a year or two ago with a new verse. Émilie gave it to me. She says her parents don't approve of it because the writer was a *Communard*. But it's pretty, isn't it?'

Pretty – no, thought Laure: for me it can never be pretty. 'I don't care for it very much,' she said drily. 'Let's go in to dinner.'

CHAPTER
NINETEEN

i

'Now, tell me. What do you think?'

Charles held the glass against the candle flame, studying the liquid it contained, its colour the pale bleached gold of summer straw. 'The colour is not bad, *madame*. It has cleared well.' Next, he sniffed thoughtfully for a few moments. 'Yes, clean and fruity.' Then he raised the glass, tipped it slowly, took a mouthful with the same premeditated care as he chose his words; and held it in his mouth, breath drawn in, his face a mask of concentration.

He swallowed, paused a little while; and smiled and nodded. 'Acceptable, quite acceptable, *madame*. I congratulate you. When the vines mature, if the weather is kind then.' He made an expressive gesture with his hands. 'I think you have every reason for optimism.'

This morning, checking the *cuves* that held the very first vintage from the new vines – the wine of 1889 – Laure had permitted herself a taste. She knew you could not expect much from plants so young, and the wine itself was still very immature; but even so, as Charles said, it was acceptable. She had tasted it herself with a sense of joy and excitement out of all proportion to its mediocrity, because at last, firmly, she could look forward with hope, even expectation. She needed patience still in abundance; but with care and cossetting and all the loving nurture she could give, one day—

So she had seized on Charles, always a sympathetic supporter of her efforts, the moment he arrived at Casseuil this morning. On holiday from his studies, he was staying again at Bergerac, and had found some slender excuse to call – a book delivered on behalf of Mademoiselle Émilie this time, Laure thought. She knew they could expect to see a great deal of him throughout September, before his term began again. Poor Charles, struggling with the intricacies of the law, had found he was taking longer to qualify than he had hoped; which meant, Laure supposed, that for some time to come he would not consider marriage. But the reverential tenderness of his manner towards Mathilde left no possible shadow of doubt that his choice was made.

As for Mathilde – Laure did not know. The girl neither encouraged nor discouraged Charles, although for the most part she was kind to him, hiding her amusement at his oddities. They had met often since the ball, for Mathilde had become a frequent visitor to the Lacroixs, just as Émilie came often to stay at Casseuil, either with the Chabrys or with themselves. And last year there had been that invitation to join the Lacroixs on a visit to the château at St Antoine de Miremont, where Charles's stately and ceremonious parents had done their best to make them feel welcome in an establishment whose restrained grandeur made Casseuil, on their return, feel positively cottage-like. Laure knew that Mathilde had completely charmed the old Comte de Miremont and his wife. Since Charles was very much a younger son, they could afford to be tolerant about her background. In any case the Naillacs were undeniably of the nobility too, if unfortunately tarnished by Protestantism and the regrettably flexible politics that had caused them, at the Revolution, to drop the aristocratic 'de' from their name. Further, although the de Miremonts were not especially wealthy, Mathilde's inheritance more than made up for that. As for Mathilde herself, all Laure knew was that something had changed in her. The sweetness was still there, but in these first years of womanhood she had grown inclined to moodiness, alternately dreamy and irritable, sometimes even depressed. No longer troubled by Victor, she did not seem any happier as a consequence.

Laure glanced at her daughter, standing beside her with a glass in her hand. She had sipped at it, but absently, as if she did not know what she was doing. Now she was gazing across the room with thoughts clearly very far removed from the *cuves* in the cool candlelit dimness, and her mother's hopes.

'What do you think, Mathilde?'

Confusedly, the girl looked round, coloured; and then sipped again, with greater attention this time. 'Yes – yes, it's quite good.'

Laure gave her an intent look and then quickly pushed aside the anxiety that rose in her at that indefinable something in Mathilde's face. She turned back to Charles and laid a hand on the *cuve* from which the wine had been drawn.

'So, let it lie there and age a little, but not much for this one. The day will come when we'll have a true Château de Casseuil again, one to lay down for years and bring out for the family feasts, like the old great wines.'

'And here's to that day!' Charles raised his glass and drained the last drops and Mathilde, unsmiling, did the same. She had that look still, a strangeness, tense and very serious, but with eyes bright and full of suppressed excitement.

As they returned to the house, emerging into the drenching heat of the sunlit courtyard, Charles said, 'Mademoiselle Naillac tells me that you expect Monsieur Brousse this evening.' After a tiny pause, he added, 'And a Monsieur Petit also.'

Was he anxious about possible competition for Mathilde's affections? Laure too wondered what this friend of Frédéric's was like: what indeed Frédéric himself was like now, after almost two years. There had been only the one single letter (if you did not count the formal expression of condolence to Henri on Victor's death) until last week, when he had written not to Mathilde but to Laure. He had finished his studies, he told her, and now planned a holiday. A new law had removed all previous exemptions to military sevice, and he and Félix were just young enough (as Charles was not) to be caught by it. In November the army would claim them; until then they intended to make a tour of Italy.

'May we be permitted to pass a few days at Casseuil on our way, *madame*?'

Reading the letter, Laure had thought, What was it I said to him all those years ago? 'You know this is still your home, for as long as you wish it to be so.' She could not refuse him a short visit now, when he asked so courteously and came so rarely. Besides, time had passed. In Paris there were many women, more exciting by far than Mathilde; it was more than likely that the painful emotions of that New Year had faded now and troubled him no longer. After all, surely he would not come, if seeing Mathilde again would only open an old wound?

It was only after she had written to welcome him and told Mathilde of his coming visit that the doubts of those days, long quiet, had come sharply to life again. She had fought them, repressed them. Of course Mathilde was excited and happy. Would she herself not be happy at the prospect of seeing Marcel again? The girl had many friends of her own age, visits, picnics, dinner parties, balls and the quieter activities of home to fill her days; but life must be a little dull sometimes, and she was fond of Frédéric. What more natural than to welcome his coming? Yet—

No, I must not even think of it. It's only my imagination, she told herself.

'Yes,' she said aloud to Charles. 'They are to pay us a brief visit.' Quickly then she sheered away from the subject. 'Will you stay for lunch, Monsieur de Miremont?' She knew his answer, of course: he never refused any invitation whose acceptance would keep him near Mathilde.

'Thank you, *madame*.'

Perhaps, she thought, his presence will distract Mathilde, keep her mind on something other than Frédéric's coming. She did not know whether or not she wished Mathilde would come to love Charles, as perhaps he deserved, certainly as Laure wanted her daughter to love the man she should eventually marry. There was no urgency now, far from it. Yet for her to want to marry soon, to settle for some kindly and eligible young man like Charles, would be reassuring, a sign that her heart had been, until his coming, secure and untouched. Laure wanted that reassurance so much, though she told herself she did not need it, not really.

There was not much comfort for her today. Mathilde had just asked some question of Charles that Laure did not hear, though she saw the young man pause – physically, mentally – coming to a standstill and gazing at Mathilde in that gravely considering way of his; and she heard Mathilde say after a moment, in exasperation, 'Monsieur de Miremont, why do you always take so long to answer even the simplest of questions?'

There was, of course, no immediate reply, although Charles smiled faintly, as if aware of a certain deficiency in that direction. Then, grave again, he said at last, 'Because, *mademoiselle*, I believe that nothing should ever be entered upon lightly. Every word is important; the wrong word may hurt, or deceive, or give offence. Of course, one may still make a wrong choice of words; but to consider before speaking lessens the risk.'

Mathilde stared at him with marked incomprehension. 'Do you *never* do anything on impulse, Monsieur de Miremont?'

'Very occasionally, I suppose. But not often. After all, everything one does involves a moral choice. Perhaps I have a greater need to take care than most; I do not know. But that is how I see it.'

Later, when he had gone, Mathilde said to her mother, 'Do you think he knows how funny he is? He can't do, or he'd not say such things. I can't bear a man with no sense of humour. He gets on my nerves.'

So, thought Laure, with anxious weariness, did everything today. For her too the hours could not pass too quickly until Frédéric came and the waiting was over; since he *was* coming, whatever happened.

Félix Petit, they discovered, when – delayed by a late train – the guests eventually arrived, was large and dark and very far from well. Frédéric, obsessively anxious about him, spared scarcely a greeting for anyone before hurrying his friend upstairs and seeing him to bed with a soothing remedy for the agonising headache that had afflicted him most of the way from Paris. Only when Félix was asleep did he come down to join them belatedly at the dinner table.

He was not good company. Having apologised briefly for his friend's indisposition, he answered their questions in monosyllables, initiated no conversation himself, and ate very little. Mathilde subsided ever deeper into silent misery; Laure could see she was very close to tears. She had longed so much to see him again, and now she was faced with this morose stranger.

Next morning it was like the clouds parting after a storm; or perhaps, more appropriately, Laure thought, like the dramatic breaking of a storm after hours of oppressive silence. His headache gone, Félix appeared at breakfast all talk and laughter, a huge vital presence suddenly shrinking everything about him to half life-size, as if only he was quite real and everyone else a little pale and insignificant. At his side the slight, vivid Frédéric of that memorable Christmas re-appeared, only this time with Félix as his partner in wit, so that jokes and laughter darted between them like lightning, swift and dazzling, at once bewildering and exhilarating their listeners.

It did not take Laure long to regret an impulse that had led her to invite Charles de Miremont, with the Lacroixs and the Chabrys, to dinner two days later. The strange new atmos-phere Félix had brought with him, which seemed to fill every corner of the château, was something alien, in which Charles would be quite out of place and probably very uncomfortable. There was nothing definable on which she could put her finger, but Laure had an unmistakable sense of some kind of dangerous and threatening enchantment. It had already enmeshed Mathilde, who hung fascinated about the two young men, to be absorbed soon into their company. They became a trio, singing and playing music together, laughing over cards, talking endlessly. Laure had a word with Nanon and asked her to remain with Mathilde, a discreet chaperon, whenever she herself could not be present; although it seemed to make no difference, for they behaved as if she were not there.

Charles came, with the others, and took his place at table; and, as was his custom, bent his head for a moment of prayer before beginning to eat. He always did it discreetly, not like Madame Naillac used to do, murmuring grace aloud in a manner calculated to act as a rebuke to her companions; but Laure saw the laughter pass in silence from Félix to Frédéric and then to Mathilde, and heard the murmured comment that brought a muffled explosion of mirth, and felt pain for their pious young guest. It was not that he did not amuse her too, but her amusement was always kindly, for there was no malice in him and she could bear none towards him. There was, on the other hand, a world of malice in Félix's dark eyes and Frédéric's thin-lipped smile, and even reflected in the expression of her once kindly daughter. As the meal progressed it grew, though never quite openly, the remarks veiled somewhat from their victim's rather slow understanding, but clear enough to the quicker witted Mathilde.

'A veritable Tartuffe, don't you agree, *mon vieux*?' Félix said to Frédéric as Laure returned from seeing their guests on their way. Laure knew the reference quite well: Tartuffe was the ingratiating religious hypocrite of Molière's play. She broke in angrily before Frédéric could give voice to the witticism that was clearly on his lips.

'He is nothing of the kind!' she said indignantly. 'He is a little eccentric perhaps, but entirely sincere and very good hearted, which is more, I feel, than can be said this evening of either of you.' Or you, Mathilde, she added sadly to herself; although at least Mathilde, alone of the three, had the grace to blush. Félix merely grinned charmingly and said with a careless gesture of the hands, 'Ah, but you see, *madame*, we do him a service. How can he hope to shine, without darkness about him?'

As if in reaction, Félix subsided next day into a mood of silent black depression which ended in another crippling headache for which the only remedy was bed. Frédéric fussed anxiously over him, releasing Mathilde to seek her mother's company, for the first time since their arrival.

'Moïse is to start preparing the *chai* for the *vendange* today,' Laure said, her tone rather more brisk than was usual towards Mathilde. 'I want to see that he does as I instructed. I suggest you come with me.'

Mathilde recognised the note of command in that 'suggest' and came meekly enough, as if aware that she had some ground to recover in her mother's esteem.

In the *chai* the air was heavy with the smell of the sulphur candles used in cleaning the *cuves*. It had a grim appropriateness, Laure thought, in keeping with the atmosphere within the château. This morning at breakfast, before the others came down, Henri had said to her, 'There's something not quite healthy about those two.'

Because she never found it easy to agree with Henri, she had merely replied, 'You never did like Frédéric, did you?'

'Do you?' he had returned; to which she could only say, quite truthfully, 'I don't know.'

But she knew about Félix. Against her will he made her laugh, she found his talk exciting and she could not deny that there was something intoxicating about his presence. But she did not like him; and she feared the poison of his influence upon her daughter. That he had Frédéric in thrall beyond hope of release was obvious enough. She did not want Mathilde to go the same way.

'*Chérie*,' she said gently now to Mathilde, as they made their way past the *cuves* to the further room where Moïse was looking over the barrels, 'don't allow your sense of humour to overcome your consideration for others.'

Mathilde glanced at her. 'Of course not,' was all she said; and then she coughed and held her handkerchief to her nose to shut out the choking fumes.

She was restless that day, and bored, as if drifting along rudderless and without any driving force, waiting for life to take her up again. No, not life: Félix and Frédéric. She did not consciously allow them to *do* anything; yet she could not help what was happening to her. A sense of excitement like nothing she had ever known before seemed to seep through her pores and run through her blood, catching her up and carrying her away without the power or the wish to resist or turn aside. Even today, out here with her mother, she felt them, saw them, bore them with her, those two young men: Frédéric's slight fairness, his strange compelling eyes, his dear familiarity changed, transformed by the dark hypnotic presence of his friend. Félix was Frédéric's hidden life made manifest, a shadow become reality. Frédéric had told her once that Félix had taught him to reach out for happiness, to dare to allow himself to feel. He had told her too how they had first become friends and a part of her had loved Félix from that moment, for his generosity. Now she understood that without him Frédéric had in some way been only half himself, that they were somehow essential one to another, part of a whole. She too wanted achingly to be a part of that whole and today, shut out, she was left with a terrible sense of emptiness.

Nanon was worried about Mathilde. She had long thought her precious girl was lovesick. She knew the signs well enough, but whether the cause was nice young Monsieur de Miremont she could not be sure. Now it was only too clear that Monsieur Petit had driven all thought of anyone else out of her head.

Nanon did not like Monsieur Petit in the least. He was one of those young men – fortunately rare in her experience – who gave you the feeling they were laughing at you, whatever they said or did; and that not kindly either. There was always a sneer lurking somewhere behind his slightest gesture. Monsieur de Miremont might be a bit on the solemn side, but Monsieur Petit took nothing seriously at all as far as Nanon could see. She was quite sure he lived an immoral life up there in Paris. She wished very much that he'd stayed there.

Her feelings for Frédéric were rather more ambiguous. As a child he had aroused in her a maternal wish to make up to him for all the neglect and abuse of one kind or another that he had suffered; but she had never been able to do anything about it, and besides Mathilde had always been her first concern. Now she was angry with him for bringing Félix here.

Today, quite early, Madame Laure had come up to the comfortable room on the third floor where Nanon had lived since her mother's death and explained that she had to go to Bergerac. 'I've found faults in four of the six new barrels that were delivered the other day and I want to see them personally about it. One can make a much stronger impression that way.' Nanon did not doubt it, having seen Madame Laure in one of her rare but terrifying rages; though mercifully they had never been directed at her. 'But,' Laure had been frowning a little then, from anxiety, 'I don't want to leave Mathilde unsupervised. She's not up yet, but she soon will be. I'd be very grateful if you'd keep an eye on her for me, at least as long as they're indoors.'

So of course when Mathilde did come down to breakfast Nanon was already seated quietly in a corner of the dining-room, knitting away as if nothing could be more natural. Mathilde, growing accustomed to this new sign of her mother's concern, if just a little irritated by it, was unsurprised and went cheerfully to kiss Nanon before taking her seat at the table; but there was none of the happy chatter Nanon might once have enjoyed. Not, that is, until the young men joined her.

Then of course it was not chatter at all, but a fast-moving laughing exchange of wit and schoolboy humour that Nanon, for all her carefully learned French, could scarcely follow. She did know, though, that Monsieur Petit's first remark, accompanied by a bright glance in her direction, was in some incomprehensible way an allusion to herself, and it made her feel uncomfortable. She was almost angered at the way – a little shamefacedly, it was true – Mathilde laughed at the remark.

There had been a storm in the night and it was raining still, so after breakfast the three young people adjourned to the *grand salon*, followed, at a cautious distance, by Nanon.

'Come and make a fourth at cards, *chère tricoteuse*!' Monsieur Petit invited her. She knew a *tricoteuse* was a lady who knitted and that this was how Monsieur Petit always referred to her, but she did not see why it never failed to reduce them to such extremes of mirth. She was afraid there might be some hidden and perhaps indelicate meaning behind the word, and she blushed.

'No thank you, *monsieur*,' she said stiffly. 'I'll just sit here.' And she took her seat in the furthest corner possible.

'Ah, she waits for the heads to roll! Then let us commence, *mes amis*.' Félix led them with a sweeping gesture to the card table, ignoring Mathilde's murmured protest at his teasing of her old nurse – for which Nanon was grateful, though it seemed to have no effect. Félix began to shuffle the cards and then stopped suddenly and laughed. 'You must keep Tartuffe away at all costs, *mademoiselle* – let him beware: *la Tricoteuse* awaits him! He may yet suffer the fate of his ancestors – *à bas les aristos!* as they used to say, those old women at the guillotine.'

Mathilde laughed a little reluctantly, glancing towards Nanon as if to show that she meant no harm. But Nanon was hurt all the same and disliked Monsieur Petit the more.

They soon forgot about her. The card game proceeded

harmlessly enough – if with many interruptions while Félix
held forth – until eventually the cards were abandoned
altogether, forgotten as the players became involved in an
intense and gloomy conversation about death, and whether or
not there was a God or an eternal life. Serious enough matters,
Nanon acknowledged to herself; but even at his most passionate, eyes flashing, arms wildly gesturing, Monsieur Petit
seemed to be rather the centre of his own drama than someone
expressing deeply held convictions. His views were, in any
case, rather shockingly unconventional, and became more so
as they moved on to art and poetry and, at last, to love. Nanon
wondered whether to intervene and put a stop to it, but
decided against it: talk could do no harm after all.

'Love is a myth, you know,' Monsieur Petit maintained
with the overwhelming note of authority that characterised
his pronouncements. 'It is a mask invented by the bourgeoisie
to conceal the lust that they dare not admit to feeling, which is
the nearest they come to sensuality. The senses now, they
alone are the true reality. That is where the true power lies
. . .' Mathilde, facing Monsieur Petit across the table, sat very
still with her eyes raised to his face, as if she were spellbound.
'Take away the senses, deny them satisfaction and what do we
have left? Nothing – only boredom, a void. Follow where
your senses lead and you will be liberated, enriched, fulfilled –
there is life, *real* life. Like love, marriage is a bourgeois
invention, a cage, a prison forged of property and money and
convenience and lust, designed to confine the senses and to
shut out the earthy reality of life. You will say, but is not lust a
thing of the senses? Indeed no, *mes amis*, for lust is born of a
desire for power and domination, a cruel and hurtful thing.
Sensuality—' His voice became warm, caressing, stirring
something uncomfortable and unwanted to life even in
Nanon's stolid uncomprehending person. 'Sensuality now is
the yielding of oneself to the deepest reality in union with
another – there, nothing wished for can be evil, not pain itself,
if both desire it – for what matters is to follow the deepest and
truest instincts, to explore them to their ultimate limits . . .'

Mathilde felt at once dazed and fascinated, and a little sick.
She had not heard Félix talk quite like this before and, excited
and alarmed, she did not understand it even now. For a

moment he shifted his gaze from her face and transferred it to Frédéric, who sat nearby, as still as she was. She saw their eyes meet, held for a moment, gravely. Then Frédéric turned his head and looked at her and smiled his faint thin smile; it was like a touch of his hand, gentle and reassuring. You have nothing to fear from us, it said.

Then he stretched and yawned, gracefully as a cat, and rose to his feet. 'You're nothing but a weather vane, *mon cher*,' he said. 'A new argument for every wind. You know you don't believe half of what you say.'

Félix grinned, all at once relaxed and easy. 'You're right – or only half the time at least.' He came to stand before Mathilde, towering over her; then he stooped to take her hand and raise it slowly to his lips. 'Did I frighten you, *mademoiselle*? Pay no heed. Do you not know that the thing we revile is the one we most fear – the more it threatens, the greater the fear, the fiercer the resistance? I defy love – because I sense that I am touched by it.' He paused, watching her intently; and then he went on in the same low voice, too low for Nanon to hear, 'You believe that love exists, *mademoiselle*. You believe too in marriage, I think – but for you it must be, not a contract of convention, but a joining of hearts and minds and bodies – is that not so?'

'That is what it ought to be.' The words sounded prim – like Charles de Miremont at his most worthy – yet her tone was breathless and she felt almost as if she were repeating what she had been told to say, as if, held by those dark eyes, she would follow wherever Félix led. If she disagreed with what he had been saying before, it was somehow because he wanted her to do so. 'Yes, I believe that love exists.' She knew she was blushing and carefully refrained from looking at Frédéric, though she felt sure too that Félix knew everything about her, more than she did herself. He is not handsome, she thought, almost with surprise; but then there was something about his overpowering presence that rendered ordinary judgements meaningless. He was Félix, above such banal concepts as beauty and ugliness, right and wrong. He frightened her a little, but fascinated her too. She understood completely the ascendancy he had over her half-brother.

'What do you think, Frédéric?' he went on after a moment,

without looking at his friend. 'You told me she was like no other woman, this sister of yours. You were right. Can you imagine her transplanted to Paris?'

Frédéric turned away and went to look out of the open window near which they sat. 'No,' he said abruptly.

'It is like imagining a lily amongst orchids – orchids grown on a dungheap, perhaps. You are right, I am sure. One ought not to think of transplanting a lily from her pure native soil to a dungheap. Purity is sterile, a dungheap is full of life; but—' He broke off, released her hand, shrugged. 'There we are. It would be a crime.'

'It's stopped raining,' said Frédéric. 'Let's go for a walk.'

So they went, and the clear sweet air blew away the sulphurous fumes of those strange hours of talk; and Nanon, disturbed without quite knowing why, returned to her room.

Mathilde was haunted by Félix. That night as she lay in bed she could not rid herself of the thought of him – his fluent irresistible talk, his dark eyes feverish in their brilliance, his arms flung out in lavish gestures or draped about Frédéric's slight shoulders, or spread along the back of the sofa where she sat, behind her, not touching but very near. She found herself imagining them about her and shivered, though not with fear.

iii

Mathilde had loved the song 'Le Temps des Cérises' from the first moment she heard it, for its wistful simplicity and its poignancy. Unfortunately, she did not feel able to play it very often, because – for some unexplained reason – her mother could not bear it and would leave the room the moment its first lilting notes rang out. But at present Laure was upstairs still, dressing for dinner, and Mathilde, alone in the *grand salon* with the door closed – the men of the household were not down yet either – sat at the piano and sang softly, from the heart, giving to the words all her own little experience of joy and longing and pain.

'J'aimerai toujours le temps des cérises—
c'est de ce temps-là
que je garde au cœur
une plaie ouverte—'

She knew before she heard or saw them when Frédéric and Félix came in, but she did not falter in her singing. They crossed the room quietly, Frédéric to stand beside her, joining his cool tenor voice to hers; Félix to lean on the piano, facing her.

She came to the end, the notes falling silent beneath her fingers, her voice dropping away into nothingness. Frédéric stood very still, one hand resting lightly on her shoulder; Félix, motionless too, watched her steadily, with his intent dark gaze. She glanced round at Frédéric, saw that his eyes were on Félix, looked back at the other man; the three of them bound together by some power deeper than consciousness. Félix said suddenly, his voice very soft, 'If I were to ask you, Mademoiselle Mathilde, would you marry me?'

She stared at him, scarcely understanding, not thinking he could be serious, though he was not smiling. The silence continued as if it had never been broken.

Then she felt Frédéric withdraw his hand from her shoulder and walk away, somewhere across the far side of the room, leaving the two of them almost alone. She did not take her eyes from Félix's dark face.

'I am in deadly earnest, *mademoiselle*,' he said at last, as if in answer to her doubt. 'Would you come to Paris as my lover, my companion, my wife? We should be all three together, you and me and Frédéric; would you need more than that, ever? I should not, nor Frédéric.'

She shivered, as she had in the night; and at that moment heard the door close softly and knew that Frédéric had left the room. 'You and me and Frédéric . . . together . . .' She felt mesmerised, heard the phrase echo round and round in her head, felt what it meant. There was something here, in what Félix held out to her, that was utterly beyond her experience or her knowledge, something dark and hidden and scarcely guessed at, and yet infinitely alluring.

'Yes,' she whispered at last. 'Yes, I would.'

He leaned right over then, slid his hand behind her head, pulled her to her feet, towards him; and then he kissed her, slowly and thoroughly and for a long time. No one had ever kissed her like that and she found it at once exciting and terrifying. She could scarcely breathe.

When the kiss came to an end and he had retreated a little, she said unsteadily, 'We ought to tell Maman, and Monsieur Séguier.'

It sounded so silly, so irrelevant, so trivial and banal, that she wondered what had made her say it. She was not surprised that for a moment Félix looked utterly blank. It was more surprising that, after a time, he should say abruptly, 'Yes, of course – there can be no question.'

Then the next instant he was matter of fact, all smiles. 'I shall waste no time. Where can I find them? Upstairs?'

'They will be down in a moment.' She felt strange now that the spell had been broken by the brisk ordinariness of his manner; even more by the thought that someone outside the charmed trio should know of this. She did not want it to become common property, a matter of convention and custom and family arrangements; she did not, for some inexplicable reason, even want her mother to know.

Laure, coming down rather at the last moment for dinner, was a little surprised to find only Mathilde in the *grand salon* standing near the window, rather pale and unnaturally still.

'What's happened? Where is everyone?'

Mathilde shook her head slowly, as if she had only half heard the question. 'Monsieur Petit is in the library with Monsieur Séguier.'

'And Frédéric?'

A faint colour touched her cheeks. 'I don't know.' She turned away, but Laure saw with concern that her hand, resting on the window sill, was trembling.

'Is something wrong? Tell me, Mathilde.'

'Nothing is wrong, Maman.'

There was rejection in every line of her daughter's stance. Laure stared for a little time at the rigid back, and then sighed and shrugged and made her way to the library, in case there should be some solution to the mystery there.

The sound of raised voices reached her even before she opened the door and found Henri and Félix facing one another across the hearth in an atmosphere thick with cigar smoke and rage.

Almost purple with fury Henri turned on her as if eager to

find some other outlet for his emotions. 'Do you know what this – this vagrant dares to ask? No, you could never guess at his presumption – marriage to Mathilde Naillac, *par exemple*! A penniless nobody, and you'd think he was the Emperor come back to life to hear him talk.'

Laure paused just for an instant to take in the startling revelation. Then she closed the door and touched his arm. 'Henri, wait – tell me—' She hesitated, looking from her husband to the dark glowering face of Frédéric's friend. 'Does Mathilde know of this?'

Félix looked both astonished and angry at once. 'Of course she knows. It was decided between us.'

So Mathilde was in love, must be in love! For a moment, Laure's relief was so great that she almost seized Félix's hands and told him that they could be married at once. And then, abruptly, she knew it was not as simple as that, not so unambiguously desirable a state of affairs as she wanted it to be.

With that momentous choice just made, Mathilde had said nothing of it to her mother, and that was not like Mathilde. Had she kept silent from anxiety as to what Henri's reaction might be? Surely not, for then she would have rushed to enlist her mother's support. Uneasily, Laure said, 'You have known each other for five days at the very most. How can you possibly know you wish to marry?' Her tone was quieter, more reasonable than Henri's, but not much less hostile.

With a theatrical gesture Félix laid his hand on his heart. 'I know, *madame* – believe me, I know beyond all doubt. As for Mademoiselle Mathilde, I beg you to ask her.'

Summoned at once, Mathilde, all innocent simplicity, acknowledged gravely that she had indeed accepted an offer of marriage from Monsieur Petit. At that, Henri exploded.

'You have done nothing of the kind! You have the consent neither of myself nor of your mother. Without that, you have no right to accept such an offer.'

Paler than ever, Mathilde opened her mouth, closed it again, murmured faintly, 'But—'

'But nothing! What would you live on pray, *mademoiselle*?' He left her no time to reply. 'This young man professes to be mortally offended that I should call him a fortune hunter, but

I don't doubt he knows what he's doing. I ask him what he has to offer, and he talks of newspaper articles and poetry! As for how he's lived all these years, I know the answer to that one – your precious brother has kept him, that's how! *mon Dieu*, what a husband for you! What a catch!'

Again Laure laid a hand briefly on Henri's arm. 'Calm yourself. Remember there is no urgency.' She turned to Félix, who looked close to exploding with fury. 'After all, you have a year's military service to do before you can consider marriage.'

'Of course! That's it!' Henri broke in again. 'Marry Mathilde, and you'll be exempt. I might have known! That's your type all over – anything to get out of your duty to your country!'

'You lie, *monsieur*! You insult me! I am neither a fortune hunter nor a shirker! I will take her without a *sou* if that is what you wish. But I will not stand here—'

'Be quiet, both of you! Henri, I imagine it is too late now for Monsieur Petit to avoid military service by marriage – is that not so?' She glanced towards the young man and was surprised that, momentarily, he looked almost confused.

'No – yes – I shall not – I am listed only for the reserve, *madame*.' He said it so quietly that she heard him only with difficulty. Before she could question him further he went on with passionate urgency, 'Love will not wait, *madame*! You have a heart, you have loved – you *must* have loved! Do not come between us now!' His eyes seemed to see right into her, reading there her love for Jean-Claude, the pain of his loss; and pleading with her not to inflict that same bitter suffering on her daughter. Laure gave a little shake, as if to free herself from the force of his will upon her.

'Leave us alone, please – both of you.' She glanced from one to another of the two men. 'I should like to speak to Mathilde by herself.'

When the door had closed behind them, Laure turned Mathilde to face her, at once daunted by the oddly resistant look in the brown eyes. '*Chérie*, I want your happiness above everything. For that reason I am very uneasy about this. You scarcely know this young man. What makes you think you wish to marry him?'

'I do; I know I do.' There was more obstinacy than passion in her tone.

'He is fascinating, I know – and very different from anyone you have ever met. I can see the attraction. But marriage is another matter. Can you really see him settled here at Casseuil in quiet domesticity?'

'Oh, but we were to go to Paris!'

'To do what? Monsieur Séguier is right – he lives pretty idly there. I cannot imagine you would have much of a life.'

'But Frédéric—' She broke off, biting her lip.

A little chill settled somewhere inside Laure. 'What has this to do with Frédéric?'

'They live together, he and Monsieur Petit. I would live there too.' She spoke with a naïve simplicity, but her colour had risen uncomfortably.

What do I say? Laure thought. Does she know what her words suggest? Does she understand *anything*? Something held her back from confronting Mathilde with the implications of what she had said. She did not want to face the possibility that her daughter would confirm for her all the doubts that had gnawed at her through the years. In the end, she said only, 'And what does Frédéric say to it all? Or doesn't he know about it?'

Mathilde bent her head. 'I don't know. He may not have heard.' Then, asserting herself again, she went on, 'Monsieur Séguier is wrong: Monsieur Petit is not interested in my money.'

'No, I don't believe he is. But what I do doubt is that he really loves you, or you him . . . No—' She put up a hand to silence Mathilde's protest. 'I am not sure why he wishes to marry you, though I admit I mistrust him. As for you, you are dazzled by him, of course; that I understand. But it is hardly a basis for marriage.'

'What would be a better one then? The one that made you marry Monsieur Séguier?'

Shock caught in Laure's throat, stilling her breath. My child, my little one – to throw that in my face, now when I most want to help and guide her! Yet – mature, wise, mindful of Mathilde's needs – she must not show that she felt the cruelty of the attack.

377

'It is because of that,' she said, unsteadily yet with force, 'that I know better what makes a good marriage and what does not.' She read the hostility in Mathilde's eyes, and could find no other defence than to repel it with coldness. 'I am not going to argue about it any more for the time being, Mathilde. If you or Monsieur Petit insist on an answer at once, then neither I nor your stepfather will consider for a moment giving our consent. I think it unlikely that we ever will. What I am quite certain about is that we all need time for reflection – a great deal of time.'

'That shows that you know nothing of love, nothing at all! All you care about is money and convention. I hate you, Maman, I hate you!' Her fierce dark eyes full of tears in her white face, Mathilde turned and ran from the room, leaving her monsieur standing there alone, trembling with shock.

Running head bent across the landing Mathilde collided with Frédéric as he came downstairs. His hands flew to her shoulders, hovered there as if about to move on, to embrace her, and then tightened their grasp and stilled, steadying her.

'Mathilde, what is it?'

She raised her head, gazing at him from a tearstained face blotched and unattractive with emotion. She said nothing for a long time, simply gulped to restrain the tears and let her eyes run over his pale delicate features, troubled now, for her. And then she said, hesitating, 'They say – I may not – even Maman—' She saw that she did not need to say what it was they had refused; and she saw something else. 'You do not want us to marry,' she added wonderingly.

He shook his head. 'No – no, I do not – yet, I don't know—' His hands moved, momentarily caressing. She ached to move closer, to be held by him in a safe familiarity wholly unlike what Félix had to offer. Yet it would be only an illusion of safety and it was not, simply, safety or comfort that she would be seeking.

'I don't know either,' she said in sudden misery. 'I don't know what I want.' But I do, I do, said a part of her. She pulled herself abruptly free, the tears flowing again. 'I wish you had not come, either of you,' and she turned away, knowing that she only partly meant the words.

*

Downstairs, when Mathilde had gone, Laure's first instinct was to summon Félix and order him to leave the house without delay. Her hand was on the bell, ready to call Françoise to bring him to her; when she was assailed by doubts.

What am I doing? she thought. What, after all, has he done, to be sent unceremoniously away? Slowly, she let her hand fall and moved to a chair near the empty hearth and sat there, trying to understand both her daughter and herself.

On the surface Félix Petit was an interesting, if rather wild, young man who had found himself infatuated with her daughter and wished to marry her; a wish that was, apparently, reciprocated. It might be undesirable, but it was entirely natural.

And yet – the whole thing left her feeling sickened and disturbed, as if underneath lurked something evil and corrupt and polluting; something she did not want to see or to know about, yet could not ignore.

It is irrational, foolish; I am giving way to idle fancies, she told herself. But was not her instinct telling her a truth that Henri, with his talk of fortune hunters, his practical business-man's mind, could not be expected to see? And, after all, even Henri had sensed something not quite right about their guests.

But putting aside her unease and her instincts, trying for a moment to look at it all without emotion, she still could not see in Félix anything but the most ineligible of men. He had neither a job, nor money, nor prospects, nor apparently much sense of responsibility. He was also clearly in an uncertain state of health, his brilliant flights of fancy as well as his sombre moods hinting at some rooted instability that augured badly for the future. Furthermore, Laure did not believe that Mathilde loved him and even the least element of common sense suggested that the two young people should be required to wait and see how time and separation affected their feelings.

After a silent dinner – for which Mathilde did not appear – Laure took Félix on one side and told him, politely but without warmth, that he must leave Casseuil first thing tomorrow.

'I do not believe my daughter truly knows her own mind. While you are here she has no hope of doing so. I must ask you not to write to her or try to communicate with her in any way. If indeed her feelings prove to be deep and enduring I may be induced to reconsider the matter, in which case you will be told — although I suspect that you too will find you have misjudged your own heart. And there is one thing more—'

'*Madame?*' He was as cool as she was, and as correct.

'If ever you do both decide you love one another and wish to marry, then unless you have settled and secure employment elsewhere, you will be expected to live here, and not in Paris. This is Mathilde's home. Bear that in mind, please.'

He gave a little bow, saying nothing.

Next morning, coming down early to breakfast, Laure heard voices coming from the dining-room, and paused with her hand on the door, listening. Clearly, Félix and Frédéric, obeying her instructions, were already up. She was about to open the door when Frédéric's voice, raised in anger, made her hesitate again.

'No; no you must not! Leave her alone!'

'I thought you said she wouldn't come anyway. Why should you mind then if I ask her?' Félix's tone was teasing and derisive. 'I know why — because you know that if I go and ask her to run away with me, I can make her do it. She won't give a thought to her parents or marriage or anything else — she'll drop everything and come. And you don't want that, do you?' There was a little silence. '*Do* you?'

'Of course I don't. You'd destroy her. She's not like your other women.'

'Oh yes she is, underneath. Come now, admit it, *mon ami*, it's not the morality of it that troubles you. You didn't want me to marry her either, did you? Can't you see what you'd gain from it if she was in Paris with us, whether as my wife or my mistress?'

'Shut up! Shut up, damn you!' Frédéric's voice was high-pitched with anguish.

Laure heard the scrape of a chair on the floor, the sound of footsteps; then Félix spoke much nearer, in a tone that was both soft and contemptuous. 'You disappoint me, Frédéric. You're no different from the rest of them, after all. A narrow spineless little bourgeois — I'm right, aren't I? Admit it!'

'You know that has nothing to do with it. You know that all I care about is Mathilde.' After a tiny pause he burst out, 'You hurt Mathilde; and I swear by our friendship, by everything there has ever been between us, that I shall kill you!'

Even outside the door, Laure could feel the tension. It held her rigid, waiting, her breath stilled, every nerve strained, for what would happen next.

Then, suddenly, Félix laughed, as easy and casual as ever. 'Don't excite yourself, *mon très cher ami*. Never fear – your immaculate Mathilde can stay and yawn herself to death in perfect peace in her provincial desert – we shall go on our way. Italy must have more to offer than this!'

Laure retreated hurriedly to the stairs as they emerged from the dining-room, and tried to look as if she had just that moment descended.

Much later, when they had long gone and Mathilde, full of questions, woke up, Laure staved off any manifestation of grief with unsympathetic briskness. 'Get up quickly – pack your things. We're going to Paris.'

iv

Oh, it was good to be back! Laure leaned over the balcony rail and breathed in the long forgotten smells of Paris in the autumn, smoke and horse dung and drains, falling leaves, food and perfume, wine, the hundred and one smells of a populous prosperous city.

It had changed, of course, as she knew it would have done. The splendid new houses of Haussmann's rebuilding had mellowed a little from their first rawness, although superimposed on that triumph of the Empire there were still, lingering, the scars of war and revolution: the fading scorch-marks on stonework, the great emptiness in the Tuileries gardens where once the royal palace had stood, the grandiose new Hôtel de Ville that had replaced the ancient gothic structure, the trees not yet mature that had filled the spaces left in the avenues and boulevards and the Bois de Boulogne by those cut down during the siege. And then there was the stark novelty of Eiffel's tower, about which she agreed with Frédéric's verdict: it was an eyesore.

But this was her Paris still, beautiful, alive, self-assured; and it was wonderful to be here again.

She turned her head as, with a smile, Mathilde came to join her. Yes, it had been right too for her. The hardness had gone from her eyes, and the harassed look was fading; she was fast becoming herself again. Laure put an arm about her and drew her to her side.

'What do you say, *chérie*? Shall we see if we can get tickets for the Opéra tomorrow night?'

'Will I be back from Neuilly in time?'

'Ah, I'd forgotten about that; perhaps not.' At Neuilly, on the edge of Paris, lived a former schoolfriend of Mathilde's, whom she had contacted as soon as they arrived in the city; the invitation to call on the family had followed. 'Never mind, we can go another time.'

Mathilde hugged her. 'Shall you mind being by yourself all afternoon?'

'Of course not, *chérie*. You know there were one or two business matters I had to attend to; I'm afraid I'd never get them done without that. It's so tempting just to enjoy being back in Paris.' She looked up at the hazy blue of the sky, and then down again to the street below, its heat tempered by the dappled shade of the trees that lined it. 'Let's go out again – just to walk. There's so much I want you to see.'

So they went out, and found themselves near the Opéra, where they were able by chance to buy tickets for that very evening; and then wandered on looking in shop windows, making an occasional impulsive purchase, following whichever turning looked most inviting.

'I don't think I should like to *live* in Paris always,' Mathilde said reflectively, as they left a milliner's carrying an attractive little hat safely in its beribboned hat box. 'There is too much noise and too much traffic – but it's lovely to visit.'

Laure glanced at her; and at that moment, as if only now aware of what she had inadvertently revealed, Mathilde looked round too and coloured. 'I know, Maman; that's not what I thought I wanted. But, I think—' She paused, as if wanting to be sure what she did think before putting it into words. 'I don't know, but I think I was not quite myself at home, before we came away. Félix' – her colour deepened still more – 'was so different, so exciting, I could think of no one else; or almost no one. It's strange though; now it's like looking back on a bad dream.' She quickened her pace a little and deliberately changed the subject. 'Look – an art exhibition. Let's go in.'

The shop they were passing had been given over entirely to a small exhibition of paintings by a number of different artists, the kind of modern works that still did not always readily find hanging space on the conventional walls of the official Salon. But the modest exhibition had attracted a good deal of interest, for the room was crowded, full of people jostling to see the paintings and commenting upon them with a lively and noisy interest. Many of the varied works hung here were already sold; for quite respectable prices, Laure thought. She made her way about the room slowly, paying these – to her – unknown artists the compliment of finding the best position from which to view each painting, in spite of the throng. A gentle rain-washed landscape caught her eye, reminding her a little of Marcel's style; she turned to draw Mathilde's attention to it, and found they had somehow become separated.

She stood on tiptoe and looked about her, reflecting ruefully that it was a great disadvantage being short; it was just as well perhaps that Mathilde was a little above the average height. Even now she could only see across the room momentarily, by chance, when a head bent or a tall man moved aside. One such instant, and she glimpsed a face, far off; and knew it instantly, devastatingly. Wide cheekbones, small cleft chin, sensuous mouth, wild dark hair; and the eyes, dark browed and smoky grey blue – she sank down again onto the soles of her feet and stood there, held to that place, quite still.

He had seen her, for a moment later the crowd parted a little and they were looking at one another.

She had thought that the years of Henri's brutality had destroyed all her sensuality for ever, that passion was something she would never know again, never want to know. Yet here she stood and felt it all flow through her again, a great flood of desire that turned her knees to water, set her aching to melt into his arms, shut out all that milling crowd about her so that she was aware only of her hungry body; and of him.

'Maman, come and see this—' Mathilde touched her arm; and then, her gaze following Laure's, clasped it more tightly. 'Maman, who's that man? He reminds me of someone.'

'He came to Casseuil once,' said Laure faintly, as if in a dream. He was looking at her still, then at Mathilde. Had he recognised her, or was he thinking: I've seen that woman somewhere before – now where? It was ten years since that golden spring, and at her time of life ten years could make all the difference. They had been hard years, full of anxiety and pain; she knew they had left their mark on her. The beauty that still at thirty-two had the power to charm a man ten years her junior, at forty-two was marred by grey hairs, and little restless lines about her eyes and mouth and across her forehead, and a figure that, neat and exquisitely clothed, had yet lost much of its youthful grace. She was slim still and skilful with the discreet use of makeup and knew how to dress to make the best of what she had; but she was over forty and even Henri no longer desired her.

She turned to Mathilde. 'Show me what you were talking about.' There was a painful constriction in her throat, so that her voice sounded half-suffocated. She wanted desperately to leave; and yet she longed to stay. After all, when she remembered on what terms they had parted – and yet; and yet—

He was, suddenly, beside them, smiling; but warily, without warmth, though there was still the echo in her memory of the dazzling boyish grin that had so enraptured her – and would now, she knew, for the simple reality of his nearness made the ache of desire unbearable, as fresh and painful as it had been all those years ago when she had watched him paint in the stable yard.

'Madame Naillac? It is, isn't it?'

That hurt, the formality, and the doubt; but she forced a smile, polite as his own. 'Yes, Monsieur Arnaud; that's right. Only it is Madame Séguier now.' She held out her hand to him, trying to look assured, and he pressed it briefly. 'You remember my daughter, Mathilde.'

He bowed his head to Mathilde – that golden loveliness, how could he not be struck by the contrast? – and then turned back to her. 'You have married again then, after all?'

'Yes.' It was awkward, painful, and she wished desperately that it had not happened. All these years the memory of their weeks together had been something to treasure, to hug to herself; but this, today, cast a shadow over the golden sweetness of it, reminding her of the bitterness of their parting, of the reality that had followed. In her thoughts, time had stood still, holding Jean-Claude for ever imprisoned in those far off days, for ever young and laughing and loving beneath the cherry trees. Better it had stayed like that, than this now, this meeting between two people who could think of nothing to say, because one of them had long ago passed beyond the reach of an enchantment once felt.

After an uncomfortable little silence, Laure asked abruptly, 'Have you any paintings here? I did not see—'

'Yes, two – over here.' His tone was not encouraging, but he made it clear all the same that he expected her to go with him; so she did, Mathilde following with a fascinated and speculative light in her eyes that her mother was too distressed to see.

The paintings, bright country scenes full of vitality, in a style that was familiar yet richer, full of the assurance of maturity, hung together at the far side of the room. One was already sold, the other marked with a price that made Laure open her eyes in wonder. She looked at the painter again, taking in the fashionable cut of his coat – bohemian but expensive – the air of prosperity. No longer a very young man, a boy, but a man full of vitality, confident, content with his lot. 'Things went well for you then?'

'Yes.'

She looked down, fumbling with the white lacy gloves that, because of the heat, she had removed. At this moment she hated her hands, still roughened by years of hard work, lined now with the lines of age. As she looked at them she saw, from somewhere beyond her range of vision, his two broad brown hands reach in to close about hers, holding them captive.

'Laure.'

She looked up, met his eyes, felt her heartbeat quicken painfully. What was in his expression made her hold her breath.

'I have been very angry with you sometimes, looking back.' He glanced at Mathilde as if, but for her, he would have said more; then he went on, 'But to see you now, like this . . . You have not changed; it could have been yesterday . . .'

It was not true, yet she believed him. She felt laughter tremble on her lips; or was it tears? Both perhaps, hope and sadness bubbling up in her, beyond reach of words.

'Have you a little time? There is a café just round the corner.'

Mathilde, forgotten, went with them, too alive with curiosity to feel resentment. She remembered, not very distinctly, the painter who had come, and she had a dim sense that in the atmosphere of his coming had been something strange affecting her mother, something she had not then been able to understand. Now, looking back, she saw that time illuminated by what she recognised now in her mother's eyes, the agitation of her manner, her heightened colour.

They ate ices, extravagant confections of cream and enticing flavours, with sweet little wafers shaped like fans; and Laure and Jean-Claude talked, and fell silent, and talked again, their breathless hesitant sentences, all little rushes and inconsequential pauses, saying more by their tone than was in the words, constrained as they were by the presence of a third party. Mathilde knew the signs well enough: the foolish smiles, the sudden gravity, the abrupt looking away, the trivial remarks that meant so much more than they said, the ferment beneath the surface that gave such a brightness to the eyes and colour to the cheeks; above all, what she knew so well herself, the ultimate, final coming to a halt, the holding back, on the threshold of something yearned for yet forbidden, deliberately placed out of reach. They said and did nothing remotely improper, nothing that could be expected to betray them; except that their whole manner gave them away.

Afterwards, Jean-Claude escorted them back to their hotel. 'I never did paint you,' he said to Laure. 'I should still like to do so. Would you allow me to?'

Laure hesitated, coming briefly to a halt. 'Perhaps,' she said and glanced at Mathilde.

Jean-Claude reached inside his coat and pulled out a card. 'It has my address. You can contact me there.'

And that was all, apart from a brief kiss on the hand when they reached the hotel.

On the way upstairs Laure knew Mathilde was watching her with more than a mild intentness. I shall have to tell her something, she thought. After all, she is not a child any more, to be shielded from the truth.

Inside their room she said quietly, very matter of fact, 'We wanted to marry once. Your grandmother prevented it.' She was uncomfortably aware of the parallels Mathilde must draw with her own situation; perhaps she was still too young to know that with Jean-Claude it had been very different.

In Mathilde's expression there was only compassion, underpinning her surprise. She had not somehow suspected it had gone as far as that. Or had it been only like her and Félix, a momentary enchantment that absence destroyed? No, for what she had observed today had not been like that. It was herself and Frédéric she had seen in those two people exchanging trivial words over their ices; and that went deep, to the roots of her being, eternally – she coloured suddenly, and deliberately closed that door in her consciousness, as she had learned so often to do. 'Why – why should she want to do that?'

Laure, standing before the mirror to remove her hat and tidy the pale coils of her hair, smiled ruefully. 'He had no money. He was much younger than I was. His family was scarcely even respectable, in your grandmother's eyes at least. Perhaps most of all she could not accept that I would allow anyone to replace your father.'

'Surely she could not stop you marrying, not if you really wanted it? You were a widow, not a young girl – and she wasn't your mother.'

Laure's hands fell to her sides and she stood very still, her head a little bent so that she could not meet her own eyes in the mirror. 'You forget: I had a daughter, whom I loved more than anyone else in the world. Your grandmother threatened to take you from me. I knew it was in her power to do so. So, I had to choose.'

Mathilde felt a little chill growing within her. 'So you chose me.'

'Yes.'

'You must sometimes hate me for it.'

Laure gave a tiny inarticulate cry and came and gathered her into her arms. 'Oh, never think that – never for a moment! There was never any question, any regret – I would make the same choice, always. The only person, ever, that I could not forgive was your grandmother, for that, and for so much else.' For Frédéric, she thought: for taking him in and making him what he is today; for the need that drove me into marriage with Henri; for wearying, endless battles I should not have had to fight. 'No, *chérie*, I love you first, always – even—' She broke off for a moment, and then resumed, 'But it hurt of course.'

'It hurt, of course': all that pain, unsuspected. The pain of a love deliberately renounced that was like a gaping wound – *une plaie ouverte*, as the song had it – always there beneath the quiet everyday surface, the part of oneself that kept going as if everything was always as it had been, hiding the endless hurt – unhealed, beyond reach of healing – that must not be allowed to show. It was that which, in her own case, had brought Mathilde at last to a kind of feverish delirium in which, scarcely knowing what she was doing, she had turned to Félix, lured by him not to healing, but towards the very heart of her pain, as if by plunging into it she could somehow end it for ever. And when her mother, perhaps guessing more than she would admit, had pulled her back from the brink, she had almost hated her for a time, even while she sensed that Laure had saved her from herself. What had she cried out in that moment of agony? 'You know nothing of love!' Yet all along her mother had known an anguish as deep as her own, and a renunciation as cruel and as lasting; worse perhaps, because time might have made it unnecessary, if only she had known or been able to wait.

Until now Mathilde had never thought of her mother except as the strong assured loving woman who was always there, always supporting, caring, in control. It was strange to think of her as a woman who had suffered terribly, who had lost a husband in appalling circumstances and known the torment of conflicting loves. Sometimes – often – Mathilde had blamed her for that calculating marriage to Henri Séguier; but had that too been a matter of renunciation, of putting some other need above herself? – We are two women who have suffered, in our own separate ways, Mathilde thought. Because of that, we can understand one another and be friends.

Tenderly she returned her mother's embrace and kissed her. She felt tears prick at her eyelids. 'Why do you think it is so hard to be happy?' she asked chokingly.

Laure's voice was gentle, her eyes steady. 'Sometimes it is easy, in spite of everything. But you must never strive for happiness; that is the surest way to lose it.'

She found the street without difficulty, a sunny steep street on the southernmost fringe of Montmartre; and then the house. There, standing outside looking at its tidy anonymous front-age, she thought, Will he be there? Was I foolish to come?

In her mind, yesterday was a mass of confused impressions. They had talked so much, yet what had they really said of the things that mattered? 'Yes; I was married six years ago . . . Madame Naillac would have approved, I think, but she was dead by then . . . Yes, I like your paintings; tell me what work you have done lately . . .' All conventional, safe, public things, keeping at bay the thoughts and feelings crowding for attention after the long years of absence and silence; and always, underneath, lay the recollection – which must be Jean-Claude's also – of how they had parted, of all that had gone before. Had he ever been able to understand or to accept the reasons for her renunciation of him? She had wanted so much to know; she wished she knew now, because it might help her to decide whether or not to cross the street, to enquire the way from the *concierge* and to find the door that might perhaps admit her to Jean-Claude's flat. It might tell her what she could expect once – if – she found herself alone, face to face, with this man who had meant so much to her.

What was he to her now? A memory, still with the power to attract? She would never know if all she did was to wait here undecided and stare at his house and wonder which of the ascending rows of windows lit his rooms.

His flat was right at the top, high under the roof. The *concierge*, puffing and grumbling, led her up the spiralling stairs and knocked on the door. Laure stood behind her, holding her breath, stilling every limb, every pulse as if only so could she be sure of hearing, if there should be anything to hear.

It seemed long hours, long tense silent hours – There's no one there, the flat's empty – no, he will come in a moment – I knew it really, he isn't here. Yesterday is all we shall have this time. And then, so clearly and distinctly that it startled her, she heard steps inside, a key turn; and the door opened. And there stood, not a servant (suddenly she had feared that) but Jean-Claude himself, smiling, laughing even, quite unsurprised, but full of apologetic gestures and thanks for the *concierge's* efforts; and then standing back to admit Laure into the little hallway.

Beyond, as he secured the door behind her, she took in somehow a wide sunlit room – lit from above, she saw – hung with oriental rugs and ornaments and exotic plants, where a great bed and carved stool and a silk-covered sofa deep in jewel-bright cushions jostled with the austerity of easel and paints set out in ordered informality where the light was strongest; and the stacked rows of completed canvases and half-done portraits.

'Let me take your cape.' He came from behind and, as he slipped it from her shoulders, bent and pressed a kiss on the nape of her neck beneath the heavy coils of her hair. His mouth was firm and warm, its message beyond denying. She turned then and there into his arms.

No more talk, no preliminaries; hungrily, kissing and caressing, they moved to the bed and fell there together on the richly coloured bedspread, and there made love. Oh the joy, the unutterable delight of a mutual passion answered with tenderness, which asked nothing but passion in return and an equal happiness at the end! She had forgotten that it was possible for her body to feel so deliciously fulfilled, that it was possible to be so happy.

Afterwards they lay for a long time gently touching one another until stirred again to passion; and it was much later before at last Jean-Claude gave a faint laugh and said softly, 'I suppose you came to have your portrait painted.'

Before replying, she leaned over and lingeringly kissed him. 'Do you really want to paint me?'

He smiled, lying on his back gazing up at her, and ran a caressing hand over her breast and down the still-firm line of waist and belly and hip. 'I should like best to paint you just as you are now, naked and beautiful, *ma chère* Laure.'

'And so content—' she murmured, nestling close to him, held in the curve of his arm.

'I would need more than one sitting, of course – many of them.'

'I only wish I could.'

'Can't you?'

'Mathilde is with an old schoolfriend this afternoon. But she has no other engagements planned and we came to Paris together.'

The arm twitched beneath her and he turned his head sharply in sudden anger. 'Mathilde again, always Mathilde! She came between us once – is it to be like this for ever?'

She sat up. 'Don't Jean-Claude! That was long ago.'

'Do you know how much it hurt, and for how long?'

'Of course I know; I felt it too. I still feel it, the more so today. But I am Mathilde's mother and she is my daughter, and I am still responsible for her.'

He sighed. 'I know; I know. I understand more now than I did then, when I was so young. But that does not mean I concede her right always to be first with you. She's a woman now, *chérie*; can't you see that?'

'She is a very young one, and so vulnerable.'

'As I was young and vulnerable. She must be about the same age as I was when we met.' Softening again, he nibbled at her ear as he always used to do. 'Come now, you must find a way. I want that portrait, of course – but you know what else I want. Or do you have scruples about deceiving your husband?'

'None,' she said emphatically. 'None at all.'

She told him then a little about her marriage and those dark things she had never spoken of before, to anyone. She knew he was appalled and angered and deeply hurt for her sake, his only consolation being that the worst was over now.

'You love that vineyard, don't you? To do that for it—'

Her expression was rueful. 'I didn't know all of it before-hand, or perhaps I could not have gone through with it; I

391

don't know. But, oh, I'm so glad we've met again like this! It makes up for everything – *everything*.'

'Come again. You must – then I can make you happy, as you ought to be, always.'

'You must never strive for happiness,' she had told Mathilde; but she knew she would do all she could to seize at this possibility unexpectedly offered to her and hold it tight before it could elude her again.

In the end it was Mathilde herself who made it possible. A little hesitant, for fear that even the suggestion might hurt or offend her mother, she told Laure that her friend had invited her to spend a few days – 'as long as you like, as long as you can, *chérie*!' – at Neuilly. She was tempted, greatly tempted. The hours of girlish confidences, the relaxed comradeship with someone of her own age, had been wonderful; but she had told her friend that she did not think it was possible, for after all she was her mother's sole companion.

And then as she recounted all this to Laure she realised suddenly that there was something new in her mother's face, something she could not quite remember ever having seen there before: a warm secret look, whose origin she guessed. What she felt about it she was not sure. She wondered, What is it like, the thing that brings that look? And she thought, through a confusion of feelings in which there was perhaps a faint trace of disapproval (or was it envy?), Why should she not be happy? And she guessed that her absence might not after all be so unwelcome.

So Mathilde went to Neuilly, and Laure went daily to sit for her portrait, although the work progressed very slowly indeed. Jean-Claude did not after all paint her in the nude, but in the summery sky blue cloth dress – embroidered in navy and shaped, in the new fashion, to skim her hips and give emphasis to the smallness of her waist – which she had worn in the gallery that day. But he kept his promise to make her happy, abundantly and with a generosity that matched her own.

There had been other women in his life since that first meeting, she knew that, though she did not ask. Once, she said, 'You did not marry then,' and he grinned and replied, 'I value my freedom too much.'

'Then you are glad perhaps that things turned out as they did between us.'

He considered the matter carefully for a moment. 'We would have been happy together, I'm sure of that. But things would have been different, of course. Yes, perhaps after all I am not sorry you refused me, though I would not have thought it then.'

She did not think of the future, and scarcely of the past, except when they relived together some lovely moment. All she knew was that here in Jean-Claude's safe and secret world she could shut out everything and take the joy that was offered to her and savour it to the full; and give no thought to the inevitable pain that must come at the end.

CHAPTER
TWENTY

Moïse Delmas and his nephew Lucien had spent the night tending the little stoves set to warm the air between the rows of vines. It had been cold and clear yesterday and Madame Laure, fearing a frost, had ordered the stoves to be lit. In the event it had grown warmer towards dawn and a damp mist had settled over the hills; but that was the way of things. A good *vigneron* had to be ready for anything. The sturdy, flourishing young vines with their newly opening flowers were too precious to be risked for the want of a night's vigilance.

'I'm keeping this one alight until Madame comes,' Moïse said, as Lucien rejoined him after checking the cooling stoves along the further rows. Lucien nodded and stretched his hands gratefully towards the hot black surface of the little iron stove.

'We could go now. She'd not mind.'

'Don't you want your wage to take home?'

Lucien grinned. 'Aye; I was forgetting.'

Moïse gazed at him with incredulity and then slowly shook his head, as if such an unconcern with worldly matters was beyond his comprehension; but then Lucien was young and new to the work and did not, like Moïse, have a whole growing family dependent on him.

Madame came as the angelus rang out, looking neat and fresh and pretty, not at all like someone who must only just this moment have crawled out of bed. In the grey unfriendly light of the May morning the rich red of her dress, the gold of her hair, brought a sense of warmth and life. These days, Moïse thought, she looked more beautiful than ever, as if middle age had brought a new bloom of maturity.

She smiled as she reached them, greeting them warmly. 'Thank you for your trouble. I'm glad the vines are safe.' She took the two neat wage packets from her pocket and handed them to the men. 'An extra seven *sous* for each of you, as we agreed. If you want to warm yourselves before you go home, Nanon has some soup ready in the kitchen.'

The men shut down the stove and stretched, yawning with a slightly modified vigour, scratching themselves. 'Do you want the stoves taken in, *madame*?'

'No thank you – leave them for now. We'll see how the weather goes today. If this mist lasts I'll get someone else to do it later. You've done enough for now.'

They agreed, and were thankful to turn towards the house, Madame Laure at their side, her presence inhibiting them a little in their talk.

'What news of Aubin these days, Moïse?' she asked as they went.

Moïse looked round and grinned. 'Oh, he has another little one now, *madame* – the third, and a boy again. The last, he says. We were all there last week for the naming – Paul, they called him.' He shook his head. 'There they are with three boys in a row, and all we've got is girls. A pity we can't swop one of them, but there it is.'

It was a complaint Laure had heard before from Moïse, so she merely smiled sympathetically and asked, 'Is Madame Lambert well after the confinement?'

'Aye, well enough; she was about again in two days. But then they can't afford idle hands.'

'I thought things were going quite well for them?'

'They are that, but they want to keep it that way.'

In the kitchen Laure saw the men settled to their soup, conferred about the day's menus with Louis-Christophe; and then made her way upstairs to her tranquil room to write some letters. She had heard from her mother yesterday, another happy chatty letter, full of the doings of Marcel's son, now fourteen and clearly a paragon, in his grandmother's eyes at least.

In the doorway of her room she came to a halt, suddenly irritated. Henri had intruded on her sanctuary and was standing near the window immersed in a copy of '*Le Figaro*' which she had brought up with her last night, but found herself in the end too tired to read.

'Good day,' she greeted him, the stiffness of her tone expressing her disapproval of his intrusion.

He looked round briefly, quite unconcerned. 'I came to get the paper. Have you had breakfast?'

'Of course. I've been out to the vineyard since then.'

She waited, motionless by the door, for him to go; but he merely returned his attention to the paper, ignoring her. After a moment, he muttered aloud, 'Arnaud – Arnaud? Where have I heard the name?' A pause, then a note of recognition, sharpened with something else. 'Wasn't that the name of the painter fellow who hung around here some years back?'

The total unexpectedness of the question took her breath away and deprived her of all power of replying. It was just as well, she thought, that Henri had not looked round, for she knew her colour had risen. She watched him, seeing how avidly he read on, and felt that there was something ominous in the intent concentration of his manner.

Then he lowered the paper, turned, and came slowly across the room.

'He's caused quite a stir, it seems,' he said with studied casualness. 'Just had a new exhibition in Paris – and one painting's offended a good few respectable people. A portrait of a woman, so it says here.' He shook the paper. 'Fully clothed and so forth, but she might as well not be with that look on her face. Immoral and brazen they're calling it. Though the critic here doesn't think so. What does he say now—? Some pretentious intellectual twaddle.' He raised the paper again, holding it crushed out of shape in his hand, the article face uppermost. ' ". . . A triumphant monument to the sensuality of Woman." I suppose he fancies her. She sounds a fine piece – a blonde woman, mature but still in her prime. The painting's called "Laure".'

The critics were right, she knew that: Jean-Claude's painting had captured her in all the sleek contentment of gratified desire. The glow on her face, the smooth relaxed curves of her body, everything had been alive with sensuality. She had seen it herself and they had laughed about it, she and Jean-Claude, as they rolled together, kissing, teasing, onto the bed. But she had not somehow thought that it would be so blatantly obvious to everyone else, still less that the sensation it caused would be so great that its ripples would be felt even at Casseuil. Henri did not read the art reports, not usually – she did not remember him ever having done so before.

He was no fool. He ran his eyes over the blonde woman called Laure who faced him across the room, and demanded, 'Did you meet him in Paris last year?' She said nothing, though she knew her pallor gave him some kind of answer; and he flung down the newspaper, came to push the door shut and then stood looking down at her. 'Tell me! Did you meet him?'

'Yes.' She tried to meet his angry gaze steadily, without flinching. 'We met by chance at an exhibition.'

'And what then?' He seized her arm. 'What then, modest little wife of mine? You don't have that look on your face for me, not ever.'

'You know what those critics are like.' She tried to speak lightly. 'They see all kinds of things in a painting that were never there in the first place.'

His grasp tightened. 'Really? Then why are you blushing? Come on, admit it. He painted you like that because that's how he saw you, fresh from his bed, his willing little whore. It was you, wasn't it?' He twisted her arm, so that she cried out. 'Tell me – tell me!'

He twisted again; and suddenly reckless, angry because of the pain, she shouted, 'All right then, it was me! I loved him; I loved him years ago and I love him now – I would have married him if I could. And, yes, I did see him in Paris, more than once. But it's over, and I shall never see him again.'

'You can be damned sure you won't!' His hand came up and then descended sharply, this way and that across her face. 'Dirty whore! That's all you are, all you were ever good for! Too old for such things – that's what you let me believe. So pure, so innocent, such a poor tired creature – and then you go off to Paris and jump into bed with some worthless painter and let him flaunt his triumph all over the town!' He pulled her close, thrusting his face into hers, though she tried to struggle free. 'Do you know what, my pure little wife: I've been going to Libourne to get what I need – paid for, to spare you – and then I find I have my very own whore here in my house all the time. Do you want payment then? Is that it?' He paused and she shrank, but could not free herself. 'No, because I've paid you already haven't I? Quite a price too – all these comforts: house, vineyard, education and trinkets for your pretty little daughter. And what do I get? Nothing any more, not even my dues as a husband! Well, that's going to change I can tell you. You sold me your body and I want my money's worth. I've been soft with you, too damned soft—'

She knew what was coming, knew with a cold drenching terror. She shook her head fiercely, murmuring, 'No – no—', tried to back away from him. But he only slapped her again and flung her down on the floor; and there brutally and successively raped her.

There was no pretence at all of desire or love, no passion to excuse his importunity. He took her in anger, venting his hatred and rage on her body until they were satisfied and she lay limp and bruised and shivering beneath him. Then he raised himself on his knees, still arched over her, and placed his hands either side of her head, pinning her to the floor by her hair.

'From now on you will welcome me to your bed every night – no more coyness, no headaches, no locked doors. You're my whore, remember, my paid whore; and you will be at my disposal, whenever and however I want you.'

From somewhere within her crushed and battered spirit she called on some last reserve of defiance. 'No, not that – never!' She tried to free her head, but it hurt her too much to move.

'If you defy me, Laure, then it's over – my part of the bargain as well as yours. I'll go back to Trissac and live there, and sue for divorce. I'll find some way to prove your adultery, never fear. You know what that will mean – prison maybe, for you and very likely for that lover of yours too; at the very least your name dragged in the dirt. It wouldn't do much for the marriage prospects of your darling Mathilde, would it? I can't see any respectable family wanting to link their name with a convicted whore.'

I shall run away, she thought, run away, so you'll never find me. But she knew that was no answer. He would hunt her down with all the vindictiveness of his offended pride; and if she still evaded him he would have his revenge all the same, through Mathilde.

Perhaps we can go together, me and Mathilde. But this was Mathilde's house and she wanted so much to see her child happy and well married – not a fugitive, caught up in this evil.

She felt tears rise chokingly in her throat and fought them with all her power, so that Henri should not be able to savour his triumph. Though he was savouring it, of course. He knew he had won, without any shadow of doubt.

And Laure had no illusions to shelter behind about what was to come. It had been bad before; now it would be worse, for she would be the object, not of a brutal and demanding passion, but of anger and hate fed and nurtured through the years. She wondered, fleetingly, with a bleak irrelevance, if he had ever loved any woman with tenderness; if, in fact, he really liked women at all, or had any respect for them.

So that was that. Bitterly, Laure accepted the need to hide her misery and conceal as best she could the bruises on her body, the raw wound to her spirit. As bitterly, she wondered if it had been worth it, to have those few blissful days with Jean-Claude, if this was how she must pay for them. On the whole she thought not.

One hope only remained for her to cling to; that soon – it could not be too soon – Mathilde would fall in love with a young man who would care for her and Casseuil with equal devotion. Once she was safely married, beyond being irrevocably harmed by any scandal caused by her mother's behaviour, then Laure would be free – free to leave behind all she loved in the world, because only then could she release herself from the torment that her life had become. It would be a bitter liberation, but it offered the only hope.

Somehow it made everything worse to know that Mathilde was too old now, too much the young woman, not to realise, for all Laure's efforts to conceal it, that something had gone badly wrong for her mother. She had seen the glow that had lit Laure's face in Paris; now she observed the pallor and strain behind the brittle light-heartedness, heard the edge of venom in Henri's voice when he spoke to her mother, and drew her own conclusions, which one way and another came as near to the truth as her inexperience could bring her. It made her protective and tender towards Laure, as if their positions were reversed, and she the mother and Laure her child; but though it comforted Laure a little, it troubled her more that Mathilde should have to share any of this burden.

CHAPTER
TWENTY ONE

i

Charles de Miremont hated July 14th. It made him feel like a
stranger in his own country, and an unwelcome one at that.
As a student at Bordeaux he had always spent the day indoors,
mostly on his knees, trying to shut out the distant sounds of
merrymaking, and thinking with regret of his home. At home
– at least since the declaration twelve years ago that this day
was to be set aside as a public holiday – it was always a time of
solemn remembrance, even of mourning. The shutters of the
château would remain closed, the day would begin with mass
and continue with activities of a suitably sober kind, reminding them all that it commemorated the opening of a Revolution that had struck fatally at their nation, their family and
their Church. At school it had been much the same, a day for
reflection, prayer and penitence. He had thought that, this
year at least, he would be at home again by the 14th; but by his
own decision, taken at long last, he had made that impossible.

Of course, his cousins at Bergerac, if not as strict as his
parents, shared their views. They did not go so far as to close
the shutters, and only he and his aunt – a de Miremont herself
– had attended mass this morning; but since then the day had
passed quietly enough. No one had ventured outside, except
to church, and no one had suggested any activity more
frivolous than the playing and singing of a number of wholly
serious songs, mostly Royalist in sentiment. It was entirely by
his own doing that Charles should now be riding from
Bergerac to Casseuil; but that did not prevent him from
feeling painfully guilty to be setting out on so very pleasurable
an errand on this day.

If there had been time to reply to Madame Séguier's letter,
arriving only this morning, he would have done so, and

suggested another date. 'If you are to arrive in Bergerac on the 13th,' she had written in reply to his carefully worded request, 'then why not come on the 14th? I am sure you would prefer not to delay. If you come about five-thirty, then you will be able to spend a little time with Mathilde before we go to our festive dinner, for which we very much hope you will join us. You know, I am sure, how happy I shall be to welcome you on such an errand – and Monsieur Séguier too of course – but in the end, as you say, the final word must be Mathilde's. I shall of course say nothing to her of the reason for your visit, since that is what you wish.' The words 'festive dinner' had made him a little uneasy, but the tone of the rest of the letter had been so encouraging that he had refused to allow it to disturb him; it was in any case too late to change things now. But he could not escape his feeling of guilt.

Once out on the road it was not guilt that troubled him most. He knew, of course, that most villages and towns had their celebrations on this day, organised by the officials of their commune. He imagined them to be rather drab, dry affairs, laid on at public expense for an unenthusiastic but obedient population (lacking its true leaders, as his father always said). What he had not expected for one moment were the signs everywhere of jubilant and wholehearted popular rejoicing. Every public building had its tricolour flag, bunting hung across every street; crowds bright with holiday clothes sat eating and drinking in the shade of trees, whilst others – mostly children – ran races, climbed greasy poles, danced and sang; bands played; and in many a village street Charles made his way only with difficulty past citizens busily setting up tables out of doors for the evening's 'Republican repast', or making preparations for a firework display or a ball. Riding past them in his sober clothes, full of disapproval and unease, he felt like the skeleton at the feast, an unwanted and unwelcome visitor from another world.

It was quiet, blissfully quiet, on the steep, winding road up to Casseuil, the only sounds the chirping of the crickets in the vines and the gentle rhythm of his horse's hooves. It was also – despite the lateness of the hour – uncomfortably hot still, and Charles looked forward with relief to the coolness of the château and the company of people who were not caught up in the general hysteria; and of Mathilde in particular.

His Mathilde (if he could dare to call her his) in all her gentle purity – he imagined her sometimes as a kind of ethereal Joan of Arc, mounted on a snow-white charger with the white and gold banner of the old true France billowing out above her head as she inspired her devoted followers to fight to the death for God and their country.

He realised, abruptly, that he had reached the courtyard and that it was already nearly seven o'clock. The unforeseen obstacles on the road had made him very late. Flustered, distressed that this important visit should start so badly, he dismounted, knocked, was admitted to the hall; and found Monsieur and Madame Séguier standing there, as if about to go out.

'Oh, Monsieur de Miremont – we were so afraid you were not able to come.' Madame Séguier held out her hand and he bent over it courteously, murmuring an apology for his lateness. 'Please don't worry. You are still in time to come with us. We are just waiting for Mathilde and then we shall be ready. Afterwards, you will have time to talk together. Will it be too much to rush you away at once?'

He stared at her, rather stupidly. 'Away, *madame*—?' But before he could finish his question, Mathilde had come down and he could think of nothing else.

Mathilde – his Maid of France, his angel – lovelier even than his most tender memory . . . in a close fitting gown of lace-trimmed taffeta, the exact blue of the wild chicory just coming into flower in the fields, with a little train that, held to one side, revealed a froth of flounced petticoat and the daintiest of creamy kid boots. Bereft of coherent speech, he coloured fiercely, touched her hand – he would not presume to kiss it – and, not quite knowing what he was doing, went with the three of them out of the house, across the courtyard and through the little wood towards the village.

There, long cloth-covered tables filled the market place, and it seemed as if all the men and women – and most of the children – of the commune were gathering, talking and laughing as they took their places on the benches at the tables,

403

calling to friends to join them, joking, teasing, full of holiday high spirits. At Mathilde's side, Charles, realising what was happening to him but quite unable to decide what to do about it, made his way in miserable confusion through the happy crowd, awash with a babble of patois and French, which today seemed equally incomprehensible to him; not even taking in what Mathilde herself said to him, as if he were indeed a foreigner unable to speak her language. Sensations crowded in on him, the rustle of Mathilde's petticoat, the noise, the fierce heat whenever they emerged from the shade of the trees, the mingled smells of hot dusty earth and of Mathilde's sweet elusive perfume, the animal odours of hot, crowded peasant bodies, the rich garlicky fragrance of the soup already being set out in tureens upon the tables and the sharper smell of the rough red country wine in the opened bottles.

He found himself somehow where he should never have been, at Mathilde's right hand on a hard bench, only too conscious of the luridly bright tricolour bunting in the chestnut trees overhead, lit by the lanterns hanging there; and of Mathilde helping him to the soup with which this celebratory meal was to begin. He thought the hot liquid would choke him as he sipped unhappily from the spoon; his taste buds acknowledged that it was good, whilst his appetite resisted all its blandishments.

There was no escape now. He was here, and without making a scene – which would be hurtful to Mathilde as well as discourteous to her parents (though he was astonished that they should have been so unaware of his feelings as not to realise how offensive this gathering must be to him) – he could not leave. Slowly, reluctantly, he ate, raising his eyes from his plate only to rest them now and then on some point way above the heads of the happy diners: on the tumbledown roof of the presbytery, for instance, and the mossy tiles of the house next to it; or the sturdy prosperous frontage of the *mairie* with its flag hanging limp in the heat above the door and the adjoining school building still prominent in its newness. Did it never occur to these thoughtlessly feasting people, he wondered, to criticise their municipal council for spending so much of the commune's money on its public buildings in these difficult times? And what did Mathilde think about that; and especially about today?

He glanced at her and met her eyes just as she turned to speak to him. Smiling her entrancingly artless smile, she was offering him wine – 'For the *chabrol*,' she said. He had no particular objection to following the country custom, but he wished it had been anywhere but here. However, he poured wine into the dregs of his soup, stirred it round and drank from the bowl; next to him Mathilde did the same. What was she thinking? Was she, naïvely, from the girlish innocence of her heart, enjoying the simple pleasures to which her parents (who should have known better) had introduced her? If so, then she was guiltless certainly, but in need of the guidance of a wiser friend or companion, a husband perhaps . . . That must be it, he decided. His Mathilde had allowed herself to be wrongly led, but had never thought about the implications of what she was doing. He must believe that, for otherwise he ought in all conscience to leave her today without putting to her the question he had come all this way to ask.

Course followed course, and time and again he forced himself to eat what he could, to make some kind of conversation with Mathilde, and with others at the table who spoke to him (they were good people too, at heart; only, like Mathilde, lacking the right leadership). Even so, it seemed hours – and was in fact a good two – before the last of the food had almost gone and word went round for silence, and Charles realised that the Mayor – in that offensively bright sash – had risen to address them.

Robert Martin was proud of his eloquence, and this evening, full of wine and good food, he was at his most fluently emotional. In low ominous tones he described the great fortress prison of the Bastille in the Paris of a hundred and three years ago; its emaciated, half-starved prisoners unjustly shut away from the world at a tyrant's whim; the long years of groaning oppression that had led at last to the glorious day of liberation, on July 14 1789. 'On the ruins of that symbol of a barbarous servitude, *mes très chers amis*, were laid the foundations of our beloved Republic. Let us carry that thought always in our hearts; let us never forget.'

Charles – thinking, It's all lies, all lies – sat with his head bent as the speech went on and on, interrupted now and then by clapping or even cheers. The phrases rolled grandly over him, less offensively now, as the Mayor moved away from the Revolution, and appealed instead to a patriotism that Charles would have shared, on another occasion.

'Our dear sisters, the lost provinces of Alsace and Lorraine, whom we long to fold again to our bosom . . . Our brave youth, serving the flag of France.' (He meant, Charles knew, the small contingent of conscripts from the commune at present forcibly absent on military service.) 'Each of us devotes himself anew to the service of our beloved nation.' Glasses were filled again, and Charles realised there was to be a toast. Could he, like the rest of them, drink to the Republic? He compromised, murmuring, 'To France!' as he sipped, and tried to ignore the cries of '*Vive la République!*' all around him.

It was over, thank goodness. The people were relaxing into groups, some leaving the tables, others beginning to clear away; a group of children, temporarily unsupervised, chased one another, squealing, in the growing darkness under the trees. Charles turned to his companion. '*Mademoiselle*—'

Mathilde was looking at him with an excited light in her eyes. 'There'll be the fireworks now – and then the ball – oh, I'm glad you're here to dance with me!'

So it wasn't over yet! And while she spoke to him like that he no longer wanted it to be, not really. In any case he had not spoken of what was in his mind, and he could not speak here, amongst all these people. And he ought not to speak without first finding out what was in her heart – what she thought of today in particular.

He stayed, while the tables were cleared and folded away, and chairs were set up for the small village band, and the darkness deepened and everyone gathered beyond the church with eyes turned up to the deep velvet blue of the sky near the windmill.

The fireworks exploded in stars and cascades and blooms of brilliant light, to the accompaniment of 'Oohs!' and 'Aahs!' and laughter and applause; and ended with rockets of blue and white and red shooting their tricoloured fires into the dark. And Charles realised suddenly that everyone around him had begun to sing, joined very soon by the notes of the band from the market place. The singing swelled, grew, rose in a great wave of emotion and crashed at last over Charles's unsuspecting head, and he knew what it was: the 'Marseillaise', that most detested of all songs, work of the very devil himself. Bringing to mind, shudderingly, that the 'impure blood' with which the song writer had wished to drench the furrows of his homeland had been that of his own great-grandfather, amongst others, Charles turned to look at Mathilde.

She had forgotten him, forgotten everyone around her. With unselfconscious abandonment she was singing with all her heart, her dark eyes, shining in the starlight, fixed on some far point in the night sky, her voice pure and clear and passionate in those terrible words; and, unmistakably, a tear gleaming on her cheek.

He watched her hungrily, painfully, full of cruelly conflicting emotions. All the sweet fervour of his Joan of Arc poured out for this unworthy cause – but how, seeing her, could he blame her for it? Through three long verses he watched her, and ached to gather her into his arms and ride away with her far into the night where the taint of this day could no longer reach her. His father had said, 'You know you will have my blessing. Mademoiselle Naillac is a delightful young woman, all one could wish.' But what would he say if he could see her now? Uneasily, Charles felt he knew quite well what he would say, and what he would want his son to do.

But Charles did not do it. Instead, as the singing ended and the crowd began to make its way back towards the market place for the dancing, he hung back, keeping her talking – he didn't quite know how, or what he was saying – and only when they were almost alone did he begin to follow the others. Monsieur and Madame Séguier (deliberately, he supposed) had gone on ahead.

'*Mademoiselle*,' he began now, 'you know perhaps that I have at last completed my law studies.'

Mathilde gave a little exclamation. 'And I meant to congratulate you! Oh, forgive me, *monsieur* – I am so glad for you.'

He smiled, a little ruefully. 'It has been a hard-won battle, *mademoiselle* – but at least it is at an end. I have reached a new stage in my life.'

'Can we call you *maître* now?'

'Call me what you will; but I shall not practise as a lawyer. No, *mademoiselle*: you see, I have never really believed that my path lies with the law.'

'Oh, where does it lie then?'

Now was the moment, if he was not to let it go for ever; and he knew, in spite of everything, that he could not do that. He came to a halt, looking gravely down at the dim pale loveliness of Mathilde's face.

'As I told your mother in my letter, now that my examinations are over I am on my way home, and I shall in fact leave for there tomorrow. But I shall not remain there, as you might suppose. On Saturday I shall go to the house of a religious order near Grenoble, there to make a retreat. You see, I have a great deal about which to seek guidance concerning the future. There is, also, something that I would ask you to think about in the meantime, if you would.'

His talk of retreats and religious matters had misled her and she looked up, only to read in his face what he was about to say; so she looked quickly down again, confused, her colour high, and wondered how she would reply, and how she wanted to reply.

'I think you must know what I have long felt for you. It is hard to find the words; it is not enough, not for me, to say simply that I love you as deeply, as reverently, as a man can love a woman. Yet I am not able to say more—' He paused to clear a throat constricted by emotion. 'There is in all the world no one beside you whom I have ever wished to make my wife, or ever shall. That being so, if you are unable to answer in the affirmative to what I ask, then I shall turn to the religious life as the only possible alternative for me. Once I thought, unequivocally, that I was called to it. I know there are those who would say that it is in fact the higher calling; but I have given the whole matter a great deal of thought, and I do not think that is true for me. If I am wrong, then your decision will show me that error. So, I ask you to consider whether you feel able to become my wife.' As she looked up again he raised a hand to silence any possible reply before it was spoken. 'Say nothing now, *mademoiselle*. You know how I mistrust the impulse of the moment. You have three weeks until I shall come to know your answer; in that time you will be able to give to what I ask the fullest and deepest consideration. Then I will know that your answer comes from the heart.' He bent to take her hand and raise it to his lips, with more than his customary reverence; and then he went on very earnestly, 'Whatever you decide, *mademoiselle*, I beg you not to be afraid to tell me with honesty and openness. I shall respect and honour you for it, and I know that your choice will point the way for me, to tell me the direction my life ought to take.'

Which, she supposed, as – rather dazed – she allowed him to lead her back to the market place, was his somewhat convoluted way of saying that he did not mind whether she said yes or no; or, rather, that he would accept her decision without going into a decline. She did not know whether to be encouraged or offended by the assurance.

With more vigour than accuracy, the band was playing a polka. Under the trees the couples danced, not always gracefully, often uncertainly, but with whole-hearted enjoyment. Mathilde, who loved dancing, felt suddenly totally disinclined to dance.

'I think, *mademoiselle*,' Charles was saying beside her, 'that I should return now to Bergerac. I am sorry about the dancing, but I feel, in the circumstances . . .'

She understood him, for at this moment he must feel much as she did. 'I will come and see you on your way – let me find Maman first.'

Laure, full of questions but unable to ask any of them, went with them through the wood to the stables. Only when Charles had gone was Mathilde able to tell her exactly what had happened.

'He was so solemn about it,' she concluded, 'as if I were some holy image on a pedestal, and not flesh and blood at all. Do you think he has any idea what I'm really like? Can you love someone if you don't know anything about them?'

'They say love is blind,' Laure reminded her tritely. 'But he has known you for some years now; he must have learned something about you in that time.'

Mathilde sighed, but lightly, and with a gleam of amusement resting on her face. 'He's so very pious – I wonder if he knows how extremely worldly I am. We are not at all alike, you know.'

'He is kind, gentle, very considerate; that's a great deal.' I am pleading his cause, Laure thought; pleading for my freedom. She felt ashamed; after all, she did not want Mathilde to marry without love. And the girl had never given the slightest hint that she might be in love with Charles. But Charles was indeed kind; and he cared about Casseuil and its vines: she could entrust him with that as well as with Mathilde, the two most precious things in her life. Yet she had wanted the greatest possible happiness for her child, a marriage, freely and lovingly entered upon, that would give her all the joy and fulfilment her mother had never known.

'If only he could laugh at himself sometimes – if only he were quicker witted, more lively – if only, just now and then, he would go wild and do something foolish, just because he felt like it suddenly . . .' She paused and sighed. 'No, Maman, I think I shall have to refuse him. I think I should go mad, having to live with him all the time. What do you think?'

'If that's what you feel, then obviously you must refuse him. But at least you have time to think it over very carefully. As Charles himself would say, don't rush it.'

Mathilde grinned at the admonition and then said, more soberly, 'No, he's right in that at least. If you rush into something like this you could regret it for ever.'

Laure wondered if she thought of Félix and that strange impulsive proposal; or of her mother, locked in a misery without end.

'I don't want to go back for the dancing. I think I shall go to bed – you don't mind do you, Maman?'

'Of course not; perhaps I shall do the same.'

Laure could not escape an uneasy sense that there was something strange about this conversation, something very important that was lacking. It was only as, momentarily silent, they went into the house, that she realised what it was. Not once, not for an instant in all their discussion of Charles's proposal, had Mathilde spoken of passion or love – or not for herself, at least. It was almost as if she knew she could not expect to find them, that for her marriage must offer less profound consolations.

The implications of that, disturbing as they were, had no opportunity, then, to reach Laure's consciousness, for as they stepped into the hall Marius said to her, '*Madame*, Monsieur Brousse is here.'

Laure could not fail to hear, behind her, Mathilde's sharp intake of breath. 'Monsieur Brousse! When did he come? I did not know—'

'He came about half an hour ago, *madame*. He went straight upstairs. He said he did not wish to be disturbed.'

'Something's wrong, Maman! It must be—'

'Hush, Mathilde.' Beneath her restraining hand, she could feel the trembling of Mathilde's arm. 'I'll go up and see.'

She was cursing Frédéric as she mounted the stairs, watched from below by Mathilde's anxious eyes. Why had he come? Why could he not leave them in peace? Whatever there was between him and Mathilde, whatever his intentions towards her, his visits always ended, somehow, in some kind of unhappiness for her.

Laure knocked on his door, that same door that once had been his grandmother's. She had to knock twice before he opened it; and then she was so shocked by his appearance that for a moment she could think of nothing to say.

Mathilde had been right; something was indeed badly wrong. His face was grey and drawn, with great dark shadows about eyes that looked at once remote and haunted. Eventually, after a long silence during which they both simply stood there, Laure stammered, 'Why did you not let us know you were coming, Frédéric? We could have had your room ready.'

'I apologise, *madame*; there was little time. Félix is dead. I came here from the funeral.' His tone was expressionless, as if he was saying something learned by heart but not understood.

She gave a little cry and took a step towards him; but he put out a hand to keep her away.

'I have all I need, thank you, *madame*. I should like to be left alone.' And then, quietly, he closed the door.

For a little while Laure stayed where she was, wondering whether to go after him, to try and offer comfort; she had an uneasy feeling that he should not be left alone. But she was hardly the right person to help him, in the circumstances, and he had in any case made it clear enough that he did not want help. Except, why otherwise had he come to Casseuil? Perhaps, she thought at last, because the Paris lodgings were too full of memories and he simply had nowhere else to go.

Troubled, she went back downstairs to where Mathilde waited outside her bedroom, and told her what Frédéric had said. As she spoke she saw the tears fill Mathilde's eyes.

'Oh, Maman, what can have happened? He was only twenty-three! Did Frédéric not say?'

'No, I've told you all he told me. Quite clearly he didn't want to talk.'

'Do you think I should go to him?'

Laure shook her head. 'If he wanted to see you he would have come down, I imagine. He made it very clear he wanted to be alone. Perhaps he'll feel more like talking in the morning. Go to bed now, *chérie* – try to sleep, in spite of everything.' She kissed Mathilde and watched until the bedroom door closed behind her; and then took a few steps towards her own room.

Bed, alone, without Henri – it was infinitely tempting. But she knew Henri. On every possible public occasion he insisted that she should be at his side, the model of a happy and compliant wife. The least sign of weariness or discontent or ill humour and he would find some way, later, in private, to punish her for it. Tonight he expected her to return to the dancing, and so she would return; it was not worth defying him, even for an hour of two of uncertain peace.

But as she made her way through the wood back to the village, hatred raged in her with a fierce intensity. He was the poison at the heart of her life, destroying every pleasure, every hope: Henri, who openly enjoyed her humiliation and her pain, even though he would never allow anyone to guess at its presence beneath the orderly, conventional surface of their marriage.

He must have been watching for her, because he came to her the moment she stepped through the gate; and pulled her arm through his. 'You were gone a long time,' he murmured accusingly. 'I hope that means that fool de Miremont has got to the point at last.' He turned to smile at Aubin Lambert, who stood beside a nearby bench where his wife sat with their

412

infant in her arms and the two older boys, five and six, leaning sleepily against her.

Aubin ran his eyes critically over Henri – as vigorous and young looking as ever – and Laure, who had aged deplorably in the past months. She must, he supposed, be over forty by now; certainly tonight she looked all of that and more. It surprised him a little, for he had always taken her youthful beauty for granted.

She smiled at him warmly enough, however, stooping to speak to the little boys; and then straightening again. 'And you, Monsieur Lambert, and you, *madame* – you are well, I hope?'

'Very well, thank you, *madame*.' Then: 'They say your vines are doing nicely.'

'We have had three harvests now, each one a little better than the last. And you – how are your new vines?' He had told her last year that he had replanted his land with Merlot and Malbec and two varieties of the Cabernet grape, all grafted onto American rootstock. When they were ready, he would be making a full-bodied red wine.

He smiled one of his rare smiles, which generally reflected some more complex emotion than simple good humour. 'They are flourishing, *madame*. This next year I propose also to plant a couple of hectares with Sémillon, Sauvignon Blanc and Muscadelle. I think I shall try a little Casseuil wine, just a little.'

She smiled too at that, and her eyes lit suddenly with a combative sparkle. So he intended to fight her on her own ground, did he? She knew of course how well qualified he was to do so. 'I look forward to tasting it some day,' she said. She felt Henri's hand close painfully about her arm, underneath, where Aubin could not see it. Trying to sound nonchalant about it, she took her leave of him.

'You don't have that pleased look on your face when you talk to me,' Henri muttered into her ear, as the band began unevenly on a waltz.

'Are you surprised?' she retorted. But her momentary excitement had gone. What use was it to plan for the future, to hope for a great wine, if everything was to be soured for her by Henri's presence? The vineyard no longer had more than a

413

superficial charm, offering an occasional short-lived respite. What she longed for above all was to see Mathilde safely – and happily – married, so that she could leave Casseuil, and Henri, for good. She looked no further than that, apart from knowing that she would make some kind of new life, somehow, because she must. There was Paris, of course, where Jean-Claude was; but they had agreed, when they parted, that this time it was for ever, that to hope again to find such joy together would be to ask too much of life. They had the sweetness of their memories to brighten the years ahead; and that must be enough. But Laure had not known then what horrors would come between her and those memories, so that they no longer had any power to cheer or comfort her. She could not even find any consolation or hope in wondering if, in spite of everything, she and Jean-Claude might yet meet again. In a strange way she had almost ceased to believe that Jean-Claude had ever existed, or that her body had ever known any kind of joy or satisfaction. What she wanted now was not fulfilment or ecstasy or even love, but escape from Henri: that alone, no more and no less. And to make that possible, Mathilde must marry. The girl had seemed glad to see Charles de Miremont today, and had not immediately rejected his proposal. If only Frédéric had not come to distract her, just when she might have been willing to take Charles seriously as a suitor, then perhaps it would all have been happily settled – soon, within the next few days, before her mother was forced to some desperate and irrevocable act.

Around her in the lantern light the couples moved in a blur of soft colour over the dusty ground, while the band lilted lumberingly on; faces shone with untroubled happiness, figures in the shadows laughed softly; and in the midst of it all Laure turned and turned in Henri's hot embrace with a deadly misery, cold and hard, knotted somewhere deep inside her.

Mathilde lay for a long time listening to the hypnotic chorus of the cicadas and the distant sound of the band, which once might have lulled her to sleep, but tonight had no effect at all except to irritate her over-strained nerves. She had left all her windows open – the two here in her bedroom, and those in her sitting-room as well – but the air was hot and heavy and nothing stirred, except when she turned in the hot bed seeking that elusive repose.

In the end, she gave up the search. She slipped out of bed, pulled a lacy wrap about her over her nightgown, lit the lamp in her sitting-room and sat down to read by its light.

When, a little later, there was a faint knock on the door, she was somehow unsurprised to find Frédéric there, for she had been thinking of him so constantly that it was if her thoughts had simply taken shape before her. He was dressed only in trousers and a shirt whose whiteness simply emphasised his look of fragility. It was as her mother had said, he looked ill, with a frightening remoteness about him. Mathilde wanted to fold him into her arms; but she did nothing, only waited for him to say what he needed to say.

'May I talk to you?' he asked softly, his voice without expression. She stood back to let him pass, and then closed the door after him.

He went to stand with his back to the fireless hearth with its great vase of roses scenting the room. Mathilde sat down on her little sofa facing him and gestured for him to be seated nearby, but he shook his head. For a long time he said nothing at all, just stood there watching her from the far cheerless place where his spirit had gone, beyond her reach. In the end, she spoke first, choosing her words with great care in case anything she said should only drive him further into himself.

'I did not know Félix was ill.'

'No.' That was a start, she thought. 'Nor did I for a long time – or not what it was.' He spoke as if with great difficulty, every word disjointed, edged with pain, yet flowing ever faster as if forced out by some inner compulsion. 'Thank God you did not marry him! . . . I only found out then; he had not told me – they turned him down for the army because of it . . . I can't bear to think what might . . . It was those women, I'm sure it was. He went to them so often. One of them, long ago – she must have infected him.'

She had not lived so sheltered that she did not know what he meant. They said that syphilis was a scourge, an epidemic poisoning the manhood of France. And she had known, if she thought about it, what kind of man Félix was, the risks he took – she shivered, like Frédéric thinking of what might have been; and then of what it must have been like for Frédéric himself these past months.

'He went mad, Mathilde – he killed himself—' He turned from her and rested his forehead on the mantelpiece, and after a long silence went on in a voice progressively less controlled, more unsteady. 'He got much worse while I was away . . . He had strange, wild moods, more than usual, but I couldn't get him to see a doctor – when I came back from the army I tried to look after him myself. It was hard and I didn't know if what I was doing was right. But then he'd be better for a while and I'd think it might be over. It was like that when – that night – I came back late from the theatre. I'd left him asleep, and quiet I thought, or I'd not have gone. There was a sound as I came up the stairs – he must have waited until he heard me.' He seemed to be holding his breath, and she held hers with him. After a moment he turned back to her, his face distorted with grief, and burst out in a flood of anguish, 'He had cut his throat. He was lying there on the bed with a great open gash, all red and the blood coming out in bursts like a flood – I tried to stop it, I held on to him, I shouted for help – there was blood everywhere, pouring out, all over the place. It wouldn't stop, there was nothing I could do, nothing – by the time they came, he was dead—' He stretched his hands towards her as if to show her how the blood had soiled them, how he could see it still; she saw it too with his eyes, running back down his arms, soaking into his clothes, on his skin and his hair, his friend's lifeblood pouring over him.

She took hold of his hands and drew him gently down beside her and reached out very tenderly to touch his hair. He stared at her half-dazed, as if just emerging from some appalling nightmare, and a shudder seemed to go right through him. The next moment he had flung himself forward and was clinging to her with a kind of urgent desperation; and then at last he began to weep, in hard, dry, painful sobs that gathered pace and force until they were incessant, anguished beyond his control.

She drew his head down to lie against her breast and held him, and stroked his hair and his back and murmured to him, low meaningless little words like a mother comforting a child.

For the rest, she knew she must let him weep until he had found release for the grief and horror and guilt he had for so long kept fiercely shut away inside him.

She did not know how much time had passed when at length he grew quieter: it might have been minutes, more likely half an hour or even longer. She only knew then that something had changed – was changing still – between them. Until this moment, she had been the comforter, meeting his need, as if he were her child; but now it was not like that any more. His arms about her had ceased to cling, but instead were holding her, the hands moving over her in a way that seemed to awaken the whole surface of her skin and reach down to what was hidden deep inside. His head stirred against her breast, she felt his mouth warm and urgent through the thin fabric of her wrap. She became achingly aware of how his body felt against hers, its slightness beneath the fine shirt, the hard angular line of bone and muscle, the quickened breathing, like her own. She wanted him to come closer still, to become part of her, flesh of her flesh; she wanted it desperately, with a devouring hunger that possessed her completely.

Somewhere, some tiny lingering remnant of her conscious mind sent out a warning, told her, No, this must not happen, this is forbidden – but it had no power over her, scarcely registered at all before the sheet of flame that consumed her swept it up too and shrivelled it to extinction. She fell back and drew him after her and gave herself up to the piercing sweetness of his coming.

Flesh of her flesh: he was that now, as in some sense he had always been, linked for ever by the shared blood in their veins that should have made this impossible, unthinkable. She felt him come slowly back to that realisation as they lay quietly together afterwards in the tiny interval of peace before understanding returned. Above her, within her arms, he tensed and she heard him draw in a sharp sudden breath. She moved her hand, slow with contentment, and ran it over his hair.

'Quiet now, *chéri* – it doesn't matter—'

She wanted to cry out at the sudden emptiness she felt when he slid away from her and knelt on the floor by her side, staring at her with a new anguish in his eyes. He touched her cheek hesitantly, almost as if he wondered how he could ever have dared to do more.

'It matters very much. Forgive me, if you can.'

She turned on her side to face him and took his hand and folded hers about it. 'Whatever we have done, it was done together. If there is any guilt, then it is shared, completely, by me as much as by you. What was your fault is mine. But it did not feel wrong . . .'

He bent his head so that his mouth rested against her fingers. 'Not then . . . but now—'

'Hush, don't think of it. What is done, is done. We can't bring back the past.' A moment ago she would have added, 'Nor would I want to.' But the conscience she had thought burnt out was coming slowly to life again, and she knew it would not be true, or not wholly and simply true, without qualification. Yet for those few minutes she had known an intensity of joy so great and so complete that nothing in all her life before had ever matched it. How could she wish that undone? Only, now she must face the consequences – and for Frédéric it meant that in consoling one grief she had replaced it with another. She knew that somehow she must convince him that he had no cause to grieve, as she did not. 'I want one thing only,' she whispered. 'For you to know that I love you and want you to be happy.'

He looked up. 'Happy?' He gave a bitter little smile. 'Happiness is an illusion, Mathilde; don't you know that?'

'Is it?' Had he not known it, just this once, if never before nor since?

He understood, but he would not acknowledge that she was right. 'Joy has wings, and sometimes for an instant they brush us in passing, as they did tonight. As for happiness – that's something else. I have never known it and I never will. But I hope that you, one day—' He kissed her hand again, as if to seal his wish for her; then, when he resumed, his thoughts had moved on. 'I suppose I must go away.' His tone said, bleakly, that there was nowhere to go, nowhere apart from her that was not a howling wilderness.

'Where would you go? I couldn't bear to think of you alone somewhere with no one to turn to. Besides, what is there to run from now? All that could happen has happened.'

*

418

So he stayed; and to every outward appearance it seemed that much of the old ease of manner had returned between them, sobered and restrained by his grief for his friend. They walked together in the garden or through the vines, they read together, played music together, talked and were silent together with a grave calmness that Laure found rather touching, both because Frédéric's desperate look had been replaced by a more temperate sadness, and because he was behaving towards Mathilde, and she to him, exactly as a brother and sister should in such circumstances.

Frédéric was vague about his future plans, but Laure gathered that he had given up the Paris flat and intended, for the time being at least, to remain at Casseuil. He asked no one's permission to do so, but Laure felt no inclination to drive him away. He was so unlike the Frédéric of the threatening partnership with Félix, so quiet and indeed gentle in his manner, that she found nothing disturbing about it. And after all, Casseuil was all the home he had.

Mathilde for her part knew that Frédéric's apparent calmness was rather the exhausted acquiescence of someone in a state of shock. Too dazed by grief to think for himself, he was content to lean on her and be guided by her, following wherever she led. Gently, because she knew that it would help him, Mathilde encouraged him to talk of Félix. She learned a great deal about Frédéric's past which she had not known before, some of it painful – even shocking – some surprising, and almost all of it, since his thirteenth year, centred with intensity upon Félix.

'You never had women friends, as Félix did,' she observed one day, a little wonderingly.

'I never wanted them. There has never been any other woman but you, not for a moment. There never will be.' She knew there was nothing false or conventional about that assurance; he was quite simply stating a fact.

They did not seek seclusion or privacy, nor did they deliberately avoid it. Sometimes, when they knew they were alone and unobserved, he would hold her hand, put an arm briefly about her, even, softly, kiss her; but always with a certain restraint. Without putting it into words they both knew why. In a way, Mathilde thought, they could keep any sense of guilt at bay like this, knowing that the one overpowering moment of passion – excusable, understandable, surely even forgivable – was the only one, a single experience, transfiguring but isolated. They drifted along now on a cloud of self-abnegation, desire and love and tenderness controlled and diffused, made safe, disarmed by a love that was deeper and more enduring than the physical simplicities of bodily longing.

We could stay together like this for ever, Mathilde thought. Sometimes it would be hard, but we have known one moment of complete joy, and we have so much else, so much more. She felt somehow exalted, happy in a strange kind of way. She told Frédéric what she was thinking, and he kissed her and murmured loving words, but made no comment; and she was troubled because just for that instant she sensed that they were not quite in tune. Then he distracted her with some thought of his own and she forgot the momentary cloud. 'All that could happen has happened,' she had said. They had no need to fear anything any more, least of all from one another.

It took little more than a week for her to realise that she might be wrong; horribly, terrifyingly wrong. Another week, and it was as if a great dark chasm had opened suddenly in the quiet sunlit path that lay before them, from which there was no turning aside, no going back. Mathilde became irritable, edgy, inclined to snap at everyone – even at Frédéric – and given to long inexplicable silences. She was clearly not sleeping well.

Concerned, Frédéric observed her closely for a day or two, and when she seemed no better, tackled her about it as they walked one morning through the wood towards the village. 'What's wrong, Mathilde?'

'Nothing,' she returned morosely; and then she stood still and looked at him. He halted too.

'Well?'

She held out her hands towards him and he came and clasped them. He could see that her mouth was trembling. 'I think I'm pregnant.' She spoke in a tiny whisper, but he heard every word. She could see them reach him one by one, sucking the colour from his face.

'You must be mistaken – it's too soon, much too soon—'

'I might be wrong, it might not be true – but it is, I know it is! Oh, Frédéric, what can I do?' She began to cry like a frightened child, and he held her, not knowing how to begin to comfort her when he was so frightened too.

In the end he seized her by the shoulders and said earnestly, 'You must come away with me – that's the only way.'

'But where could we go?'

'Somewhere – anywhere. We can set up house together. I'll care for you; I've money enough. No one will think anything of it, a sister and brother living together.'

'And a child; their child.'

'Oh God.' He shut his eyes for a moment; and then he said, 'They'd not know that, if we went somewhere quiet, where we're not known; abroad perhaps.'

'What about my mother? It would break her heart.' To leave Laure, and this place she loved, all that was dear and safe and familiar – even for Frédéric; and for Frédéric as a fugitive like herself, with a child dependent on them both for everything. 'We'd always be afraid someone would find out, never be sure—'

'What else is there then, tell me that?'

'I don't know,' she whispered. What was joy, if it dragged this in its wake? 'Do you know, is it against the law? Could they punish us for it? I couldn't bear it if they took the child away.'

'I don't know.' He gave a bitter little laugh. 'You should ask Tartuffe.' She stared at him. 'You know, your lawyer friend, Charles de Miremont.'

'I know. I wasn't thinking of that.' She was silent for a little longer, fighting her way through the turmoil of her thoughts to some inevitable conclusion. Then she said, 'I know what I must do.' She spoke as if she had chosen to face a firing squad.

In two days Charles de Miremont was back and had called at Casseuil. Frédéric disappeared somewhere as soon as he was announced, and the young man spent an ecstatic afternoon in Mathilde's company. When he had gone, Mathilde came to find Laure, who was dressing for dinner upstairs; she was alone, for she always dressed without servants, and Henri was at Trissac and would not be home until later.

'Maman,' she said quietly, 'Monsieur le Comte de Miremont will be calling on you tomorrow, if that's agreeable, with his wife. I have accepted Charles's proposal.'

Laure swung round from the dressing-table, all smiles and astonishment. 'Mathilde! I never imagined! You—' She stopped suddenly, struck by the gravity of her daughter's expression. She did not look like a newly engaged girl. 'Are you sure that's what you want?'

Mathilde nodded. 'Yes, Maman. And I – we want to be married soon, as soon as possible. Please.'

Puzzled, Laure stood up and came to look more closely at her daughter. 'What is it, *ma mie*? Something's not right.'

She had not meant to tell her mother. She had wanted no one to know but herself and Frédéric, their secret for ever. Only she found she could not keep silent.

'I'm pregnant, Maman.'

She wished the ground could have opened and swallowed her up before she lived to see that look on her mother's face, knowing she was the cause of it; but then she had wished that on the day she had first realised what had happened, and here she still was, living through it all, somehow.

Laure stared at her with incredulous horror. 'He did this to you? Charles, that devout kind man – I would never have believed it of him!'

'Not Charles, Maman—'

'Then who?' The next moment something seemed to die behind her eyes, some faith, or hope. She whispered, as if fending off a blow, 'No!'

Speechless with misery, Mathilde nodded. But Laure came and grasped her shoulders, almost shaking her, grimly demanding. 'I want it in words, Mathilde, out loud, in the open. Let's have no more pretence. Who is responsible for this?'

'I am, Maman; and – Frédéric.' His name was breathed in an undertone, but it was there and Laure heard it, beyond any possibility of doubt.

The next moment, unexpectedly, a note of relief had crept into Laure's voice. 'But he's been here scarcely three weeks – it's far too soon; you couldn't be certain yet. Are you sure you've not imagined it all? I know you're fond of him, more than you ought to be; but to make a child it is necessary for a man to—' She was infinitely gentle, wanting to believe what her tone implied, that her daughter was an innocent child still, dreaming a child's dreams.

'I know that, Maman; it happened. The night he came here – he was unhappy and – we did not mean to; it was an accident.' Her mother drew back, hands falling to her sides. 'I'm sorry, Maman. I know it's very soon; I know I could be mistaken. But I know I am not.'

'I thought it was over,' Laure cried brokenly. 'You seemed so natural together, not like before. And all the time that had happened, and you knew and said nothing—'

The bitterness in her tone stung Mathilde to anger, because of the hurt behind it.

'It's not the sort of thing you tell everyone!'

'It's not the sort of thing that should happen, ever!' And then she sighed, with a terrible weariness. 'Oh, what's the use? It has happened, God help us!' She broke off again, trying to make sense of it, to understand. 'And this is your solution is it then – to trap a good man into marriage?'

'I haven't trapped him. He wanted to marry me – you know that.'

'But he does not know you are carrying another man's child – or what man. You know what he's like. You know he thinks you little short of an angel. Certainly he has no doubt you are a virgin. What do you think it would do to him if he were ever to find out? Have you thought of that? Or if you are wrong and you marry him and only realise too late that there's no child – you can't turn back then.'

'What does it matter? I can't marry Frédéric, can I?' She saw that Laure was shocked that she could even say that, and so bleakly, as if it were a matter for regret. 'Besides, we went over all that, Frédéric and I.'

'Oh, so you've told him, have you? What did he have to say? Was this his solution then?'

'No. He wanted me to go away with him.'

'I might have known. What kind of life would that have been, living like criminals, always afraid of discovery? And for a child!'

'I didn't go, did I, Maman?' Mathilde pointed out quietly. 'Why do you think I said yes to Charles?'

'In desperation, because you could think of nothing else; yes, I understand that. But it won't do, Mathilde.' She had her emotions under control again, her brain working quickly, looking for solutions. 'We'll go to Paris – I know people who will help. We'll take steps—'

'No!' Mathilde backed away. 'No one's going to murder my baby!'

It was Laure's turn to be shocked. 'I didn't mean *that*,' she said more gently. 'God forbid! But before it becomes obvious we can take some discreet lodgings somewhere and make enquiries for a decent family – a childless couple, perhaps, who'd be glad to bring up the child as their own. They need know nothing of its origins.'

'Maman, I *want* this child.'

The passionate conviction of the words startled Laure, who cried in return, 'But it's the child of incest! You don't know—' She broke off, unable to put that fear into words. She did not know whether or not to be glad that Mathilde appeared to have no idea what she had been about to say.

'I know what I want, Maman,' the girl said with emotion. 'Oh, of course I wish it had not happened. But now it has, I want to hold my baby in my arms and care for it and love it and have it with me always.' Her voice grew rough, emerging in the end as a tremulous whisper. 'I know it's wrong, but I love him – I cannot give away his child.'

Laure spread her hands in despair. 'Oh, Mathilde!'

And then she stepped forward and gathered her daughter into her arms and they clung together weeping for a long time.

In the end Laure too came to believe that there was no other way than the one Mathilde had chosen. If it had been anyone but Frédéric – only it *was* Frédéric, and the child would be not just a bastard but the outcome of incest. She could not ask Mathilde, her own beloved daughter, to face the consequences of that. Once she knew there was no question in the girl's mind of adoption, the conclusion was inevitable.

She felt like a conspirator, locked in deceit with Mathilde and Frédéric, their innocent victim that guileless and good young man. She knew that what they were doing was ugly, inexcusable; she knew it more than Mathilde, who was desperate and unhappy, and Frédéric, who was, she thought, nearly unbalanced by such a succession of griefs. She hated the façade they all put up, all smiles and good humour, basking – apparently – in the approval of Henri and the de Miremont parents, and warmly welcoming to the man they so deeply wronged.

ii

'A brandy before you go, Monsieur de Miremont?' Henri, standing by the sideboard in the *grand salon*, looked round at Charles, who was seated as close as possible to Mathilde, talking to her in a low voice. The wedding was to take place on Thursday, two weeks after the proposal had been accepted. This afternoon the young couple had spent two hours at the presbytery, receiving instruction from the *curé* on the duties and responsibilities of the married state. Afterwards, Charles had stayed for dinner, delaying his return to Bergerac for as long as possible. He had been reminding Mathilde that there were only two full days still to go, when Henri's interruption brought to mind how late it was. He looked round.

'No thank you, *monsieur*. I think I really must take my leave of you.' He smiled tenderly at Mathilde who, pale and quiet, raised her eyes briefly to his face and then looked away again almost at once. He rose to his feet.

'Will you come again tomorrow?' Henri asked. 'I imagine my wife will want to give you some instructions about the vineyard before Thursday.'

Laure, standing aimlessly near the window looking out on the darkening landscape, glanced sharply round at Henri; Charles looked puzzled. 'I do not see—'

Henry's face had a malicious little smile upon it; or at least to Laure it looked malicious. 'Since you're not indulging yourselves with a wedding journey, there's no reason for my wife to delay putting the vineyard in your hands. We intend to take up residence at Trissac from Thursday evening, immediately after the wedding.'

Mathilde gave a little cry, hastily stifled. Laure controlled herself better, but not because she felt less. Alone at Trissac with Henri, with not even the vineyard to console her – no, it was a horrible, unbearable prospect! She was about to speak, to try and form some kind of calm and rational protest, when she thought, But as a step towards leaving him, might that not be best? However great her longing, she could not simply leave Henri the moment Mathilde was married, or not without a scandal that would only add to her daughter's unhappiness. But by going to Trissac she would at once be distancing herself from Mathilde and Charles, so that after a little while her going would be the less likely to reflect upon them. A few weeks, perhaps months, at Trissac, and she would be free. She supposed she could endure that, if she had to. Then she realised Charles was saying something.

'Oh but, *monsieur*, I had assumed Madame Séguier would remain here, for the time being at least. I am very ignorant of the craft of the *vigneron* – I depend upon her to continue the wonderful work she has already begun. I beg of you both to reconsider your decision.' He glanced towards Laure, as if he assumed it had been her decision too.

Laure, too confused to know what to say, heard the two men argue the case, politely; and was aware at last that Henri had given way. She had spent too much emotion in the past days to have any left to spare now; wearily, she did not know whether she was glad or sorry.

Charles, pleased with his small victory, took his leave of them. 'Good-night, *madame – monsieur* – please convey my good wishes to Monsieur Brousse and tell him I hope he will be fully recovered by Thursday.' Frédéric had retreated to his room the moment Charles had arrived this morning, returning untouched the meals Laure had sent up to him; and she had put in a not wholly untruthful plea of sickness on his behalf. He had looked ill enough, after all, ever since the dreadful day of Charles's proposal.

Charles kissed Mathilde's hand. 'Don't come with me to the door, *chère* Mathilde. You look tired – you must take care of yourself.'

It was Henri who went with him, leaving mother and daughter alone. Mathilde ran at once to close the door and then came to clasp Laure's arm.

'Maman,' she pleaded urgently, 'don't let him take you to Trissac. You mustn't leave me, not ever! When Frédéric's gone

426

you'll be the only one who knows. I need you!' She was close to tears, almost hysterical.

Laure laid a hand over hers. 'I shall stay, Mathilde,' she said, but her voice was dry and hard. She had thought Mathilde's marriage would set her free; now she saw that it had only trapped her more securely than ever. I suppose it serves me right, she thought grimly.

Mathilde managed a tremulous smile and then released her mother and went to run her fingers idly over the pile of music on the piano, as if she did not quite know what she was doing. When she spoke again she was quivering with emotion, but her voice was bright, too bright. 'You know, Maman, Charles has been singing my praises today. He says I am just what a young bride ought to be. No great fuss, no demands for a huge grand wedding – all I want is a quick, quiet, private ceremony. Charles said everyone should be like me, knowing what things really matter, above everything. He says we want only the essentials, not the unnecessary trappings. *Monsieur le curé* agrees with him. Long engagements and elaborate weddings are for people who are only interested in making a show; that's what they both said. We don't need such things, of course, because we're quite sure of one another. That's good, isn't it, Maman?'

Laure, hurt unbearably by the brittle tone, could not endure, either, the pain in her daughter's eyes, and looked away. 'This is not what I wanted for you, Mathilde,' she said in a bitter undertone. 'Not this sham, based on deceit. I wanted you to love and be loved in return, to marry for that alone, to be happy for ever.'

'That was a dream, Maman,' said Mathilde starkly. 'This is life.'

CHAPTER
TWENTY TWO

i

Frédéric stayed for the wedding, for appearance's sake and because Mathilde asked it of him; and the next day left Casseuil. They had one last moment together before he went, when they clung to one another for a long time in silent agony; and then he told her she would never see him again. She knew he meant it.

It took Charles three nights to consummate the marriage, so fearful was he of hurting Mathilde. After that, he made love to her two or three times a week, but never on Fridays or fast days, and always with the utmost gentleness. She submitted to him with neither distaste nor pleasure, which was perhaps what he expected from a woman of her supposed purity. There was nothing in his lovemaking to remind her of the blissful abandonment of those moments with Frédéric. In any case, once he knew she was pregnant, Charles left her alone altogether, for fear of hurting the child.

She told him about the baby when they had been married for a month, assuming the shy happiness of a young bride who has done her duty. She was becoming an appallingly good liar. Charles was delighted, and protected and cossetted and fussed over her until she could have screamed with irritation; which she did not, of course.

Gradually, in a dull sort of way, she grew used to his constant presence in her life, his oddities. He set up a prie-dieu in their bedroom, at which he knelt night and morning, though mercifully he did not seem to expect her to do the same – rather to her surprise, he accepted her lack of piety without question or reproach. She wondered ruefully if he thought her too good to need such a careful routine. She went to mass with him once nearly every Sunday and holy day, but that was all.

Charles went daily, and generally to vespers as well, and the Abbé Lebrun was a frequent guest at their table. When he was not there, Charles himself said grace aloud before meals.

To Mathilde it was all somehow a little unreal, as if she were suspended outside herself, observing the quiet well-behaved young bride going through the routines of her life with Charles, as if none of it really had anything to do with her.

Once she had told Charles she was pregnant, she went with Laure to see Doctor Bonnet, who confirmed it, of course. 'I'd have said it was a little more than four weeks,' he commented casually; and then apparently saw some evidence on Mathilde's face of the frozen dismay that had filled her. He grinned, all easy reassurance. 'Oh, I know it can't be. These things are very hard to judge. I wish I had ten francs for every time I'd got it wrong – I'd be a wealthy man by now.' Mathilde realised that he did not indeed have the faintest suspicion that this time he might be right; or she hoped he did not. He sent her on her way with instructions to rest and eat sensibly and not to worry about anything.

She said nothing to Laure on the way home and, once in the house, went straight to her room to remove her outdoor clothes. Charles had gone out after breakfast; she could not remember where, though she supposed he had told her. Perhaps he was shooting with Louis Chabry.

She went to the window of her sitting-room and stood looking down on the wet gravel of the courtyard (there would not be much of a harvest this year), the well with its ornate decoration, the low stone *chai* with its tiled roof weathered to a soft coral and tinted with the grey and gold of the lichen, the delicate wrought iron fence that linked *chai* to stables and led the eyes through it to the track and the wood beyond.

Suddenly, as clearly as if it were happening to her now, Mathilde was taken back to the morning when she and Frédéric had stood there together under the trees and confronted the consequences of what they had done, which had brought her to where she was today. Just over six weeks ago – was it really only that?

And this is where I am now, she thought; married to Charles and carrying a child who will be born too soon.

Until now she had been swept along only by a desperate

need to conceal her secret by whatever means and so protect herself; nothing else had been quite real to her. She wished at this moment that she was still hemmed in by that protective single-mindedness; but it had gone, and a chill wind seemed to have blown in after it and carried her to this point, where she stood at the window and saw everything with icy clarity, as it really was. She remembered with anguish how she and Frédéric had clung together that day in the wood, seeking comfort from one another. But they had found none, and now here she stood with her spirit stripped naked to the elements that battered it, and knew that she was alone, utterly alone –

No, she thought abruptly, that is not quite true, though it feels as if it is. I have Maman, who knows everything, and Nanon, who I think guesses something, and would go on loving me even if I were to tell her the truth. I am not in fact alone – not like Frédéric, who has no one left at all. At some conscious level she had accepted his assurance that she would never see him again. Now, for the first time, she felt it right through her, as a bleak and bitter truth. He had gone away from Casseuil and from her, to become a solitary wanderer without a home, because of what they had done. And she would never see him again as long as she lived, or hear his voice or feel his arms about her; or even have news of him by a word or a letter. He might as well be dead – except that if he were dead then there would at least be a grave she could visit, to take flowers and weep and remember. Now, this way, she had lost him completely.

Slowly, tears formed in her eyes and she began to cry; but after a little while, because she could not hope for any kind of comfort, she stopped and blew her nose. Outside, a carriage had turned in under the arch and come to a halt below her window: Catherine Chabry and Émilie Lacroix had come to call. She glanced quickly in the mirror to check that her face gave nothing away, and then went downstairs to welcome her visitors.

ii

The liquid in the *cuve* was quiet beneath the residual scum left from the wild frothing activity of the past weeks. Laure ran off a very little into a clear undecorated glass and held it up against the light of the candles set in the simple chandeliers that hung at intervals from the vaulted stone roof of the *chai*. She gave a little nod and then lowered the glass to taste.

Moïse must have met someone on his way out of the *chai*, for she could hear him talking, although she had not been aware of anyone coming in. She could not quite catch what he was saying, but though he was speaking French he sounded cheerful and animated: it was probably Charles then. She had been a little surprised at how quickly Moïse and the other workers had taken to the new master of Casseuil. They had been suspicious of him at first, even resentful, and clearly they still found him a somewhat comic figure. But they all liked to talk to him and there was, Laure recognised, a real affection growing beneath the amused tolerance of their attitude towards him. Perhaps after all it was not so surprising. Charles had that rare enough gift, of appearing to be deeply and wholeheartedly interested in the person in whose company he happened to find himself; probably because he was genuinely so interested.

She glanced round. Yes, there he was at the foot of the steps, his head tilted very slightly to one side and a look of concentrated attention on his face. Moïse, however, had work to do and soon freed Charles to make his way across the *chai* towards her. He looked a little sombre, she thought; and then she noticed with alarm that he was wearing a black armband.

'What's happened? Have you had bad news?' He had gone out early this morning, before even she was up – to mass, she supposed – and she had not seen him since.

She touched the armband, and he smiled faintly. 'No,' he reassured her. 'That is for the King.'

Laure, who had already clashed several times with her son-in-law's thoroughly reactionary politics – she had only lately realised just how reactionary they were – tried to suppress a feeling of impatience. 'Which King is this? I lose track of all your pretenders.'

'King Louis XVI, *madame*,' he told her, the gravity of his tone rebuking her a little for her disrespect.

'Oh, Charles, he was executed a hundred years ago!'

'Precisely, *madame*: a hundred years ago today, on January 21 1793.'

431

'And this is 1893! Why can't you accept that things have changed a little since then?'

'But not for the better, I think. Read your newspapers, *madame* – can you really claim that the corruption of which you read daily is desirable in those who govern us?'

Since the papers were at present full of the financial irregularities of government ministers involved in the recent collapse of the Panama Canal company, Laure knew she was not – unfortunately – in a strong position. 'There have been corrupt kings, you know, Charles,' she pointed out. 'Besides, wishing the Revolution hadn't happened isn't going to help us now, is it? Why, even the Pope wants us all to be good Republicans. Surely his word carries some weight with you?'

'The Holy Father can be wrong, on occasions,' said Charles stiffly. 'It is not a matter of doctrine.'

Laure sighed with exasperation. 'Oh, Charles, sometimes I despair of you!' She looked up at his offended expression and regretted her tone. In the circumstances he deserved more than ordinary consideration from her. 'Have you come to see how the wine is progressing?'

His face lightened at once. He showed little practical aptitude as a *vigneron* (although he had shown himself reasonably efficient in the management of other aspects of the estate's business, such as the woodlands bordering the vineyard); but his enthusiasm was genuine enough. 'Is it ready? Has the fermentation finished?'

'It's stabilised for the time being. It's ready for racking – but not today.'

'Why not?'

'One doesn't rack wine at the full moon: it's too unstable then. We wait for a waning moon.'

'Really? I didn't know that.' He stared in fascination at the cloudy liquid remaining in her glass, as if half-expecting it to do something dramatic at any moment; and then he said, 'I have been intending to ask – do you allow a secondary fermentation? I know that in Bordeaux it is usual, and Monsieur Lambert uses it too – he described the process to me one day. But he is not yet making white wine, of course.'

So even Aubin talked to him! Laure was momentarily silenced by surprise; then she said, 'No, if there is too much

fermentation we'd find all the sugar was used up – we'd have
either a dry wine, or (worst of all) vinegar. That's partly why
it has to be racked so often, to keep it under control – as well
as clearing the wine of impurities of course. Sometimes, if
necessary, we add sulphur.'

'That halts the fermentation? But does it not affect the
taste?'

She smiled. 'Have you ever noticed any difference? No, we
use just as much as we need and no more. The very best years
don't need any, of course, because then the high sugar content
of the grapes produces so much alcohol that it knocks out the
yeasts and prevents them working any more. The better the
year, the more we can leave to nature. The other thing that's
important in controlling fermentation is the temperature – if
it's too warm, it goes much too fast; too cold, and it stops
altogether.'

'Then no wonder it has stopped today!' said Charles with
feeling. It was certainly very cold; this morning as Laure had
crossed the courtyard she had thought it might well snow by
nightfall.

'That reminds me – Moïse was telling me something this
morning. I gather you've been arranging to rent some land.'

She saw him colour a little. He cleared his throat and said
rather awkwardly, 'Oh – yes – that. I had meant to tell you.'

'You are master here, of course,' she reminded him gently.
'You are not obliged to tell me anything. But I did think two
francs a week for about half a hectare of land was more than a
little excessive – after all, we can't graze many beasts on it, and
the output of manure will be minimal. And very expensive at
that rate.'

She had not thought he could blush any more deeply, but he
did so. 'I suppose you think I am misusing your daughter's
inheritance?'

'I don't think that at all. Though I do gather Monsieur
Vergnolles is delighted. He's telling everyone how he's pulled
a fast one on you. After all, two francs a week for a poor piece
of land he's too infirm to do anything with – it's beyond
belief. In the long run he'll get far more out of it this way than
he ever could if he had either farmed it or sold it.'

'He doesn't want to sell. He hopes his son will come back

433

one day and take over. It's sad, don't you think, that so many young men never come home again once they have completed their military service? Conscription is eating away at the fabric of family life.'

'Charles, stop trying to sidetrack me.' He looked at her with a limpid innocence in his blue eyes; and she shook her head ruefully. 'Even you are not quite so simple-minded as to think that piece of land is worth so much: I know that quite well. Just as I know why, when you got there yesterday and found old Monsieur Vergnolles outside chopping wood, you set him talking about the best manure for vines, and then while he rambled on you finished off the wood for him.' Not very efficiently at that, Moïse had reported; but old Monsieur Vergnolles had been pleased all the same. Charles was young and strong and quicker at the work than he would have been.

'I know I should have asked you about the manure.'

'Don't be silly. You weren't in the least interested in manure, were you? What you cared about was that those two old people are alone and poor, and have no one to care for them. And two francs a week is going to help a great deal. But you know they'd never take it from you, not as a gift.' She smiled at him gently. 'You can be quite clever when you want to be.' She saw that, uncomfortable and embarrassed, he did not know what to say; so she went on, 'What I can't understand is, why them? Don't you know Madame Vergnolles is Monsieur Martin's sister and they're both as anti-Catholic as it is possible to be? They must hate all the things you care most deeply about. It is one thing repairing the presbytery, you know, but quite another to help people who won't dream of thanking you for it.'

'They are still human beings,' he said quietly; then, as if as an afterthought, 'Besides, if they receive acts of kindness from members of the Church, will they not be drawn towards her as a consequence?'

'Not if they think the Church is populated by gullible fools,' retorted Laure bluntly; and regretted her words almost at once. 'I'm sorry, Charles, that was unjust. You are a good, kind man—'

Fiercely he shook his head. 'No, *madame*, please – I beg you, don't talk of it any more.' He seemed so distressed that she relented and dropped the subject. What she could never say, of course, was how much his devious act of kindness had stirred her conscience, reminding her painfully how she more than anyone had imposed upon him; unforgivably, so it seemed to her. She tried to shake off the depression that the reflection brought with it, and looked past him towards the door. 'Where is Moïse? He's taking a long time. I'd better go and see what he's up to—' She set off, but Charles caught her arm.

'*Madame*, one moment please!' She turned. 'There is something I wish to talk about – that's why I came.' She saw that the sombreness which had been on his face when he first came up to her was there again. 'It's Mathilde.'

'She's not worse?' Just before Christmas Mathilde had become very unwell, exhausted and constantly dizzy, tormented by persistent headaches, her hands and ankles painfully swollen. Doctor Bonnet had insisted that she retire immediately to bed, where she had remained ever since with little sign of improvement.

'No, thank God; or not as far as her body is concerned. It is her unhappiness that troubles me.'

'I know. I feel the same. But these moods take pregnant women sometimes, you know. It will pass once the baby's born.' Strange, she thought, how I tell the most blatant lies and deceive and conceal the truth day in day out, yet I never blush as Charles did when I caught him in a kindness.

'Yes, I expect that is true. But yesterday I was talking of it to Catherine Chabry. She says that there is nothing unusual in a woman weeping often after the birth of her child; but she thought it rare beforehand. And she has had four children.'

Laure wondered with a little chill what Catherine Chabry had made of Charles's report. She only hoped it had seemed no more to her than an interesting medical phenomenon. 'I think it takes everyone differently,' she said vaguely, and was not surprised that Charles failed to be reassured.

'I want to help her, *madame*. Sometimes I think there is something troubling her, but she does not seem able to talk to me. I think she talks to you more. Perhaps you know; perhaps you can help.'

'I can only try.'

He bent his head, and she saw that he was twisting his hands anxiously together. 'Sometimes,' he went on in a low anguished voice, 'I am afraid I shall lose her. I know I must accept God's will, but—'

Only under extreme emotion did Charles ever fail to finish a sentence; Laure, moved and full of compassion, clasped her hands about his. 'Be patient, *mon cher*. There are only two – three – months to go now. I am sure all will be well in the end.'

But she was by no means sure. She knew better than Charles what a black depth of depression had swallowed up her daughter, because – as he said – Mathilde talked to her; when she talked to anyone, that was.

When she returned to the house, she looked in on Mathilde, but found her asleep: she often slept in the day, because she was rarely able to sleep at night and when she did was afflicted by terrible nightmares. Coming downstairs again, anxiety turning within her as it had done so often lately, Laure found there was a letter waiting for her. It was a moment or two before she recognised Marcel's writing, so long was it since he had written to her; and then, afraid that some disaster had struck her mother, she swiftly tore the letter open.

All was well. Her mother had even written the first part of the letter herself, describing a theatre outing in honour of her seventieth birthday; but Marcel had taken over, because he had a proposal to put to Laure. 'I hope you will quickly recover from the shock of hearing from me in person, *ma chère sœur*. You see, your account of your daughter's wedding (how astonishing to think little Mathilde is old enough to be a bride!) and the photographs that helped us to share your happiness with you, just a little – all that set me thinking how much I should like to see you again – how much we should all like to see you. Maman has always said she would never return to France so long as the province of her birth remains in German hands – but now I think she begins to fear that if she waits until it is free again she will be too old to come (I tell her she will never be too old if she lives to be a hundred, but she will have these fantasies). My son Michael is fifteen now – he is at school still, of course, and doing well – but when the time comes for him to leave, then I think it will do him good to visit Europe, before he settles down to a career. He has relations in Ireland too, of course, as well as in France. So, what do you think? Shall we plan a grand tour to take place in a year or two? May we come to Casseuil and try your new wine? I hope it will be ready by then. Your son-in-law sounds a most agreeable young man, who would I am sure make us welcome. Shall we come?'

Marcel himself might have been there in the *grand salon* with her, pleading his case, his voice full of the note of teasing affection she remembered so well. But did she want him here in person, facing her across the hearth, where his shrewd eyes could see the harsh lines that the past two years with Henri had scoured into her once-youthful face, where his quick ear could hear the hate in Henri's voice when he spoke to her, and his knowledge of the world and its ways would set him wondering about Mathilde, and her unhappiness and the baby—? No, she thought; no, I don't want him to come, nor Maman, nor any of them. I couldn't bear it if they were ever to find out how much every part of my life here at Casseuil is a lie, how all the surface happiness is an empty sham.

But she could hardly say that, of course. For the moment all she could do was to write and tell them that Mathilde was not well and that they must all wait and see. She wished, desperately, that it was over – but not too soon, not so soon that their secret would be betrayed. Would Charles – innocent, inexperienced, not very quick-witted – would he suspect anything, if Mathilde gave birth in March to a large healthy baby quite clearly not in the least premature? Would Doctor Bonnet give them away? She did not know, and at the moment she could almost think it was the least of her worries. What mattered much more was that Mathilde should be well again. Charles was not alone in his fear.

For Mathilde it was not a fear at all. 'I shall die when the baby's born, Maman. I am glad.' She said it in a dry matter-of-fact voice as Laure sat at her bedside that evening, holding her hand; Charles had been sleeping in her sitting-room since she had been ill, and he was there now, with the intervening door firmly closed. It was, Laure supposed, one advantage of having so relentlessly upright a son-in-law that she could be sure he was not listening at the keyhole.

Laure's hand tightened about her daughter's. The look in the dark, weary, red-rimmed eyes frightened her, because it was so steady and sure and unafraid. 'Don't talk like that, *minou*. You don't want your baby to be motherless, do you now?'

'It will have you and Nanon, and Charles I suppose. That's enough.' Then there was fear in her eyes, real and terrible, so that Laure wanted to reach out and clasp her and comfort her; but she had to be so careful with Mathilde these days, with her moods. 'Maman,' – her voice came in a whisper now – 'do you think – I've heard—'

'What, *ma mie*?'

'They say, sometimes – a child like this; you know, when the parents are related . . . Don't they say it will be wrong somehow, deformed or sick in its mind? Like a curse, because it was a sin.'

Laure stroked her hand. 'Not a curse, *minou* – that's silly. It's only a very slight possibility, you know – not inevitable, not at all. Frédéric is only your half-brother – I'm sure everything will be all right.' That particular fear had haunted her from the very beginning, but she had thought Mathilde had at least been spared – as if she did not have enough, with everything else.

'I had a horrible nightmare about it last night, Maman . . . I hope it dies too, when I do.'

Laure did what she could, but when she left Mathilde she knew she had brought her no comfort at all. But she supposed that at least she had helped some of the long night hours to pass; it was well after midnight now.

When she reached her room she found that Henri was still awake; or if he had been asleep her coming disturbed him. He sat up, and she shrank at the anger on his face. 'Where have you been all this time? What do you mean by keeping me waiting?'

'I've been with Mathilde, as you know full well.'

'You spend far too much time with her. She's Charles's responsibility now, not yours. Your duty is to me, first and before all. It's time you realised that.'

Laure went to the dressing-table to unpin her hair; these days Henri insisted always that she undress in the room with

438

him. She knew he was watching her, and she waited with dread for him to come to her, as he would any moment now.

'Mathilde is very ill. She needs me.'

'I don't know what's the matter with the girl. Most women have babies without making such a fuss – and she's so miserable. God knows why. She's got everything a girl could ask for, I'd have said.'

She heard the bed creak and the steps cross the floor towards her; and then Henri's broad figure loomed up in the mirror behind her, filling the frame, making her own candlelit image look very small and defenceless.

Much later, when he lay snoring beside her on the bed, she moved at last, easing her aching body out from the covers into the cold cleansing air. Softly, she pulled a wrap about her, put slippers on her feet and crept out onto the landing. There at last she felt as if she could breathe again.

'Oh, I hate him, I *hate* him!'

She had thought she hated Philippe's mother, all those years ago; but that had been nothing beside this, which consumed and tormented her through every moment of each day and most of all through the terrible night hours. How long must she endure it? How long would it go on? For years and years, apparently without end? She had thought she would be free, once Mathilde was married; she had thought she could see a way out. But here she was, bound more firmly than ever.

There was a bright moon tonight, and it shone through the unshuttered windows on the half-landing, lighting the stairs. She went down, seeing nothing, thinking only of Henri with a loathing that set her trembling. He was nearly sixty now, but as strong and powerful as ever, as healthy and vigorous as he had been at forty. There was no escape that way, barring an accident – like what had happened to Victor perhaps . . .

She came to a halt, her hand tight about the handrail, her eyes staring into the darkness below; but seeing something else, clear, unmistakable, starkly lit.

She had blamed herself for Victor's death, believing it was the result of her own neglect, almost as if she had deliberately willed it. After all, such things could be arranged, if one chose: a carefully judged incision in the leather of a girth, somewhere not too obvious; a clumsy moment of jostling at the top of a stone staircase – this very one, for instance . . . There were many possibilities; but few of them sure, or irrevocable.

On the other hand, Henri lay up there on the bed, his head flung back on the bolster, his mouth a little open as he snored. Nearby, her pillow (he scorned a pillow), square and soft, lay where she had left it. If she were to creep back up there now, and take the pillow in both hands, and ram it over that hated face and hold it there and hold it there, on and on until she could be sure, absolutely sure . . . Would anyone ever know?

She caught her breath, pressed her hand to her mouth. Murder: she, Laure Séguier, was contemplating murder, deliberately, carefully, without any other emotion than an intense and overpowering hatred—

She forced herself to go on, down the stairs, into the darkness of the hall; as if there, where the shadow swallowed up her dark thoughts, she could find safety from them.

Another thought came then, quite unbidden: Wait a little, just two months; if Mathilde dies you will be free . . .

What am I thinking, oh what am I thinking? Appalled, shivering, she ran to the front door and pulled back the bolts and opened it, and ran out onto the little bridge, across the courtyard, round to the garden; fleeing in horror past the fountain, along the paths, to the low wall that edged the slope. And there at last she halted; and the cold night air quickly penetrated her thin clothes and forced out, somehow, the dark imaginings from her spirit, leaving an exhausted stillness behind.

She began slowly to take in what lay before her. It had not snowed after all, and the silver on the landscape came from the moon hung high in the velvet darkness of the sky, extinguishing the stars, transforming everything below. Vineyards, tobacco fields, rooftops, pools, the distant river; all were marked out, line by line, in the cold lovely clarity of the light. Here and there, deep shadowed and black, was the shape of a wood or a small valley, the lee side of a building, the thin vertical line of a poplar tree. A beauty that was relentless, merciless and yet of a perfection that took the breath away—

Long, long years ago she had believed that some fate had

brought her here to Casseuil, some purpose; that it was right for her. Yet when since then, except for the smallest interval of time, had it ever seemed right, or easy; when had she been happy, for more than a moment? Just now she had thought only of escape, at any price—

Only – here just below her feet were the vineyards she had planted and tended with such care, the vines now six years old, not so far perhaps from the time when they would be mature enough for her to hope for a good wine; and behind her, lying wakeful in her bed, was the daughter she loved, who might not die after all, and who was carrying her grandchild, who might be born whole and unblemished . . . Was that enough to tempt her to stay? To persuade her not to risk everything by some rash and violent act? To give her the strength to endure the worst that Henri could do, without breaking?

Madame Naillac had been unable to drive her away; was she to allow Henri to succeed where Philippe's mother had failed?

She folded her arms about her, hugging herself, trying to shut out the cold and to give herself courage. She *would* hold on, taking one day at a time, in the hope that tomorrow might be better – or the day after, or the one after that. It was how she had survived all these years since Philippe's death, how she had come as far as she had today. She must not allow herself to feel for a moment that all she had achieved was nothing, set against Henri's brutality and Mathilde's grief.

She drew in a long deep breath of the cold air and turned and walked back towards the house.

iii

The baby, when he came, was a little late, a week perhaps; but Mathilde was so ill that it was easy to believe that the child had arrived too soon. The labour was slow and agonising and lasted for nearly two days. At the moment of birth Mathilde was scarcely conscious and Doctor Bonnet had nearly given up hope both for her and the child.

Aware at first only of a cessation of almost unbearable pain, and of a weariness beyond words, Mathilde lay without moving, her eyes closed, waiting until at last the darkness should swallow her up for ever. Then there came, from somewhere very far away beyond her reach, a thin thready cry, slowly gathering strength. With an enormous effort of will she opened her eyes; and saw Charles's face bending over her. She thought he was holding her hand too, and he was smiling, though there were tears in his eyes. She wanted to ask about the baby, but it was too difficult for her to frame the words; only, somehow, he seemed to understand.

'We have a fine son, *chérie*,' Charles murmured tenderly. 'He's a little small, but then he did come early.' He shook his head and gave a soft laugh. 'So hasty and impulsive – who would think he was a son of mine?'

She shut her eyes quickly, because she found all at once that she could not bear to look at him. She was aware of a little bustle of activity, as if they were anxious about her. When she opened her eyes again her mother was there, holding a small white bundle in her arms.

'Here he is, *minou* – for you to see.' She laid the bundle by Mathilde's shoulder, so that she could turn her head to look at it. He was tiny, Frédéric's son, unbelievably tiny, with a fuzz of dark hair on his head and unfocused dark blue eyes blinking at her, and funny wrinkled little hands just visible above the folds of the shawl; which, in a moment, Laure turned back, so that her daughter could see the whole of the small creature lying there.

He was perfect.

CHAPTER
TWENTY THREE

The children would be out of school at any moment: Laure knew that, because little Paul Lambert, Aubin's youngest son, was standing by the school gate, his face pressed against the railings, waiting for his brothers to emerge. He could almost always be seen there at this time of day. He looked round and smiled at her as she passed, before returning to his vigil; he was an engaging child, more open and friendly than the two older boys.

In the market place, Laure met Aubin himself, coming out of the new post office (opened just last year). He greeted her politely. 'I see they've begun on the tobacco.'

'Yes.' Henri had been at Trissac all day today, busy with the harvest. 'Not long now to your *vendange* – the vines looked good, as I came by just now.'

'I'll be making my first Casseuil wine this year, all being well,' Aubin said.

'I can only wish you a good harvest then,' Laure admitted with a smile. 'After all, if it isn't good for you then it won't be good for me either.'

'Would you want to wish me anything else in any case, *Madame*—?' he returned, grinning.

'Ah, now that's a difficult one!' Then she added, more seriously, 'I still haven't quite grown used to having *any* kind of harvest, after so long.'

Aubin nodded. 'We didn't last year, did we? But compared to the phylloxera, what is a little spring hailstorm?'

'A mere nothing, of course – but I wouldn't want to have to face any more like that for a long time.'

'No. Still, at least they can't blame the weather on the Jews – only on God, and he can look after himself, I reckon.'

Laure looked a little puzzled.

'Haven't you heard of the latest scientific discovery?' Aubin's tone was heavy with sarcasm. 'I had it last week from Jean Frangeas, ignorant old fool that he is: the phylloxera was introduced deliberately to France by the Jews.'

'By the Jews? But why?'

'To destroy the French wine trade, I suppose.'

'How utterly ridiculous! I never cease to be amazed at what people will believe! Why should the Jews want to destroy the wine trade, in any case?'

Aubin shrugged. 'As you say, *madame*, it is ridiculous. But he lost everything when the disease hit his vines – I suppose he wants someone to blame. Since no one can say a good word for the Jews at the moment, there it is.'

'Captain Dreyfus has a lot to answer for.'

'Well, he's paying for it, isn't he?' The Jewish army officer had been found guilty last winter of passing military secrets to Germany, and was now serving a life sentence at the remote Devil's Island penal settlement: it had been the latest in a series of spy scares during the past years, all accentuated by the general mistrust of Germany.

'Poor man,' Laure commented then. The phrase must have struck some other chord in her consciousness, for she said next, 'Still no news of Madame Delmas?'

Aubin shook his head. 'Not a word.' The clatter of sabots along the street behind them made him turn his head. 'There are the children out. I'd better go.'

Laure made her way down through the wood to the château, walking slowly and enjoying the freshness of the little breeze that stirred the air. It had been a good idea to go out for a walk: it had cheered her a little, to be alone and away from the house for a short time; but not as much as she had hoped, not enough to lift the general undefined sense of depression from her spirits. Though of course it was not undefined at all, having a very specific cause. As always, it went back to Henri, and the secret misery of her life with him; or so she supposed. She would never again – she thought, she hoped and prayed – feel as she had on that January night two years ago, when there had been murder in her heart. She had come near it again, once or twice, since then, but only for a moment and never with such a desperate intensity of feeling. There was after all more to live for now than there had been at that dark time: the vineyard still, of course, but also two healthy grandchildren, and Mathilde restored to some kind of calmness, if a rather precarious one. Her daughter was, sometimes, even happy. Laure remembered how she had looked when she first held the infant Joseph to her breast: rapt, entranced, with a world of adoring love in her eyes. 'She is like the Madonna herself,' Charles had whispered to Laure, in awed tones. But Laure, with some foreboding, had seen only a young mother whose whole happiness would now be entrusted for ever to the fragile grasp of her child. Still, better to have so uncertain a cause of happiness, than none at all. It was as much, perhaps, as her mother had.

In the *chai* Laure found Moïse giving the '93 wine its final racking.

'Go home now, Moïse,' she said gently. 'I'll finish off for you if you like.'

He shook his head. 'It's nearly done, *madame*.' He looked round at her. 'It's better to have something to do.' Then he added, 'Two weeks now, she's been waiting. It was never like this with any of the others.'

'Perhaps that means it's a boy then,' suggested Laure cheerfully. 'I've heard it said boys are always late.'

Moïse shook his head again. 'It'll be another girl, *madame*, you'll see. Alive or dead, all our little ones have been girls.' He looked anxious, Laure thought; as well he might. His wife had borne seven daughters, of whom three survived; but for some years now they had assumed there would be no more children. By peasant standards, Madame Delmas was old, and this unexpected pregnancy might well prove more dangerous than most.

When he had gone Laure went into the house, with a trace of reluctance of which she was ashamed and which – though it had been growing in her for some months now – she could not quite explain. After all, Henri was there less often these days than at any time since their marriage.

Further, the only sounds to greet her as she came in were happy ones: the contented gurgling of a baby, a child's laughter, Mathilde's gentle voice, and Charles's, warm with tenderness. They were all in the *grand salon*. Laure opened the door very softly, so that they did not hear her coming, and stood watching them. Before the hearth – which was masked by a great vase of flowers – a round, rosy blonde baby lay kicking and laughing on the rug: Charlotte, ten months old, and Charles's only child, had he but known it. He had not wanted Mathilde to become pregnant again, after witnessing the agony of her first confinement. Laure knew that, because Mathilde had told her so one day, adding, 'But there *must* be another, Maman – so I know I have done my duty by him, in spite of everything.' Exactly how she had managed to overcome his fears Laure did not know, but Charlotte had duly arrived, as easily as was possible, and had been healthy, happy and trouble-free from birth. It was just as well, perhaps, because her mother – though she cared for her with genuine affection – had little love left over for her infant daughter. Charles adored her; but then he adored Joseph too. He knelt now at the foot of Charlotte's rug with his arm about Frédéric's small son, and talked tenderly to his little daughter. Beside him, Mathilde sat on a stool with her eyes on Joseph and her hand caressing his dark curls; she was already four months pregnant again, the swelling just visible, if one knew. At the moment, she shone with happiness.

A devoted family, united in love, Laure thought wryly; and realised at last what it was that made her feel so little at home beneath her own roof. It was not that Charles and Mathilde were so happy and united that they excluded her; on the contrary, she knew with certainty that Mathilde's need of her would keep her tied to her daughter's side for the foreseeable future. Because Laure was the one other person who knew the truth, the only person to whom Mathilde could talk of the secret that gnawed at her, she had to stay, for the sake of Mathilde's sanity. But in every other respect Laure felt almost a stranger in her own house – more so even than she had in all the years of marriage to Henri, who had never made the château fully his home. If she had not felt the need to defer so much to Charles – because she knew the wrong they had done him – it might have been different. Not that he showed any wish to usurp her position, or to dominate the household of which he was now legitimately master. But he could not help leaving his mark on everything he did, if only because he was, in all he stood for, so very different from any other member of the family; and because Mathilde, full of guilt, submitted meekly to him on every occasion when he chose to express his own wishes. Charles treated Laure with the greatest respect, Mathilde clung to her; and there were two grandchildren for her to love. Yet somehow she still felt shut out. Perhaps if Charles had shown more than a rather ineffectual enthusiasm for the vineyard, she might have felt closer to him; if, for example, he had proved to be the very person into whose hands she would have been happy to entrust its future; but he was not, and Mathilde had never had very much interest in it, so that was that: Laure must go on alone, as she had done for so many years already. Only it was hard, when life had few other solaces to offer her, and little hope of any in the future.

Joseph had a ball clutched in his hands, which he had been studying for some time with careful attention. All at once he laughed, glanced over his shoulder at his mother and then raised the ball above his head, ready to throw it.

'No, *mon chéri* – no, you must not, not indoors.' Mathilde's voice was so soft and unconvincing that Laure was not surprised that Joseph took little notice, only laughing the more. Charles intervened, rather more firmly, 'Joseph, *mon cher*, why don't you let me have your ball.' He extricated it gently from the child's grasp. 'See, we'll put it away until the morning, then you can play with it outside.'

The last part of what he said was almost submerged in a great wail from Joseph, rising quickly to a high, wild hysterical crying which they all knew only too well by now. He tore himself free from Charles and flung himself on the floor, drumming his heels, his face purple, his mouth wide, shrieking and sobbing until he could scarcely draw breath. Mathilde tried to hold him, close to tears herself; Charles looked round rather helplessly for something to distract him – in a moment, Laure knew, they would return the ball to him. She stepped forward quickly.

'Joseph, what a noise!'

He shut his mouth, opened his eyes, and for a moment stared at her in surprise. The next instant he scrambled to his

447

feet and came running to her as if tears had never been further from his mind.

'You little rogue, Joseph,' she said, laughing, and gathered him up. He linked his plump little arms about her neck, his dark eyes very bright as he smiled at her. 'He's so like you, Charles!' – so people often said; but Laure thought she already saw in him a strong physical resemblance to Philippe; which, since her first husband was his grandfather on both sides, was perhaps hardly surprising.

Mathilde came over to them. 'It is high time you were going to bed, *mon petit*,' she said, reaching out to take her son from Laure; meekly, he allowed himself to be given up.

Charles got to his feet. 'Yes, we must be getting ready for dinner, or our guests will be here before we are. Let me take Joseph, *ma chérie*.'

Mathilde shook her head. 'No – I'll carry him upstairs.'

'But he is much too heavy!'

'I can manage. Ring for Nanon, and she will take Charlotte up.'

But Charles lifted Charlotte himself, and the two of them went upstairs, carrying the children. Laure, following them, saw how slowly Mathilde walked, burdened by the weight of the child; but she knew that her daughter would never admit to any difficulty.

Bedtime for the children was always a happy affair, especially when (as was usually the case) Charles was present. Mathilde would sing to them both, Charles would tell Joseph a story – some simple tale he had heard from his nurse long ago – and there would be a good deal of gentle laughter; then would come the nightly prayers, and each in turn would kiss the children, as would Laure, who generally had no other part in the bedtime rituals.

The three adults were dressed and ready in the *grand salon* in good time before the guests arrived for dinner; although Charles noticed an absence, as Laure (a little apprehensively) had known he would. 'Has Monsieur Séguier returned yet?' he asked quietly.

Laure, feeling uncomfortable, tried to look casual and unconcerned. 'I'm afraid he's unable to be here. He asked me to apologise to you.'

Henri had, in fact, done nothing of the sort, when he had told her at breakfast that he would not be in to dinner tonight. Faced with her protest – 'But it's Charles's birthday. There will be guests!' – he said, 'Exactly: the Chabrys and the Lacroixs and the *curé* and all the rest of Charles's pious and illiberal friends. No thank you. I prefer my own kind. A prior engagement, at the Masonic Lodge in Bergerac – you may tell your son-in-law.' He had spoken with a certain malicious pleasure, knowing Charles's horror of freemasonry. And then he had left for Trissac.

His early approval of Charles as Mathilde's husband had not survived three years of daily proximity. By now, when they met, he found it difficult to conceal his contempt for the young man; when they were apart, he did not even try. His attitude had one beneficial effect: it made Laure more tolerant than she might otherwise have been of Charles's more uncongenial opinions. Even when her son-in-law had tried (as he had the first summer after his marriage) to persuade her not to attend the July 14 celebrations in the village, she had refused him with patient good humour; and had forgiven him for having persuaded Mathilde to stay at home – but then for Mathilde the whole occasion must have all kinds of uneasy associations, which she would be glad to relinquish.

But tonight, Laure knew, her tolerance would be strained to the utmost. Although they were family connections, the Chabrys dined rarely at the château; only their womenfolk – Catherine, and her sister Émilie, married now herself – visited with any regularity, calling sometimes to see Mathilde. More often, Charles would be invited to their house, spending – Laure supposed – long hours in talk of a religious or political nature the very thought of which filled her with dismay. There would certainly be talk of that kind at dinner tonight, causing her to feel more excluded than ever. She had often thought that between them the Chabry brothers made the *curé* look positively left wing: their father, César Chabry, had been just as bad, but that bitter and cantankerous old man had died a year ago, and his sons now managed his property. It was not that Laure did not enjoy a political argument – on the contrary, such talk had been a part of her Paris girlhood, and even with Charles, sometimes, (so long as she kept her temper and chose her words with due care for his susceptibilities) she could argue quite pleasurably. But, unlike Charles, the Chabrys never listened to an opposing point of view, and regarded all who held one as utterly beyond redemption. There was no pleasure in discussion in such company.

They had been only a few minutes at table when Eugène Chabry said, 'I see the Dreyfus family won't let the matter alone – they continue to protest the man's innocence.' His tone suggested that such blind partisanship amounted to a crime.

'That seems natural enough to me,' said Laure. 'Whether he was guilty or nor, his trial was hardly a model of fairness and impartiality.'

Louis Chabry was clearly shocked. *Madame!* he exclaimed. 'He was lucky not to have been shot out of hand; a Jew, promoted to such a privileged position, trusted, and then to betray that trust!'

'What has his being a Jew to do with it?'

'Everything, naturally. Can you imagine a Frenchman behaving as he did?'

'May I remind you that Captain Dreyfus *is* a Frenchman,' said Laure quietly. 'As surely as you, or Charles, or – or indeed General de Miremont.' That was the name of Charles's cousin, who had stood as godfather to Joseph at the magnificent christening two and a half years ago. Her remark had not, she saw, disturbed Charles at all – he even nodded his agreement – but it deeply offended Louis Chabry.

'I am astonished to hear you speak of them in the same breath, *madame!*'

'Why? Do you think it impossible that there should be wicked or treasonable Frenchmen?'

'Alas, no – but in the army—'

'Which is the repository of perfection, I suppose?' said Laure with a sarcasm which was lost on her hearer.

'Of the patriotic virtues, certainly – or so it should be: one of the three pillars of France's greatness, would she but realise it – together with the Church and the King. Is that not so, Charles?'

Charles nodded gravely. 'So I most firmly believe. In all

three we see the principles of order and hierarchy that are so necessary to France's well-being. So necessary, may I say, to counter the dangerous and deluded doctrines of liberty, equality and fraternity, which have done so much to weaken France and to destroy her national character.'

'I am surprised you think liberty such a dangerous idea,' said Laure drily.

'When it degenerates to licence, certainly,' said Charles. 'But of course none of these ideas is intrinsically evil.'

'Even equality?'

'Are we not all equal in the sight of God?'

'All Catholics? Or everyone – including Jews?'

Out of the corner of her eye, Laure saw Eugène Chabry open his mouth to speak; but Charles replied more quickly than usual, 'Everyone, of course – was Our Lord himself not a Jew?'

Laure was quite sure that this time Charles had shocked his friends, though he appeared not to notice it; and (rather to Laure's surprise) they said nothing.

'It is when the notion of equality is distorted and made use of for worldly ends,' Charles went on, 'that the danger emerges. When it is claimed that every man is equally competent to vote, to govern, to defend his country, to manage industry – that all are endowed with the same gifts and powers of understanding – it is *then* that it becomes dangerous, for no one is willing to acknowledge the need for good leadership, for some individuals to hold a more humble position in society than others. It is a corrupting doctrine, eating away at the simplicity of country life, the security of the family, the respect accorded by the peasant and the worker to the landowner and the master, as well as the paternal affection which those in authority – from the monarch to the lowliest artisan – should feel for those under their command. It brings discontent and envy and atheism in its wake, and threatens the very foundations of society.'

'But who is going to decide who is fit to be the landowner and the master – still more the King – in your orderly society? Those who are the strongest, I suppose—'

'Not if society and government are firmly founded in religion – then it will be clear what kind of hierarchy God has ordained for man's happiness.' Beside him, the Abbé Lebrun was nodding, clearly happy to be in such congenial company.

'I am sorry, Charles,' said Laure briskly, 'but it seems to me you are talking complete nonsense. Human society just does not work like that.'

'Because the good and natural order has been all but destroyed by revolution and corrupting ideas: that is why.'

'And let me tell you,' intervened Louis Chabry, 'if the old order is not restored – and soon – then it will be the worse for France! Her punishment will be greater than anything she has suffered in more than a hundred years of bloodshed and unrest.'

For several minutes Louis Chabry's apocalyptic vision flickered luridly over the dinner table, and Laure fell silent, knowing from previous experience that she was powerless to counter it in any way. After a time, leaving the men to their gloomy prophecies, she turned to Catherine Chabry and asked after her children, though she knew what a flood of tedious personal anecdote that would bring. 'Louis-Albert is so clever, you know – a brilliant pupil, one might say. His examination results this year . . . Vincent is so popular at school, everyone likes him; why just yesterday . . . I must tell you what Marie-Jeanne said last week . . .'

Laure was sitting there, smiling, nodding, giving the occasional murmur; and hearing very little of what was being said to her, when Eugène Chabry's voice suddenly pierced her consciousness, '. . . we've pulled down the house at La Borie – it was long past being any use to anyone: we never could see why Papa left it there. The next thing is to clear the land around it – there must be a full hectare, but all such a tangle of undergrowth. It was an orchard once, but the cherry trees are too old to bear good fruit and the seedlings have been allowed to grow unchecked. It's a veritable jungle, I can tell you. The whole place is just an eyesore. It will improve the whole of that field to have the extra land under tobacco.'

Laure heard him and went on smiling fixedly at Catherine Chabry, and hoped that no trace of distress was visible in her expression or her manner. She had not been back to La Borie since she had last lain there in Jean-Claude's arms. But to think that now she never could, that soon every trace of it would have vanished – that was horribly painful, putting a seal somehow on her loneliness, as if to remind her that all her happiness had indeed gone for ever and could never come again, in any form.

Henri came home very late that night, so drunk that he fell into bed and went instantly to sleep. Laure lay for a long time listening to his snores, grateful for the unaccustomed respite that his state had given her, but with the burden of depression still heavy on her spirits. To have been reminded so forcibly of Jean-Claude tonight somehow only made it worse. In the past – before Henri had found out about their affair – she used sometimes to think of Jean-Claude as she lay in bed, remembering the joy they had shared; but in recent years she had found it difficult to disentangle the happy memories from the horrors she had endured so often since. Now, what she remembered was not so much the physical delight of their union, but the shared laughter, the companionship; and to think of that only reminded her more strongly than ever how rare such joys had been in her life. In the darkness of the night she felt a sense of loneliness more acute than anything she had ever known before. Old age was not so very far away now; and she could see no prospect that anything might improve. The best she could hope for was to outlive Henri, though at present that seemed an infinitely remote possibility. Sometime towards dawn she began to weep; and then she rebuked herself for her self-pity and briefly fell asleep.

Henri left for Trissac again, the moment breakfast was over. A little later, crossing the hall on her way to the vineyard, Laure heard the usual morning sounds from upstairs: Charlotte's gurgling, Joseph's incessant chatter, rising once to a high-pitched note of protest, to which Nanon's loving, scolding voice soon responded; and Mathilde's, as always low with tenderness. By the time Laure reached the door the adult soothing had clearly failed, for the full-bodied fury of one of Joseph's tantrums burst upon the house. It was natural enough behaviour for a two-year old; but Laure was of the opinion that Joseph needed a firmer hand than anyone seemed prepared to give him. Unfortunately, Mathilde would not hear of it and Charles – though he claimed to agree – seemed incapable of exerting quite the right degree of firmness. Laure closed the door on the noise and made her way over the courtyard – a grey morning, but hot, she noted: it might rain later – to where the women worked among the vines, removing the yellowing lower leaves to allow the maximum amount of sunlight to reach the fruit.

She had not quite reached them when Moïse came running down through the wood, his face rosy with an agitation she could not read.

'*Madame* – I am late – forgive me.' Then, unable to contain himself, he burst out, 'We have a son – a boy – at dawn today. Can you believe it? I think it must be a dream!' His voice was husky, his eyes full of tears. Moved, Laure clasped his hand.

'That is wonderful, Moïse. I am so truly happy for you. But why are you here? You must go home and stay with your wife.'

He stared at her. 'I thought—' Then he grinned suddenly, and opened his mouth; but was unable to continue.

'Go home, Moïse.' She gave him a gentle push; and then the next moment held him back. 'Your wife – is she well?'

He nodded, his eyes still bright with unshed tears. 'She is very well – they both are.'

'Then go home, until she is fit to be about again – really fit, that is. We can manage here. I'll come and see the baby tomorrow, if I may.'

He thanked her warmly and went back through the wood.

His happiness cheered her – such a little thing, the birth of a child; yet so momentous too. Though she herself had not known that joy, when her own daughter was born; and her strongest sensation at Joseph's birth had been one of relief – that he was unblemished, that he looked nothing like Frédéric, that apparently no one saw anything worthy of comment in the timing of his birth. Little Charlotte's coming had been, comparatively, a matter of unclouded happiness – though even that could not match Moïse's joy this morning. She was truly happy for him, not because she set any particular value on a baby boy, as opposed to a girl, but because Moïse had been a part of her life at Casseuil ever since she had come here, and he was by now a good and loyal friend, and she wanted him to be happy.

She made her way to the *chai*, to see what needed to be done there in Moïse's absence. If nothing else, there would be the barrels of maturing wine to be checked and the press to be cleaned and made ready for the *vendange*.

Nanon passed her in the courtyard, with Joseph's hand clasped tight in her own as he skipped and darted about, restless and full of mischief. He called to Laure and waved, and she waved back and stood watching as the two of them walked out into the vineyard. There Nanon paused to speak to Moïse's sister-in-law, working at the defoliation. Joseph, quiet now, stood watching the women at work – the quick neat fingers moving through the leaves – with a close attention that was evident even at this distance. Laure smiled to herself and went into the *chai*.

She had finished the checking and topping up of the barrels and had set to work on the *pressoir*, to clean it and thoroughly test the mechanism, when a sudden sound behind her made her turn sharply. There, full in the long dazzling rectangle of sunlight that fell through the open door across the steps and the hard earth floor of the *chai*, stood a tiny figure, his curls gleaming in the sun, his bright intent gaze on the great dark mass of wood and metal that formed the *pressoir*.

He smiled happily and trotted to her side. 'Doing, Grandmère?' he asked. For a moment, thinking of that flight of stone steps, and of her grandson descending them unseen and unaided on his unsteady infant legs, Laure caught her breath. She wanted to scold him, cry out, demand to know how he came here and where Nanon was; and then the eager curiosity of his expression drove out every other consideration, and she smiled down at him. 'I'm cleaning the pressoir, *mon chéri* – so that we can press the grapes here when the *vendange* comes. You see this great arm here—' She explained it all to him, simply, yet aware that it must all be way beyond the understanding of a two-and-a-half-year-old. But he listened with a concentration she had never seen in him before, as if he understood every word. Delighted by his interest, she took down implements from the shelves and showed them to him, lifted him up to look into the empty *cuves*, led him through each department of the *chai*, telling him about everything; and he went with her quietly and attentively, watching all she did with those bright intelligent eyes.

Laure did not know how long they spent together – an hour perhaps – for they were so happily absorbed in what they were doing that they did not notice the time pass. It was only when they came at last to the office, and she was holding the child up to look at the map of the vineyard and telling him the names of the grape varieties, that an entirely new realisation came to her with sudden force, like a revelation: 'Here, in my arms, today, is the future of Casseuil.'

A great joy surged through her; and in a kind of panic, she fought it. Don't be foolish – it's natural for a two-year-old to be inquisitive, about all kinds of things – he's little more than a baby. But some part of her, already convinced, would not accept the warning to be cautious, to protect herself against disappointment. Every trace of depression suddenly left her. I am not alone, she thought. I shall have my great wine, one day; and when I do, then this child – a man by then perhaps, but that will not matter – *he* will share the triumph with me. And when at last I die, he will be here still to carry on the work that has been my life. For this – for the years of his growing while he learned from her; for the years of his manhood, when he would be her companion and friend – for this, everything she had suffered and endured was worthwhile, and had a purpose after all.

Don't hope so much – you mustn't, the voice went on, warning her; but it could not suppress her joy.

'Joseph! Joseph!' *That* voice – Nanon's – was frantic with anxiety. Of course, she would never have allowed him to wander into the *chai* if she had seen him go; there were too many dangers. But two-year-old children had a phenomenal gift for vanishing, as Laure well knew. Feeling a little conscience stricken that she had not returned him long since, she carried him out to where Nanon – and by now Mathilde and Charles too – were searching and calling around the garden and the outbuildings.

Mathilde saw them and came running. She seized Joseph, clasping him to her and kissing him and exclaiming, while he wriggled and tried to escape.

'I'm sorry,' said Laure. 'I did not think that you might be looking for him.' But she was not really sorry. As Mathilde, defeated by his squirming, set him down again beside her, he turned and looked up at his grandmother and smiled, exactly as if he shared her happiness to the full.

CHAPTER
TWENTY FOUR

i

'Yes, I like the '93 – it's the first one so far that has brought to mind the old pre-phylloxera Casseuils. Very slight by comparison, but with such young vines that's only to be expected. I'll take some of this one – I could sell six crates, I imagine.'

He set the half-empty glass down beside the others ranged on the office table, amongst the bottles brought out for him to sample, only the two most recent of which bore the Château de Casseuil label. Laure, who had been watching tensely as he tasted, trying not to let him see how desperately she wanted him to approve, smiled and relaxed. Until today, young Monsieur Teyssier – whose firm had once been their largest buyer – had found nothing to tempt him about the new wines.

'What of the years after this one? I might consider taking a barrel or two and bottling it myself, if it was good enough.'

Laure shook her head. 'No, I'm sorry. I know my late husband used to come to that arrangement sometimes, but I prefer to keep full control of the bottling. That way I know exactly what is going out under our label. I intend no reflection on your integrity, you understand – but not everyone is as scrupulous as I know you to be. Of course, if you wish to taste what we have in barrel, you may be able to judge its potential, and I would be willing to consider an offer at this stage, for delivery later. When it's mature, should it prove to be better than we hope, you would find yourself very much at an advantage.'

'Perhaps. I will consider the matter.' He moved glasses and bottles to clear a space on the table, and leaned forward with his arms folded. 'Now, *madame* – what about the '69? I gather you still have just a little of that one, and I have a customer most anxious to lay his hands on some. He will pay a very good price – an excessive price even, I believe.'

Laure smiled. 'I rather think no price can be regarded as excessive for a '69 Château de Casseuil. Or at least not until we have a new wine to match it.'

'Do you think you ever will? What of the years since '93? Is there anything promising there – anything worth my while tasting?'

'In '94, as you know, we lost everything to the hailstorm in May. The '95 isn't bad, but will not, I think, improve very much more. '96 and '97 were frankly, disappointing, although we may find ourselves pleasantly surprised in due course. Last year's, the '98, was better again – that I do recommend you to taste.'

'And this year? What is '99 likely to bring? Will the century end with a vintage to remember?'

'If this fine weather continues, who knows? But it's only September and we need a good many more misty nights like last night if we're to have any hope of a really good wine. I'm not so rash as to make predictions as early as this. The red wines are going to be good, I gather.'

The broker nodded. 'Yes, I have great hopes. They're whispering that this will be the best year for Bordeaux since the crisis hit them. Some even predict a wine worthy of comparison with the pre-phylloxera ones. But that's taking it too far, when the *vendange* is only just under way. We shall see.' He rose to his feet. 'Well, what about the '69? I'm sure we can come to some mutually satisfactory arrangement.'

They did, and he left an hour later a happy man. Laure recognised that it was for the old wine that he had come, and not for the new. But he had bought some of the new, and that was another step on the road forward. So far the sales had been small and mostly very local, through acquaintances or to chance buyers, with most of the wine going for blending or distilling. Few of their old customers had been interested, until now.

'A most agreeable morning, *madame* – and how pleasant not to hear the word "Dreyfus" for once!' said Monsieur Teyssier, as they parted.

Laure laughed. 'How did we manage to talk so long without

mentioning him?' The affair of the unfortunate Captain had not after all ended with his condemnation and exile nearly five years ago. Recent disclosures – and a fierce press campaign – had cast grave doubts on the whole question of his guilt. For more than a year now the debate had raged, dividing a large part of the French population between those (mostly anti-clerical and left wing) who demanded a new, and fairer, trial and those (mostly Catholic and right wing) who believed that the army could do no wrong and insisted on the man's guilt.

'Perhaps now the trial's over it will all quieten down; but somehow I doubt it.'

Laure shook her head. 'It was all far too inconclusive for that, I think. It wasn't the fair and open trial everyone had hoped for.'

'Not quite everyone, *madame*. After all, some did not want the case re-opened in the first place.'

'As I know only too well,' admitted Laure ruefully.

'Another divided household? Ah, you are not alone in that, *madame*.'

'We shall just have to restrict our conversation to wine – an agreeably uncontroversial subject.'

'Don't you believe it, *madame*! I have known men come to blows over it, I can assure you!'

When he had gone Laure made her way down the steps to the *chai*, where Moïse was cleaning out the *cuves*; he paused and grinned at her, sharing her pleasure in a good morning's work. Then he said, 'I've been asking around, *madame*. I reckon I can get eleven more to come for the *vendange*, if you pay them what you said. With me and Lucien, and my wife and my two sisters-in-law and my niece that would make seventeen, eighteen if you gave a hand too – and there's Monsieur de Miremont, perhaps.' His face softened suddenly, in a way that had become only too familiar to Laure during the past four years; she knew what was coming before he spoke again. 'Pity my Jean-Marc's only four. He's good with his hands already – you'd be amazed to see him! So neat and careful. We'll have to bring him with us, of course.'

Laure suspected that the infant paragon might be rather more of a hindrance than a help; but Moïse so adored this longed-for son of his old age that she had to be very careful not to hurt his paternal pride. 'I expect we might even be able to find a little job for him to do,' she said kindly; and then could not resist bringing in the other child who was her own special delight. 'This year Joseph will be old enough to learn a good deal – he may even be a real help.' Then she thought, This family boasting is all very well, but it doesn't solve our problems. Aloud, she added, 'But we can't depend on children, can we? If we do have a good harvest, we'll need far more labourers than that. I've heard there are Spaniards in the area, looking for work. Didn't Aubin take some on at Le Petit Colin?'

'Yes, he did. But you might have a problem there, if you couldn't make them understand what they were to do. It's not like picking at Le Petit Colin, where you just gather the lot at once. Here, you've got to know what to take and what to leave. And you've got to take proper care of what you do pick – you can't risk losing the juice there is, through carelessness.'

'I know.' She smiled. 'Well, we'll see. We've a good few weeks to go yet. It's ridiculous, isn't it? When we had no harvest to gather there were men everywhere desperate for work. Now that we need good skilled labour again, there's none to be had.'

'That's the way it is, *madame*.'

Laure returned a little early to the house, about an hour before lunch-time. There was not a great deal to occupy her today, which was a pity, because she was impatient for the time to pass quickly until evening, when Mathilde and Charles would return with the children from St Antoine de Miremont, where they had spent the past five weeks. The heat had been so intense here, and Mathilde so thin and exhausted since the stillbirth last year, that Charles had thought a change would do her good. The forests round his home were dense and cool, temptingly so in this weather. Laure hoped very much that she would see an improvement in her daughter; but she knew only too well that Mathilde's nervous irritation had its roots much further back than last year's illness. She had been painfully thin long before that, and the look of strain was not new either, even though the anguish of bearing a dead child at the end of a long and difficult labour had made matters much worse.

461

Laure glanced into the *grand salon*, to check that Henri was not there, before entering herself; she did not think he had returned, but she wanted to be sure. The room was empty, quiet and cool. She went to look at the newspapers laid out on the table. They took a great many at the moment, both local and national; among them, '*L'Aurore*', and the local '*L'Indépendant*', for herself and (sometimes) for Henri; '*Le Gaulois*' and '*Le Journal de Bergerac*' for Charles. There was also '*La Croix*' – with an expression of distaste Laure put that particular paper aside, concealing it beneath the others. Its tone of hysterical anti-semitism nauseated her, the more so since it was produced by the Catholic Assumptionist order, who ought surely to know better. At least Charles did not take quite that tone himself, however certain he was of the guilt of Captain Alfred Dreyfus.

Laure wondered what her son-in-law would make of the latest developments; he had been away when the court had shown how suspect was the evidence for conviction. She would enjoy a lively argument with him when he came home.

There was not much that was new today. She turned pages idly, put down one paper and took up another. She did not know what it was that made her linger a moment over the columns of births, marriages and deaths in '*Le Figaro*'; as a rule they interested her not at all. But she knew why, the next instant, her attention was caught and held, numbed, scarcely taking in what her eyes read: it was the name, which might have been marked in fire so fiercely did it draw her eye. 'Jean-Claude ARNAUD'.

It was not the usual elaborate paragraph stating that Monsieur and Madame This, and Monsieur and Madame That had the happiness to announce the marriage of their children, so and so, at such a church, on such a date. No, this was simplicity itself, a brief notice that Geneviève Sorel and Jean-Claude Arnaud, painter, had celebrated their marriage on August 14, in Montmartre. That was all. Nothing to indicate who she was, this stranger he had married, or where she had come from, or whether she was young, or old . . . Old, like Laure, to whom he had said long ago, 'I shall always love you.'

She put down the paper at last and went, trembling, to stand by the window, looking out but seeing little. She had known she could hope for nothing from him, that they were unlikely ever to meet again, that the intoxicating passion they had shared was just a memory now, no more. Yet – something must have lingered, some faint shadow of a hope that one day she might be free, and that they might meet again, and that he might want her still, against all the odds. Now, in a shattering instant, that hope had died. She did not know what she felt, not exactly, though it was a bleak enough sensation; and by some curious association of ideas she thought suddenly of the damp long-dead ashes in the hearth of the cottage at La Borie on the day she had first waited there for Jean-Claude. That golden lovely day of spring sunshine when she had discovered a new world of bodily delight and happiness . . . She began, silently, to weep.

'*Madame*, Monsieur Meynel is here, asking for Monsieur Séguier.'

Laure brushed a hand rapidly across her eyes and then turned round. 'I thought Monsieur Séguier had gone to Trissac this morning.' Monsieur Meynel was the *régisseur* from Henri's estate, where, presumably, they ought to have met already today.

'I don't know, *madame*. Monsieur Meynel hasn't seen him, and he doesn't seem to be at home either.'

'Thank you, Marius. Show Monsieur Meynel into the study and I'll come.' That would, she thought, give her time to make sure all traces of tears had gone from her face.

Monsieur Meynel had a look of impatience. 'I thought I'd find Monsieur Séguier here – I supposed he must have been delayed. I've been expecting him since first thing this morning, and I can't get on with anything until I've seen him.'

'I'm sorry, *monsieur*. He did not tell me where he was going, but he went out some hours ago. I assumed he was going to Trissac. I can't help you, I'm afraid.'

When she had at last convinced him that Henri was not in the château, Monsieur Meynel moved to the door, clearly thoroughly irritated. 'I really can't be expected to go on like this! He insists that I consult him at every stage, but just lately he seems to have lost interest altogether—' He broke off, glancing at Laure, and seemed to realise that this complaint against his employer was perhaps a little indiscreet. Laure went with him to the front door, while he quickly found another target for his ill-humour. 'I think I should warn you, that son-in-law of yours is causing a good deal of ill feeling in some quarters.'

'Oh?' Laure was genuinely surprised. Since his marriage Charles had so disarmed all the initial suspicion towards him that he had last year been invited to stand with Louis Chabry's party for election to the municipal council, and to his astonished delight had – alone of that list – been duly elected. He had few enemies in the commune, even amongst his political opponents.

'Yes – our notary at Trissac is not at all happy. Monsieur de Miremont has been poaching on his territory, you know. It's all very well for a wealthy man like him to go giving free legal advice, but some people have to make a living that way. It's not right.'

'I hadn't heard that your friend at Trissac had any difficulty making a living,' said Laure drily. The notary combined his legal practice with money lending, and for a long time had lived comfortably on the interest from debts which many of the peasant families would never be able to pay off. He was, on the whole, very much hated. Laure knew there had been one or two occasions when a little timely advice from Charles had kept some hapless individual from his clutches. Charles's hard-won legal knowledge had proved useful after all, and it was regarded in the neighbourhood as a useful asset, to be drawn on in need. 'In any case,' Laure continued now, 'my son-in-law only gives his advice when asked, and then only in the most difficult and needy cases. He has no intention of setting up in opposition to any professional lawyer. It's just that some people simply cannot afford proper legal advice. And I'm afraid that sometimes in the past those are the very people who have been most imposed upon, in a deplorable manner.'

The *régisseur* went on his way with his temper at boiling point. The intensity of the midday sun would not help, Laure thought without sympathy, as she closed the door on its glare.

The visit had at least distracted her from the pain of that chance-met news item. She held it at bay still, thinking instead

464

of Henri, and of what Monsieur Meynel had said. One or two
things, apparently unconnected, began to fall into what might
be a kind of pattern, if only she could see it clearly. There was
that business two weeks ago, which had brought her such
immeasurable relief. Coming to her in bed as usual, Henri had
heaved his bulk onto her body, while she lay with closed eyes
waiting for it to be over; and then all at once she had realised
that the harsh quick breathing had quietened, and he had come
to a halt of some kind. Opening her eyes she had seen that his
face had a faintly puzzled expression, as if he did not quite
know what he was doing there. Then he had dragged himself
off her, rolled over and gone suddenly to sleep. Before that,
now and then, he had found himself impotent, but that had
only made him angry and more violent than ever with her, in
other ways. This, now, was something new. What was more,
he had shown no interest in her since, beyond a passing
absent-minded grope.

She still avoided him as much as she could, of course, not
trusting him at all. Even so, she could not help noticing that he
seemed increasingly inclined to be forgetful; he had even
asked her, two days ago, where 'that fool of a Charles' was.
However, one expected a little forgetfulness in old age; it
would doubtless be afflicting her too before long.

Henri came back at lunch-time, wandering into the dining-
room with a vague, almost blank expression, which was quite
unlike his usual look of firm decisiveness.

'Where have you been?' she asked.

He stood still beside his chair, frowning a little. Then he
said, 'Bergerac – I went to Bergerac.'

'But why? You were expected at Trissac.'

'Was I?' He sat down and began at once to eat.

'Why did you go to Bergerac?' Laure persisted, not because
she really wanted to know, but because she had an uneasy
feeling that it was important.

'Bergerac? Why did I go to Bergerac? Why should I want to
go to Bergerac?'

'I don't know. You tell me. And why you didn't go to
Trissac.'

He stared at her, shook his head, raised a spoonful of soup
to his mouth; and then for no apparent reason dropped the

spoon, splashing hot liquid over the table cloth. Frowning, he fumbled a little, retrieved the spoon and began again to eat. He never did answer Laure's question, although once lunch was over he rode to Trissac; or Laure supposed that was where he went.

ii

Joseph bounced up and down on the seat of the coach carrying the family south from Bergerac. He knew he was irritating his mother and his father and his sister Charlotte, and disturbing little Marie-Françoise, who was trying to sleep with her head on Nanon's lap; and Nanon had twice told him to sit still. But he was much too excited to obey her. Besides, no one was ever really angry with him, whatever he did. He knew he had only to smile at his mother or turn his eyes imploringly upon her, and she would kiss him and cuddle him and forget all about his misdeeds. His father was not quite so predictably indulgent, but he rarely scolded any of his children, and if he ever felt the need to do so would immediately follow the scolding with the warmest of hugs, as if it hurt him to be angry. Even Nanon only scolded very lovingly, in the tone of one who didn't quite mean what she said.

His grandmother now – she was another matter. She always made it quite clear that there were bounds beyond which he must not pass, not under any circumstances. What would happen if he were to do so he was not quite sure, because he had never dared to try. Yet he was not afraid of her. On the contrary, he had missed her terribly while they were at St Antoine de Miremont. His other grandparents, though they would occasionally talk to the children and smile at them and pat their heads and give them sweets, were rather remote beings, a little frightening and very grand. One had to be on one's best behaviour, always, at their house, and remember not to chatter and ask questions. He had no nice warm feelings when he was with them.

Grand-mère Laure made him feel warm all the time, as of course did his parents and Nanon; but with Grand-mère there was something more, something special, a unique feeling of being completely where he belonged, in the company of someone who knew what he was thinking and what he wanted

466

even better than he did himself. It was best of all when she took him into the *chai* or the vineyard and let him see what was going on, and told him all about it, not as if he was a little boy, but as if he were in fact quite grown up, as she was.

There, at last, were the Casseuil vines, marching up the hill away from the road in the shadows of late afternoon. He gave a final massive bounce and stood up and went to press his nose against the glass. 'Look! Look – we're home!'

His mother gave a cry of alarm, and his father's arms closed about him, pulling him away from the door. 'If you lean on the door, *chéri*, it may fall open, and then where would you be?'

'Outside,' he said cheerfully, at which Nanon tut-tutted and his mother gathered him onto her knee and rocked him.

'You'd be hurt, *mon petit* – badly hurt, perhaps even killed. You must never do that, never—'

Sometimes the urgency of her anxious love irritated him a little, as it did now. For just a moment or two he allowed her to kiss him and stroke his hair, and then he wriggled free and jumped about among the feet on the floor of the carriage. Charlotte kicked him; his father, suddenly stern, said, 'Joseph, sit down and be quiet – at once!' He did so, very meekly, though his dark eyes, peeping at them all beneath long lashes, were brimful of mischief. His father laid a hand caressingly on his curly hair. 'A little patience, *mon fils*. We're nearly home, and then you may run all you like.'

He did run, the moment the carriage door was opened, as fast as he could towards the little figure of Grand-mère Laure on the bridge before the château door, neat and trim with her grey-gold hair and the grey dress prettily embroidered in whorls of red. He wanted to reach her before anyone else did, and he was sure she wanted it too. She held out her arms, laughing a little; but he came to a halt just a short way off, suddenly remembering his manners.

'*Bonjour*, Grand-mère,' he said politely, and then stood on tiptoe to kiss her on both cheeks. She gathered him into her arms and he forgot about manners and clasped her about the neck and laughed. Then she set him down and looked at him.

'I do believe you've grown, *chéri*.'

After that, of course, she had to welcome the others. Joseph watched her and jumped from one foot to the other, full of impatience. Why did adults always talk so much, about so many silly things? It wasted so much precious time.

'Grand-mère, can we go the *chai, please*?'

The imploring gaze that would have melted his mother's heart had no visible effect upon his grandmother, although he was sure she would have liked to agree to his request. But she simply smiled and laid a hand on his head and said, 'Not just now, Joseph. It will be dinner-time soon. Tomorrow, I promise—'

With that he had to be content. At least he knew she always kept her promises.

Laure took his hand as they went into the house, conscious as she talked to the others of his slim, graceful, upright little figure at her side. She loved Joseph with a quite astonishing intensity: not, of course, like Mathilde, because he was Frédéric's son; nor yet, like Charles's parents, because he was a boy; nor even, simply, because he was her grandson, though she loved his sisters too. But for her Joseph was more than just her grandson, because she had been right, on that late August day four years ago, when she had suddenly seen in the inquisitive toddler a future for herself and for Casseuil. Day by day, year by year, she had seen his interest in the vineyard grow, rejoiced as he spent every free moment at her side, answered his eager questions with delight, felt her heart sing as he carried out some simple task, effortlessly and perfectly, after being shown once how to do it. She had not after all been foolish to hope for much. On the contrary, it had been better even than she had dreamed it might be. From that first day a special affinity had grown and developed between them, a closeness that was deeper now than that which linked her with any other human being. Sometimes she thought it even made up for all the miseries of her life with Henri.

She was almost able to forget Henri at dinner that night, though he fumbled with his cutlery, dropped bread on the floor and spilled food down his front. The family was complete again. Mathilde – still looking dreadfully tired, Laure thought, with a little tremor of anxiety – was at least calm and seemed glad to be home. But there was now a constant reminder of how she once had been: her daughter

Charlotte, at almost five as lively and happy and sweet-natured as her mother at the same age, and extraordinarily like her, with that heavy golden hair and creamy complexion, and only the blue eyes to distinguish her in any way from the carefree Mathilde of long ago. From the moment they sat down to dinner she chattered incessantly, full of all the things they had seen and done whilst they were away.

'You really must not talk quite so much, Charlotte,' said Mathilde at last. 'You must allow other people an opportunity to speak occasionally.'

Charlotte hunched her shoulders and hung her head; but at the same moment peeped mischievously under her lashes at her father and then at her grandmother, and they both smiled back, consoling her for the enforced silence. Then, as the conversation became more general, she whispered something to her little sister, who began to giggle, her small exquisite fair face suddenly all dimples: Marie-Françoise at three was a quiet and generally rather solemn child, with the cloudy dark hair and deep blue eyes of the de Miremonts. The giggles – quickly becoming uncontrollable – spread to Charlotte and before long threatened to overwhelm the adult conversation.

'They are tired,' Charles excused them, though without much conviction; but the giggling then infected Joseph too and – in spite of Mathilde's disapproval and her wholly unavailing attempts to control it – put an end to any hope of reasoned and civilised talk. Laure was amused, but quite glad all the same when dinner was over and the children came for their good-night kisses before going to bed. All three, Laure noticed, shrank a little when it came to Henri's turn, as they had not done in the past, as far as she could remember.

'I'll take them up,' Mathilde said to Charles. 'I think they'll settle more quietly if I see them to bed by myself.'

Charles and Laure and Henri went to the *grand salon*, where Charles seated himself peacefully beside the empty hearth, with the look of a man who is glad to be home again; while Henri wandered about the room picking up an ornament here, a book there, and then putting them down again. Occasionally, some object would fall to the floor.

'Have you lost something?' Laure asked, irritated by his restless movements. He looked at her and shook his head.

'No – no, I don't think so.' Then he added, 'I shall go to bed,' and slowly left the room.

Laure saw Charles watching her intently. 'Do you think he's behaving oddly, or is it just my imagination?'

'No, I'm afraid not; I saw it at once. He seems – distant, even confused. There has been a great change, I think. Perhaps you should consult Doctor Bonnet.'

'Perhaps I should.' Now Henri had gone she felt, as always, a great strain fall from her; his present strange behaviour made no difference to that. She drew a deep breath and prepared herself for a pleasant evening of friendly argument. 'Did you read of the verdict in the Dreyfus retrial?'

'Yes.' He sounded a little wary. 'I did not like it.'

'Nor did I – but for opposite reasons to yours, I suspect.'

'Perhaps not, *madame*. It was wrong of course to find him "guilty with extenuating circumstances" when it is clear that he is either guilty or not guilty. But it seems to me' – here he looked just a little shamefaced – 'that the evidence showed his innocence beyond any possible doubt. I regret that there has been what is clearly a widespread conspiracy on the part of many in high places within the army to falsify the evidence.'

Laure was astonished. Charles had many relations in the army, two generals among them (one of whom was Joseph's godfather), and his blind support for the military hierarchy was, she had thought, only to be expected. It seemed that it was not so blind after all.

'Does your father take that view?' That might explain it, for Charles had certainly inherited most of his political views from his father.

'No, as it happens he does not.' He smiled at her, acknowledging her pleased surprise; and then went on thoughtfully, 'It is a curious thing that when one returns to a place one knows well, after a long absence, one sees it – so to speak – with new eyes.' He spoke even more slowly than usual, as if struggling to put into words something that was of great importance to him. Laure forced herself to be silent and wait patiently for him to finish. 'I have thought before that there was a difference between the people at home and the people here. This time I think I saw what it was. At home the peasants are not welcoming, they do not talk to one readily, they are even hostile – apart, that is, from those who have served my family as servants for many years, and those who farm our lands. Yet even they are deferential, one might even say obsequious. Once, that seemed to me to be entirely normal. It was strange to come here and find that there was no respect, or none for rank and position, none that was automatic or could be taken for granted. It is as if the people here believe that respect must be earned. There is a freedom, an equality of bearing between people of all ranks, which in fact I have come to like very much. My father, I know, would not. Why do you think that there are these differences? They are real, I assure you.'

'I expect it has a good deal to do with history. They were nearly all Protestants here once, united by persecution. And Protestantism is in its way a very egalitarian creed, remember. There was none of the hatred of the nobility that you find elsewhere, because they were Protestants too. They all saved their hatred for the Catholic church, and probably for the King as well.'

'But my father has always been the most considerate and devoted of landowners. His relations with his dependants have always been excellent, fatherly one might say. My grandfather was the same, I believe. To them, servants and labourers were as children, to be loved and protected.'

'But if you treat people as children then you must expect deference, not equality; that goes without saying. Besides, perhaps your great-grandfather wasn't so scrupulous, or your great-great-grandfather. People have long memories, as you should know very well.'

After a moment he understood her, and answered her teasing smile with one of his own, a little rueful. He said, carefully, 'Perhaps there comes a time when one ought to try to forget – in part at least.'

She laughed and reached out to pat his hand. 'We'll make a Republican of you yet, *mon cher*.'

He pulled a face. 'There are limits, *madame*! No, I am convinced still that the only hope for stability in France lies in a return to monarchy and religion. But perhaps I am beginning to believe that there may after all be some value in a limited democracy, as once I did not.'

Mathilde came in then and Laure, struck by how thin she still was, and how tense, remembered too her own troubles, and the relaxed mood left her.

But Joseph is back, there is that at least to be thankful for, she thought as she went upstairs that night, clutching that consolation and holding it to her, as she lay beside Henri's snoring and twitching figure and realised in the loneliness of the night that she would never again lie with Jean-Claude's arms about her and a blissful peace in every limb.

Joseph had to wait until mid morning before Laure could fulfil her promise to him. Before that, she followed Charles's advice and went to see Doctor Bonnet, who agreed to come to dinner that evening, so as to observe Henri under the cover of a purely social visit. Laure had tried, first, to encourage Henri to see the doctor of his own free will; but he seemed not to understand in the least what she was trying to say. He was apparently quite unaware that there was anything wrong with him.

That duty done, the rest of the morning was pure pleasure for Laure and Joseph. 'You said I could see the old wine,' the child reminded her as they crossed the courtyard hand in hand.

'So I did,' Laure agreed. She reached into her pocket and pulled out a bunch of keys, linked by a chain to her belt. 'You see, I have come prepared.'

They descended the steps into the *chai*, passing the *pressoir* and the *cuves*, cleaned and ready for harvest, and the scrubbed shelves on which were ranged the implements used in the various stages of wine making – pipes and nozzles and tubes, for tasting and racking and bottling, apparatus for filtering and corking, all shining with polished brass and silver. 'No other metal must ever touch the wine,' Laure had told Joseph once. 'It would react with it and ruin it:' He loved to watch her at work with this jewel-bright equipment, but today he scarcely gave it a second glance, for Laure had lit a lamp and was leading him on into the furthest depths of the *chai*.

Beyond this room the next – cooler and dimmer – held the barrels in which the new wine lay ageing, the vintage marked in chalk on each one. They stretched away in ordered ranks into the darkness, smelling deliciously of mingled oak and wine, the most exciting smell in the world, Joseph thought, sniffing the chill air with delight. At the far end of the room, Laure unlocked a low door and led him through into the storerooms dug most deeply into the hillside.

Here, in the arched stone alcoves built by Joseph's great-grandfather lay row upon row of bottles, the newer wine in this room, the old wine – the great wine – in the deepest recesses of all. 'This wine is about as old as your father,' Laure told him, as they came to a halt before the alcove where lay what remained of the '69 Château de Casseuil. To untutored eyes it might look like nothing more than a stacked array of bottles, only the bases visible, with nothing but a tiny peeling notice to indicate what they were. But to Laure, and to Joseph standing awed at her side, it was as magical and wonderful as hidden treasure, gleaming richly gold in the lamplight, with a depth and quality of colour quite unlike that of the new liquid in the first bottles they had passed.

'And here – this is older still. This wine is older even than I am, just a tiny bit.'

Beside her, Joseph gave a little shiver; only from happiness and excitement, but Laure was immediately concerned. His hand in hers felt cold.

'One day you shall taste some of these wines,' she promised. 'But now let's go and warm ourselves outside. I want to see how the grapes are doing. We can't just live in the past, you see – we must make great wine for the future too, wine as great as this.'

Joseph did not always understand precisely what his grandmother was saying to him, but something inside him always seemed to know and to respond. He went obediently with her out into the fierce heat of the morning, across the courtyard, under the arch to the vineyard.

They walked along the rows between the vines, Joseph chanting over and over to himself the lilting names of the grapes, his skipping feet keeping time with their rhythm: 'Sémillon, Sauvignon Blanc and Muscadelle . . . Sémillon, Sauvignon Blanc and Muscadelle . . .' Sometimes he would break off and recite like a litany the things Grand-mère had taught him about them, which sounded as magical and mysterious as the names themselves, 'Sémillon for colour and body and unctuousness, *pourriture noble* and long, long life . . . Sauvignon Blanc for aroma and acidity . . . Muscadelle for the fragrance of musk . . .'

Now and then Grand-mère came to a halt and bent to examine one of the bunches of grapes, minutely, with great attention. After a time, Joseph stopped his chanting and asked, 'What are you looking at, Grand-mère?' She looked round at him, with eyes brighter even than usual.

'Here, *chéri* – look.' She crouched down and Joseph squatted beside her. 'These are Sémillon grapes – you can tell by the very thin skins – and they're bigger than the Sauvignon grapes over there. But look here – you see those little specks?' Joseph saw, and nodded. 'If we have lots more like that on the grapes, and then they all turn brown and wrinkled, *then* you will know we are going to have a good harvest. So we shall have to watch, shan't we?'

Joseph sensed her excitement. 'Can I help when the *vendange* comes, Grand-mère?'

'Ah now, there we shall have to see. But if you promise to be very careful and do just what you are told, then I might let you help.' He grinned up at her, and knew she would say yes.

Doctor Bonnet was very grave when he spoke to Laure in the hall before leaving the château that evening.

'I am afraid it doesn't look good, *ma chère madame*. I fear a progressive and degenerative illness, which will be very hard for you all. Mercifully, Monsieur Séguier himself seems quite unaware that there is anything wrong, for which I suppose we must be thankful. But I need to examine him fully, of course. I will come again tomorrow.'

By harvest time Henri was much worse, changing in those few weeks from a vigorous man in his prime to the oldest of old men. He took to getting out of bed in the middle of the night, dressing haphazardly in whatever was to hand, lighting candles or fires at great danger to himself and everyone else; and wandering about the countryside in an apparently aimless manner. Sometimes he would be found by a kindly neighbour and returned gently to the château. In the end Laure had to make sure that he was never left alone; when she could not be with him, then Michel his manservant had to be there. For the comfort of them all, he took his meals in his room (from which Laure had removed herself; for ever, she hoped) and was allowed outside only for a closely supervised hour or two of exercise each day.

iii

The harvest that October drove all thought of Henri and of the other heartaches of the year from Laure's consciousness. At last, at long last, the weather favoured them. Misty dawns, warm, moist, gave way to hot sunny afternoons, and day by day the grapes ripened, speckled, rotted, filling the air with their fragrance. Time and again the *vendangeurs* – just enough of them, after all – moved along the rows, carefully gathering the most rotted fruit. The spores rose like dust from the *comportes* as the baskets were emptied into them, and again in the *chai* as the men poured the grapes into the *pressoir*. That peculiar, distinctive, heady aroma, which Laure had forgotten until now, tingled in her nostrils, sweeping her back to the long ago autumn of 1869, so full of mingled joy and pain; for when, after all, was life not like that? She had learned long since that joy never came without alloy.

But it was almost untarnished this year, as she worked in the vineyard in the constant company of Joseph, who asked eager questions – but never unnecessarily or at the wrong moment – and took in everything she said to him, learning quickly which fruit to pick and which to leave for another day, proud of the grapes rapidly filling his own small basket. His piping treble joined in the singing, humming the words when even his quick intelligence could not follow them: these days, when all the children learned French at school, the patois was no longer the first language of any but the oldest of the country people, but they still sang the old songs in the vineyard. He even proved useful in controlling the erratic wanderings of Jean-Marc Delmas, who after the first day attached himself to the older boy and followed him wherever he went, fortunately without getting too much in Joseph's way; Laure saw how patient her grandson was with the persistent and devoted toddler. It was Joseph who found Jean-Marc a job at last, carrying small buckets of pressed

475

grape skins out from the *pressoir* to the cart in the courtyard, in which, once the *vendange* was over, they would be carried to the vineyard to be spread as fertiliser beneath the vines.

'Well, *mon petit*,' Charles said proudly to Joseph at the end of the first day, 'you have the makings of a fine *vigneron* – is that not right, Grand-mère?'

Laure smiled at the child. 'Absolutely right,' she agreed, with pride and happiness swelling together inside her and her eyes on the rosy shining face of her grandson: Casseuil's future, assured for them all when she should be long dead. For fathering Joseph, she could forgive Frédéric all the pain he had caused them.

The weather held, the grapes continued to rot and were gathered and pressed; and the wild fermentation began as the coach house echoed to the singing and dancing of the harvest feast. It was like the old days at last, château and vineyard alive again after the years of struggle, in a perfect climax to the long and troubled century that was drawing to its close. It was as if a new age had dawned.

CHAPTER
TWENTY FIVE

There was a fresh wind blowing as Laure rode to Trissac, but it was a bright clear day and she enjoyed the feel of the wind in her face and the brisk trot along the drive and up into the village. For a little while she could forget the inevitable forthcoming difficulties with Monsieur Meynel – their problem was not any great difference about the running of Henri's estate, for which she was responsible since he became ill, but rather an intense and irrational mutual dislike. Laure did her best to put personal feelings aside, but the *régisseur* had no such scruples and Laure would leave every meeting with him feeling exhausted and irritated. It did not help that she could summon up no enthusiasm at all for the growing of tobacco. But there was no putting it off any longer, for in March the final preparations had to be made, if sowing was to begin in April. She must check that the ploughing had begun (she could be reasonably sure of that, for the *régisseur* was competent enough) and see that the materials needed for this year's crop were ordered and the money made available to pay for them.

As she passed Le Petit Colin Aubin called to her from the vineyard where he was working, and she drew rein to speak to him.

'A good year, last year,' he said with satisfaction. 'The red is my best yet; but the Casseuil now – that's really something. We'll have to compare them when they're ready, you and I.'

'I shan't be bottling until around 1904,' she replied. 'I want to give this one a good long time in the oak. Nearer the time we'll fix a date for a tasting.'

'A pity it won't be ready for the Paris Exhibition this summer – a medal now, that would be something.'

Laure laughed. 'Ah, but which of us would win it? My vines have maturity on their side.'

'We shall see – we shall see! I'm hoping for something in the departmental competition next year as it is.'

It was all very friendly, a neighbourly rivalry which they both enjoyed. Laure asked after his sons, who were of course at school today, and answered his equally polite enquiries; and then continued on her way.

There was no one else about this afternoon, except a derelict old woman whom she passed near the windmill, trudging up the hill with her head bent and a bundle on her back.

Poor old soul, Laure thought compassionately; although the stench that rose from her almost overthrew her pity.

The Abbé Lebrun's arthritis was bad today and he had a miserable cold. At the end of the quiet weekday mass, at which he had as usual been the only worshipper, Monsieur de Miremont had asked sympathetically after the *curé* and walked back across the market place with him to the door of the presbytery. 'I should take yourself to bed if I were you, *mon père*,' the young man advised. 'Joseph can have a holiday today.'

Lying in bed, fortified by a large brandy and gazing contentedly up at the solid newness of his bedroom ceiling, the *abbé* regretted only the cancelled lessons. When first he had been invited to teach the six-year-old boy he had accepted with reluctance, and then only because he was grateful for all the changes for the better that Joseph's father had brought into his life. He had remembered his only other experience of teaching and thought that at nearly seventy he was much too old to be faced with so heavy a task. But he found to his surprise that teaching Joseph was pure pleasure. True, the boy was lively and full of mischief, undoubtedly a little spoiled, but he was warm, generous and good-hearted. The only likeness between him and that reserved and uncongenial pupil of many years ago lay in the keen intelligence they shared. 'He doesn't get his brains from me, that's for sure,' Monsieur de Miremont had said with a wry smile, when the *abbé* praised Joseph's work.

But there would be no lessons today and the *curé* lay in bed and reflected that after all his years of struggle a small measure of success had come to him at last – though not, he had to admit with some faint chagrin, through his own efforts at all. If his congregation had increased a little, and church and presbytery were in good repair, and few people now shouted abuse at him in the street, it was Charles de Miremont he had to thank for that. Still, since it had the desired effect, he accepted it all gratefully and as humbly as he was able.

Warmed by the brandy and the fire that his new house-keeper had lit in his room, he drifted contentedly through the day.

Mathilde was not contented at all. Much as she loved Joseph, the wild high spirits which the combination of windy weather and an unexpected holiday had stirred up in him tried her patience sorely. The peace of her morning lessons with the little girls was constantly interrupted; her son would not read or draw or do anything at all quiet or orderly. In the end Laure took him with her to the *chai*, where he was very quiet and very still for more than an hour while she and Moïse racked last year's wine, a process that he watched with fascinated absorption and the occasional apt question. Unfortunately he came in to lunch with no visible sign that he had used up any of that excessive energy; and in the afternoon Laure was going to Trissac and could not take him with her.

'Perhaps you would like to ride with him,' Mathilde suggested to Charles, when they had finally banished Joseph from the lunch table, as the only means of ensuring five minutes' peace.

'I should, very much, but I am afraid I have promised to call on Louis Chabry this afternoon.' He looked genuinely regretful.

'More plotting I suppose,' said Laure provocatively.

Charles would not allow himself to be ruffled. 'To discuss peaceful ways of combating the government's policies to-wards the Church is hardly plotting,' he returned with dignity. 'The threat to the religious orders is very real.'

'Considering the way the Assumptionists behaved over the Dreyfus affair you can hardly blame them.'

'That was one case only. Our fear is that the government

threatens the whole existence of the Church. It will be the Church schools next, so Chabry believes – and then where will we sent Joseph for his education?'

Laure resisted the temptation to suggest an alternative and deftly changed the subject. She wished that Charles's apparent inability to see the imperfections of others did not extend to Louis Chabry, whom she disliked and mistrusted.

After lunch it was usual for the little girls to lie down and rest for an hour or two; but with Joseph wide awake and unoccupied they soon became as over-excited as he was. In the end, exasperated, Mathilde bundled all three children into their warmest clothes and took them down to the garden to run off that superabundant energy.

An hour of this, and she was thoroughly cold. She called the children and ushered them into the house, asking Françoise to bring a *goûter* of bread and chocolate to the *petit salon* for them all. Meanwhile, they went upstairs to change, Charlotte and Marie-Françoise holding her hands (they were warm anyway), Joseph striding ahead two steps at a time, something he did with difficulty but with determination. Mathilde supposed he thought it was manly, and he wanted very much to be a man, like Papa. Not that Charles ever did anything so wild and uncalculated as to run upstairs two steps at a time, she reflected with amusement.

They had reached the half-landing when the bell clanged. Mathilde heard Marius hurrying to answer it; and a woman's voice, rather harsh and punctuated with coughing, saying something she could not hear. Then some kind of argument seemed to have broken out, for Marius was protesting angrily.

Mathilde took two steps back down the stairs so she could see better.

The woman who had come in was not a prepossessing sight. She was fat, dressed in clothes that once had been vulgarly flamboyant, but now were torn and dirty, almost in rags. Her grey hair still bore the traces of a blonde dye and framed a puffy, pasty, lined face over-coloured with rouge. Her manner veered between uncertainty and brashness.

Mathilde sent Joseph and the girls on their way without her and descended to the hall. 'What is it, Marius? Can I help?'

Close to, the woman smelt unappealingly of dirt and stale

urine, inadequately masked by an over-use of perfume. 'I want to see Madame Naillac,' she said, evidently seeing more hope in Mathilde than in Marius.

'I told her there's only Madame de Miremont or Madame Séguier, and she says that's not who she meant.'

'Madame *Laure* Naillac,' the woman intervened.

Mathilde smiled, more politely than she felt. After all, the woman was old and none too well, if the frequent cough was any indication. If nothing else, Charles was always very firm about caring for the unfortunate, even the most unpromising vagrant. 'You must mean my mother, Madame Séguier. She is not at home at the moment. Perhaps I can help.' A small hand slid into her own and she glanced round; Joseph, overcome by curiosity, had crept down to the hall behind her, but was now clinging to her hand as if he rather regretted his disobedience. She was about to scold him when the woman's voice broke in.

'You must be Mathilde!' In the unhealthy face the brown eyes were still bright and alert, full of enquiry. She smiled too, as if suddenly sure of her welcome. 'You were just a little thing when I saw you last – but pretty even then. Who would have thought—!' Her gaze moved to Joseph and he shrank back a little; but not quite enough to avoid the none too clean hand that patted him on the head. 'Is this your little boy? But it must be – he's Philippe all over again, to the life. Fancy that, Laure a grandmother! I wonder—'

'I'm sorry, I don't have the—'

'Of course, I don't doubt I've changed a bit.' She patted her hair with a gesture that might once have been appealing, but was now merely pathetic. 'Madame Brousse – Madame Rosaline Brousse.'

Mathilde stood very still. She had only the dimmest recollection, not enough even to bring a picture to mind; but if she could have done so it would have borne little relation to this near derelict old woman, of that she was certain. How could this blowsy pathetic over-painted creature ever have given birth to the slender elegant young man she still thought of almost every day, who even in his moments of deepest despair had never lost his look of self-contained neatness?

Frédéric's mother, here at Casseuil – but why; why after all these years?

She had the answer almost at once. 'I had no reply to my letter, so I decided I'd have to come and see for myself,' said Rosaline.

'What letter? There's been no letter as far as I know.' Could her mother have heard from Rosaline and said nothing?

'Just last year I wrote.' There were, Mathilde saw, tears springing to her eyes. 'It's natural enough at my time of life to want your nearest and dearest about you. I asked after Frédéric – I hoped he'd write, but I heard nothing. Maybe he's grown too proud for that now, ashamed of his old mother.'

The note of self-pity was worse than her previously ingratiating tone. Mathilde broke in quickly. 'There was no letter, to my knowledge. It must have gone astray. As for—' She paused, for she had not spoken his name once since he left and to do so now set her heart twisting painfully, as if she were deliberately opening an old wound. *Une plaie ouverte* . . . No, not that, not that – 'As for Frédéric, he's gone away, we don't know where. We've heard nothing of him for eight years now.' Was that all it was? It seemed a lifetime, looking back. She felt suddenly very tired. 'You'd better come in,' she said; and turned to Marius. 'Show Madame Brousse into the *grand salon*. You would like some refreshment perhaps – a little tea?'

'A nip of something stronger wouldn't come amiss,' Rosaline returned.

'Marius will attend to you,' was all Mathilde would say, a little coldly. 'My mother will be home soon.'

She was trembling as she mounted the stairs. Yes, the wound was open again, raw and quivering within her. Or had it never really been closed, in spite of the passing of time and Charles's tenderness and the births of three loved children? She had so much; she knew she ought to be happy, or at the very least content. It was an ingratitude beyond words to have, always, this sense of emptiness, just because one person had gone from her life.

'Maman, was that Uncle Frédéric she was talking about?'

She looked down at her son, wondering if the painful rapid beating of her heart showed in her face. 'What do you know about Uncle Frédéric?' She did not even know he had heard of him.

'He's in the wedding picture – he looks cross. I don't think he liked having his photo taken. Grand-mère told me it was him.'

'Did she say anything else?'

'No. Papa says he went away, a long long way away.' The words had, to Mathilde, a weary terrible sound.

She decided that the children should have their *goûter* upstairs, under Nanon's supervision; and returned alone, full of an apprehension tinged with curiosity, to see what Rosaline was doing.

Slumped in the most comfortable chair at the fireside, a glass in her hand and a rapidly emptying brandy bottle at her elbow, Rosaline was examining the family photographs – or rather, one of them, a wedding group elaborately posed. 'I heard your boy say Frédéric was in the wedding photo. Is this him?'

Mathilde came to look, bending over – at as great a distance as possible – to see that Rosaline was pointing to a short plump fair man in middle age who bore no resemblance at all to Frédéric. She is his mother, she thought, and she does not even know what he looked like!

'No, that's my Uncle Marcel. That's his son's wedding.' Three years ago the young man's sudden meeting with the very beautiful daughter of a millionaire railroad magnate had ended his father's long-cherished plan for a visit to Europe. Michael Frémont had insisted on being married instead, and this photograph was the only compensation Laure had received for the cancelled reunion with her family. Mathilde had been surprised that she did not seem to mind very much.

Mathilde reached over to the back of the ranged photographs. 'Here he is.' He looked, not cross, she thought, but blank, his face a pale mask amongst all those strenuously smiling countenances. She hated the photo, *hated* it!

Rosaline laid the photograph on her lap and studied it intently, fortifying herself with a further glass of brandy. 'My little boy!' she murmured with a regret that sounded real enough. The brandy did not seem to have affected her speech and manner at all, which indicated to Mathilde how habitual such heavy drinking must be. She wondered fleetingly what Rosaline's life had been like since she left Casseuil, to what depths of degradation she had sunk; but she did not really want to know.

Rosaline told her all the same, breaking at once into a long, rambling account of how she and Achille had set up house together, but how very soon Achille had tired of her and gone away; and how she then found someone else, 'A real gentleman he was, and didn't he make a fuss of me!' – but he too had tired of her. She recounted them all, the succession of affairs that grew ever briefer and more sordid as she aged, until she no longer had anything to attract any but the most desperate. When no one would keep her, or even pay for an hour of her still skilful lovemaking, she was reduced to finding any work she could to keep herself alive, scrubbing floors, taking in washing, anything. For a long time a lingering remnant of her old buoyant optimism had kept her believing that one day all would change, that she would meet the generous, rich and kindly man who would assure her comfort until the day she died. And then her health began to break and hope faded and she grew frightened, suddenly seeing the stark reality of her own death waiting just a short step away, a solitary, squalid death without any last trace of dignity left to her. So she had thought of the son she had so readily abandoned, and written to ask for news; and when none came set out on foot for Casseuil.

It was a sad, sordid story, and Mathilde could not help but pity her, though she could feel no liking for this poor derelict drunken woman. She knew what kind of mother Rosaline had been, how what she was had somehow damaged Frédéric beyond repair; yet when all was said and done she had given him life, and for that alone Mathilde could not quite hate her.

She was relieved when Laure came home and took control. She saw her mother's astonishment and dismay, but saw too how quickly she concealed it and turned to the practical aspects of the situation. No, there had been no letter, she assured Rosaline; and they had no idea where Frédéric had gone. 'I suppose you turned him away too, just as you did me,' Rosaline accused her with bitterness. 'You always hated us for coming here. If it hadn't been for the old woman you'd have sent him packing long ago, wouldn't you?'

To Mathilde's surprise, Charles – who had come in soon

after her mother – intervened gently, 'Your son left of his own free will, *madame*. I think he felt that once I was master here then it would be easier for us all if he were no longer to live under the same roof. He valued his independence, and we had little in common, I believe. Furthermore, he told me before he left that he had a great desire to see something of the world. He had adequate means; I imagine he is indulging that desire to the full. You need have no anxiety on his behalf.'

So that was what Frédéric had told Charles! Mathilde had often wondered what explanation he had given for his sudden departure, since Charles had accepted it without curiosity.

Not needing to consult one another on the matter, the three of them knew that there was no question of sending Rosaline packing, now that she was here. She had no money, and nowhere to go. At the very least – so Laure assured her – she must remain at Casseuil until she had decided what to do next. Rosaline heard her with a pathetic look of relief which she tried hard to conceal.

Quickly, Laure gave orders for a room to be made ready, the bed prepared and warmed, arrangements to be made for dinner to be taken up to Rosaline once she was installed there by the freshly lit fire.

At dinner, when the children had left the table and the three adults were alone again, lingering over the last remnants of a good pre-phylloxera Bordeaux, Laure said reflectively, 'I wonder now – if I had not sent Rosaline away – no, because I had to, as things were . . . But if I had not gone away myself, so she had no opportunity to do what she did – things would have been very different. Perhaps she would not then be in the state she is in today.'

'You could not be expected to foresee everything,' said Charles. 'When you sent her away you saw that she was amply provided for. I think that you have nothing with which to reproach yourself.'

It was not self-reproach that was in Laure's thoughts, but rather an awesome sense of responsibility. There were so many interweaving threads going far back into the darkness of the past, and on into the future, their twists and turns unseen and unforeseen, their ends unknown. Each day was in some respects a step into the dark. 'Such little things can have such profound effects on our lives and on those around us – even the tiny things we forget to do or say. We suddenly find they were not little at all, or unimportant; but by then it is too late.'

'That is why our lightest word or action must be considered and weighed before we speak or act,' Charles put in, understanding – as Mathilde could not – that she was thinking now of Victor and the worn girth. 'But even taking everything into account, we cannot expect to see every consequence. After all, we are none of us alone when we make a choice; the choices of those around us have a part to play as well, and the consequences they will have must be unknown to us.'

'I find that a frightening thought.'

'It is only so if you are not able to understand that there is a power from whom nothing is hidden, who holds every one of the tangled threads of our lives in his hand. He knows of us what we do not know ourselves, sees our every motive, reads our hearts, and foresees the end of our every smallest word and deed. We are never entirely alone.'

Laure looked away from his earnest blue eyes, and shivered. 'I do not find that reassuring at all,' she said, aware that she risked shocking him by the remark.

'I am sorry if that is so,' was all he said, very gravely; and Laure felt more uncomfortable than ever. She caught a fleeting glimpse of Mathilde's face and saw how very still and pale it was. This sort of talk could hardly help to calm the feelings stirred to life today.

With studied cheerfulness, Laure changed the subject. 'You were right, Charles. Monsieur Meynel doesn't think it a good idea to replant with vines at Trissac, while ordinary wine prices are so low.'

On her way downstairs next morning, Laure tapped gently on the door of Rosaline's room and, receiving some kind of grunted reply, pushed it open. She thought at first that their unbidden guest was suffering from the inevitable effects of last night's brandy, for she groaned as the light from the door reached her eyes, and turned her head away. But as Laure stepped nearer she saw the unnatural brightness of the eyes and the hectic colour on the muddy pallor of the face, and heard the harsh painful breathing. She put out a hand and was alarmed by the burning heat of Rosaline's forehead.

She brought her water to drink, smoothed the bedclothes, propped her up until she indicated that she was more comfortable; and then she hurried downstairs and sent at once for Doctor Bonnet.

When he came, they understood that she must already have been ill when she reached Casseuil, and for some days beforehand. Lack of food, too much drink and the bitter weather had made sure that she was in no state to resist the onset of the illness.

'Her lungs are inflamed,' the doctor told them. 'I don't hold out much hope for her, not in her present condition. But perhaps with careful nursing—'

She had all the care they could give her. Mathilde in particular, remembering always that to her Frédéric owed his very existence, took most of the nursing upon herself, brushing aside Charles's anxious concern – which was the easier to do because of all of them he was the most insistent that Rosaline should have the most devoted attention. 'The poorest and most unfortunate must demand the greatest love from each of us,' was one of his frequent dictums. It would have sounded self-righteous and priggish, had he not always been the first to put it into effect.

Despite all they could do, it became very clear after a few days that Rosaline was not going to recover. 'Her heart's not strong enough,' the doctor told them gloomily. He hated losing his patients, which meant that since few people sent for him until all other remedies had failed, he had ample cause of unhappiness.

They sent for the *curé*, who rose from his own sickbed to administer the last rites; and waited for the inevitable end. Rosaline seemed to have given up, accepting her fate quietly, with resignation. Perhaps, feeling so ill, her only other sensation was relief at being so tenderly cared for, her every pain eased as far as was humanly possible, her every need met as if she were not an intruder with no possible claim on their kindness, but a beloved and welcome member of the family. Perhaps that unaccustomed sense of having all the burdens taken from her stirred to life some lingering remnant of a conscience that had never been more than a blighted shoot; certainly she seemed calmed and consoled by the *curé's* ministrations.

After he had gone and Rosaline had been made reasonably comfortable, Mathilde sat as usual at the bedside sewing quietly, with the spring sun flooding through the window onto her back and the little fire crackling to itself in the grate. Rosaline seemed to be asleep, the only sign of life that difficult breathing and the occasional twitch of her pale, puffy fingers on the silk counterpane. Mathilde herself had almost been lulled to sleep by the quiet and the warmth, when she was startled into full wakefulness by a sound from the bed.

Rosaline's brown eyes were wide open and fixed on Mathilde, perfectly clear and intelligent. 'I want to see Laure—' the old woman croaked. 'Ask her to come.'

Mathilde rang and sent Françoise in search of Laure; and when she came moved to sit on the window seat leaving her mother to occupy the bedside chair. Rosaline was still fully awake and alert, and seemed to need to talk, though she found it hard to do so.

'There's something I must tell you, before—' she began. 'I did wrong – not much, but it was wrong for all that – you were most hurt by it, so you should know.'

Laure leaned over and took her hand, holding it gently. 'If it's to do with that time when I was away and Achille came here, then don't think of it.' Very likely Rosaline was remembering some petty theft, some deceit. Laure knew there had probably been many such incidents she would never know about. 'That was all so long ago, and in the end it made no difference.'

'No . . . no, it's not that . . . Philippe . . .' She was already tiring. The words struggled out in a whisper and then faded into silence.

'Don't trouble about that either. I understood long ago that I was partly to blame, or he would not have needed you – and it wasn't your fault that he loved you. He knew you before ever we met, and you gave him a son.'

'That's just it . . . Frédéric . . . He wasn't . . .'

Laure heard Mathilde stir suddenly behind her; for herself,

she felt frozen, braced for something already guessed at, and dreaded.

Several seconds passed before Rosaline was able to speak again, but when she did so the whole room seemed to be holding its breath in readiness.

'There was someone else, another man . . . Philippe hadn't been for a week or two, I went out . . . He was in a bar, a sailor maybe, I don't know . . . A foreigner though, English, perhaps Dutch – he didn't speak any French . . . He had nice ways, and I liked him . . . It was just the one night; I never saw him again after that. I told myself – it might have been Philippe, I didn't know . . . But Frédéric was like him, very like, so I knew he wasn't Philippe's . . .' She sighed, as if glad to have the truth told; and then added into the continuing silence, 'I suppose it doesn't matter much now . . . Philippe loved him, and it made the old woman happy . . . But I'm sorry now it hurt you . . .'

Laure heard Mathilde give a tiny stifled cry and, a moment later, run softly from the room. She wanted desperately to go after her, but she could not leave Rosaline alone. The woman was still watching her, waiting for forgiveness and reassurance. It must have seemed so easy to her.

In the end, Laure did it; spoke the comforting lying words that would smooth the last unease from Rosaline's conscience, and that were so very hard for her to say.

'It was all over long ago, Rosaline. As you say, it doesn't matter now. You were a mother, you had to protect your son; I can understand that so well. How could I, a mother too, hold that against you?'

But it was just because of that motherhood that she could not forgive, because of the bitterness and pain that Rosaline's little lie had brought into Mathilde's life. The choices we make, the tangled threads—

Then she thought perhaps she had forgiven, unknowingly. What had Rosaline done, but protect herself and her child as best she knew how – just as Mathilde had done too, with Laure's help? Yet if Rosaline had told the truth there would have been no need for Mathilde's lie, no need for any of it – everything, right from the start, would have been utterly and completely different. Her chief feeling as Rosaline drifted into sleep was not of bitterness or anger, but of a terrible sadness at the haphazard messiness of life.

Rosaline died that night, slipping deeper into an unconsciousness from which she never woke again. She was buried in the cemetery at Casseuil, not far from the ornate tomb where Philippe and his mother had been interred. Laure told Charles quietly of Rosaline's confession, suggesting that Mathilde might be a little sad to know that the brother she had loved was in fact no blood relation at all. Charles nodded gravely and said, 'Yes, that would be understandable.' Then: 'Poor woman, carrying that burden of guilt all these years. In the end it solves nothing, to enter into deceit.'

Laure doubted that Rosaline had been greatly burdened even at the last; it was Mathilde's burden that grieved her, made worse by her daughter's complete refusal to talk about it.

For Mathilde it was as if a storm had broken over her, washing away all the landmarks, leaving no trace of the familiar to help or guide her. For several days she was torn all ways, veering wildly between the guilt that had been swept away and one that had grown and intensified beyond words; and a horrible anguished realisation of what might have been, if only she had known.

Joseph, her child and Frédéric's, was not a child of incest, conceived through a sin so appalling that its name could hardly be spoken aloud. That one simple realisation brought her the first rapturous sense of relief, of a shadow gone for ever. There had been a sin, of course; but only a little, ordinary, everyday one. She could think of the night of Joseph's conception, remember the fleeting joy of it, without a shrinking sense of horror, even with sweet regret.

Only then she saw the other side of it, the inevitable corollary. If that guilt was the less, then the other, the one she still lived through every day, was the greater. What was there in that simple act of passion, even in its consequences, to justify the lie of her marriage to Charles, the terrible deceit she had practised on him? That she had been entirely successful in her deceit somehow only made it worse.

First and last and always, she came back to the realisation

that everything – the shame, the lie, her marriage to Charles – all had been unnecessary; for there had been no real barrier to her love for Frédéric. If his mother had only told the truth, they could have loved and married as freely and happily as any other young couple.

Only then of course they might never have met at all, for everything would have been different right from the start.

It was all such a tangle, of guilt and relief and regret and bitterness, and through it all the hopeless longing, somehow, to let Frédéric know the truth, wherever he was. Except that of course the truth was no help to them now, in any way.

Round and round in circles went her thoughts and her emotions, reaching no resting place, tearing her apart. She could talk about it to no one, not even to Laure, for she could not find the right words to express it all without ambiguity. After all, how can you tell what you feel when you do not know yourself what that is?

She had to keep herself under some kind of control, of course, or she would betray herself to Charles. She doubted if he would ever be able to understand or to accept the enormity of the truth even if he was one day to be confronted with it in all its starkness; but she did not even want him to guess that Rosaline's confession had any deeper effect than to make her a little sad. It was not easy, but she had learned very well during the past years to keep her feelings firmly shut away.

Only now they were in such a ferment within her that she could not suppress them without real danger to her health and sanity. Laure watched in anguish and saw the signs: an almost total loss of appetite; an inability to sleep; a frequent uncontrollable trembling; the inconsequential, trivial, too bright remarks, begun and then broken off with a nervous little laugh; the constant restlessness; the sudden tears, explained to no one as she fled to the sanctuary of her room.

'Sometimes it seems that since our marriage she has never known any happiness,' Charles said one day to Laure, in evident distress. 'Before, sometimes, she used to be happy. But I have failed her, I can see that now. I love her so much, more than I ought, I think. I want to help her – but she seems so far from me. I realise now that it has always been so—' he broke off, not trusting himself to go on.

Laure wondered helplessly what she could say to comfort him, when she guessed that his very tenderness towards Mathilde only made his wife's anguish the more intense. When she was silent, searching for something helpful to say, he went on, 'What do you think – shall I take her away for a holiday? Arcachon is quiet at this time of year and she has never been there. I know of a comfortable hotel with an excellent restaurant, not far from the sea. They say sea air has a restorative effect. If we were to leave the children here and go alone, perhaps—'

Laure knew he had a vision of establishing a new warmth between them, the closeness that, for all Mathilde's dutiful efforts, he still had not found, which in the early days of their marriage he had not even sought, thinking himself too much beneath her. Only Laure knew that such an enforced companionship might have the very opposite effect on someone in Mathilde's highly strung state. 'I don't know,' she said at last. 'You must ask Mathilde what she would like.'

Mathilde accepted Charles's suggestion with something like enthusiasm, because in her nervous restlessness any change was better than to stay here and face the unvarying routine of each day. 'Yes, let's go,' she said; 'at once, tomorrow.'

'Tomorrow!' He looked horrified. 'Oh, but *chérie*, we cannot possibly.' She turned a frown of impatience upon him, tapping her foot; and he spread his hands resignedly. 'Very well, we shall go tomorrow.'

She packed with wild urgency, as if the whole business was of the utmost importance, pausing only to rush from one person to another giving last-minute instructions of no particular significance. Laure tried to calm her, to take her on one side for a quiet talk, but Mathilde brushed her aside with the brusque impatience that had become so characteristic of her these days. It was only when she went to say good-night to Joseph that any sign of the sweet warm Mathilde of the past showed through. She embraced him fiercely, kissing him, stroking his hair.

'Joseph, *mon petit, mon chéri*, you must be very, very good while I am away, and do just what Grand-mère tells you. And write to me and to Papa – you have the address safe, haven't you? – and don't go out in the fields by yourself, and when you go in the stables mind Barbarossa's hooves – and never, never ride alone, will you?'

Joseph only half listened to the catalogue of unimpressively obvious instructions, and then lay down and closed his eyes and wondered what all the fuss was about.

Nanon was waiting on the landing when Mathilde emerged from the bedroom.

'I want to talk to you, *floreta*,' she said. There was something in her voice that penetrated even Mathilde's shell of painful emotion, a certain grim authority quite unlike her usual comfortable tone. 'Upstairs,' she added.

Mathilde followed her to the tidy sparse little room, but waited in the doorway as if anxious to be away.

Nanon sat down by her fire and patted a nearby chair. 'Come and sit here, *floreta*.'

Mathilde closed the door and came, sitting there with her mouth shut tight and her hands twisting in her lap. Nanon laid her own hand over them.

'Now, here's what I want. I've seen a lot of things I've said nothing about. For years and years I've seen, and kept my mouth shut. You didn't want to tell me, so I let it go. But I know you very well – didn't I nurse you myself at this very breast? I know you didn't marry Monsieur de Miremont for love, though how anyone could help but love him I don't know. I think I know where you gave your heart, too; and it wasn't to that Monsieur Petit either – that was just a sickness. One thing I didn't think of, not until later, was – well, I'm not going to say it if you don't want me to. But if you're going to be alone, just the two of you, you and Monsieur Charles, then I think it's time we had a little talk. Otherwise there'll be trouble. You can't talk to him, I can see that. And your Maman says you won't talk to her.'

'Did she ask you to speak to me then?' Mathilde's tone was hostile, hardened against Nanon's probing sympathy.

'No, *floreta*. Only it's bad if you won't even talk to her. She knows, doesn't she?'

'Knows what?'

Nanon ignored the defiant manner. 'She knows why what Rosaline had to say upset you so.' Suddenly she held out her arms, with all their memories of comfort given in long-ago troubles. 'Come, *floreta* – come to Nanon!'

Mathilde slid from the chair to her knees and allowed herself to be enfolded in that angular embrace; and there began at last to weep. And after a time, slowly, piece by piece, she told Nanon everything.

At the end there was a little silence, while she waited for the soothing words that had never failed her, healing the hurts of her girlhood like a salve on a wound. But, instead, Nanon's caressing hand fell from her hair and she felt herself pushed away, just far enough so that her old nurse could look into her face. There was nothing in the least soothing in her expression; she looked stern, even disapproving. Oddly, Mathilde felt an infinitesimal touch of relief.

'Well, *floreta* – have you been to confession?'

Mathilde looked puzzled.

'You know what I'm talking about,' Nanon went on. 'You did wrong. There was the baby, like me with my Jacques. And then there was Monsieur Charles – deceiving a good man like him, that was bad, worse than the other maybe. But I guess you'd find it hard to go and confess those things to the *curé*, being as he knows you so well.' Mathilde bent her head, unable to think of anything to say. Nanon continued earnestly, 'You'll be staying in a place where you don't know a soul. Find a priest there, *floreta*. Tell him everything, put it all right with the Good Lord. When that's done, you can give your heart to your husband and there'll be nothing in the way any more. You see if I'm not right.'

The practical simplicity of Nanon's remedy, as if she were offering a well-tried and infallible cure for a minor illness, was unexpectedly comforting to Mathilde. If only it could be as easy as that, a single action to put an end to all the torment and misery!

It was not quite so easy, of course. But she did follow Nanon's advice – giving Charles the slip one afternoon, by means of yet another small lie – and, afterwards, felt a kind of exhausted peace. The Church said it was over, once confession had been made and absolution received; so she trusted the Church, clinging to that assurance to carry her forward.

She went from the church to meet Charles at their hotel, reminding herself all the way back that there was now nothing between them, that she could give her heart to him without the reserve that came from guilt. It was what Nanon had told her, but she did not at the moment feel any different when she thought of Charles; she did not in fact feel anything at all. She had loved Frédéric so intensely and so completely, and for so long, that ridding herself of the guilt of their union could not begin to tear that love out at the roots. She tried not to think about it, but she knew it was there still, as it always had been.

Charles was standing on the hotel steps as she approached, and he had not seen her, for he was gazing out at the sea. His face had an unusually sombre look, as if he was troubled or unhappy. She halted for a moment, watching him. If he is unhappy, she reminded herself, then it is my duty to help and comfort him. She went up to him and laid a hand on his arm. 'Charles,' she said gently.

He looked round, startled; and then smiled, his manner and expression all at once entirely normal, sober and calm and good-humoured. They went in to change, for their usual walk before dinner.

It was a brisk windy afternoon, with a wild sea rushing into the bay. They walked slowly, and Mathilde – true to her new resolution – tried to be everything she had so often failed to be: warm, tender, light-hearted. She had never, in all their married life, tried so hard to please. Yet she had the impression that she had never before been so far from succeeding. Charles smiled at her little jokes, put his hand over hers when she made some loving remark, responded briefly to her exclamations about the weather or the scenery; but she sensed under it all a reserve which she was sure was quite new. By the time they returned to the hotel for dinner she was aware of a slowly rising sense of panic. What had happened? Had all the years of guilt and misery, which had kept her from being the loving wife she ought to have been, at last turned him against her? Had she allowed her guilt to dig so deep a gulf between them that nothing she could do would ever bridge it again?

She was nervous as they sat at dinner, chattering incessantly and drinking a little too much, conscious all the time that Charles was becoming more and more silent. Afterwards, they made their way to their comfortable suite of rooms and Mathilde, pleading tiredness, undressed and put on her nightgown; and returned to their bedroom to find Charles standing at the uncurtained and unshuttered window looking out into the night. The sound of breaking waves came softly into the room, countering, with its hint of wildness, the gentle solitary light of the bedside lamp. Mathilde closed the dressing-room door and went to stand beside her husband. He did not move. She felt suddenly frightened, and very alone.

'Charles—' Her voice was quiet, a little desperate. 'Hold me – please!'

He turned then, at once, and put his arms about her, gently and carefully. She reached up to clasp him, aware of a need in herself such as she had never known before with Charles. She drew his head down and pressed her mouth to his; and felt it unmoving and cool, making no response at all. She slid her fingers into the thickness of his hair, caressing him, and moved her body closer to his, and kissed him softly on both cheeks, on his chin, all around and then back to his lips; and this time he did respond, almost warily at first and then, suddenly, with an urgency that came close to abandonment. 'Come to bed,' she whispered; and then wished she had not spoken, for he raised his head and looked down at her in surprise, and she was afraid she had lost him again.

'But I am not ready – I am still dressed.' He sounded breathless and unsure of himself.

'That doesn't matter.' She took his hand and led him to the bed and they sat down there, while she began to take off his jacket. But before she had finished he had his arms about her again and was kissing her as he had never kissed her before, with passion and eagerness and longing. He lay down and pulled her after him and she closed her eyes, whilst her fingers swiftly and neatly unbuttoned, and pushed clothes aside; and then they were together, with no thought for anything but their need for one another.

Afterwards, when they lay quietly side by side, sleepy and content, Mathilde thought, It was not like Frédéric – but I have never before been so nearly happy with Charles.

CHAPTER
TWENTY SIX

Moïse cycled into the courtyard an hour early to help with the preparations for the wine tasting. His new bicycle was the object of great pride, only the fourth in the village, polished and cared for with almost as much tender concern as he showed towards his son. It brought him smiling to work and took him whistling home again and enabled him – at least when they were not very busy – to go home for lunch and return for the afternoon's work, instead of eating in the *chai* or the vineyard. Once, soon after he had bought it, he had suggested Laure might like to try it. With skirts tucked up in a most undignified manner (a good thing the modest Charles was not about) she had wobbled over the gravel of the courtyard, far more frightened for the safety of the vehicle than for herself. She had rather enjoyed the sensation, the promise (with practice) of undreamed of speed. 'But I think I'd better stick to two legs – or four,' she had told Moïse laughingly. She had however urged Charles to buy himself a bicycle. 'I am considering the matter,' he had admitted; and then, to her surprise, had added with an unaccustomed note of longing, 'What I should really like is one of those new automobiles.'

Today, however, Moïse wheeled the bicycle into the coachhouse and left it there without a backward glance or an approving comment, and went with Laure to the *chai* where the tasting was to take place.

'I think we shall need three large tables,' Laure said. 'We'll have to bring some chairs from the house – the benches don't seat quite enough.'

'Just like one of the old harvest feasts,' was Moïse's comment.

'From what I hear, we'll be more than that today.'

Aubin's simple neighbourly challenge had somehow grown into a major communal event. A month ago, bottling the first of the wine of 1899, ready to send off an order for Monsieur Teyssier – who had been eloquent in his praise of its quality – Laure had remembered her promise to arrange a competitive tasting with Aubin and had duly contacted him.

From that point the whole project had taken on a life of its own. Aubin, of course, would bring with him his wife and sons, his sisters and brother-in-law and their families. Then three other *vignerons* who made Casseuil wine were invited to come with samples of their own versions of the 1899 vintage, and naturally they would bring their own families and friends. In addition, of course, there must be some entirely neutral judges of the wine, so the schoolmaster and the doctor, unrelated to any of the commune's vine growers, were invited too. After that, Laure, recollecting just in time that Charles was after all the owner of the vineyard, suggested he might wish to invite some friends of his own – so (rather to her regret; but then they were family connections, when all was said and done) the Chabrys were coming, and one or two others. In fact, it looked very much as if almost the entire village would be present.

Laure had chosen a date in Easter week when she knew Joseph would be home for the holidays. Since the Abbé Lebrun's death two years ago there had been no priest at Casseuil, so Charles had decided to send the boy rather earlier than he had intended to his own old school. To everyone's relief Joseph seemed happy and settled; and furthermore, he had lost a good deal of the wildness that had begun to worry them all. Sending him away from his mother's doting over-indulgence had been the best thing they could have done, Laure thought. This morning Joseph had gone with Charles to mass at Trissac, but as soon as he returned he would come to help them in the *chai*.

It was like a solemn ritual, Joseph thought. Cool and dim beneath its simple vaulted roof, lit only by the candles overhead and set out here and there on the tables, the *chai* had something of the atmosphere of a church about it. Even the stillness was like that of a rapt congregation, except that this was the stillness of eager anticipation rather than of prayer. Joseph felt a little awed himself, although he had been full of excited chatter all morning, as he helped his grandmother – and Papa and Moïse and Lucien – with the preparations. He was proud that he alone of the four grandchildren should be allowed in the *chai* this morning, though Charlotte and Marie-Françoise had helped his mother and Nanon to pick flowers and arrange them in vases, for him to carry from the house to the *chai*. The two little girls had then had to go and rest, so that they would not be too tired at lunch-time. Joseph, meanwhile, had polished the glasses (or most of them) and cut up bread for the tasters to eat between wines to clear their palates and covered the tables with clean white cloths and carried plates and bowls and cutlery from the house, ready for the lunch afterwards. Louis-Christophe had been busy in the kitchen for several days, preparing the food.

Then, just before everyone began to arrive, Joseph had hugged his grandmother. 'You will win, Grand-mère, I'm sure of it.' They had both glanced up at the bottle standing on the shelf behind them, the tawny-gold wine glowing through the clear glass.

Now there were four other bottles beside it and Joseph was not quite so confident. Two of the wines looked very pale and insipid, which was, he knew, not a good sign; but the other two of Grand-mère's rivals had an ominously impressive appearance.

All the preliminary chatter of welcome ceased. The only noise now came from outside, where the laughter and shouting of children echoed about the courtyard, from all those too small to be involved in the tasting, left to play in the sunshine. At a word from his grandmother, Joseph took the first bottle, which Monsieur Durat the schoolmaster had already opened, and carried it to the table and there poured a little of the wine into each of the glasses (clear and unadorned, so as to set the wine off to fullest advantage). He knew everyone was watching him (especially Monsieur Bertaud, whose wine this was) and he took the greatest possible care, pouring very gently and slowly, so that no one could later accuse him of favouring his grandmother by treating the rival wines at all roughly. When he had finished he looked up at Grand-mère Laure and they exchanged smiles, full of understanding.

The tasters took up their glasses. Joseph went to stand beside his grandmother – he was still too young to taste so many undiluted wines, she had told him – and watched the circle of grave faces, deep-shadowed in the candlelight. Here and there the strong line of a cheekbone or a jaw or a nose (Monsieur Martin's was far and away the most prominent) was thrown into sharp relief; eyes gleamed in the dimness, studying the pale wine with the shrewd attention of men and women who had lived by wines all their lives and knew exactly what they were looking for. The light shone on the hands curved about the stems of the glasses, gnarled, bent, work-worn hands, most of them, or well on the way to being so; some (like Eugène Chabry's) pale and a little puffy; or his father's, thin, nervous, long-fingered, with a certain grace in the way they held the glass; or those of Paul Lambert, Aubin's youngest son (who was evidently, at thirteen, quite old enough to be tasting, to Joseph's great envy), still small and soft and marked only by the accidental scars of childhood.

They raised the glasses to study the wine against the light; they swirled it in the glasses and sniffed, carefully, with an occasional indeterminate murmur of comment. Monsieur Bertaud watched anxiously for any sign of approval.

They tasted. Joseph studied the faces, concentrating on that odd distortion of the features inevitable during the correct tasting of wine, the breath drawn in, the wine held on the tongue.

Some swallowed the wine, some spat on the earth floor of the *chai*. There was some nodding (not much) and a general if slight stir of relaxation. Robert Martin was the first to speak, turning to Monsieur Bertaud. 'I'm sorry, *mon ami* – this is pleasant enough, but there's no body to it. Maybe you harvested too early.'

The man made a brave attempt to conceal his disappointment, but could not quite raise a smile. 'You can't get the labour these days, to take the trouble over it like we used to – and I've more land under these grapes than, say, Monsieur Lambert there, and only two boys. I have to get them in all in one go. Maybe you lose the great wines this way, but at least you get something and make a bit of a profit too. I don't ask for any more.'

You could tell, thought Laure with an inward stir of amusement, that Robert Martin was standing down as mayor at the municipal elections in May; otherwise he would not have risked stirring up the resentment that she could see in the face of Monsieur Bertaud, and even more in those of his sons.

Hands reached for the bread; Joseph took the second bottle and refilled the glasses. Much the same verdict was passed by the company on this wine. The next came off a little better. 'More body, but perhaps too assertive and lacking in finesse for a true Casseuil,' commented the schoolmaster, himself from a winegrowing family near St Émilion.

Then it was Aubin's turn. Joseph knew this wine was different, even before he poured. That wonderful colour, the subtle fragrance rising from it – Grand-mère had once let him taste her own '99 wine and he knew, looking at this, that it was going to be a dangerously close rival to hers – too close for happiness. He watched apprehensively as the glasses were raised.

It was good, and the immediate outburst of enthusiastic praise underlined it. It was not just the colour. It had a powerful bouquet, honeyed and heady, which immediately set it apart from the others; but it was the taste that drew the most eloquent flow of approving adjectives.

'It is excellent, Monsieur Lambert,' said Laure generously, wondering now with a sense of disappointment how hers would compare to this; it was some weeks since she had tasted it. After the other wines it was easy to recognise the very qualities that for so long they had all striven to find again. This was, recognisably, triumphantly, a Casseuil. She allowed Joseph to take a sip from her glass.

'It will be better for a few more years in the bottle. But yes, I am pleased with it.'

More than pleased, said Aubin's face; delighted, and proud.

Laure's was as good. In what way exactly it differed from Aubin's it was not easy to say, but it was different, although it had the same full-bodied lusciousness of texture and taste. There was a little more depth to the colour – more amber, less topaz – and a faint but distinct hint of vanilla. 'That will be the oak, of course,' said Aubin. 'You keep yours in the cask longer than I do – that makes a difference.'

'I think I can honestly say that I find an equal merit in these two wines,' Charles said. It sounded diplomatic, but Laure knew he meant it; Charles was never merely diplomatic.

Not everyone agreed with him and in the end two more gave their vote to Laure than to Aubin; but it was close enough for honour to be satisfied. The tasters relaxed and began to discuss other wines they had enjoyed (or not), arguing their merits among themselves. Laure put up a hand. 'A moment more, *mes chers amis* – I have one last wine for you.' She smiled at Joseph, who was in the secret with her and went to the office and brought out a tray on which three bottles stood, the labels stained with age. 'The '69 Château de Casseuil,' explained Laure. 'Now let us see how our new wine compares with the best of the past.'

This time Laure poured, and the reverential silence fell again, more complete than ever and lasting long after the first sips were taken. At last Robert Martin said, 'Now, *there* was a wine!'

Laure knew exactly what he meant. The new wines had been good, infinitely better indeed than those of the earlier years since replanting, and rich in the qualities that had made Casseuil great. But set against this they were mere pale ghosts of the great years, like a dream of what once had been.

'I suppose it's the ageing that makes the difference,' said Doctor Bonnet thoughtfully.

Moïse nodded, rather as one seizing thankfully at the nearest excuse. 'That'll be it.'

'No,' said Aubin. 'It's more than that. I remember now – even when this wine was young it was different. It is the difference between a great wine and a merely good one.'

The glow of pride had left his face; and Laure felt the same disappointment within herself. I have not done it yet, she thought, as she divided the last of that wonderful wine amongst the company. The '99 is better, much better. But the great wine is still to come.

Once the serious business of tasting was over, the children were called in from the courtyard, the food was carried out to the *chai* and spread on the tables, and everyone sat down to eat. The laughter and discussion expanded, grew more animated, filled the usually hushed atmosphere of the *chai* with noise. Joseph, thoroughly satisfied by the happy outcome (and not quite understanding why his grandmother should be looking so downcast about it), sought out Paul Lambert and became involved in a lively if unsubtle argument as to the relative merits of Le Petit Colin and the Château, as far as wine was concerned. Good-natured at first, it became rather heated after a time and might even have ended in blows, had Joseph not caught his grandmother's eye on him. Paul, quickly assessing the situation, moved the conversation into rather more nonsensical channels and they sat giggling together, with Jean-Marc Delmas – attached to Joseph as usual – trying to understand what was so funny about what they were saying. André, Robert Martin's grandson, soon joined them, and a number of other youngsters, until they formed an uproariously noisy group over which their elders occasionally shook their heads in mock despair.

The Chabrys seemed to be the only guests to remain aloof from the general conviviality. Trying to make it clear, perhaps, that as family – not mere friends – they were somehow rather above the rest of the company, they occupied seats at one end of a table, well into a corner, ignored by everyone except a few of their own particular friends. No one (with the possible exception of Charles) was sorry when they left early.

Charles returned to the *chai* when he had seen them off, resuming his place near the empty seats.

'Come on now – more wine for *monsieur le maire*!' called Robert Martin, filling Charles's glass.

Laure, surprised out of a gloomy reverie, cast a questioning glance at Robert Martin, and then at Charles, who had coloured very deeply and was murmuring something incoherent about, 'A long way off . . .' and '. . . not decided yet.' A chorus of encouraging comment and laughter drowned most of what did emerge of his words: but when at last he found an opening, Charles waved his hands and burst out, 'Not now, *mes amis* – not now, I beg of you!'

Fortunately for him, Mathilde chose that moment to come

in with Nanon and the younger children and effectively diverted attention from her husband.

'I am so sorry we're late, *mon chéri*,' she said, kissing Charles lightly on the cheek. 'Philippe would not wake in time.' The little boy, looking sleepily round at the company from Nanon's arms, was the result of that impulsive holiday in Arcachon.

Mathilde sat down beside Charles. Charlotte and Marie-Françoise went dutifully to kiss the closest family friends amongst the company; then Charlotte – nine and a half now – took her seat with all the dignity and assurance of a young woman, though her eyes were very bright with excitement; and Marie-Françoise's delicate, exquisite face had a happy glow to it, so that it looked almost rosy. It took only a few moments for the gravity of the little girls to dissolve in the cheerful atmosphere: they ate heartily (there was still ample food left, fortunately), whispered together, and giggled a great deal; and when the other children left at last, joined Joseph in a noisy game of chase about the *chai* until their mother and Nanon rounded up all three of them and herded them back to the house.

It was not until all the guests had gone and the clearing up was completed, and Moïse had mounted his bicycle and ridden away, that Laure, walking back across the courtyard with Charles, was able to ask him about Robert Martin's mysterious remark. Again, an embarrassed colour spread over her son-in-law's face.

'It's simply this – they have asked me to stand for election as mayor.'

Laure came to a halt and stared at him in astonishment. 'They? The Chabrys I suppose?'

'No – it was Martin himself who suggested it. I had thought Monsieur Lambert would wish to stand, but he says he cannot spare the time for all the mayoral duties.'

'But your politics are nothing like theirs! If you stand you'll trail all your Royalist Catholic friends with you – Louis and Eugène Chabry and the rest – isn't that so? Then Martin's friends will have to choose their own nominee to oppose you – and *he*'ll become mayor, even if you're elected to the council, because no one will vote for the Chabrys and you'll be in a minority. That's right isn't it?' She wondered if perhaps Robert Martin was deliberately trying to undermine Charles's position by this device, forcing him to demonstrate how closely he was linked by his beliefs with the unpopular Chabrys. Until now she had thought the Mayor rather liked Charles, concealing a genuine respect beneath his constant teasing remarks at the expense of the younger man's religious and political views.

'Perhaps,' said Charles slowly. 'Yes, I know the Chabrys are not popular. People are sadly blind to their good points. Yet, many of the existing members of the council are good men with a real desire to serve the commune; I have learned that since I served with them. I could, I think, include several of them in my own list without any uneasiness of conscience.' He smiled a little ruefully. 'Martin told me he knows I can be trusted to choose the best men to stand with me – by which of course he means his friends. I don't know; I shall have to consider very carefully what I ought to do. I have agreed to nothing yet. In any case, I have a much more serious doubt about the whole matter.'

'Oh?'

'Yes – I have to ask myself if I could consider undertaking many of the duties that would be expected of me as mayor. For example, the Mayor must conduct marriages, the godless civil marriages required by the state. How can I in all conscience act so contrary to all I believe of the solemnity of the sacrament of marriage?'

'It's not contrary to it, but simply an addition, in conformity with the law. I don't see anything difficult about that.'

'But what of those who have no religious ceremony? The Church teaches that a civil marriage is no marriage. Am I to connive at living in sin?'

'Better surely that they have a civil contract than none at all, don't you think? You can always offer up a prayer for them on the quiet while you hear their vows.'

He smiled with happy relief, quite clearly taking her remark rather more seriously than she had intended. Then, grave again, he objected, 'But how at this time can I think for one moment of allowing myself to become a representative of a Republic so godless, so much the enemy of all I hold dear?

That would be to live a lie, a terrible lie. I, Charles de Miremont, to wear a sash in the colours of a Republic more defiantly atheist than any since 1792? That is not conceivable, surely?'

'But you would be the representative of the people who elected you, not of the government.'

'The Mayor is still obliged to carry out the decrees of the government. What, for example, if the present moves to separate Church and State were to succeed? I might find myself required to confiscate church buildings on behalf of the commune.'

'Since they're already technically communal property I think that's unlikely,' said Laure a little impatiently. 'Besides, if you find yourself faced with something you really cannot stomach you can always resign, can you not?' She paused, studying his troubled face; and then asked, 'Have you discussed this with Louis Chabry? What does he think?'

'He thinks I should stand; they all think so. They believe I can thus best serve the interests of the Church.'

'Ah! – then you shouldn't stand.' Charles seemed surprised. 'The Mayor should serve the interests of all the people, not simply one faction,' she explained.

'Robert Martin did not.'

'No, I agree. Yet he represented more than you would, if you served only the Church. There are few enough Catholics in Casseuil. The mayor represents Protestants and Atheists and Freemasons, Republicans and Royalists – everyone.'

'I could not do anything else but put God first.'

'That's another matter. That *does* mean serving all the people, doesn't it?'

He regarded her thoughtfully for a long time; and then he said slowly, 'Does it? I shall need to think about that.'

As they stepped into the hall Laure remembered with a sinking of the spirit that she had promised Henri's manservant a free evening today. That meant that she must spend the next few hours upstairs, tending her husband. She hated every moment she spent with him, fighting the repulsion she felt as he dribbled over the food she spooned into his mouth, or lay half asleep, mumbling and snorting and grunting, a great ungainly mass that was hardly a human being any longer, in any sense she recognised. Lately he had grown much worse, deteriorating steadily, until now he lay all day in bed, unable to feed himself or wash or talk coherently, incontinent, apparently unaware of where he was or who was with him. Laure had hated the man he had been, and she hated the thing he had become. I wish he would die, she thought, often, and felt no guilt that she should do so. If she had loved him she would have felt the same, for this vegetable existence was no life at all.

'I will have your dinner sent up,' Charles said, as usual, as she left him in the hall. She knew that, as usual, she would be unable to eat it in that close, evil-smelling atmosphere.

She had brought a book with her, but she could not read either. When Henri had been fed and changed (for perhaps the fifth time today) and had settled again into the noisy stupor in which he passed the hours, Laure installed herself in a chair, as far as possible from the bed, where she could look out of the window – open just a crack – on the sun setting over the valley.

So, here she was at the end of a day from which she had hoped for so much! She had thought she might be able to look back on it and say, 'It was all worth while, all of it, for I have done what I set out to do at last.'

But she could not say that, about the wine or anything else. Things were, certainly, a little better. Mathilde had been restored to calmness and to health. Sometimes during the past four years she had been able to talk of Frédéric quite openly, even in front of Charles, without too much inappropriate emotion. She lived a life of apparent contentment, almost wholly absorbed in her children, a devoted wife and mother. But Laure knew that beneath the surface the sadness was still there; that very likely Mathilde would take it with her to the grave. Even for her, that was coming nearer every day.

I am an old woman, Laure thought, an old woman. So much of my life has gone, so many of the people I knew and loved are dead or gone away. I only ever wanted two things, Mathilde's happiness and a great wine; and they are both as far away as ever. I am old and I am tired and I do not want to go on and on like this, for ever and ever. She felt her eyes fill with tears, weak self-pitying tears that angered her because she could not suppress them.

There was a gentle tap on the door. Laure took out a handkerchief and blew her nose, vigorously, as if to rebuke her weakness. 'Come in!'

Charlotte crossed the room, glancing with nervous fascination at the figure on the bed and wrinkling her pretty nose. 'Papa asked me to bring this letter, Grand-mère – you'd missed it downstairs.'

Marcel, Laure thought hopefully – recounting with his new and unaccustomed expansiveness the doings of his two small grandchildren, just as once her mother had done; but her mother was dead now, since last year.

Laure looked at Charlotte, so fresh and pretty, untouched by the tainted atmosphere of the sickroom. She felt a little cheered. Yes, she understood Marcel, as she had understood her mother. It was good being a grandparent, one stage removed from the painful ties of responsibility . . . She kissed the girl. 'Thank you, *ma petite*. Good-night.'

The letter was not from Marcel after all. In fact she could not tell who had sent it. A Bordeaux postmark and handwriting that was not familiar and yet stirred her memory? She opened it carefully.

'Bravo, *madame*! Casseuil has risen from the grave, and I honour you for the faith and courage which I know you must have spent upon it. A little more faith, a little more courage, and we will, I know, taste the very greatest wines once more.'

Laure turned the letter over and studied the signature. It was a moment or two before she could decipher it; and then, with a sense of wonder, she read, 'Jean Delisle.'

Jean Delisle, after all this time! A warm glow of affectionate recollection swept her. Her friend and teacher, to whom she owed so much, without whom she could have achieved nothing. And, yes, I *have* achieved something, she thought now, remembering with sudden clarity the bleak days when he had left Casseuil, seeing no future for it. Much, much more than I could ever have hoped for.

Her old friend had retired now, to live with a married niece in Bordeaux; and coming by chance at a friend's table on a bottle of the '99 Château de Casseuil he had been astonished and delighted, and made further enquiries. So he had learned a little of Laure's life after his departure – her own second marriage, and Mathilde's marriage too, and that it was Laure herself and not her son-in-law who controlled the vineyard still – and he had decided to write.

Laure read the letter through twice and then let it fall to her lap and sat gazing out of the window with a new optimism coming to life within her. Fifty-six was no age after all, no age at all, when you were fit and well, as she was. A little more faith, a little more courage . . . That was all she needed, and she did after all have it in abundance. Thank you, *mon ami*, she murmured in her thoughts to the old friend who had reached out of the past to strengthen her failing spirit.

CHAPTER
TWENTY SEVEN

'Friday 21 June 1907. Topping up of barrels (Moïse). Hoeing. *Le palissage* continuing. Mildew spraying.'

Laure blotted the ink and shut the book and rose, ready to go and see that the tasks were progressing as they ought (no need to check on Moïse, who had been at work in the maturing room for some time now). And then, half-way to the door, she paused, listening. Surely that was a sound she should not be hearing this morning – the clink of bottles?

She opened the door that led to the *chai* and descended the steps, feeling the coolness gathering around her as she did so. At a small table at the far end of the room, Lucien Delmas was at work attaching labels, one by one, to the bottles stacked against the wall – they should already have been labelled by now, but Laure had wanted to wait for the new labels, redesigned to include the proud declaration that the Château had won the gold medal for its wine at the departmental competition in 1905; they had only arrived from the printer in Libourne yesterday.

'Lucien, what are you doing? I said those were to be left. You should be helping the new man – I don't want any mistakes with the spraying.'

Lucien shrugged. He did not look round, but she could see that his mouth had a stubborn line to it. 'I'm not working with Pierre Frangeas.'

'Why ever not? You were at school with him, weren't you? And in the army together? What has he done that you should suddenly turn against him?'

'He insulted me. Besides, I've always hated him.'

'You should be grateful to him – if I hadn't had to pay him so much to get him to come here, you and Moïse wouldn't

510

have had a rise either.' The necessity to make that increase still rankled a little with her.

He looked round then with an angry light in his eyes, and she realised she had said exactly the wrong thing. 'That's just it! I'm not going to be taunted by that pig for not being worth a fair wage!'

'Oh, Lucien, you know that's not how it was! It's my fault for not having seen that you were due for a rise – it's so easy to take people for granted when they go quietly doing their best from day to day.'

'Then you won't be doing it again, you can be sure of that!'

'Lucien, surely I've shown how much I value you, by paying you even more than Pierre and the others are getting? Doesn't that satisfy you?'

'Not if you had to be forced into it.' Angrily he pushed the newly labelled bottle aside and reached for another, banging it down on the table; and then hastily checking to make sure he had not damaged it.

Laure drew a deep breath and tried again. 'I relied on you to keep an eye on him today. You know how behind we are with everything.'

'Then let's hope he keeps at it all day, not like yesterday.'

'What happened yesterday?'

'Oh, he sloped off to the café for an hour or two while you and my uncle were in Bergerac.'

'Didn't you stop him?'

He stared at her. 'How was I supposed to do that?'

It was a reasonable question. It was also clear, Laure thought, that relations between Lucien and the newcomer were beyond repair, at least for the time being. She gave in.

'Very well. You finish off here then.'

It was with a feeling of exasperation that she crossed the courtyard. She was in no mood this morning for coping with temperamental differences amongst her work force. She had spent all last night sitting up with Henri, who had been unusually restless, and she felt tired and irritable. Pierre Frangeas had seemed like the answer to her present problems – being that increasingly rare phenomenon, a young man looking for work on the land. She had thought him competent and willing and quick to learn. But if he was going to make things difficult with Lucien, whom she relied upon as much as she did his Uncle Moïse, then perhaps he was not worth the high wage she had been forced to pay to get him to come at all. On the other hand, she needed labourers desperately. Moïse had been off work sick for two weeks in May and everything had fallen behind as a result. They were only just beginning to catch up.

She made her way to the plot near the bottom of the hill where (she hoped) the new man would be at work. Not far away – in an adjacent plot – she could see the women (Moïse's wife and daughters among them) busy at the *palissage* – training the young vine branches on to the supporting fence. The other regular labourers, Mathieu Bertaud and Georges Lavergne, neither so skilled nor so reliable as Moïse and Lucien, should be hoeing to clear the ground of weeds somewhere on the far side of the château, beyond the woods – she would go and check on them later. She was uneasy about Pierre Frangeas, who had after all worked only for one day under Lucien's supervision.

The leaves of the nearer vines in the plot were already shaded with blue from the spraying: copper sulphate, slaked lime and water, the combination known as Bordeaux mixture that had proved so effective against mildew since its introduction several years ago. Laure felt relieved – it looked as though Pierre could after all be relied upon. But when she came within sight of him she found that he had abandoned the spraying equipment and was carrying on a rather one-sided conversation with Moïse's daughter Anne, who looked as though she did not much appreciate what he was saying to her – she at least was continuing to work.

Pierre saw Laure before she reached him and hastily returned to the spraying, with all the air of one who had never left it. Laure felt annoyed. In general the odd pause for a talk or a rest did not trouble her, but at the moment they could not afford such luxuries, if the work was to be done at all. She watched the young man for a little while, and then went to him and brought up the matter Lucien had mentioned: she knew Moïse's nephew well enough to be quite sure that he would not have invented such a story.

'Please make sure you reserve your visits to the café for

outside working hours,' she said, mildly enough, she thought, in the circumstances.

He nodded in silence, but his expression was thunderous and, as she turned to make her way back up the hill, she heard him mutter something ferociously uncomplimentary about Lucien. She was too weary to take it up with him.

At the top of the bank that ran down to the road beside the *caveau* the roses were in bloom; on impulse, Laure went to cut a few blossoms with the little pruning knife she carried in her pocket, and laid them on the tomb. It had a neglected look, with weeds growing in the cracks in the stonework and grass almost obliterating the gravel. When they had a quiet interval, she decided, she would come and tidy it up. She pulled out one or two of the more obvious weeds and then turned sharply as a passer-by greeted her from the road.

It was Aubin, pushing his bicycle up the steepest part of the hill. He nodded towards the *caveau*. 'It's been needing that,' he commented of her weeding. He sounded neither approving nor disapproving, as if his mind was occupied with other more pressing considerations.

'Well, *monsieur*, you can come and put it right then, if you've nothing else to do,' Laure returned with mock ill-humour.

He did not take the remark in his usual spirit of raillery. 'I have to be getting back. I've already given up more of the day than I can spare, but Marie would have wanted me to go – you know how women are.' His wife had died last year and, though he showed few signs of it, Laure suspected he missed her deeply. When she looked puzzled, he added, 'I've been to Bergerac, to the station, to see the regiment on its way.'

Laure knew that Aubin's second son was doing his military service at the barracks in the town. 'Where are they off to then?'

'Narbonne, of course.'

'Oh! The wine troubles – yes, of course. I suppose the authorities are not going to risk sending in more local troops, after the mutiny.'

'No, though a good many in the 108th are not happy about it either, my Jean among them. When your father's a small *vigneron* too you understand why there's been all that unrest in the Midi. He has no wish to go firing on people much like his own kinsfolk who only want a fairer deal for wine growers.'

'I don't expect it'll come to that. Things seem to be quietening down, from what one hears.'

'The government's too slow to take measures to put things right. Clemenceau's way is to send in troops first and listen afterwards – if he listens at all.'

'You don't take the view then that the chief reason for the low wine prices is overproduction? After all, wine-growing in the Midi had expanded enormously in the past few years.'

'And so has fraud by the merchants. If every hectolitre of wine is treated with sugar and generally adulterated, then of course there's going to be even more on the market and even smaller profits for the *vigneron* – or no profits at all. I tell you, if it wasn't for the little bit of Casseuil I produce, I'd have gone under too these past months. The price I get for my ordinary wine doesn't even cover the costs of production. But at least people are prepared to pay for a good Casseuil, as you'll know.'

Laure nodded. 'On the other hand, if you produce it on the scale I do you need labour, and not just at harvest time either. Do you know the wages that are being demanded now?'

'Well, labour's scarce in the countryside – and since the laws legalising unions we've all learned how to get together to further our interests, *vignerons* as well as labourers. There were injustices before, you must admit.'

'I know.' She sighed. 'Perhaps I'm getting too old for all these changes.'

'You, *madame*? Never!' He paused, and then went on, 'I see Pierre Frangeas is working for you.'

'Since last week, yes.'

'You know his brother's with the Chabrys? They say he's up to the neck in their intrigues, the brother I mean. They're all out to make the most of any trouble – they'll stir it up where they can't find any, and they don't mind how dirty their hands get in the process. But maybe *monsieur le maire* has told you all about that – he should know.'

'He takes the view that the Socialists are behind the troubles, in the Midi and elsewhere.'

'The Socialists only want the best for the workers and the poor. Chabry and the rest of those reactionary crypto-Royalist types just want trouble for its own sake – anything to upset the Republic. You know Chabry's eldest had a hand in smashing up Jewish shops back during the Dreyfus affair?'

'Louis-Albert? No, I didn't. But wasn't he away at the time?'

'Yes, in Bordeaux, filling in time between school and military service with a lot of other young hooligans. But he was the ringleader, by all accounts. It came to court, but the family pulled a few strings and he got off lightly. What's more, I heard Eugène Chabry himself say the boy did well, acting on his own initiative like that. They're a nasty lot, the Chabrys, under all that piety.'

Since his words only confirmed her own uneasy feelings about Charles's friends, Laure did not quite know what to say.

'Just keep an eye on Pierre Frangeas, that's all,' Aubin advised.

'There's not much harm he can do here, I'd have thought – but thank you, all the same.'

'Perhaps you should tell Monsieur de Miremont. He's not like the rest of them, I know.'

'No,' agreed Laure. Unfortunately Charles had always found it very difficult to believe ill of anyone, least of all his fellow Catholics. Perhaps presented with something more concrete than feelings of unease—

'Looks as if you're wanted.' Laure turned and saw Mathilde hurrying towards her. 'I'll be on my way. Good day, *madame*.'

'Maman, Michel thinks you should come.'

'Henri?'

'Yes, Maman.'

Michel, Henri's manservant, had been right to think there was some urgency. All trace of the restlessness of the night had gone, in fact almost all sign of life of any kind, apart from a faint infrequent breathing.

'Shall I send for Charles, Maman?' Mathilde whispered.

'Where is he?'

'At the *mairie*. But he was going on to lunch with the Chabrys.'

'No, leave it, *chérie*. I doubt if there's any need for anyone but the doctor.'

It was, Doctor Bonnet said, just a matter of time. Laure sat by the bed, because she felt she ought to do so, though she did not quite know why. For much of the time Mathilde kept her company; Laure suspected it was as much for her own sake as for her mother's.

'There wasn't a letter today then?' she asked quietly, observing Mathilde's anxious frown.

'No.'

Laure laid a hand over hers. 'You must remember, *minou* – he'd have written if he was still unhappy. I'm sure everything's fine again and he just hasn't had time to write.'

Mathilde smiled faintly, without conviction. Two weeks ago a letter from Joseph at school had overturned all her usual resigned calm. It had been a long letter, full of an undefined misery that was quite unlike his previous cheerful accounts of school life. Mathilde had thought at once of Frédéric's tales of his own early days at school, the bullying and fear from which Félix had saved him. Was his son suffering the same horrors now, unable to find words to describe them even to the mother who loved him so deeply? 'Oh, Maman, I want to come home. I hate it here; I'm so unhappy . . .' She had wept to read it, and expected Charles to hurry at once to rescue his beloved Joseph from school.

But Charles had only said, sympathetically but without alarm, 'I expect he's in trouble for some misbehaviour, otherwise he'd have said what was wrong. We'll write at once to console him. I imagine it will blow over in no time.'

But there had been no reply to their tenderly consoling letter. Frédéric would have brought him home at once, Mathilde thought accusingly. He would have understood. But she could not say it of course, though her manner towards Charles expressed her resentment. He only put it down to her anxiety for Joseph, and was especially kind to her.

After a moment, Laure said very gently, 'Mathilde *chérie* – try not to depend too much on Joseph, not for all your happiness. It is good for neither of you.'

516

'Did you not do that with me, when I was a child?'

Laure gave the matter a moment or two of careful consideration. 'Not quite as you do, no I don't think so. The vineyard meant a great deal to me too, and took more of my time than you did, I think – certainly it kept me awake more. And there was Jean-Claude – even though in the end I chose you.'

'But for me there is no Jean-Claude,' Mathilde reminded her. 'Only Charles, and he—' She broke off, biting her lip.

'I know, *minou*,' said Laure gently. 'But you have three other children.'

'And I love them, you know that.'

'Not as you love Joseph. I understand, *chérie* – I know your reasons, as no one else does. But for your sake you must be on your guard. It is painful enough to be a mother and feel every trouble of your child without binding yourself closer than nature ever meant you to be, so that when your child grows and wants his freedom then you cannot bear to allow him to separate himself from you – and if he does all the same, the pain is more than you can bear. That can be a terrible and destructive thing, and very dangerous to your happiness and Joseph's. Either he will be destroyed because he is never able to grow, or you will lose him altogether because that will be the only way he can free himself. You must learn to find happiness apart from him, before it is too late.'

Mathilde bent her head so that her mother could not see her face. 'How can I, as things are?'

Laure laid a hand over her daughter's. 'You are not always unhappy are you, *chérie* – even now, with Joseph away?'

'An absence of unhappiness is not the same thing as happiness, Maman.' The moment of passion between Mathilde and Charles that evening in Arcachon had not been the last; but it had not, sadly, brought an end to all the difficulties between them. Mathilde had tried very hard for a long time to show Charles the love that was his due, and he had seemed grateful for it. But the reserve she had sensed in him on that same memorable evening had not gone; on the contrary she sensed its presence again and again, and though she knew he tried to hide it, she never failed to be frightened by it. She had not realised until then how much she relied on Charles's love for her as the one small justification for the wrong she had done him. She could tell herself that he had gained something from their marriage, in spite of everything. But if he no longer loved her as he once had done, then that was not true any more. Charles was never anything but tender and loving towards her; but it was only in their occasional moments of mutual passion that she truly found reassurance; and they did not last.

Henri died early that evening, just before Charles returned.

'I'm so sorry I was not here,' he said warmly, taking Laure's hands in his. 'Did you send for the *curé*?'

Laure shook her head. 'I don't think Monsieur Séguier would have wanted that.'

But Charles insisted on a Catholic funeral and Laure let him have his way. Henri had never had any connection with the Church, but she could not feel that it mattered very much either way. Charles went next morning to see the new *curé*, Père Paviot, who was unlikely to refuse his request, in view of what he owed to Charles. Since the separation of Church and State the parish priest was no longer paid by the State but depended wholly on his congregation; which in Casseuil meant only a handful of people. It was fortunate for the *curé* that Charles was generous.

Laure would not be expected in the vineyard today. Everyone knew how Henri had been during the past years and no one would be surprised if she showed little sign of grief at his passing; but there were limits. So she resigned herself to staying quietly at home and leaving the arrangements to Charles. She sent Marius to tell Moïse to see that work continued as usual today (they could not afford any more delays) and after breakfast settled down in the *petit salon* to write to Marcel with the news.

Marius returned almost at once, in a state of considerable agitation. 'Madame – I regret – you should not be disturbed – but it seems—' His hands gestured wildly, expressing the failure of words to meet the situation.

'Calm yourself, Marius. What is wrong?'

'Monsieur Delmas, *madame*—'

'Which Monsieur Delmas?'

'Both, *madame* – Monsieur Moïse and Monsieur Lucien. Oh, this is so difficult! If only it had not happened now!' He paused, just long enough for her to hear beyond the shuttered window the sound of voices raised in argument somewhere across the courtyard; very angry voices. She stood up quickly and went to push open the shutters to look, Marius at her shoulder.

'Oh, *madame*, Monsieur Frangeas is there too now!'

And if something wasn't done soon they would all be at one another's throats – Laure had never seen the usually phlegmatic Moïse so enraged. 'I think I'd better go and investigate,' she said, ignoring Marius's protests.

The appearance of her black-clad figure silenced everyone at once, as if they remembered what an inappropriate moment this was for a quarrel. She looked from Pierre's sullen scowling countenance, to Moïse's; and then to Lucien's – where she stopped.

'What's happened to you?'

His right eye was sunk in a mass of purple red flesh, his swollen lip split and still oozing blood a little; the way he cradled one arm suggested further injuries.

It was Moïse who answered for him. 'It's this – this, *salaud*!' He jerked a furious thumb towards Pierre. 'Him and his brother – they lay in wait for my nephew last night and beat him up – see, see what they did!' He paused, suddenly recalling Laure's newly widowed state, and said uncomfortably, 'I'm sorry, *madame* – it's not the time, I know.'

'Never mind, Moïse – it can't be helped. Lucien, have you seen the doctor?'

'No, *madame*. It's not necessary,' said the boy, with difficulty because of his damaged lip.

'Nevertheless, you should. Moïse, will you go with him to Doctor Bonnet's at once? Refer any costs to me. As for you, Monsieur Frangeas, I'd like a word with you.'

Her new labourer denied nothing; in fact he seemed to feel that his behaviour had been entirely commendable in the circumstances. 'No one goes sneaking on me, no one!' he said. When Laure remonstrated with him, he was unpardonably rude to her, and she had no choice but to dismiss him at once. *That leaves me with three and a half workers, I suppose,* she thought ruefully. But perhaps better three and a half willing workers than half a dozen grudging ones. In any case, there was nothing she could do about it until the funeral was over.

The funeral on the following Monday was a muted affair, since to the community at large Henri had ceased to exist many years ago; most of his friends were dead and all of his relations. Laure even felt a little sad that there should be no one left at all to mourn him, though she made small pretence at doing so herself. She put on an appropriately solemn expression and dressed as a widow should, but that was all.

She was surprised to find how exhausted she felt at the end of the day, when at last she was free to relax in a chair in the quiet of the *grand salon*. Charles, who was as attentively concerned in his manner as if she had been the most devoted of wives grieving a loving husband, sat down near her.

'It is, I think, worse when there is nothing left to do,' he said. 'It is only then that one is able to realise fully what has happened.'

In which case, thought Laure ruefully, I should be jumping for joy. But she only said, 'I still have the appointment with the lawyer on Wednesday. He left me Trissac, you know.' She hoped that her very genuine astonishment at what the lawyer had told her at the funeral did not show on her face. Had Henri forgotten, long ago, to change his will? Had he simply had no one else to bequeath his property to? Or had he perhaps after all felt that she could be trusted to take good care of Trissac; or even that he owed her some compensation for all she had endured at his hands? She would never know.

Charles, of course, thought it all entirely proper. 'So I would have expected,' he said. 'It's a substantial property.'

So it was, Laure had to admit: forty hectares of land, and a beautiful house whose serene classicism should have made it the most delightful of living places. But she could never step into one of those light, exquisitely proportioned rooms without thinking of Henri, hearing his steps outside the door, feeling his presence. 'I think perhaps I shall sell it.'

'Oh no, that you must not do!' He sounded quite shocked. 'I know you do not need to live there – indeed, I hope you will never feel the need to do so. But the land will provide you with a very good income – you can always replace the steward, if you wish. It is in any case a bad time to sell, with land prices so low. As for the house, if you do not need it yourself, you may one day be glad to have something to pass on to your grandchildren.'

She knew he was simply being practical and was not offended, although on her other side Mathilde gave a disapproving exclamation. 'I shall see what the lawyer has to say, and then think about it.'

'Would you like me to drop you off in Bergerac on my way on Wednesday?'

'Oh, I'd forgotten you were going to Périgueux – yes, please.' That made her feel better at once, for she thoroughly enjoyed travelling in Charles's shiny new Panhard automobile. It amused her to observe how much Charles loved that noisy temperamental machine, in which he roared through the countryside scattering chickens and setting dogs barking. It was so at odds somehow with his staid and cautious personality, a reassuring sign that he was after all subject to common human vanities. 'Will you allow me to drive then?'

He grinned. 'A little, perhaps.'

Mathilde, who had still not overcome her fear of the new vehicle, shuddered. 'I wish you would go by train. Périgueux's such a long way.'

'Ah, but that wouldn't impress the Prefect so much,' Laure pointed out.

'What does he want to see you about anyway?'

'Various things; and I have one or two matters on which I need to consult him myself. I think too that in these unsettled times he likes to be reassured that all is well, at least in one corner of his jurisdiction.'

'Oh yes, that reminds me,' Laure put in. 'Aubin was telling me something the other day.' She reported Aubin's view of the Chabrys, and watched Charles frown a little.

'I cannot believe it,' he said at the end. 'These men are my own kinsfolk, by marriage if not by blood. I know them as well as I know myself. I know their beliefs and their aims, which are the same as my own, in every respect.'

'Come now, Charles, you must know that isn't true, whether you believe Aubin or not. I can't see Louis Chabry –

still less Eugène – being so conciliatory a mayor, or so popular a one.'

'I'm not sure that being conciliatory is a virtue. It sounds too like compromise.'

'Or peace-making, perhaps? There's nothing wrong with trying to encourage what unites everyone, instead of emphasising the divisions. Can you imagine Louis Chabry making a July 14th speech? He wouldn't try and appeal to everyone's patriotism and loyalty, or talk about the love we all share for our commune and its people. He would harangue us all with a catalogue of our sins against the Church and the Monarchy and probably urge us all to blame the Jews for everything. Am I not right?'

Charles hesitated for a moment before replying. 'There may be slight differences between us, but not fundamental ones, not of the kind Monsieur Lambert has suggested, of that I am sure. After all, we talk freely together whenever we meet.'

'Freely, as members of the same family, not as political allies. How often are you present at their meetings? Not so often since you became mayor. Perhaps you should ask them outright what they talk about when you're not there.' She knew he was becoming irritated – and trying very hard to suppress it, out of respect for her – and so she gently changed the subject.

Charles was right in one thing, she thought as she reached her bedroom that evening: only now, with the funeral over, was she really able to feel that Henri had gone. All these years come to an end at last, over, behind her—

She went to the window and pushed it open and leaned out, breathing in the sweet, soft evening air. Somewhere in the wood a nightingale was singing, the haunting sweetness of the sound emphasising the tranquillity that was seeping through her.

Soon, another realisation came to her: for the first time in her life she was wholly and completely independent. Trissac was hers, to do with exactly as she pleased. No one had the right to control or command her, or even advise her, if she did not wish them to do so. She had the means now to do anything she wanted – *anything*. She loved Casseuil, and all her hopes

522

and ambitions were centred on it and on the wine she had still not quite perfected; but it was not hers and never would be. Until now she had owned almost nothing of her own. Now, free of Henri, she was a woman of means, her own mistress at last. She did not want to change any part of her life, but she could do so now, at any time, if she chose. She felt so exhilarated by the sudden realisation that she almost burst into song, but realised just in time that it might sound more than a little shocking on the day of her husband's funeral.

'If you wish me to stay at home tonight, *madame*, I shall be happy to do so. They will understand, I am sure.'

'They' were the Chabrys, with whom Charles was engaged to dine tonight, by an arrangement made before he knew of Henri's death. He stood in the study, where he had come in search of Laure, holding her hand and looking gravely down at her. Laure herself was impatient to finish sorting Henri's papers – ready for tomorrow's visit to the lawyer – and was not in a mood to be tolerant of Charles's wholly unnecessary scruples.

'You know quite well that my objections to your drinking with the Chabrys have nothing to do with my widowed state,' she said briskly. 'They have never stopped you before, so I see no reason why they should now.'

Charles frowned, just a little, and then said very carefully, 'This is not the time to discuss such things, *madame*.'

'No, I agree.' She forced a smile. 'Go to your dinner, with a clear conscience – if you can.' Then she added, 'But I suggest you ask a few probing questions for once. You might be surprised by the answers you get.'

'I doubt it,' he returned, trying not to sound offended. Then he kissed her hand. 'I expect I shall be late. Good-night, *madame*.'

Laure had rarely felt so out of humour with Charles. She was glad to hear the door close behind him and the car drive away – though she could not resist the impulse that drew her to the window to watch its noisy and dramatic exit from the courtyard.

Once the papers had been put neatly ready for tomorrow she went upstairs, to tidy herself for dinner and to say good-night to the children. She looked first into Henri's room, where the windows had stood wide since the funeral, so that the soft summer air could drive out all the long lingering odours of the sickroom. She drew a deep slow breath: empty – the room was empty, free at last of Henri's presence. One day perhaps she would even be able to enter it without thinking of him. She closed the door again and went to brush her hair and pin it once more high on her head; and then she pushed open the door of the pretty little room which Marie-Françoise shared with Charlotte, when her older sister was not – as now – away at school. There was a little scuffling sound: a book being hastily closed and concealed beneath the pillow, Laure thought, with a smile. By the time she reached the bedside Marie-Françoise was lying very still with closed eyes trying to look as if she had been asleep for hours. Laure bent and kissed the soft cheek.

'Good-night, *ma chérie*.'

The deep blue eyes fluttered open, the child rubbed them slowly with her small hand, and yawned ostentatiously. Laure laughed.

'Poor little one – have I woken you?' The mocking tone was not lost on Marie-Françoise, who giggled and sat up and clasped her thin arms about Laure's neck.

'Good-night, Grand-mère.'

She was all skin and bone, at that awkward ungraceful age just before puberty, but charming still in her own way; more charming perhaps because at eleven a streak of mischief had begun to reveal itself, now that Charlotte was no longer there to overshadow her younger sister. Marie-Françoise was not after all so unvaryingly docile as Laure had always thought her.

'Are you sad, Grand-mère?' the child asked after a moment.

Startled, Laure sat down on the edge of the bed and looked at her. 'Sad, *ma petite*? Should I be?' Then, with a sense of horror, she remembered Henri. Of course she should be! And to show this child that she was not; worse, to put herself in a position where she might have to try and explain why she was not – that was unpardonable. She searched for some way out of the predicament; and then saw that Marie-Françoise was smiling triumphantly.

'I knew you weren't, Grand-mère. I'm not either; I'm glad!' And with that frank admission she seemed to regard the matter as closed, for she hugged and kissed her grandmother again and then snuggled down in the bed, ready for the nightly ritual of tucking in.

Laure – still a little shaken – found Mathilde and Philippe kneeling side by side on the floor by the boy's bed, while he said his prayers. 'And don't forget Joseph,' Mathilde was prompting him. 'Ask God to take great care of him.' She raised her eyes for a moment to look across at the achingly tidy bed at the other side of the room, where Joseph had not slept for so long.

'Yes, Maman.' Philippe bent his fair head more earnestly than ever over his folded hands and murmured a further prayer. An Ave, a Pater Noster, and then he crossed himself, kissed his mother, murmured, 'Good-night, Maman,' and climbed into bed. Inclined to be slow on the uptake, and rather humourless at times, Philippe was, Laure suspected, much like Charles must have been at his age; a nice enough little boy she supposed, in his way, if unexciting. But he was her grandson and she loved him, so she went to kiss him good-night all the same. Then she and Mathilde went down to dinner, and Laure carefully avoided the subject of Joseph and his absent letters, not wanting to make the effort to be sympathetic yet again. As a result, dinner was a largely silent meal and Mathilde ate very little; and then went almost at once to bed, pleading exhaustion.

Laure softened enough to say, 'Don't worry, *chérie*; I know he's all right,' before Mathilde left the room; though her words seemed to have no effect at all on her daughter.

I do know too, Laure thought, when she was left alone. Joseph's an open, confiding child. He'd have written at once if he was still unhappy. But that argument had already failed several times to convince Mathilde.

Laure sat on in the *grand salon* for an hour or two, reading contentedly and enjoying the consciousness – always there somewhere at the back of her mind – that the only responsibilities left to her now were entirely pleasurable ones. She was still downstairs when the car roared back into the courtyard, just before midnight.

Shortly afterwards Charles looked into the room. Laure laid down her book and stood up. 'Did you have a good evening?' she asked, a little guardedly.

She saw the answer before he gave it. He stepped further into the room, closing the door, and his expression was sombre in the extreme; even miserable, she thought.

'No,' he said abruptly. Then he came and sat down near her and she resumed her own seat, knowing he wanted to say more.

'You were right, *madame*,' he said at last. 'I have been blind. Perhaps I did not want to see.'

She had no need to ask him what he was talking about. 'Aubin was right then? I'm sorry.' As she was, in a way; although only because of Charles's evident distress. 'What happened?' she prompted gently, when he had been silent for some time, only staring gloomily down at his clasped hands.

He rose to his feet again and wandered restlessly about, occasionally pausing to look at her; he was frowning, and looked anxious and troubled. 'I do not like gossip – I try to pay no attention to it when it comes my way.'

'Aubin doesn't gossip as a rule – after all, if he did then I suppose we'd have heard the story before. But that's why I thought it was so important.' She saw that he was moving away again. 'I'm sorry, I interrupted you. Go on.'

'I did not repeat what I had heard. I tried to put it from my mind. Yet – all that was said seemed changed tonight, because of it – though there was nothing new, just the usual things. Until—' Abruptly he sat down again. 'You know of the *"Revue de l'Action Française"*, I suppose?'

It seemed such an irrelevant question that Laure was startled. 'Yes – yes, of course. It was started partly as a result of the Dreyfus business, wasn't it? Very right wing, Royalist, but not in your sense, I think. It is, unfortunately, intellectually acceptable in some quarters. Or so I've heard. I've never read it. But I don't understand—?'

'No. Nor did I. Louis Chabry takes it, and has for some time. I find now that Eugène has some close connection with the Paris group that is behind it. You know he is often in Paris?'

'I didn't, but it doesn't surprise me.'

'He had just returned today. He said little about his trip, except to express his disgust at the immorality of life in the capital – which of course is something of which I have no experience, though I fear he is probably right. After all, it is not peculiar to Paris . . . But I digress—' He drew a deep breath and went on, 'I think it was then I first had the impression that there was something not said, that Eugène had concerns and interests – even news of some kind – of which the others had some knowledge and expectation, and I did not. There were a good many others there, you see – men who have not been present when I have dined there before. I know they meet regularly together on Tuesday evenings, but I have rarely attended these meetings, having so many other duties to attend to. But they were very pressing that I should be there tonight; and so I went. You advised me to ask probing questions: I did not need to do so. It was only necessary for me to listen and to notice what had formerly escaped me. I think if you had said nothing to me, then I should have noticed nothing, and should not have stayed.'

'Stayed?'

'Yes. At dinner the talk was general, as it is so often when I am there – we deplore the corruption and irreligion of government, the decline of patriotism, the breaking down of the natural bonds which link man to man within society and the family – you know the kind of thing.' He smiled very faintly, and Laure nodded; then, grave again, he continued, 'But there were hints that this was not to be all, which I would not, I think, have noticed previously. Afterwards, there came a moment when it might have seemed natural for me to leave; but Eugène Chabry said, "Are you with us, *mon ami*?" I realised then that there was to be further talk, of a more private nature. Some of the party had left – the *curé* among them; one or two others had newly arrived. It has happened before, I realise that now, but I am not a man for late nights and I have never considered staying. Tonight I stayed.'

He was silent for so long then, his head bent, his fingers restlessly linked, that Laure wondered if he had realised that after all he could not tell her what he had learned. Perhaps, suddenly, it seemed too much of a betrayal.

'It was not what you imagined then?'

He looked up; the anxiety had cleared from his face, leaving an unusual degree of determination and even a spark of anger. 'I do not know what I imagined.' His tone had a crispness she had never heard in it before. 'What I found was a seditious gathering – I use the words advisedly, not lightly, as you have done on occasions. Eugène Chabry has returned from Paris with a mission, *madame*. His aim, and that of his friends, is to gather support for the cause in which he believes. That cause is not, after all, the one in which I believe. Oh yes, they are Royalist in sympathy, or so they claim. They seek an ordered society, based on religion, respect, proper authority, and above all a consuming love of France. So they see it at least. But what I had not known – no, what I had chosen not to know, not to hear, or to see (though how I could have failed to do so I do not understand, for it was always there, always) – that love of France, of order, of monarchy, is not love at all, but hatred; hatred for all that is not as they are: for Germans, yes, but also for very many they regard as aliens within France herself – for Jews, for Freemasons, for Socialists, for Republicans, even for Protestants – for everyone, in short, who does not think as they do. It is not simply intolerance that they preach, but violent action – action against these groups and against the government itself which, as they see it, embodies all that they most detest. They hope to build up their support into an organised network throughout France – above all, to mobilise the young in their cause: there were young men there tonight, eager to play a part. What kind of part that would be was only too clear – the story Monsieur Lambert told you is true in every respect, it seems. Louis-Albert himself was there; he boasted of the incident, unashamedly, holding it up as an example of what might be done – a small example, to be developed and enlarged upon. He was loudly applauded. I can only say that I was sickened almost beyond words to hear such talk, amongst men whom I regarded as my friends.'

'So you left them?'

He looked surprised, even a little shocked. 'Indeed no, *madame*! I say I was sickened almost beyond words – but not quite, I am glad to say.'

Her eyes widened. 'You mean you told them what you thought?'

528

'Of course. What else could I do?' He reddened a little, as if the recollection made him uncomfortable. 'At first they took it for a joke.' Laure, pitying him, imagined how unkindly they must have jeered at him; but not for long, it seemed. 'Then they realised I was in deadly earnest. Things became – a little heated.' He coloured more deeply still. 'I regret to say, I lost my temper.'

The thought of Charles so abandoning all constraint was so incongruous that Laure laughed aloud; and then instantly regretted doing so, and laid her hand gently over his. 'Forgive me, *mon cher* – it is only that I have never seen you angry, and cannot imagine it.'

'It was not amusing, not at all. There was a great deal said, on all sides, that should not have been said. We – some of the company, that is – came very close to blows.' Then a rueful light shone in his blue eyes. 'I think if I had not been so large a man, I might have had cause to fear – in particular when I told them that I should have to lay these matters before the Prefect, when I see him tomorrow.'

'You told them *that*?' Laure stared at him in an amazement tinged with admiration.

'Naturally. I would not do it in an underhand manner.'

'And will you make a report to the Prefect?'

'I must. There can be no question about it. I have a duty to do so.'

'But – your own friends—?'

'No longer, *madame*. We are linked distantly by ties of marriage, but that is all. So I told them, and so it must be from now on.' He leaned back in his chair, and the decisive, angry air fell away from him, leaving him looking suddenly completely dejected. 'I hope I do not have to live through such an evening ever again,' he said with feeling.

There was still no letter from Joseph. By the next morning Mathilde was almost beside herself with anxiety. Laure, feeling more than a little impatient with her daughter, was glad to set out early for Bergerac, and soon forgot Mathilde's troubles in the sheer delight of being allowed to drive the Panhard.

Mathilde, unable to settle to anything, sought out Nanon's company, desperate for any distraction. But Nanon's attempts to soothe her did not help at all. How could they, when she knew Joseph was in trouble and no one else would even acknowledge the possibility? What, she thought, if he should run away and come to some harm – or try to kill himself? He was only fourteen, but it was not unknown, even in one so young.

Wanting activity and voices around her, she took Marie-Françoise and Philippe into the vineyard when their morning lessons with their tutor were over (Charlotte was at boarding school now, like Joseph). But somehow the children could not distract her either. They ran in circles round her, laughing and chasing one another until she cried out in exasperation, at which they ran off among the vines. She did not call them back, but wandered on by herself along the track.

She knew she wanted Joseph to come home; and not just because he was unhappy. He was everything to her, her world, her reason for living. No matter how much she loved the other three, they could never mean to her what Joseph did, because he alone was the son of the only man she had ever loved. When he was away, she felt as if she were only half alive; she counted the days until he could be home again. And to endure his absence knowing that he too was desperately unhappy – that was an agony beyond words.

Oh, Frédéric *chéri*, you would not have let it happen – oh, where are you now, where are you? Why don't you come back? It could not hurt as much as this does. She began to cry softly and miserably.

She was aware as if from a long way off that a voice called, but she walked on. It was a moment or two before she realised that the call was being repeated fiercely, urgently; had become almost a scream. 'Maman!'

She looked round. Philippe was running towards her through the vines, his face chalk white. He came nearer, the words tumbling out incoherently, but she understood enough to go with him back towards the *caveau*.

'Someone's smashed it all up – we called, but you didn't come. Marie-Françoise climbed on a stone to see, and it fell.'

The solid stones of the *caveau*, loosened in places by some ferocious premeditated attack, had indeed given way. Beneath the defaced headstone the blocks were broken and scattered; and among them lay Marie-Françoise, white and still with a smear of blood on her forehead.

'Go and fetch Monsieur Delmas – *quickly*!' Mathilde knelt by the child, feeling for a pulse, although she was not quite sure where to find one. 'Oh *chérie*, wake up – please wake up!'

It seemed hours before Moïse came. He glanced quickly over the scene and then knelt down too.

'Is she alive?'

He nodded. 'She's alive. Let's get her to the house. Monsieur Philippe, can you run for Doctor Bonnet, there's a good lad?'

Philippe ran off and Moïse lifted Marie-Françoise into his arms: she was light for her eleven years.

They carried her to her room and laid her on her bed, and Mathilde, in a kind of daze, thanked Moïse and tried to explain to a distraught Nanon what had happened; and wished the doctor would come; and thought all the time, It's my fault – Maman was right, I was thinking only of Joseph – I didn't take care.

Marie-Françoise was still unconscious when the doctor came. He examined her thoroughly and then looked very grave. 'Is Monsieur de Miremont at home, *madame*?'

Mathilde felt cold, terribly cold. 'No, he won't be back until tomorrow. Oh, is it bad? Tell me!'

The doctor patted her hand. 'She's had a severe blow to the head; she may well be unconscious for some time yet – for many hours perhaps. But there's little visible damage. Let us hope—' She knew what he hoped; it was what was unsaid, the thing he feared, that chilled her through and through.

'You have the telephone. Could Monsieur de Miremont be contacted that way?' He saw the look on her face and added quickly, 'To give you support, that's all.' But she did not believe that was all.

They did telephone and Charles, who had only just reached Périgueux, agreed to return at once. It would still be a long time before he was home. Even Laure could not be back for a while yet, though they sent the trap to meet her; but in a way that was a relief because Mathilde did not really want to see her. She held her daughter's hand and gazed at the quiet still face, watching achingly for any sign of life. She refused to eat or to give up her place to Nanon.

What have I done? she thought. Why can I never learn? Always, always another wrong to pile on the first terrible deceit – and now Marie-Françoise is to pay for my neglect. I did not love her enough, because she is only Charles's daughter.

When Laure came home Mathilde shook off her attempt at consolation, and Laure, a little hurt, went to occupy herself with more practical matters. She examined the broken *caveau*, questioned Moïse and Lucien, and very soon reached her own conclusions.

It was well after midnight when Charles returned, but Mathilde had not gone to bed.

'I am sorry, *chérie*, I had trouble with the car.'

She turned; and ran sobbing into his arms. 'Oh Charles, it was all my fault!'

He held her, rocked her, a great comforting embrace, something safe and dependable in a suddenly frightening world; hearing, and not judging. 'Gently, *ma chérie*, gently. Don't blame yourself.'

'But if it had not been for me – and now I'm punished for my neglect—'

'Hush, never say that – suffering is not a punishment, it is not God's will, not ever – only something we can use with his help, and learn from. Now, quiet, *chérie*, and tell me what the doctor said.'

They sat down side by side, though her hands clasped the sleeve of his coat as if she was afraid he might go away again. He heard her in silence, his face grave but tender; and then he said, 'We must wait patiently, and pray. We can help each other.'

It did help her to have him there, sharing her vigil, holding her and soothing her. When, from time to time, he knelt to pray she did not feel irritated or amused, but only hoped that somehow the faith that sustained him would work some miracle that was beyond her, with her hopelessness and her guilt.

*

The doctor came again in the morning, and concealed nothing from Charles, telling him all that he had kept from Mathilde, to spare her. Marie-Françoise might wake suddenly, restored to her old self at once, whole and uninjured; but the longer she lay unconscious the more likely it became that there was some deeper damage, that her mind might be clouded and her limbs affected; that she might never wake again.

The hours dragged interminably. Mathilde would not leave the bedside, and Charles refused to leave her. Laure filled the time as best she could, smothering anxiety in activity. There was one constructive result of that, which she was able to communicate to Charles and Mathilde when she looked in at dinner-time.

'I think I know who was responsible for the damage to the *caveau*,' she said. 'In fact the whole village seems to know. I'm told the Delmas family were out in force all yesterday looking for the Frangeas brothers – but, wisely perhaps, they were lying low: Moïse thinks they've gone for good. But it seems that everyone heard them swearing revenge the night the *caveau* was damaged – both for Pierre's dismissal and for what his brother called "*Monsieur le maire*'s defamation of the character of Monsieur Eugène Chabry". He must have heard of your break with them somehow.'

'Yes,' said Charles grimly. 'He was there.' He turned to draw Mathilde into his arms. 'You see, *ma chérie*, we are all responsible for what happened, one way and another.'

She smiled weakly up at him and laid her head on his shoulder; it looked as though she might sleep at last after more than twenty-four hours of anxious watching. Laure softly left the room.

It was much later and fully dark when Charles shook her abruptly awake. 'Look, Mathilde.'

She looked; and saw that Marie-Françoise's eyes, clear and blue, were resting on her father's face. The child moved her head, moaned a little, and managed a faint smile. 'Papa—' she said.

Mathilde began very quietly to weep. Charles went to put his arms about the child, kissing her and stroking her hair. Through her tears Mathilde watched him and knew that for the first time in their married life she was glad he was there.

*

The next day there was a letter from Joseph, matter-of-fact and cheerful and saying not a word about his former misery, beyond a passing reference to a temporary disagreement with his best friend.

'There, you see,' said Charles to Mathilde. 'Did I not tell you there was nothing wrong? It's an excellent school. I knew there was no reason why he should be unhappy. Don't you think that if I'd seriously believed there was anything wrong I would have gone at once to bring him home? I love him too, you know.'

There was nothing she could say to that.

CHAPTER
TWENTY EIGHT

i

'Come on, *mon caporal*, let's see you.' Charlotte turned her brother round so that she could examine the brand new stripes on his sleeves. 'Oh, how handsome you look, Joseph!'

She's quite right, thought Laure, gazing fondly at the elegant figure of her grandson. On some men the infantry-man's tight-fitting blue tunic and full red trousers looked unflatteringly bulky; but Joseph's tall slim figure set them off to their greatest advantage, aided by the high polish of his boots and the jaunty (and not quite regulation) angle at which the blue and red *képi* sat on his dark curls. He looked absurdly young still, much less than his twenty-one years, for all his considerable height and the narrow black line of the mous-tache above his sensitive mouth.

Joseph in his turn regarded his sister; tall and fair like their mother, she looked up at him from the combined shade of a wide plumed hat and a frilled parasol, her eyes very bright and blue. 'Now, let me look at you,' her brother said. 'A new dress, is it not? Very pretty too – is it *mousseline de soie*?' He fingered the soft white folds, with their trimming of blue ribbon. 'As for you yourself, you look radiant, *ma chère*. Did I not say marriage suited you?'

She stood on tiptoe to whisper something in his ear; and in response he laughed and hugged her. 'Oh, that's wonderful! So I shall be an uncle!' He reached across to shake the hand of Charlotte's husband of five months. 'I am so glad for you both.'

'Ah, but today the congratulations must be for you,' said Samuel Bonnet: son of their own Doctor Bonnet, and now his father's partner, his courtesy and intelligence and obvious devotion to Charlotte had in the end overcome Charles's

535

considerable reservations about his Protestant beliefs. 'Only eight months in the army, and already a corporal – that's quite something, is it not?'

Joseph shrugged modestly. 'Not in the least, *mon ami*.'

Charles, his face full of tender pride, ignored the disclaimer and embraced the young man. 'Well done, *mon fils*.'

They had arranged to meet Joseph after mass in the Square des Mobiles in Bergerac, where, shaded by the elms of the Jardin Public, a statue commemorated the Gardes Mobiles of the Dordogne killed in the Franco-Prussian war. As they waited – Joseph had been a little late – Laure had studied the familiar carved figure of the young soldier brandishing a rifle and thought back to those eventful anxious months of 1870 when her whole world had changed. Forty-four years ago – so long, that no one of those around her could remember them, for even Charles had been little more than a baby. France, crushed and humiliated, had after all risen triumphantly from that terrible defeat; not to wreak the long-talked-of revenge on Germany (strange, how that was hardly mentioned nowadays), but to bring her people decades of peace and prosperity. For Laure too, all that turmoil had resolved itself at last into this July Sunday, full of the promise of simple pleasures in the company of those she loved, and of Joseph in particular – who was her future, and her hope.

Even now that he was doing his military service they met often, for he had resisted all Charles's suggestions that he should join a more prestigious branch of the army – the dragoons or the light cavalry, perhaps; his godfather the General would put in a word for him – and had been happy to be assigned to the infantry regiment in Bergerac. 'Now I can come home as often as possible,' he had said; and had done exactly that, whenever he had leave. Today, though, Charles had suggested a picnic, and so they were meeting here – all except Philippe, who was away at school.

They set out – with much laughter and singing – along the Périgueux road, Laure driving Mathilde in the Panhard, Charlotte and Marie-Françoise rather cramped in the de Dion Bouton driven by Samuel; Charles and Joseph following on their bicycles. All the way passers-by turned their heads to stare at the noisy happy procession of vehicles; until, a few kilometres beyond the town, they reached the still heat of a wood and turned to the right along a shaded track to park close to a glade.

There, on the fragrant grass and lichen of the forest floor, they spread a tablecloth, scattered cushions, opened folding stools and carried plates and glasses from the cars; and then wine, red and white (in an ice bucket); and hampers packed with pâté, chickens, salads, bread, cheese, strawberries, peaches, some exquisite pâtisserie and a good deal else. Joseph threw off his képi and tunic and flung himself down on the grass in his shirt sleeves, with a great sigh of contentment. 'Now, this is better than the barracks!'

Laure, perched on her stool where the shade was deepest, watched them all; and felt a sudden longing to paint that idyllic scene – except that her small talent could never do justice to it. Marcel now – or better still, Jean-Claude (she thought of him with more nostalgia than pain) – he would have been well able to capture the play of sunlight and shadow on the glade, to convey exactly the quality of the light and the heavy incense-like sweetness of the midday heat, the varied greens of the foliage that filtered the sun – pale feathery acacia, the brilliant gold-green of oak, the long shining leaves of chestnut – and the subtle silvery green and grey and brown tones of the lichened trunks.

Held within that natural enclosure, where the cars and all the trappings of modern life were hidden from view, there he would have caught the patterned movement of the happy picnickers; the flesh tones of faces and hands shining in the gentle woodland light, the soft pastel shades of the girls' dresses, and Mathilde's pink-ribboned grey, falling in drifts of silk and muslin over the bright grass, their hazy folds emphasised by sharply defined blocks of darkness and colour: the sober Sunday suits of Charles and Samuel; the jewel-like glow of Joseph's red trousers and discarded blue jacket.

Here and there, one detail echoed another: the folded parasols laid aside; the decorations on the ladies' hats – blue plumes, a cluster of pink roses, loops of green satin ribbon – the sheen of golden hair, or black, or Samuel's bright chestnut; the inviting earth tones of the food on the tablecloth, all browns and reds and greens and golds. And above it all, where the light slanted through the trees, full of dancing atoms of golden dust, a dragonfly darted suddenly, dazzlingly blue, and then was gone. Oh yes, it asked for Jean-Claude's eye for colour, his vitality and optimism.

'Wine, Grand-mère?' Joseph was reaching towards her with a bottle of one of their own lesser vintages in his hand. She took a glass and held it while he poured. 'What were you dreaming of there?'

'Oh, I was thinking what a fine painting you would all make.'

He laughed. 'Then you must put Louis-Christophe's *pâté aux truffes* right in the centre – that is a work of art in its own right!' He kissed his fingers towards the pâté and then reached for the dish and a knife. 'Let me help you to some, Grand-mère. You wouldn't believe how often I dream of it!'

'Poor hard-done-by soldiers, starving in your barracks!'

'You can mock, Charlotte – can you imagine, after hours of drill and polishing your kit and performing endless boring and strenuous and wholly pointless exercises, coming in to some uninspiring stew – all right perhaps for those who have never known Louis-Christophe's *pâté aux truffes*, but for me—! Just imagine!'

'What suffering! Poor Joseph – my heart weeps for you! And I don't believe a word of it. Aren't you always out on manoeuvres, playing at mock battles like a lot of silly schoolboys?'

'Not quite always, alas – but yes, that I do enjoy, I must admit.'

'What exactly do you do on manoeuvres?' Marie-Françoise asked. 'Do you use real weapons?'

'Oh yes. We charge the enemy and vanquish him at the points of our bayonets.' He gestured ferociously with his knife. 'But then afterwards we set up camp in some pleasant field and cook our meals out in the open – food always tastes better out of doors, you must admit. As you say, Charlotte, it's much like being boys again.'

'Do the smaller boys end up as Germans or Englishmen then, like in the playground?'

'Of course not – we're all Frenchmen!' He poured wine for his sisters and for himself.

'*Ma chérie*, England is an ally now – do you forget that?'

Charlotte smiled at her husband. 'Of course not – but I don't imagine anyone takes all these war-like antics very seriously – do you, Joseph?'

'Then they should,' Samuel put in before Joseph could reply. 'When one looks at the massive build-up of military forces all over Europe – and especially in Germany – one can no longer believe that war is unlikely.' The sober tone of his remark threw a momentary little chill over the company. Charles intervened quickly to counter it.

'I think it is less true than it was, *mon cher* Samuel. We have built up a good network of allies – Russia, Italy, Britain. And since three year military service came in our army is at last being brought up to strength.'

'I doubt if poor Joseph appreciates that,' Samuel observed with a wry smile at his brother-in-law; but Joseph was too absorbed in his enjoyment of the pâté to do more than smile in return.

'One has to accept what is in the interests of France,' said Charles austerely. 'The balance between our forces and those of Germany is now about equal; that is the best possible protection against war.'

'Things don't look so settled in the Balkans since the assassination.'

'What assassination is that?' asked Marie-Françoise, as she heaped her plate with salad.

'Don't you read the papers? A future soldier's wife should be well informed, you know.' Marie-Françoise pulled a face. She had recently become informally engaged to the brother of a schoolfriend, Nicolas de Presnoy, about to begin his training as an officer at St Cyr, the élite military college near Paris; they could not, of course, consider marriage for a long time yet.

Samuel shook his head teasingly. 'The papers have been full of it, you know. It must be about two weeks ago now – the Archduke Franz Ferdinand of Austria and his wife were assassinated at some little place in the Balkans – Sarajevo, in Serbia.'

'Oh. Is that bad? Well, it is for the poor Archduke, I can see that. But for us, I mean?'

'It's the way things have always been in the Balkans,' said Charles soothingly. 'It has been a trouble spot for years. I have no doubt there will be bad relations between Serbia and Austria for some time to come, but it is all a very long way from France. After all, apart from a few extremists like Eugène Chabry, we all want peace. In fact, in my opinion the present government is if anything too ready for peace at any price – they're almost as bad as the Socialists.'

'I think this is one time when we should banish politics altogether,' Laure broke in. 'If we go on like this you'll be discussing the income tax proposals next, and then we shall all have indigestion. Joseph, will you be able to come to Casseuil on Tuesday?'

Her grandson looked regretful. 'I'm afraid not. I have to take part in our own parade. It's a pity you can't all come to that – though I suppose then Casseuil might be deprived of Papa's speech, and that would never do – July 14th wouldn't be the same without it.' He exchanged an affectionate glance with Charles. 'I had that from Paul Lambert, you know . . . Oh, you must tell Monsieur Lambert when you see him – I'm now in Paul's section; he's my sergeant.'

'Really?' Laure's smile was rueful. 'That will please Monsieur Lambert – in fact perhaps we should try and keep it quiet or we'll never hear the end of it. But doesn't he finish his service this autumn?'

'No – he got caught by the three year law. He'll finish in 1915 now.'

'And you not until 1916.' Laure sighed. 'I shall be almost seventy before you come home. I had hoped to see you take over from me before then.'

'Take over from you! You'll never give up, Grand-mère – not to anyone. But don't you think I'm just as eager to be back at Casseuil? After all, it's what I've always wanted to do, ever since I first toddled into the *chai* at your heels. As a matter of fact, I've been thinking about it a great deal lately.'

Something in his tone caught her attention. 'Oh?'

'You remember you once said that these days a *vigneron* has to be something of a scientist, if he's going to keep up with all the developments?'

'Perhaps; but instinct and skill and experience still count for most in the end.'

'Of course. But don't you think it would be good for Casseuil if you had someone with a scientific training to work alongside you? I mean a really thorough training in viticulture or some related subject. There are several places where one can undertake such studies.'

Laure looked down at his eager face and the bright dark eyes gazing so earnestly up into her own. 'You mean you think of going on to University?'

'Better still, to somewhere like the École Nationale Supérieure at Montpellier – that is *the* place for wine studies of every kind. I have begun reading around the subject as much as possible already. Time hangs heavy sometimes, and it's a good way to fill those idle moments.'

'How long would it all take?'

'Supposing I could gain admission to Montpellier on leaving the army – and it's by no means certain, of course – that would be another two years, more probably three. By 1919 I could be back at Casseuil for good.' He glanced at his mother, who had made a dismayed murmuring sound. 'It's a long time, I know; but in the end it would be worth it, I am sure.'

'Except,' said Laure mournfully, 'that I shall be seventy-one by then – if I live so long, that is.'

'You will!' he told her confidently. 'Of course, I should spend all the vacations at Casseuil. In the end I'd be much more use to you – truly, I'm sure that's right.'

'It does make sense,' put in Samuel. 'In fact it sounds an excellent idea to me.' Charles too nodded approvingly.

'You're always saying that a *vigneron* must constantly look to the future, Grand-mère.'

'Yes, and plan and act as if he would live for ever. And have patience to wait and wait – I know. But—' Laure stopped. She would not say it – that she would not live for ever, that she had waited so long already for the crowning moment of her life when this charming young grandson of hers would be working at her side, sharing her enthusiasm and her hopes.

541

After all, he did share them in full, for why otherwise would he think to commit himself to future years of study? Like her, he wanted the very best for Casseuil; like her, he was prepared to look forward, to plan for a distant and better future, whatever present inconveniences he might have to endure. Courage and trust and patience had brought her through so much already; they must carry on just a little longer.

'I think it is a good plan, Joseph,' she said at last, steadily and with approval. 'After all, old age has one great advantage over youth – time passes so very much more quickly. Five years – that's nothing!'

'And I shall be at Casseuil whenever I can. If the autumn manoeuvres don't clash with the *vendange* this year, I intend to negotiate for some leave then. That's if things don't suddenly become very difficult under our new Colonel – you know what they say about the fervour of a newcomer.'

'What's he like?' Charles asked.

'He hasn't arrived yet. Colonel Aurousseau doesn't officially retire until the end of the month. But I shall start working on everyone as soon as I've sized up the new situation.'

Laure laughed. 'You'll probably succeed too.' Joseph had the ability to charm anything out of anyone, as she knew full well. He was, perhaps, still a little spoiled; but experience of life and his own warm and generous nature would remedy that in time, she was sure. Sometimes she wondered if any love of any kind between a man and a woman had ever brought as much joy as did the loving companionship that bound her to her grandson. She could even accept with equanimity the possibility that it might be Joseph and not herself who would eventually nurture into life the great Casseuil wine she had sought for so long.

'Never mind the *vendange*,' said Marie-Françoise. 'I heard from Nicolas this morning – he's coming to Casseuil to stay, and Agnès is coming with him – you know she said she'd like to meet you again.' Her dear friend Agnès had been very taken with Joseph at their only previous meeting. 'We must arrange something – try and get leave for three weeks today, the first Sunday in August.'

'I'll see what I can do. We shall have to plan another picnic. Why don't we take a boat on the river for a change?'

They began, enthusiastically, to discuss the possibility.

ii

There was no picnic on that first Sunday in August, because all leave had been cancelled some days before and the de Presnoys abandoned their plans to come to Casseuil. On the Saturday, notices appeared on every public building, white posters headed with crossed tricolour flags, announcing a general mobilisation; and each man of military age received his instructions.

Four days later Mathilde stood with Charles and Laure and Marie-Françoise and Philippe at the edge of the field that served as a parade ground for the regiment; and felt as if her heart was being torn from her body.

Overhead, a grey sky mocked the cheerful surface of the scene: the grass browned by summer and marching feet, the regimental colours swaying at the head of the weaving columns of men in their bright red and blue; the officers' gleaming horses stamping their hooves and tossing their heads; old Colonel Aurousseau – snatched back from the briefest taste of retirement – seated motionless and proud on a shining chestnut stallion to review his troops; the band – drumsticks flying, bugles glistening and sparkling as the men marched – playing music that was joyous and martial and triumphant, heart-breakingly so to the ears of so many in the watching crowd. They looked on in a concentrated silence, broken only now and then by a suppressed sob – a mother's cry, thought Mathilde; and wished she too could weep. But she felt frozen right through, except for the anguish at her heart.

She was aware of Charles's arm moving about her shoulder, as if he understood and wanted her to know that he shared her feelings; which of course he did not and never could. She stared and stared, but she was not even able to make out Joseph in all those changing patterns of marching men. It was a nightmare, come on them suddenly, appallingly, from a clear sky. 'It will be over soon', they all said; but she could only wish that she might wake up and find that it had not happened at all.

On her other side, Laure's hand closed about hers, squeezing it tight. Mathilde looked round and caught a faint smile on her mother's face; but there were tears brimming in her eyes. 'Just a few weeks and they'll be home,' Laure murmured. At that moment she had a horrible feeling that she was reliving the past. The suddenness of it all, the coming of war from nothing, so unexpectedly; the assurance that it would soon be over: it had been like that in Paris in the summer of 1870.

The next morning at the station where they went to see Joseph on his way the feeling of repetition was intensified. There were the weeping wives and mothers and sweethearts clinging to the departing soldiers; the slogans – '*À Berlin*!' – scrawled on the carriages; the garlands and flags; the crowds singing the 'Marseillaise'.

But it was not quite the same. This time no one in France had wanted the war. Certainly no one had sought it, hoping until the very last moment to keep it at bay, until German troops simultaneously marched into neutral Luxembourg and stepped over the French border near Belfort; and the Kaiser declared war. Then they knew they no longer had any choice but to fight. This time there was no jubilation, no wild cheering, only a quiet sense of purpose and determination; and a unity Laure did not remember from before, when the war fever of Paris had found no echo in the countryside. Suddenly it seemed as if there were no longer any political or religious differences, no Catholics or Protestants, Jews, Unbelievers, Republicans, Socialists or Royalists, but only French men and women, united against the invader.

The greatest difference of all for her was that this time it touched her most nearly, right from the beginning, as it touched almost everyone. Joseph was going, and the Lambert boys, and Samuel Bonnet and Louis Chabry's sons, and Robert Martin's sons and grandson, and the *curé* and the schoolmaster's son and Monsieur Meynel from Trissac and Lucien Delmas and Marius and Louis-Christophe – all the men from the commune of Casseuil who were not too old or too young, too infirm or reserved for some other occupation;

more than a hundred in all. From every part of France trains were carrying the soldiers north and east to confront the advancing German armies; just as this train now carried Joseph and his comrades away from Bergerac to an unknown destination.

Laure stood fixed to the spot and watched the departing train puffing and rattling on its way, and the forest of waving hands and handkerchiefs that impeded her view. She felt sad, her throat constricted with emotion, and anxiety stirred the surface of her mind; but it did not go very deep. Joseph was her future, the whole purpose for which she had struggled so long. Casseuil needed him; and soon – she had no doubt – he would come safely home.

A faint moan beside her broke into her thoughts. She looked round and saw that Mathilde, white-faced, had fallen against Charles, who was struggling to support her. 'She's ill – help me! Oh, she should not have come! I was afraid it would be too much!'

They half-carried her to the car, while Laure tried to reassure Charles, who was almost beside himself with anxiety. It was not until they had lain Mathilde on the seat and rubbed her hands, and seen her open her eyes and slowly sit up, that Charles became to the slightest degree calmer. Then Mathilde began to weep and it seemed as if she would never stop; and it was Laure who had to drive them home, since Charles could not be persuaded to give his attention to anything but his wife. 'She'll be better once she's lying down in bed,' said Laure sensibly.

Mathilde wept all the way to Casseuil, whilst Charles held her hand and Laure repeated soothingly again and again, 'Just a few weeks, that's all – then he'll be home.'

But all the time she heard the mocking reminder that so they had said in 1870, only to be proved so bitterly wrong. That war had lasted almost a year, to end in the bloody civil battles of the Commune; but it was different this time, quite different – it must be different.

They saw very little of Charles during the following days. When he was not in his office working his way laboriously through the mounds of official directives which the postman brought daily to the *mairie*, or explaining to anxious enquirers how some new regulation applied to them, he was occupied with the requisitioning of horses and vehicles, or making frequent journeys to Bergerac for consultations with the Sub Prefect.

Out in the heat of those early August days the horses of the commune – from Charles's own Barbarossa to the Vergnolles' curiously-put-together nag – were lined up in the market place and then led away in a sad procession to the station. Mathilde, whose own gentle mare had gone too, wept once again and hoped that the poor creature would be treated kindly. She was calmer now, on the whole, but still pale, and constantly weary from sleeplessness.

'We're all going to have to manage somehow, until the war's over,' said Laure. 'Let's hope the men are back for the *vendange* – it's going to be very difficult with only ourselves and Moïse.'

Nanon, like a restored monarch, resumed her old position in the kitchen. Françoise gave notice and left for a more lucrative post in the chemical factory in Bergerac, where, in the absence of so many men, they were suddenly crying out for female labour. But on the whole life indoors continued with little inconvenience.

Outside it was another matter, for though Jean-Marc Delmas, on holiday from school, came to give them temporary help, Moïse was by now too old and infirm for the heaviest work, and rather slow whatever he did. It will be like the old days, Laure thought ruefully; except that then, of course, she had not had to manage twenty hectares of flourishing vines and Trissac's huge tobacco fields. The only positive aspect of the matter was that Mathilde would have plenty to occupy her, to keep her from brooding until Joseph was safely back in Bergerac.

On the day when the horses departed, one of the newspapers printed a map of the north-eastern area of France, which Charles duly pinned up in the hall for them all to see. They made little flags – blue for the French army, black for the German, red for the tiny British expeditionary force at present aiding the Belgians in their gallant fight against the enemy now invading their territory – and pinned them to mark the front lines of the opposing forces; or what they supposed to be the front lines from the rather uninformative newspaper reports.

'Well, we have our first victory to record,' said Charles happily that morning. 'Mulhouse is liberated – Alsace is French again.' Triumphantly he set the blue flags marching across that debated land.

Laure was more cautious. 'Mulhouse is only one town,' she pointed out.

'By now they may well have taken Strasbourg too.'

He was singing quietly to himself as he left the house, for yet another meeting in Bergerac. Amused, Laure realised that the tune was the 'Marseillaise'; he had never until now brought himself to sing it, even on Bastille day.

The happiness had left his face by the time he came home for lunch. Laure, in the *petit salon*, watched him cycle into the courtyard, noting the gravely pensive expression; and then remembered with a little tremor of anxiety that he had set out this morning in the car.

'What's happened to the Panhard?' she asked, coming out to him as he crossed the hall.

'I decided that the army needs it more than I do,' he said, almost brusquely, and made his way upstairs. Perhaps only Laure knew how great a sacrifice he had made that day.

iii

'Fancy a bit of shooting, *caporal*?' Sergeant Lambert aimed his rifle at a squirrel glimpsed distantly fleeing over the tree tops away from the troops crashing through the forest; and then let it fall again.

Joseph laughed. 'It might liven the war up a bit.'

'You'll have shooting enough in time,' Second Lieutenant Mercier, overhearing, assured them.

'My feet will be worn out by then,' grumbled Private Baudry beside Joseph; who thought he had a point.

They had been marching now for two long hot weeks, ever since it was realised (so Paul Lambert claimed) that the small German advance across the eastern borders of France had been only a diversion. 'They're marching into France through Belgium,' Paul had said. 'We'll have to cut them off there.' So they had followed the line of the river Meuse from near Verdun (where the train had left them) to the Belgian border. Yesterday they had crossed from the hilly, densely forested countryside of France to the almost indistinguishable forest of the Belgian Ardennes; a foreign land. Joseph had sensed a stir of excitement amongst the men of his squad, which he had shared.

It had soon faded. Weighed down in the fiercest summer heat by a heavy blue greatcoat and a pack crammed with all the articles regarded (by someone who had never had to carry them all at one time, Joseph assumed) as essential for the soldier on the march – not to mention a rifle and its necessary ammunition – every one of the weary men was rapidly losing his early enthusiasm for the promised action. Besides, they had none of them so much as glimpsed a German soldier.

Even here in the forest it was stiflingly hot. Joseph tried not to think of the now long-absent pleasures of a bath, or cool light clothes, or swimming in the soft green waters of the pool at Casseuil. He had not even had time to shave this morning before they set out again; he fingered his stubbly chin and reflected ruefully that he would very soon (like the rest of his fellows) justify the nickname *poilu* (it meant 'hairy') given to the ordinary French foot soldier. It seemed a very long time since the breakfast of bread and coffee eaten in haste as the first dawn light crept into the forest; he realised he was hungry, almost as hungry as he was thirsty. He reached for his water bottle and drank – when he left home it had been filled with wine, but now that had all gone.

'Something's up,' said Paul, glancing ahead. Joseph looked too, aware that the by now rather half-hearted singing (it had been enthusiastic during the first days) had become merely intermittent, and even stopped altogether in places, while a murmuring ripple of excitement was making its way back towards them through the columns of men.

'I'll go and see,' said Paul, and his short, fair figure disappeared from view. He reappeared very soon. 'The cavalry's spotted them,' he reported, his eyes very bright.

'The Boches?' That was Baudry again.

'That's right, at some place called Nevraumont – Uhlans and infantry, on the way from Neufchâteau to Bertrix.' He spoke with the knowledgeable air of one wholly familiar with the geography of this foreign land, although Joseph was quite sure he had never heard of the places until now. 'We'll see some action at last.'

Joseph felt a curious sensation in the pit of his stomach and all at once it was not too hot any more, but cold, so that he shivered, momentarily but quite distinctly. His skin felt alive, as if little insects were running all over it. Excitement, he thought; but he knew that in part at least it was fear. He glanced furtively at the men near him and saw something very similar reflected on their faces. They looked both grave and bright-eyed, and very alert, as if every nerve was tensed. They marched with a new firmness, in a silence broken only by an occasional low-voiced exchange, a brief burst of laughter, a breathy whistle, quickly ended.

The final hour of that morning's march passed for Joseph in a blur shot through with occasional images of unusual clarity. He was, above all, acutely conscious of his companions, in particular the sixteen men who, like him, were marching to battle; who shared so many of his feelings and yet were full of emotions and sensations and experiences that he could only guess at; and whom he was to lead. He felt at once both very young and full of an invigorating sense of responsibility. He caught Paul's eye and grinned, warmed by a new sense of comradeship. They had always got on well, but this was different, a unique bond peculiar to this day and this moment and the thing that waited for them both out in the midday heat beyond the forest.

The village of Nevraumont, approached through a wood straddling a small river, greeted them with a scattering of shots. Confusedly, Joseph was aware of orders being shouted, somewhere ahead, coming swiftly his way. About him, men halted, shuffled and stumbled uncertainly, stared about. 'Get into line!' – Paul's voice, commanding. Following not conscious choice, but some reflex ingrained by months of training, Joseph took up the order and passed it on to his squad.

In moments the disordered columns had resolved themselves into orderly ranks, drawn up with all the precision of the final review at Bergerac. There was an instant of calm – no,

549

not calm, rather of waiting, alert and in readiness. Company commanders, mounted – all gold braid and fringed epaulettes – moved white-gloved hands to draw their swords, brilliant in the sun. Before the eyes of the massed battalions, the regimental colours unfurled slowly in the summer heat, proclaiming battle honours going back to the days of the great Napoleon.

Joseph felt a great lump in his throat. If he was afraid, that was nothing against his pride in this moment, in the knowledge that he was about to fight for France. It was a reality at last, all his ideals, his sense of honour, brought to this place and this time. To him, France was civilisation, set against the barbarous power of the aggressor; the values of the mind and the heart and the spirit against the glorification of military might. France was literature and philosophy and inventiveness, food and wine and music and art; above all, for Joseph, France was Casseuil, the château, the vine-covered slopes, the family he loved: for them, for their safety and their future happiness, he would fight today, and die if it was asked of him. He bent his head for a moment in prayer.

The bugles rang out, their high silver notes setting his pulses racing. 'Forward – forward for France!' The band struck up a heart-stirring march.

They began to move off, steadily, purposefully, their feet keeping time to the music. Rifle fire burst out in front of them, and the toneless rattle of a machine gun; here and there a man staggered, cried out, fell; more and more as they advanced, staining the bruised grass with a pattern of red and blue. Joseph scarcely noticed, as if it was all a dream.

'Fix your bayonets!' The bugles sounded the charge. They broke into a run. Ahead of him Paul was singing the 'Marseillaise'; they sang together, all of them, straining to out-sing the guns, running and singing towards the shadowy grey shapes of the enemy waiting among the houses.

iv

Laure, returning to the house from an early visit to Trissac, was surprised to find that Charles had not left already for the *mairie*. Normally he would take a light breakfast after mass and then go at once to his office, where Laure had planned to meet him this morning. But instead he was standing in the hall reading a newspaper with great attention; beyond him, through the open dining-room door, Mathilde and Marie-Françoise and Philippe were visible, seated about the table, their eyes on Charles.

'Is there any news today?' Laure asked, thankfully closing the door on the already dazzling heat of the late August morning.

She had to repeat the question before Charles at last looked round. 'I beg your pardon, *madame* – I did not hear you come in. Good day.' He glanced once more at the paper. 'There is nothing very definite – another bulletin – but I think there must be a mistake, a misprint perhaps. *'Le Figaro'* may have something different.'

Laure reached for that paper, which lay on the chest nearby, and turned to the main news item, the most recent bulletin from the Commander-in-Chief, General Joffre. 'The situation from the Somme to the Vosges remains today as it was yesterday. The German forces appear to have slowed their advance . . .' She read aloud, while the words slowly reached her understanding. 'That can't be right, Charles. What does yours say?'

Charles let his paper fall, his face grave. 'The same – exactly the same.'

'The Somme to the Vosges, Papa?' Philippe, overhearing, had come to the dining-room doorway. 'But that's right inside France!'

They gathered, all of them, about the map pinned to the study door, and stared at it. The blue flags marched north-west through Belfort (Alsace had not after all fallen to France) and Verdun, on across the Belgian border, through Charleroi into Flanders; the red flags, wavering a little, had moved back after a recent battle just inside the French border at Le Cateau, leaving the actual allied line somewhat uncertain. But the Somme!

They stared at the river, from the point where it flowed into the Channel many kilometres south of Boulogne, giving its name to the surrounding *département*; and then their eyes moved on, steadily south-east, ever deeper into France, nearer to Paris. A line linking that river to the Vosges mountains that

bordered Alsace would leave five or six northern *départe-*
ments unprotected; and would indicate a sudden and dramatic
German advance on a wide front. Laure shivered. Was Paris
once again to be encircled?

'Does that mean,' whispered Mathilde, 'that the Germans
have occupied everything above that line?'

'Our soldiers wouldn't retreat so far – they wouldn't!'
Philippe burst out. 'Joseph wouldn't, I know!' To his thir-
teen-year-old eyes Joseph was a hero, still spoken of by the
teachers at school with affectionate approval, and now
answering his country's call with high courage and a light
heart. 'Someone's telling lies,' he suggested after a moment.

Charles shook his head and, in silence, moved the flags
south and west; Laure saw that his hands were trembling.

'What a good thing the Russians moved so quickly,' she said
brightly. 'If they continue victorious in the east then the
Germans will have to send more troops against them – that
will help us a great deal.' She tried to sound entirely confident.

Charles gave a faint brief smile, and then straightened a little,
as if to throw off the burden of anxiety. 'Let us give some
thought to our own communal problems – if it is convenient
for you now, *madame*?' Among his other duties, Charles was
responsible for ensuring that all the crops of whatever kind
were safely harvested. 'I should be glad of your help in the
matter,' he had said to Laure yesterday. Now, she said,

'Of course – as soon as you wish.'

'Then I will delay going to my office a little longer. Let's go
to the library.'

There, he said, 'I have already made a number of enquiries,
to find out exactly what help is needed. Some families are able
to manage, I gather – many have made their own arrangements with neighbours – but I have begun a list here of those
who have expressed a wish for extra help, and another of those
who have said nothing, but I believe are likely to want it –' He
smiled across the table at Laure. 'You are on that list.'

'For Trissac? Yes, the tobacco's ready, and there are only
Madame Meynel and her youngest boy, and they are not very
willing to help. Of course, any extra labourers will be paid, as
necessary – but that isn't the problem.'

'A good thing it's the school holidays – that gives us more

hands immediately. We have Jean-Marc Delmas. Monsieur Durat has expressed a willingness to do whatever may be asked of him, but of course his health is not very certain. You see my list of possible labourers here – Mathilde has asked to be included, and Marie-Françoise and Philippe, and I shall do what I can myself of course, as my duties permit. I have an impression that everyone is most willing to make every effort the circumstances require of us. But we must be sure that all needs are covered. Who else grows tobacco?'

'Monsieur Chabry – his will be ready too.'

'Of course, down at La Borie – I was forgetting. I must try to see him and assure him he will have the help he requires.'

'I can call on him if you like – we are lunching with Charlotte if you remember, and it's on my way. I can see if he needs any more labourers and let you know.'

'Excellent – if you would – thank you.' He made a note or two and then went on, 'Now, the crucial thing is to have the tobacco harvested before the grapes are ready – then we really shall need every hand out in the fields. Our chief difficulty will come in October, when the children are back at school and the Casseuil *vendange* begins. There'll be the maize to harvest as well, and possibly some late hay. But please God the war will be over by then.'

'Do you think the soldiers will be demobilised in time?'

'If not, I'm sure the authorities will organise leave . . . Let's return to the present. Have we forgotten anyone?'

The discussions over, they rose to go; but as Laure reached the door, Charles said, '*Madame*, have you given any further consideration to your brother's suggestion?'

'That I should go to America?' She smiled. 'He included us all in that invitation, if you remember. I know what your answer would be, even if you didn't have your duties to keep you here. Do you think mine would be any different?'

'Not really, no. In fact, I am a little surprised that he as a Frenchman should even suggest it.'

'He is more American than Frenchman now; the war must seem very far away and insignificant to him. But there you are. I shall be happy to consider a visit when all this is over – but for the time being, my place is here.'

*

Late that afternoon, as the heat lessened a little, Laure and
Mathilde returned home from their lunch with the Bonnets,
driving slowly in the trap pulled by the ancient pony who was
(like Moïse) too old for active service. On the edge of the
village they saw Charles ahead of them, walking slowly with
bent head. Laure halted the trap beside him.

'May we offer you a lift, Charles?'

He looked up, and for a moment she was shocked: he
looked dreadful, pale and exhausted and thoroughly
unhappy. Mathilde cried out, 'Oh, what is it, *mon chéri*?'

He forced a faint smile. 'I am quite well – don't alarm
yourself. But I think I would prefer to walk home, if you
don't mind.'

Laure began to drive on, but they had gone only a short way
when Mathilde clasped her arm. 'Maman, what if there was
news – about Joseph – bad news? Oh, Maman, stop, I must
go back—!' She was already half out of the trap, so Laure was
forced to stop for fear she would hurt herself. She turned and
saw Charles, clearly anxious, hurry towards Mathilde and
take her in his arms.

'Charles, it's not Joseph – please say it's not Joseph!'

Gently he kissed her. 'No, *chérie*, I promise you there is no
news of Joseph. Thank God he was not – his name was not—'
He stopped, and Mathilde looked up into his face. Laure
could see that there were tears in his eyes.

'What has happened?' Mathilde asked. 'There has been
some news, hasn't there?'

He nodded. 'Yes, I am afraid so.' He paused, swallowing
hard. 'I had not expected – they send the names to the *mairie*,
you see – the names of the dead. It was for me to break the
news.'

'Oh, *mon cher*!'

Laure stepped down into the road and led the pony nearer
to him. 'Names, you said – were there many? Who are they?'

'The second Bertaud boy – I have just come from there.' He
gestured towards the nearby house. 'Young Monsieur Fronsac – you know his wife is just delivered of their first – their
child . . . Then there is Robert Martin's grandson—'

'Three – three in our little commune!' Mathilde sounded

disbelieving and appalled, as if the nearness touched her as much as the number.

'André Martin was with the 108th wasn't he?'

'Yes, *madame*, and Monsieur Fronsac too. Étienne Bertaud was with the 50th. He fell in Belgium, on the twenty second, as did Monsieur Fronsac. André Martin was gravely wounded and died next day, just over the border in France, I believe.'

'A week ago,' said Mathilde slowly, 'and they were in Belgium. Then Joseph was there – and he is alive, or we'd have heard.'

'Have you seen all the families?' Laure asked.

'Yes – yes, I have now . . .' he paused, while a shadow seemed to pass over his face at the recollection of the afternoon's visits; then he said abruptly, 'I will accept your offer of a lift after all. Thank you.'

A little later, whilst he and Mathilde changed for dinner, Charles came and stood beside her as she sat brushing her hair before the mirror. 'Mathilde—'

She rested her hands on the dressing-table and looked up at him. 'Yes?'

He did not continue at once, but bit his lip, frowning, as if unsure how to go on. Then he said, 'I did not do it well – what I had to do today.'

She smiled consolingly. 'I'm sure you did, as well as anyone could.' There was something in her tone which suggested that he did not have all her attention. She added, 'At least Joseph is safe. Oh, if only it would all end soon!'

He clasped her shoulders, caressing them; but she had not diverted him from his more immediate anxiety. 'I wish I could be sure that I had said the right thing. What if I made it all worse for them?'

'Just be thankful it was not Joseph,' Mathilde said, with a trace of impatience.

'I am afraid it is not as simple as that. I must know what is best. I pray I may not have to do it again; but if I do—'

She put down the brush and stood up and turned to face him, taking his hands in hers. 'Don't torment yourself, Charles. It's bad enough to have Joseph away, without trying to carry everyone else's grief as well.'

He said no more and simply took her in his arms; but above

her bent head, where she could not see it, his expression was more troubled than ever.

After dinner Mathilde went early to bed and left Charles and Laure alone in the *petit salon*. Charles sat in silence for a long time, unaware of the furtive glances his mother-in-law was directing at him from time to time. At last, she said, 'It must have been very difficult for you today.'

He raised his head, and she saw his strained features relax a little, as if he was relieved to be given the opportunity to talk. 'I fear I am not fitted for so terrible a task. Do you not think I should be able to walk into the house of a fallen soldier and say, "*Madame*, your son has given his life for France. His country is proud of him"? Something like that, so that even in their grief they can hold their heads high and find comfort. But I cannot – today I could not. I could think only that it might have been Joseph. What use is that, if all I can do is weep too?'

Laure took his hand in hers. 'More consolation perhaps than any fine words, *mon cher*. If it were Joseph, would it help you to be told of it in high-flown phrases?'

'I don't know – I don't know. Perhaps not. But it is better to know that it was a noble and heroic death. To believe it to be simply a waste, without sense or purpose – that would be terrible.'

'No one will think that. We all know why they died.'

'If there . . . if things go badly, then it will seem as if it was all in vain.'

'Don't think of it, Charles,' she said gently; but she knew that was advice she would not herself be able to follow.

'You know,' he said next, in quite another tone, 'it's said that the government's preparing to move to Bordeaux.'

v

Dusk brought cold, as a relief from the baking heat of the day, and a dew to lay the dust; but it brought no easing of the chaos that, even on this side of the river, choked the roads. Through the night the carts and wagons rumbled on as best they could, each one creaking and lumbering beneath the weight of a haphazard heap of household goods and children and captive animals – cats meowling in boxes, caged birds mute with terror, agitated hens struggling in a sack or a crate – the whole great untidy mass dragged by a stumbling donkey or the desperate strength of an aged peasant. They forced their way somehow through the exhausted ranks of the soldiers, who no longer formed anything so orderly as a column, were no longer visibly an army. Their own carts laden with guns or (horribly) with a stinking blood-drenched jumble of dead and wounded, added to the tangle on the roads. The cries of men in pain mingled with the noises of animals, the cursing of peasants trying to wring another tiny mite of strength from their beasts, the wailing of children, the occasional shouted order rising with a kind of hopelessness from some officer trying to keep his men together, to keep them moving; and beneath it all the rumble of cart wheels, the thudding of hooves, the endless slow trudging of booted feet.

Overhead the round moon, wan and sickly looking, darkened from time to time as a haze of oily black smoke drifted across it from the leaping orange-red flames that lit the horizon and the plain in a kind of lurid pattern, marking the path of the German advance. Far off in the north-west, Reims burned, and the whole vast plain of the Champagne, from the west to the Argonne forests in the east, was dotted with the lesser fires of countless towns and villages. From them all the people fled with whatever goods lay closest to hand, to be swept up and carried along like so much driftwood in the great southward-flowing rivers of the French army.

In the rear of the retreating forces Joseph's regiment marched – or rather, dragged one exhausted foot after another, and prayed that soon they might hear the order to halt and rest – just for a few hours, a few minutes even, here by the road, anywhere – that tomorrow, by some miracle, the Germans would not attack, that they might even melt away with the dawn like the early mist.

They had attacked incessantly during the last baking August days, all the way from the Meuse to the Aisne, and on into this first week of September, sudden fierce attacks, which were fought off only with difficulty and at bitter cost by men who had no strength left, except what anger gave them, or fear; and whose numbers and ammunition dwindled daily. Crossing the Marne this morning they had thought that at last (perhaps) they had left the enemy behind them; but they all knew that just over there, a kilometre or two across the water, the Germans were marching into Vitry-le-François, until a week ago the General Headquarters of the French army.

The worst of it was that Joseph and his comrades had not been ready for a retreat, or even expected one; they had not ended their first day of fierce fighting in Belgium with a sense of defeat. Rather, they had driven the Germans out of the village of Nevraumont, back to a defensive series of trenches in neighbouring Rossart; and then, in a second desperate, costly assault, had taken that village too. Later, savouring the bitter-sweet taste of victory, looking forward to a well-earned rest, they had not at first been able to believe it when at dusk the order came to withdraw. But the bugles had sounded the clear unmistakable call, which they had been taught to recognise but had never expected to hear in the field; and they had obeyed, muttering and grumbling amongst themselves. 'Why? Why give up, just when we're winning?' . . . 'All that, for this!' . . . 'We've been betrayed, that's what it is!'

Joseph, full of bitterness himself, had kept silent, because an officer ought not to encourage criticism of his superiors, or questioning of their orders; but he could think of no defence – and nor could Paul, who was less restrained. It had only gradually dawned on them, from murmurs heard, word passed on from senior officers, that their little victory had been only one tiny moment of glory in a whole unending series of failed or inconclusive actions along a battle line stretching from Mons to the Vosges.

So they had marched south on those roads choked with terrified refugees, where by day the dust filled eyes and nose and throat, quickly turning a tormenting thirst to agony, and coated hair and skin and clothes. With no more than the briefest of pauses for sleep, short of food and water, sweating beneath the heavy thickness of their greatcoats, unendurably burdened by their knapsacks, many had flung away blankets, spare boots, cooking pots, spades, anything that seemed in the hopelessness of retreat simply a useless encumbrance; a few, breaking all the rules (but what use were rules now?), rolled the whole pack into a ditch, and sometimes even sank down beside it themselves, falling at once into an exhausted sleep.

Joseph, his feet rubbed raw inside his boots, had constantly to resist an almost overwhelming temptation to do the same. With the other N.C.O.s he ceaselessly encouraged, consoled, argued, commanded, threatened; anything to get the stragglers on the road again and into what was left of the ranks. Sometimes, he had been forced in the end simply to leave a man to his fate. If the fear of falling into German hands was not enough to get him moving again, then there was little else to be done.

'Here, *camarade*.' Joseph looked round. Paul was holding out a bottle, nearly emptied of the sour red wine it had contained. They were skirting the great Champagne vineyards, but this was all Paul had been able to find. Still, it was quite an achievement to have found anything at all. Paul had negotiated fiercely for it with a woman at a farmhouse they had passed last night: it must, Joseph had thought at the time – with some admiration for Paul's bargaining skills – have been the fastest successful transaction ever made. The country people were only too inclined to put up their prices the moment the soldiers appeared, but Paul could match anyone in peasant cunning.

Now, Joseph shook his head, but forced a faint grateful smile. 'No thank you – I've some water still.'

'It won't be up to much by now.'

'It'll do. And you might be needing that later.'

'We'll be stopping soon.'

'Do you think so?'

'I know so.' Even retreat had not quite dimmed Paul's unflagging optimism; nor his ability to know what their superiors had in store for them long before everyone else. Joseph was not sure if it was due to lucky guesswork or a keen sense of hearing; both perhaps.

'*Mon caporal*, Baudry's dropped out again.' The words were spoken tonelessly, with all the indifference of exhaustion.

'Shall I come?' asked Paul.

Joseph shook his head; and then, automatically, in a kind of plodding daze that had nothing to do with will or choice or decision, he turned and made his way back towards the slumped figure at the roadside, pack half-off, face grey beneath the coating of pale dust, eyes closed. He might have been dead – perhaps indeed he was. He had been wounded five days ago, as they fought off a furious German attack not far from St Hilaire-le-Grand – a slight wound, hastily treated by one of the regimental surgeons; but the heat and the endless marching and the lack of food and water were no treatment for a wounded man. He was bleeding again, Joseph saw, noting the dark stain on the sleeve of the greatcoat.

He touched the man's shoulder. 'Baudry – come on, *mon ami.*'

Baudry did not stir, but at least he seemed to be still breathing. Joseph turned him a little, just enough to loosen coat and collar; and then he reached for his own water bottle, in which a few drops still remained – warm and pretty unpleasant by now, but water all the same.

'Baudry!' The man's eyes opened; he stared dully at Joseph and then, unimpressed, closed them again.

A cart rumbled by, pulled by a gasping pony. Without thinking, Joseph moved back, out of the way; and then on the impulse of the moment scrambled to his feet – swaying a little as dizziness swept him – and seized the arm of the old man who led it. '*Monsieur*, allow this man to ride on your cart, I implore you!'

The man paused for a moment, eyeing what he could see of the sweating, dust-stained, unshaven young man before him; and then spat in the road. 'Why should I, tell me that? You can't even defend us. Some army – retreating, always retreating! Why can't you stand and fight like men? Because you daren't, that's why – you're cowards, all cowards, the lot of you! Traitors, worse than Germans! I remember 1870, let me tell you, and this is just the same, the same old story!' Grumbling, cursing the soldiers, he spat again and went on his way; the cart caught Joseph's arm as it passed, jolting him backwards so that he almost fell.

Baudry had been watching the exchange, though with no sign of interest. When Joseph knelt again beside him, he muttered, 'Leave me – go on, *mon caporal*—'

Joseph, saying nothing, gave him water to drink; and then became aware of a horse looming up beside him, of trembling sweat-darkened legs coming to a halt. He looked up into the white weary face of Second Lieutenant Mercier, in command of the company since the deaths of both Captain and Lieutenant at Rossart.

'Get his wound bound up again, *caporal*. Pass me his pack – I'll carry it. Then get him on his feet as fast as you can. Another two kilometres and we should get a halt. If he can last out until then.'

He rode back to the front of the column with the pack, while Joseph tied his last clean shirt about Baudry's arm and helped him to his feet. They struggled on together, Joseph not entirely sure who was the supported and who the supporter; but somehow they came up at last with the straggling tail of the regiment.

Paul did not look round as Joseph reached him, but nodded towards a scattering of houses away to their right. 'That's Courdemange. The next place is Chatelraould – and that's where we stop.' Ahead, lights glimmered faintly, soft domestic lights looking pale and ineffectual against the fiercer glow of the towns burning behind them.

Somehow, Joseph got his men into the barn allotted to them for what was left of the night; or those of them who could make it so far. Many simply collapsed into sleep on their way across the farmyard and lay motionless on the hard stony ground. In the end he did the same, dropping his rifle and falling on top of it, asleep before he could feel its angular line against his body.

From some deep black core of warmth and nothingness, Joseph felt himself dragged towards the light. He resisted, grunted, tried to shake off the hand roughly grasping his arm; and then came achingly back to the chill reality of cramped limbs, the hardness of the surface on which he lay, the seeping dawn mist; and further off, the sound of horses stamping, men shouting, bugles calling. '*Merde!*' he muttered.

'Precisely, *camarade*,' agreed Paul's voice in his ear. 'Get the men up. We're needed over the river.'

Joseph rolled over and accepted Paul's hand to drag him the last distance to his feet, where he stood for a moment with his eyes still closed and wondered how he would ever find the strength to stay upright, let alone fight. Then he turned and ran stumbling and yawning to stir his squad to wakefulness.

Five kilometres away across the river the Germans had marched out of Vitry on to the exhausted remnants of the 107th regiment at Frignicourt. Desperately trying to fight off the attack, the regiment had sent for help, and the 108th was called in to provide a supporting diversion. Dimly, distantly, Joseph was aware of marching at what seemed an inhuman speed through the misty woods to the river, of orders called and passed on, of leading his men forward; of a stumbling rush onto a bridge under drenching fire; of firing and firing himself until at last his cartridge pouch was empty – but by then (thank goodness!) the 107th had been able to withdraw in reasonable order and the Germans had not followed; and they themselves could plod wearily back along the sun-baked road – obstructed now by the little two-wheeled hand carts that carried the wounded to the dressing stations – to Chatelraould and a hastily prepared meal. It was by now well into the afternoon.

'Monkey again,' said Paul, as they sat propped against a wall in the corner of the farmyard with the hot but rather unappetising-looking stew in their mess tins before them.

Joseph took a few mouthfuls of the 'monkey' (it was tinned beef) and then gave up; he was, he decided, too weary to eat. He passed his tin to Paul, who simply shook his head and the next moment dropped, suddenly, asleep. Joseph closed his own eyes and rested his head on the wall, and knew that sleep was beyond him. His mind wandered undirected amongst this random image and that, pausing here and there for no apparent reason. I suppose it's Sunday today, he found himself thinking; and a little vision followed, of the church at Casseuil, a cool quiet refuge from the cicada-loud heat of the day – of the monotonous intoning of the priest – of his father kneeling with bent head, wrapped in a consuming intensity of prayer – of his mother in her soft blue Sunday dress (so he had seen her last) and a pretty hat with a veil, her face very still, her gloved hands fidgeting a little – of Grand-mère, alert as always to everything around her, opening a sharp disapproving dark eye on Philippe as he shuffled and knocked his missal to the floor – of Marie-Françoise very conscious of a new hat, holding her head at an appealing angle; and Charlotte, all aglow with happiness.

He was aware of no sense of nostalgia, not even of a longing to be with them again. He felt rather that he was looking at them from a long, long way away, a vast distance in time and space, as if at some mythical interlude in an age long gone: an age that bore no resemblance at all to this, where he was existing now. Yet even this did not seem quite real either, for a grey miasma hung around him, shutting him off from the burning sun that beat down on the white earth and reflected back a dazzling light to hurt the eyes; while the noise – guns, voices; wheels turning, turning on the road – rumbled on and on in his head . . .

Again that hand, shaking him urgently. 'On your feet, *camarade* – orders to fall in.'

They fell in, untidily, in the farmyard, unbearably hot in that confined space, too weary even to be very curious about the reason for the order. The setting sun fell on Second Lieutenant Mercier as he rode into the yard, and Joseph was instantly aware of some difference, some new vitality, lighting the man's tired face from within. He became suddenly attentive, and was conscious that around him a similar listening silence had fallen.

'*Mes chers amis*, tomorrow will be a decisive day for France. In an hour from now we leave for Courdemange, there to take up our positions; by dawn we must be fully ready. It is with pride that I tell you that to our regiment has fallen the honour of holding the front line. I will now read to you the Order of the Day just issued by General Joffre to the entire French army.

' "As we commit ourselves to a battle on which the safety of our country depends, it is vital to remind you all that there must be no more looking behind you. Use your whole strength to attack and drive back the enemy. A troop that is unable to make any further advance must defend the territory gained at whatever cost and die where it stands rather than give way. In the position in which we find ourselves today no lapse of any kind can be tolerated." '

'*Vive la France!*'

As the men took up the cry, Joseph felt all his exhaustion and despondency fall away from him, and a new hope sprang to life in its place. The retreat is over, he thought. We are going on the attack, at last.

vi

After breakfast, Laure discussed domestic matters with Nanon and set Moïse to work on the day's tasks; and then she returned to the house. In the hall, Mathilde and Philippe and Marie-Françoise, sensibly dressed, like herself, in loose comfortable working clothes, were gazing at the map.

'No change,' said Mathilde flatly. She had hoped that Charles, reading the papers before leaving for his office, would have been able to advance the line of flags a little; but it remained exactly where it had been for nearly a month now. In that first week of September they had held their breath as the line had held; and then advanced, swiftly, steadily, sweeping the Gemans before it, from the Marne to the Aisne – and on, they had supposed, and expected, daily; but no news had come, none at all. The victorious end of the war was not after all upon them, not quite yet.

'Where are we going today?' Marie-Françoise asked.

'Monsieur Frangeas's vineyard,' said Laure; and they went out into the grey cold morning. 'I'm afraid we may be held up by the rain again today.' It was a blessing in a way, she supposed, that the cold wet weather that had followed the hot summer made it certain there would be no good harvest this year. With such a shortage of labour it would have been tantalising to be faced with a great harvest to gather.

Under the trees the soft earth was sticky, caking their shoes, but they hardly noticed. They reached the market place just as the bent, lined figure of the postman emerged from the Post Office. Along the village street doors opened and women came to stand waiting on the doorsteps for his arrival, sometimes exchanging a remark with a neighbour, as if to make it plain that they were only there by chance and did not greatly care whether the postman stopped at their house or not. Mathilde quickened her pace, but Laure laid a warning hand on her arm and she slowed again.

'I don't *expect* a letter,' said Mathilde, in the tone of one trying to convince herself.

564

There had been no news from Joseph since his one letter in August. They were well used by now to the consolations shared by all the villagers, to account for absent letters – 'They've been busy, of course; they won't have time to write.' 'I expect they're short of notepaper.' 'The post will have been held up by the fighting.' 'They'll be keeping the letters back until after the next offensive, in case word gets out too soon.' No one ever said, 'Perhaps he's been wounded,' though sometimes a long silence ended at last with a letter from a hospital, which would arouse mingled anxiety and relief – anxiety, because so many later died of their wounds, or were permanently maimed; relief, because he was at least alive and out of the war. Least of all did anyone speak of the worst possibility of all, that the tall figure of the Mayor might appear one day at the door with distress in every line of his body; and they would know that for them there was to be no more waiting, not ever. Nine families in the commune had already suffered that terrible visitation, nine in two short months.

'Ah, Madame de Miremont, three for the château this morning – two for you, *madame*, and one for Mademoiselle.' Mathilde and Marie-Françoise seized the letters as a starving man might snatch bread.

'Nicolas! Oh, it's from Nicolas!'

'Two – two at once, from Joseph!'

'There, you see – the post was held up.' Laure knew her comment went unheard, except by Philippe, who was as impatient as she was for his mother to finish reading and pass the letters on.

'Oh!' Marie-Françoise had gone white. 'Maman, Nicolas has been sent to the front!'

'But he's younger even than Joseph,' said Laure. 'He can scarcely have started his training yet.'

'He says they're short of officers.' Her tone was full of misery. 'Oh, why do they have to send him now? The war must be nearly over – surely they could manage without him! What does Joseph say, Maman – will it end soon?'

'He thinks so, yes – but this is his first letter – the 15th of September, it says – when was that? Nearly a fortnight ago. It's from somewhere called Wargemoulin – that's in Champagne, he says, just near the Roman road north of Châlons sur

Marne. They drove the Germans back from the Marne in just three days – "More than eighty kilometres, of which we covered forty the second day – spurred on by what we saw on the way of the devastation the Germans had left behind them – burned and ransacked houses and churches, so many bodies – but I will spare you the details; except to say that we thought only of revenge, seeing it. But for today revenge must wait. We are resting here, and we feel we have earned a rest. Sadly, our losses during the battle were high – Colonel Aurousseau fell mortally wounded." '

'Yes, poor man,' murmured Laure. 'I heard that.'

' "And very many others, among whom was the Second Lieutenant of our company and so many of my good friends of the past weeks. But we can be proud that we held our ground and turned retreat to victory, as did the whole French army that day. A breathing space here, and then the pursuit will recommence. A few weeks, and I am sure it will all be over. Tell Grand-mère, I shall be at Casseuil for the *vendange* I am *certain*." ' Mathilde looked up, smiling ecstatically. 'Oh, that's wonderful—' and then, 'But of course, it may be different now.' She tore open the second letter and began to read; and after a moment disappointment clouded her face. 'This was written just last Friday, the 25th – they were south of Aubérive, only about 20 kilometres west of Wargemoulin. "The Germans have established themselves in well-defended trenches along a front some few kilometres to the north. While the Generals decide how we are to drive them out, we try to make ourselves comfortable here. We have begun to establish a network of trenches ourselves, which helps to keep us warm and will, we hope, provide a starting point for a new offensive. Sometimes we fire a few shots to remind the Germans we are still here, and they do the same. Oh, I must tell you – I have been made a sergeant—" ' Mathilde's voice rose briefly with excitement, and then fell again. ' "I have command with Paul of the second section of our company (that means we each have about thirty men under us – or we would in normal times). We have rigged up a wattle shelter – all we sergeants gather there to talk and eat and drink and play cards, when there's nothing else going on – the trick is not to be last inside, or you end up with the place where the rain trickles off the roof onto the back of your neck – though you can put your *képi* on back to front so that the peak affords a little protection . . . Your parcel reached me, and better still the news of you all, for which I thank you . . . I am sure it will not be long before we shall all be rejoicing that the Germans have been driven out of France . . ." ' Mathilde's voice tailed away into silence, and she passed the letters to Laure, so that she could read them for herself. After a little while they went rather soberly on their way, saying little.

It was perhaps as well, Laure thought, that they were all kept so busy with the demands of the various harvests; without the distractions of work the long wait for victory would have been unbearable.

But no harvest this year could be like the harvests of other years, and not just because cold winds and rain had damaged most of the crops. There was no singing among the *vendangeurs* this year, no laughter, no dancing and piping in the meal breaks. They talked, but gravely, exchanging news, fears and consolations; often during the breaks someone would produce a newspaper and read aloud to those who could not read, and then there would be a long and often heated (but never acrimonious) discussion as to what it all meant.

Today, when a shower forced an unscheduled break, Madame Frangeas said to Laure, as they crowded into the kitchen, 'I've got some clothes for you, for the Belgian refugees – I heard you were asking. They need a bit of mending here and there.'

'That won't be a problem,' said Laure. For some weeks now – ever since she had offered Trissac to the refugee committee in Bergerac as temporary housing for Belgian refugees – a party of ladies had met at the château each Sunday afternoon to sew and mend on behalf of those unfortunates, most of whom had left almost everything behind when they fled their homes. 'If you remind me before we leave, I can take them with me.'

They left sooner than they had intended, for the shower showed no sign of easing and after an hour Monsieur Frangeas said, dejectedly, 'There'll be no more work today, *mes amis*. Thank you for coming. If it is fine tomorrow I shall be happy to welcome you again.'

As they set out together for home, Mathilde said, 'Did you hear them say Lucien Delmas has been wounded?'

'Yes, but not too seriously, I gathered. They think he'll be home soon, to convalesce.'

'I envy them – I know I shouldn't, but I do. I don't want Joseph to be hurt, but—'

Laure was about to make some bracing remark designed to indicate her disapproval of Mathilde's sighing anxiety about Joseph; but at that moment she caught sight of a young woman in black coming along the road behind them. 'There's Madame Fronsac. I want to see her about baby clothes. You go on – I'll catch you up.'

The young widow had offered her own infant's outgrown garments for a baby born to one of the refugee families at Trissac; but it took Laure some time to accept the offer and make the arrangements, for Madame Fronsac was eager to talk. When at last she was able to free herself, everyone else had long gone.

She made her way home and washed and changed, and went downstairs to find Mathilde settled by the fire in the *grand salon*, working at her sewing.

'I wondered what had become of you, Maman. Is Marie-Françoise with you?'

Laure, thankful to be off her feet (these days she did sometimes feel her age, just a little) sat down. 'No. Didn't she come on with you?'

'I haven't seen her since we stopped work. I was sure she must be with you.' She paused in her sewing, suddenly full of anxiety. 'Where can she be?'

'I expect she ran on ahead to change. Or perhaps she wanted to write to Nicolas – yes, I'm sure that will be it.'

'But she's not in her room, and no one's seen her.'

'Not Nanon?'

'No.'

'But she must be somewhere. She was in the vineyard, at least until it rained ... Though I don't remember ... Perhaps she's gone to call on Charlotte.'

'Without saying anything? She has never done that before.'

'She's eighteen now, *chérie*.'

'And a young unmarried girl. She ought not to be out

alone.' She snipped at a thread and spread out the shirt she was sewing, gazing frowningly at it; then she laid it aside and stood up. 'I shall telephone Charlotte, to see if she's there.'

Charlotte had seen nothing of her sister; nor, when they made enquiries, had Charles or Madame Frangeas or anyone else.

'I expect she's simply gone for a walk,' suggested Laure. 'You know how soothing that can be when one is troubled about something, and she was upset by the news from Nicolas.'

Marie-Françoise returned to the château just as Charles came in that evening. She was soaked, the ribbons of her hat dripping over the brim, her hair more wildly curly than ever, her boots and the hem of her sensible serge skirt caked with mud; but her pale face was glowing with some internal light and her eyes were bright with excitement.

'I'm going to train as a nurse,' she announced proudly to her astounded parents. 'I heard the Red Cross are training people – I've been to Bergerac to see about it. I shall begin on Monday. I told them you would give your permission.'

Mathilde stared at her in horror. 'But you're quite unused to anything like that – there may be all kinds of dreadful things—'

'You are only eighteen, *chérie*,' said Charles gravely. 'I am not sure that an unmarried girl should be exposed to—'

She did not wait to hear the end of her parents' protests. 'I can't bear to sit at home any longer, just waiting for the war to be over. I know there are things to do here, but they're not enough, not nearly enough – and now Nicolas has gone—' She bit her lip, and then went on, 'I want to go where the help's most needed. I might be sent to the front – and if not there are the hospitals in Bergerac – they need more staff for the temporary ones, they say.'

Charles and Mathilde, apparently unable to think of anything to say, simply gazed at her. Laure went impulsively to put an arm about her.

'You've done the right thing, *chérie*, I am sure. I commend your courage.' Her motives might be a little mixed, Laure thought, but then whose were not? And it pleased her to discover beneath the gentle pliant surface of her granddaughter such unexpected resolution. Gentleness and pliancy were all very well, but if Mathilde had been born with a little less of her father's acquiescence and rather more of her mother's steely determination then perhaps she would not have been crushed so readily by life's unhappiness.

Charles said, with sudden decision, 'Your grandmother is right, Marie-Françoise. You have done well, and I am proud of you.'

Later, when they were alone in their room, Mathilde turned on him angrily. 'How could you say that to Marie-Françoise? Why did you not forbid her to go – you could, you know you could!'

Charles put his arms out to hold her, but she shook him away. 'Do you want me to lose all my children? First Joseph – no, Charlotte first, then Joseph, and next week Philippe goes back to school – and now Marie-Françoise! What if none of them ever comes back? Charles, I couldn't bear it! Leave me one, one at least, I beg you!'

He gestured helplessly. 'How can I agree, when France needs all her children, more than you or I?'

That seemed only to set light to her fury. 'You only say that because it eases your conscience! You feel guilty that you're not in the army – that's it, isn't it? So you let them all go, and you can feel really proud and pretend you've nothing to be ashamed of. I'm right, aren't I?' She knew she should not say it, and she was appalled at the cruelty of her outburst; and she knew that what she was really saying, from some painful, angry part of herself, was, 'Joseph has gone and may never come back, and you are still here; and I wish – oh, I wish! – that it was the other way round!'

'Mathilde!' She sensed his shock and dismay. He had gone very white and stood transfixed, staring at her as if he could not believe what he heard. 'I promise you, I . . . If I believed, for one moment . . . Mathilde . . .'

She burst into tears. 'Oh Charles, I'm sorry, forgive me! I didn't mean it, really I didn't!' She clasped his arm, pleading for him to understand. Then she looked up at him and whispered, 'I'm so afraid, Charles; so afraid.'

'Do you think I'm not afraid too?' He spoke with such anguished vehemence that she was startled. 'All the time, afraid for you and the girls and Philippe and above all for Joseph . . . and—' his voice dropped to a harsh undertone 'and for myself, because I do not want to go on day after day like this, seeing the way people look at me when they open the door to my knock – to know that I am the agent of grief and despair in so many homes . . . It is almost more than I can bear.'

She stared up at him, astonished to hear him talk like this. She could not remember that he had ever in all their life together spoken to her so personally, and with such pain. She had not even guessed that he could feel so deeply, about anything. That he found it hard to be the constant bearer of bad news – that she accepted; it was only natural, after all. No one – even the most insensitive – could have been untouched by it. But that Charles – stolid, controlled, unimaginative, sustained by a firm religious faith – could be suffering such torment beneath the calm exterior; that astonished and dismayed her.

She saw then what she had not observed before: how his expression and his bearing were not in the least calm, or only so to the casual glance. He was controlled, certainly – or had been until this moment – but every line of his face was taut with strain, his hands clenched tight, his body rigid as if braced to meet some new and certain blow. She realised too that none of this was new; it was simply that she had chosen not to see it. And she knew why she did not want to recognise what unbearable strain he was enduring; because to do so would be to acknowledge that he needed her, at a time when her fear for Joseph left her no room for any other emotion.

'You must teach yourself not to think about it,' she urged him. 'Do what has to be done, and then put it out of your mind.'

'Could you do that?' he retorted, still with that pain in his voice.

'I would tell myself: It's not Joseph; and be thankful.'

'You would not – I know you would not! You *could* not.'

'Yes I could.' Her eyes were accusing. 'You make yourself suffer, because it's the only way not to feel guilty about being left behind. That's true, isn't it?' Somehow, she knew, this was worse than her other outburst, much worse, because it

571

was said not in the unthinking heat of the moment, but calmly and deliberately, in the full knowledge that it would hurt him. She wished it unsaid at once; and yet she knew she had meant to say it.

If it was intended to hurt, then it had succeeded, she could see that. His hands fell to his sides and he looked crushed, shrunken into himself. Part of her wanted to go to him at once, to beg his forgiveness and to comfort and reassure him, as she knew she ought to do. But if she were to do that, then it would not end there. Once she had reached out to him and made herself available to him, then she would have to be there always, whenever he needed her; and that would, she realised, be a good deal more often than she had suspected before she had glimpsed that hidden vulnerability which alarmed her so. She wanted him to go on being her strong comfort and support; and if she were to allow him just this once to reverse the process, then there was no knowing where it would end. Perhaps, when Joseph was safely home again, it would be different . . .

So she stayed where she was and watched him step back a little and say, soberly, his voice flat and without life, 'You are right in one thing, Mathilde. I am ashamed to be spared all that Joseph and the others are suffering.'

She was exasperated that he accepted her cruelty so meekly; yet relieved too, for she could then offer him a tiny measure of reassurance, without committing herself to anything more. 'It was wrong of me to say that,' she admitted. 'I'm sorry. I know it's not easy for you.'

He drew a deep breath, and she saw the great effort he made to bring himself under control. She recognised now – as she had never done before – how resolutely he pushed his own troubles aside, so as to be able to give her what she needed. But then, she told herself, he could always go and pray about it afterwards; like Nanon, he believed very firmly in that particular source of strength. She had no such certainty to help her.

He took her hands in his and said quietly, 'Let us be practical, shall we? We can do nothing for Joseph, except pray. But, like you, I have been thinking of Philippe. I too am not happy that he should go so far away from us at this time. I have been making enquiries about somewhere nearer. Since he has long felt he has a vocation for the priesthood, a seminary might be the answer: we shall see. But wherever it is it will be near at hand, I promise you.' Then he kissed her gently on the forehead and drew her into his arms. 'My poor Mathilde – it is worse for you than for any of us, I know. The sword that pierces the heart – it is the price of motherhood. I wish I could bear it for you.'

Mathilde clung to him in silence and hated herself for what she had done to him; all she had done, ever since the first great wrong of their wedding day.

CHAPTER
TWENTY NINE

i

'Go now, Maman?' Louis Chabry's little grandson, who had been fidgeting very audibly for some time, had come to the end of his small patience. Two rows in front of him, Laure reflected that of late mass had indeed become a gloomy business for a child. The growing list of names solemnly intoned week after week could mean nothing to him; even the 'Chabry, Vincent,' must have been heard so often since it was added to the list in February that it could no longer make any impression on the dead man's nephew. In any case, at three years old, it was unlikely that he even remembered the uncle who had gone away a year ago; to him these were names, just names, lengthening the service and plunging everyone into a sombre silence.

Just names – but each of them, for Laure, brought to mind an individual, liked or disliked, a member of a family, whose life had been inextricably bound up with her own for so many years. '. . . Bertaud, Étienne; Bertaud, Mathieu . . . Chabry, Vincent . . . Delmas, Lucien . . . Durat, Jules . . . Frangeas, Pierre . . . Jabot, Marius . . . Martin, André; Martin, Lazare . . . Paviot, Jérôme, priest . . . Vergnolles, Daniel . . .' Laure counted them off on her fingers one by one: seventeen this week, one more than last week – seventeen in a single year of war; and that was without counting the wounded already prayed for, many of whom, like Lazare Martin today, would be promoted all too soon from one list to the other.

A little guiltily, Laure wished (like the child) that mass was over; not because it bored her, but because it left her with a dreary sense of misery. All that grief, all those homes touched by the pain of loss – she hated even to think of it. In the early days she had been able to look on the war simply as an irritation: a large one, which roused her sometimes to fury, because of the inconveniences it brought with it; but nevertheless merely something to be endured with a certain degree of patience, since one had no choice about it and it must – surely – soon be over. Only with each day that had passed, that 'soon' had receded a little further into the future. Who would have dreamed, a year ago, that it would still be going on now, nearly thirteen months later? In 1870 ten months of war had seemed interminable . . . Now it had become, she thought (with a degree of shame) rather like being constantly present at a very long funeral, in which one was not most directly or immediately involved, but was forced for decorum's sake always to maintain the correct expression of solemnity, to give voice to the appropriate sentiments, sympathetic or morally (and patriotically) uplifting. Inwardly rebellious, she felt sometimes that the constant demands on her compassion and her capacity for grief were both unreasonable and excessive; one could not live like this all the time, one ought not to do so. It was all becoming more than a little tiresome . . . Shocked (not for the first time) at the direction of her thoughts, she forced herself to concentrate on the prayers for peace to which the priest had moved; and to which, disobeying the promptings of Rome, he always added a plea for the defeat of Germany – the neutrality of the Pope in the matter was a very sore point with most French Catholics.

It was a relief to be out in the bright late-morning heat of the market place, full of the little ordinary Sunday incidents and activities of Casseuil in summer-time: a group of children playing under the trees; three geese, very white, waddling home across the street; a dog lying in the shade, stirring only to scratch itself, half-heartedly, before dropping with a sigh to sleep again; a woman coming from the baker's with bread; and the café – but there the outside world broke in again. There were no argumentative groups about the tables, noisily (and not too seriously) putting the world to rights: only three very old men concentrating in silence on a leisurely game of cards; and Jean Chassaing, son of the village postmistress, sitting alone and apart, frowning at nothing in particular with his glass of wine untouched before him, the disfigured face and empty sleeve showing only too clearly why he had returned home.

Abruptly, Laure turned towards the gate and the inviting tranquillity of the wood, walking quickly so as to avoid having to talk to the others (she too felt inclined to solitude at the moment); but they soon caught up with her.

'Lazare Martin's funeral takes place tomorrow,' Charles said after a moment.

As if I could have forgotten, thought Laure crossly. She tried not to listen to the sad reflective conversation that followed between Charles and Mathilde.

Passing through the hall ahead of them she glanced – from habit only – at the map. The little flags had remained almost stationary since September last year; there had been only the most minor changes, including a tiny advance in Lorraine, where Joseph's regiment had moved up after the attack to occupy and organise the newly captured German trenches. 'They are positively magnificent,' he had told them in his next letter. 'This is luxury-living indeed!' Then he had added reassuringly, 'It is a quiet sector – we do not expect to be kept very busy;' just as – he had claimed – the sector in Champagne where they had spent the months of autumn and the bitter winter had been quiet – but Lucien Delmas (recovered from his wound and returned to the front) had died in Lorraine, and Vincent Chabry in Champagne. The worst casualties, though, had been in Artois, where a major offensive in May had failed horribly; and where Joseph now was.

After lunch, Laure left the others to linger over their coffee (promising to return in time to join the ladies' sewing party) and changed and made her way to the *chai*. There she began to pack three crates with bottles of the '99 vintage, taking her time, not simply because one must be careful with such valuable wine, but because the carrying out of the simple routine task was wonderfully soothing to her spirit, and also put off a little the moment when she must return to the house and its troubles.

Not that the war did not touch her here. On the contrary, these three crates – to be carried tomorrow on the ox cart to Bergerac (thank goodness the Casseuil oxen had not been taken to feed the army, as had happened in some areas nearer the front!) – had been ordered as a direct result of the war. Sales had been very poor since last August: it was an unfortunate fact that in wartime the most enthusiastic connoisseur seemed to feel guilty about enjoying good wine. 'But' – so Monsieur Teyssier (too old for active service) had said acidly, when he called yesterday to make arrangements for delivery – 'Limoges is clearly a paradise, where guilt is unknown.' It was to that town that many generals and other senior army officers had been banished by General Joffre to a comfortable semi-retirement, following last summer's disastrous Battle of the Frontiers, with its appalling losses. The victory of the Marne had, apparently, been a direct consequence of that weeding-out process, although, sadly, without reducing the casualty rate. A year later it looked a less decisive transformation, though now and then another General would be quietly 'Limoged'. Still, if the retired officers now had nothing better to do with their time than drink a '99 Château de Casseuil and dream of past glories, that was all to the good; far better than to be responsible for sending young men like Joseph to their deaths.

But I must not think of that, Laure told herself; and she began to sing. '*Quand nous chanterons le temps des cérises . . .*'

Her thoughts went back to the past, tinged with an agreeable melancholy which no longer had any power to hurt her.

Next morning before dawn Charles helped her to pack the ox cart. Moïse would not be at work until later, and in any case was now quite incapable of such heavy work. He had been very ill through the winter and his slow recovery had not been helped by Lucien's death; but at least young Jean-Marc was on holiday again and able – temporarily at least – to provide another pair of hands in the vineyard. He would be twenty before November, and that put him in the class of '15, the young men technically due for military service in 1915; and the class of '14 had already been marched away last autumn – if victory did not come soon, the army would need a new transfusion of young men.

Laure enjoyed the slow ambling journey to Bergerac, as the

night gave way almost imperceptibly to the grey stillness of dawn. She was, for some reason, more than ordinarily aware of every tiny shift of light, every smell and sight and sound. She watched as, slowly, the sun rose, sending rays slanting along the valley, dispersing the mist, which minute by minute rose from the river and fields to lie suspended in threads over the woods, pale and insubstantial against the dense foliage. Between the rows of vines the fine grass was silvered with dew, giving the vine leaves overhanging it a dark robust heavy look by contrast; the grapes clustered amongst them were still quite green, held back by a cool and changeable summer and too little sun.

As the cart rattled noisily past the pool, the still green surface – until then scarcely distinguishable from the close-cropped greenness of the surrounding field – became suddenly full of rippling life as startled frogs leapt into the water from the bulrushes that edged it; a faint plopping filled the air, and Laure smiled. It was good to be alive, with every sense keenly awake to one's surroundings, to be able to smell and to hear and to see.

The sun rose higher, its warmth reaching down even into the bottom of the valley. Alongside the road as it levelled out the tobacco fields stretched, dense, glossy and almost ready for harvest. Over there, the brilliant yellow and brown of a field of sunflowers stood out against an orchard where the peaches hung red and gold in the trees. Here, passing through a wood, the light was soft and dusky, the air a little chill, but on the low-growing elder the fruit was massed like black jewels (or gigantic caviare, thought Laure fancifully) and blackberries ripened lusciously, tempting the birds; and beyond, in the sun again, flowers patterned the verges with the purple of knapweed and loosestrife, the vibrant blue of viper's bugloss; with yellow daisies and the tiny pink flowers of the thyme. Ahead, the road ran on towards the river, pale and stony, its dewy stickiness turning quickly to dust in the growing heat.

All so peaceful, so untouched, so beautiful . . . Who could look at this and think of war? – of men fighting and dying, the clamour of bugles and neighing horses, the murderous firing of rifles, the flash of bayonets – all those things she had read about in the papers, or seen hinted at in Joseph's letters, and today wished only to put from her mind. But she reached the next village and the postman was going from house to house, watched from their doorsteps by women weary with anxiety and the weight of too many burdens and responsibilities . . . No, she could not escape.

She was home again in time for the funeral. Dressed in black, she walked to the village with Mathilde and Nanon and Philippe; Charles, his tricolour sash about his waist, had gone on ahead, so as to be at the Martins' house in time to greet the pastor, when he arrived from Bergerac to conduct the burial service.

The street was already packed with women and children and old men, as if, in mourning this first of the commune's sons to be brought home for burial, they were also remembering all those others who would never come home. They watched in a silence heavy with grief as the hearse, draped with flags, came slowly past, accompanied by the pastor, and behind it, side by side, upright and dry-eyed, the dead man's parents, their feet keeping time (as far as possible) with the thin uncertain notes of the band. Further back walked other members of the family, old Madame Vergnolles, and Aubin and his sisters and his daughter-in-law; and then Charles, leading the few remaining members of the municipal council. Behind the band that brought up the rear the villagers followed the little procession along the street to the Martin *caveau* in its prominent position overlooking the former mayor's small vineyard. There – once the religious ceremonies were over – Charles made an emotional little speech, and a very young bugler played, and the band broke into the 'Marseillaise', which a few voices, husky and wavering, attempted to sing.

It was over. Laure, turning away, overheard Robert Martin say to one of the many well-wishers who had gathered around him, 'He did his duty.' His voice had an odd rasping sound, which struck at her heart. Suddenly it was all too much for her. Half-blinded by tears, she fumbled for a handkerchief; and in so doing almost collided with Aubin.

'Oh, I beg your pardon!' She blew her nose vigorously. 'Why should I be weeping, if he does not – even Madame—'

She stopped, and they both looked at the former mayor and his wife, still outwardly calm and controlled, their whole bearing proclaiming, We are proud of him. They were talking to Charles now; and it struck Laure with sudden force that of the two men one would have supposed Charles to be the one ravaged by grief. He had retained all the freshness and vigour of youth well into middle age, his face full of an innocent openness that had kept it young; but the war had changed all that. Today, she thought, he looked almost haggard.

Beside her, Aubin said, '*Monsieur le maire* has aged a great deal lately. I think his present duties fall heavily on him.'

'Yes,' agreed Laure. 'He feels it all very much.'

'Perhaps it would have been better if it had fallen to a tougher character – someone like Robert Martin himself, for instance.'

'Oh, but just imagine how dreadful it would be if you were to find your own son's name on the official list, coldly, just like that!'

Aubin gave her an odd look, and seemed to be about to say something; but then clearly thought better of it, for he remained silent.

'Paul could not stay for the funeral then?'

'No. They don't get much leave. A whole year to wait, then blink and you'd miss him. But there it is; better than nothing, I suppose. Jean hopes to get home before long, then we'll have seen all three of them at last . . . Paul seems to have struck up quite a friendship with your grandson. He spoke of him a good deal.' That sounded what was, for Aubin, an unusually warm and personal note, which Laure acknowledged with a smile. 'He was telling me they had quite a discussion one day, about the prospects for wine sales now the soldiers get a daily ration.'

'You sold some of last year's to the army yourself, didn't you?'

'That's right. I'd been afraid I'd have it left on my hands, the way things were. There's not much call for the Casseuil of course, as you'll know. But ordinary wine prices look set to rise. If you think about it, half a litre per day per man – that's quite a tidy lot of wine. And as Paul says, think of all those cider-drinking Normans and Bretons getting used to their daily wine ration, and you can see there could be quite a demand building up for when this is all over.'

Laure smiled. 'He has a shrewd head for business, your Paul – like his father.'

'He's a good lad.' He was visibly pleased by the tribute. 'I thought he might be angry I was doing well out of it – they can be so touchy, these soldiers on leave; there was no pleasing Jacques when he was home. But Paul saw it my way – if we've got to suffer all the rest, why shouldn't we put a bit of money by too? It does no one any harm. Your tobacco will be the same, I suppose?'

'If the war goes on much longer, yes. But I'd rather see an early victory than make my fortune.'

'That goes without saying.'

The evenings had their own routine, once the simple evening meal was over. In the *grand salon* Mathilde would knit, endlessly, and rather tediously, Laure thought, making socks and gloves and scarves for the poor *poilus* suffering in the bleak north-eastern climate. Last autumn, as the cold intensified, Joseph had put in a plea for warm clothing; and Mathilde had abandoned her refugee sewing (the Belgians were in any case quite well supplied by then) and taken up her knitting needles. Laure told her that she must have provided for the entire regiment by now; but she was not deterred.

Near her, Charles would sit in a comfortable armchair, sipping slowly at a brandy, talking little, trying to relax and put the cares of the day behind him; something that he had never yet quite succeeded in doing.

Laure would install herself at a table, catching up with the paperwork she had no time to work on during the day. When – as now – Philippe was home from the seminary he attended near Périgueux, he would read (though he was not very scholarly by inclination), or chatter rather exhaustingly, until sent to bed. On the few occasions when Marie-Françoise was off duty (she was still, to her frequently-expressed chagrin, confined to light nursing in one of the hospitals in Bergerac), then there might be a game of cards, or some music; but tonight, as usual, she was absent.

Laure was beginning to close her books, fold her papers, and say good-night to them all; when the telephone rang. Charles, the harsh little lines appearing again between his brows, went to answer it; and came back very soon with such a shining look of joy on his face that Laure almost expected him to announce the wholesale collapse of the German army.

'That was Joseph,' he said. 'He had no time to speak longer. He's got leave – he's coming home at last! Tomorrow night, he hopes; if not, the next day.'

Laure thought there had never been such preparations. Mathilde arranged great pots of flowers in every room (and especially in Joseph's) and sang joyously as she did so; Nanon sang even louder as she concocted the most enticing dishes in her range (Mathilde's one regret was that Louis-Christophe's skills were not available to welcome Joseph home); Charles had a new spring in his step as he went to and from the *mairie* – and mercifully no bad news came to spoil his mood; Laure rushed around cramming as much activity as possible into the hours that were left, so that she would be free to enjoy Joseph's company once he was home – she insisted on the help of the reluctant Philippe, who was exasperating everyone else with his excited high spirits.

That evening they were all five restless and on edge. They told one another time and again that it was unlikely – wartime train services being what they were – that he would be home tonight. Nor was he; and the next morning Mathilde looked exhausted from sleeplessness.

It was an uncomfortable day, for none of them could concentrate on anything, breaking off frequently to look out of the window or listen for the sound of approaching feet; by the evening they were all trying (with varying degrees of success) to control their irritability. At midnight, when Joseph still had not come, Laure went up to bed. She knew that Charles and Mathilde stayed up very much longer, for she had been awake for a long time when she heard them cross the landing outside her room. Mathilde was weeping, and Charles talking to her in a low consoling voice.

The following morning Laure woke early, conscious of work to be done; it was no good allowing anxiety to get in the way, as she had done yesterday. She ought to begin cleaning the *cuves*, because with so few workers and everything consequently taking so much longer to do, she must have as much completed as possible before the Trissac tobacco harvest claimed her attention, and the various other harvests that would follow; otherwise the château *vendange* would be upon her before she was ready.

She opened the shutters and dressed, and made her way downstairs to the kitchen, where Nanon already had coffee prepared and was cutting bread for her own breakfast. She smiled and cut some for Laure too, not needing to ask.

'He didn't come then – not last night.'

'No, he didn't. But you know what the trains are like.' Nanon did not, never having been on a train, but she nodded all the same.

Laure ate there in the kitchen with Nanon, because it was convenient and comfortable. Then she went up to the *grand salon* to collect the papers left there last night. She heard the front door – heavy, with its solid latch and circular handle – open and close again; and then someone took two steps – slow, booted steps – on to the stone flagged floor. Her heart gave a great thud and she rushed into the hall; and there stopped, suddenly struck with doubt.

It was a stranger standing there in the stillness of exhaustion, looking at her: tall, heavily bearded – a great black beard, unkempt as his hair – the uniform indescribably stained and worn and dirty, with such a stench coming from him that she could smell it even at this distance.

Then he moved a hand, just a fraction, extending one grimy palm towards her; and she knew the hand and, looking up again to his face, met the dark eyes.

'Joseph!' She ran to him and put her arms about him. He laughed a little, shakily, trying to hold her off.

'Keep your distance, Grand-mère – I don't want to share my little companions of the trenches with you.'

She ignored him completely and reached up to pull that dirty bearded face down, and kissed him again and again. In the end he gave up trying to deter her and hugged her in return. She found she was crying, from sheer joy at seeing him.

Philippe must have heard something, for just as Nanon emerged panting from the kitchen, all tears and tender little exclamations, Joseph's brother appeared on the half-landing, shrieked 'Maman! Papa! He's home!' and came running down to fling himself on Joseph, ousting both Nanon and Laure.

An instant later, he recoiled in disgust. 'Pouah! You stink, Joseph!'

Joseph laughed. 'Fine soldier you'd make, *mon petit frère*.'

Then Mathilde was there, wrapped in a curious assortment of garments pulled about her as she stumbled out of bed; and Charles, his eyes full of tears and his voice husky with emotion. Both embraced Joseph at once, full of endearments and questions and loving concern.

'We were so afraid something had happened to you – when you didn't come—' Mathilde sobbed at last.

Joseph stroked her cheek. 'There were difficulties with the trains, that's all.'

'Have you been travelling ever since you telephoned?'

'Yes, Papa.'

'Then that's enough questioning,' Laure broke in, all brisk practicality. 'Except to find out which you want first – food or a bath?'

He smiled at her gratefully. 'A bath, if you please, Grand-mère, and a change of clothes, then I'll be fit to sit down with you.'

But when, after a long time, Joseph did not come down for the tempting breakfast set out for him in the dining-room, Charles went up to investigate and found him stretched out on his bed, bathed and half-dressed; and sound asleep.

'If that's what he needs most, then so be it,' said Charles; aware, as were the others, of some disappointment.

Joseph slept for twenty-four hours, which was trying for all of them, torn as they were between concern for his well-being and a desire to waste no moment of his leave. Nanon spent the day vigorously cleaning and mending his uniform as best she could. 'Too much brushing, and this will drop to bits,' she commented to Laure, who passed her in the courtyard as she was shaking out the blue greatcoat. In the afternoon Charlotte called with her infant daughter, lingered for some time, and eventually went away again, with an invitation to come for lunch tomorrow. Mathilde crept upstairs at regular intervals to look in on Joseph and reassure herself that he was still there, alive and whole and unharmed; and hoping a little guiltily that the tiny sounds of the door opening and her tiptoeing across the room, or the touch of her hand on his hair, might wake him.

He came down for breakfast next morning clean and tidy and without his beard, and ate like a starving man. Though trying hard not to be too demanding, Charles and Mathilde plied him with questions, since he seemed unwilling to talk unprompted; but he answered them so briefly that they were not much the wiser afterwards.

'Where have you come from?' Charles asked. 'Artois?'

He nodded. 'Yes – just north of Arras, near Vimy.'

'Isn't that the one point where there was some success during the May offensive?'

'Yes. With General Pétain's corps.'

'Do you know if there is anything else in the offing?'

'It's being talked about, for the autumn. That's all I know.'

'Will you be going back to Artois?'

'Yes. I must be back by Sunday night . . . What day is it today?'

'Friday.'

'Then I shall have to leave first thing tomorrow, at the very latest, if I'm to be sure of being in time.'

Mathilde gave an anguished cry. 'Joseph, no! It's a whole year since we saw you – you *must* stay longer, you must!'

Unmoved, he shrugged. 'If you want me to risk a court martial—'

She began to weep, caressing his hand as it rested on the table near her. 'No – no, of course not, *mon chéri*.'

After breakfast Charles took him briefly on one side. 'Is there really no way you can stay longer – no one you could contact, to explain how long it took to get here? Would they not be sympathetic?'

Joseph gave a faint smile. 'I am not at school now, Papa. Besides, the regiment moves back to the front line on Monday – I must be with them.'

'I thought that's where you'd left them?'

'No. We only have four days at a time in the front line; then four days in the second line and eight days behind the lines – that's what I've missed, which is no loss, as you'd realise if you saw the places we stay in.'

Charles studied Joseph's face, tanned except where the beard had been, all the soft curves that had given it such a look of youthfulness gone, replaced by harsher lines. One would almost think he had aged a year for every month he had been away.

'Joseph, you know – I have no wish to influence you – but your godfather, General de Miremont . . . He is stationed at Limoges, as perhaps you will have heard. He would be happy to find you a place on his staff, were I to ask him. It would be such a relief to your mother.'

Joseph said only, 'No thank you, Papa,' in a tone of devastating coldness; and then turned and walked away, out to the *chai* where Laure, trying to be tactful by absenting herself from the house, was topping up the maturing wine in the barrels, replacing what had been lost by evaporation.

She looked round as he came down the steps and stood in the doorway of the maturing shed, leaning against the door-post. She said nothing, simply smiled and gave a little nod. For the first time she could ever remember, Laure saw in Joseph a resemblance to Frédéric, slight but unmistakable; in the set of his mouth and the withdrawn expression, which hinted at a pain that he had no intention of revealing. It was all she could do not to run to him, but she knew that would have been the worst possible reaction.

'Do you mind if I smoke?' He had never smoked before the war.

'Not at all,' she said, watching the way he lit the cigarette and drew on it with all the slow concentration of a man who has long sought relief that way.

'I imagine you'll need a good autumn, if the harvest is to pick up.'

'Yes.' She moved on along the rows of barrels, pretending to give them her attention, but aware only of Joseph; and acutely conscious too that there were so many things she must not say or ask, if she was not to drive him away. He had changed, gone through experiences of which, for all her eventful life, she had neither knowledge nor understanding; it

586

was almost as if she had to get to know him again, cautiously, sensitively, avoiding false steps. She knew she would reach him more easily by her silence than by risking the wrong words.

'I haven't seen Moïse about. Is he still working for you?'

'In theory, yes,' she said ruefully. 'In practice, very little. I wonder sometimes why I keep him on. Because there's no one else, of course – and also because he needs to do something, to keep him from brooding, poor man. He's worried about Jean-Marc, of course – if they call up the '15 class, he'll be going. He's been giving us a hand here in the mean time.'

'He's left school now, I suppose?'

'Yes; he's just passed to train as a teacher. You know that's been his ambition for a long time?'

'Yes, I remember something of the kind.'

Laure took a risk and asked, 'Do you think it will end soon?'

'The war?' He shrugged. 'Who knows? I don't any more. If there's an autumn offensive – if it succeeds—' He threw his cigarette stub to the ground and crushed it with his foot. 'Have you time for a walk through the vines? You can see if I remember which ones are which.'

'Of course.' She tried not to sound too pleased, and walked as calmly as she could to join him.

For about an hour they wandered through the rows, saying very little (and none of it of any great significance), but enjoying the tranquillity of an old companionship restored; it was there still, diminished perhaps, but fundamentally intact, in spite of everything. By the time they returned to the house, the look that had reminded Laure of Frédéric had gone.

At lunch Joseph was relentlessly light-hearted, almost his old self; but not quite, for there was something brittle about his teasing of Charlotte and Philippe, his attempts to cheer his mother, a kind of desperation even, Laure thought. Below the surface lay something much darker which she had glimpsed this morning but which he had now pushed firmly out of sight.

He spent the afternoon in the *grand salon*, admiring Charlotte's little daughter (quite dotingly, to his sister's delight); parrying his mother's questions; and trying hard, by his warmth of manner, to make up to Charles for the cloud that had come between them that morning.

Charlotte stayed for dinner, and Marie-Françoise came home. There was a great deal of laughter and no one said anything that might even hint at fears or serious emotions; despite the fact that it was those deeper things that were uppermost in all their minds.

Very early next morning, they assembled in the hall to say goodbye to Joseph, already a little separated from them by the lovingly refurbished uniform in which he had dressed. He embraced Nanon first. 'Thanks to you, *chère* Nanon, I am fit to be seen again. It may even hold together until they issue our new uniforms.'

'I didn't know you were getting new uniforms,' said Charlotte brightly. 'What will they be like?'

'A most ravishing pale blue – with just a hint of grey: *horizon bleu*, they call it. It is supposed to make us less conspicuous, but against what I am not sure.'

'Perhaps they will drop you from the sky from aeroplanes, to terrify the enemy – angelic visitants falling into battle.'

He laughed. 'Who knows? They come up with something new every day. We're also to be issued with very practical and unromantic steel helmets. So you see, Maman,' he drew Mathilde into his arms, 'we shall all be invulnerable in future – quite indestructible.'

She clung to him, quite unable to match his light tone; and began to weep. It was a long time before he could turn to Philippe and Charlotte, and then to Laure for a final, silent embrace. Then he was in the trap with his younger sister perched beside him and Charles driving them. They left Marie-Françoise at the hospital and went on to the station.

There, as they waited in the cloudy dawn light for the train to arrive, Charles said awkwardly, 'Forgive me for what I suggested yesterday. It was not intended as a slight upon your honour. I know you would never choose the easy way. I spoke from love – but I should not have said it, I see that now.'

Joseph kissed him. 'I know that, Papa; there is no need to tell me. I am sorry I was angry. It was not because I am some kind of hero, like you read about in those terrible lying newspapers; but – oh, there is no time to explain. Just be assured that it's over, and I shall never think of it again.'

For some time after the train had gone Charles stood staring along the line.

ii

There was yet another hold-up ahead. The double file of men slithering and floundering its way along the half-submerged duckboards in front of Joseph jolted to a halt, bumping one against another and grumbling fluently. Joseph made the halt official and pushed past them along the communication trench to the head of the section, where, round the bend of the traverse, he found Paul Lambert and a corporal deep in angry altercations with a struggling heap of men: someone had lost his footing and others, too close behind in these slippery conditions, had stumbled over him, with chaotic results.

When the tangle had been sorted out (it did not take long, after all) and the column was on the move again – their new uniforms by now even more thoroughly coated with a layer of pale thin Artois mud – Joseph walked for a time beside Paul; who said after a moment, raising his voice above the noise of their own artillery, bombarding the German lines, 'Promotion prospects looking up again, I'd say.'

That rather tasteless joke had been Paul's invariable observation for some time now, whenever they had been involved in what promised to be a costly and probably unsuccessful undertaking.

Yesterday morning had been different; it had seemed as if the turning point had come at last. For once they had all been full of hope. Weeks of preparation and apparently careful planning, the digging of new trenches and communication lines, the distribution of new uniforms and steel helmets, replenished stocks of ammunition; all the signs that those in command had at last taken into consideration the lessons learned in fourteen months of war, that at last they had devised an offensive plan that could succeed: all these had led to a revival of confidence in men who were becoming not only resigned but disheartened by months of bloody stalemate. Their own particular part in the new offensive had been to support an assault on the familiar Vimy ridge, for so long the target of their floundering efforts in the trenches; but this time, they had been sure, destined to fall into their hands.

They had been wrong. Their artillery – hampered by faulty shells – had failed to break the German front line and the advance had come up against a German resistance that had been heated and only too effective. By nightfall all they had to show for the heavy losses of the day was a portion of captured German trench. Fortunately for Joseph and Paul, their regiment had been in support and their casualties not as great as they might have been.

Today was another matter. Before dawn, as the bombardment began, they had been marched from their position south of Neuville St Vaast, to make their way first west, then north, then in a south-easterly direction, around the village to where an attack could be launched over open ground on the German lines, which here ran almost at right angles to their own. Their objective, Joseph knew from Paul, was a German trench called *Cinq Saules* (five willows). Now that they were nearing their destination Joseph wondered idly which (if any) of the stunted shell-blasted remnants of trees visible through the smoke of the bombardment indicated where the willows had once been.

'We're well behind schedule,' Paul commented. 'We should be in position by now, or we'll be attacking in the dark.'

'They didn't allow for this stuff underfoot, I suppose,' said Joseph. 'It's two steps back for every one forward. Now, if someone would only invent a machine to give our legs a bit of extra impetus—'

'Funny you should say that. I was thinking of just such a thing this morning. I believe I have the very gadget – in my head as yet, you understand; but a little time to mature the idea, and you'll have it – standard issue for all our troops. I envisage a sort of propeller, one to be attached just above each knee – can't you imagine it?'

Joseph laughed. 'I'd invest every *sou* of my savings in its development. There, I can't say fairer than that.'

'What, all ten *sous* of it? I'm overwhelmed! We shall make our fortune!'

'Keep working on it then.' He gripped Paul's shoulder. 'I'd better get back to my place.'

'See you later, *camarade*.'

iii

At Le Petit Colin, Anne Lambert, wife of Aubin's eldest son Jacques, was scrubbing the kitchen table. It was a satisfying task, one that used up some of the irritation and anger that she could not decently express in any other way (though she did, sometimes; only to regret it afterwards, for her father-in-law did not take kindly to opposition). With Jacques away, her bed unbearably solitary, and only Aubin for company, the time seemed to pass with agonising slowness. Only the occasional letters from her husband, uninformative though they were, broke the monotonous tension of her days – not that she was ever idle, with so much to do.

It was hot today, the sun falling through the open door onto her bent back, comforting after the cold and rain of the past weeks. Perhaps the white grapes would ripen well after all; but then that would only mean more work, when the *vendange* came.

She look a long time over the table, because afterwards she would have to go out to the *chai* and help her father-in-law with the racking of this year's red wine, a task she would not have minded if Aubin had not been so unvaryingly critical of all she did. She scrubbed more vigorously than ever.

A little chill fell over her, a shadow as someone came through the door behind her, blotting out the sun. She turned quickly; and then stood quite still with one hand pressed to her breast. '*Monsieur le maire!*'

It was Death, stepping over the threshold in the guise of this tall man, stooping a little, his kindly eyes troubled below the now permanently furrowed brow.

Anne groped for a stool and sat down.

'No – no, *madame*, it is not Jacques.' The quick reassurance set her shaking with relief. 'Where can I find your father-in-law?'

591

'In the *chai* . . . Shall I come?'

He shook his head. 'Not yet, I think. Later perhaps.' He knew, she supposed, that she and Aubin were not always on good terms. She watched him go, and did not ask whether it was Jean or Paul. She would know soon enough.

Aubin looked round as Charles entered the *chai*, which formed an annexe to the main body of the house. He took his hands from the bellows with which he had been pumping the wine from the *cuve* along the tube to the barrel, and straightened. He stood quietly waiting, his face impassive. Charles came up to him and stood bareheaded before him, the words emerging with the simple fluency of experience; which could never quite conceal the emotion beneath.

'I am deeply sorry, Monsieur Lambert. Word came this morning that your son Paul fell near Vimy in Artois on September 26.'

Carefully, Aubin laid his hand on the rough oak surface of the *cuve*, as if steadying himself, though he looked steady enough.

'Paul . . . Paul, is it?' He sounded a little dazed; he spoke very slowly, almost reflectively. 'I am glad his mother isn't alive to see it. He was always her favourite – you know how women are, with the youngest.'

Charles placed a hand on his shoulder. 'I do not know what I can say – except—'

Aubin looked up at him, with something almost like a smile twisting his mouth. 'That you are glad it isn't your boy, if you're honest.' He saw Charles flinch, and added, 'No, I do you an injustice, I think.'

'I don't know . . . Each time, I think: This could be Joseph. I am grateful – and yet ashamed to be spared.'

Aubin raised his hand and laid it over Charles's. 'It's not of our choosing, *mon ami*, not yours, nor mine. We have to take what comes.' For a moment he bent his head, as if with his best efforts there was something on his face that he would rather Charles did not see. 'Was your boy there too, do you know?'

'We have heard nothing. But I suppose so; they were in the same company.'

'Yes . . . You'll tell me if you hear.' His tone became

politely dismissive, and he freed himself and bent again over the bellows. 'The work has to be done, just the same. Wine for the troops – they can't get enough of it. I negotiated a good contract for this: money in the bank, to keep the winter cold away.' There was a bitter note just discernible below the apparently casual words.

CHAPTER THIRTY

i

As usual, Laure felt a great surge of relief as she climbed into the trap and took the reins in her hands and turned the pony's head towards the drive that led away from the Château de Trissac towards the road.

The Belgian refugees had long since been found more modest and private accommodation elsewhere, and last autumn Henri's old home had become a hospital for crippled soldiers. Laure visited the château frequently, with great conscientiousness, doing all she could – with (she hoped) appropriate tact and sensitivity – to help in any way, either financially, or by giving her time. But though she was quite untroubled – except by a quite proper compassion – when meeting a disabled individual, whether here or elsewhere, it was quite another matter to be faced with row after row of appalling injuries: men without legs or arms, scarred and disfigured, lying or sitting in those lovely rooms (that somehow only made it worse) wherever she turned her eyes. It was a kind of nightmare, and one often repeated and becoming progressively more unendurable. It brought shockingly home to her the devastating scale of injury that this war had inflicted upon them all, just as did the lengthening list of Casseuil's dead – thirty-one, this morning at mass. The papers might be silent on casualties, but one would have to be very stupid not to be able to make some approximate calculation based on what one saw in this small corner of France; only she did not want to make that calculation.

Out in the brightness of the late April day, with the two captains who were her guests for the afternoon in the trap beside her as she drove up the hill, between vines coming

594

slowly into leaf above ground that was no longer so scrupu-
lously cleared of weeds, she felt better at once.

She liked Captain Maupin, a small dark lively infantry
officer who had become a regular visitor to Casseuil. He had
only stumps left where his legs had been (he had to be lifted
into the trap), but nothing seemed to repress his high spirits.
Such courage made Laure ashamed of all her trivial discon-
tents. Captain Baillie, a large Chasseur who had lost one leg
and had other less visible injuries, had not visited them before,
having only recently come to Trissac.

'You continue to have good news of your grandson, I trust,
madame?' Captain Maupin asked courteously, once he had
brought to a close his exuberantly expressed delight at leaving
behind (if only for an afternoon) one of the more formidable
nursing sisters.

'Thank you, yes. We heard again yesterday. He is very
much better and hopes he may be allowed to leave the hospital
within the next few days.'

'Then you may perhaps see him at home?'

'I'm afraid he thinks not. He may be allowed a few days
leave, but not a pass to come as far as this. It seems they want
him back with his regiment as soon as possible.'

'Ah yes, of course.' Laure could sense his sympathy. She
heard him explain to his companion, 'Madame Séguier's
grandson is a lieutenant with the 108th. They were sent to
Verdun a few weeks ago, where he was wounded – but not
seriously, it seems.'

'Bad luck, that,' said the Chasseur Captain gruffly, to
Laure's astonishment. What could he mean? That to be
injured as he was himself, and so out of the war for good, was
preferable to being returned to the front? Surely not.

'He has a charmed life, your grandson, that's clear,' put in
Captain Maupin brightly, as if to cover the other man's
blunder. 'Baillie here was at Verdun himself – in the first days,
in February.'

'That was bad, I imagine,' said Laure. The newspapers had
reported 'Artillery activity of considerable intensity' in the
Verdun area on February 21. What that had meant, they knew
now, was that the Germans – for so long on the defensive –

had suddenly launched a meticulously prepared and devastating attack on the neglected fortress city of Verdun, and, ever since, the French army – pouring in battalion after battalion – had been fighting for its life. It was no longer possible, even for Laure, to feel resentment or irritation at the demands of the war; things were far too desperate for that.

'I got out of it,' said Captain Baillie now. 'That's more than most of us did.'

There was a gloomy little silence. After a moment, Captain Baillie said to his fellow officer, 'Did you hear, they've appointed Nivelle over the head of Pétain?'

'I'd heard something of the kind – but dear Madame Séguier must wonder what on earth we are talking about.'

'On the contrary, I know that General Pétain has been in command at Verdun since February, and that he is much respected by the army – or by the ordinary soldiers at least. Joseph says he is the one general who hates to see men killed. But I didn't know he'd been replaced.'

'Not replaced exactly,' Maupin corrected her; 'just moved down the road to Bar-le-Duc. General Nivelle is now the man on the spot.'

'And General Nivelle likes plenty of action,' said the Chasseur grimly. 'We'll be seeing offensive tactics with a vengeance, no matter what the cost.'

'Will we have the pleasure of the company of Mademoiselle de Miremont this afternoon?' asked Captain Maupin quickly. It was obvious that he was only anxious to prevent his companion from saying anything more that might alarm their hostess, for which Laure was grateful to him, even though she was not particularly alarmed.

'We hope so, although she had not arrived when I left. Madame Bonnet will certainly be there.'

'And little Mademoiselle Marie-Laure?' Laure smiled and nodded. 'There, *mon ami*.' He nudged his companion. 'I promised you the most delightful female company this afternoon, did I not? That little one will capture your heart. Such irresistible charm at one year old; what will she be capable of at seventeen?'

*

Charles was waiting in the courtyard when they arrived, and Marie-Françoise was with him, the warmest of smiles lighting her small pale face. (She works too hard, Laure thought, observing that pallor.)

'Ah, *mademoiselle*, you are spring itself today!' exclaimed Captain Maupin, his bright dark eyes running approvingly over her slight exquisite figure, set off as it was by a new frock of the fashionable shorter length, all soft folds of ivory chiffon, scalloped and layered, and fastened to the waist with tiny pearl buttons. Laure was a little surprised to see her wearing it. 'I shall keep it for when I go to Paris,' she had said when she first bought it: she planned a visit to Paris to coincide with Nicolas's next leave. Laure watched her face as she talked to Captain Maupin and wondered if there was anything there, beyond a young girl's enjoyment of a light flirtation.

Charles helped Captain Baillie to descend (he had an artificial leg and could walk reasonably well with the aid of a stick); and then he and Marie-Françoise went to lift the other Captain on to the chair on which he would be carried into the house. He protested vigorously – and with some embarrassment.

'No, *mademoiselle*, I beg you – I am much too heavy for you – it is not right.'

'I am a nurse, *mon capitaine* – had you forgotten?' Efficiently – much more efficiently than the clumsy and nervous Charles – she did what was necessary, talking all the while about something quite trivial, so as to distract the Captain from the awkwardness of his situation. When he was at last safely installed in a chair in the *grand salon*, he kissed her hand.

'You are an angel, *mademoiselle*,' he murmured.

She drew her hand gently away and went to help Nanon with the tea tray; as she turned Laure glimpsed her face and surprised upon it an expression so different from the sweet brightness of a moment ago that she was puzzled. Had she really seen her granddaughter's lip trembling, as if tears were very near? Yet the next instant she was smiling round at the company. 'Tea, Catherine?' I must have imagined it, thought Laure.

The ladies of the sewing (and knitting) group had laid their work aside and stayed to tea. These Sunday afternoons entertaining the men from the hospital had become a regular and agreeable diversion (repeated, one way and another, in many houses in the commune). There would be tea and cakes, much talk and laughter, and – afterwards – a performance or two on the piano from one or other of the more accomplished ladies. It was enjoyment without guilt, since it was all done for the sake of the soldiers.

'You know we are planning another little concert for you?' Catherine Chabry said to Captain Maupin when everyone had been served with tea. 'It is to take place next month, in the hospital gardens we hope.'

'Oh, then you must engage that delightful soprano again – the one who sang at the New Year.' The Captain's eyes were full of merriment. 'What was her name now? It doesn't matter. I do remember her rendering of the "Marseillaise" – *such* a presence! Many a time since I have asked myself what manufacturer was able to supply a tricolour of a size adequate to drape that splendid physique.'

'Large, was she?' Captain Baillie was clearly beginning to cheer up.

'Oh, *mon ami*, *inconceivably* large – you cannot imagine! *Chère* Madame Chabry, you must engage her again. To be fair, she had a wonderful voice.'

'Who was she?' Charlotte asked.

'Jeanne Bourbarraud,' said Marie-Françoise. 'You know—' And suddenly she broke into a dramatic full-voiced rendering of the 'Marseillaise', standing there in the centre of the room, her tiny figure somehow – in the way she moved and gestured – conjuring up for them the vast, tricolour-draped soprano of the New Year concert.

She was watched first in an amazed silence, and then with growing laughter. Afterwards, Captain Maupin cried, 'Bravo, *mademoiselle*!' and clapped enthusiastically.

Marie-Françoise went first very white, and then coloured deeply and abruptly sat down again on a stool half-hidden by her grandmother's chair.

'I don't know what things are coming to!' said Catherine in a disapproving undertone (but quite loud enough for Marie-

Françoise to hear). 'When I was her age I would not have dreamed of making such a display of myself – and to make a mockery of our most sacred anthem, at a time like this!'

'I wasn't mocking anything, except the soprano,' Marie-Françoise protested.

But Catherine swept on. 'Everything that was good about our national life seems to have vanished with this war. I was just saying before you came in, *chère* Madame Séguier: even decent peasants are losing their traditional values. Look at all the new clothes they wear on Sundays – women whose husbands are away fighting for their very freedom, mark you! Then there are all the little luxuries they buy for their houses, useless ornaments, all kinds of unnecessary frivolities. No longer, it seems, are they content with simplicity and frugality. The government should never have paid those separation allowances – all that money is rotting the fabric of country life!'

'That's unfair of you, *madame*,' Marie-Françoise broke in indignantly. 'Why shouldn't people enjoy a little comfort, to make up for all they're suffering? You don't have to live in poverty because your husband's away – why should they?'

'Marie-Françoise!' Mathilde was clearly appalled at her daughter's behaviour; but she merely found that the girl's wrath was turned on her instead.

'What do you want them to do then? Weep?' And then she did just that, wildly, hysterically, and fled from the room.

There was an astonished silence; then Laure said, 'Excuse me,' and went after her.

She found her granddaughter in the library, sitting on the floor with her head on one of the old armchairs and sobbing in a desperate, abandoned outpouring of grief.

Laure sank on to the floor beside her and put her arms about her. '*Chérie – mignonne* – what is it? Tell me!'

For what seemed an interminably long time Marie-Françoise said nothing and continued only to weep, while Laure caressed her and murmured tenderly and wondered what to do. She was beginning to think despairingly of going for Nanon, who could generally be relied upon in an emotional crisis; when Marie-Françoise suddenly sat up, gulped, and burst out starkly:

'I heard from Agnès yesterday. Nicolas is dead – at Verdun – on the 9th.' Then, all at once as rigidly controlled as she had been uncontrolled a moment ago, she rose to her feet, pulling the folds of her pretty skirt into shape. 'I shall go to nurse at the front – I must go now! If he is old enough to die for France, then I am old enough to work for her, where I'm most needed. Don't you agree, Grand-mère?'

Laure rose too, and placed her hands on either side of that pale, tear-stained, fiercely determined little face. 'Yes, ma chérie; I think I would feel as you do.' And then she drew the girl into her arms. But Marie-Françoise had finished with weeping.

She held tight to Laure for a moment and then she said, 'We'd better go back. Can you lend me a handkerchief?'

ii

For the last part of his journey along the vehicle-crammed eastward road they were calling the 'Voie Sacrée' – the Sacred Way – which formed the sole link between Verdun and the outside world, Joseph could hear the boom of constant shelling, and became aware once more of the familiar reverberations beneath his feet, steadily increasing with every step. He could not see the city yet, hidden as it was by the lie of the land; and around him the woods and meadows (at least where the boots of soldiers had not trampled them) were alive with the shining green of May, beneath a sky brilliantly blue. A deaf man, turning his back on the ceaseless flow of traffic, might have imagined himself in pastoral tranquillity. But Joseph was not deaf; and already he could feel his nerves bracing themselves, tautening in preparation for what lay ahead. He forced himself to take a deep breath and concentrate on the immediate moment: the spring woods, the slow jerky jolting progress of the vehicles on the road, the passing columns of soldiers moving towards the battle; and, now and then, coming the other way, the grey-faced remnants of a battalion or a division marching like ghosts into the sunlight.

Over the city and the hills that encircled it smoke hung in a dense pall, shot through with tongues of fire. Descending the long hill towards the Meuse, where it wound roughly southward along its valley, Joseph felt the reverberations increase, like the rumblings of an earthquake, a constant shuddering growl that echoed the deafening roar of the guns.

They were with him still even in the gloomy subterranean casemates that tunnelled their way beneath the great two-hundred-and-fifty-year-old citadel of Verdun, though here they were overlaid with other sounds: the faint, far off echoing voices of men, most of whom he could not see, that washed towards him as he passed the ends of the galleries that ran at right angles to the one where he walked, the rattle of the little train that serviced this underground world, doors clanging, water running, the banging of cooking pots, the endless tramp of feet.

The first time he had come here the vaulted galleries had reminded Joseph, fleetingly, of the *chai* at Casseuil; but that impression had faded quickly. There was something essentially transient about this place, with its constantly changing population of soldiers moving to and from the battle zone, each man claiming his own little temporary space, scattering it with the few personal items he had been able to squeeze into his pack. It was a place in which to pass time, with talk or cards or drinking, or carving some little trinket out of a remnant of shell casing or some other piece of battle debris. Even the occasional burst of laughter or singing could not give it a sense of life. The *chai* was all of a piece, a fruitful place, designed and used over hundreds of years for a single pleasurable purpose; a wholesome thing, its vaulted roof guarding the mysterious, miraculous processes of growth within from any harm – from heat and cold and too much light – nurturing them to maturity. This place, vaulted too, and as old and as strong, gave only temporary shelter to men and equipment moving on in a day, two days, next week; it was a kind of limbo, from which the only path of release lay through a region of desolation and torment.

Beginning to feel already acutely depressed that he should be back here again (foolish, when he had only just arrived), Joseph wandered on, quite lost, looking for a familiar face. When at last he found one, bent over a table somewhere in an angle of one of the galleries, in the shape of an officer playing at cards with three fellow lieutenants, it belonged not to someone from his own battalion, as he had hoped, but to a Lieutenant Girardet, whom he knew slightly and who was with another of the regiments attached to the XII Corps, to which the 108th belonged. The other men were evidently members of Girardet's headquarters' staff, whose office door was half open behind them.

Girardet saw him coming and stood up. '*Mon Dieu*, whom have we here?' He came to give Joseph a friendly slap on the back. 'Have you lost your way, *mon vieux*?'

Joseph smiled faintly, feeling just a little cheered. 'No, I'm back off sick leave. My battalion's here somewhere.'

'Not until the day after tomorrow, *mon vieux*, or so I believe. They're still in the Marre sub sector. But no point trying to make your way up to them – if you didn't get yourself blown up, you'd probably pass them in the dark. This isn't your first time here, is it?'

'No – I was here last month, but got hit by shrapnel soon after – it wasn't much.'

'Badly managed that. A few more weeks and we might have been out of this lot – you never know. As it is, I think the fun's just beginning. Still, there we are. Find yourself a corner for the night and then come and join us for dinner – if these lofty fellows aren't too grand for you.'

The 'lofty fellows' denied it warmly, and one of them offered to show Joseph where he could leave his belongings.

When they had gone, one of the others said, 'Who's that then, Girardet?'

'Sorry, I should have introduced you. Lieutenant de Miremont. We were on the same officer training course last winter.'

'Any relation to General de Miremont? Why isn't he sitting with his feet up in some nice cosy headquarters' job?'

'Like you, you mean?' The other aimed a blow at his head – well out of range – while the third said,

'De Miremont? Aren't they the people who own Casseuil – *the* Château de Casseuil?'

'Yes, that's right. That's where he comes from.'

'Ah – now *there*'s a wine – pure ambrosia!' He closed his eyes ecstatically. 'Oh, to be sitting in a sunlit garden, with a beautiful woman by my side – the most superb *pâté de foie gras* before me – and a glass of '99 Château de Casseuil in my hand . . .'

'Better still, strawberries and Casseuil – have you ever tried—?'

'What was that you were saying?'

The three young men jumped, turned their heads, and immediately sprang to their feet, very much as if they had been surprised in some irregularity. The officer who had come on them so suddenly, unheard, did not appear to notice their consternation. He was a slight man, impeccably groomed despite the battle-worn uniform. The severe lines of his face had at the moment an oddly high colour, suggesting an unusual degree of emotion.

'We were just discussing the delights of '99 Château de Casseuil, *mon capitaine*,' said one of the young men, in a poor attempt at a jocular tone.

'Lieutenant de Miremont, who was here just now – he comes from there,' Girardet explained quietly.

The Captain, now looking rather pale, turned his penetrating gaze on the last speaker. '*Who* did you say?' He spoke in scarcely more than an undertone.

Girardet repeated the name, and explained how he had met Joseph, and what he was doing here; and then waited while the Captain simply stared at him for a long time and at last said, 'I see,' and went on his way.

The three young men exchanged glances, sighed with obvious relief, and returned to their abandoned game.

Joseph felt – unreasonably perhaps – a certain disappointment that he would have a day to wait before he could rejoin his battalion. It was not that he wanted to return to the scenes that he remembered – from the far side of the chaos and squalor of dressing station and hospital – in the miserable cold and rain of early April. But since, sooner or later, he had to return, it was better that it should be sooner. It was, he felt, less trying to endure an evil now, than to wait for it to come upon one, knowing it was on its way, and constantly feeling a need to brace oneself to face it.

Still, he had the promised dinner to help him pass the time. He tidied himself, left his belongings in as orderly a manner as possible on the bunk allotted to him, and set out to find the junior officers' mess, to which he had been invited.

The dinner was not at all bad, and the company light-hearted and friendly, becoming more so as time passed and the contents of three bottles of wine – not the regulation *pinard*, but a decent Burgundy – steadily diminished. It had almost all gone, when one of the staff officers turned to Joseph. 'Here, do you know Captain Brousse?'

Joseph thought for a moment (something stirred in his mind, but vanished before he could grasp it); and then shook his head. 'No, I don't think so – should I?'

'Not if you can help it!' said one of the others, with feeling.

'It's just that he overheard us talking about you this afternoon and seemed curious about you. I wondered, that's all. I wouldn't recommend his acquaintance – he's a *salaud*.'

'Oh, come now, that's not fair!' Girardet broke in. 'There's no one I'd rather follow in an attack, I can tell you. He's my company commander,' he added for Joseph's benefit. 'And a brave one at that.'

'Courage is just a matter of being noticed.'

'You don't get the *médaille militaire* for nothing, *mon vieux*. Three times wounded, and four citations too – that's quite something. Oh, I agree he's not a man whose company I'd seek away from the front line, but I respect him all the same.'

'Someone was saying he'd seen colonial service before this.'

'I believe so – Morocco, I heard. But he didn't come over with any of the colonial regiments.'

'A shady past!' commented the first speaker, dividing the last of the wine amongst the glasses. 'You mark my words, he has some dark secret from which he fled to Africa.'

Joseph, listening in silence, felt that stirring of memory again, as if somewhere deep in his mind there had been a flicker of recognition. 'What's his first name, do you know?'

'You don't get on first name terms with Captain Brousse. But come to think of it, I did see it somewhere once. What was it now? Let me see – it began with 'd', I think – Daniel? Dominique? – no . . . I know: Frédéric!'

There was a chorus of derisive laughter, while, in the midst of it, Joseph sat unheeding as everything at last fell into place.

He had a sudden clear picture of himself – a young schoolboy – coming on his mother one summer afternoon, leaving the little group of rooms on the third floor, which faced Nanon's; and seeing her face, very pale and quiet, when he asked what was in there. She had taken him inside, and he had been rather disappointed to find just three very ordinary rooms, simply furnished, with nothing personal or particularly interesting about them. But in answer to his questions, she had told him that these had been his Uncle Frédéric's rooms, before he went away. Later, downstairs again, he had told his father about it, just in passing, and had been a little surprised by how grave he too had looked, even a little sad. Joseph had carried with him from that episode a sense of something more important by far than the apparently trivial surface would suggest. There was some kind of mystery about his mother's half-brother, who had not after all been her half-brother (he had learned more recently about Rosaline) and who had gone away before he was born. But that his name had been Frédéric Brousse he knew perfectly well. Was it possible—? The man had asked after him; and he had been living overseas.

He broke abruptly in on the conversation, which by now had moved on to something quite different. 'Where can I find Captain Brousse?'

They stared at him.

'Why?' asked Girardet. 'Do you think you know him after all?'

'It's possible. I'd like to find out.'

'You can't go calling on him at this time of night!' someone objected.

'Oh, he doesn't sleep much – that's no problem. But don't blame me if he sends you packing. He's not one for socialising.'

Captain Brousse had a room to himself, outside which an orderly dozed, stirring only to see who had passed before lapsing into sleep again. Girardet knocked on the door; and opened it to the crisp '*Entrez*' from within.

On a camp stool at a folding table Captain Brousse sat reading by the light of a lantern. Behind him, a mattress lay on the stone floor, at its foot a few impersonal belongings –

sword, boots, binoculars, revolver, the various items of an officer's equipment. Otherwise, the tiny room was bare.

Joseph found himself subjected briefly to an uncomfortably penetrating glance from a pair of greenish eyes, before they were returned – sharply and with obvious irritation – to Girardet.

'Well, *lieutenant*?'

'I apologise for disturbing you so late, *mon capitaine*, but this is Lieutenant de Miremont. He'd like a word with you, if you feel able to spare him a moment.'

The eyes shifted back to Joseph, and the man at the table became very still. There was, suddenly, a formidable tension in the atmosphere. In front of him, Lieutenant Girardet moved his weight unnecessarily from one foot to the other and back again. Joseph began to wish he had not come.

Then the Captain laid his book aside – very carefully, almost with precision – and rose to his feet. 'You can go, Girardet,' he said curtly.

With an apologetic glance at Joseph, Girardet went, obviously relieved. He closed the door behind him.

The small room seemed even smaller, although there were only the two of them present now. The Captain stood with his back to the light, saying nothing; Joseph, looking down on him, was only too conscious of being scanned from head to toe with disconcerting intentness. He felt he ought to say something – he had after all initiated the interview – but found himself quite unable to do so. At last, into the silence, the other man's voice broke with clipped emotionless precision. 'So – you are Mathilde's son.'

Joseph cleared his throat. 'Yes, *mon capitaine*; her eldest son.'

'You do not look like her.'

'I believe I resemble my grandfather, *mon capitaine*.'

There was another little silence, during which Joseph noticed that the Captain's hand was clutching the edge of the table so harshly that his knuckles showed white. Was he as nervous as Joseph himself?

'You must be – what? – twenty-three?'

'Yes, *mon capitaine*.' It occurred to him that if, as he suspected, Uncle Frédéric (he could not imagine himself ever

606

addressing this man with such familiarity) had left Casseuil under some kind of a cloud, he might well resent the way Joseph's arrival had forced him to confront it all again. I should not have come, Joseph thought once more. Not knowing the whole story, I should have left well alone. Then, trying to break through the awkwardness, he said, 'I heard you were asking – I thought – I believe we may be related.' He remembered that they were not after all in the least related, but that Captain Brousse did not know this; and fell silent again, not quite knowing how to go on.

The man moved at last, pulling the chair clear from under the table. 'Sit down, *lieutenant.*' It was an order, so Joseph did so. Captain Brousse perched himself on the edge of the table with a grace that had nothing casual or relaxed about it; and the light now fell on him.

Joseph saw a slight, spare man, whose taut skin was bronzed and threaded with lines, and whose hair was an odd mixture of sun-bleached brown and grey; his mouth thin, a little hard, his light eyes apparently missing nothing. His 'uncle' must be about his mother's age, he supposed, but he had none of her still youthful bloom and softness. He looked as if life and experience had battered everything out of him, leaving only a certain steely energy behind. Joseph was not surprised the other officers had spoken of him as they had; he felt himself that he would not like to make an enemy, of however slight a kind, of Captain Brousse.

Suddenly unable to endure any more of the new and apparently interminable silence, Joseph burst out, 'What an extraordinary coincidence, to meet you like this!' Even to his ears the observation sounded false and clumsy.

Captain Brousse might not have heard it, for all the reaction he showed; but when he spoke next there was a just perceptible tremor in his voice, which had suddenly lost its decisiveness of tone. 'You . . . she . . . you said you were the eldest son. There are others then?'

'Four of us, *mon capitaine.* After myself, Charlotte and then Marie-Françoise, and Philippe last of all – he is still at school.' He knew he was now talking too much, but some demon had his tongue and he could not stop. 'Charlotte is married to a very good man – he is working as a surgeon at one of the clearing stations at the moment. They have a little daughter, the most delightful little thing, Marie-Laure – so you see, I am an uncle myself. Marie-Françoise, now, she—'

'Yes, good.' The interruption was brusque and indicated a complete lack of interest in Joseph's siblings. The next moment he asked with a grimness quite at variance with the words, 'Your mother – is she happy?'

'Yes, of course.' It was a question that had never occurred to him to ask; he realised it was something he had always taken for granted. 'With my father, of course – they are very close.' Something even more forbidding in the man's face silenced him.

Captain Brousse abruptly stood up, half-turned away so that Joseph could no longer see his expression. Wondering if he ought somehow to extricate himself from this uncomfortable situation, but not knowing quite how to set about it, he reached without thinking towards the book the Captain had been reading and turned it towards him so that he could see the title. 'Anatole France: *Les Dieux ont Soif*.' Then, realising he had read aloud, he coloured fierily.

Frédéric sat down again on the table. 'Do you know it?' For the first time he spoke naturally, with a genuine interest in his tone.

'Yes, I read it before the war – two or three times. I thought it very fine. But it's not very cheerful reading for such a time as this.'

'I don't know; one can escape from the inhumanities of the present day to those of another age – it is almost consoling. It certainly confirms my impression that men and women can be relied upon in any circumstances – even the most apparently elevated – to act with the utmost inhumanity to their fellow creatures.'

'Oh, but do you think that really is what the book is saying? There is so much individual goodness – even in the terrorist, Gamelin – at heart he is not evil – his motives are good.'

'The highest motives can lead one down the worst paths. But perhaps you haven't learned that yet.'

'No; it's true, of course. But I don't agree that men have not changed. Surely the terrible things that were done by men like those in the book – at the time of the Revolution – in the name of liberty and fraternity – surely we have learned enough now not to let them happen again?' Joseph spoke very earnestly, as if he had to convince himself as well as this other man.

'Have we? Have we indeed any choice at all, whether to allow this to happen or that? Have we ever had a choice? I doubt it. Listen to those guns – they're going on late tonight.' They listened to the constant booming reverberation that had formed a background to their meeting. ' "The Gods are thirsty", that title says – and there they are still, malevolent as ever, the old gods, great parched mouths open wide – a vast emptiness demanding eternally to be filled with blood. An endless sacrifice required to quench an eternal thirst – no, *mon enfant*, nothing has changed.'

Troubled, because he felt the force of that grimly pessimistic vision, Joseph said, slowly, 'I know. Somehow it isn't as if men were doing it to one another, not as individuals – it's as if there was something out there beyond the control of us all – some power that is drawing us in, and we have no choice about it.' He shivered suddenly, though even here deep in the earth the night was warm.

'Yes, it is exactly like that,' said Frédéric. Then he added quickly, 'I am sorry – I have no right to force my pessimism upon you. The young ought to retain their ideals.'

'Before the war I had them in plenty. Perhaps I do still. My father always taught me to believe in two things, above all others – the loving Fatherhood of God, and the Brotherhood of Man. What I have seen in these past months has made me doubt the one – more than doubt it sometimes. But as to the other, I can no longer even look on the Germans as an enemy, not all the time, not as individuals. When I was home last I wanted to talk to my father about it, but there was so little time – and I was afraid of hurting him. It means so much to him that we should share his faith.'

The Captain had withdrawn into himself again. He said rather unpleasantly, 'Yes, I remember – he was always pious, your – father—'

Flinching a little at the tone, Joseph found himself brought by it to a sudden realisation: there had quite clearly been a rift of some kind between his father and this man – a quarrel perhaps, made the more painful because his mother had loved both men. It was difficult to imagine his father quarrelling with anyone, but clearly he would have little in common with a man like Captain Brousse. Perhaps there had been a disagreement over the marriage. Whatever it was, Joseph felt a sudden wish to heal that rift, to bring them all closer together again.

'He is a good man,' he said gravely. 'The best I have ever known, I think. I mean that quite sincerely. Not the quickest witted perhaps, but that doesn't matter. He is the only man I have ever met who is ready, unfailingly and without hesitation, to admit it when he is in the wrong. He is also a man completely without hate or malice of any kind. I know, I am certain, that he would welcome you at Casseuil, were you ever to come there again. Of course, my mother would be overjoyed to see you again. They will be delighted to know we've met, when I write and tell them.'

He hoped he was right about that; but if he thought his plea on Charles's behalf would soften Frédéric, he was mistaken.

'No! No, they must not know!'

Joseph was astonished at the vehemence of the reaction. Captain Brousse stood up, visibly trembling, voice and expression full of an icy intensity. 'On no account are you to mention our meeting, or to speak of me – I insist upon it!'

'But why not? You are wrong if you think—'

'No! I have my reasons – leave it at that!'

His tone was so forbidding that Joseph did not dare to protest any further. He felt crushed and rather miserable. Just for a little while he had begun to feel at ease with this man, enjoying their discussion (for all its dark implications), aware even – surprisingly – of a certain affinity; but that seemed to have been destroyed beyond recall, if it had ever been there. He rose to his feet.

'It's getting late, *mon capitaine*,' he said stiffly. 'I will say good-night.'

The older man put out a hand and touched his arm, briefly, but with a kind of entreaty, which as suddenly entered his voice. 'No, I beg you – I did not intend—' He spread his hands as if he could not find words for what he wanted to say; and Joseph – touched by the helplessness of the gesture – relaxed a little and (rather warily) sat down again.

'I've some brandy somewhere, I think,' said the Captain casually. 'Would you like some?'

They drank and talked, and before long Joseph was as much at ease as if Frédéric was indeed his uncle and they had known one another all their lives. He realised he liked the man, that behind the cynicism (which in some ways rather appealed to him) was a mind akin to his own, with similar preoccupations, a similar delight in argument; even, he found, a similar taste in literature and philosophy. They were still very different, of course, but they had enough in common for Joseph to find himself, once, on the point of saying, 'One could almost believe we really were related, after all.' Then he remembered that Frédéric had no reason to believe that they were not. He wondered whether to tell him of Rosaline's confession (he had told him of her death, which apparently left him quite unmoved); and then decided against it. After all, Mathilde was the only family Frédéric had ever cared about; why take that from him unnecessarily, especially in these uncertain times?

He found himself confiding a great deal in Frédéric about his own life, his interests and ambitions – or such of them as still remained to him – and found his companion surprisingly interested in what he had to say; though he could not be persuaded to be similarly communicative about himself. Once, Joseph said, 'And what of you? What became of you when you left Casseuil? Lieutenant Girardet said you had been in Morocco.'

'Amongst other places, yes. I wandered around. Then I returned to France when war broke out. An inglorious period of my life, of no interest whatsoever . . . Tell me, where did you go to school?' And that was as much as he could be persuaded to say about his past.

They had been laughing together over some witticism of Frédéric's at the expense of their commanding officers; when Joseph happened to glance at his watch. '*Mon Dieu*; it's five o'clock! We've talked all night.'

Frédéric scanned his face. 'And you're not long out of hospital – it was selfish of me to keep you from your bed. You'd better go and get some sleep now.'

'Oh, it doesn't matter – I've nothing to do today, except wait.'

'I suspect we'll be going up the line tomorrow night, which means a busy day – but I'll find a moment to look you out, I promise.' He laid a hand on Joseph's shoulder and said with unusual warmth, 'Thank you for coming.'

Joseph stood up. 'I'm glad I came, too. Good-night.'

It was early evening before Frédéric found time to come in search of Joseph. He found the young man seated cross-legged on his bunk, writing with great concentration. Frédéric halted inside the door of the cavernous dormitory, watching him through the passing figures of soldiers making ready to leave.

At this distance the lines and shadows that the war had marked on his young face were no longer visible, and he seemed just a boy, his slim body vigorous and graceful, his curly hair emphasising the softness of an expression which was at the moment remote and faintly smiling. What was he writing so busily? Frédéric wondered. A letter? To his mother—? He tried to see her reading it, but in his mind there was only the elusive memory of the girl he had known, slender, pure, golden-haired, sweet with infinite tenderness. Now, like him, that girl would have changed, matured, lived through many experiences of which he knew nothing. He felt a sudden terrible longing to see her again, to give in to Joseph's plea that he should go to Casseuil; to hurry across to him now and tell him that after all he might write to Mathilde of their meeting. But he remained where he was, knowing that he must not do any of those things, for Mathilde's sake as well as his own; and watching the boy who was, beyond any doubting, his son.

His son; his and Mathilde's . . . Astonishing to think that from the mess and muddle of his life had come this fine and immensely likeable young man; it almost seemed to make some kind of sense of an existence that until now had seemed entirely without point or purpose. But for that to be true Joseph must somehow survive the butchery of this apparently eternal war and return unscathed to Casseuil, and to Mathilde.

Placing no value at all on his own life – wishing rather that it might very soon be brought to an end – Frédéric had not once during the course of the war felt afraid for himself, apart from the inevitable instinctive flinching of any animal confronted with danger; but he knew that he was, now, wholly, devastatingly, afraid for Joseph. He had not prayed since childhood, had never even thought of doing so; but now he was almost moved to prayer as a straw to clutch at in a suddenly dissolving and terrifying world.

At this moment Joseph, sensing something perhaps, turned his head and saw him. He smiled – a warm, boyish grin – and waved; and laid his writing materials aside and uncurled himself from the bunk. Frédéric, conscious of joy and love and pain in equal and quite appalling proportions, went to him.

'I came to say goodbye. We leave for the Thiaumont area in an hour.'

Joseph's smile faded; much of the youthfulness left his face. 'Where's that?'

'Somewhere along the ridge north-west of Fleury, up from the Ravine des Vignes, so my map indicates. It sounds positively bucolic, doesn't it?' They discussed the geography of the area for a moment or two, and Frédéric felt that they were neither of them hearing what the other was saying; which was not surprising, since it was all so trivial. It was stupid, he thought, to be talking so inconsequentially, when there was so much unsaid that clamoured for speech. But he had never been good at expressing his deepest feelings, and for years now there had been no reason for him even to try. Suddenly faced with an overpowering flood of feeling, which had in an instant swept away all the careful defences he had built up against ever feeling again, he could find no words even to say the few things he was free to say. He could not, of course, say, 'I am glad you are my son,' or 'Tell Mathilde I love her still'; but he ought not to be wholly tongue-tied.

In the end, it was Joseph who said, 'I am so glad we have met. Perhaps one day you will allow me to let them know at home – I think it would give them pleasure.' As if reading some imminent rebuff in Frédéric's expression, he went on, his tone now very earnest, 'I think we shall be going to the front line too, very soon. If anything should happen to me, and you hear of it – then will you get in touch with them? Please.'

Frédéric stood quite still; he knew he had gone very pale. He had no idea how to reply, not because he dreamed of refusing the request, but because even to think of it hurt him unendurably. Eventually, he said, 'I—no—nothing must—' and then gave up, gesturing helplessly.

After a little while, terrified that Joseph might take his near silence for a refusal, he drew a deep breath and said, drily, with great difficulty, 'I promise.'

Joseph came with hands outstretched to say goodbye, and was visibly surprised when Frédéric suddenly embraced him, reaching up to kiss him on both cheeks. A moment after, he released him, with equal suddenness. 'Take care, *mon enfant*.' He laid a hand on his son's arm. 'I hope Charles de Miremont's God exists, after all; for then He may protect you.'

'Both of us,' Joseph corrected him, 'and then you will be able to come with me to Casseuil.' All at once his voice was as husky as Frédéric's.

iii

Joseph's company had both shrunk and grown younger while he was away. It had never, in all the time he had commanded it, been up to full strength; but now many of the faces he had known had gone, and one hundred and thirty two men had been reduced to one hundred and seven – and that despite the addition of a group of new conscripts of the '16 class, many of them still only nineteen. They looked, to him, extraordinarily young, mere children even; he felt at once protective, and miserable that they should be brought into all this. They in their turn seemed to regard him as positively ancient, a veteran worthy of awed respect, an attitude that amused him.

The rumours he had heard as to the regiment's next move proved to be well founded; it was also very clear that General Pétain's carefully devised system for ensuring regular rest periods for troops between short spells in the line had been largely abandoned. After two days in the citadel, the battalion Commandant called his officers together and informed them that the next night they would be moving up under cover of darkness to the front line. Each company commander was supplied with a little sketch plan, with his position marked upon it and a note of the unit he was to relieve; and then the Commandant passed on his more general instruction. 'You will hold all the territory assigned to you at all costs; you will immediately retake any lost trenches; you will be ready to go forward to the attack the instant you receive an order to that effect.'

The same tired old phrases, Joseph thought wearily. At the Marne that command to 'hold the ground at all costs' had seemed wonderfully inspiring, putting new heart into them all; but then it had been fresh, and they had not all learned by bitter experience exactly what it could mean. However, he did as was expected of him, and carried the words back to his company and passed them on, wondering what the youngsters of the '16 class would make of them.

As they marched at dusk in double file through the suburbs of Verdun, a fresh-faced lad, who looked closer to sixteen than nineteen – Borderie, Raymond, Joseph thought, placing him in his mind – finding his commanding officer beside him, said, '*Mon lieutenant*, I hope you don't mind my asking – perhaps I seem very stupid – but I don't understand how, if we all hold our ground, there can be any lost trenches for us to retake?'

Joseph did not go so far as to admit that French troops had, now and then, been known to give way; instead he said as matter-of-factly as he could, 'Holding at all costs can mean there is no one left to defend the ground any longer. Then another unit must come in and retake it from the enemy.'

'Oh.' The boy swallowed. 'Yes. Of course.' His eyes had an odd glitter to them; Joseph recognised that look of mingled fear and pride. How long it seemed since he had felt it himself! 'One thing I'm glad about,' the boy went on, in a shyly confiding tone, 'it will be better to be able to see the enemy. I didn't much like it where we were before, just digging and putting up fences and things, and at any moment a shell could come from nowhere and – ' He demonstrated the upward movement of the shell blast with his hands. 'But you'll know about that of course.'

Joseph merely smiled. He was by no means certain that young Borderie would find any great change for the better where they were going, but there was no point in disillusioning him – he would discover the truth for himself soon enough.

'*Mon lieutenant*, have you ever been in a gas attack?'

'Once or twice. Why do you ask?'

'Do the gas masks really keep it all out?'

'Oh yes, so long as you put them on in time.' The gas masks – cumbersome and uncomfortable – were the most recent addition to the heavy pack the soldiers already carried. 'You've been trained in their use, haven't you?'

'Yes, *mon lieutenant*.'

Out here the earth seemed in constant motion, quivering and trembling beneath their feet; whilst overhead the sky was alight with a mad Olympian firework display: the cascading pink and orange blossoms of bursting shells; the brilliant greens and reds of rockets and flares – slowly opening, tinting the drifting haze, throwing lurid colours on the landscape – the quickly repeated yellow flash of gunfire along the undulating horizon.

The air was heavy with smoke; and as they crossed the river and left the suburbs behind, moving out on to the track that rose towards the eastern hills, that smoke, acrid with the odours of explosives, was soon underlaid by another smell, which approached and receded and approached again, ever more frequently, until it became at last permanent and overpowering: the sickly sweetish nauseating stench of putrefaction. On either side of the track, lit by the ceaseless lights from above, lay the bodies of horses – they had stopped using them now on the supply routes to the front, because the losses had become so great, so these corpses were old, soft and bloated and horribly decayed. More often, as they moved further away from the city, the corpses were those of men, whose burial was a last priority in this constantly bombarded battlefield.

Here and there in the column a man retched and coughed; one of the newcomers, Joseph supposed, though even he felt his stomach heave as the first wave of the smell hit him. But he had already grown used to it, in Artois; except that there it had been a faint additional aroma, only occasionally really offensive – not like this, which filled the nostrils, left a taste in the mouth, was unavoidable, pervasive, very soon becoming an

616

integral part of drawing breath, flowing into the lungs and out again, seeping through the pores. It would, he knew, only grow worse the closer they came to the front.

Other debris scattered the track and the land to either side – helmets, broken waggons tipped sideways, indeterminate rags of muddied cloth, handcarts no longer any use for bringing the wounded over this potholed terrain, oddments of equipment lost or thrown aside. Here and there they had to make a detour to avoid a shell hole, although – their guide assured them – this track so far behind the lines was rarely hit.

Further on they came to the beginning of a communication trench, scarcely more than knee high and before long shallower still, so that it became no more than a scrape pitted by half-filled-in shell holes: it could not conceivably offer any kind of shelter.

Sometimes they were overtaken by stretcher bearers, hurrying to bring in the wounded under cover of darkness, and – increasingly – slower parties met them, returning, burdened with groaning heaps of humanity; or an *homme-soupe* hurried by, encumbered with great circular loaves of army bread threaded on a string about his neck, and bottles of *pinard* tucked beneath his arm, making his way to supply some hungry unit; or a frightened runner carrying messages to or from headquarters.

The trench ran up into the foothills, on through the darkness of a ravine, full of blasted trees, like a steep, blackened outsize stubble field. Here and there, faint reminiscent smells of earth and vegetation lingered, stabbing with concentrated and swiftly vanishing sweetness through the pervasive stench. In other places, someone stumbled over some unseen obstacle, and a groan or a cry would indicate a wounded man, fallen there who knew how long ago, lying helpless across their path. They would move him aside, but left it to others to get him to safety. Only some of the youngsters were much troubled by it.

Further on still, coming into the open again, the trench disappeared altogether and they could do no more than follow their guide, blindly, picking their way around tangled heaps of barbed wire, shell holes whose precipitous sides slid down beyond sight, great black lumps of shell fragments, and more

617

and more of the weird distorted shapes they knew to be fallen men only by the intensifying of the smell.

Ahead and over them the shelling was subsiding, not to silence, but to an occasional isolated burst of noise and flame; the earth steadied and stilled. Joseph could sense that everywhere over those darkening slopes and along the shadowed ravines, men were emerging from trenches and shell holes, like nocturnal animals from their lairs, to the few brief hours of frenzied activity that the short night allowed them before the shelling began again at dawn. Their own path became as busy with passing groups as any country high road.

They knew when they had reached their destination not by any sign of trench or dugout, but because, just below the crest of a ridge, their guide told them to halt and pointed out to Joseph where the officer he was to relieve waited for him with the handful of exhausted men who were – at last – to return down the line. So this is it, thought Joseph wryly. Our home for the next few days.

More than a month later, as June burned towards its close, they were still there.

iv

Darkness came late, bringing little lessening of the heat. The guns pounded on, and now and then a shell burst near them, but the bombardment tonight was intent on other targets. Joseph crept out of the hole where he had spent the day and instructed his sergeant to collect together a trenching detail. He despatched two reluctant privates back down the lines for supplies (perhaps tonight they would get through), checked on the condition of the wounded (one more had joined them that day and two had died; another – haemorrhaging badly – clearly hadn't long to go) and wondered fleetingly when they would next see a stretcher party; he had too few men left to spare anyone to carry the wounded away. Then he gave the day's reports – casualty list, a handful of identity tags, equipment returns, urgent requests for ammunition, an uninformative account of the unvarying bombardment – to a man whose shoulder wound needed attention but who could at least walk; and sent him on his way to the command post at Quatre Cheminées, back on the edge of the Ravine des Vignes which ran down from their sector towards the valley. 'Don't try and come back,' he told him, and saw the man's face relax a little with relief. 'Get yourself to the clearing station afterwards. They can send someone else with the ammunition.'

The shelling had died down a little by now. Joseph emerged on to the open land just in front of a random series of holes and dips where the company had cowered beneath the shells, and took a length of white tape from his pocket and laid it in an impeccably straight line across their position, to show where the digging party should begin work on a new trench. Seeing them quickly setting to work on the nightly task (looking up now and then, fearful that a flare might shoot up to mark their position for some hidden machine gunner) Joseph had a sudden momentary recollection of one of the kitchen maids scrubbing the kitchen floor at Casseuil and grumbling fluently at him as he tramped muddy shoes across it from the garden. 'Always to do again, that's the trouble with this job,' she had said. 'You just finish, and someone messes it all up again.' But he pushed the thought quickly aside. It was unwise to allow memories to intrude out here; or any thoughts, apart from the superficial practical questions that had to be dealt with from day to day. Anything else, and one would quickly go mad.

The sound of the digging replaced the noise of the guns. They might have been peasants at work in the fields; except that the men never sang – or even spoke – as they worked, and the sound of the spades, striking stones or metal fragments, then slicing through some softer matter, seemed to Joseph to have something horrible about it. Perhaps it was only in his imagination, because he knew from experience what lay embedded in that tormented earth, how often the spades would come up against some dissolving remnant of a corpse. In the early days here they had tried to avoid the corpses, moving to another spot if the ground was too encumbered; but they had quickly realised that this was impracticable and the dead had become – like every other kind of debris – just an inevitable part of the trench wall. They were all by now inured to the unpleasantness of it, though it made things particularly uncomfortable during the baking heat of the June days.

By dawn there was a semblance of a trench for them to

crouch in as the bombardment revived. No peepholes here, or sandbags or duckboards or dugouts or latrines or any of the other features with which even the most basic of the trenches Joseph had known in two years of war had been supplied: this ditch, inadequately protected by a haphazard and tangled barbed wire fence, was scarcely half a metre in height – but there was nothing he could do about it. By evening it would almost certainly be reduced once more to a churned-up line of dips and hillocks.

By day the battlefield bore no trace of the sinister magic of the night-time display. The sun rose on a world without colour, a scarred and pimpled landscape of drab greys and browns, and the sickly greens of the rapidly reducing pools of thick, scum-covered, foul-smelling water lurking in the bottom of the older shell holes. If evil could take physical shape, Joseph thought, then this was it, this endless dreary stretch of poisoned land on which the bursting shells alternately buried and disinterred the bodies of the dead, adding incessantly somewhere or other to their number.

'Each one of us,' his father would say sometimes, 'each man and woman and child, is sacred, made in the image of God, a temple of the Holy Spirit.' This morning, as he crouched low watching the shells do their work, the words came to Joseph as a kind of harshly ironic commentary on the scene before him. 'The image of God' – here at the mercy of the shells, God's image, these fragile human bodies, had become mere playthings, mice to a giant unseen cat, battered, dismembered, torn, tossed high over the battleground, thrown down again in fragments that sometimes became missiles themselves. It was, Joseph thought in a rare interval of conscious revulsion, the ultimate in blasphemy – or a bitter demonstration that in the moral void of the universe there was no longer any limit to the horror that was possible, if there had ever been.

The sun rose higher, piercing the smoke that drifted across the shuddering ground, setting Joseph's head throbbing beneath the heavy rim of his steel helmet. He could not remember when he had last slept, and he was parched with thirst; they all were. No supplies had got through to them for four days now, not since the last inadequate ration of foul-smelling water – 'tastes of corpses,' one man had said in disgust; but he had drunk it all the same – and *pinard* (only a little, for most of the bottles had smashed on the way up) – and dirt-encrusted bread. What, if anything, was left in their flasks had to be carefully conserved, as far as was possible. Somewhere about him Joseph had the remains of a bar of chocolate, oozing out of its wrapping in the heat, but hungry though he was he did not eat it; he would only be the more thirsty afterwards.

There came a long rushing whine and a shell burst just in front of the trench, across the barbed wire; the blast flung them back, scattering earth and fragments over them. One man, hit, gave a cry which subsided very soon to a continual low moaning, but there was nothing anyone could do to help him before nightfall. They crept back to the trench, bent low, protecting themselves as best they could with their packs, faces close to the foul stinking earth.

In the afternoon great bloated bluebottles buzzed around them, feeding on the corpse fragments; the stench was appalling. Beneath the noise of the bombardment someone began to cry, miserably, like an abandoned child. Joseph heard it with indifference, as just one more sound in this place of evil noises. Here one came not to acceptance – how could this ever be acceptable? – but to a kind of moral torpor, a state in which every normal sensitivity was deadened and repressed. It was the only way to survive.

Suddenly, to his left, there was a scream, repeated again and again. A figure leapt out of the trench and began to run, laughing now, wildly, between the screams, back towards the distant uneven line of the next position. Behind him, others were scrambling to their feet, following raggedly; the whole of that length of trench was full of movement. Joseph jumped to his feet, hurriedly drawing his revolver as he ran. 'Get back! Get back at once, all of you!'

They paused, turned frightened eyes upon him – those terrible blank, dazed eyes in the gaunt, dirty, bearded faces – saw the gun pointed at them, and stumbled resentfully back to the trench; even the first man followed them, with Joseph's hand at his elbow, directing his steps – it was young Borderie, Joseph realised. He went with them into the trench, stationing himself watchfully beside them. Borderie, shivering and whimpering, was quieter now; the others gave him curious sideways looks, but left him alone.

The next moment, Joseph had no time to do more than think, This is it . . . before a shell burst full in the trench. He felt the heat of it, the blast forcing the breath from his body; felt himself flung back; heard the patter of fragments, earth, stones, other debris, falling round him like rain; and opened his eyes in the tiny silence that followed to realise, with some astonishment, that he was shaken but unhurt, come to rest on the lip of the crater that had opened where the trench had been. Raising his head he saw that the rest of the line was still intact, marked by the grey gleam of steel helmets.

All that remained of his immediate companions, however, was a scattering of scarcely recognisable pieces of flesh and torn clothing; a gas mask and a helmet; two men lying at the far side of the hole. Joseph edged his way cautiously towards them. One was dead, half his body blown away; the other lay staring at the sky with a bloody froth bubbling out of his mouth. Joseph held his hand until, very soon, he too died; then he collected the identity discs and retreated to what he hoped was the safest side of the crater. The bombardment beyond sounded tremendous, incessant now. He flattened himself against the earth.

After a time he heard voices shouting, feeble below the din; a handful of blue figures appeared outlined against the sky, wreathed in smoke, and then were as suddenly blasted away. One man, supporting another, tumbled with a cry down the slope, dragging the other with him. He rolled against Joseph and lay still. Joseph sat up, keeping his head low, and looked at them. They were not men of his company, or even of his regiment; from what he knew of the French positions, they should have been somewhere to the south-east of here, along the ridge. Clearly, behind the barrage of shells, the Germans had moved in to the attack, driving these men before them. It had become common enough in the constantly fluctuating fighting of the past weeks, first one way then the other, a German advance, a French counter-attack – though all the time the German lines had edged, under the deadly cover of their artillery, just that little bit further forward, across the

French positions, infiltrating a ravine, overrunning a ridge, met always by a desperate resistance – or almost always.

The man nearest to Joseph was quite obviously dead; the other, a Captain (wounded some time ago by the look of him) was still alive, but only just. Almost certainly, left without leadership, reduced to a mere remnant, the company had retreated suicidally through the bombardment until none of them remained. They would have done better to have abandoned their Captain to the Germans, rather than risk their lives carrying him, since he was unlikely to last long, if the bloody mess of his body below the waist was anything to go by. Joseph's mind registered that the number on the collar was that of Girardet's regiment – and Captain Brousse's . . . His gaze moved to the still grey face beneath the helmet; and recognition slowly reached him. Beneath the rough grizzled beard, the dirt – it was Frédéric, surely?

The light eyes opened, unfocused for a moment, and then settled on him. He was not sure whether or not they knew him. He bent closer and took the tensed fingers in his. '*Mon capitaine* – uncle – do you know me? Joseph, Mathilde's son.' He thought then that there was just the faintest shadow of a smile on the thin lips. Frédéric had heard him then, even through the din of the bombardment; and he knew him.

Here in the shell hole the heat was caught and held, intensified. Conscious of his own thirst, Joseph reached for his flask and moistened Frédéric's lips with a little of the *pinard*; afterwards – though he heard nothing – he thought the man murmured, 'Thank you.' Then he closed his eyes and lay so still that Joseph wondered if he had died. He felt for a pulse – no, not yet; there was a faint flicker of life.

He did not know how long he crouched there, except that somewhere beyond the smoke, far over the rooftops of Verdun (not visible from here) the sun was sinking in the sky; but he did not want to disturb Frédéric by moving his hand to look at his watch. He became aware at last that the dying man's eyes were open again, fixed intently upon his face. There was a look of fierce concentration about Frédéric's whole demeanour, as if he had drawn all his resources together for some crucial purpose, not yet achieved. Perhaps there was something he wanted to say; if so, he must wait for a moment of quiet, or all his efforts would be wasted – but that might be a long time coming. Joseph bent towards him. 'What is it?' he asked as clearly as he could. Frédéric said nothing, did not move, but retained that look of waiting and listening.

A silence did fall, a sudden lull. The thin lips moved, and with a final tremendous effort of will Frédéric forced out a few faint gasping words. 'Mathilde – tell her – her son is a – credit to – his – father . . .'

'I will, of course I will,' Joseph whispered, painfully moved to realise that here at last was the gesture towards the reconciliation he had so wanted to bring about. He realised that it was unlikely that Frédéric had heard him, for, exhausted by the effort, he had closed his eyes and appeared now to be scarcely conscious.

It had not been merely a lull. The bombardment had ceased altogether. The air was still, but for the rumbling of their own artillery somewhere along the ridge towards Fort Souville.

Joseph did not want to leave Frédéric while he still lived – the protective indifference had temporarily left him. But the unexpected stilling of the guns, especially in daylight, was often the signal for a major attack, and his responsibility was to the living men in his care, not to the dying. Gently he freed his fingers from Frédéric's clasp, bent to kiss the still face, gently, on the forehead, and then, with painful regret, scrambled up the slope to investigate.

A handful of men were emerging from their holes and from what was left of the trench, a little warily, watching the eastern horizon for signs of life. A sergeant said, 'Our guns have stopped!' Joseph realised it was true. The utter silence should have been welcome, but it was not, for it was so inexplicable as to be sinister. Then just as – a little absently – he noticed near his feet a cluster of flies buzzing in their death throes on a piece of rotting flesh, he became aware of a new smell, pungent, sickening, a little vinegary; and a choking sensation in his throat.

'Gas!' he shouted. 'Get your gas masks on!'

He fumbled for his own, fastening it quickly in place. Then he thought of Frédéric, there in the hollow where the poison would seep down and linger for days. If he was conscious still – he must not die like that.

He slithered back down the crater; but he was too late. Gasping, retching, Frédéric lay convulsed by a kind of agonising intensification of a death rattle. Joseph could do nothing at all, except take him in his arms and hold him there against his breast until, a moment or two after, he died. Joseph slid the identity tag from Frédéric's wrist and put it with the others in his pocket.

Only then, as he turned and made his way laboriously up the slope once more did he realise that he was himself gasping painfully. It was never easy to breathe in a gas mask, but it should not be this difficult, with each breath struggled for through a constriction like a strangler's fingers about the throat. He coughed and fought desperately for air, stumbling a little as he reached the others. There must be something wrong with his gas mask.

Two men, too late in getting their masks on, were already dead; but near him a third, anonymous behind that grotesque disguise, clutched at his throat and fell; and another further off. He saw in the masked faces now turning towards him the realisation that was dawning, horribly, on him: that this was some new kind of gas, something from which their masks had never been designed to protect them.

They were lucky, if it could be called that. If the gas filtered through their masks it still lost some of its concentration on the way; and it was clear (since they had seen no sign of the deadly silent shells) that the force of the attack had not been directed at them. By dawn, when the gas had cleared, lingering only in the hollows, there were, mercifully, few fatalities amongst the company. But beyond the ridge the French guns were still silent. 'That's where the gas attack was,' the Sergeant said. 'We just got the edge of it.' Joseph thought he was probably right.

The next morning the enemy shelling began again in a great sweeping barrage that heralded the massive German assault for which the gas had cleared the way.

v

'Reading between the lines, I'd say the first day of the British attack on the Somme was a disaster,' commented Laure, as she sat in the *grand salon* turning the pages of a newspaper while they waited for lunch. 'They use words like "courageous" and "heated German resistance".'

'There was something about a French advance,' Mathilde pointed out, her knitting needles stilling for a moment.

'Yes,' said Laure drily. 'They "gained all their first day objectives", it says – which probably means they advanced a couple of metres. Besides, there was only a handful of our troops involved.'

'Charles says the offensive was designed to relieve the pressure on Verdun. Perhaps it's succeeded, in that at least.'

'Let's hope so.' Laure read on a little, then said more cheerfully, 'At least there can be no doubt that the war in the air is going our way. It's strange isn't it, when you think about it, that men should be fighting up there far above our heads.' She raised her eyes to the painted beams, as if she half-expected to see aeroplanes there. 'What time do you expect Marie-Françoise tonight? I'd like to prepare myself for the usual assault. I must say, I do wish they'd let her go to the front. She will continue to be impossible until they do.'

'But they are quite right, she is much too young,' said Mathilde. She laid the knitting aside. 'Where is Charles? He promised to be back for lunch today. He can't go on overworking like this, and not eating properly. He'll be ill.'

'He's always home for dinner,' Laure pointed out. 'I don't think he is likely to suffer seriously from malnutrition.' She glanced keenly at her daughter. 'However, I wonder sometimes if there are other things that he lacks . . .'

'Oh?' There was a note of reserve in Mathilde's voice.

'I could be wrong. I just have a feeling sometimes that he is carrying all your burdens as well as his own, and that perhaps you don't give him a great deal in return.'

Mathilde coloured very faintly. 'I am sure you are wrong,' she said firmly. 'That's why I want him to look after himself – because I care about him . . . I wish he would come home.'

'Perhaps some more names came in this morning,' suggested Laure.

'Oh, I pray not! It's only two days since the last ones . . . Poor Madame Delmas – she looked so ill when I saw her after mass yesterday.'

'Yes, Moïse is frantic with worry. With two nephews lost

626

he's sure Jean-Marc will be next.' She folded the newspapers and said, 'I think we should begin without Charles. You know he could be hours late. I'll go and tell Nanon.' She left the room, closing the door behind her.

She had almost reached the kitchen stairs when she realised there was someone behind her, standing quite still in the middle of the hall. She swung round.

'Charles! We didn't hear you come in—' She stopped: he had his hands pressed to his eyes. 'Charles, what is it?'

He let his hands fall and stared at her, but she was not sure if he really saw her. In all the years of the war he had never looked so ill as this, so white and haunted. He remained where he was, saying absolutely nothing, though his mouth opened and closed again, slowly. Laure realised that he had been crying – for a long time perhaps, for his eyes were rimmed with red, his skin blotched and swollen. She laid a hand on his arm.

'Charles—' she prompted, very gently.

He stirred, focusing his eyes on her. 'I came – I was home on time – but I couldn't—' He stopped and swallowed hard.

'Were there more names?'

He nodded. 'One, yes.'

Poor Charles, Laure thought. Then, 'Who is it, *mon cher*?' She was ready to try and console him, as best she could.

He held out a hand – it was trembling slightly – the fingers closed about something, which he dropped into her palm. She looked at it: a metal disc, dented and scratched and blackened, though the name and number engraved on it were still legible. It was some time before the words registered in her mind.

She raised her eyes to his face, aware only of a complete disbelief. 'There must be some mistake. It can't be his.'

'There is no mistake. He – fell – on the 23rd of June, at Verdun.'

She stared at him. Behind her the door opened. Mathilde said, 'I thought I heard voices,' and then, faltering, 'Charles—'

'It's Joseph,' he said quietly, and opened his arms to her. She gave a terrible anguished cry and ran past her mother to Charles's embrace.

Laure stayed exactly where she was, gazing into space and shaking her head again and again. 'No,' she murmured, 'no, it can't be true – no—'

CHAPTER
THIRTY ONE

i

For Mathilde that July day closed a door, for ever, on a part of her life that once had been its core.

In a perverse kind of way, the news of Joseph's death came almost as a relief, because some instinct had told her right from the beginning that she would lose him, one day; and it had been agonising, waiting for that day, wondering how long she still had. Now, finally and to eternity, everything that had linked her to Frédéric had gone. All she had left was Charles and his children; nothing came between them any more and – surely, at last – the penance had been paid in full. There was nothing more to fear, because the worst had happened. There was a kind of rightness about it.

That did not make her grief less real, but it made it somehow tolerable. She turned for consolation to Nanon, whose view of things she so strongly shared, and to Charles, because she could comfort herself by helping him, unreservedly, as she had never done before. The force of his grief appalled her, not least because of her knowledge that Joseph was not his son. Once, she thought, If I were to tell him the truth, would he be able to accept Joseph's death more easily? But she knew the answer quite well. His love for Joseph was too deep-rooted to be destroyed by learning that he had not fathered him. In every sense but that – the simple biological fact – he *was* Joseph's father, who had loved and nurtured the boy from infancy; more truly so than Frédéric had ever been. No, to tell him the truth would only bring him still more pain, of another and perhaps more tormenting kind. So, tenderly, lovingly, Mathilde gave all she had to Charles and his needs.

For Laure, alone and unneeded by any of them, it was

another matter. At first, disbelieving, she refused to accept Joseph's death at all; refused, until she saw the official notice with his name and the stark details, and the letter that came to Charles from Joseph's battalion commander, speaking of him in the warmest terms and describing how – with a handful of men – he had held off a German attack until all of them had perished. The next day, retaking the captured position, a relieving force had found the company's remains. The Commandant ended by saying that he had recommended Joseph for a posthumous *Croix de Guerre*.

That promise – which brought tears of sorrowful pride to Charles's eyes – impressed Laure not at all; what use to anyone was a dead hero? Convinced at last that Joseph had gone, she found herself possessed by a consuming rage. She wanted to scream and shout and stamp and fling herself to the floor with fists and heels drumming in defiant anger against the providence that had done this thing to her, whoever He was, wherever He was.

It was as if some tacit agreement, some unwritten contract, had been irrevocably and independently broken by one of the parties, on a cosmic scale. For this (some part of her had bargained), for this I will endure everything you throw at me, all you ask, every pain and hardship; for this I will resist the darkest temptation – even to murder itself: for the sake of the goal which you will undertake that I shall reach at last. And that goal, taking a beloved human shape, had been Joseph, who had embodied all the hopes and dreams and ambitions of her life. She had never really been afraid for him, however grim the news of the war, because she had been so convinced, so utterly certain, that he was meant to come back.

And now this had happened. After all she had gone through, all she had done. It was unjust, cruel, senseless. In the *chai*, in the vineyard, in her room, she cursed the power that had so betrayed her, all her bitterness pouring out in a white-hot flow of words, unspoken, or cried aloud in some lonely place.

And then when that brought her no relief, no answer, she knew why at last; it was because there was no power, no providence that could shape her life. She had bargained with an illusion, with something that did not exist. Any sense of purpose was a mirage, and she had fooled herself. Life was a random series of incidents leading only to extinction, and no more. Beyond the animal that was Laure Séguier, her senses, her mind, her emotions, the beating heart that had loved Joseph so, there was only emptiness.

The rage left her, but what followed it was far worse, for there was nothing to take its place. What she felt now was not grief exactly, because she did not really feel anything at all. No loss or pain in her life before this had left her so devastated, in the most literal sense of the word: her spirit had been crushed, destroyed, blown to the winds. All that remained was her body, going somehow through the motions of daily life with the thoroughness of habit, but as dead and cold and empty inside as the hearth in the deserted house at La Borie long ago, with its damp black ashes.

The third winter of the war was a bitter one, in every sense. Snow fell and lay for days, coating the hills and the valley, and piercing frosts threatened the vines. Laure did what she ought to protect them, but did not really care whether they died or not. A slight cold, ignored and neglected as she filled her days with pointless activity outdoors and in, turned to a fever and then to pneumonia.

Old Doctor Bonnet called daily; and Mathilde and Nanon, the more anxious because they could not remember that she had ever been ill before, even very slightly, sat by turns at her bedside. Laure, dimly aware of what was happening, assumed it was the end, and was glad.

She did not die, or not immediately. Slowly the fever and inflammation lessened, and finally left her altogether. But she recovered so far and then no further. Weak and tired she lay day after day in bed, showing no interest in anything, taking the food or the medicine that were offered, but making no improvement at all. Doctor Bonnet was clearly deeply concerned.

Then, in January, Marie-Françoise passed her twenty-first birthday and was at last old enough for the serious nursing she so passionately wanted to do. She came home for a few days before leaving for a front line hospital, and established herself in Laure's room, taking over there with an unsentimental briskness that daunted them all.

Laure opened her eyes one afternoon to find her grand-daughter sitting on the edge of the bed looking down at her, as if willing her to wake up and pay attention; she had a very determined expression on her small face. Laure's first instinct was to close her eyes again, but some faint stirring of curiosity prevented her from doing so. She waited, returning Marie-Françoise's stare, but not otherwise moving.

'You know, Grand-mère,' said Marie-Françoise, 'there is absolutely no reason why you should not get well. It is up to you.'

Laure did not waste her energy denying it. 'Then I choose not to,' she said stubbornly. 'That is my right.'

'If you like,' said Marie-Françoise; then she added, 'The world didn't come to an end just because Joseph died, you know.' There was not the least concession to gentleness in her tone.

'Yours may not have done,' returned Laure, trying to match her granddaughter's astringency. 'As far as I am concerned I see no possible point in going on. What is there left for me now, tell me that?'

'A great deal. The vineyard still – I think that's worth something, even if you do not. And then there are all the other people who love you and who don't want to lose you.'

'Do you expect me to believe that I matter that much to anyone? Who really cares whether an old woman lives or dies?'

'Now you're being self-pitying, and that at least isn't like you, thank goodness. You know quite well that we care, if you're honest with yourself.' She concluded airily, 'If nothing else I want you to live long enough to see me qualified as a doctor. You'd be so proud of me.'

Quite against her inclination, Laure found herself struggling to sit up, suddenly intrigued. 'What's this? I've heard nothing about this!'

'Of course you haven't – you've been lying there feeling sorry for yourself. Though to be honest I've only just decided – or, rather, I've only just taken some firm steps about it. Now I know. I shall get all the experience I can in nursing and then as soon as the war is over I shall go and train as a doctor.

It seems to me the world's had more than enough of destruction; we could do with a few more people devoting themselves to healing. Don't you agree?'

Laure did manage to sit up (Marie-Françoise, watching her, had made no effort to help). 'Yes, yes I do. What does your father say?'

'He was surprised; but once he got used to the idea I think he was pleased, and Maman too – but then she always agrees with him in the end.' She laughed. 'Nanon thinks it's all very improper – a *girl* wanting to be a doctor: what is the world coming to!'

Laure smiled faintly and reached out to clasp her grand-daughter's hand. 'So – you think I should hang on, just to see what becomes of you?'

'Curiosity's as good a reason as any for living, isn't it?'

Perhaps it was, thought Laure; and in any case it was the only reason she had at the moment.

Gradually she regained her strength, until on the day Marie-Françoise left for the north she was able to see her off from the front doorstep (afterwards, Charles closed the door on her quickly, because of the cold). After that, piece by piece, she picked up the threads of her life, steadily resuming her old routine. It still seemed to her largely without point, but she tried not to dwell on that too much. A day at a time, that was enough to be going on with; better not to think any further ahead.

ii

A year of uncertain weather drew towards its end with an autumn of warm clear days opening and closing in mist. It was the autumn that, for years, Laure had dreamed about. The vines were fully mature now – there were even new generations, some already well grown, planted alongside to assure the future of the vineyard – and the frosts of last winter had done no more than encourage them to fight the harder for survival; which meant the most luscious fruit, ripening gently and turning day by day through that lovely autumn to a perfection of rottenness.

Only there was no labour to be had. That year the older men had been sent home from the army to work on the land, but most of them were exhausted by years of war, and of little use; and since everyone over eighteen (and a few unlucky seventeen-year-olds) had been called up in their place it meant in effect less help and not more. It also caused Mathilde renewed anguish. 'Oh, Maman, Philippe will be eighteen in two years – what if it goes on as long as that?'

'It won't,' said Laure staunchly, 'not now the Americans have come in.' But she was speaking from habit rather than conviction. She was not sure about anything any more.

The smaller vineyards, dependent largely on family labour, could gather the Casseuil grapes without too much difficulty, so long as a neighbour or two gave a hand. But for Laure with her twenty hectares it was another matter. Even Charles, doing his best to organise the commune's workforce, could do little for her. 'I am so sorry,' he said, as if he were somehow personally responsible for this failure. They were standing together in the entrance to the courtyard, looking out over the vines, whose golden leaves were gloriously lit by the morning sun slanting through the mist.

'It's not your fault,' said Laure quietly. 'I have a choice, I suppose. I can do what we did the last three years, and just go through the vineyard once, picking everything that's even passable. That way, we shall have a pleasant enough wine – sweet, perhaps quite good, but no more. Or I can try and do several pickings – which will mean we may have a superb wine, but with so few *vendangeurs* there'll only be the tiniest bit, and most of the grapes are sure to go to waste.' She looked up at her son-in-law. 'What do you think?'

'I don't know, *madame* – I really don't know. I am only sad that it should come to this.' Laure could read in his face something of the same feeling she had: 'It is sad; but, set against everything else, such a little thing.'

'I think I shall have to compromise, that's all,' Laure decided.

In Philippe's day it had taken eighty skilled pickers to harvest the grapes. More recently, Laure had been forced, often, to manage with many fewer – as few as fifty sometimes. But this year, in spite of ridiculously high wages, she could find scarcely fifteen workers to come. It was not just the absence of the men of course, but the fact that the women –

who had always formed the bulk of the *vendangeurs* – had so many extra tasks to do at home that they could not spare the time to work at the château. Even those who did come could often give only a day or two here and there. Laure herself – like all the members of her household – worked through every daylight hour, as strenuously as if she cared deeply what became of the harvest.

Meanwhile, day by day, an ever larger number of grapes, purple-brown and dusty with spores, decayed and fell to the ground, because there was no one to pick them.

Early in November, his own harvest over, Aubin came to help her. They worked together along the rows, talking little. It was a slow and depressing business, because by now few grapes were still fit to be gathered. Late in the morning exhaustion forced them to take a break. They perched on the coping around the *caveau*, looking over the valley, where the scent of roses was wafted towards them on the lightest of breezes.

'We're getting old, that's our trouble, you and I,' said Laure after a moment.

'We're all getting old, every one of us,' Aubin said. He had rested his head on the fence behind him and closed his eyes. 'And we're all that's left. It's taken everything else, this war – our youth, our future, our life blood, everything. Even the young are only young in years. A country of the old and the maimed—'

Laure had never known him so fluently bitter before, but then like so many he had never until now had such good cause for bitterness. 'How is Jacques?' she asked, following his train of thought.

'Oh, not so bad in himself now. But when he's at home he just sits around the house like a ghost. Not that he's at home much. He spends more time in the café with the other disabled soldiers. He comes to life there all right – all political talk, and angry at that; with reason perhaps.' He shifted his position restlessly. 'You know what he told me? He says there were serious troubles in the army back in May.'

'I heard rumours of failing morale.'

'It was more than that, it seems. He heard of whole regiments rounded up and shot – that was when he was in hospital of course. He says they had to send Pétain in to sort things out, but by then it had taken firm hold. Infected by the Russian troubles some said. But I reckon it takes more than a few soldiers singing the "Internationale" to break an army.'

'Three years of war and yet another bloody, pointless offensive to tickle a General's vanity – yes, I know.'

'You mean the Nivelle offensive? Yes, that was the last straw, I understand. But there's one thing I can't get out of my mind—'

'Yes?'

'Jean died in May. What if he didn't die in battle, as they said? What if he was shot, for mutiny? They wouldn't have told me that, would they?'

'What does Jacques say?'

'He says the 108th was sound, all through. But then he would, wouldn't he? There are some things you'd never admit, especially not to your own father.'

'Believe him. You can't do anything else. You'll only torment yourself otherwise.'

'I have to believe him. But I don't, even so – not completely. I suppose I'll never know.' He sighed; and then observed casually, 'They say there's been more trouble in the chemical factory in Bergerac.'

'Workers singing the "Internationale" again, I suppose. Or is it another strike?'

'Not this time. Just some who'd like one.'

'I can't say I blame them, any of them, even if I wouldn't do it myself. As you say, we've given everything to this war, all that we care about, all our strength. Yet victory seems as far away as ever. If some people want peace at any price, short of outright defeat, then who can blame them?'

'It'll still come too late to give us back our future. That's gone for ever; the present too, for the most part. All we've got left is the past, and that will die with us.'

Laure's mood was too much in tune with his for her to be able to disagree, or to say anything to cheer him; though in fact after a moment she did think of something.

'You may have a future yet – there may be grandchildren.'

'I doubt it,' said Aubin bitterly. 'Jacques hardly speaks to Anne these days. No.' He stood up slowly. 'It's the way things are – money in the bank, good land, and no one to pass it on to . . . Shall we get back to work?'

They worked and worked, and poured the dusty grapes into the press, and set the must on its wild fermenting course. But by the end of November the rain came and Laure watched the greater part of a wonderful harvest turn finally to a mass of common rottenness, and could do nothing to save it.

She felt a great sadness, but it was a dreary, accepting kind of sensation. She had done her best and she had failed. It was a pity – a terrible pity – but she could not feel that it mattered very much any more.

CHAPTER
THIRTY TWO

i

Several of the little flags had fallen out of the map, but for a long time now no one had bothered to put them back: until recently, because there was never any significant change in the lines; in the past few days because the change had been too terrible to be marked so starkly.

After so many years of stagnation, to be faced with this, a sudden concentrated German offensive that had broken right through the Allied front, forcing the British towards the coast and the French, fighting desperately all the way, back on Paris. Was it all to end like this – after all they had gone through, all the blood and pain and loss – in total defeat? The very thought was unbearable.

Laure did not look at the map as she passed it on her way outside. From the courtyard she could see Mathilde and Philippe walking through the wood towards the village, on their way to confession, in preparation for tomorrow's Easter celebrations. She had no intention of following their example. She continued to go to mass on Sundays only because to have explained her reasons for not doing so would have distressed Charles, who had quite enough cause for unhappiness already. But she knew it was all a sham, quite meaningless.

She made her way to the vineyard, where there were some small jobs requiring her attention – Moïse was sick again, so she had been without help for some days. It was quite warm today, with an occasional gleam of sunlight, a gentle spring day: she enjoyed the time she spent making repairs, where necessary, to the fencing on which the vines were trained. Afterwards she walked along the rows gathering up the twigs left lying there after the pruning, which no one had found time to clear, and piled them beside the track and set light to them. She stood watching the little fire smouldering and crackling away near her feet, sending up a sweet-smelling smoke into the soft air.

She became aware, without much interest, that someone was pushing a bicycle slowly up the hill; that he (or she) had stopped at the top of the hill – as well he might, for it was a steep climb. Then she realised from the sounds that the cyclist had turned on to the château drive. She looked round and for a moment her eyes seemed to have transferred the flames of the little fire to some point half way up the pale stone walls of the stable, alongside which the track ran. Then she blinked, clearing her vision, and saw that the colour was the same, but that it belonged not to a fire but to a young man with fiery coloured hair who was coming slowly her way.

She watched him and wondered who he could be; he was certainly no one she had ever seen before in her life – she would have remembered that hair. She smiled to herself – one could almost imagine being able to warm one's hands at its brightness.

He was not very tall, slightly made, dressed in civilian clothes of a rather unusual cut, and he was pushing the bicycle with one hand. He had no choice about that, she saw, for his other sleeve was pinned, empty, across his chest. His face – freckled, with eyes (blue, were they?) that looked eagerly about him as he came – was marked with a long burn scar down one side, puckering the skin a little, and very pink, as if not long healed. One of the soldiers from Trissac perhaps.

Then he saw her, propped the bicycle against the wall, and came over to her, smiling and removing his hat, so that his hair shone more brightly still. '*Madame*, I am not sure if I have come to the right place. Is this the Château de Casseuil?'

She was intrigued. He spoke fluently, but with an odd accent – American, was it? 'Yes, that's right, *monsieur*. How can I help you?'

'I am looking for a Madame Séguier.'

'Then look no further.'

He grinned delightedly; in spite of the scar, he had a most

attractive smile – and, yes, his eyes were blue, bright lively eyes. He held out his hand towards her.

'Mike Freeman, *madame* – though it should be Frémont, I suppose. My grandfather always thought we'd let the family down.'

She took his hand and he began to shake it vigorously, while she stared at him, doubting, questioning, hoping, all at once.

'Your grandfather?'

'Marcel Frémont – your brother I believe, *madame*.'

She gave a little joyous shout of laughter. '*Marcel*? You're Marcel's grandson? Oh, how wonderful! Stand there, let me look at you – oh, I can hardly believe it!' She looked him up and down, chattering on without quite knowing what she was saying, and then she embraced him; and then she linked her arm through his and said, 'Come in and meet everyone – tell us all about yourself – and Marcel – and all of you.'

They met the others in the courtyard, returning in a solemn silence from the village; Charles was with them now. They halted and looked questioningly at the strange young man, and then at Laure's radiant face.

'Let me present Mike Freeman, my own – what is it now? – great-nephew, that's right.'

There were exclamations and embraces, rather more subdued perhaps than Laure's had been, but warm enough for all that. Mathilde hurried to tell Nanon that there would be one more for lunch, and another bed to be made ready. 'You will stay for some days, won't you?' Charles and Laure, with Philippe an interested third, went with Mike to the *grand salon*, Laure questioning him eagerly all the way. 'How is Marcel? How does he look now? Is he well?'

'Very well, *madame*. Like you, he does not show his age. He misses my grandmother of course – they were very close; but I think that if two people have been happy together then at least there are good memories, when one of them dies: it makes it easier to bear. And he has his painting – that keeps him interested.'

'Painting? Then he has taken it up again?'

'Oh yes, since he retired that has been his whole life – wonderful paintings they are too – very different from his early style, I believe.' 'Thank you,' he said to Charles, who had quietly indicated a comfortable chair to their guest, since Laure seemed to have forgotten about such trivial matters. Mike sat down. 'Yes, he and Rose think of nothing else. They are two of a kind, you know.'

Laure sat down near him. 'Rose?'

'My sister – she's nearly nineteen now, two years younger than me. She was painting – drawing, anyway – oh, before she could walk, I should think. They get together, her and my grandfather, and you can't get any sense out of them for hours, unless you talk about painting too.' He grinned, with a warmth that hinted at a lively affection for his sister. 'But she's good company, all the same. Maybe you'll meet her one day. What she really wants is to come and study in Paris, when all this is over.'

'When,' he said; and cheerfully, as if that day would come soon, and not with defeat. Laure found his confidence consoling, as was his presence, and the flow of first-hand news of her beloved brother.

It was only as they went in to lunch that she realised she had not asked after Mike himself. 'What brings you here?' she enquired as they took their seats at table. 'We had no idea you were in France. How long have you been here? Why didn't Marcel write?'

'Well, posts aren't very easy, especially since the U-boat attacks started.' Then he smiled a little ruefully. 'To tell you the truth there was a bit of trouble about my coming over here. You see, they were saying Americans enlisting in a foreign force would lose their citizenship – that was long before there was any talk of the States coming into the war, of course, back in '16. I'd done a bit of flying and some friends of mine were coming over, so it seemed a good idea to come along too.'

'Flying?' Laure broke in. 'Then you're a pilot?'

He nodded. 'I was, at least. My father was dead set against it from the start – he never liked me flying, even at home. My grandfather stuck by him, of course, saying I was too young and it was too dangerous. There was one hell of a row. But I came all the same, as you see.'

'You must have been with the Lafayette Squadron – is that right?'

'That's right. They wound us up last month.' He grinned. 'We'd have been transferred to the American Air Corps, but not one of us was passed medically fit.'

'We read all about you.' Laure's eyes shone. 'It meant so much to us, all you young Americans flying for France.'

'It was said to be one of the things that turned the scales at Verdun,' put in Charles quietly. To Laure, the name of that battle sounded always like the tolling of a funeral bell, full of muffled reverberations of grief.

'We did what we could,' said Mike. 'But there you are – I find myself surplus to requirements. There didn't seem much else for it but to go home. Only I thought first I'd come and take a look at my long lost relations. So I bought myself a bicycle – good healthy exercise – and here I am.'

'And what will you do when you go home, do you think?' Laure asked.

Mike shrugged. 'I don't know. Something with planes, I suppose – it's the only thing I'm any good at. I couldn't face working for my father – no head for business, he says—'

'Is he in the bank, like your grandfather was?'

'Well, it's a bit more than just the bank, you know. My grandfather had expanded a good bit before he retired, and there are my other grandfather's railroad interests. My father loves it – he lives for his work. I think I'm a disappointment to him – Rose too. But we've enough to live on, and more – we can neither of us see the point in going on making money just for the sake of it. We could all live comfortably just on the interest from investments. Still, we all have different ways of being happy, I suppose.'

He spoke as if happiness was a natural part of the human condition, to be expected even in wartime; and certainly he seemed happy, Laure thought, in spite of all he must have seen and suffered. It was an infectious quality, cheering even their troubled household; if he did not quite make them happy, his brief stay at least brought a lightening of the dark, and a hope that the dawn might not be so far away after all. By the time he left – promising to keep in touch – Laure felt, not revitalised exactly, but certainly refreshed. She gave him a long letter to take to Marcel, full of praise for his grandson and telling him how his visit had delighted them.

ii

By the end of May Casseuil's losses had reached fifty-five and the German breakthrough was still not complete. The reckless courage of the new American forces – so like their own in those far-off days of 1914 – seemed to have revived a spark in their weary allies, and fired them with a new will to resist, and to go on resisting. But everything still hung in the balance. They could only go on holding their breath and hoping.

With Moïse, Laure rarely discussed the war; it depressed and worried him too much for that. She suspected he might even have welcomed a defeat, if it brought Jean-Marc safely home. Last year's tiny quantity of wonderful wine was ready for racking again, so she set Moïse on the first spraying with Bordeaux mixture (a relatively light task) and began on the racking herself, a little regretfully, because it was a beautiful morning and she would have liked to be outside. If nothing else, she was more likely to sleep well after a day in the fresh air, instead of lying awake for much of the night haunted by griefs and regrets which in daylight she could keep well under control.

The smell of the wine rose in her nostrils as she worked; the exquisitely subtle aroma that held such promise. Yet what would there be to show for it? Ten hectolitres perhaps – a hundred or so cases; and the knowledge that this might have been the greatest of all vintages if she could have gathered more than a fraction of the grapes at the peak of their perfection.

She heard someone come into the *chai* behind her and looked round: it was Mathilde. Laure could not see her face, for the light was behind her, but that some kind of extreme agitation had taken hold of her Laure realised at once. She saw that she held a piece of paper in her hand.

'What is it, *chérie*?'

'Look.'

Laure took the paper, turning it towards the light so that she could read it. 'What is this? From Germany? Who would write from Germany? Who is this, Mathilde—? I can't read the signature – Jules, Jean – and is that Simon, or what?'

'It doesn't matter, Maman. *Read* it!' Mathilde's voice was sharp with impatience, and also vibrating with some more intense emotion.

Laure read, her eyes skimming the words, while she murmured them aloud with an interrogatory note in her voice. '*Chère madame*, I have undertaken to write to you on behalf of a friend, like me a prisoner here in Germany. He was concerned that you might not have had news of him, but until now has been unable, through sickness, to communicate with you. I am now writing on his behalf, and at his wish, to let you know (should you be unaware of it) that your son—' Laure stopped. 'Your son – your son, Mathilde—' She could hardly breathe.

'Go on!'

'Your son, Lieutenant de Miremont, taken prisoner at Verdun in 1916, is alive and, now, quite well again. He left hospital finally a week ago, and came here, where we met.' Laure let the letter fall. 'Oh, Mathilde—!' She felt faint, full of a sudden whirlwind of emotions, way beyond her control. She felt Mathilde's hand on her arm.

'Sit down, Maman – you've gone quite white.'

She found herself somehow on the bench against the wall. 'I don't understand – how can—? Why did we not hear?'

Mathilde knelt on the floor beside her and took her hands; and Laure could see now that she was both weeping and smiling at once, as she had been doing all along.

'Does it matter, Maman? He's alive, that's all. We'll know the rest one day. Maman, he'll be coming *home*!'

Laure did not dare to allow herself to believe it, to accept the little voice that crowed jubilantly, 'I knew – I knew all the time!'

'How do you know it's true? What if it's some kind of mistake – a horrible trick perhaps?'

'Why would anyone play a trick like that?'

'Then why hasn't Joseph written himself?'

'Perhaps his hand's hurt. Perhaps—' she faltered, evidently quailing before the possibilities of disablement that might

643

explain the deficiency; then she said earnestly, 'Nothing matters, so long as he's alive. Don't you see that, Maman?'

Laure clutched Mathilde's fingers, still not believing. 'Yes – yes, of course,' she whispered. Then, 'Does Charles know?'

'I'll go to the *mairie* now, if you're fit to be left.'

'Of course I am. Hurry, *chérie*!'

Mathilde ran all the way, reaching the steps of the *mairie* just as Charles came towards it along the street. She recognised the look on his face and knew from what kind of errand he was returning.

'Jean-Jacques Martin,' he said to her, before she could speak. 'In Italy. I think it makes it worse that it was so far away. They have no one left now, those two old people.'

Mathilde realised that an outpouring of joy was hardly appropriate at the moment. She laid her hand on Charles's arm. 'Come inside, *mon chéri*. I have something to show you.'

In the *chai*, when Mathilde had gone, Laure sat where she was for a long time, while the first shock passed, and with it all her doubts. Then she sank to the floor with her arms stretched out along the bench, and bent her head on them and wept for joy and thankfulness.

iii

They rang the church bell, until the rope broke. They hung flags in the trees and for the first time in more than four years there was dancing and singing in the market place at Casseuil.

'It's over! It's over at last!' people said, again and again.

But as there had been no wild enthusiasm when they went to war, so now as it came to an end the celebrations were muted too. There was relief, yes, and thankfulness; but they had all lost too much for unrestrained jubilation.

In the château that was particularly true, for two days earlier they had heard that Marie-Françoise had been struck down by the virulent influenza that had been sweeping Europe since August and was adding daily to the monstrous total of the dead. Mathilde had wanted to go to her at once, but both Charles and Marie-Françoise's superiors at the hospital had insisted that she must not; there was no sense in risking the infection for herself.

644

So on that November day of the Armistice the three of them, with Nanon, sat very soberly in the *grand salon* and toasted the ambiguous victory in champagne, rather in the manner of participants in a solemn religious ritual.

Marie-Françoise recovered, but turned down all offers of leave and remained at the hospital where – as she was presumably immune to further infection – her services would be the more valued.

Three days after the Armistice was declared, a letter arrived from Joseph himself, the only one he had written in reply to the long tender messages they had sent him the moment they knew where he was. His letter – and it was from him, Laure accepted joyously, looking at the familiar neat handwriting – delighted them all, but was, undeniably, just a little unsatisfactory, since it said not much more than, 'I am well; I hope to be home before long.' A few observations about the revolution that had broken out in Germany, a final rather stiff and conventional expression of his affection for them all; and that was it.

'There'll be time enough to talk when he's home,' Charles said consolingly.

They heard no more until a wet dismal day in January, when Charles returned from a meeting of the municipal council, called to discuss the provision of a war memorial; and crossed the hall just as the telephone rang.

They heard him answer it, listen, catch his breath; and then say, in a voice sharp with emotion, 'Where are you? . . .' There was a pause; then he went on, 'Yes, yes of course—' and at last hung up, rather abruptly, as if someone had broken off the call sooner than he had expected. He came into the *grand salon* where they had assembled for lunch.

'That was Joseph,' he said huskily. 'He'll be arriving at Bergerac at five.'

Charles drove himself and Mathilde to the station that afternoon in the newly acquired Renault: a sober, utilitarian vehicle, it would never replace the Panhard in his affections.

Laure did not go with them. She wanted to, with a desperate longing, all the more perhaps because it was touched with a faint tinge of apprehension. But this first moment of Joseph's return belonged by rights to Charles and Mathilde, so she saw them go and tried to still her nervousness by helping Nanon with her preparations in the kitchen: they had not yet acquired new staff to replace her.

At the station Charles parked the car and then he and Mathilde walked slowly onto the appropriate platform. They were much too early, and would have perhaps half an hour to wait. It had stopped raining, but the wind was cold and it was already dark, and Charles suggested they go and pass the time in a café, but Mathilde would not hear of it. She installed herself on a bench and sat nervously twisting her hands together, while Charles paced up and down before her.

The train did come at last, after what seemed hours, pulling slowly, with much groaning and puffing, into the station. Mathilde stood up and grasped Charles's arm very tightly. He closed his hand about hers and they stood together, scanning the passing carriages for a tall young soldier.

The train came to a halt. Doors opened, people got out, and were greeted and went away. Charles and Mathilde walked along, looking and looking.

And then far off near the rear of the train they saw him, holding awkwardly to the side of the door as he lowered himself very slowly on to the step that broke the fall to the platform. Charles began to run and reached him just in time to help him in the final descent. Then Joseph turned into his embrace. Mathilde caught his arm and he put it about her too and they clung together in an emotion-charged silence.

Then, still saying nothing, the three of them walked back towards the car, Charles carrying Joseph's few belongings.

Their eyes never left him as they went. His appearance had none of the grimy unkempt look of that long ago return on leave; on the contrary, he had shaved (apart from the moustache) and his hair was tidy, and the ill-fitting suit was at least clean. But the change in him was the more marked for that. It was difficult to see in this haggard veteran any trace of the young man who had gone away. He was painfully thin –

beneath her hand, even through the thickness of his sleeve, Mathilde felt only skin and bone – his eyes were set in great dark hollows, and further hollows marked his face from cheekbone to jaw. His mouth – once so ready to laugh – had a taut, hard look about it, and his skin, stretched too tight over the bones, was an unhealthy grey colour. He walked very slowly, with a severe and obviously painful limp. Mathilde's joy in his return was quickly tempered by an anguished dismay that he should look so ill.

On the way home, Charles asked, 'Did the Germans treat you well?' It seemed a fairly safe question to begin with.

'In hospital, yes. In the prison camp—' He spread his hands. 'They were correct.' His voice seemed changed too, deeper, the tone without joy and lifeless.

Mathilde moved as close to him as she could. 'Did you know they told us you were dead?'

He looked sharply round at her. 'No, I didn't. I'm sorry.'

'They sent us your identity disc,' said Charles.

'I see. I knew I'd lost it.' He moved his right arm to reveal a badly scarred wrist. 'I was hit there, as you see. It must have fallen off then. I'm surprised anyone found it.'

'We thought they'd taken it from your body,' Mathilde told him, with all the horror of the thought in her voice. 'We didn't think they'd tell someone their son was dead, without seeing a body.'

'That wasn't unusual, at Verdun.' Joseph's expression darkened still further.

'What happened exactly, when you were taken prisoner?' Charles asked.

'I don't remember much. I was hit. Later, they told me I'd been taken behind the German lines some time before they were driven back again from our position.'

'Why didn't the Germans let us know you were a prisoner?' persisted Mathilde.

Joseph shrugged. 'There was some confusion as to who I was.'

'For two years?'

'I'm here now, Maman. Let it rest.' He sounded so weary that she could only do as he wished.

*

The celebratory dinner to welcome Joseph home was a dismal failure. He sat at the table picking half-heartedly at what had once been his favourite dishes, speaking only to give brief or evasive answers to their questions. The meal was punctuated by long awkward intervals when no one could think of anything to say. Afterwards, Joseph said, 'I'd like to go to bed, please,' and half-supported by Charles made his slow way upstairs.

Next morning he looked just a little less exhausted, but he was no more cheerful or communicative. He returned to his room after breakfast and did not emerge again until lunch-time.

'You would think he was sorry to be home again, not glad,' said Mathilde with a break in her voice.

'Give him time, *chérie*,' said Laure gently (though last night she had herself shed a few tears to find Joseph so changed). 'I suspect he's been through a great deal more than we'll ever know.'

Charles nodded gravely. 'I think we have to remember that this is not an end, but a beginning; a new beginning, for all of us.'

After lunch, for which he still seemed to have little appetite, Joseph fell asleep stretched on the sofa in the *grand salon*, and was still there when the Bonnets arrived for tea. Little Marie-Laure – three years old now – toddled over to him and regarded him speculatively with her head on one side; and then gave him an experimental poke in the eye.

Charlotte ran to her in horror; but Joseph sat up, and even laughed. 'Is that how you welcome your Uncle Joseph home?' he demanded in a voice rough with sleep. The child shrank a little, and he held out his hands towards her. 'Come, *mignonne* – a kiss for your uncle?'

She gave him one, rather solemnly, and then ran to clutch her mother's hand. After that, for a time, there was a good deal of laughter and talk, which Joseph was clearly making a considerable effort to join in. To Laure, he looked as if he was struggling to remember patterns of behaviour from some long-forgotten past, bringing them out with all the awkwardness of disuse. But, as Charles said, this was a new beginning.

He asked after old Doctor Bonnet (very frail now) and

answered Samuel Bonnet's knowledgeable questions about his own injuries: 'The hip and thigh mostly – it took them some time to put it right' – and was suitably (if rather superficially) brotherly towards Charlotte and Marie-Françoise, who had only recently returned home herself.

Later, when they were all comfortably seated about the room, and a little silence fell, Joseph began abruptly, 'A strange thing happened at Verdun—' They all looked at him, except for the child who, her fears allayed, sat at his feet laboriously tying knots in his shoelaces. 'I met Uncle Frédéric there.'

Laure watched Mathilde put down her cup, very slowly and carefully, as if she could not trust herself to hold it without dropping it. Behind the surprised exclamations from Joseph's sisters, she knew that Mathilde, like herself, had caught her breath, and did not know what to say.

'Really? How astonishing!' exclaimed Charles. 'How did that come about?'

Joseph told them, simply and briefly; and said how much he had liked the uncle who was not an uncle at all. 'Though I didn't tell him he wasn't, of course. I thought it better not.'

Then he said, very gently, 'We met again later, the day before I was hit. He was mortally wounded. I was with him when he died.' He looked as if he had somehow returned in spirit to that dark place, and for a little while he said nothing more. But at last he stirred – they had waited in silence for him to go on – and said, 'I don't know why he left here, and he gave no hint of it to me. But there was one thing, the last thing he said – I think it had something to do with that. It doesn't sound much, but I am quite sure it was important to him.' He moved his gaze to his mother's white face. 'He said – now let me get it right – yes, that was it: "Tell Mathilde, her son is a credit to his father." ' Then he looked at Charles.

Mathilde gave a little gasp and pressed her hand to her mouth; and then, shuddering, rose to her feet and ran from the room. Dismayed, Laure saw Charles go quickly after her; and was too late to prevent him.

In her room, Mathilde crouched by the bed, weeping with great searing sobs, fed almost as much by the mixed emotions of Joseph's return as by the news he had just given them. She did not hear the door open behind her, but she felt the hands on her shoulders and turned more by instinct than deliberate choice into Charles's arms, since there was nowhere else to go. He held her close, stroking her hair, while she wept against his shoulder. And then he murmured, 'I know, *chérie*; I know . . .'

It was a little while before the sense of the words reached her; and then, abruptly, she stopped weeping.

'I know,' he had said; and Charles had never in his life spoken on impulse, without being exactly sure of his meaning. If he said, 'I know,' then it was not an idle meaningless soothing phrase, but something deliberately intended.

What did he know? She knelt there with her head bent against his shoulder, and felt her heart beat painfully fast.

He continued to hold her, gently and consolingly. After a time, he said, 'We'll have a mass said for him, if you wish.'

'Yes,' she whispered. Perhaps after all the words had merely been said to soothe her; perhaps he believed he understood her. She would never know, for she could not ask him. She could only, meekly and thankfully, accept his loving consolation.

The *curé* said a requiem mass for Frédéric in the church where, long ago, he had made his first communion under the proud austere gaze of his grandmother. Now his son knelt there with the others to pray for his soul.

Mathilde listened to the solemn words of the requiem and felt her whole heart rise with them in fervent prayer.

'*Requiescat in pace*' – may he rest in peace. Peace for Frédéric, at the end of a tormented life. Peace for his son, after so much suffering. Peace for Casseuil, for France, for the whole world.

Let there be no more wars; let there be peace for ever.

CHAPTER
THIRTY THREE

i

It was like waking from a long nightmare and finding that, in the meantime, the familiar surroundings had changed beyond recall; and there could be no going back.

'A new beginning,' Charles had said. But for none of them in those first months after Joseph's return was there any sense of renewal. The man who had come home was a stranger, only fleetingly bringing to mind the boy who had gone away from them. Worse, he was a stranger they could not learn to know, because he did not seem to want them to know him. A silent gloomy man, often irritable and withdrawn, he would not let any of them near him.

He hurt Charles by refusing – without explanation, and simply by absenting himself – to come to mass; and then made matters worse by faithfully attending any religious observance, of any kind, connected with the war – to remember a dead soldier; on Armistice Day.

He grieved Mathilde by evading all her questions, rebuffing her tenderest gestures, shutting her out of all but the surface of his life; and emphasised his rejection of her by spending hours in the café, day after day, deep in conversation with the other ex-soldiers.

He distressed Laure by showing not the remotest interest in the vineyard, as if the boyish enthusiasm that had meant so much to her had been no more than a figment of her imagination. She tried very hard. She asked for his help sometimes, and he gave it, politely but with reserve. When she told him about the *vendange* of 1917, which should have been so wonderful but was not, he merely said, 'Poor Grand-mère,' and moved on to something else; he declined an offer to taste the wine. She was infuriated that his main – his only –

concern in the weeks after his return seemed to be to assist Jacques Lambert to win election as mayor (from which post Charles, with immeasurable relief, had resigned). When Aubin's son succeeded, heading a list of ex-soldiers who were unashamedly Socialist to a man, Joseph even looked, briefly, quite pleased. He went to join the celebrations afterwards in the café, where – Laure supposed – they all talked about the war, yet again.

'The war, always the war!' she exclaimed in fury one day. 'We're at peace now, thank God. Can't you forget the war?'

He looked both sombre and a little shocked. 'No, Grand-mère. It must never be forgotten – never!'

After one particularly hurtful episode, Mathilde said to Laure, 'Sometimes he reminds me so much of Frédéric it frightens me. But Frédéric would talk to me, even when he would talk to no one else. I can't reach Joseph at all.'

Laure had been struck by the likeness too. Did the years of Joseph's happy childhood count for nothing, she wondered? Had the war blotted them out for ever?

Then Samuel Bonnet, observing the situation with a doctor's eye, said, 'In my opinion that hip needs attention. I'm sure it's giving him far more pain than it ought.' He arranged an appointment with a specialist of his acquaintance, and they all felt hopeful. If Joseph was in pain (but why had he not told them?) then he could hardly be expected to be patient and good humoured.

The specialist advised immediate surgery and Joseph spent several difficult months alternately in and out of hospital, followed by a long period of convalescence; at the end of which he began, at last, to make a steady improvement – physically, at least. He forced himself to take increasing amounts of exercise, willing himself back to health and strength. But emotionally there was no change at all. He was as morose and silent as ever.

'I'm afraid this sort of problem is not uncommon, amongst returned soldiers,' Samuel Bonnet said sadly. 'All we can hope is that time will bring healing.'

Laure, deeply depressed by it all, wondered how much time it would take. It was by now 1921, she was seventy-two, and she had no wish to go on carrying all the burdens of the vineyard for ever, alone and with no prospect of handing on her responsibilities to a fit successor. She found herself thinking that perhaps they had after all lost Joseph as surely as if he had perished on that summer's day at Verdun.

In the spring a letter came from Marcel. His granddaughter Rose, not quite twenty-two, was to complete her art studies by coming to Paris. But first, she would like to visit them. Perhaps August would be convenient?

Two days before she was due to arrive, Joseph announced his intention of travelling to the Pyrenees to set out on a solitary walking tour lasting several weeks. Mathilde was appalled.

'You'll injure yourself, Joseph. It's much too far to go alone. What if you need help, and you're in some remote place where no one will ever find you?'

'I shall not injure myself. The weather has been perfect, and is likely to remain so, I think—'

'It's too hot for walking.'

'Not for mountain walking. If I feel tired, I shall rest for a few days. But I shall not feel tired.'

'And what,' Charles put in, 'about your cousin from America?'

'What about her? You will make her welcome, I don't doubt. She does not need me here.'

'Don't you want to meet her?'

'Frankly, no.'

So that was that. Nothing they could say had any effect and the next morning – light knapsack packed with the bare necessities – he set out. Mathilde cried when he had gone, and Charles's disappointment was almost as marked.

So was Laure's. This fine hot summer held out a promise that all the losses of the past might finally be redeemed. Before the war – before that great aching abyss had opened in their universe – Joseph would have wished as eagerly as she did for the heat to last into the autumn, tempered then by mists, bringing just the right conditions for the *pourriture noble* to spread over the grapes. Before the war he too would have scanned the sky each morning to see if the weather would hold another day, and another. He too would have walked between the vines, watching the grapes swell and ripen, holding his breath with hope and expectation. The summer was too hot for the finest red wine, which would have that unmistakable scorched taste; but – crowned by a perfect autumn – it might be just right for the very best Casseuil.

But Joseph went on his way without once commenting on the weather (except as it affected his walking) or the vines.

Rose was small-boned and slender and a little like her brother, except that her delicate creamy-complexioned face was set in a mass of curls even redder and brighter (if that was possible) than Mike's had been, and her eyes were as green and sparkling as the pool below the vineyard on a breezy spring day.

She was warm, impetuous, high-spirited, and in a moment had captivated them all. She asked endless questions, but always listened with flattering attentiveness to the answers. She talked of art to Laure, and showed a very encouraging concern about the prospects for the *vendange*. She discussed religious ideas with Charles in a tone of sweet seriousness; she was a good Catholic, and went to mass with them every Sunday. She made Mathilde laugh, as Mathilde had not done for a very long time, with her eccentric French accent and her eager enthusiasm for everything and anything. Little Marie-Laure adored her, which was the surest way to Charlotte's affections; and Marie-Françoise – briefly home from her medical studies – found a keen intelligence beneath the lively exterior, which pleased her. Poor Philippe, about to begin his theological studies in earnest, lost his heart to her completely and, in a turmoil, wondered if he had been quite wrong to think he had a vocation. Gently and tactfully, she made it clear that though she liked him his passion was not returned; so it seemed that the priesthood would win after all.

They took her for rides and drives and picnics, for boat-trips on the river, visits to châteaux and churches and forests and favourite restaurants, to Bordeaux and Arcachon; and she enjoyed them all. She was equally happy when they simply stayed at home, dozing in the garden shade through the long hot afternoons, sketching, singing, dancing to the records she had brought with her, talking, just living: she had a great zest for life.

'She should be exhausting and tiresome,' said Laure to Mathilde one day, when Rose was out of earshot (they could hear her infectious laughter carrying across the garden). 'I wonder why she isn't? That enthusiasm is in fact surprisingly refreshing.'

'Yes, that's true.'

'Perhaps it's because she's so completely fresh and innocent. She knows instinctively how to please, because she's interested in everyone and cares about them – but there's nothing calculating about her. She is the most natural person I've ever met.'

'Do you think all American girls are like that?'

'If they are, then poor Philippe must never go to America.'

Mathilde thought then, by an inevitable progression, of her other son; and sighed. 'I do wish Joseph were here.'

'I wonder how she'd behave to him?'

They found out after all, for she was still at Casseuil when Joseph came home at the beginning of September. Burned brown by the sun, glowing with health and fresh air, he was as remote and sombre as ever.

Washed and changed for dinner that first evening he came into the *grand salon* and stood grimly silent while Charles introduced Rose. She smiled and held out her hand. 'I've wanted to meet you so much,' she said warmly, although with rather less than her usual ebullience.

He took her hand for the shortest length of time compatible with good manners. 'I hope you have enjoyed your stay, *mademoiselle*.' After that, he paid as little attention to her as he did to everyone else. Somehow the brightness of the past weeks died a little, shadowed by Joseph's presence.

Later, a little reluctantly, Mathilde took him on one side. 'You weren't very polite to Rose, Joseph. She's a delightful girl – you ought to be pleasanter to her.'

'She's too – bright—' he said shortly, and refused to discuss the matter further.

His first sight of her advancing on him had reminded him in some way of the moment of leaving the battlefield after weeks in the front line, with its grim colourless monotony; and coming, behind the lines, on the forgotten landscape of fields and woods and hills and villages, so dazzling in its colours, so vibrantly green and blue and red and gold, so brilliantly alive that it hurt his eyes, painfully assaulting his senses with its look of sheer blazing unreality. Rose, with her bright hair and sparkling eyes and warm lilting voice, was like that, too much for his bruised spirit to bear; it would take time to grow used to her, and he had no wish to make the effort to do so. He avoided her as much as he could.

After dinner two days later, Mathilde murmured to Laure, 'I think Rose is trying to attract Joseph. Did you see how she kept looking at him across the table?'

'Yes, I did. But then he's a good looking young man; I suppose it shows she's human. I doubt if she'll get very far. He doesn't seem to like her much.'

They would have given Rose every credit for persistence had they seen her the next morning, setting out at a run, sketching materials under her arm, in pursuit of Joseph as he walked through the wood, along the village street, towards the windmill.

'Do you mind if I walk with you? I want to sketch the view from up here. My drawing needs practice, you know.'

He shrugged, not looking round at her, though he could not help but be aware of the flamboyant brightness of her hair and the dress green as her eyes. 'You are free to walk where you please, *mademoiselle*.'

'Oh, please don't be so formal! Everyone calls me Rose.'

'That is no reason for me to do so, is it?'

'No, I suppose not.' She tried again. 'Do you draw at all?'

'I have no talent for it.'

'Have you tried?'

'Not since I was a child.'

'Then you should. You might find you have a talent after all.'

'I doubt it.'

Beside the windmill – disused now – she came to a halt and turned to look across the valley, as it lay shimmering in the heat, a soft pattern of lovingly cultivated land stretching into the hazy blue distance, where it merged at last with the sky.

Joseph hesitated, as if wondering whether to go on without

her and then – clearly deciding that manners required him at least to wait a moment or two before doing so – halted too.

'Isn't it beautiful!' she exclaimed, but softly. 'Not wild or dramatic, but quietly beautiful, just tamed enough to suggest safety and tranquillity – man and the land in harmony, working together.' Joseph said nothing. She glanced at him, and then asked, 'Do you think your grandmother will have her good vintage this year?'

'That depends on the weather.'

'The vines are beginning to change colour, just a little – can you see from here? There is more gold in the green, even a little red in places.'

'They're pure gold in the autumn.' He instantly regretted the momentary near-enthusiasm of his tone. 'If you're going to sketch here, I'll go.'

She looked about her. 'Let me see – yes, here I think.' She perched herself on a bank commanding a clear view of the valley, and began to pull sketch pad and charcoals from her bag. From the corner of her eye she saw that Joseph had not yet moved away, but had remained where he was, watching her. She did not look at him, but turned the pages of her sketch book, seeking an empty page.

The next moment he was beside her, reaching down to lay a hand on the book. 'May I see?'

She looked up, all the full sweetness of her smile turned upon him. 'Of course.'

Frowning a little, he turned the pages, pausing now and then to gaze a little longer than usual at one sketch or another; and then, abruptly, he became very still, his expression intent and sombre.

'Which one is that?' She stood up to look. 'Oh.'

Beneath the stark lines of the sketch she had written, 'Fleury village, Verdun, July 1921.' There was no village, no sign that there had ever been one, only a rubble-strewn expanse of battered ground. In one corner a little clump of poppies raised frail heads in defiance of the surrounding desolation.

'You didn't say you had been there.'

'I went on the way here. It was a private thing. You see, Mike and I have always been very close, and he wanted me to go.' She looked up at him very earnestly. 'I wanted so much to understand. It made such an impression on him, that battle. He tried to tell me about it, but it's hard to feel it too when you haven't lived through it yourself.'

'It was different for Mike.'

'I know; he told me that. He said it was more dangerous for the pilots, but at least they were free, up in the air, in some control of what was happening to them. He told me how he used to look down through the smoke of the bombardment and see the men crouched in holes like animals, only just distinguishable from the earth around them. He said some pilots despised them, but he didn't, because he knew it was much harder for them. They had no excitement to help, no sense of adventure – only endurance of what ought by rights to have been beyond enduring. He said that simply not to run away, in those conditions, took more than human courage . . . There's something else he's found since – that it's very hard to return to ordinary life, because nothing seems so real as the war. He says there will be a whole generation who will feel like that.'

'Yes.' Joseph continued to look at the drawing, the few simple lines, the economy of shading, which presented before him that too well-remembered landscape. 'Perhaps you have understood something. This is what you felt, not just what you saw.'

'I think you would have to be very strange not to feel something in that place.' She reached out to take the book and turned the page to show him the next sketch, of a similar starkness. 'I did that the same day, and the next one.' He looked at them in silence, but she could see the emotion on his face. 'I met an old man there, whose son had died in the battle; he said it was a glorious victory.'

'He would not have said that if he'd fought there.'

'A waste then? A terrible, senseless waste of life?'

'Yes. Yet – oh, I don't know. There was no glory there, nor pride nor honour. We were reduced to something less than animals. It degraded and corrupted us. For those of us who were there some of the poison of that place will inevitably go with us to the grave. But if one came to believe that all the suffering went for absolutely nothing, one would soon go mad. If it had no purpose in itself, then one has to find a purpose, if only a personal, individual one.'

'That must be hard . . . I suppose, that it should never be allowed to happen again – that would be some kind of purpose to carry away from it. Not much, but something.'

'No, it's a great deal,' he said with sudden vehemence. 'As an ambition, it towers over the puny world-conquering dreams of Generals and Kings. Think of it—' He was gazing intently at her now, his eyes very dark and his hands moving quickly to give fluent emphasis to the impassioned words. 'To create the conditions where there will be no more war, not ever, then you must transform humanity itself. War has been a part of the human condition since Cain first turned on Abel. All that has changed in all the centuries is that the weapons of destruction have become steadily more terrible and more powerful, so that once they are unleashed we are helpless before them. If we go on like this, there will come a time when men will be in a position to destroy the whole universe, just like that, in a moment. So it is up to those of us who have felt what war means – who can see what it might yet mean, in the future – it is for us to do all in our power to bring it to an end, now, before it is too late.'

'So everything that is not a means to that end, seems utterly trivial.' She gave a little smile. 'Such as the making of wine.'

Even Joseph grinned at that, ruefully. 'Yes. Of course.'

'But if you work so hard at doing away with war that everything else is cast to one side – what then? You'll have a wonderful peace, but it will be the peace of the grave. Human beings need something to live for. If it isn't to be honour and glory and patriotism and power, then it will have to be something else. Life in all its richness perhaps – love and laughter, food and wine, singing and dancing.'

'Now you're being naïve. I'm not advocating a return to an Arcadia that only ever existed in some poet's imagination.'

'Nor am I. But while you work for your perfect peaceful world you can still encourage the good things to grow and flourish – in fact, you must, or they will die and life won't be worth living any more.' She saw that he was frowning. 'Think about it,' she said.

He moved suddenly, as if stirring into wakefulness from a

long sleep. Then he said abruptly, 'I'm keeping you from your sketching. I'll see you at lunch-time.' And he went to meet his friends in the café.

It was Sunday next day and, while the others were at mass, Joseph took a book to the shadiest corner of the garden. He was exasperated when, after what seemed far too short a time (surely mass could not be over already?) he looked up to see Rose coming towards him.

Behind her the spray of the fountain glittered in the sun, somehow adding an extra dimension of flamboyant unreality to her bright hair and troublesome presence. He did not want her; she disturbed the rather uncertain equilibrium he had so carefully built up for himself, threatening to touch him in ways that he was by no means ready or willing to entertain. He wished she would go away, even more that she had not come in the first place. He wondered whether to fend her off by some expression of wholehearted rudeness, but in the end took the lesser course of giving his whole attention, pointedly, to his book. Not that, in fact, any of his attention was really on it; he could not have told anyone what was written on the page before him.

'I've been looking for you everywhere, Joseph. Would you like to come for a walk?'

The directness of the question rather astonished him, but he merely said, 'It's too hot.'

'That's what they all say, but there's still some freshness in the air. It will be worse this afternoon. Besides, you've been out walking in hotter weather.'

'I don't go in for ladylike little ambles, with pauses for sketching from time to time. You'd soon get tired.'

'First it's too hot to walk, then you'd be too energetic for me! Which excuse do you mean me to accept? Besides, I'm no ladylike walker either. I'm an American, remember – all those wide open spaces . . .'

In exasperation he threw down his book and looked up at her. 'Why can't you leave me in peace? Can't you see that's what I want?'

She studied him with her head on one side. 'I'm not sure,' she said reflectively. 'Besides, I like you. I want to know you better. And there's not much time left.'

He looked as if for a moment she had taken his breath away. 'You're very frank!'

'Of course, why not?' She was smiling, her eyes bright and full of warm laughter. Joseph felt utterly unsure of himself before her, as if something over which he had absolutely no control was sweeping him up and threatening to carry him where he did not want to go – and he suspected that it was she who was in control, surely, confidently, completely.

'I am not good company,' he said a little unsteadily.

'Never mind – I don't. And I promise not to chatter all the time. I want to look, not talk.' Her smile became infinitely coaxing. 'Do come, please.'

He came, though quite how and why he did not know, since he felt at the moment that it was the last thing he wanted to do. Then, very soon – again, he did not quite know how – he found that he was actually enjoying himself, in a quiet way.

Rose was quite right; she was no ladylike ambler. She walked briskly, with vigorous strides that kept pace quite easily with his own (he deliberately made no concession to her small size and shorter legs). She did not say much, but her eyes moved constantly about her, observing, admiring, noting this detail and that. She did not need to say anything for him to know that her artist's gaze missed very little. Against his will he found himself beginning to talk. He confided in her things he had told no one else, things about the war, moments of weakness, degradation, fear, some particular horror that had haunted him ever since. He did not want to tell her, if only because such things seemed wholly at variance with the languid heat of the day, the lovely summer landscape and her bright and happy personality. Yet she listened without evasion or reproach, saying little, but when she did speak somehow finding exactly the right words, so that he had no sense of intrusion or of failure to understand.

When at last he came back to the present, he realised that they had walked very much further than he at least had either expected or intended. Worse, it was lunch-time and it had taken them two hours to reach this place, on the northern bank of the river upstream from Bergerac.

'We can't possibly be back in time,' said Joseph, troubled.

'Then we shall just have to be late, or go hungry,' returned Rose easily.

'No – I know! We'll find a restaurant somewhere and telephone Casseuil from there to say we'll not be home. I've enough money on me to pay for a meal.'

They ate in a little garden behind an inn near the river, with a vine twining green and cool through a trellis over their heads. The meal was simple, in the local style: a richly flavoured soup (he showed her how to *faire chabrol*, which she did with much laughter), crusty country bread, a pâté with truffles, trout, a casserole of mutton and haricot beans with a salad, cheeses and fruit and an apparently inexhaustible supply of wine.

They ate very slowly, savouring each mouthful, talking now not about anything painful or too serious, but about the food and the wine – and other food and wine they had enjoyed before – and about Rose's hopes for the future (she was a little vague) and her painting, her own and that of her favourite artists, about America and how different it was from France. Joseph forgot all about being uneasy, and they laughed a good deal over nothing in particular, and more than once he found himself simply gazing across the table at that fair lively face in its bright cloud of hair, taking pleasure in watching the play of light on the flawless skin, the way her mouth seemed always warm, close to laughter, her eyes sparkled – but not coldly – infinitely tantalising. He found more than once that he was forgetting to eat, forgetting everything but her.

They lingered at the table for a long time after the meal was over, sipping the last of the wine, talking idly, sleepy and replete. Then, when the afternoon heat had begun just a little to decline, Joseph paid for the meal and they set off to walk home.

It was still hot, and where possible they took a path through a wood, or lingered in the shade of a building or a tree. They walked side by side, and Joseph was acutely conscious of her presence, of her arm almost touching his, so that with just the tiniest movement he could have reached out and taken her hand in his. He did not do so; but in some odd way it was almost as if they were touching, as if her nearness had set up some impulse to run through him from her fingers to his. He began to find it more and more difficult to know what to say, because her presence filled him with a sensation too overpowering for words.

Within sight of the château, where the road swung upward between the vines, Rose came to a sudden halt. 'Joseph.'

He turned to face her. She looked very grave, and something in her expression took his breath away and set him alight with a wild confusion of fire and tenderness.

'Thank you,' she said softly. 'It's been a wonderful day.' She stood on tiptoe, put her hands on his shoulders and kissed him. One tiny moment of shock and hesitation, and then his arms were about her and they were kissing as if it was what they had longed to do all day, this and nothing else; as indeed – he recognised now – it was.

When they came to an end, still holding one another and breathing quickly, he said, 'That was a mistake. Forget what happened. I have nothing to offer.'

Though his arms had fallen away from her, she continued to clasp his neck, looking steadily up into his face. 'You have, *mon cher*. You just don't know it yet. But I can wait.'

He did not believe her, but he did not argue. She let go of him and they walked on up the hill.

Next morning she left for Paris.

ii

The weather held, with no more than the softest and briefest scattering of rain, just enough to swell the grapes to perfection. Week after week the sun shone, through September and on into October; and with the autumn came the mists.

It was half-way through October, and it ought to be time at last. Laure went out early to examine the grapes; and met Joseph coming towards her through the mist. His face had on it an expression she had not seen for years, and had feared she would never see again: a wholehearted boyish excitement. She felt as if her heart had leapt into her throat for joy.

'Grand-mère, they're ready. Come and see.'

She went with him; and he led the way to the nearest plot and there bent to push the leaves gently aside, just as Jean Delisle had done long, long ago, when she was just a silly ignorant girl who could not understand his excitement. Now, seeing the grapes turning brown and purple, dusted with spores, smelling the heavy sweetness that filled the air, she knew exactly what it meant – and this time there was no bitterness in the knowledge.

She straightened, and Joseph did the same, and they looked at one another with shining triumphant eyes. Then she hugged him, and he pulled her clear of the vines and swung her round, almost as if she were Marie-Laure.

'Oh, just let the weather hold, Grand-mère!'

She laughed and freed herself, rather breathless and dishevelled, but so happy that she did not care. 'I'd better go and find Moïse. We must begin at once.'

Even now, labour was not plentiful in the countryside – probably it never would be again; but by paying huge wages Laure had managed to attract the most skilled workers. And Joseph was there of course, sleeves rolled up, back bent, singing with the others as he gathered the grapes; or leading the oxen back to the *chai*; or working the *pressoir* – and, always, sharing her anxious hope as one sunny mist-bounded day succeeded another.

The weather held, on into November, until the last sweet rotting grape was picked. The air in the *chai* was pungent with the smell of fermentation, the customary stillness troubled by the living bubbling sounds from the *cuves*. In the kitchen everyone – workers and family together – sat down to a feast as lavish as any in days gone by. Afterwards, Moïse's one remaining nephew, who was an accomplished accordionist, played for the dancing – town dances for the most part, becoming popular since the war, when the old *bourrées* and other country dances had fallen into disuse. But the dancing was still vigorous and happy and went on far into the night; and Joseph partnered Laure in the very first waltz as proudly as if she were the loveliest young girl in the company and not an old woman whose life was nearly over.

'Now we have only to wait,' she told him, when at last – exhausted – she allowed him to see her to her room.

He kissed her. 'A lifetime of waiting, rewarded at last.'

She reached up and touched his cheek. 'This has been a rich harvest in every way, *mon chéri*. I am so thankful, so happy—' She broke off and pulled out a handkerchief; and then laughed ruefully. 'Truly happy, I promise you!'

He kissed her again. 'Good-night, *chère* Grand-mère.'

iii

Rose was invited to Casseuil for Christmas, and accepted warmly. She had written two or three times that autumn, long lively letters for them all to read, full of her enjoyment of student life, and the sense of wonder at every new thing that was so much a part of her.

At lunch on Christmas Eve – snatched hastily in the midst of all the preparations – Joseph said with apparent casualness, 'I'll go and meet Rose, Papa.'

'Oh, there's no need,' Charles replied. 'I'm not busy this—' He felt Mathilde's hand on his arm, exerting an unusually strong pressure. 'Come to think of it, that's a good idea, Joseph.' He cast a slightly sheepish smile towards Mathilde.

Joseph drove alone to Bergerac, parked, made his way to the platform. He watched the train come in, with a heart beating so fast that he could scarcely breathe. Where was she? Would she be the same as he remembered? He had known her such a short time—

And then she was there, jumping down from the train with her hair flaming out beneath a jaunty little black hat; and she came running towards him laden with bags and parcels, which she dropped unceremoniously on the platform at his feet. Then she was in his arms, sweet and warm and laughing and even more wonderful than he remembered.

She raised her face for his kiss; but he remained quite still, looking down at her. Then he took her face in his hands and even frowned a little. 'I can't wait any longer, Rose. Will you marry me?'

'Of course I will – what a silly question!'

Then he did kiss her, softly, on each cheek; and at last full on the mouth, very slowly, very thoroughly, lingering there for a long time, and utterly heedless of the interested glances of the passers-by.

CHAPTER
THIRTY FOUR

i

The station staff at Bergerac were becoming well used by now to the comings and goings from the Château de Casseuil; and, knowing the family, had generally worked out what each arrival and departure implied even before it had taken place.

At Christmas, of course, the pretty American cousin had become engaged to Monsieur Joseph. A tearful but passionate parting had followed after the New Year; to be succeeded by an ecstatic reunion at Easter. The next parting, a week later, had been the most painful, because Mademoiselle Rose was returning to her parents in New York, to prepare for her marriage – for which, to everyone's delight, she was to return to Casseuil in the summer.

There were many interested bystanders at the station on the August day when Madame Séguier's brother and his family were due to arrive at Bergerac. They saw the two cars from the château drive up to the station, watched the family emerge onto the platform, happy, nervous, excited, and stand there in a group gazing along the line as the time approached. Above all, they saw Madame Laure's small upright figure, in front of them all, waiting for this reunion with the brother she had not seen for so long; and wondered what exactly she must be feeling now.

Laure watched him step down from the train, a little round sprightly old man with white hair and a rosy face; and the brown eyes that had not changed at all in the forty-six years since they had last met.

Poised to run to him, she waited just long enough for Joseph to find Rose in the tangle of descending passengers; and then she darted forward. 'Marcel! Oh, Marcel!'

Laughing in happy breathless bursts, they fell into one

another's arms, all joyful exclamations and endlessly repeated kisses.

Then at last they both drew back and stood just far enough apart to be able to look one another over with critical affection.

Marcel saw a tiny old lady, lined and white-haired, but with all the fine-boned slender beauty he remembered, and the way of wearing the simplest of clothes – like today's low waisted black crêpe dress – with undoubted style. 'How *elegant* you are, *ma chère* Laure – there is nothing in the least provincial about you, even after all these years in the country. And you look so *young*!'

She laughed and prodded his conspicuous belly. 'As for you, Marcel, I see you have been accruing interest, like the good businessman you are!'

He grinned at her and drew her arm through his. 'I didn't realise how much I'd missed you, until now. It is wonderful to see you again. Now, you'd better introduce me to the audacious young rascal who's stolen my granddaughter. Then I'll see if I shall ever be able to bring myself to forgive him.'

She led him to where Joseph stood with his arms about Rose, holding her as if he did not intend ever to let her go again.

Gradually the babble of greetings, laughter, welcome, subsided a little, and they all made their way to the waiting cars and the taxi, that were to take them back to the château: Marcel and Laure, arms still linked; Joseph and Rose, wrapped in a world of their own; Marcel's son Michael (how had her brother managed to produce so very dull a son? Laure asked herself) and his nervously smiling Irish wife (she spoke little French); Mike (now running his own commercial airline business) and his pretty, lively wife and their two small children; Marie-Françoise, that decisive, stubborn, much-beloved granddaughter now nearing the end of her medical studies and home for the wedding; Philippe, rather grave, hiding (Laure suspected) a wistfully envious heart beneath the black folds of his *soutane*, as he walked behind his brother and the young woman who would soon become his sister-in-law; and Charles and Mathilde who must between them be feeling a confusing tangle of emotions at the changes the next few weeks would bring to their lives.

There was little time for them to dwell on their emotions during the three weeks before the wedding. The château was alive with noise and activity from dawn to dusk, not just with the wedding preparations, but with the running and shouting of children (Charlotte's two little ones were often there, to add to the clamour), endless talking and reminiscence, and more laughter than had been heard within these walls for decades.

Laure still found time in all the bustle to show Marcel over her domain, the *chai* and the vineyard – or rather, hers and Joseph's; but for the time being, naturally enough, Joseph had other preoccupations.

She and Marcel had a long and pleasurable tasting session in the *chai* (not last year's wine, for she had other plans for that); at the end of which her brother said feelingly, 'It certainly is good to be back in a country where enjoying wine is not regarded as either a sin or a crime! This prohibition business does so take the edge off one's pleasures at times. André's vineyard – you remember him? His son runs it now – he's reduced to producing non-alcoholic grape juice, apart from a small quantity of sacramental wine. Terrible!'

'You'll have to come back to France, *mon cher*. Can you imagine a French government ever *considering* Prohibition?'

His hands flew up. 'The very idea! The stupid thing is, it doesn't even work. It's just driven it all underground – the criminals are doing magnificently out of it. But no – when all's said and done, America is my country now. Don't misunderstand me – I am very glad we agreed to hold the wedding here. I am happy beyond words to see France again – and to see you – but I have no wish to stay for ever.' He looked round the dimly lit *chai*, at the barrels stacked high in long rows stretching away into the distance; and back to the little smiling figure of his sister standing there with a glass in her hand and her bright brown eyes on his face. 'You said to me once that you felt you were meant to come here. I see now that it was quite true. I could not imagine you anywhere else.'

All morning the lawyers had been busy with the legal details, but by lunch-time the marriage contracts had at last been completed, ready for signature. The meal was noisy and chaotic, with so many people of all ages about the table; and afterwards, as they rose to leave, Joseph came to lean over the back of Rose's chair, his mouth very close to her ear. 'Come outside, *chérie*.'

She went with him and, once in the courtyard, he seized her hand and ran with her out under the archway and down the hill between the vines, and did not stop until they were out of sight of the house.

'I had to get you away,' he explained, putting his arms about her. 'I have hardly seen you since you arrived. All that chatter! I couldn't stand it a moment longer.'

'It will be better after tomorrow,' she said sweetly. 'And – who knows? – you may decide that having me to yourself all the time is not quite so wonderful after all.'

'Don't say that! You know I shall never think that.' He pulled her closer. 'Oh, Rose, I wish so much that it was tomorrow already, and you were my wife!'

'Just a few hours, that's all.'

'But so long. What if something should come between us, something terrible?'

She laughed softly, standing on tiptoe to rub her nose against his. 'Don't be silly. What could ever come between us?' She saw that he was still afraid, and recognised that for him there could never be any certainty of happiness. She reached up to take his head between her hands and bring it down for her kiss, all tender reassurance.

Then hand in hand they walked on beyond the vines, past the pool and into the wood beyond. It had begun to rain, just a little, enough for them to hear the soft patter of moisture on the leaves overhead, but not to feel it here in the shelter of the trees.

'It's just a shower,' said Joseph. 'We'll wait here until it stops.'

'No great vintage this year, I suppose.'

'One can't expect a miracle two years running.'

'Not the same one anyway.'

They talked without quite knowing what they were saying,

as if holding something at bay, their voices soft and breathless. They did not look at one another.

Joseph suggested they sat down until the rain ceased, and knelt to spread his jacket on the ground. 'Come.' He reached up, took her hand and drew her down beside him.

She knelt there facing him, held by his grasp on her arms, looking gravely into his dark face; and then at the same moment they moved together into a single fierce embrace, which carried them down on to the spread coat, mouths joined, hands, bodies, all seeking one another, wanting the unity that tomorrow Church and State would require of them. It was a kind of unacknowledged battle, a fierce conflict of mind and will against the overpowering passion and need that engulfed them, a battle they neither of them at the moment wanted either to fight or to win.

Rose at last pulled away, sat up a little and looked down at Joseph with her hair in disarray and her fair face unusually flushed. 'Oh dear – I do so want *not* to wait until tomorrow!' she admitted ruefully.

He sat up too and drew her – dangerously yet carefully – into his arms again, holding her so that he could rest his mouth on the living warmth of her hair. 'I know – for me it's the same, I want you so much – so desperately.'

She moved her head so that she could look into his face. 'But we must wait, and not spoil it. We've waited so long; it makes no difference, a few hours more. We shall have a lifetime together after tomorrow. You are the first and only one for me, and I want it to be perfect.'

'And you for me, *ma bien aimée*.'

Her eyes widened with astonishment. 'But you're a Frenchman!'

He laughed, a little unsteadily. 'Rose, you must learn not to generalise. I am myself first, and my father's son. Even in the war, I could never bring myself to use any woman, however willing, just as something for my own gratification – it would have been against everything I have ever believed in. And I have never loved until now.' His hold tightened about her. 'Which is not to say I never wanted to – and perhaps if I had not been wounded and taken prisoner – but, oh Rose, I want you now!'

670

She knew that if they stayed any longer in the wood they would both of them be beyond anything that their weakening powers of self-restraint could do. It was not that to give way now would blight their lives for ever; but it would be a pity, taking the shine off something that her devout Catholic mind saw as a good and precious thing. She jumped up, holding out a hand to pull him to his feet.

'Come, Joseph – let's go back, before we do anything we might regret.'

He stood up, gathering up his jacket, grinning ruefully. 'I thought the Irish were wild and impulsive and rash – what's become of your Irish blood?'

'Now who's generalising? I am myself, as you would say. And yours too, for ever – from tomorrow.'

They ran back through the rain, hand in hand and laughing, thinking of tomorrow, warm with happiness and anticipation.

Laure, from her window, saw them come running across the courtyard and disappear from sight into the house. She smiled to herself and turned back into the room. Their love and happiness were transparent, and they had come through so much to find them, Joseph especially – but Rose too, for she had known what she had to fight, and had set out to win that battle with all the calculating understanding that love gave her. She would be good for Joseph, a strength and support through all their days together.

Marcel's granddaughter: she smiled to herself at the unexpectedness of life. So long since she and Marcel had walked through the misty vineyard, fifty-six years ago – she had been so young then, so ignorant and foolish; quite unlike Rose, with her instinctive wisdom, her generous enthusiasm. She had thought herself in love, thought life had to offer only comfort and luxury and a kind of heedless happiness.

She wondered what kind of person she would have become if Philippe had not died, if the phylloxera had not struck the vines, if she had indeed been faced with years of the uncomplicated comfortable life she had imagined to lie before her. Oddly, she was glad now that it had not turned out that way. Not that she would have wished on any of those she loved the suffering that so many of them had been forced to endure. But for herself, without her own terrible struggle for survival and love, her failures and victories, life would have been the poorer in every way. If nothing else, success was the sweeter for having been reached through so much pain.

Now, at seventy-four, she held in her hands at the moment all the happiness an old woman could hope for. But she did not clutch it to her, selfishly, fearful that it might escape her. Somehow, she had come to see that joys clung to only evaporate and slip away through the fingers. No, this moment was to be savoured, enjoyed, with gratitude for what it gave, without either fear or hope for tomorrow. If sorrow were to come again – as it would, for it was as much a part of life as joy – then it would be the less bitter for the happiness she had enjoyed today.

Mathilde too had seen Joseph and Rose return, passing them in the hall as they came in, so absorbed in one another that they did not notice her.

Thoughtfully, she went on her way through the *petit salon* to the library to find Charles, wishing to consult him about some final detail of the seating plan for tomorrow. He was alone, she was glad to see, reading in the first little interlude of peace he had found all day. He looked up as she came in and smiled tenderly and put out a hand to draw her down to sit on a chair beside him.

'I'm glad you've come, *chérie*. I have been wanting to talk to you, so much.' She gave him a questioning look. 'You agreed it was right, I know – but will you mind very much going to live at Trissac?'

She shook her head. 'No; or only a little. And I know it's the right thing, for me and for Joseph – and Rose too. They must be able to start their married life without his mother always breathing down their necks. They'll need Maman here of course – but then in many ways she's so much wiser than I am.'

He stroked her hand, his head bent so that she could not see his face. 'Loving can be such a painful thing,' he said slowly.

'But good too,' she murmured. He looked up; and she added in a whisper, from the heart, 'I love you, Charles.'

She was astonished at the extent of the disbelief she saw then on his face; and, afterwards, at the emotion that set his mouth trembling a little. She watched disbelief turn to hope, and then to wonder; and then he raised her hand to his face and held her palm against his cheek. She moved her fingers caressingly. 'Didn't you know that?'

'It hasn't always been true, has it?'

She held her breath, feeling her heart beat faster.

'I thought you loved me, when we married. I thought that was why you married me. I don't know exactly when it was that I began to realise I was wrong. I am not always very quick to see things. I think perhaps I only knew the whole truth, finally, in full, after Madame Brousse died.'

Mathilde could not speak; she could scarcely breathe. She knew she had gone very white, and the room seemed all at once to be spinning round her. But Charles was not looking at her now and – holding her hand as if he had forgotten that he was doing so – he went on, 'Then, I tried to understand, but I found it very hard; very hard. Now I have been brought only to wonder at your courage – and his, Frédéric's. It must have been so painful, for both of you. One cannot guard against loving, of course; there can be no blame attached to you for loving where you ought not to have loved. But to turn your back on temptation so firmly, as you both did – for him to choose to go away from everything he valued, for you to choose marriage to a man you did not love (nor, to be fair, did you pretend to love him) and then to try as far as was in your power to make him a good wife – that took courage of no common order, more courage perhaps than I should have had in your circumstances. The worst thing of all must have been to discover that there had after all been no barrier between you, when it was too late.' He did see then how pale she was. 'I am glad we had Joseph so soon, and the others. That must have helped. But I know that the regret must always have been there.'

Swept by relief – he did not know then, not all of it! – she sank on the floor at his feet and clasped her arms about him. 'Not now, Charles – not any longer. I am quite sure, completely sure, that no one else – no one at all – could have made me so happy as you have done, or been so patient and loving through it all. I do not deserve you – you cannot know how very much I don't deserve you!'

Moved by the passionate sincerity of that declaration, he gathered her close to him, cradling her head against his shoulder. '*Ma très chère* Mathilde! We have both made mistakes, so many mistakes. But we can try to begin again, a new life, together.'

iii

The little marriage procession made its way up through the wood to the market place, emerging from the dappled shade into the bright September sunlight. Past the war memorial, with its weeping statue of Marianne – symbol of the Republic – and Frédéric's name third of the fifty-six engraved upon it; and across the street to the *mairie* – its doors, like that of the church, decorated with flowers and greenery – where Jacques Lambert waited on the steps to welcome them.

The brief civil ceremony over, they returned across the road to the church, Joseph and Rose, their witnesses and parents, and a little knot of bridesmaids. The Mayor went with them too, the first time that anyone could remember a Lambert setting foot in the church. There were four Lamberts there today: Jacques, of course, and his wife Anne with their infant son asleep in her arms, and Aubin, very spruce in his best suit. Near him sat Moïse, bent and tired but visibly proud of the young man at his side – soon, Jean-Marc would be no longer just a student, but a fully qualified teacher. The Chabrys were there, and the Lacroixs from Bergerac; and a scattering of de Miremonts, including the General, Joseph's godfather, in his magnificent uniform and a splendid array of medals; and Nanon, openly weeping in her place beside Laure, among the other members of the family. In fact so many people wanted to come that the little church could not accommodate them all and the marriage procession had to pass through a considerable crowd on its way from the *mairie* to the church.

Laure turned her head as they came in and through a sudden misting of tears saw the young couple coming towards her: Rose in a softly draped frock of creamy chiffon and lace, with a long filmy veil over her bright hair, held in place with a wreath of orange blossoms; and Joseph, very tall and thin and dark, but with a look of expectant happiness glowing – hesitant still, but there – in his eyes.

Afterwards, they returned to the château not, now, in an orderly little procession, but with bride and groom swallowed up by a great happy crowd, making for the courtyard where almost the entire village (and certainly all who wished to come) were to be welcomed to the long tables set out as if for a gigantic and extravagant harvest festival – emergency arrangements had been made indoors, in case of rain, but happily they were not needed.

Fourteen elaborate courses, a wonderful wedding cake, champagne and the '99 Château de Casseuil, speeches and toasts, laughter and singing, much kissing and embracing and fervently expressed good wishes: it all went on until evening came and the little lamps were lit in the trees and along the roof of the *chai* and the stables. Then the tables were cleared away and the dancing began.

It was only then that Laure put into effect her own little cherished scheme. She slipped past the dancers and – as if by some happy prearrangement – found Joseph and Rose pausing for a moment of quiet conversation in a corner of the garden, with Charles and Mathilde and Marcel.

'Come with me,' she said softly. 'There is something I want to share with you all.'

As unobtrusively as possible, they went with her to the *chai*.

There, with the door closed behind them and the candles flickering over their heads, they gathered round in silence while Laure drew off a little wine from one of the *cuves* into a new bottle and went to the table where glasses were already set out. As she moved, the light caught the liquid, sending sparks of gold darting from its clear depths.

'The vintage of 1921,' she said softly. 'Very young and very new, scarcely born, one might say. But today I want you all to taste.'

They watched as she poured a little of the liquid into each glass, and then signalled to them to take one. They did so and then stood there, looking at her: Marcel, plump and beaming and content; Charles, with his free hand holding Mathilde's, as it had been almost all the time since the moment when Joseph and Rose had exchanged their vows; Rose herself, with her hair that lit the dimness and her pale shining face; and

Joseph, on whom Laure's eyes rested, holding his gaze with her own.

Still looking at him, she raised her glass, and spoke the words so carefully rehearsed, very slowly and solemnly, in a voice a little rough and tremulous with emotion. 'This wine began its life as your love was born. I pray that the two will grow and mature together with the years, and grow richer and more wonderful day by day, and that your happiness will outlive even the very greatest of our wines.'

She swirled the glass, and sniffed, and the others did the same; and then they tasted. Sweetness first, almost too much, for only in maturity would the other complexities of scent and flavour assert themselves; but they were discernible even now, as a promise lingering on the tongue after the wine had gone. And the hugeness of the wine was there already, the unctuous texture, the powerful honeyed aroma: all the richness of summer, its essence drawn into this golden liquid which, over the years, would darken to amber, mature to an intense, harmonious, opulent wine to be spoken of with awe long after it had become no more than a memory.

It was Joseph who broke the gravely appreciative silence. He set down his glass and stretched his hands towards his grandmother. 'It is like you, Grand-mère,' he said tenderly. 'Enduring and generous and infinitely consoling to the heart.'

She laughed and patted his cheek softly with her hand.

'You are a flatterer, Joseph, and your tongue's far too sweet for your own good. But be happy, both of you – that's all I ask.'

JUBILEE
CLAIRE RAYNER

THE POPPY CHRONICLES

An enthralling historical saga . . .

Mildred Amberly – suffocating in affluent Leinster
Terrace – doomed at 28 to be an old maid. Lizah 'Kid'
Harris – a Jewish boxer from London's East End –
living from one fight to the next. Worlds apart . . .

But one rainy night Mildred takes a cab across London
into Lizah's world – a world of drama, excitement and
teeming life. But if she has escaped Leinster Terrace,
Mildred can't get away from its values . . . And
Lizah's family exerts pressures of its own. The past
will tear them apart . . .

Yet out of all this conflict comes Poppy – with her
mother's strong will and her father's boundless
appetite for life. Poppy, whose first memories are of
Queen Victoria's jubilee, who will live through two
world wars, and witness a century of change . . .

0 7221 7292 3   GENERAL FICTION   £3.50

THE
Distant Kingdom

DAPHNE WRIGHT

For twenty-six-year-old Perdita Whitney, life in India with
a father she hardly remembers seems just like a fairy tale.
His generosity and affection gradually heal the wounds in
her soul. And her new-found happiness is crowned when
she marries the man of her dreams – Lord Beaminster, the
dashing hero of the regiment.

But dream turns to nightmare when her husband becomes a
stranger. And as the army battles its way through the
treacherous passes of Afghanistan, Perdita must fight her
own heartbreaking battle . . .

'Difficult to put down.
Daphne Wright has a brilliant future'
CATHERINE GASKIN

'A vivid read, an imaginative story' *PUBLISHING NEWS*

0 7474 0090 3   GENERAL FICTION   £3.50

ALEXANDER
CORDELL

THIS PROUD
AND SAVAGE LAND

A vivid saga of passion, turmoil and heartache in
nineteenth-century Wales

Hywel Mortymer is just sixteen in 1800, when a family feud
leaves him orphaned, dispossessed and hunted even to the
grim coalmines of Blaenafon, where he flees to seek survival
below ground.

There he finds the elfin beauty Rhian, who labours with him
at coal face and iron furnace to safeguard their love against
pit disaster and vengeful cousins alike. But a harsh land
lives by harsh laws and, by the shining waters where they
snatched their brief joy, Hywel must confront his
tormentors and their bitter, brutal vendetta . . .

Set amid the dark tangle of danger and corruption of the
early days of the Welsh coal industry, *This Proud and
Savage Land* is an enthralling saga of love, of treachery, and
of the very land itself.

Also by Alexander Cordell in Sphere paperbacks – don't
miss
TUNNEL TIGERS

0 7221 2573 9   GENERAL FICTION   £3.99

A selection of bestsellers from SPHERE

FICTION

KALEIDOSCOPE	Danielle Steel	£3.50 ☐
AMTRAK WARS VOL. 4	Patrick Tilley	£3.50 ☐
TO SAIL BEYOND THE SUNSET	Robert A. Heinlein	£3.50 ☐
JUBILEE: THE POPPY CHRONICLES 1	Claire Rayner	£3.50 ☐
DAUGHTERS	Suzanne Goodwin	£3.50 ☐

FILM AND TV TIE-IN

WILLOW	Wayland Drew	£2.99 ☐
BUSTER	Colin Shindler	£2.99 ☐
COMING TOGETHER	Alexandra Hine	£2.99 ☐
RUN FOR YOUR LIFE	Stuart Collins	£2.99 ☐
BLACK FOREST CLINIC	Peter Heim	£2.99 ☐

NON-FICTION

MONTY: THE MAN BEHIND THE LEGEND	Nigel Hamilton	£3.99 ☐
BURTON: MY BROTHER	Graham Jenkins	£3.50 ☐
BARE-FACED MESSIAH	Russell Miller	£3.99 ☐
THE COCHIN CONNECTION	Alison and Brian Milgate	£3.50 ☐
HOWARD & MASCHLER ON FOOD	Elizabeth Jane Howard and Fay Maschler	£3.99 ☐

All Sphere books are available at your local bookshop or newsagent, or can be ordered direct from the publisher. Just tick the titles you want and fill in the form below.

Name _____

Address _____

_____

Write to Sphere Books, Cash Sales Department, P.O. Box 11, Falmouth, Cornwall TR10 9EN

Please enclose a cheque or postal order to the value of the cover price plus:

UK: 60p for the first book, 25p for the second book and 15p for each additional book ordered to a maximum charge of £1.90.

OVERSEAS & EIRE: £1.25 for the first book, 75p for the second book and 28p for each subsequent title ordered.

BFPO: 60p for the first book, 25p for the second book plus 15p per copy for the next 7 books, thereafter 9p per book.

Sphere Books reserve the right to show new retail prices on covers which may differ from those previously advertised in the text elsewhere, and to increase postal rates in accordance with the P.O.